WAR FOR THE GRAY KINGDOM

M.N.M. Abbott

ISBN: 978-0-9897008-3-2

ACKNOWLEGEMENTS

A heartfelt thanks to my mother, Sandy for her strength and my sister, Mia for her creative guidance. I would love to give a loud thank you to Cody Roecker. Thank you for the honest reviews. They motivated me more than you can imagine. Honorable mentions go to Aaron Hooker, Gabriel Kelly, Alexander Sterling Kent. Finally, thank you Vance Kovacs for being a huge artistic inspiration

KING'S PEAK
JENKIRK
ELF WOODS
OVERLOOK
DARGADIA
CASTLE GAILERIEN
BROAD RIVER
GREAT WASTES
WHITE SEA DESERT
LORRISAN TERRITORY
BEBIDIN TERRITORY
ULA LAKE
ZSU TERRITORY
ESKRANA
KATI JUNGLE
ILITHIAN SEA
MAGICAL REALM
N
E
S
W

INTRODUCTION

The demons had vanished. For three years since the Holy Hounds' victory over Melanin in the world of magic, none showed itself. Not even what remained of the Red Cult was seen. The last of the demon lord's forces scattered, disappearing as if they had never been.

In their absence, Dargadia and the other kingdoms flourished. King Lorvan and his daughter Princess Eyrie led their people to a new peace. Toth and Tamis had no small part to play. They could never have renewed their world without the help of the Order of the Master Knights and the new Order of Mages. Arch Mage Balefire proved himself in keeping the peace between commoners and those with even a little magical power. The king and both orders worked tirelessly, never wavering. They knew that any day, Adwen and her Holy Hounds could return.

For three years, the Holy Hounds did not come to the world of magic. Adwen and Oryn made certain Jack reunited with his wife, Ashley. When the chaos of Jack's return to the police department was sorted out, Adwen and her knightly companion left to unknown places. Alexander remained with his friend and in hiding. He was still wanted for murder with no way to prove his innocence. Regardless, Jack and Ashley did what they could to give him a home.

In time, Jack and Alexander learned they could not truly rejoin human kind in the non-magical world. They were Holy Hounds. With that came many difficulties. Yet there were many more benefits. If they could not be human, they could do something else.

Chapter 1
OMENS

Late at night, two sport motorcycles screamed down from San Bruno Mountain on a dry dirt road, kicking up dust. Northbound, the pair chased each other as they sped through San Francisco. On a dark straightway with no traffic cameras, the smaller biker tipped forward, balancing on the front tire. The larger biker shook his head as his friend came alongside, maintaining balance. Helmets muffled their chuckles.

In the shadows and trees of Golden Gate Park, they hid their bikes side by side. Although the bikes had no license plates, they did have custom paint jobs: the side of one read Big Dog and the other Bad Dog. Certain their bikes were well hidden in the brush the duo went to work.

A small team of thieves broke into the park's art museum as if it were child's play. Five black-clad men took control of the upper floors. Two security guards lay unconscious with zip-tie bonds on their wrists and ankles. The plan was going perfectly, using tech and finesse to claim priceless carved masks. While one intruder hacked into the security system behind a wall, the others monitored the hall using their own devices to stabilize the display case.

They spoke softly through headsets: "The magnets are in place. Everything is reading green. Is the inside prepped?"

Their ear pieces carried another voice from beyond the wall. "Almost. Give me a few more seconds."

"We're on a tight schedule."

"Yeah, yeah. I'm focused. Just wait a minute."

Seconds ticked by as the four waited on the fifth. When everything should have been ready, they waited a little longer. Finally, their leader lost patience.

"Are you ready to go?" No answer came. "If you're not ready, say so or you're alone on this job and we're gone."

More silence filled their headsets, changing frustration to unease. This was unlike their companion. In case the channel was tapped, they turned off the headsets.

"Eric, go check on him."

The man silently obeyed. Going down the sprawling hall, he rounded the corner and disappeared. Again, the team waited. A few seconds passed, and an odd sound echoed outward. It put the remaining three on edge, exchanging looks.

They followed their boss's lead. As he took out an electrical weapon, the other two prepared their own weapons. Reaching the corner where Eric had rounded, they saw the two guards still unconscious. Eric and the other two thieves were nowhere to be seen, so they continued forward. The door to the security room sat open. Going closer, more footsteps joined theirs. Someone came out, and it was neither Eric nor their companion.

A figure in black, blue and red leather stepped out and turned to face them. His features were completely obscured by a shiny motorcycle helmet. As he stood waiting, the thieves stopped, staring back. How this stranger had gotten past their surveillance was confounding.

One scoffed, "How'd this clown get in here?"

Before any could reply, the stranger moved. His speed was blinding. He seemed to fly along the hall at them as if fired from a cannon.

One cursed in dismay and another fired a Taser. Adding to their shock, the strange biker displayed unnatural reflexes, dodging the flying pins and wires. The biker darted to the side, running across the wall. They shouted, raising crackling electrical gadgets, backing away while the man pounced from above. As a thief jabbed with a snapping set of prongs, the biker ducked low. His shoulder struck the thief in the stomach, launching him into Plexiglas windows, where he bounced to the floor. As the thief crumpled up on the floor, gasping, the man with the spent Taser fled.

The third thief faced this anonymous adversary alone. He

lunged, shouting in outrage, but no matter how hard he punched or tried to zap the stranger, it was no use. For the stranger, this was no more difficult than corralling a clumsy toddler. After a while, the thief paused to catch his breath, staring incredulously. How was this guy so fast?

Then the man in the biker helmet made a rude gesture, taunting the thief.

Enraged and losing all sense, the thief bellowed and lobbed the Taser.

It sparked and snapped, hurtling through the air. When it was about to connect with the stranger, the Taser abruptly stopped moving. The biker chuckled at the dumbfounded thief as the Taser hovered midair. Then the weapon spun around and aimed at its owner. In the blink of an eye, it flew at the thief. The prongs found his ribs as he turned to run. He wailed and fell, convulsing on the floor.

Whistling a catchy tune, the biker approached the downed thieves. He used some of their own zip ties to bind them like the guards. Nearly finished, a sensation coursed down his spine, making him pause. He knew right away that his fellow biker needed help.

The last conscious member of the team ran out the hacked security door, fleeing for their van. His hands shook as he fumbled to open the door and put the key in the ignition. He turned it hard. The engine refused to even growl. Then he noticed the corner of the van's hood. A patch of the painted metal had been peeled away. When he scrambled out of the vehicle to see what had happened, his stomach did a somersault. The battery sat on the ground, the two cables severed and still bolted to the posts. Panic set in as he cursed aloud and fled for the darkest reaches of the park.

After escaping the illuminated palm trees and walkways, the thief huffed and panted. He had run far into a dense forested area. Taking a minute to think, only one thing made sense: He needed help. He pawed through the many pouches in his black clothing and found his cell phone. Placing the SIM card and battery back inside, the screen powered on as he begged the device to load faster. The glow of the screen illuminated his strained features.

"Come on! Come on you, worthless piece of garbage!"

A gasping sigh of relief burst from his lungs when the phone was finally ready. He selected a number on speed dial. Holding it to his ear as the dial tones chimed, he hoped the call would be well received. After a few more tones came and died off, a stick snapped loudly somewhere close by. The thief whirled around, beginning to feel eyes watching him. Forgetting the phone by his face, he listened, terrified that something was lurking amid the trees. Crunching footfalls distracted the man entirely even as a masculine voice came across the line at last.

"I thought I told you not to call."

Terrified, the thief murmured shakily. "I gotta go."

The phone beeped as he ended the call and started running again. The ground gave way to one of the parks' ponds. Surprised by the fall and then the water's cold, his small cry of shock sounded across the pond. Whatever was chasing him was right behind, so he swam, ignoring the fact that the water likely destroyed the phone. If he could escape through the forested side of the park he would be free. It was not much farther.

Finding solid ground and crossing an empty paved path, he bolted toward a meadow lying between him and escape, then paused to catch his breath. This was as safe a place as any for now. Sopping wet clothes clung to his limbs, water squelched in boggy boots. His lungs burned, aching for more rest. Only as his labored breathing slowed did his eyes catch movement ahead. Transients frequented the park at night, so at first it was no surprise when a burly figure emerged from the shadows. Yet the homeless seldom wore clean black, brown and yellow leather. Light from distant lamps lanced over the figure's shiny biker helmet.

Freezing at the sight of another silent biker, his eyes widened with horror. His breaths became ragged. The figure was large, muscular and strolling closer. Wheezing, shuddering and desperate, the thief patted his pockets and pouches. His fidgeting fingers grasped a folded knife. The thief flicked it open, brandishing it where the biker would clearly see it.

This did nothing to halt the stranger.

He swiped the knife through the air angrily, shouting. "Back off! If you don't back off you're dead! Do you hear me, freak?"

When nothing the thief said or did mattered, desperation drove him wild. He bellowed and lunged. His knife hand swung in fast. A small thud followed at the meeting of metal and flesh.

At last, the big biker stopped.

Holding the knife in the stranger's ribs, he panted, staring in disbelief that there was no reaction. The biker simply stood before him, staring from somewhere inside the helmet. The longer the thief stared back the more confused he became. Twisting the knife and stabbing several more times, only a little blood came out on the blade. The stranger bled for a moment as if from a simple paper cut. Nevertheless, he showed no reaction of pain.

Again, the thief stabbed him, but this time the biker moved, taking a firm grip of the thief's wrist. Slowly drawing the knife out, the biker's gloved hand squeezed. The pressure was immense, crushing bones. A sick series of snaps met their ears, and the thief screamed in terror and agony, buckling over. The knife fell to the ground.

Every miserable cry went ignored. The biker grabbed the thief by the back of his shirt and dragged him across the lawn back into the park.

The man sobbed and cradled his shattered wrist. Tears swelled, blurring vision. Not giving up, there were a few more tools left in his pockets. Taking out a tiny stun gun, he clicked the button, urging it to come to life. The instant it crackled, he jammed it into the biker's leg. The thief did not expect a reaction but hoped it would do something. To his surprise, voltage had a strong effect on the almost unstoppable stranger. Yet he was not prepared for everything he witnessed.

At the instant the weapon struck the biker, he paused and shuddered, resisting the electrical shock. Then he toppled over, shuddering as the thief held the device to his leg. The clothes on his body became like smoke as did the helmet, swirling and rippling wildly. To the thief's astonishment, the clothes transformed into a set of leather and metal armor, like that of an ancient warrior. As the armor settled and solidified the helmet vanished, revealing a blond man with a short chin beard. He had pointed ears and his pale blue eyes glowed in the dark, flashing like the prongs in his leg. Growling and snarling, sharp fangs in his mouth clenched tightly.

Scrambling away and to his feet, the thief gasped and panted, taking out the Glock stowed in his soggy boots. Gunfire was his last resort because it would alert police and make escape even harder. Aiming at the creature shuddering on the grass, he was transfixed by its eerie glowing eyes. The knife had done nothing to this thing. An electrical jolt just made it angry. What would a bullet do?

A muffled voice from behind frightened him into whirling around. "You're kidding me, right?"

The gun went off the moment the thief turned and saw the biker from the museum. A tiny hole appeared in the leather jacket where his heart was. To the thief's mounting horror and astonishment, the short biker staggered but only a little. The biker seemed more surprised than wounded. The sight of the unfazed figure left the thief stunned, jaw agape and gasping.

Walking up to the thief, the biker took the gun from his weak grasp and tapped him on the side of the head with it. The casual blow knocked the thief out. Dropping the gun on the unconscious criminal, Jack made the motorcycle helmet vanish, brushing at the red and black hair on his brow.

He smiled and shook his head. "Come on, Jarhead. I warned you they use Tazers. You had one job to do."

Climbing to his feet, Alexander transformed his appearance back to that of a leather-clad biker. Not bothering to form a helmet with the rest of the disguise, the former Marine rolled his eyes. "Shut up, Toto. He swam through a lake. How was I supposed to know his gear was waterproof?"

Jack clicked his tongue, teasing his best friend. "Don't give me that. Marines should know better than to underestimate the enemy. Knowing's half the battle, right?"

He was incredulous. "Don't start, Short Stack."

"Awe well. Anyway, Jarhead, how about you carry him back since it was you who dropped the ball this time?"

To this, Alexander could not help but shake his head and chuckle. "Yeah, sure."

Strolling through the trees and avoiding potential witnesses, they made their way back to the museum. Their glowing eyes flashed with amusement at the relative success of their mission.

"Did you have any trouble disabling the van?"

Alexander hefted the limp thief a little higher on his shoulder. "Nope, but I got zapped a bit cutting the wires."

"When you followed him, did he make any phone calls?"

"Yeah, I made sure he heard me so he wouldn't say much. He ended the call right after someone answered."

"Perfect! When my department gets a hold of them I'll make

sure everything goes just right. His phone is wet, but our techs are pretty good. We'll get to who hired them. Going to nail that manager this time."

"Huh?"

"My partner and I have this investigation in the bag. While interviewing, I got to read the thoughts of one of the thieves. Without saying a word, I got him to tell me almost everything."

The Marine scoffed. "Too bad reading minds isn't admissible evidence."

Jack rolled his eyes. "Preaching to the choir."

"Speaking of partners, how are things with Officer Grigori?"

"Not bad. He's been wearing different deodorant. He's also on a diet that doesn't make me want to vomit when I smell him in the car. This Holy Hound nose picks up everything."

Alexander sighed. "You know that's not what I meant."

"He's still searching. Mr. Grigori is fascinated by the elusive bikers who are seen at random before a case gets cracked. He doesn't like vigilantes, and he is very interested in the occasional wacked-out eyewitness testimony."

"Like what this moron is going to say when he gets interrogated at the station."

Jack glowered, "Yeah. Since someone forgot to knock out the little wimp before picking him up. If we keep going like this we'll have to stop completely. You especially can't afford to be identified."

"As if it would be any better for you? A vigilante cop? We would both be in trouble."

Jack frowned. "Don't remind me. They wouldn't be able to hurt us, but Ashley would not be able to handle it. Things have been hard enough."

Alexander grimaced.

Jack's and Ashley's marriage had been stressed over the last three years since the two men returned from the magical realm. Jack's transformation into a Holy Hound kept them from going back to the way things were. There were things they could no longer do together, but both were far too devoted to cut ties. They mutually carried on through the strain.

"I'm lucky she loves me. That's all I have to say."

"Why don't we call this the last one?" Alexander tried to cheer up his friend. "I can be the secret family pet, and you don't have to risk your career and relationship with Ashley."

Jack threw back a skeptical look. "You would be okay with playing the Fido role?"

He was not. "I am if you and Ashley are willing to keep giving me raw steak dinners every week. Tell her to stop getting tri-tip. I like to chew on bones."

Jack knew the truth but smiled. "Honestly, I wouldn't be able to handle a normal life. Well, as normal as I can have. The vigilante gig keeps me sane."

Alexander smiled back. "We could always keep working on the bikes?"

"True, but that doesn't replace all of the running up walls and jumping across rooftops. Anything normal that compares is illegal or too expensive."

They walked toward wider lighted pathways. As they were going to transform their magical garments into biker helmets, a foul smell hit their noses. The vile odor triggered their keen sense of smell, forcing them to stop and sniff. Staring out into the city, Jack and Alexander growled.

"Is that what I think it is?"

Jack growled loudly, becoming alarmed. "That's not vampires or werewolves. We've cleared out most of this city. They don't smell quite like this though. Drop that sack of potatoes and put your game face on."

When Alexander laid the human on the pathway, their enchanted garments shifted into magical armor. Their pointed ears lengthened, and their bared teeth formed sharp canines. Jack summoned dual daggers and Alexander his short sword. The gold and silver blades glinted in the lamplight. The warriors bolted, running nose to the wind, tracking the scent as fast as they could. Both knew what was ahead. Demons had come to their city.

A small mob of man-sized fiends bounded across rooftops north of the park, heading westward. Jack and Alexander stopped to stare in disbelief. Observing the nasty gecko-like monsters with shark teeth, they remained at a distance. Safely hidden on a fire escape, the warriors began to debate.

"We should kill them quickly before they cause any damage."

Jack snarled back, "No, we need to know why they are here. I can't get anything from their pea brains this far away. I need to get closer."

"If they aren't killed quickly, who knows what they will do? You're willing to risk that?"

"I don't want to; we have to! Those are soldier-class demons. They don't do anything without a boss giving orders. That's the only explanation for them popping up. When Adwen killed the demon lord, they should have all gone back under the rock they crawled from. I'd like a deep look inside one's head if we can catch it. Then we'll know what's happening."

Alexander's battlefield instincts did not like this. "And if this turns out to be a trap?"

Jack tossed him a wry smile. "Guess we're about to find out. Come on, Big Dog. Let's see how stealthy you can be."

As he vaulted up from their hideaway, the Marine grimaced before doing the same.

Powerful winds blew from the ocean. The demons went farther west, then turned steadily northwest. Jack and Alexander followed, careful not to be seen by the demons, as well as humans on the streets. While the monsters they chased were all but invisible to city denizens, both Holy Hounds had to put effort into going unnoticed.

The vividly colored demons scrambled and leaped from roof to roof. In their wake, Jack and Alexander gained. Their hands gripped ledges where they dropped into cover before quickly climbing up again. His telepathy tapped the monsters' minds, but they felt out of reach. Instead, he found those of the humans all around them. Alex's thoughts of frustration with this plan was an added distraction, gradually making Jack irritated as well. If he could lock onto the thoughts he wanted to hear, he would be free to block everything else out again.

To the aggravation of both warriors, they approached the edge of the city where they would lose the cover of buildings and side streets. Beyond lay many trees and craggy slopes before the rocky shore. Ducking behind another rooftop ventilation unit, Jack growled to his friend.

"Screw this. I can't get a bead on them. Time to make purple paint out of these things."

"Roger that, Bad Dog."

No longer concealing themselves, the warriors moved at their full potential. Their speed far surpassed that of the demons. In seconds, Jack's daggers flew like missiles, ripping through bounding monsters, turning them to purple muck. Alexander pounced others, their heads cleaved off.

Several Clown demons shrieked at the attack and quickened their pace, fleeing from the Holy Hounds. The gaggle reached the trees, escaping the lights of the city for the dark of the woods.

The warriors closed in on them. Jack snarled as he killed another. This was the first time he had seen demons running for their lives. More likely, they were running toward something. At this thought, Jack redoubled his attack.

Watching Jack's back in their chase through the forest, Alexander caught up to a few more demons. In the midst of slaughtering the colorful fiends, he smelled Jack's fear. Now both Holy Hounds alerted for the unexpected. The land's edge was just ahead, the scent of ocean brine thick in the air.

Three demons darted from the cover of the forest, speeding toward the rocky shore. Jack sent his daggers flying, guiding them with telekinesis. First the blades sliced through a demon, then turned for a second. The remaining demon retreated toward the trees, bounding and hissing, long claws scraping across rock and dirt. Alexander went around the other side of the rise in the earth, cutting off the demon's escape. Together, the warriors hemmed the last fiend into the lower cliff shelf near the shore's labyrinth of stones.

Waves crashed against the rocks below where the demon finally stopped, turning to show the warriors rows of serrated teeth. It watched them stalk closer with weapons drawn.

Jack and Alexander panted from the running.

"Can you hear its thoughts?"

Studying the ugly creature, Jack was leery. "Yeah, but I'm not hearing what we need yet."

The surface thoughts of the demon were primitive, taking in smells and sounds. To find the information it was trying to hide, Jack would need to touch its head. While the stupid thing stood brandishing wicked claws and teeth, the monster seemed entertained. As Jack sensed this emotion in the demon's mind, a sick feeling swelled in his stomach.

"What are you waiting for?" Alexander growled nervously. "Grab it!"

As Jack was about to lunge, they heard many feet landing on the ground behind them. A small army of the same weak demons covered the cliff, cutting them off from escape. The only way out was to jump into the ocean, but even that route was not guaranteed to save them. When the horde stepped to the edge of the rocky out-cropping they stood. Like the one facing Jack and Alexander on the ledge, they stared, hissing.

"Hurry!" Alexander snarled.

Jack faced the demon once more, ready to lunge. To their combined horror and confusion, the demon screamed and began to writhe. Then it burst, purple slime forming a puddle on the earth. The warriors recoiled.

Every demon started to scream and yowl, contorting before exploding into a shower of foul fluids. Puddles frothed, turning black as pitch. Mist formed high upon the cliff and flowed down to their feet. A strange sound like boiling water gurgled from the mist.

Out of the black on the upper ledge rose a giant standing al-most twenty feet tall. Black liquid splashed and dripped from all over the emerging figure, showering everything nearby that was not already covered. It stretched out four long arms before opening bright glow-ing eyes. The red pupils focused on the Holy Hounds and an arm moved in a swift downward motion at the stunned warriors.

Seeing the enormous spear fly, Jack and Alexander dodged sideways, landing together in the muddy mess. They jumped to their feet as the monster threw another spear. The Marine leaped clear, while Jack ducked and rolled the other way.

The powerful demon laughed atop the ledge, throwing spear after spear. When each of the four claws hurled a spear, black muck slithered up from the ground to create another. Again, the demon chuckled, throwing a well-aimed shaft.

Jack dodged, but the ground was slick from the flood of slime. He could not avoid a strike. He yelped a high-pitch cry and fell. The pain from the evil weapon's touch was indescribable.

Alexander saw his friend go down and heard his cry. Desper-ate, the Marine charged up the slope. He could not allow the demon to throw another at Jack.

Grinning, the monster took great pleasure at the fallen warri-or. The demon honed its aim to try to finish the job. Noticing Alex-ander's advance to higher ground, the grin turned more sadistic. The demon laughed mercilessly before throwing the spear at Jack.

Yielding no room for distraction, Alexander refused to look where the spear landed. Leaping at the demon, Alexander transformed. His body grew massive, the magical armor reforming to fit the beastly warrior. The yellow hound creature swung his golden sword through the air, while he heard Jack yelp in anguish below.

The demon backhanded the hound warrior out of the air, sending him rolling across the ground. Each step the Demon Colossus took toward Alexander shook the ground and it summoned two more spears, leaving a pair of hands empty to rip the warrior apart.

When the yellow hound warrior found his footing, his clawed hand gripped his holy weapon tighter. His muzzle wrinkled in a tight snarl, white fangs glinted with saliva. His tail arched, bristled from intense anger.

A lightning-fast spear thrust threatened to impale him, but Alexander's reflexes were faster in his true form. The claws on his pawed feet gave him traction in the muddy ground. He avoided a second spear thrust. When the Colossus swung both spears to rend the warrior in half, Alexander's agility and strength enabled him leap and tumble closer to the giant. Alexander leaped to his feet, slicing deep into the closest leg, letting purple and black spray forth.

Angry, the lame demon roared, swiping at Alexander with enormous hands. As the warrior swung for the monster's other leg, it swatted at him and lost fingers to the blessed sword. Another deafening roar shook the air on the windy cliff. Before the hound could slice again, the demon kicked, catching Alexander in the chest plate.

The warrior careened yards away, tumbling across the ground. By the time he was alert and on his feet, a spear was moving in fast. Instinctively, the warrior bounded aside only to be snatched by an uninjured hand. Alexander roared, resisting the fingers and long claws that held him fast, arms pinned to his sides. The hand squeezed tighter, raising him high.

The demon laughed heartily, opening its toothy mouth wide, ready to bite off Alexander's head. This hound creature was fun to defeat and smelled delicious.

A whistling sound came before purple and black sprayed in all directions. Alexander fell with the dismembered hand as it began to liquefy in midair. Two silver and gold daggers sailed about, dancing around the demon, slicing at the gaps in the fiend's armor. More springs of vile filth erupted, making the monster wail.

A black and white hound warrior with a curled tail limped at the base of the outcropping. One injured arm braced a wound on his side as he held the other high, helping to focus on directing the daggers. Flexing fur covered fingers with claws, Jack snarled, urging the daggers to cyclone around another arm. The limb broke away at the elbow and the demon continued to cry out as the warrior began slicing another arm.

Alexander advanced again, carving into the Colossus's legs.

It swayed, roaring and wailing. Seeing Jack on his feet controlling the flying daggers, the demon filled with outrage. It bellowed, lobbing a spear while it could still hold one. Jack was barely able to step aside in time. Slime and mud exploded from the ground where it struck and stayed.

This bought Alexander enough time to take down the demon at the leg, forcing it to kneel. With a crash, it fell, bracing itself with stumps for arms. Before the Colossus could react, Alexander ran up one arm like a ramp. In the blink of an eye the yellow hound warrior swept his sword down. Dark liquids spurted from the seam he created around the demon's neck. It fell quiet just as its head dropped, landing on the sullied earth.

The body collapsed, letting the hound jump to the ground and rush to his friend's aid. Alexander transformed into his more human shape as he dashed to the bloodied hound warrior.

Bracing his injured companion's shoulder, he asked urgently, "How hurt are you? Take it easy."

Jack reverted to more human shape as well. He smiled and scoffed, "We've both been hurt worse." Stealing a peek at the missing chunk of flesh in his side where the enormous spear clipped him, he winced. "Can't remember which time was worse, but I'll be okay. Let's get the bikes, Ol' Yeller."

Alexandre could not help but chuckle. "Shut up, Rin-Tin-Tin."

The way back to the park had to be taken slowly. Blood wept from Jack's wounds, especially from his side. A trickling trail lay behind across many rooftops. It was hard to jump and climb over the city, but they needed to avoid being seen in the streets. Their enchanted armor could not hide wounds made by evil weapons. When they returned to the park they washed stinking demon fluids off in a pond before departing.

Heading back to San Bruno Mountain, they rode the bikes at a more lawful speed. Every so often Jack swerved.

"Ashley can't see you like this so bring some beer and we'll wait on the mountain. Sunrise will patch you up fast."

Jack winced at the seizing of his shredded flesh. Over the sound of their bikes, he called out in reply: "I like the sound of that. Better she never knows this happened."

"I told you it was a trap."

"No, you didn't."

"Yes, I did. And you still didn't find out what the demons were up to."

"Oh, yes we did. They have a leader; that's what we learned. Those slimy scum buckets don't have two IQ points to rub together. Someone or something with real brains is behind the operation. What was that thing we killed anyway?"

"Never seen one before. Don't want to see one again, either."

Jack chuckled, and it hurt, making him shudder and swerve on the road.

"Hey! Pull over a second. Rest a minute before you kiss pavement."

Jack did not argue. The pain was terrible and riding the bike did not help. Pulling over at a curb, his breaths were laborious. Jack panted, shuddering like a leaf and gripping the handles tightly.

Alexander pulled alongside and waited for his companion to recuperate. If Jack's hunch was right, and they usually were, then there was only one thing they could do. He spoke with a grim tone. "We need to find Adwen. She needs to know."

Sitting upright in his seat, Jack sighed, "Yeah, she does. We'll need to take off soon. I'll put in a leave of absence tomorrow at the station. Grigori can get through the paperwork on his own." Then he frowned. "I'll have to tell Ashley something before we leave."

Alexander rolled his eyes. "First we need to figure out where we're going. We don't know where Adwen and Oryn went, let alone whether we can get there. We assumed that if trouble came she would find us."

"I know, bud. Just give me a chance to think."

"Think this one out: Adwen can use her sword to open portals to anywhere, including the other world. For all we know they went back to Dargadia. Here, the demons have the upper hand, and they're hunting us."

Jack restrained a laugh. "I doubt they're in Dargadia." Enjoying Alexander's confusion, Jack pointed over his friend's shoulder.

An electronic billboard glowed overhead with brilliant colors, advertising a band for an upcoming tour. In the bright image, a stern man with short brown hair and bangs made a deadpan glare, bright green eyes glowing. Beside him, holding a guitar, stood a girl striking a wild pose. Her hair was silvery white with golden, side-swept bangs. Her blue eyes gleamed, and her black lips parted in an ecstatic grin. The woman's copper skin looked flawless on the screen.

While the Marine gazed up at their friends' images in disbelief, the injured cop shook his head. It was so like Adwen to drag Oryn into an over-the-top adventure.

"Looks like we'll be taking a trip to Los Angeles. Red Lily is kicking off their tour in a few days. Come on, Rufus. Let's get some beer."

Chapter 2
PREMONITIONS

Sunshine gleamed over the desert. Rusty mountains crouched in the north basking in the heat of the day as hot air percolated, making the scenery dance. Pitiable growth stood dry having not seen rain in many months. Rushing past the desolate wastes filled with cactus, a huge white van careened along the interstate highway.

Inside the cabin there was laughter and talking over loud rock music. Gavin, the wiry drummer, cackled as he grappled with James, their bass player. Both fumbled on their seats, laughing hysterically.

"What did you say to me, you hairy hobbit?" Gavin laughed harder as he struggled to speak. "Say it to my face. Say it again!"

James sputtered, sniggering while fighting him off. "Your mom's lips taste like sea-salt caramel!" He cackled harder when this incited more rough-housing.

A loud masculine voice shouted from the back. "Enough of that!"

The men paused and stared, panting.

Green eyes glowed brilliantly at the pair. Oryn's brown bangs framed his serpentine glare as he stared them down. He sat back, resting beside Adwen and holding a thick book open. Wearing a black and green collared shirt with slacks, he propped his feet on one of the band's gear bags.

"Put a stop to the nonsense before I put a stop to it for you," he told the pair. "I'm reading."

This yielded a nervous gulp from James, and Gavin was apologetic. "Our bad. We'll stop."

Adwen shook her head, rolling her eyes at the knight beside her. "The music is louder than they are. You've already read that book anyhow."

Looking up from his copy of The Art of War, Oryn raised an eyebrow. "It is more a study than a pleasure. If the writer even existed, this is a noteworthy work to revisit."

Ted, the band backup player and singer, sniggered nearby. Oryn shot him a deadly look, making his eyes glow bright.

"You don't scare me anymore. Why are you really reading that again?"

Oryn ignored the question as he resumed reading.

Adwen answered for him. "He just likes it. We traveled the world together, and war history books are his favorite."

"As one cannot exercise sword play in a van, reading of combat is a compromise." The green-eyed warrior added coolly, "Now if you do not mind, I'm busy. Stop pestering me."

She smiled at her companion. "Do I have to stop pestering you?"

He was silent. A few seconds later, a faint smile appeared on his face, and he gave a discreet look. She could not possibly pester him.

Adwen giggled then turned to the rest of the band. "Guys? The manager said we are staying at a nice hotel in Malibu. We are booked starting tomorrow evening. Everybody going to behave?"

Gavin gave a skeptical smile. "Look who's talking? Are you going to behave, dog girl?"

"Going out for a late-night swim like last time?" Ted smiled. "Skinny dipping doesn't get the right kind of attention. You're lucky no one recognized you."

Rolling her eyes, Adwen huffed, smiling back. "I don't know. Can you keep from leaking information to obsessed fans that we are magical? We let you all know what we were in confidence that you would keep quiet."

"Come on! It's not my fault that your boyfriend can heal people in the crowd with his voice. The rumors started on their own. I'm just helping a little."

"Help by not feeding the fire, Teddy. If you can't stop, then be more discreet."

The man sighed. "Okay, okay. I'll give it a rest."

"Thank you."

"Hey, Adwen!" James held out his smart phone, displaying a

weather app. "Looks like rain for the next two days in Southern California."

Gavin and Ted groaned.

She looked confused. "I thought it was supposed to be clear skies?"

"Well, yeah. It's clear on the show date, but cloudy and a chance of rain before that."

Adwen sighed. "You scared me for a second. That would suck for our first big venue to get rained out."

"Tell me about it. Setup on the Santa Monica Pier would suck."

"Either way, sound checking is really going to suck there. Rest up. Two days to zero hour."

Late the following day after they arrived at the hotel, the human members of the band went out together for a night on the town. Adwen and Oryn chose to stay in. They laid together on the hard mattress sharing warmth, enjoying the silence. Eventually the Holy Hounds drifted off into a deep sleep.

Shadows flitted to and fro in the near darkness. Human screams and demon roars echoed all around. Adwen saw a human in the chaos fighting back. A figure turned this way and that, taking swipes at fiends that came from every direction.

As she saw through the dark more clearly, the armored warrior continued to fight. He had no weapons. To fight back, razor sharp fingertips ripped enemies apart. Somehow, the warrior's armor was darker than the surrounding blackness. His eyes were red, yet human. They glowed in the gloom, flashing with emotions of desperation and determination. No matter how long he fought, hands drenched with evil blood, the dark warrior refused to tire or give in.

Another monster attacked from his side, and he killed it with a flick of his wrist. Then he saw Adwen. He froze, red eyes wide, pupils dilating in fear. Becoming like a statue, the strange warrior could not breathe as he stared at Adwen.

When she took a step forward he recoiled, still staring with wide eyes. Adwen was only curious, studying the black armor that hid him so well. The more she looked at the frightened being, the more she felt an urge. Gently, Adwen extended an open hand to him.

The warrior was stunned, confused. Looking to her hand and up again, he blinked, wondering. For a long moment, the dark knight stared in disbelief.

Adwen woke in Oryn's arms. She gazed at the clean, white walls of the sterile hotel room. Raindrops pattered against the windows hidden by thick curtains. For a while she lay still, glowing blue eyes shifting in thought. There had been no visions from the Light Spirits since their adventures in the magical world. She wondered what this could mean. Foreboding filled her heart.

Minutes passed, and Oryn woke as well. Holding her tighter, he smelled the silvery hair on the back of her head and sighed contentedly. Realizing she was awake, the knight also caught onto a faint scent of fear. He held her closer in hope of being a comfort. When a moment went by and she said nothing, Oryn could not guess what was wrong.

His voice murmured softly behind her ear, "What is it?"

Adwen hesitated to answer, gazing out at nothing. "I had a vision."

This was grim news. The Light Spirits would only provide such guidance if she were needed; if she were needed, then something was terribly wrong. Oryn's mood turned dark, but he kept fears from changing the kind tone in his voice.

"What of?"

She thought hard to understand the vision. That warrior alone in the dark was a complete mystery. Why had he been so afraid of her?

Her brow furrowed. "I don't know."

Both were quiet as she slipped her hands into his, lacing their fingers. They looked out into nothingness, holding each other. Neither wanted to believe it, but both knew that this could be their last peaceful evening together. That thought alone was painful to consider.

Resting his chin over her shoulder, he took a deep breath through his nose. Closing his eyes, Oryn smelled her skin. The knight very much wished to stay there forever. Wishing not to make things any more difficult, he refrained from kissing her neck. Gently taking his hands from hers, he felt it was time for a walk.

Feeling him pull away and get up, she was a little surprised. Adwen wondered what he was doing. When his hand reached the door handle, he heard her soft voice coo and a small dog whimper accompany it.

"Where are you going?"

The sound tugged at his heart, which longed to return to her side. He so wanted to hold her until the sun came up again. Glancing over, his face forced a confident expression and a faint smile. "I won't be long. Rest yourself." Oryn went out into the downpour and closed the door behind him.

Adwen was shocked that he would leave at this moment. With the new vision and his sudden departure in the night, there was no chance she would get peaceful rest. Her bare feet padded on carpet on her way to the window. Drawing a curtain and peeking through bamboo blinds, she looked out from the scenic hotel over the beach. Her bright stare followed him down a path that led to the shore through the deluge.

To keep out some of the rain, Oryn willed his magic garments to return to being armor. Scaled metal flowed over his body, limbs, feet and fingers, coming to sharp points like claws. A leathery hood formed up and over his head, shielding him from the rainfall. The glow in his green stare grew intense as he neared the sandy beach stalking the surf.

Patches of volcanic rock peeked out from yellow, shifting sand. Wind ripped and pulled at everything, sending salty foam into the air to mingle with falling droplets. It threatened to pull the hood back from the warrior, but it stayed in place fluttering with the folds of the capes on his elaborate armor.

Letting his human ears and teeth go, fangs grew out as he growled, sneering at the dark ocean. Tussling waves splashed, reaching his boots, then recoiled without having touched them.

Something was coming. It was a sense that would have excited him several years ago when he was captain of the Order of the Master Knights; now it frightened him. Oryn Conrad had nothing to lose before Adwen came into his world. Exchanging his fear for resolve, the knight summoned the large, spiked sword into his grasp for the first time in weeks. The Rose Thorne glinted in the shadows amid the storm, catching light from far inland.

Heightened senses let him hear and feel every raindrop that

hit the blade. Tiny vibrations penetrated his armored glove. The lungs in his broad chest filled, then released, beginning the rhythm Oryn had been taught. The focus that the breathing brought intensified, shutting out the clamor of the stormy beach, and he started to spar alone.

Slowly at first, his sword swept and swung up, back and around. He took disciplined steps, leaving precise patterns in the sand. Traveling the world with Adwen introduced him to forms of combat never taught to the Order. Taking what he learned abroad, the talented swordsman practiced a mixed combat style. Swinging and whirling about, moving and stepping faster and faster, Oryn and his sword became a blur.

Sand and raindrops flung from his feet and his blade, flying outward from his imaginary training arena, footprints flattening the sand in a perfect ring. At his fastest, the precise moves of his blade stopped the rain from finding the ground. The strength and power imbued into his body allowed him to practice for several minutes without rest.

Waves lapped closer. When a wave finally rolled far enough to wipe away the sand he had trodden down, Oryn concluded his exercise with a mighty swing. The knight spun, sending pale green magic into his hands. Then he roared, swinging fast and hard at the rumbling water. The force of the sword cutting the air sent the wave and a vast patch of sand flying far beyond the next breaking crest.

He was a little tired from the intense practice, but pleased. For a time, he watched the tumultuous water, listening to the wind tugging at his hood. He relaxed his grip on his sword. Making it vanish in a small flash of light, Oryn felt a little better. He had become stronger and more skilled than ever. Whatever came, he was ready.

Chapter 3
SWEET SORROW

"What is this?" the police chief asked.

Jack sat in the chair by the chief's desk, taking a sip of coffee. "It's a notice for a leave of absence. I'm going away for a while."

The burly, middle-aged chief grimaced more the longer he looked at the paper. "There's no mention of how much time you're taking, Officer Towers. Is something wrong at home?"

"No, no, nothing like that. Ashley and I are fine. I need to do some soul searching."

A frown formed on the chief's face. "Then it's the job?"

Jack smiled and shook his head. It would be easier to just read the chief's mind. However, he had grown to miss true conversation, hearing spoken words and not knowing every thought spawning it.

"I wish I could say it was."

"Soul searching sounds like a euphemism for something, Jack. Why are you being so mysterious with me?"

"If you're wondering if I'm coming back at all, don't worry about it. I already talked with Grigori." Jack had needed to read his partner's mind to avoid a full-blown argument. He was secretly thankful Chief Wilken was being less inquisitive.

"Will you tell me where you're going?"

He shrugged and smiled. "No idea. I'm hopping on my bike and going for a ride." Jack sensed the chief was growing suspicious. Just this once, he opened his mind to hear the man's thoughts as a precaution.

"Hmm," Then the chief pondered. < He says it's not his wife or the job, but she's not going with him. Soul searching? Wish this bastard would be clear. If he's involved in something illegal, I don't want to know. Heaven help us all if he is and gets caught.> After considering Jack's vagueness, he nodded and feigned a smile. "Well, I hope you call soon to let us know you're coming back. Can't keep you if you mean to go on an endless vacation."

Jack watched the human sign the paper, stand and shook his hand.

"Stay safe, Mr. Towers. You know how dangerous it can be out there. Enjoy the trip."

Getting up to go, Jack replied. "Thank you, sir."

"Tell me, what is that beautiful wife of yours going to do? Do you know what she thinks?"

Smiling kindly, Jack lied. "We've talked about it already. She's not worried. In fact, she thinks it's a great idea."

Jack had yet to tell Ashley anything. Two days passed since the battle by the northwestern shore. He knew it was best to tell her soon but found himself procrastinating. By the time he talked to Grigori, it seemed better if she were told a little later. The sooner she knew he was going, the more of their remaining time would be spoiled. Based on his experience with the gigantic demon, this could be a journey to his death.

Alexander slipped into the house by the back yard and was seated at the dinner table. While Ashley put dinner together, Jack rested by the table conversing with his friend using their animal language.

The Marine growled, "You haven't told her yet? You are a total dirt bag."

Jack growled back, "I'm telling her tonight, so back off. Has it occurred to you what she's going to think when she knows what's going on?"

"I don't have the luxury of knowing what goes through her head. But I do know that waiting until the last minute is wrong."

A short snarl came from Jack as he glared. "Reading her mind is not a luxury; it's punishment. It's taken a long time for me to get good at not doing it by accident."

Alexander made his baby-blue eyes glow brighter as he frowned, showing how strongly he felt on the subject.

"Listen to me, soldier-boy," Jack growled in frustration. "When you got shipped out into the desert to fight with guns and hand grenades, how were those last days at home? How scared was your wife?"

He remained stoic but felt a twinge at the bitter-sweet memories.

Jack sensed his empathy. That softened their animal tones to low, rumbling growls. "I didn't want the last hours together to be ruined. You and I both know there is a chance we might not make it back. No matter what I tell her, she's going to know that. Capiche, Jarhead?"

Alexander huffed and growled softly, "I get it. I still don't like it."

The lovely blonde carried in two serving plates of food, and Jack quickly darted to help. She gave them both an incredulous look. "Boys? You've been at this for a while now. If I'm not supposed to know what you're saying, then it means you're discussing me."

After sniffing the warm, steamy roast before putting it on the table, Jack was reassuring. "It's nothing to worry about. Some wild work stuff came up a few days back, and we were arguing over it." He shot Alexander a hard look as she was distracted taking a seat, warning to play along.

The Marine rolled his eyes.

Jack sat near her, and she gave him an accusing stare. "Really? I can never tell with you, but your friend is a bad liar. Should I ask him if that's what the argument was?"

He acted playfully taken aback. "What? You're calling me a liar? Please, Ashley, cut me some slack."

She saw through the ploy, shaking her head. "Alex, what were you two growling over?"

Jack struggled to hide apprehension as their guest was put on the spot.

Alexander's piece of roast was barely on his plate when the question was put to him. This had happened many times before, and it was nothing new. "Hold on, don't drag me into this. He's your hubby!"

Ashley wore a clever smile. "What's Jack up to? He's been acting weird lately."

Finally, Jack sensed it was time to give in a little. Holding up his hands, he was submissive. "Okay, okay, I'll tell you what's going on. It will have to wait until after dinner."

This shocked her. He rarely ever admitted to telling white lies without putting up a fight. This was pleasant, but made her strangely uneasy.

"You promise?"

His glowing mahogany eyes sparkled sweetly. "Promise and cross my heart."

The unease dissipated as she looked at him.

Their last dinner together was cheery. Everyone shared stories from their day. Alexander had limited access to normal life, hiding away in the forests and foothills of San Bruno Mountain. Every so often, he saw funny goings on with joggers, or dodged being sighted. Ashley worked two jobs, mainly as a photographer for marketing companies. Often there were days she worked for herself, providing stock photos online. It was during these outings when Ashley had more interesting experiences. These stories were the ones Jack cherished the most over dinner. This evening, he soaked in every syllable more diligently, trying to imprint the image of her joyous expressions on his memory.

Once he realized their plates were clear of food and their glasses empty, his heart sank. Ashley started to get up from the table and take the plates, but he stopped her.

"That can wait, sweetheart. Sit a bit longer." Jack gave his friend a serious glance.

The Marine nodded and made a soft growl when he got up to leave, "You shouldn't have waited this long."

Alexander went out to the small back yard. After the door closed, Jack could see Ashley knew this conversation was not going to be pleasant. Both tried hard to appear happy. Nevertheless, the couple looked apprehensive even before Jack spoke.

Worry showed in Ashley's eyes while her face wore a sweet smile. "Are you going to tell me what you two were arguing about?"

Jack's eyes glowed, giving away that he was internally conflicted, in contrast to his warm tone. "Yes, I am."

"Was it really about me, or was it about your late-night adventures?"

He did not want to see her smile disappear. "A bit of both. Alex and I are going on a road trip. All the snarling was over waiting so long to tell you. We need to take off soon."

This did not seem like something to have such a serious, private talk about. Her face showed surprise. "That's all? Where are you going?"

"Far away."

At first Ashley was confused, but then she began to understand. Fear gripped her as she felt sick. Her hands were suddenly clammy and her mouth dry. A metallic taste was on her tongue from the blood rushing away from her face. "Why do you need to go?"

Jack hated to see her this scared. "We had a scuffle with a few monsters ..."

"Don't tell me." She cut him off, realizing he had seen more demons. She still had nightmares from when their first house was demolished by a flying creature she could barely see. Its eyes were red and its body shadowy and elusive to her human sight. The thing almost killed Jack right in front of her. "Do I need to pack?"

"No. You can stay here." The truth was that Jack thought it would not matter. If the demons wanted to kill her to get at him, there was nowhere she could run.

Ashley felt a little calmer, but not much. "For how long?"

He thought about it. "Not sure. I wish I knew."

They fell silent. Ticking clocks in their home measured the tension.

"When do you plan to leave?"

"In the morning. We're taking the other bikes with us."

When she raised her gaze to meet his, her stare was difficult to read. She seemed resolute. "You should go now."

Jack refused to read her mind, certain she was angry and wanted him gone. This put a knot in his throat, choking him while his stomach felt full of worms. The surge of prickly emotions caused his stare to glow brighter than ever, lowering to the cluttered dinner table. He worked his jaw, fighting to regain control of his feelings.

He uttered weakly, "Okay." When he got up slowly from his chair, she stood also.

Ashley made him stop, touching a hand to his cheek to make him look at her. She had a pained smile, but her stare was no longer afraid. There was admiration there. "Your friends need you, baby. If those ... things are back, then I can't keep you."

Jack's heart leaped as she took one of his hands, fitting her fingers between his. She kissed the back of his hand, holding tight. He could tell without telepathy that Ashley did not wish him to go. Seeing it was true made leaving so much harder.

Staring deep into him, she fended off tears with another smile. "I love you, Jack Towers. Before you go, do one more thing for me."

"Anything."

She choked back a sob. "Tell me that you're coming back."

Firmly pulling her into himself, Jack held her close. "I'm coming back. I promise I'm coming back." He felt her shudder, smelling salt on her skin. For a little longer, they held each other. Then it was time to go.

They released each other after exchanging bitter-sweet kisses. Their fingers pulled apart as he backed away for the door. When he stepped out into the dark, Ashley Towers finally dropped to her knees, leaning against the wall to cry.

Standing outside with the door at his back, Jack's supernatural ears heard her. Then the scent of his companion grabbed his attention.

Alexander leaned back against the siding, arms folded. His face was hard but no longer disapproving. His eyes were bright in the gloom between lit windows.

Jack found a way to shut out the pain. Staring back, the warrior made his garments change from casual clothes into biker leathers and a shiny helmet.

Alexander did the same. He nodded to Jack, light rippling over the visor.

The companions vaulted over the high fence and ran into a thicket. They uncovered their hidden bikes, started the powerful engines and sped on their way. Once the tires found smooth pavement, their speed increased. Jack and Alexander rode through the night planning to reach Los Angeles by dawn.

Chapter 4
MERELY PLAYERS

Sunset Boulevard blared with the voices of traffic. Shopping districts filled with milling people, as well as pigeons fluttering to and from the ground, scavenging crumbs dropped beside vendor islands. Bright sunshine breathed more life onto the paved landscape. Humid air vibrated from the voices of person, engines and café music.

Jack and Alexander attempted to track down the leaders of their magical team. After several unsuccessful hours, they resigned to find them at the pier before the concert. The Marine had to keep his helmet on almost everywhere. This was the region where Adwen had broken him out of jail. Of all places on Earth, this was where he needed to go unrecognized. The cop and the fugitive Marine did their best to enjoy the day, finding things to distract themselves from terrible tension and anticipation. Raw steaks from a butcher shop helped. They ate on an isolated patch of beach north of Santa Monica.

When the day began to wane, they rode to an inconspicuous place. They hid their bikes in a tiny fold of a vast beach rock. Summoning the tactical Ghillie camouflage blanket from his collection of magically stored items, Jack tethered the foliage-mimicking blanket over their bikes with Alexander's help. The sun sank toward the deep blue horizon as the pair walked south along the coastal waters.

The Twilight Concert commenced. Hundreds of moving bodies gathered on the beach flocking closer to the pier. A Ferris-wheel covered in lights turned lazily, and a roller coaster rested by the stage scaffolding. Lights shined on performers as massive speakers blasted over the heads of a crowing crowd. Loud, wildly musical minutes passed with every song as bands rotated in and out of the stage light.

Excitement ran high backstage among bands preparing to perform, including the members of Red Lily. Gavin and James were riled. The two cousins talked nonsense, joking and laughing with musicians in other bands. Ted watched from beside Adwen and Oryn, occasionally adding a quip of his own. Theodor noticed that their supernatural singer and lead guitarist had not been themselves lately. In the past, Adwen joined getting hyped alongside Gavin and James. Tonight, she and her knight were quiet. Oryn did not snap at the rowdy boys even once.

As Adwen methodically tuned her guitar, even after it was ready, Ted cleared his throat to get their attention. "What's eating you guys?"

She feigned a giddy smile and it was unconvincing. "Just a bit nervous. We'll be revved once the lights are on us, Teddy."

Oryn looked away, staring into the distance, unreadable.

The young man frowned. "You're crap at lying, sweetheart. You're freaked about something. You two are fearless with stage performance! Why would this one be any different?"

She tried to reassure their band mate. "Don't worry about us. We'll be fine."

The cousins carried on nearby, oblivious, as Ted grimaced. If his weird friends were going to confide in him, they would do so eventually.

"Alright, you two know you can trust me. Talk when you feel like it." He went over to do a triple check on the equipment.

When he was gone, Oryn growled softly, "He and the others should be told."

Adwen was quiet for a moment. "They should. We will tell them after this show. I've been considering how to break it to them – that I want to cancel the rest of the tour."

"That would be wise. However, they would not be pleased. So much of their time and effort has been invested. Their livelihoods are placed in this."

"I know they would put up resistance. Believe me, I know Gavin and James would. Hopefully, Teddy would understand and help them deal with it. If we do decide to shut this down, I don't want to do so without consulting them. That wouldn't be fair."

Oryn frowned. "Nothing is fair. What is important what is right and wrong."

She glared at him, her sapphire eyes glowing hot. "If I can make it fair, I shall. If I am not allowed the chance to try, then I will do what is necessary."

The knight's frown softened when he saw how upset she was beneath the anger. "Of course."

Adwen loved this life with the band. It was exciting, Adrenaline boosting and full of adventure. She did not want that to end, though she knew in her heart that it would sooner than anticipated. What frightened her most was not knowing on what terms it would come to a screeching halt.

Two familiar scents passed under their noses, prompting them to glance around a nearby corner. Dressed in a full leather bike suit, Jack strolled inside smiling, opening his arms wide at the sight of them. This was a pleasant distraction for Adwen and even for Oryn.

"Hey, Adwen! Cujo! Long time no see! Saw the billboards and fliers and had to see if this was for real."

She darted over to share a big hug, ecstatic to see her mouthy companion. Alexander stepped forward, also in a biker disguise, helmet still on. The visor was up, letting his eyes show.

"I'm so glad you saw the ads! Thank you for coming! This is amazing! You guys look great! How has it been?"

Jack scoffed, tossing Oryn's firm gaze a sly smile. "Crazy, but not too crazy. Having a little fun living in San Francisco. Hey, Jarhead? Tell her what we've been up to."

Alexander was not in the mood for swapping stories and irritated that Jack did not get to the point. He would not allow his friend to draw this out as he had done with Ashley. The blond warrior made a rumbling growl inside his helmet, staring grimly.

"We've seen demons."

All four held their breaths. Adwen was frightened by the news and studied the dark grimace forming on Jack's face. Pondering, she gave a solemn sigh and stared at the ground. From behind, she heard Oryn growl softly.

"It appears the tour shall end tonight."

"It definitely looks that way."

Jack rumbled, uncertain, "What are your orders?"

After a long pause, she spoke with confidence. "We see this show through, and I break the bad news to the others. Right after the load-out, I'm taking us to Dargadia. It's time to find out what is going on."

Just then, a pair of very angry security guards came charging in. One was drenched from head to toe in sea water. The other smelled of garbage and beer. Particles from a waste bin stuck to his uniform. Ted joined the small gathering just in time to see them lunge for Jack and Alexander.

"You ruined my radio, punk! Come on! Fun is over. You and your friend are meeting with the cops."

Before there could be a scuffle where the humans would lose, Adwen got their attention. "Hey! Let my friends go. They are here to see me, and I want them here!"

The men paused, and Jack gave them a cocky grin.

"They don't have tickets or passes, and this one assaulted us! They have to go!"

Adwen cocked her head, wearing a curious smile. "How did he do it?" She had a funny feeling Jack was more tactful than the average party crasher.

Both guards stammered and exchanged looks. "I don't know! All we know is he did it. He threw me over the rail into the ocean!"

Jack grinned, folding his arms. "How could you say it was me if you don't know how I did it? Looked to me like you were scared and jumped."

The guard held his tongue as he was on the verge of exploding with rage.

"He dumped a trashcan over me!" the other guard said. "I don't need to call cops; I just want to know how he did it."

Everyone present who knew Jack rolled their eyes or shook their heads.

"These guys, huh?" Jack pointed a thumb at the disheveled men, proud of himself.

Adwen restrained laughter. "If you didn't witness him doing anything, then it wasn't him. Leave my friends alone. I'll keep an eye on them."

The sopping wet guard fumed and stomped off, but the other lingered a moment longer. Very curious and confused, the man frowned. "I know you did it. Tell me how you did that."

Jack shrugged, still smiling.

This disappointed the human, and he walked away, flicking pieces of garbage off his dark uniform.

Ted returned from checking the equipment. Recognizing the eerie glow of the strangers' eyes, he started to laugh. "Adwen! Are these the others you told us about?"

"Yes. This is Jack, and this is Alex."

Oryn folded his arms and frowned. "And best not forget all I've told of the first of them."

"Aw, Cujo, you did miss me! I'm touched."

For an instant, Oryn shot Jack a small, clever smile.

"You boys are welcome to hang with the bands backstage. Don't break anything or you're as good as dead."

"Thanks, Theodor."

The young man stared. "How do you know my name?"

Adwen sighed. "You didn't believe me, did you? The trouble maker can read minds, among other things."

"He's not going to start anything, is he? We can't have any fights back stage."

Jack patted Ted's shoulder as they passed. "It's okay. I'm on my best behavior tonight."

This did not console Ted. "What is his best behavior?"

Adwen and Oryn shared an incredulous glance.

"That's not good, is it?" Ted did not like the lack of an answer.

"Teddy? We need to talk to you and the boys. Something's come up."

"What is it?"

"Demons are back."

Theodor's face turned pale.

"We don't think there's reason to panic yet. Just be aware that the first sign of funny stuff, aside from Jack's behavior, run – run and get as many to follow as you can."

His stomach felt sour, as if he might vomit, and his eyes shifted nervously. "Uh, what kind of funny stuff should I look for?"

Oryn answered. "Lights and electricity acting strangely – flickering, sparking and such."

"If we are nearby, we will alert you. Can you let Gavin and

James know we can't finish the tour?"

"I'll take care of them. Don't worry about us. At least now I know why you guys are off tonight."

"Ted?"

"Yeah?"

She wore a kind smile. "We're sticking around for the performance before we go."

He looked hopeful. "Really?"

Her smile was beaming. "Yes, Teddy. The show must go on."

Ted sighed happily. "That almost makes up for the demon thing."

A shout from the MC reached them. "Red Lily! Where are you guys?! The first band just loaded out! Set up now!"

Ted called to the distressed voice of the Master of Ceremonies, "Grabbing the gear now! We've got it under control!" Turning to his friends, he was flustered. "Totally forgot that was why I came back here. It's time to break a leg."

Oryn was irritated. "That is a rather foolish thing to fail to mention."

"Leave him alone and help rein in the cousins."

His eyes flashed dangerously, and he smiled. "That shall be done."

Thanks to Ted's thoroughness in pre-checking the gear, the rushed pack-in went smoothly. People started clapping and whistling at the sight of them setting up. When Adwen practiced a familiar riff, loud screams erupted.

The crowd's roar dispelled the dark cloud in her mind, bringing a care-free smile. She jammed harder as Gavin tested the drums then James did the same with his black electric bass. Ted began to join in testing the connections on his guitar when Oryn entered. Taking his place by Adwen under the front spotlight, he set the mic stand the way he liked it and addressed the audience. He shed his knightly mannerisms, adopting the guise of a confident showman.

"Good evening, Santa Monica."

Another eruption of clamor answered. It gave him a rush to hear it, making his heart race. "We're grateful you are here for us tonight. How loud do you want it?"

The roar of the crowd was the loudest yet.

He made an ominous chuckle into the mic. "Then let the show begin."

Gavin smashed the drums and pedals like a madman, cuing Adwen to lay into her guitar, making it scream with the sea of people. Then Oryn used a little of his inhuman side, roaring into the microphone. At this, the gathering of humans cheered, witnessing the first song from the band's hit album.

They were animated. Lights flashed many colors, illuminating thousands of waving hands over the pier. Hundreds more on the sandy beach enjoyed what was projected on a big screen. Oryn sang the songs the band wrote together, letting his voice rattle the air with every powerful tone. At times, Adwen caught his attention, dancing while she jammed. He loved to see her that way.

Adwen felt the fire in her body ignite. She had to keep her eyes closed. Her gaze was glowing brighter than the overhead lights. Silvery spirit flesh beneath living skin swirled and churned, playing the guitar as if it were part of her body. White and gold hair furled in the ocean winds, fluttering the folds of her stage costume, driving her crazy with joy. Being near Oryn made the experience more wonderful. At his side, the scene felt complete.

Before the start of the next song, Oryn addressed the crowd again. "Had enough yet?"

A din of voices replied with wild screams.

Oryn had a prepared response, but forgot it. A strange feeling crept up his spine.

Adwen felt the same. Alarmed, she moved closer to Oryn and growled covertly. "Be ready for anything."

He showed her a warm smile. Of course he would be.

Stage lights began to flicker. Big and small sporadic flashes spread across the pier. People in the audience murmured, fidgeting with disobedient phones. The speakers on stage started to squeal when something immensely heavy came down on one corner of the scaffolds. Screeching metal made some people gasp, recoiling as the lights on half the stage burst, showers of sparks falling like dying stars.

Adwen and Oryn looked up in shock and dismay, staring at a set of bright red specs against the sky. Oryn dropped the now useless microphone and stood close to Adwen, who took off her guitar, staring firmly at the winged figure.

A chilling, deep voice spoke, and only the two understood.

To human ears, there was a gurgling garbled series of sounds like a scrambled recording.

"Hah! Heir of the Neverborn. It is good to see you ... again."

Adwen called to the horror-frozen bandmates. "Run! Get out!"

They scrambled off stage and out the back. Oryn bellowed at the crowded pier, "Run, all of you! It is going to attack!"

Many started to scream and run, but even more stayed, trying vainly to make their smart phones record. This frustrated the Holy Hounds and entertained the demon.

The dark figure's broad, leathery wings flicked in anticipation. "Such dumb creatures with their toys. They really should listen to you, Sir Oryn. How does it feel to be made the fool?"

In a flash of violet light, the tall being with long horns summoned a black, serrated sword. A second later, he turned and opened his mouth, belching black and purple flames down at the people. Screams of agony and odors of burning flesh, hair and wood filled the air, spurring the remaining witnesses to flee.

Before the demon spat another plume of fire, Adwen screamed in outrage, summoning her ivory sword. The white and blue fire on the blade blazed to life. She swung up at the monster, sending a fireball at his perch.

Panicked humans on the pier and the beach rushed for the city or farther down the shore. Only the few devices far enough from the demon's disruptive magic were able to record the purple and bluish-white flashes.

Jack and Alexander joined their friends as the demon soared skyward and then swooped low, breathing more fire on the humans and the pier, cutting off escape. Adwen reacted as fast as she could to save a few people, throwing her fire to snuff out the demon's and opening an escape path.

Jack summoned his daggers and sent them flying after the fiend's broad wings. Cutting them off would bring the aerial attacks to an end.

To everyone's dismay, the demon struck the short warrior's daggers with his enormous sword, driving their blades deep into the pier's wooden planking. Laughing sadistically in mirthful guffaws, he landed atop the highest loop of the roller coaster. Out of the reach of the Holy Hounds, the demon goaded them.

"None of you can save the humans. No one in either world shall survive!"

Adwen's enraged voice sounded across the distance: "Who are you? Name yourself!

The monster's head tilted to one side. "You do not recognize me? I suppose not."

Then the demon's face contorted, shifting into one that was very human. Its eyes remained black and red with no pupils at the center. He smiled at the horror on Adwen's and Oryn's faces.

Oryn was the angriest and he roared like a lion. "Jacques!"

A sickening chuckle echoed through the wind. "Not anymore." The human face melted away, revealing the abomination's true form. "I have been given power and a new name. I am Impurus, you little dogs of light."

Adwen snarled and transformed into her true form. Seven feet tall, the armored white hound with the gold emblem barked and snarled. "You will always be Jacques, worm!"

The demon sneered.

In reply, the white Holy Hound swung her fiery sword, lobbing another ball of flame.

Impurus took flight to dodge it, then dived toward them and the burning stage, grinning.

Jack transformed. His tail curled and swished with excitement. As anticipated, the creature believed that Jack's daggers were irretrievably stuck in the planks. With a burst of telekinesis, Jack took hold of the weapons and hurled them straight at the monster.

At the last second, Impurus saw the projectiles and roared in surprise, rolling in midflight. One dagger flew harmlessly past the demon, but the other clipped a hole through a wing membrane. The wound burned and bled, making Impurus wail and gnash pointed teeth. Then it spewed evil fire at the Holy Hounds, making the warriors scatter.

Only Oryn stood his ground, reassuming his elaborate suit of armor. He projected a pale-green light shield. It held the demon's flames back as they engulfed the rest of the collapsing stage. Oryn saw the monster making another pass, and the knight summoned his holy sword. It blocked the jagged demon blade, but the monster's swing was powerful, sending Oryn careening through several layers of backstage set. Oryn controlled the fall and landed on his feet on the other side.

Jack and Alexander stayed by Adwen. They watched the two wings soaring back round. Evil fire encircled the warriors as the stage and pier crumbled to ash, and flames licked at their feet. The twin daggers whirled in the air beside Jack's clawed hands. He panted, jaws twitching in a vicious snarl at the thing in the sky.

A growl from Adwen made the others give pause. "When he comes, get clear. Understand?"

They gave her alarmed looks.

"He's going to breath fire again. Just get out of his way. I'm going to try to finish this here."

Alexander nodded firmly. "Roger."

The flying monster announced his return with a mighty roar, making Alexander and Jack tense up. Adwen stared the fiend down, preparing for the next deadly exchange.

Impurus spat a broad stream of dark fire.

As they were ordered, Jack and Alexander leaped to safer positions.

Adwen made white fire from within her chest pour out of her mouth and eyes, cloaking her armor and white fur coat. She roared, heat radiating in the air before her fangs. Pointing her sword at Impurus, she made dark and pure fire collide. The two intense opposite energies met, exploding and quenching each other, and hurling debris in every direction. Black and white smoke engulfed the pier.

Though blinded, Adwen could hear and sense Impurus. He was still flying straight for her through the cloud. She raised her sword again to block him as he closed in on her.

The instant she could see him, she saw his grin widen more insanely than ever. His sword was not in his hand. When she swung to block him, instead of meeting his sword she glimpsed a ball of black stone in his grasp. Impurus threw it past her sword. She was helpless to stop the evil sphere, glowing with vile symbols.

It struck her neck, unfurling into plated links, burning on contact. Impurus swooped away, laughing manically, leaving her to howl and claw at the thing wrapping around her neck. The weapon burned like demon fire, making it impossible to think.

Oryn found her amid the flames in time to block a slice from Impurus's sword as he swooped again. Jack and Alexander joined in her defense as she began to buckle to her knees.

To escape the demon and the burning pier, Adwen used her sword, pointing off the structure's edge nearby. She commanded the ancient blade to form a portal and a wreath of flames burned reality, tearing a hole for them to leap through. The other side was too dark for even their eyes to see. Regardless, she darted through with the others at her heels.

When the gateway closed, and they vanished, Impurus landed on the pier smiling.

Chapter 5
FALLEN INNOCENTS

In the dark, Adwen wailed and fell to the ground, her body glowing brightly. Jack and Alexander stood by while Oryn pried at the demon's device wrapped around her neck. His hands burned and blistered, making him snarl, but he would not give up. Adwen screamed, her form losing definition amid the glow of her body. Then, to their horror, her form shrank into a blur, dwindling as she cried out, "Oryn! Hurry!"

Desperation drove him mad, and he recalled his sword into his hands. He raised it high and swung down at the black ring. It shattered in an explosion, knocking them back on their heels. Pieces flew like shrapnel, leaving shallow cuts. The demonic device was destroyed.

The bright light around Adwen went out, and she fell quiet at last. Her small white form lay still. Going closer, Oryn knelt low to look her over as he reached out a hand. The warriors felt how weak she had become. Whatever had shrunk her and drained her power also had sapped their strength.

Now a small, frail creature like a nymph, she lay at their feet breathing in small, weak gasps. She had the guise of a child. Her body was pale white. Fine, soft fur covered ears folded on the sides of her small head. Adwen looked as if both her human and Holy Hound forms had merged, forced into a single shape and in a weak state. The magical garments of blue, white and gold were simple wrappings on her meek body and frail limbs. She remained unconscious.

Oryn scooped her up, cradling her. With Adwen's head resting on his shoulder, he felt reassured by the feeling of her breath on his neck. Turning to the stunned faces of Jack and Alexander, he clenched sharp fangs, green eyes hot with rage. "Find a place to take her."

They nodded and darted off in different directions. A few minutes passed as Oryn stood in the dark and mist struggling to contain his anger. Jacques was a powerful demon now. Oryn should have killed the man when he'd had the opportunity. Adwen also could have killed him, sparing everyone from this attack. What a vile creature he had become. No, Jacques had always been vile.

In the quiet of the dark landscape, Jack called out through the fog, "Over here!"

They found him and a deep cave he had discovered behind a boulder. Darting inside, Oryn sat back to rest with Adwen against his chest. His arms held her tightly, providing warmth. The fire in her mystical golden heart was too weak to keep out the cold.

"How long do we wait?"

Oryn looked up to their weary gazes. "Until daybreak or she wakes. We need her to guide us in this place where she has brought us."

Jack was confused. "You don't know this place?"

He stared at the dirty rock wall of their sanctuary. "I do not know it."

Questions ceased. For a time, they rested, but none could sleep except her.

The roguish cop and the tough Marine traded watches at the cave entrance. The night was still except for rare gasps of wind. Without the sun or stars, there was no sense of time or direction. The scents of dust, dirt and ash were prevalent, but they often caught whiffs of a sickly-sweet odor. None of the warriors recognized it.

Jack sat by the entrance searching the gloom for signs of life. When his senses of smell and sight found nothing, his telepathy reached out as far as he could muster. Nothing lay within the range of his abilities – not even the mind of an insect sparked to his. This was more disheartening than being surrounded by tiny demon spawn.

Looking around for any source of light, Jack saw only black and fog. Fed up not being able to tell the time, Jack took a chance and summoned a wristwatch. Not everything brought from one world to another would last long before disintegrating. Unlike his old pistol years ago, the watch worked fine. It ticked; the fine whisker-thin hands moved. According to the watch, it was the dark hours before dawn.

The warrior in his mystical armor fitted the band on one wrist. As he checked the time again, he did a double take. Jack felt sick as he saw the hands spinning in reverse for a moment, freezing up, and then acting normally at random intervals. Either time was broken or the watch was.

He growled and swore under his breath.

"What's wrong?" Alexander asked from nearby.

"I'm getting tired of waiting. Hey, Cujo?"

Oryn growled, "What is it?"

"I want to scout the area. I have a sneaky suspicion that the sun isn't coming. For all we know, Adwen will stay knocked out for a lot longer."

The knight considered the suggestion. "Not smelling or seeing danger does not mean there is none." He took a moment to check her. She remained unconscious, and he sighed ruefully. "Go. Take Alexander with you. Do not stray too far in case we have need."

Leaving the quiet cave for the equally quiet wasteland, Jack turned to his friend. "How are you holding up?"

"Glad we ate before this happened. Other than that, looking forward to killing that Impurus if we find him again."

"I second that motion, Big Dog."

"Got any idea where we are?"

He pondered for a moment, glancing at rocks and boulders through the fog. "Don't know, and I'm afraid to find out. Remember how I'm usually right with these things?"

"Yeah."

"I really don't want to be right this time."

Alexander grimaced. "Then do me a favor: Don't say it. Figured out where we're going yet?"

"Think so." He sniffed the air. "That weird smell."

"It smells good and bad at the same time, like watery, decomposing wood."

The odd smell led the warriors deeper into the foggy doldrums. A few miles later, a subtle breeze started, slowly lifting the black mist. With each passing second, their sight extended farther out. They continued up a gentle hill, and the odor thickened. Weak wind blew it directly into their faces until that was the only scent it carried. Then when they saw something other than rocks, they stopped and stared. A white, oblong mass lay on the ground at the edge of their vision's reach.

Alexander studied the motionless object, summoning his short sword. "What is that?"

With the same morbid curiosity, Jack watched the shape. It never moved, but it was not part of the ground. "I don't sense any thinking. Even undead can think. You going to check it out, or am I?"

The Marine growled, "We both check it."

"Take it easy, Courage. Let's go slow."

Every step closer to the mass brought more clarity. The shape came into focus. At first, they thought it was a deer. When the warriors stepped within a few feet, both stopped, shock taking the breath from their lungs.

As they stared, Jack's insides churned. "Is that what I think it is?"

Alexander knew the least among the team about magical creatures, but he knew what was lying in the dust, and he knew it was something extraordinary. His heart pounded like a drum as he gazed somberly at the dead unicorn.

They walked around the pure white creature. Long black spears protruded from its back. Jack admired the silky, flowing mane. It appeared to have run after being attacked and then laid down to die, legs tightly tucked beneath as if to sleep. Its horn pointed to the ground, head curled under the bowing neck.

The blood of the dead unicorn ran blue like a wild brook on snowy fur. The blood was still fresh. Curious, Jack looked at his watch, and Alexander examined the magical creature more closely. The nearer he approached it, the more the wristwatch hands twitched frantically, never wavering beyond two seconds forward or back. Time virtually stood still over the unicorn's body.

Alexander dipped a finger in the blood and brought it up for them both to smell. It was far more intense than anticipated. They gagged. The blood smelled strongly of pollen, rotten wood and mildew. It was the odor that filled the air, and the intensity almost choked them.

A mild gust rolled through, and the Marine recoiled from the body to shield his nose from the smell, but it only grew more intense. Then he gasped, "Jack, look."

From atop the hill, Jack and Alexander stared at a valley of ashes and dust. The black land was dotted with hundreds of pure white forms as far as the eye could see. A combination of the odor from thousands of dead unicorns and the horror of the sight left Jack stunned.

"There are so many."

Staring at the dark landscaped dotted like a starry night, Alexander nodded. "There are. We should go back. I think we both know where we are."

"Roger that."

Oryn wished Adwen would wake soon. He wanted that even more than he wanted to decapitate the demon to blame. He wondered what had been done to her. There had been battles before when she was weakened, but not like this. When she awoke, perhaps she could explain where she had brought them and why. This land was dark and desolate. The sooner they left it, the better.

Checking her again, Oryn sensed her breathing was more relaxed. She drew from his warmth, resting in his arms. As much as he wanted her to wake, sleep may be what she needed most. She needed strength, but here there was no sunlight to grant it. He wondered, how were they to travel by portal with her so weak?

Shifting against the hard, dusty floor of the cave, he became aware of stones poking upward uncomfortably. As he shifted, his hand brushed against a very smooth, flat stone. It toppled over with a small clink, catching his attention. Picking up the piece, he felt it was heavy for its size. It appeared to be a perfectly carved rectangular tablet. Filth coated the plate, so he rubbed at it with his thumb, finding white marble underneath. Wiping more of the dirt away revealed letters chiseled into the surface and embossed with gold leaf. A man's name, rank and years of life were partially revealed when Oryn dropped the table as if it were hot, eyes wide in shock and disbelief.

He gasped at it laying on the ground, gold letters face up. Then he saw more tablets were strewn about, most broken into tiny fragments. They were all around, some protruding from the cave walls. Large broken marble blocks made up the cave's structure. Horrified, Oryn stole another look at Adwen, and he desperately wished she would awaken and tell him his fears were wrong.

In the stillness he could hear and sense the other Holy Hounds returning. He laid Adwen down on a soft patch of dust where no stones protruded. Then he went out to meet them.

Jack and Alexander saw Oryn standing at the mouth of the cave looking flush, skin pale and clammy. His gaze was to the ground as he braced himself on a white marble boulder. He felt ill and weak, even more so at locking eyes with the others. The knight realized what they had learned, and they could see it in his face.

The short warrior grimaced, reading the knight's thoughts. "I know, Cujo, I know. We both do. Do us a favor and don't go crazy just yet. Get Adwen. This is not a good place to stay."

Still sick to his stomach, Oryn's grief began to drive him to anger. Snarling, he spat, "And go where? If we are to find a safe place, she would know the way to it. We wait until she wakes."

Jack growled, "Don't lose your cool. Not here. Not now. Pull yourself together. You know that this is a very bad place to stay for long. We have no choice but to move on."

Oryn's anger simmered. His eyes glowed brilliantly, and he bared small fangs. "Don't presume to command me, whelp. There is no point in witless wandering with no sense of direction and no desti- nation! I say again, we wait!"

In the darker shadows of the cave, Adwen stirred, waking. It was hard to move at first. Fighting to sit up, she turned over, then pushed herself to her small feet. Barking and growling from the heat- ed argument echoed in her ears as she wobbled, barely able to stand. Adwen braced against rough, filthy walls for balance with tiny hands and clawed fingers, guiding herself to the mouth of the cave.

Finally reaching the outside, she saw her warriors go silent and stare. Then she took in the sight of the land around them. Know- ing they were not far from where the portal opened, Adwen held her breath. Large, blue canine eyes glistened and widened, tears trickling down quivering cheeks. She swayed, knees buckling. Oryn darted over to catch her from falling to the ground. Soft, white ears on silver and gold hair folded, quivering as the rest of her form shuddered. She continued to stare out into the nothingness, horrified.

"Adwen." The knight forgot his anger to console her. "Can you stand on your own?"

She uttered weakly, her voice unchanged by her strange, shrunken shape, "It's gone. Everything is gone. The city, Plexus. The Order. It's all gone." Then she held her eyes closed tight, shaking while more and more tears fell.

They were quiet for a moment, their first question answered. The warriors were indeed on the ground the Order once stood upon. It was completely razed, crushed and swallowed by the earth. If not for the tablets and rubble, there was no other way to recognize the place.

Jack broke the painful pause. "There must be survivors."

The thought finally struck Oryn as well. "Yes, there would have to be. We must seek them out. Adwen, are you strong enough to travel?"

She found the will to subdue her anguished tears, looking up into his face. He looked sad, but more concerned for her. "I'll need you to carry me. I'm still really tired."

Without hesitation, Oryn picked her up, filling with resolve. "In which direction does our path lie?"

Looking around, her sight could not penetrate the fog much farther than anyone else's. She glanced about until a warm spark lit in her heart. She pointed.

"That way. I don't know how far, but we need to go that way."

Oryn flashed a small, encouraging smile. "As you command."

As they set out, the other warriors exchanged looks. They knew what lay ahead in the dark.

Adwen was exhausted. She rested her cheek on Oryn's shoulder, one arm wrapped about his neck. His armor was cool to the touch, while his arms were pleasantly warm. The gentle cadence of Oryn's stride rocked her soothingly along their course.

Eventually, Oryn had no choice but to put more questions to her. "What has happened to you? What did that foul monster do?"

Not raising her head, she gazed out into space. "He tried to destroy me with a trap. Had I not brought us here before taking it off, this might have been avoided. It was an evil seal. I've been bound to the fate of the magic in Dargadia."

None of them were pleased.

Jack mused aloud. "You're still alive, so that must mean that the land isn't totally destroyed."

There was a paused, and Adwen was somber. "The seal was not completed before Oryn destroyed the thing on me. Any longer, and I would not be here. I can feel the magic flow in the earth now. It is weaker than I am."

"How do we fix it?"

"I don't know."

Jack sighed, and Alexander frowned. The burly warrior nudged the shorter, nodding to the top of the hill rising before them. They tensed, wondering what to do to soften the blow.

Clearing his throat failed to get Oryn's attention. Stopping, Jack cleared his throat more loudly. Once the knight perceived, he turned and made and angry frown. Adwen glanced sidelong, her cheek still pressed to the warrior's armor.

Jack struggled to form words, but the sad look Adwen wore made it too difficult to break the news. Grimacing, he gestured to Alexander to tell them what was ahead.

Alexander did not appreciate the passing of the task. Nevertheless, he accepted.

"You should know, you are about to see something over there."

Oryn was baffled, and Adwen became nervous.

Jack managed to speak up. "Just brace yourselves."

Worried by their demeanor, Oryn took her up the hill, where the fog and mist lifted. Oryn held Adwen even tighter at the sight of the first dead unicorn. She stared in pained astonishment. But once they saw the rolling hills covered in numbers beyond count, they were forced to come to a halt. The four stood together in silence.

Adwen could not take any more. She buried her face in Oryn's neck and fought the urge to sob. While they continued, her eyes remained closed or she looked away from the pale bodies.

Her warriors tried not to pay too much attention to the unicorns or the nauseating scent of their blood. Even Jack could not find the will to comment. His mental barriers were weakened by distress, letting his friend's emotions spill into his own. This drowned the psychic warrior in so many thoughts that it was difficult to discern which were his own. Jack spent the dreary march trying to consolidate the streams of words and images.

Alexander saw that Jack was struggling, his face drawn and eyes dilating wildly. The Marine placed a hand on his short friend's shoulder, momentarily snapping him out of it.

Jack forced a weak smile. "Thanks, Ol' Yeller."

"No problem."

Adwen gazed at Oryn's armor and listened to their footfalls on soft ash. "We need to get everyone back together. Tamis is still alive somewhere."

The knight nodded. "Agreed."

This fresh conversation alleviated Jack. "I hope the kid is okay."

Alexander added, "Tamis is young, but he's as tough as the rest of us. He's fine."

Adwen felt the same. "The demons were smart. They knew better than to take him down. It would have alerted us and spoiled the trap. We would have come back here sooner, interrupting whatever they've done."

Each of them began to sense a strange tingling in the air like static electricity.

Oryn growled. "Or what they are still doing. Look there."

Near the edge of the landscape of dead unicorns, the remnants of a village stood. In the center, a tall dark pillar pointed at the veiled sky. The gloom hung lower over the pitch-black monolith. They skirted around, avoiding the sensation given off by the landmark.

"What is that?" Alexander growled, unsure whether they were at a safe distance.

Adwen scowled. "It's made by the demons. It might be sustaining the darkness like a conductor."

Jack scoffed. "An evil version of a tesla coil. Great. How long do we wait to attack it?"

Learning something new gave Adwen some resolve. "Let me think about that. It will be defended. We are in no condition to storm the town yet. I think we are getting close to where we need to be."

Ahead they found a forest with trees drained of color, leafless and cracked. The black mist thickened in the deadwood. Oryn and Adwen remained at the front, leading the way, while Jack and Alexander watched their backs. Gnarled oaks provided little comfort with the cover they brought. More than ever, the Holy Hounds felt wary.

Oryn's bright green eyes scanned for any movement. Rustling dried leaves nearby made him and the others freeze. Clutching Adwen, he may need to fight one-handed. The three summoned sharp blades and listened for whatever approached.

A bulky silhouette the size of a horse trotted briskly. A tiny closed lantern hung on one side, light peeking through cracks in the rickety frame. When the form stopped, there was silence. Then a happy, booming bark came as the rusty brown creature bounded with two small riders on his back.

"Adwen! Sir Oryn! Jack and Alex! You've come back!"

They instantly recognized the voice of their fifth companion.

"Tamis!" Adwen called out, relieved to hear him again after so long. But as he came closer, everyone was shocked at what they saw.

The rusty brown Holy Hound had a black stone ring around his neck covered in demon runes. His body was that of a gigantic hound with no armor other than his fur. Their youngest fellow warrior panted, pleased to see them. The two humans astride him were short and wore flat masks painted with demon blood. Primitive cowhide leather armor also had demon blood paint to cover their human scents.

Tamis's animal speech was more hushed as he came near. "I knew you would come soon. I should have been quieter in my greeting. Quick, this way."

Chapter 6
LIGHT IN THE DARK

Tamis led the Holy Hounds into denser deadwood and then across a deep river. On the other side they continued onward, and Oryn realized where they were. Most of the kingdom's northern border was lined by high cliffs. Near one of the waterfalls from the old Elf wood far above, a cave mouth sat hidden behind natural folds of the earth. Human and other scents were strong upon entering.

It was quiet and dark in the tunnel. Farther into upper passages, a warm glow from fires and candles lit the way, and they heard murmurs and hushed conversations.

Tamis barked before entering the first chamber, filled with humans and gargoyles. "We've returned. I have a great surprise this time."

The gargoyles understood his words and looked up. The men and women did not understand, but could tell by his bark that Tamis was happy. When Sir Oryn came in with Adwen and the others, everyone inside who saw gasped and or cheered. They kept their voices low, but could not contain their excitement.

A man in the back called out, "The Holy Hounds have come! Get the captain! He will need to know."

Some shushed, urging him to whisper.

At last, the two young riders on Tamis's back climbed down and removed their masks. Two beaming smiles appeared from behind the carved wood. Now that they could see who they had brought to the hideout, the young men were thrilled.

Adwen recognized their scents and more adult features. Now teenagers, she was relieved to see her two first friends from the magical world. "Colin! Remy!"

Remy chuckled, while his older cousin was still as cautious as ever. He shushed Adwen respectfully. "Everyone must keep their voices down. This place is safe, but too much happiness spoken so loudly can help them find us. We are so very glad to see you, Adwen. Thank you for coming back."

Her heart warmed at finding the two boys and hearing Colin's words.

Remy spoke up, confused. "What's happened to you, Adwen? Did they you get you like they got Tamis?"

She and her companions looked to their youngest warrior, trapped in simple animal form.

"Tamis?"

The rusty brown hound hung his head, sullen. "It is a very long story, Lady Adwen. It is not pleasant. We will speak of it soon."

Before any could press him further, two men and a gargoyle parted the gathering crowd. The men wore scratched, unpolished knight armor with dusty crimson capes. The eldest of the dark-haired men gasped at seeing the Holy Hounds with his own eyes. The other smiled, a new scar on the side of his mouth, disfiguring a delighted smile. A grim looking gargoyle stood alongside with tattered wings flicking, showing reserved pleasure at seeing the warriors.

Oryn nodded to the knights, realizing they were the last few surviving from the Order. To his added relief, he knew them.

Raglan welcomed them warmly. He appeared tired yet alert. "Thank you, Tame One, for finding us. I wish this meeting was under better circumstances, but we need to speak with you all."

Remy piped up. "Can't we come?"

Dynic shook his head, smiling at the bold boy. "Not this time, lad. Another time."

The knights and the gargoyle led them deeper into the overlook sanctuary. Many watched the companions make their way to the upper levels in the cliff. Several chambers they passed held weapons where gold rings and chains were melted to coat silver-steel blades. It was the only way they could effectively fight the demons. Another opening led to a ledge beside the waterfalls. To Adwen's and the other's surprise, they were just above the black mist. Stars winked above the natural blanket of clouds. A subtle, pale glow emanated from the eastern horizon.

Oryn saw it right way and was glad. "Dawn."

Raglan shook his head. "We have not seen a dawn in weeks."

The Holy Hounds stared in disbelief.

"Time is twisted around the demon's desires." Dynic scowled. "The sky over our land is cursed. We only glimpse the edges of sunrise and a glimmer of sunset, but the sun never shines. The darkest night sky is all we see."

Adwen was dismayed. "How long has this been happening?"

The two knight brothers exchanged glances.

Raglan frowned. "The demons came weeks ago."

Dynic answered as well. "Perhaps the better part of three months. It has been blasted difficult to keep track of the time."

Raglan rolled his eyes. "We cannot really be sure, but it has been too long."

The gargoyle finally spoke up. His rough voice rumbled, "Why are we not discussing the cause rather than the result? Tell them what they need to know."

Adwen needed to know: "What happened at the Order?"

Raglan and Dynic became very gloomy. The gargoyle grimaced.

She was desperate to know. "Where is Sir Peregrine? Core? Malik the Phoenix? Balefire and the Order of Mages?"

Raglan sighed, dreading that he was going to relive the events. "You tell them, Geoden. You among us have enough nerve to tell it again."

The gargoyle nodded. "Malik flew away not long after your departure three years ago. He said nothing, taking wing and vanishing. We among the clan thought it was an omen. As for Core, he was the first to die."

This shocked Adwen. "He's more spirit than living or undead. How?"

"A few survivors from Tanoaks brought word that a madman had come. He walked into the temple there to slit his own throat. The more his blood fell to the ground, the more he laughed, and the more he cut himself, turning him into an abomination with wings. Whatever he did fouled the ground, souring the stones, reducing the temple to rubble. The monster he became then flew straight for the Order."

Dynic rubbed the side of his head, marred by scars from demon claws. "That happened in the same hour that the fortress started to shudder at its foundations."

Geoden nodded. "The magic seal that the fortress was built upon broke. The last of the three temples was destroyed, and so was the seal. Core must have been bound to the seal and the fortress. He shattered and faded. His dying words were for all to run for their lives. The whole time the earth quaked and groaned. The clan felt the pain it bore. Balefire and the Elders met straightaway. They argued. During their meeting the winged demon came with a flying army. Many mages stayed to fight, while Arch Mage Balefire took the rest to find the king in Deleon and warn him."

Jack interrupted, "What about Sir Peregrine?"

Ruefully, Raglan answered, "He sent us and other knights to try to lead as many people as possible away to safety. The captain was inside when the earth swallowed the fortress and the city."

The news devastated the warriors. Peregrine was a strong, dear friend, and many good people died with him.

"Thankfully, one of the mages knew of this place in the cliffs."

Another man's voice called as he joined the meeting, "And most other survivors are far north taking refuge in Jenkirk, where the sun yet shines, Lady Adwen."

Virgil joined them with a new walnut and oak crossbow on his back.

"You're late, ranger." The gargoyle showed a rare smile.

"Yes, yes, of course I am." Lighting his pipe, the skilled hunter puffed repeatedly until smoke was drawn at last. "My friendship with the once-secret shapeshifters in the north has paid off. They helped me lead a few hundred refugees to safety."

"That safety can't last if the demons aren't thwarted." Raglan shook his head. "Lest we forget the pillars of black."

"What happened in Deleon?" Adwen pleaded. "King Lorvan, Princess Eyrie and Toth? Where did they go? Did they make it to Jenkirk with the refugees?"

The three men and the gargoyle turned to look at Tamis, trapped in bestial form.

He sat heavily on his haunches, ears hanging low as he whimpered, "I was there."

"What happened?" Adwen pleaded.

His stare remained downcast at the stone floor. "The Arch Mage and the last of his Order arrived minutes before the demon assault. The city was lost in the blink of an eye. Balefire, Toth and the mages were commanded to take the princess out a secret passage and escape. I was commanded the same. I refused. I stayed to fight in the throne room. We remained to buy the others more time to flee." Then Tamis fell silent.

Her face was full of fearful anticipation. "And?"

Tamis raised his head, anger and pain in his stare. He growled, "The winged demon Impurus broke through the barricade with one swing of his sword. Those who guarded the door were killed immediately. King Lorvan used some of his fire magic, but it did no good. Fire did not hurt the monster. It might as well have been water to bathe him. And then ... Impurus breathed fire that was not within the king's power to wield. He burned. There weren't even ashes left."

Adwen clenched her little fangs in anger. "Vile bastard."

"He had knocked me aside like a child. By the time I could get up, the king was gone. When I tried to avenge him, the monster threw something. It became this ring." Tamis turned his head to try to see the black stone object fused to his skin. "It made my bow vanish as if I had dispelled it myself. Then he hit me over the head. When I woke I was locked in a cage of demon steel."

Recalling horrible events, their companion hung his head again. "They toyed with me. For days on end, powerful fiends like enormous statues came, drawing runes on the ring. Each time they did, I felt pain that I cannot describe. Sometimes something would happen to me along with the pain. After many times, I realized that they were experimenting. They were trying to find out how to make the ring do something. I do not know what."

Adwen knew. "They wanted to do this to me." The leaders of the sanctuary stared. "Impurus put a ring like that on me to bind me to the magic of the land. I almost vanished into nothingness. Oryn was able to break it before the seal could finish its work. How did you escape? They didn't let you go, did they?"

"Of course not." He huffed gruffly. "A mage servant in the castle managed to hide from the demons. She was a ... dear friend, Elena." Pained whimpers wracked Tamis, and he sobbed for a moment. "She picked my lock and set me free. We took another secret passage to get out. Demons were searching for me everywhere. She didn't make it. Elena is gone."

Oryn sympathized, but prompted him amid the creature sobs. "The princess. Where were they going with her?"

The big hound shook his head. "I cannot know. Perhaps the docks. That was where the passage they took led. It was the most secret passage in the whole castle."

"This is all we know regarding the Princess Eyrie," Geoden said. "Ever since the ranger took those unable to fight to the north, everyone here has searched for survivors, salvageable goods and more information. We knew you would come and make good use of any information."

Raglan smiled, a happy thought warming his heart. "Those boys, Colin and Remy, work well with Sir Tamis. They devised their own stealthy armor and used slingshots with pebbles coated in gold to put out demon eyes. They have gathered the bulk of our knowledge. Perfect scouts, those two."

Adwen nodded, smiling. "So, tell me about the black pillars. How many are there?"

"The boys have found three thus far. If there are more, they are beyond the range I am willing to allow them to travel. The first pillar was made shortly after the deaths of the unicorns. They are not all alike. Some are smaller. The newest is likely the one you saw. However, the first one created is in the middle of the plains. Stay well away from there."

Tamis growled, remembering the place. "The first of the black stones pointing at the sky is the largest we've found. There are too many powerful demons gathered there at its foundation. To attack that place in our condition would be futile."

Alexander spoke at last. "Do you know how to destroy the pillars?"

"Light," Raglan said. "The boys and I were able to sneak up close to the smallest pillar, which is nearby. It is also the newest and least guarded. When we shined a lantern to the surface, it cracked. Unfortunately, we were forced to run for our lives. Damaging the thing alerted every demon in the area to our presence."

Dynic was eager to finish the meeting and take the fight to the monsters. "When do you intend to attack? The dark mist is growing higher and reaching outward. Virgil has told us that the black fog now stretches far into the northern passes."

Oryn growled and spoke so the knight could understand: "Be patient. Adwen is in a very vulnerable state. We must make an effective plan before taking any risks."

Adwen tried to quell her protector and the human. "Light is clearly the key. We can begin work on a plan of attack. Does everyone agree?"

All nodded in answer.

"Good. I think you are right; the nearest pillar is the one we strike first. Let's form a plan to get me in close to use my light."

Colin and Remy rode atop Tamis's back leading Adwen and fifteen brave humans. A few knights joined them. Dynic was the only leader of the resistance who came, as per Adwen's request. Oryn agreed with her notion to avoid risking too many lives so soon. If this battle went badly, there was no telling who would make it back alive.

Three tiny lanterns were brought, one for the teenage scouts riding Tamis, and the remaining two for Dynic's small platoon. The skilled fighters were well practiced by now at facing demons in the dark. The knights trained as many as possible on how to use the breathing ritual for focus.

Tamis came to a stop and crouched low at the edge of the seemingly empty town. Remy fluttered the lantern shutter, signaling for the company to halt. They had arrived.

In the town itself, tiny green balls of light faded in and out, illuminating portions of the streets and alleys. Far more of the green wisps lingered about the pillar like ominous fireflies. The tingling sensation in the air put everyone on edge.

Dynic blinked his lantern to his lieutenant, who blinked back and took several fighters and mages around the south side. The scarred knight smiled and saluted Adwen before taking the rest around the north to await the signal from the scouts. A few minutes after Adwen and her warriors saw the adult humans go to their positions, it was their time to move.

Tamis led the way, his paws soundless on dust and dirt. Oryn, Jack and Alexander were equally silent entering the lifeless town. Adwen clung to Oryn as he carried her, both scanning for enemies when not looking at the tall pillar. The scent of demons thickened, making their spines tingle. Getting close to the town center, where an old market place used to be, they had to stop.

Wretches prowled about, four huge spikes on their backs with waving tendrils. The large bear-sized creatures were everywhere. They patrolled the perimeter of the evil monolith. Now that they were closer, the Holy Hounds could see demon runes rippling with a purple glow.

Colin looked to one side, blinking his lantern, careful not to let the demons see it. Through the narrow gap between crumbling buildings, Dynic's lantern flickered back. When he looked the other way and repeated, the second team responded. Everyone was in position. Now was the time for the distraction.

Both teams brought a small rag rolled and stuffed into a silver canister. Each team exposed their cloth bait, wetted with human blood, and threw their canisters as far into the streets as they could. Right away, there was hissing at the sound of silver metal rattling against cobbled stones. Then the scent of blood made every demon raise its head to sniff.

Adwen and the others watched as the demons sniffed, beginning to salivate. Then they darted off, bounding hungrily toward the two bait canisters. As soon as the last of them followed, Tamis and the boys took the warriors straight for the pillar. Getting close, the tingling in the air became a steady low hum.

When Oryn moved to take Adwen closer, he gestured that everyone get back. They took several steps away from the demon monument and let the pair approach it. Adwen mustered what little light was left inside her, making her heart glow in her chest. Holding up a tiny hand, golden threads of light reached up from her palm, swaying in the air. About to put the energy to the surface of the black pillar, she paused to whisper.

"Be ready to run. A lot of rock is about to come crashing down."

He smiled slyly. "And demons are about to become quite angry."

She put her hand to the stone, but there was some resistance. A force pushed back at Adwen, keeping her from touching it. A moment later, the force gave way, and the tendrils of light on her hand penetrated the black surface. Dark stone rippled like water, then loud cracking filled their ears. Pebbles started to fall. Runes on the pillar vanished, as wailing demon cries from the north and south of the town echoed to their ears.

Dynic's teams attacked the demons right away as the pillar started to fall, helping Adwen and her companions escape. Tamis bore the boys along at a reckless speed, bounding wildly with the others on his tail. A great thundering explosion shook the air. When the pillar blew, shards rained down, and the tingling feeling disappeared, as did demon battle cries. The wretches that did not die ran, allowing the humans to escape.

No lives were lost in the skirmish. Tamis waited for Dynic's forces to find them, then led the proud teams back to the sanctuary.

Colin and Remy slid from Tamis's back to the cave floor among those who had stayed behind. The resistance members clamored to find out what had happened from Dynic and Adwen. While the boys hopped up and down jubilantly, giggling with excitement, the knight removed his helm and beamed. Then everyone knew the mission was a success. Chatter erupted all around, echoing throughout the tunnels.

"Miss Adwen! You did it! I knew you would!" Remy crowed.

Colin tried to control his cousin. "Hush! Not so loud."

The boy was astonished at the reaction. "You were there. Why don't you let me make a little noise for once? The demons are not so close to the sanctuary now. We're safer."

"Better to be even safer. Adwen, are you alright?"

In Oryn's arms, she was the only one present not celebrating. Her expression was one of deep contemplation. Addressing Colin, she put on a sweet smile. "I'm doing fine. Just tired."

Dynic waved to his brother across the jovial crowd, then turned to Adwen and her warriors. "We shall meet at the overlook to discuss what happened."

She nodded and smiled at the boys again. "A little celebrating shouldn't take long."

They returned the look with plenty of enthusiasm.

After wading through many cheerful people and satisfied gargoyles, they arrived at the place where they could see over the darkness. Together in the airy overlook, Raglan, Dynic, Geoden and Virgil bowed their heads as Oryn brought Adwen near. A table and chairs were set for the meeting. The knight sat with her across from a very proud Raglan.

"My brother tells me that the dark pillar was destroyed. We have never had such a victory. But I must hear from you, Tame One. What exactly happened?"

"The diversion drew away the demons, just as planned." She paused, frowning. "There was power in the pillar. It pushed back at my light. I was barely able to break the thing."

Oryn and her other warriors frowned.

However, Dynic spoke up still smiling. "But you did break it. The pillar blew into a thousand pieces!"

She was about to reply, but Jack gasped and pointed beyond the southwest corner of the cliff. The edge of the sky began to turn pale.

Geoden shook his head ruefully. "Have you forgotten that dawn cannot shine?"

Then Virgil, puffing on his pipe, gave the glow a more calculating eye. "It has not been this bright here in a long while."

Everyone began to look. Leaving the table for the ledge, Oryn set Adwen down on her own feet so she could see for herself.

She felt warmth in her chest as the light grew. The magic in the land quickened. Then she gasped, and her body began to shine a blinding white until she could not be seen. Men and gargoyle forgot the sunrise to shield their eyes from the light radiating from Adwen. When the blinding light faded away, they smiled and almost began to laugh.

Adwen had reclaimed her elf-like form. Her garments remained simple wrappings of magical cloth. She flexed her hands, taking a deep breath. Still weak, Adwen was no stronger than an average human girl. Happy to gain some strength, she summoned the fiery sword into her grasp. The weapon bound to her appeared in her hands, blue flames licking along the edges. Since she was so weak the sword was smaller. It appeared to be a normal blade, if not for the supernatural fire.

Then the sunrise receded, and night returned. The sword vanished from Adwen's hands, making her flinch in surprise at the suddenness. It was a great disappointment to be unable to wield her sword except at dawn, but regaining her shape was a relief.

Oryn drew close to share an embrace.

A loud throat-clearing by the ranger brought attention back

to the meeting. "Now that you've gotten a bit stronger and taken a moment to relish it, it is time to discuss tactics, Lady Adwen."

They released each other, and she claimed the chair at the table. Fingers laced before her, she locked eyes with the human knight. "I am still rather weak, just so you're aware, Sir Raglan. Where were we?"

"Before that very welcome interruption from the sun, we were about to decide how to proceed. The nearest dark pillar is destroyed. How soon would you be willing to take down another?"

"Ah," she replied. She had been thinking very hard about this. A feeling in her heart told her what was necessary. "Soon, but not just yet. A few days from now."

Raglan frowned, and Dynic was aghast, speaking up yet again. "What? Why a few days?"

His older brother remained calm. "Steady, brother."

Dynic was less than steady as he turned red in the face, placing a hand on the table, glaring at Adwen and the Holy Hounds.

"We have been waiting months."

She was somber, but the others were angry at the human, growling and snarling.

"You were not here. None but Tamis was here for the entirety of this nightmare. When there is finally a means to fight for our land, you tell us to wait?"

Oryn glowered. "Mind yourself, Dynic."

"We are starving! The demons hunt us; they never sleep. I for one am not going to sit around for more than one day before taking the fight to them again!"

Adwen barked and spoke in unison, "Enough!"

The scarred knight scowled, "If you won't fight tonight, I'll take a lit candle to the next damned pillar alone if I have to."

"They are on to us now," she replied. "Now they know I am not destroyed. Attacking the next pillar too soon would be suicide. They weren't ready for us last night. Next time will be much more dangerous, especially for you and everyone in the sanctuary."

Raising a hand to prevent Dynic form speaking, Raglan answered, "What is your proposal exactly?"

"Leave; everyone go to Jenkirk."

There was quiet, while he thought then frowned. "I'm sorry. My brother and I are in an agreement: With or without your help, we will attack the next pillar after sunset."

Geoden chided the knights, "It is a very foolish thing to do, ignoring the guidance of the Heir of Darien."

Virgil stepped forward calmly while cleaning out his pipe. "You'd better listen to her."

"Go shove some dirt in that filthy pipe, ranger!"

"Enough, Dynic!" Raglan sighed heavily, shaking his head. "I am in a very hard position, Lady Adwen."

She remained silent considering his tired eyes.

"Everyone here has stayed by choice. The ranger leads some through the passes when they wish to go; that is his purpose here. Not one has asked to go in a month. Everyone, me included, cannot resign to retreat, not after everything we've sacrificed. Too much of our will to live has been invested into this fight."

Her expression became firm and calculating. "So, for pride, you would needlessly sacrifice other lives along with your own?"

Raglan flinched and frowned, a startled look on his face.

"What about the lives of your scouts?" she continued. "I've seen in your heart. You made a promise to Domus as he died. You would break that promise now?"

Both knight brothers were taken aback but would not change their minds.

Torn and frustrated, Raglan could not concede. "I am sorry, Tame One. I truly am. If you so choose to join in the coming battle, you are welcome. Bring word to me before the sun's dying light if you change your mind."

Raglan stood and turned to leave with Dynic.

As they were about to reach the passage threshold, Oryn shouted at their backs. "You fools! You trade pride for shame! The blood of those who perish will be on your hands this night, not the demons!"

They walked out as if they had not heard, and Adwen shushed Oryn. "They know. Let them go. We need to think."

"Will you let them go alone, Tame One?"

She looked up into the face of the gargoyle. He rarely showed strong expressions, but his gaze was full of pure sorrow. His kind were born as children of the earth, sworn guardians of human kind.

"What will you do?"

Virgil patted the shoulder of his winged friend. "Show a little faith in her yet. Her task is no different than your own."

Giving them a thankful smile for supporting her, Adwen shook her head. "This is hard. The worst part is that my choice is made for me. We have to go."

Jack scoffed, "And get you killed? Get everyone killed?"

She frowned. "There are people and gargoyles here that must be protected. Many of them will be the first of a new Order if we put a stop to the demon invasion."

"Well," Jack said, "they're off to a great start, aren't they?"

She raised an eyebrow. "What about how you started out?"

Jack hesitated before replying, "Good point."

"We'll wait a little before telling Raglan or Dynic. I need time to think. And so do they."

Adwen's company, Virgil and Geoden waited for uncounted hours to see if the knight brothers would come to their senses. When the brothers formulated a plan, and assumed most wanted to take part, they encountered hesitance. Some gargoyles convinced others to stay, sharing that this attack was against the counsel of the heir. Others refused to listen and instead focused on sharpening blades of pure gold as mages practiced their varied talents.

Virgil volunteered to act as envoy for Adwen, telling Raglan that she and her warriors would join the coming battle if they could not talk the fighters out of it. Oryn took Jack and Alexander to join Geoden in talking with the fighters, trying to convince more to stay behind. They could not idly wait for sunset.

Sitting on the overlook, Adwen watched the near stagnant mist under the cursed sky. Tamis sat with her, sharing thoughts between moments of quiet.

"I believe those stars to be real," Tamis said while lying on the floor beside Adwen and gazing skyward. "They must be. They move as true stars should. I've watched them for hours when not collecting supplies with the boys."

A faint smile came to Adwen. "That's encouraging to know. It would be sad if those stars weren't real. They're beautiful."

He whimpered. "I don't want to take them out to this fight, Adwen. I can barely stand it. This is foolishness."

Patting the thick fur on his shoulder, she felt the same. "They would go even if you stayed here. I really do wish I could make them all change their minds."

Their noses caught the scent of familiar humans. Turning their heads, she smiled sweetly, and Tamis gave a baleful look at Colin and Remy.

The boys proudly approached, wearing their hide armor, painted with demon's blood. As they approached, they bowed their heads to her.

Colin was concerned at finding her here. "Adwen? We came to fetch Tamis. What are you up here for? Everyone is getting ready. I thought you agreed to come destroy another pillar?"

No longer pretending to be happy, she turned dismal. "I told Sir Raglan and Sir Dynic that they should not do this. At least not this soon. Now is not the time to attack again."

Remy frowned. "So they won't listen to you?" He shook his head. "We are the best at going undetected. If we do not go, then someone else would have to do our part. They'd be found long before giving the signal."

"I don't like the sound of you not wanting to go, Adwen." Colin agreed. "But Remy is right. Are you only coming along for the same reason? No one else could do the same task you can?"

After considering it, she was grim. "No."

Even Tamis was curious as to her answer.

"I have a job to do, and it is not to follow orders from mortals. I'm here to do what the Light Spirits guide me to do. They guide me with feelings and visions. The feelings I have now are that this mission is foolish and will cost many lives. But I also feel that I must go and bring my warriors to save as many as possible. You both are sweet, strong boys who are almost men. Your real calling hasn't come yet. This is not it for you."

Colin and Remy frowned. Then Colin spoke again, his voice calm and consoling. "We're not afraid to die, Adwen."

"Death is not what we are afraid of," Remy said. "We're afraid of how others are hurt by senseless killing. So many have died. They don't hurt anymore after they die. It's everyone else who hurts. Because my cousin and I are fighting too, the others don't hurt so much. The knights, fighters, mages and gargoyles are stronger somehow with us around."

"You see, Adwen?" Colin tried to explain. "We have to go because we know how important we are."

Tears swelled in Adwen's eyes. "But what if something happens to one or both of you? What then?"

The cousins exchanged somber glances. "Don't know," Colin replied. "Trying not to think about it."

"If most of the others refused to go, we would stay behind," Remy said. "We're really sorry, Adwen."

Their bravery and selflessness warmed and broke her heart. Getting to her feet, she pulled them close, hugging them tightly. They embraced her, and she heard Remy speak near her ear.

"It's going to be okay, Adwen. You'll see."

She kissed both their heads, saying a silent blessing over them for protection. Inside, she begged the Light Spirits to keep them safe this night.

Upon paws the size of dinner plates, Tamis leaned his head over her shoulder, joining the embrace. His warm neck was soft and comforting against her skin. When they all pulled apart, he rumbled to her with a look of determination. "If anything goes wrong, I'll run them back to the sanctuary faster than I've ever run before."

She wiped her tears away, smiling back at the giant rust-colored creature. "Thank you, Tamis. I know you would."

"It's sunset," called Virgil from the tunnel. "Ah, Lady Adwen. I was looking everywhere for you. You are needed down by the entrance. I'm afraid you'll have to move quickly. Sir Oryn appears to be killing Sir Dynic."

Adwen heaved a heavy sigh, groaning, "Oh no."

Chaos filled the last chamber before the exit tunnel. Booming gargoyle shouts echoed. Men and women yelled over one another as they clamored around Oryn and the two knights. The eyes of Adwen's most loyal servant burned, fangs clenched as he snarled, slamming Dynic's back to the stone wall again and again. No matter how hard the human brothers tried, they could not overpower Oryn. Even weakened, Oryn was far too strong.

Jack barked over clamor, "Calm down, Cujo! Get a grip!"

"I have a firm grip, and it shall stay that way!" He snarled at Dynic, who glared back with equal intensity.

Raglan pried at the inhuman grasp on his brother's armor. "Release him, Sir Oryn! Control yourself before you kill him! Let go of Sir Dynic!"

Oryn bellowed, mingling growls with speech, "I think not! I've half a mind to bite his foolhardy head off for his insolence!"

Defiant as ever, Dynic sneered, "Then I have thought wrong of you all these years; becoming what you are hasn't changed you at all. You've gone from being a cruel executioner to a wild brute of a mongrel."

With supernatural speed, the enraged Holy Hound back-handed the knight. Gashes from the back of Oryn's plated fingers left three new marks on the man's face, matching the scars on the other side. Dynic gasped and shouted in pain, writhing in his suit of silver-steel armor.

As angry as he was, Oryn maintained enough control to hold back and prevent a lethal blow. Snarling, he bellowed as the agitation of the onlookers overflowed. "A brute mongrel? An angry animal would not be as merciful as I have just been. You bleed, fool! You bleed, and I will not heal you with my magic. There shall be no battle for you. The demons can smell a single drop from miles away!"

Adwen's supernatural voice called over everyone, "Stop this!"

The din instantly quieted to a few scattered whispers. They stared and made way, letting Adwen through to Oryn, who still held Dynic to the cave wall. She walked briskly followed by Tamis and the two scouts.

"What do you think you are doing? Fix his face and leave him alone."

Oryn refused. "He defies you and insults me. The first offense alone deserves the new scars I've given him."

Adwen's eyes glowed bright and unblinking. She seized control of Oryn's physical movement. A gasp of surprise escaped Oryn, and his glare became a stunned stare. Against his will, his hands shuddered and opened, dropping Dynic. Then he growled and began to glare once more, his body forced to kneel. His dangerous rumbling sounds echoed in the cave.

Raglan checked his brother to see if the cuts were deep. They were only on the skin, leaving flesh and bone unharmed. "Get a rag and some water! Clean his wounds." A mage rushed off, and Raglan stood, storming to Oryn.

Adwen stood between them, blocking his path.

"Please, Lady Adwen. Let me pass."

She glared, her voice stern. "Depends on what you intend to do to him."

The human knight remained calm, thinking before replying, "I want a word, nothing more. May I please speak to him directly, Good Lady?"

She knew he was honest. Stepping aside, she watched.

He grimaced down at the luminous glare of Sir Oryn Conrad, contemplating what had just occurred. Then he spoke with a tone of remorse. "Forgive my brother if you can, Sir Oryn. You know very well how men can become in times of hunger and desperation. We say things we should not and would otherwise never wish to say in a lifetime. Will you not heal his wounds?"

Oryn snarled, then spoke, his voice cold as ice and just as cutting. "I will not. The price for his words and for his weakness to hunger and fear shall be this: He will bear the scars and not join the battle. That is punishment enough to my taste. And when it is over, he will count those who return alive – and those who do not."

There was silence in the cave apart from Oryn's growls and Dynic's labored breathing and groans. Turning to his brother, he sighed. "I'm sorry to say that I agree with Sir Oryn's sentiments. Your head is not clear. Even if you were not bleeding, you are a risk on the battlefield. Stay here and prepare to receive any wounded. There are sure to be some who return in dire need."

Dynic was desperate. "Brother? You deny me the fight? You cannot be serious!"

"I am quite serious. You have fresh injuries. The ambush would fail."

Angry, and his pride as wounded as his cheek, the younger knight bowed his head, teeth clenched. He could never go against his brother's station as captain.

At last, Adwen let Oryn stand and she spoke. "Sunset has passed. Do you still want to do this? This is your last chance to listen to me."

Raglan faced her. "You are the heir of Darien. You carry light that cannot be doused by water or wind. If light is all that is needed, then I intend to fight. I believe you are strong enough to break this next pillar."

She frowned. "Then we had better go. It's time."

The town of Vanguard lay down the empty highway where the next nearest dark pillar stood. After fording the river, Sir Raglan, Geoden and forty-seven humans and gargoyles kept close in a brisk march. More than half of the remaining resistance fighters had chosen to go. Adwen's warriors and the winged soldiers kept watch during the journey, alert for any demon ambush.

None came. When Adwen's companions stopped and Colin flashed the lantern, several more lanterns in their small army flickered back. They had arrived and were ready. When Raglan's team split off, Jack went along. Alexander followed Geoden's group the other way, leaving Adwen and Oryn with Tamis and the cousins.

Waiting a short time before going in, Adwen and her friends gazed up through the darkness. The pillar was massive, rising almost fifty feet high. They could see the little green lights hovering about the surfaces all the way to its peak. From where they stood, the Holy Hounds felt the static radiating outward. This pillar was much stronger than the first they destroyed.

When Adwen realized its power, she became fearful. Then she felt her dearest friend place a hand on her shoulder. Adwen put her hand on his, smiling weakly. His gesture helped return a little of her nerve.

Colin nodded, cuing their time to move.

Nodding to Oryn, Adwen changed into her weakened true form: a huge white dog with a gold mark on her forehead. Adwen stood on all fours beside Tamis.

The smaller rust-brown hound led the way, slinking stealthily into the overtaken town. Right away, they saw demons patrolling the streets. With keen senses, the team skirted around buildings, avoiding detection by the monsters of many sizes and shapes. They sneaked through a network of alleys, crossing streets only when necessary.

When they drew close enough to see the base of the dark pillar, it was surrounded by much stronger demons. Oryn growled a curse under his breath. Felons were among the evil gathering. Their four long, blade-tipped tendrils swayed like those of an anemone under water. Even the gargoyles would have trouble fighting Felons. Human combatants would not last long.

Colin and Remy studied the terrible things through their masks, which hid frightened expressions. They could not give the signal with their lantern because their position gave no line of sight to other teams in this large town. The plan was to wait for the way to clear and to run for the pillar as fast as they could. Bringing it down would scatter the demons, allowing the fighters to escape.

The survival of the humans and gargoyles depended heavily on Adwen's success. With the pain of apprehension, she watched the pillar and waited. Her timing needed to be perfect.

Silent minutes passed in the nearly complete darkness, surrounded by skulking monsters and floating green wisps. A warning call from a demon to the north made those in the town center raise their heads. Then they shrieked and roared, charging toward the sound. Something had gone wrong. Raglan and Jack's team had been discovered too soon. Instead of drawing in a portion of the demons, the whole horde rushed onto them.

Shouting broke out in the south as Geoden and Alexander led a rescue charge through the town. Hot on the heels of the demons, they raced to support their overwhelmed friends.

During the chaos, Adwen and her company ran for the pillar. Demons attacked from all sides, forcing her to dodge around and past her fighters. Oryn summoned his sword and slashed at demons, freeing other fighters to continue to the skirmish to the north. By the time Adwen reached the pillar's base with Tamis, Colin and Remy, hordes of demons flooded back, mouths drenched in human blood.

Seeing the wave of enemies, Oryn had no choice but to hold them back on his own. He stood his ground and fought, giving Adwen time to reach the pillar.

She felt pain being inflicted on her warriors. It terrified her and spurred her to change quickly into her elf-like form. Willing her power to manifest as fine tendrils of pure light, she reached the golden threads from her hand and thrust them to the dark stone.

Immediately, a barrier pushed back. She tried harder and harder, bracing her wrist with the other hand, fighting to touch it to the pillar. As she continued to combat the evil barrier, an image appeared in the dark stone surface behind the runes. A face like an animated engraving stared and smiled at her with white specs for eyes.

When it laughed at her fear and weakness, the powerful being waved a spindly set of claws. A force of intense darkness struck her, throwing her backward. She screamed as she fell to the ground, scorching burns across her body.

"Adwen!" The boys shouted and Tamis yelped.

A Wretch leaped from a nearby rooftop, racing toward where Adwen lay quivering. Oryn was far to overwhelmed, so Tamis shook the boys from his back, and the young warrior hound bounded in, jaws in a tight snarl. He leaped, pouncing on the Wretch, sinking his teeth into its arm. He could do no real harm but fought regardless.

As Tamis wrestled with the monster, Colin and Remy ran to get Adwen off the ground. They pulled at her, picking her up to flee.

Tamis snarled and yelped as he was repeatedly cut and bit. Then he was tossed by the powerful Wretch and tumbled aside.

Adwen was just becoming lucid again when the sound of Remy's voice hit her ears.

"Colin! Look out!"

Looming over them, the Wretch raised a set of sharp claws. Just as it slashed for them, Remy pulled out his slingshot. He fired swiftly and deftly, aiming straight for one of its red, glowing eyes. The monster wailed.

Then the claws found Colin's torso. He was thrown, his hide armor shredded.

A scream ripped from Adwen's lungs so loud that everyone still alive and fighting heard.

Desperate and tortured by the sound that came out of Adwen, Oryn went wild. His primal side emerged, and he lost control. The knight transformed. At a height far beyond that of the other warriors and even Adwen, Oryn's black and brown hound form grew to ten feet tall. Jaws gnashing, blood matted the fur on his neck while he slashed and sliced with armored claws and holy sword. Then he leaped over the demons to reach her side. There he continued to lash out wildly, killing everything that approached.

Tamis bounded over as Colin scrambled to his feet, bracing his side. Adwen helped the boys climb onto the rusty hound's back and watched them race away. Tears streaked her scorched face and she called out at the top of her voice.

"Oryn!"

He became far less feral, panting and bleeding, splashed with demon blood. Looking deep into her face, he growled. "Could you not break it?"

"No!" she sobbed. "Tell the others to retreat. We have to run before more demons come!"

Immediately, he let loose a deafening howl. It rattled the air, reaching far out to everyone. The remainder of the fighters instantly understood that the battle was lost. Those who could fled. Fighters unable to run were cut down and fed upon by the horde of demons.

Oryn scooped Adwen up in his huge arms and ran. He carried her through the darkness as she wept. During the entire scramble back to the sanctuary, they smelled the copper scent trails left by their friends.

As soon as Oryn crossed the river below the cave entrance, he set Adwen down and reverted to his own elf-like shape. Only then was he small enough to fit through the entrance. Adwen ran through the passage with him. When they reached the first chamber, those who stayed behind were startled by the sight of their sudden arrival and then by their horrible injuries.

She was desperate to find Colin. "Where are the boys? Where are they?"

One called out. "Tamis took them higher, Lady Adwen! Hurry!"

The crowd parted to make way for the pair, letting them race to the upper chambers. Adwen's heart fluttered with fear that they may already be too late.

Virgil and Dynic were in the upper chamber by the overlook. They knelt over a sobbing Remy. Tamis sat in the far corner, shuddering, lapping at bloody wounds. Colin lay between the men as Adwen and Oryn dashed inside.

The damaged hide armor was removed, while Dynic fought to stymie the bleeding. A huge gash split Colin's middle, red springs welling up beyond control. The clothes on the boy and Dynic's hands were soaked. Remy continued to cry, holding his shuddering cousin's hand, staring into his pale, frightened face. The pain and loss of blood wracked him with waves of quaking fits. Virgil helped keep him still, allowing the horrified knight to staunch the bleeding until Adwen and Oryn brushed Dynic out of the way.

"Hold on, Colin," she urged, crying harder.

Oryn held his hands over the wound, forcing magic to reach from his fingers as currents of pale-green electricity. Wherever the magic touched was healed, but there was much damage. Oryn was himself wounded, and the effort to heal Colin stretched his strength. The injury was very deep, requiring a high cost to repair. Slowly, the missing flesh and sinews reformed.

Remy grasped Colin's shaking fist, crying. "You're almost healed. It's okay. You're okay."

Virgil and Adwen were worried. Even if healed, Colin's strength was fading from the loss of so much blood. Despite Oryn's hard work, there was no assurance Colin would survive.

When the bleeding finally stopped and the wound closed without a blemish, Colin shivered less intensely. His face remained white as milk, and his weak gaze locked with Remy's. Labored breaths became shallower and slower.

Frightened, Remy sobbed again. "Colin? Colin? Say something."

Straining for enough air, a flickering smile came over him. Then he murmured. "You're such a good shot." Colin's eyes steadily rolled back and closed.

A terrible stillness followed. Dynic stood by, barely able to watch as Remy began to scream.

"Colin? Colin! Colin!"

Virgil quickly pulled Remy to himself, shushing his cries. "Relax, boy. He's unconscious. Let him rest." The ranger held him tightly as the boy shook uncontrollably as he sobbed.

Oryn stood, and Adwen laid a hand on Colin's chest, which still drew breath. "Thank you, Oryn. Thank you so much."

He nodded and then approached Dynic, who stood by the nearest cave wall. The knight had been gazing in horror into nothingness, but when Oryn came closer their eyes locked. Oryn's scowl fixated on Dynic's bewildered expression. Neither spoke for a time. Eventually, the human could not maintain the stare, ashamed.

But Oryn finally spoke. "Go to the lower chamber."

He looked up, confounded.

The icy stare from Oryn was harsher than the boy's wound. "Count how many returned, as I instructed before the battle. Report to me the number of those who returned and how many survive this night. If you cannot watch this boy, then you will make your eyes watch every other wounded warrior. Go."

Cries of agony and woe echoed in the sanctuary. Injured lay all around, red trickling from shallow gashes as well as mortal wounds. Survivors steadily found their way back, following the river to the roaring falls if they lost their way in the dark. Oryn used what he could of his magic to heal the most dangerous wounds. He did not have the strength to repair everyone as he had done with Colin. Not every wounded fighter survived long enough to receive his touch.

Jack and Alexander eventually made it back, carrying Geoden. One wing was cleaved off, and blood poured from the severed end. Raglan followed, lucky to have suffered minor cuts. Jack had worked very hard to save lives. The two Holy Hounds were badly wounded but would survive to heal in the morning.

Oryn met them and immediately went to work on the gargoyle's wounds.

Smiling through the pain, Geoden chuckled. "Thank you, Sir Oryn." Though he would never fly again, the gargoyle was not bothered.

Oryn frowned, admiring the creature's tenacity. "At full strength, I could have healed your entire wing. You are more than deserving."

His smile grew, showing sharp incisors. Steely eyes sparkled. "I appreciate that sentiment. However, I bear the wound proudly. Its story is worth more. I shall live an eternity to share the meaning to all who will listen."

At this, Raglan bowed his head, wounded in ways he could not bleed out from.

Oryn smelled the shame. "Find Adwen and the ranger. They await your return."

Staring balefully, Raglan nodded and rushed to seek them out.

Adwen sat with Tamis by the boys. Colin now lay on a soft mat and had a pillow. Virgil was just pulling a warm blanket over him when Raglan arrived.

The moment he saw Colin, he blanched. Everyone stared at him in the passage. He looked as if he had seen a ghost. As unsettling as it was to see the older boy lying on the floor, Remy's expression was devastating. The boy was bold with a kind heart, but now his face bore the agony of betrayal; pleading eyes simply asked why.

Feeling feeble, Raglan took a step forward, then froze. He could not bring himself to go near Colin. Dropping to his knees, he bowed his head to them all, hands on his thighs to brace himself from falling on his face. Fighting his own tongue, the knight spoke.

"I've failed you. I've failed you all. I am not worthy of my station as captain. Lady Adwen, take it from me. Find one who is worthy. Please, relieve me of my duties."

Her frown deepened. "The Order of the Master Knights is gone, Sir Raglan. You know that."

Head hanging a little lower, he resisted the urge to break down and sob. "You are yet the servant of the Light Spirits. Your forebear's Order is gone, but you are here. I answer to you. I should never have forgotten my place or yours. Command me as to the will of the Light."

Listening to the still small voice in her heart, she answered the knight on his knees. "You are relieved as Captain of the Order of the Master Knights."

Raglan sighed, sorrowful.

"And you are now appointed General of the Order of the Gargoyle."

He looked up, eyes wide.

"Your brother, Sir Dynic, shall be told of his new rank as Captain of the new Order."

The knight was dumbfounded. "A new Order? General? You would have me serve?"

Adwen nodded. "I would, and so do the Light Spirits. Everyone here who lives tonight and so wishes can serve. The Order of the Gargoyle takes all who serve and protect, no matter the race or the form. Their honor, courage and compassion shall dictate that right." She lifted a hand. "Stand, General. You have a lot of work to do."

He stood like a statue, frozen on the floor, breathless.

A small smile at his newfound humility curled Adwen's lips. "Go on."

Numb, General Sir Raglan stood. Then he walked back the way he came, bewildered.

When he was gone, Virgil smiled. "Order of the Gargoyle? I

like that. It has a subtle ring to it." The ranger chuckled. "Perhaps I'll join."

Adwen almost laughed. "You? I thought you liked independence?"

Taking out a bit of smoke herbs for the pipe, he headed for the overlook. "Indeed, I do. I would take part so long as it stays that way. I'll be taking this outside. Fresh air is needed for the boy. I take my leave, Good Lady Adwen."

Tamis's bleeding stopped, and he looked up at her, growling softly. "Adwen? What will we do now? That pillar was the weakest we know of, but you could not break it. Now what is your command?"

She put a reassuring hand on his shoulder. "We will do something. Let me think a while, and by dawn you'll have an answer."

The reply did not worry him. Whatever the something would be, it would be good. At the least it would be better than this terrible night.

Over several dark, harrowing hours, survivors returned from the battle. Those who Oryn could save were partially healed. He was exhausted by the end, almost staggering. Dynic helped him ascend the tunnels to the overlook, where Adwen and her warriors met with the leaders of the Order of the Gargoyle.

Geoden, presented with a rank above Sir Dynic's, stood at the table. He beamed at Sir Oryn as he was brought in, drained from healing so many.

"Your weakness does you great credit, Sir Oryn. Well done."

Alexander took hold of Oryn, letting Dynic stand by his brother and the one-winged gargoyle. As the Marine accepted Oryn's weight, he nodded. "Thank you, Shield Captain."

General Raglan sat at the table across from Adwen and her warriors. Their faces were cut and burned, awash with emotional wounds from defeat. For a long while, no one spoke.

Virgil stepped up and broke the silence: "The first War Meeting between the Order of the Gargoyle and Lady Adwen has begun. Good Lady, do you wish to speak as guest and superior at the war table?"

"I do, Virgil, thank you. Captain Dynic?"

His tired stare rose up to meet hers. "Yes, Lady Adwen?"

"What were our losses?"

The captain swallowed a lump in his throat, recalling Colin's return in the early hours. "Twenty-five are unaccounted for, Lady. Twenty-two returned." He paused to restrain his need to vomit, turning pale. "Seventeen survived this night. The twenty-eight who stayed out of the battle are well."

Feeling a twinge of remorse for Dynic, Adwen examined his heart. He would never allow himself to forget all he had seen. "Thank you, Captain. My own are injured and weak but will endure to fight another time. Shield Captain?"

Geoden grunted proudly, "Yes, Good Lady?"

"Ensure that medicines are properly rationed to prevent infections. Surely there is need for more. Select skilled scouts to scavenge the site of the first pillar. No demons will return to that town. It is the safest place to search for now."

"It shall be done, Lady Adwen."

Finished, she nodded to Virgil. "Thank you."

He smiled and nodded back. "Turn to speak is passed to General Raglan."

The weary knight gazed solemnly, his voice soft and sad. "What does the Good Lady intend to do and how shall the new Order proceed?"

Her blue eyes glowed at him warmly, while her face was stern. "Leave this place. Do so slowly in small numbers, no more than five at a time. As the strength of the wounded permits, have them go ahead of the rest. None who are still bleeding or are bloody can leave until they are cleaned. Demons would sniff them out."

"That will take time, Lady Adwen, and time I will work hard to give. It will be done as you've commanded. But what will you do?"

"I have to go back to the other world."

As the leader of the new Order nodded, Tamis whimpered. "Shall I go with you?"

Smiling, she shook her head and growled softly in return. "No, you cannot disguise yourself as human. The other world would not be safe for you. Assist whoever the Shield Captain picks to appoint as scouts."

The huge hound nodded. "As you wish, Lady Adwen."

Looking back across the war table, her tone was more encouraging. "I don't know what we will find in the other world, but my warriors and I need to heal, and that is the safest place for us to do so. We will return as soon as we are ready. Stay safe and stay strong. This is not over."

"Yes." Shield Captain Geoden smiled and added, "The war has just begun."

In the south by the edge of the cliff, light from the distant sun reached out.

"It's time." Virgil informed them all, "This War Meeting is adjourned. Thank you for joining us, Lady Adwen."

Adwen stood and led three of her warriors to the ledge. The waterfall cascaded past one side under the stars. By the light of the incomplete dawn, she summoned the Gray Blade. Blue and white fire rippled to life on the sword. Pointing it toward empty air, a wreath of blue flames ripped through reality, showing a vacant city alley between to towering buildings.

General Raglan stood and spoke with renewed strength of spirit. "We await your return, Lady Adwen. Be safe."

"Same to you, General. Until we meet again."

The four passed through, walking beyond the flames until their feet found concrete. Then the fiery wreath closed, leaving the Order of the Gargoyle staring out into the dark once more.

Chapter 7
DARK INTO LIGHT

Sounds of traffic and strong odors from exhaust and pigeon droppings filled the air. On the other side of the portal, Jack and Alexander breathed in the many stinks and sweet smells from cafés. A vast surge of energy filled them as Adwen was cut off from the magical world. Her power returned in full. White light shone from her body until she was restored, separated from the binding to the land of Dargadia. The enchanted armor returned, and Adwen willed it to become a set of elaborate clothes. Facing her warriors, she heaved a sigh.

"This feels much better. How is everybody now?"

Able to stand on his own, Oryn nodded. "Well, but still weak."

They each willed their appearances to be more human. Alexander formed a thick brown jacket, hiding his healing wounds. "Having a bite to eat sounds good."

"I second that." Jack's stomach growled pitifully as a third reply.

The knight rolled his eyes, and Adwen could not help but smile. "Okay, who has cash?"

Their shortest member raised his hand. "I do. Where am I going?"

"Aren't you reading my mind? That's so unlike you."

He was not amused. "Things change after years of being in a marriage. Some things are better left unheard."

Surprised, she pretended not to notice his sullen reaction. "Wherever you can find enough meat to feed us all. After what happened at the pier, Oryn and I need to lie low with Alex. We'll wait on the rooftop for you. After we eat, we can figure out where to go."

The Marine was curious. "Where are we? Nothing looks familiar."

"The city of roses and bridges."

"What?"

"Portland."

"Goodie." Jack's tone was sarcastic. "I love the rain! And before I go, I had better unload a few things. This is going to be a lot of meat. I'm at my maximum load."

They stared as he began to summon many objects he had collected. Recalling scissors, staplers, a crowbar, four cans of beer, zip-ties from the museum mission in San Francisco, and a tool bag. Adwen was dumbfounded.

"I have to know: What's with the office supplies?"

Jack wore a sly smile, making his eyes shine.

Alexander answered, "He plays jokes on the other cops at the department."

Oryn raised an eyebrow. "The tools?"

"We have motorcycles. Never know when we might need the ratchet set. As for the crowbar, I almost forgot I had that. Do me a favor, Big Dog, and take the tools. You can give them back later. See yah when I see yah."

When he was gone in search of raw meat to feast upon, Adwen and Oryn gave Alexander curious looks.

Taking notice, he shrugged. "What?"

"Big Dog? Really? Are you a street thug when I'm not around?"

"It was his idea. Big Dog and Bad Dog keep a watch over San Francisco. He sniffs out perps through the police department, and we ambush them at night."

Adwen shared a smiling glance with Oryn.

Alexander and Jack had not explained their vigilante gig. "What?"

"Nothing!" Adwen said. "It's okay. It sounds like more fun than what we chose to do."

Her doting knight inclined an eyebrow. "That is a rather weak lie."

"It's not as fun as it sounds," the Marine said darkly. "Believe me, it's not."

Deciding not to push the issue, Adwen continued to smile. "Let's take this to the top of a building before we're seen."

After watching the sun rise, she and her warriors healed while waiting for Jack. Most stores selling large cuts of meat were not open until a little later, forcing him to take longer than anticipated. When he arrived, each of them had a wrapped package straight from a privately-owned butcher shop. Oryn was given the largest to restore the strength spent healing so many wounds.

With everyone satisfied, Adwen shared her plan: "We have to stay in the city for a little while. I don't know why we're here, but it should not take long to find out."

Jack patted his stomach. "I'm full, and now I'm dog tired." He chuckled at his own bad joke.

Alexander stared, unimpressed.

Ignoring the horrible pun, she agreed. "Each of us needs rest. If the demons are hunting us in this world, we should stay where they are less likely to expose themselves."

Oryn answered immediately, "A hotel."

They stared.

"It is inconspicuous, provides privacy and places for rest. Is that not what is needed?"

Jack's sly smile returned, and he inclined his head at Adwen. "So, how much money are you carrying?"

"I have a paid-off Visa card," she admitted.

"How in the world do you have a card when you don't legally exist?"

Wearing a sardonic look, she replied, "I thought you were a cop."

He chuckled. "Oh, you're a bad girl! False ID!"

"Shut up, Jack. I know a nice place. It's pricy, but we'll only be spending one night. Since I don't legally exist, how about we go to the River's Edge? My treat."

"It has a spa...?"

"Jack, calm down."

He gripped Alexander by the front of his coat, shaking him roughly, grinning giddily. "It has a spa!"

Oryn sighed and opened the front door for everyone, letting

Adwen lead them to the reception desk. She reached into a pocket of her white and blue leather jacket as she approached the receptionist.

The nicely dressed woman smiled kindly. "Good afternoon. How can I help you today?"

"Hello! I would like to know if you have any available rooms, please."

Searching on her computer, she replied, "One moment, ma'am."

Jack murmured to Alexander, grinning, "Even if they don't have rooms, we're staying."

"Shut up, Jack," The Marine growled in return.

The human behind the counter was none the wiser as she looked up and smiled. "We have a room for two ma'am. It's one of the honeymoon suites."

"Would I be able to have a room for four?"

"I'm sorry, ma'am. There are no rooms that size available."

Adwen sighed. "Then we will take two rooms in the same hall if you have them."

"Let me check. Yes! We have two rooms next to each other. They don't have a view of the river, but they are on the top floor. A lovely garden with trees is on the roof. It is less expensive than the honeymoon suite as well. Is that what you would like?"

Passing the card across the counter, Adwen smiled and nodded. "Perfect. We'll take those two rooms."

Accepting the card, she read the name at the bottom before looking up again. "And may I see a form of ID, please?"

Summoning a driver's license in her pocket, Adwen presented it and awaited a reaction from Jack. She could tell without looking that he was about to pester her.

Reading the names on the cards, the receptionist swiped the Visa card for payment. "Thank you for your business, Ms. Ana."

When the receptionist handed back the cards, Jack growled softly, wearing a sly smile, "Oh my, Ana. Is that fake ID?"

Adwen struggled against responding and just sighed.

"Here are the two keys. Would you like a tour of the facilities?"

"That won't be necessary, but thank you. I've been here before. It's amazing."

The woman blushed. "Thank you. The owner would be

pleased to hear that. I hope you and your party enjoy your stay, Ms. Ana."

They stepped into an elevator, and Adwen pushed the button for their floor.

As the doors were closing, Jack chimed, "Ms. Ana, license and registration, please."

Irritated, Adwen replied coldly while crossing her arms, "Go buy your own drinks, Jack."

This put a stop to his fun and he groaned, "Aw."

The rooms were clean and had thick, plush mattresses. Jack and Alexander went to share a drink at the bar overlooking the river, leaving Adwen and Oryn to rest in their room. They opened the curtains wide, letting bright sunshine heal the last of their aches. It was warm. The sun shined on them all afternoon as they lay with her in his arms. Sleeping was nearly impossible. Most of the time was spent feeling each other's presence, haunted by the previous night. The other world had overflowed with death.

Adwen could not forget the face she saw in the second pillar they had attacked. The white specs for eyes were like Melanin's. Whose face was that? She did not want an answer. More than ever, she wished for peaceful sleep and sweet dreams.

Holding her, Oryn could not sleep either. He was troubled by how Impurus was bold enough to attack openly at the concert. The knight concluded that he should remain awake, leaving nothing to chance. There was no way to know if the abomination could swoop into the room while they slept. Memories of that monster's face twisting into that of Jacques made the knight sick with rage.

An unexpected knock came at the door, and Oryn was on his feet in a flash. They exchanged looks before he cautiously approached the peep hole. Jack and Alexander stood in the hall, their images warped by the lens in the door. The friends had sneaked drinks out of the bar and brought them to the room. Jack held a glass of fruity liquor up to the peep hole, ice clinking against the inside.

Rolling his eyes, Oryn opened the door. The sun was setting, but they did not need lights yet. As Oryn closed the door and locked it, she sat up. "Why aren't you guys napping? We're all exhausted. You two especially."

The cop and Marine exchanged glances. "Can't sleep."

"After that massacre?" Alexander shook his head. "Too

shook up."

Crossing his arms, Oryn frowned. "It seems all of us are."

"How about a drink? Might as well, since good sleep is not on the menu."

She shook her head. "No thanks."

Jack opened up his mind to read her thoughts and became sympathetic, holding the set of icy cocktails. "Colin's going to be fine. Cujo did good work on him."

She looked up and smiled. "Thank you, Jack."

He pondered a response, but his mind was still open and picked up something else: outside the room, down the hall, in the elevator, there were deadly thoughts. Jack's face blanched, and he nearly dropped the drinks on the carpet.

The others saw him turn pale and his eyes dilate. They all sensed impending danger. Adwen jumped to her feet, addressing her psychic warrior: "How many?"

Setting the drinks aside, Jack growled, dilating eyes aglow. "Five or six. They're armed."

"With what?"

Each allowed their elf-like appearances to emerge with their armor, and Jack clenched sharp fangs. "Everything."

Oryn snarled, eyeing the door. Shadows in the hall crossed the line of light through the peep hole. "What is your command?"

She growled deeply as the room darkened after sunset. They nodded to each other.

Within seconds, the lock clicked and the door burst open. Five black-clad men rushed in with automatic rifles raised in all directions. They fanned out, searching every corner. The room was empty, but a window was ajar.

They hid in the rooftop garden, and Jack read the intruders' minds.

Adwen growled nearby. "What are we dealing with?"

"They're professionals. And they know exactly who we are. Another team is moving toward the roof."

"There's a second team?"

"They're in contact with someone outside the building. Trying to get a bead on them."

Seconds later, a door to the roof flew open and an assault team emerged. Moving as one, the humans searched the south side of the rooftop patio. They looked through night optics to scan the garden. When they detected nothing, one whispered into a headset.

"Are you sure the targets are on the roof?"

A voice replied, "They are still on site. Stay alert."

Softly, Jack growled, "They intend to kill, not capture."

Somehow, one of the humans heard the growl and pointed to a section of the garden. A branch rustled, and before any could fire a single round, a bright flash of white light blinded them through their optics, making them shout and scramble to stay in formation. The voice in their headsets shouted as well.

"Your six! On your six! Subject Ghost is on your six!"

Behind the stunned team, whose sight was beginning to return, Adwen stood in her true form. The pale fire sword came to life, flames lapping ravenously with her anger. When the first to recover saw her, he took aim, but she swung the blade, cutting the rifle. By the time the hunk of metal and plastic hit the ground, he pulled a Tazer and fired at her. The pins hit Adwen's stomach, snapping and crackling. To the man's horror, it did nothing. Adwen growled, the energy melding with hers, making her blue eyes flash in time with the nodes.

Ears pricked atop her head, her snarl twitched. "That doesn't work on me."

She kicked him in the chest, sending him flying with crushed ribs as the rest of the humans opened fire. As Adwen dodged the sprays of bullets, she sliced another gun in half and Alexander dashed out to grab a man by the head, throwing him into a wall. Just as Jack joined the fray, a sniper from another building's roof hit Adwen's chest plate. The high-caliber bullet glanced off, drawing her attention to the human who dared to shoot.

Another sniper from a second roof fired. That bullet ripped through the side of Adwen's arm, sending a spray of silver blood flying. It burned horribly. Stunned and bleeding, Adwen realized these bullets were no ordinary metal. Changing tactics, she roared at the top of her lungs as she sliced the nearest armed human in half. Blue fire reduced him to ash in seconds.

"Demon steel! The bullets are demon steel!"

Oryn roared, pouncing on another team arriving on the roof through the open door. "Leave none alive!"

Adwen pointed the Gray Blade at the first sniper, shooting a ball of fire. The human ducked behind a ventilation unit, only to be vaporized with half of the machinery.

Jack's blades finished the first team of humans, and Adwen's blue fire destroyed the evidence. More sniper fire struck near her as her flames consumed the remains of the second team. When nothing was left, Adwen turned to the next sniper, who was being joined by a third.

They trained their aim on her through scopes, while she dashed to the edge of the hotel roof. When she leaped into the air over the street, they panicked, shooting as swiftly as they could. With a blinding flash, she appeared overhead and landed just behind them. The humans shouted in fear as she aimed her sword at them. Blue fire billowed outward like hot breath. Only the evil bullets survived the fire's touch.

A human-size demon suddenly leaped from a shadow, pouncing. Adwen killed it right away, then howled to her warriors.

"Follow me! A horde is coming! Hurry!"

Dozens upon dozens of smaller demons spilled out of every corner. Adwen and her warriors bounded away northwest, pursued by hungry, snapping jaws. Taking the chase to the interstate highway, the roofs of vans and semi-trucks sped past. The Holy Hounds bounded across to the other side, their weight rocking smaller vehicles, confounding drivers. Some of the demons were struck, but most managed to keep up the chase.

A few caught up, but they were slain immediately. Their purple waste stained the ground, only to be tread upon by the rest of the monsters racing after the Holy Hounds. Headed up a mountainside dotted with small buildings, the warriors separated, splitting the monsters into more manageable groups. By the time the pursuit reached the trees, a small band of foolish demons had caught up with Adwen. Bounding between the treetops, she sliced and slashed, leaping farther ahead to await another wave of attackers.

A mighty roar reached her long, soft ears as a Wretch leaped from the boughs of maple trees. Having never seen this class of demon in the non-magical world before, she stared. More appeared and attacked. The first pounced, raking claws across her other arm. Then it died by her sword as she dashed out into a quiet, winding road lined with lamp posts.

Two more demons darted out of cover, but she twirled aside,

stabbing the first and decapitating the second. Hoping that was the last of them, she was proved wrong when a pair of human screams cut through the air. Two young girls at a bus stop cringed under a lamp, shrieking in the spotlight. They could see the silhouettes of three demons and their bright red eyes in the dark, running up the road.

Adwen was about to run to their rescue, but a lone figure emerged from the dark tree line. While the first Wretch prepared to attack the humans, a powerful fist caught the underside of its jaw. The force caved the monster's head in, launching the body into a tree, where it fell.

The stranger was tall with messy shoulder-length black hair. The figure wore a blood red leather jacket. Purple demon blood drenched his hands as he faced the girls, his back to Adwen as he had not seen her yet. The voice of the stranger was raspy and deep.

"Run! Go!"

More demon blood splattered the pavement as he swept his hand to the side, gesturing to the girls to flee. With the humans running away, he was free to fight. Facing the shrieking monsters, he roared like a lion. His clawed fingertips swiped the head completely off the next demon to pounce. Another demon sailed over him, racing out to attack Adwen instead.

She raised a hand, knifing her own claws through its chest, sending out condensed energy. An explosion of white light tore the demon from reality, leaving black particles falling like dirty snow. Adwen stared through the drifting cloud of dust and ashes, observing the stranger, who only just realized she was there.

Standing still, he stared back with bright cherry-red eyes. His fear intensified the longer he looked at her. His mouth was slightly agape, with sharp carnivorous teeth barely visible. His breath was trapped in his broad, muscular chest, which bore huge fang scars across his left breast. He stood like a statue, unable to move, terrified.

Blinking and cocking her head, she took a step forward. He took two wobbly steps backward then stopped, his stare more fearful than before. She paused, curious, studying the worn young face of the powerful alpha werewolf.

Another roar came, and they both turned to find Oryn leaping from the high boughs of a maple. His sword arced down through the air, ready to cleave the being down the middle.

In a bright flash of light, Adwen instantly appeared by the odd werewolf, blocking Oryn's blade with her own. She watched the reaction of the being, seeing his disbelief as she defended him. As he stepped back from Oryn and his raised weapon, Adwen glanced at her warrior's fearsome sneer.

Oryn growled loudly, "Why do you stay my hand?"

"Put your sword down. I think this one wants to talk."

The werewolf glanced back and forth at each of them, unsure what to do.

With great effort, the knight snarled, doing as she wished. With clenched fists he dismissed the sword while he stared down the dark creature.

Dismissing her own weapon, she moved her muzzle in close to sniff. The werewolf held still, watching her animal face show confusion. Then she cocked her head again.

"How is it that a demon can feel fear?"

His raspy voice had a distinct English accent. Speaking softly, he looked her over, uncertain. "Why shouldn't I ... knowing what you can do?"

Adwen's gaze became intense and searching. Changing into her elf-like human shape, she crossed her arms, growling, "That's not what I meant. You know that."

His red, glowing eyes caught sight of Jack and Alexander arriving. Cutting off any escape, they studied him and sniffed the air.

Jack was astonished. "Why isn't the monster dead yet?"

Looking around at them, the werewolf agreed. "I was just wondering that myself."

Huffing, Jack twirled the daggers in his hands. "I'll take care of this."

Adwen snarled and snapped, "No!"

Instantly Jack was unable to move. Adwen forced his body to stay put. Once he gave up trying, she released him, and he shuddered. Frowning, he grumbled and put away the daggers. "I hate it when you do that."

She ignored him and approached the werewolf. "What is your name?"

With no more room to recoil, he gulped, "Kale."

Looking him over, she frowned.

After a moment of tenuous silence, Kale spoke up again: "If

you're going to destroy me, please get it over with."

"I'll grant your wish." The knight snarled, eyes bright.

Adwen's eyes flashed at him, and she was angry. "That's enough, Oryn."

After hearing the name, Kale felt even more frightened than before. He glanced at the ravenous werewolf slayer for a second but did not forget Adwen. Certain he would die any moment, he resigned to the idea and calmed. No longer gaping, he waited for this encounter to end.

"How much do you know about demons?"

Caught off guard, Kale blinked. "More than I'd like to. Almost everything."

Then Adwen came to a decision, certain he was useful. "I want to ask you something."

"Yeah?"

"Will you let me look into your heart? Can you resist hiding anything from my sight?"

Swallowing the lump in his throat, Kale's skin became clammy. He nodded. "Yeah. I ... I think I can."

Oryn growled ominously, "You'll find only darkness."

She shot him a warning look. Kale smelled of pure terror, no matter how calm he kept himself. No real demon could feel such fear. She needed to see into his heart to find out his true nature.

Not sure what to expect, Kale braced for pain. None came. As with Jack, her power suddenly gripped him, holding him frozen. Adwen's strength made him gasp. He could sense her gaze searching everything, everywhere. No corner or compartment of his being was unseen. When he was released at last, the werewolf shuddered, waiting for her reaction.

Adwen looked at Kale as if she were seeing him for the first time. A warm smile made her eyes glow. "You're not a demon, are you?"

The warriors were confused. Kale was equally astonished. His brow furrowed.

"I was last I checked."

She laughed, beaming at the amusing creature. Then a thought came to her, and she knew it had to be done. Becoming more serious, Adwen was confident in the decision.

"I have something for you. You've been waiting for this for a long time."

Afraid of the answer, he looked apprehensive. "What is it?"

Light in her chest began to radiate out through her skin, making her body glow.

"A chance. You've never had one."

Watching her glow brighter in the dark, he was uncertain. "What sort of chance? Aren't you going to kill me?"

A metallic ringing blared from Adwen. Part of what glowed in her chest passed along her right arm to her hand. It glowed brightly in her palm. Extending the hand for Kale to take, her voice resonated.

"That depends on you."

Everyone observed what Kale might do. Oryn sneered and growled. A piece of Adwen's heart was being offered to this demon.

Kale knew that to touch even a part of the Golden Heart was to risk being ripped from reality. However, there was much unknown involving the core of Adwen's being; even the demons knew little of it. Whether it would bring him death or something better, there was only one way to find out.

He fidgeted, claws on fingertips scraping callus skin. Finally, extending his hand, Kale cautiously reached. When he reached hers, she grabbed him tight. The light burned, making him shake and sweat, gasping. Tiny flames sparked on the top of his skin, slowly burning at flesh. Kale looked deep into her eyes, waiting for her to burn him alive and leave nothing left.

Instead, she spoke, "Will you serve as a warrior at my side?"

Almost forgetting the pain, Kale's gaze became huge. The whites of his eyes turned black in the surge of emotions. "Yes," he gasped.

Adwen smiled. "Will you serve the powers of Light that guide me and confront the powers of darkness?"

"Yes!" He blurted out right away, eager at being asked. His hand continued to burn, reaching tendons and veins. The pain was nothing to him now. All his attention was on Adwen and her questions.

Her smile grew. "Very well."

There was a burst of light, and Adwen released him, letting Kale stumble back. Jack and Alexander recoiled, drawing weapons when he fell toward them. The three Holy Hounds snarled, watching

Kale marvel at what Adwen had done to his hand.

Flexing fingers on his healed hand, staring in confusion, Kale studied the spot of metallic gold branded into him. It showed through both sides of his hand, catching the light and glinting.

"Wha-what did you do?" He gasped as Adwen took his hand and he was not burned, showing the mark to him.

She giggled at his reaction. "This is the start. And there is more." Letting go for him to look more closely at the piece of her heart in his hand, Adwen asked another question. "Where would you like to go out for breakfast tomorrow?"

Oryn, Jack and Alexander were alarmed. Werewolves could only consume human flesh and blood. Kale gave her a perplexed expression. Then his jaw slackened. He began to shake like a leaf that might be blown over by a slight breeze. The white around his eyes turned black again, tears filling them and overflowing down his face. Falling to his knees he wept. A smile of pure joy came over him as he uttered weakly, "You took it away?"

She gave a comforting look, nodding.

He shook even more, crying and laughing softly, bewildered. Never had he known such joy. It wracked him with overwhelming happiness that poured out in fountains of tears and hushed, choking laughter. Kale hung his head, completely overcome.

Jack growled to Adwen, "What did you do to him?"

"I took his hunger away. He can eat whatever he likes now."

No one was more shocked than Oryn, who continued to watch the werewolf sobbing in the middle of the road. It was more unbelievable to witness a demon crying.

Adwen gently called to her newest companion, "Are you ready to get to work?"

His head snapped up, wearing a happy smile. The black had gone from his eyes as he blurted out. "Gladly!" Wiping his face, he sniffled and added, "Gladly, I'll serve you ... boss."

She laughed. "Call me Adwen."

He nodded. "Adwen." Picking himself up, he was thrilled. "What's the first order of business, then?"

Glancing at her friends, she admitted, "We need a safe place to hide out for the night. All of us need to get some sleep. Do you know a place?"

Shocked at the simplicity of the order, he shrugged. "Sure. It's not much, but nothing will come knocking. Come on."

Chapter 8
IMPOSSIBLE THINGS

Kale was fast, as swift as Adwen. He led them northward, clinging to the shadows. Most of the journey cut through the green forest, moist from recent rainfall. Kale made no sound and neither did the others as they followed to his secret refuge.

Racing behind the powerful werewolf, Adwen heard a stream of protests from Oryn and Jack.

"Are you insane?" Jack barked. "You want a demon to help out? This is nuts!"

She ignored Jack's criticism.

Then Oryn snarled, never taking his eyes off Kale in his bright red leather jacket: "He's dangerous. How do you expect a demon to fight against its own kind? They are controlled by the powers of darkness!"

Irritated, Adwen growled back, as she leaped down a steep mountainside after their guide. "Kale is not connected to the darkness. Now he is bound to me, not the other way around. There are no intentions he can have that I will not know. Did you completely forget that I saw his heart?"

Not letting the werewolf out of his sight as they crossed a busy highway, Oryn felt a twinge of regret for questioning her. "I remember well. I was present."

Jack was not finished expressing his exasperation. "I can't even sense him with my mind. Come to think of it, none of us can sense him except for his werewolf stench! He could stand right behind us, and we would not know it if it weren't for the stink!"

Shooting Jack a deadly glare, she growled loudly, blue fire flickering on her shoulders.

At this, Jack fell silent. Never had he made her this angry since he became one of her warriors. Her fury put a knot in his throat and he looked away.

Kale stopped a hundred yards from a drab, dilapidated train station topped by a broken clock. Signs surrounding the structure warned people to keep out, and a high fence blocked access. A police patrol car cruised past in the dark, and Kale hid around the corner of a shipping container. When Adwen and the others caught up, he turned to them pretending he heard none of the arguing. His red eyes glowed as he smiled slyly.

"Security is a bit tight. There are some cameras and sensors, but there shouldn't be a problem once we're past. I can suppress them for you."

She smiled. "It's okay. My power can suppress electronic stuff, too. And, Kale?"

"Hmm?"

"Go ahead and wait for us inside." Adwen glanced back, frowning. "We need to have a talk."

He shrugged nonchalantly. "Okay. See you in a tick."

Watching him leap over the fence and slip through a broken window, Adwen turned to confront her three friends. Her eyes glowed brilliantly as she crossed her arms. The trio wore frowns, watching her read their faces.

"Alright, let's get this over with. Everyone get off what's on your chest."

Taking a chance, Jack spoke again, but more carefully. "This is a hard pill to swallow, Adwen. That is a demon. The human soul is no longer in that body. He is running around in a stolen flesh suit. Remember when you showed me a werewolf and had me kill it?"

"Yes, I remember."

He shook his head. "I can't forget that. I never will. Then there are all of the demons we've fought. I've heard the inside of their heads a thousand times. Not being able to hear Kale's thoughts is freaking me out. He's blocking me. The only other person who was powerful enough to block me was an Elf king!"

Adwen inclined an eyebrow, knowing he was not through yet. "And?"

"I've got a question: How good is he really if he has that body?"

Recalling some of what she had seen and felt in Kale, she replied. "It was not stolen; it was given."

The three were perplexed and said nothing.

She continued: "He did not choose to be placed into the body of that poor man. So what else is bothering you?"

Oryn grimaced. "Demons lie. They cannot help it."

"Kale is bound to me. I know every truth and every lie that comes out of his mouth the instant he thinks it."

"Yes, but what of us? How are we to fight alongside this demon if we cannot know when he weaves lies?"

Adwen almost rolled her eyes but resisted the urge. "I'll make you all a deal: If he says anything you think might be a lie, ask me. Then I'll tell you if it is. How's that?"

Oryn nodded. "Agreed."

"Me, too," Jack added.

Turning to Alexander, Adwen remained stern. "Alex? You've been quiet this whole time. What do you think?"

His brow furrowed. "They both said what I was thinking."

"You're welcome," Jack murmured under his breath.

"I can't bring myself to trust a demon."

Adwen's expression became harsh. "Do you trust me?"

His tone was hard. "Of course I do. I trust you absolutely, but I can't make myself trust a demon on a moment's notice."

Her harsh look glowed brightly at the Marine. "I understand. I understand how all of you feel. This is not easy. But we need him as much as he needs us."

Jack raised an eyebrow. "How much is that?"

"Immeasurably."

They were shocked by sensing that she spoke the truth.

"And Alex? Since you say you can't trust him, I'm going to help you figure out how."

He grimaced.

"Tonight you will share a room with Kale, and you will fall asleep."

Oryn and Jack glanced at their friend, watching the growing discomfort on his face.

Adwen was unsympathetic. "Does anyone else have any problems to talk about?"

They were silent, wishing only for the long day to end.

"Good. I'm as tired as the rest of you. Let's get some sleep."

Darting through the open lot, Adwen reached out with her power to the small motion-activated cameras. The surveillance system bent to her will, failing to detect the Holy Hounds as they jumped the fence on their way to the abandoned train station. Once everyone made it through the window, she let the camera sensors return to working order.

Inside smelled of mold and toxic chemicals. The weathered wood was dark and rotten, barely standing under the weight of the structure. Kale leaned on a crumbly door frame, glancing over as they appeared. He was straight faced until they came in, and then he smiled kindly, concealing his mouth full of wolf teeth.

"Upstairs is better for hiding out, but mind your step. This place is getting torn down soon for a reason."

Adwen called after him as he was about to climb the stairs. "Kale, I'd like to introduce you to my friends properly."

Pausing, he looked over and became slightly embarrassed. "Ah! Apologies. Been a long time since meeting others on a name basis. Sure."

"This is Sir Oryn Conrad."

The knight glared at the werewolf in silence.

"Jack Towers."

He casually crossed his arms, trying again to tap into the demon's mind. It was no use.

Kale noticed the strong probe but easily repelled it. Giving a very light touch back at Jack's mind, he chuckled. "A cop. This should be interesting."

Jack felt the swift touch and was startled by the quickness that the demon plucked out a thought. This put him even more on edge.

Adwen rolled her eyes, ignoring what had just happened. "And this is Alexander."

The Marine wore a hard, unreadable expression, but nodded.

The werewolf chuckled, and responded in his quiet, raspy voice, "A good crew. Looking forward to doing business with yah."

"I'm going to have Alex spend the night with you."

The announcement stunned Kale. Then he shrugged. "Alright. You coming, bunkmate?" Going up the dark stairs to his usual sleeping place, the werewolf turned in for the night.

As he disappeared into what used to be an office on the second floor, Alexander gave Adwen a questioning look. "Can you freeze him like you can us if he tries something?"

Restraining a smile, Adwen replied, "Nope."

None of the three liked the answer, and Alexander sighed, more apprehensive than before. "Outstanding. I think I'll see you all in the morning."

"You will. I promise."

A promise from her was very reassuring, but it did not make the journey up to Kale's room any easier. He trudged up the squeaky, cracked stairs, rusted nails whining at his weight.

Adwen led Oryn and Jack to a waiting area filled with broken furniture. It smelled the least of poisonous substances. As she and the knight settled down in a corner together, Jack leaned back on some old boards by a boarded-up window.

After a minute of settling into their spots, Adwen laid her head on Oryn's chest, thinking of what happened at the hotel. "Jack?"

His voice echoed across the room. "Yeah? What's up?"

"Those men at the hotel. When you read their minds, did you find out who they were?"

He grimaced, shaking his head. "No, I didn't. I have no idea who they were or where they came from. They weren't cops; that I can promise you. Police tend to have a distinct smell. Can't say how, but they just do."

Feeling dread at a new thought, Adwen replied, "I think I've seen men like them before."

Oryn and Jack stared. "Where?"

Holding onto Oryn tightly, she frowned, blue eyes aglow in anger. "Men just like them were hunting my family, though they didn't have demon-steel bullets."

The knight stole a glance at her wounded arm. Adwen's silver blood stopped trickling a short while ago. Seeing the damage was ominous. If they were to encounter those people again, they would have to be very careful.

"We'll worry about it tomorrow."

Following the faint scent trail left by Kale, Alexander entered the dilapidated office. The furniture was gone, leaving the space almost completely bare. He did not see Kale at first but could smell him. He found the werewolf in the red jacket sitting against a wall around a corner, clawed hands in his pockets. Keeping an eye on the creature, the Marine tried to decide where to get some rest for himself.

Kale broke the quiet suddenly: "Like I said, it's not much. Mind you, don't sit on a board with splinters."

Alexander acted as if he had heard nothing, picking a wall that was not so filthy. There he sat, trying to relax, and closed his eyes.

Kale spoke again: "You might want to be careful, mate."

Alexander looked over, making his stare glow bright, expecting a threat.

Smiling, the werewolf turned his head and added, "This place is dangerous. There's a monster who likes to stay in the closet."

At this, Alexander frowned, pursing his lips. Kale was sitting inside the old office closet, chuckling to himself. Taking a breath again and hushing his laughter, he shook his head. "I'm sorry. Not my best material. Been waiting ages to use that one, though." His chuckling continued.

The Marine groaned, "Outstanding. A demon who jokes. As if we need another one of those."

"You're an interesting one. All of you are."

Alexander said nothing, making another attempt to go to sleep. To his disappointment, Kale was not done speaking.

"Where were you when she was sent to fetch yah for all this?"

He scowled. "I don't have to tell you anything."

Kale was not intimidated, but withdrew a little in the awkward conversation. "Alright, sorry. Didn't mean to offend. Trying to figure out what's different about you that sticks out to me. Can't quite put my finger on it."

Clearly this would not end until Kale got whatever he was after. Alexander decided to carefully play along with the demon.

"What did you mean by 'sent to fetch' me? She picked me."

Studying him, Kale discovered what was different in this warrior compared to the others. What he found almost made him start laughing again. "You've got to be joking. Are you having me on?"

Alexander glared back straight-faced.

Seeing that he was right, Kale shook his head ruefully. "I can't believe this. You, a warrior of light serving the Heir of Darien, does not believe the Light Spirits exist."

"What does that matter?"

"Oh, come off it. Adwen did not pick any of you lot; she was sent by the Light Spirits to offer the choice. How is that so hard to believe?"

The Marine huffed and scowled. "Why should I? Have you ever seen a Light Spirit?"

Becoming serious, Kale corrected him. "They, not A. You owe them much. I owe them much. After all they've done, the least you could do is acknowledge that they exist."

"You didn't answer my question: Have you ever seen the Light Spirits?"

The glow in Kale's bright red eyes glinted. "Of course not. Have you?"

Alexander shook his head and looked away. "If there's no evidence, then they don't exist."

A quiet moment passed as Kale stared at the Marine, studying his mind. Then he had an idea and smiled.

"Hey, soldier?"

Uncomfortable with the demon knowing he was prior military, he looked over, scowling. "What do you want from me?"

Kale continued to smile slyly. An instant later, something breathed behind Alexander's ear and a touch like a finger tapped him three times on the shoulder. He nearly jumped out of his skin, reeling and yet finding nothing there. Giving Kale a frightened, searching stare, he braced himself for the unexpected.

Kale teased, "Oh! What was that?"

Alexander took a breath to steady his nerves. "You tapped me on the shoulder."

Playing coy, the werewolf acted confused. "What? You were looking right at me, keeping my hands to myself. Why would you think I tapped you on the shoulder from way over here?"

"Because you're a demon."

Kale let the playful mood go and became serious. "That's circumstantial. All of the evidence is circumstantial in the end. For instance, there was the fact that I called for your attention in the exact moment that I had a funny look on my face, and then the tapping occurred. The truth is that I did tap you on the shoulder, but you did not see me do it and have no idea how I did it."

"What's your point?"

"You can believe that a demon tapped you on the shoulder but deny the presence of the Light Spirits, who have granted you immense power. That is my point. The evidence to their existence is all around you and within you. Your inability to believe in them is why you don't feel the sun's touch the same way as the others."

"The sunlight feels warmer than when I was human, if that's what you mean."

Kale looked down, shaking his head, smiling. "If you want to find out what I'm talking about, give this a go in the morning: When the sun comes through that window, stand there. And here's the easy part, since you are a jarhead – clear your mind."

Alexander frowned, still skeptical.

"Clear your head and open your heart while the light of dawn touches your skin. I dare yah." Kale chuckled more as he settled himself down to sleep.

Alexander Greeves did not know what to make of the last few minutes. This demon was eerie. The power to tap his shoulder without being near him was beyond even Jack and his telekinesis. Nevertheless, the Marine was tired. It was time get some sleep.

A rainstorm swept in from the coast passing up the inlet to the city. Wind whipped and tugged at everything, pelting the ground with big drops of water. Their hideout's roof leaked in many places. Tiny cascades trickled down, tapping rotten boards on the second floor. There was no lightning or thunder to accompany the storm, only cleansing rain.

Everyone slept soundly except Kale. In his empty closet space he shivered, eyes moving to and fro rapidly. Each breath was a shuddering one, while sweat collected on his brow. His nightmare was horrible and always the same. Sometimes there was more or less, but rarely did it change.

In the jacket pocket where his left hand twitched and clenched in the throes of the tortured sleep, a soft glow radiated. Gradually, Kale's breathing slowed, and his fidgeting ceased. The nightmare ebbed, and something took its place. When he was calm and still, his eyes snapped open. Fully awake, the last thing he remembered hearing echoed in his mind. The sounds from the lucid dream made his crimson eyes fill with tears again, and put a weak smile on his face. He cherished the moment that recently passed.

Noticing the light in his pocket, he took his hand out, examining the patch of glowing golden flesh. The light dimmed again as he admired it, and it resumed its metallic sheen. A tear ran down one cheek. He held the hand and then gently kissed what she had given him. Raising his gaze upward, another tear fell, and he whispered.

"Thank you."

Kale closed his eyes again, settling more comfortably against the wall. He did not go back to sleep so as not to spoil the evening with another nightmare.

There were several new puddles around Alexander when he began to wake. Luckily, none had formed where he had bedded down. Right away, he checked to see if the werewolf was still in his closet. He was, and he appeared to be asleep, bearded chin resting on his chest. The hair growing around his strong jaw looked more like black wolf fur than facial hair. The rest of his shaggy mane fell around his face and onto broad, burly shoulders.

Dim light filtered through the gaps in the planks that boarded the windows. Getting up without waking Kale, he checked to see if the weather was clear. Peering through the gap where a plank had loosened, the sky was a perfect blue between scattered fluffy clouds. Traffic packed the highway with commuters headed to work deeper in the city.

As the sun drifted out past the mountaintops, warm light fell across him. He stared at the luminous, burning orb rising higher. Kale remained quiet and still. The Marine decided to test the werewolf's harmless dare.

Alexander closed his eyes. He steadily decluttered his thoughts. When his mind was still, he relaxed, letting the light warm his skin. Wondering if there really were Light Spirits, he waited, anticipating nothing. Regardless, the light's warmth was pleasant and held him there a little longer than usual.

Then the warmth of the light on his cheeks felt strange. It felt warmer and softer, like skin on palms and fingertips. The light felt like hands caressing him so gently that he could barely feel it. It healed his weary mind and filled his body with strength.

When he opened his eyes, light was lancing through trees and distant buildings, flickering in odd shapes through the dirty glass window. The shapes formed a face and a pair of slender hands on outstretched arms. The image of a woman smiled. He gasped when he realized he was not witnessing a trick of the light. His wife's spirit sat on the windowsill, framed with pure light.

Emily stared, caressing him with the light that gave her form. She was so happy he had finally found her again.

Alexander was breathless. He tried to grasp her hands and felt great relief at finding he could. Yet when he reached to pull her close, he could not. Elated just to see her, it did not bother him. The Marine settled with what he was able to have. Emily's presence warmed his heart, filling it to the brim.

"She's still there, isn't she?" asked a hushed, raspy voice.

Emily glanced over at the slouched werewolf, wearing a thankful, beaming expression. As the sun rose higher, it was time for her to go. Unable to speak, she mouthed the words he would be able to read on her lips so easily. His eyes glazed over as she disappeared.

Kale kept his head low, eyes closed as he spoke. "She's always been there, and she always will be. Now you know where to find her."

Turning to stare at the demon, Alexander could think of nothing to say.

"The others only feel the warmth of the Light Spirits. It feels like hands, touching, feeling. It feels like love." He paused and sighed quietly. "I wish I could feel the light like that."

For a long while the room was quiet. Alexander stared at Kale, trying to understand how and why he did this. He almost failed to notice Jack coming to find them. When his friend finally entered and spoke, he quickly wiped at the dampness on his lashes.

"Hey, Jarhead. You survived the night! Where's the werewolf?" Jack saw Alexander had been crying while Kale slouched back in the closet. The cop snarled, his glare alight with rage. "What did you do, you sorry sack of ..."

"Leave him alone," Alexander said.

Jack was taken aback. "You're crying. I've never seen you

cry. What did he do?"

"He didn't do anything. It's okay."

The cop was suspicious. "It's obvious he did something."

Rubbing at the back of his neck, Alexander sighed. "It was nothing." Glancing over in the closet, he mused. "He ... tapped me on the shoulder."

Where no one could see, a small contented smile crept across Kale's face.

Alexander kept rubbing his neck, pondering as he turned to go.

As he left, Jack remained suspicious. The warrior glared at Kale's head, covered in thick, wavy, messy black hair. His intense stare glowed mahogany brown. Jack growled, speaking with his mind, knowing the creature could hear and reply.

<Leave my friends alone, demon. The next time you try to mess with any of us, remember I'm watching you.>

There was silence. Kale was unresponsive, making Jack's glare deepen. Then he heard Kale's voice whisper behind one ear and felt his breath.

"Likewise."

Jack gave a start, flinching and checking to see what was there. He found nothing. Observing Kale with more apprehension than anger, the creature started to stretch his arms.

Pretending to have only just woken up, Kale feigned a big, fanged yawn. Then he glanced at Jack's alarmed expression. "Oh! Good morning? Have you been standing there long?"

The warrior scowled.

Kale was secretly amused. "Well, thanks for coming to fetch me. It's time to move along." Picking himself up from the closet floor, he passed Jack, chuckling.

Letting the werewolf stroll ahead, he was thankful for the growing distance between them. Jack felt he could tolerate Kale less and less with every encounter.

Adwen and Oryn waited by the broken window for the others. When they saw Alexander, he was lost in thought.

She called to him, "Did you get decent sleep?"

Noticing where they were, he went closer, staring vacantly at the floor.

This worried Oryn. "Did he invade your dreams?"

Adwen rolled her eyes, knowing Kale would not do such a thing.

Alexander shook his head. "He's weird, but he's okay."

She beamed. "I know."

Even then the knight was not convinced, and he studied the Marine's demeanor.

Kale walked casually down the creaky steps, wearing a happy smile. "Morning."

"Good morning, Kale. Did you sleep last night?"

Thinking about it, he nodded. "Yeah. I actually had a dream. It was very special."

Oryn sneered. "Demons can't dream. Even if they did sleep, there would only be nightmares."

The cold remark made Kale chuckle and he teased Oryn. "Oh, look who knows so much."

Adwen spoke up in Kale's defense. "He was telling the truth. Relax already. He's on our side."

Oryn believed her, though it was hard to accept.

When Jack came downstairs, Adwen influenced the energy in the security cameras to go dormant. The group darted out and leaped over the tall chain-link fence. At a safe distance from the condemned structure, they continued at a stroll.

Adwen asked the werewolf in their midst, "Okay, so what are you having for breakfast?"

He was surprised. "You were serious about that? Give me a minute. Need to think."

The knight and the police officer exchanged suspicious looks, waiting for what he would answer.

A thought occurred to Kale that pleased him. "I'd like ... a Happy Meal."

They stopped, and everyone stared.

"Really?" Adwen shrugged. "That's not even filling."

Kale was undeterred. "Nah. It's the principal of the matter. I've been eating nothing but psychos, murderers and sadists for the last five years. I want a damn Happy Meal."

She almost laughed. "Okay, Happy Meal it is. Shall we walk to pass the time until the lunch menu is up?"

"Sure." He chuckled to himself, amused and glad that this was happening.

Meanwhile, Oryn and Jack continued to keep a close eye on the werewolf. Alexander did as well, but not with the same hostility as his friends.

At a table with a curved padded bench, a warm steamy meal in waxy paper products lay before Kale. For a long moment he looked at the wrapped cheeseburger, French fries and tiny soda. The smell was appetizing for the first time in his five years in the living worlds. It was not glorious, but it was liberating.

Adwen and the others watched him pick up a single fry with two sharp claws. He tossed it back, chewing before swallowing. Kale licked his lips, considering the taste. It was a far cry from the flesh and blood of humans, along with their feelings and emotions. He could hardly believe he'd just eaten something that was guiltless. Laughing quietly, he smiled. "That was so salty."

"Eat the fries before they go cold," Adwen advised. "They don't taste as good after that."

"Good to know. Thanks." Consuming them in threes and fours, he gradually emptied the cardboard carton.

Alexander watched, seeing the glimmer of joy in Kale's red eyes. "What kind of demon are you?"

Adwen shushed him. "Alex!"

Kale heard no animosity in the question. Washing down the last mouthful of fries, the soda was saccharine sweet and bubbly. "It's alright, Adwen. There's no direct translation from the demon language for what I am. Some others have called me a rogue."

Oryn raised an eyebrow. "A rogue demon?"

"Yeah, right? Sort of an oxymoron. My kind try to kill me every chance they get once they learn what I am."

The Marine wanted to know more. "Why?"

Sighing, Kale's mood diminished with this conversation topic. "I'm a liability. I know too many secrets the darkness wants to keep from the living. I am a weak link in their perfect chain. They can't stand for it."

Adwen smiled. "Glad we found you."

He scoffed. "Yeah, so am I. Even if you had chosen to destroy me, better you than them. They would lock me away in eternal torment instead of making me disappear. There's a special place in the Void for rejects like myself. They never get out."

"Are there many like you?" Alexander asked.

"Doubtful," Oryn said, earning a cold look from Adwen.

"There aren't." Kale frowned. "Rogues are an anomaly. They can only be spawned from a lost soul. None can come from the black lake in the center of the Void. A lost soul that can become a rogue is resistant to the darkness, retaining their elements of light. They're usually very careful not to pick such a resistant soul for making a demon. I'm an accident."

Adwen asked a question of her own: "Do you know of any others who got out of the Void?"

"Any that the darkness discovers are quickly hunted down. I only know of one other who ever got out. She was able to briefly serve Darien."

"Impossible," Oryn said, shaking his head. "There was never any mention of such a demon."

Reading the hatred in Oryn's eyes, Kale coolly replied, "There was, and her host was swiftly killed by another demon, stopping her from providing more secrets. If too many people knew that information about how to fight demons had come straight from the mouth of a demon, Darien would have been in a tight spot. It had to be kept very hush-hush."

The knight clenched his jaw, mulling over the concept. Adwen was nodding, indicating that Kale spoke the truth.

He returned some of his attention to the meal, which was starting to cool. Kale opened the cheeseburger wrapper and took a deep sniff before taking a bite. It did not impress his changed sense of taste, but it was heavenly for being so simple.

"Well," Adwen began, "we need you to do the same thing. None of us really knows what we are up against this time."

Wolfing down the meaty cheeseburger, Kale sucked some mustard from one claw. "Sounds good to me. Let's get on with it. What's the disaster?"

They all exchanged dark looks. "Dargadia has been overrun."

Kale had only been half joking and he frowned. "Oh ... sorry. Well, I'm afraid I'm going to need some details. What's going on exactly?"

"The Order is destroyed, and the sky over the kingdom is

eternal night."

At hearing this, Kale's eyes became wide, and he sat back in his seat. "It's the time then."

"What?"

"Ever heard of the Darkening Time?"

Oryn replied, "Darien's guardians mentioned such a thing."

"Hold on," Jack cut in. "We took care of the Darkening Time. That was when we fought the demons a couple years ago."

Kale wore a solemn expression. "I'm afraid not. What you experienced was the precursor. This is the Darkening Time. One of the visions from the Elf King Arianwyn told of Darien's Heir and four warriors riding into the Darkening Time. The fate of worlds would rest in their hands to either restore the balance or fall into chaos for eternity. That time would come when the sky sleeps and the innocents cover the hills like snow."

Adwen added grimly, "They killed the unicorns."

The werewolf's face drained of color. Feeling as if he may vomit the Happy Meal, his expression was baleful. "How many?"

Jack studied his reaction. "No point in counting. And time is frozen around them. Everywhere is ash and dust around ruins and dead trees."

Kale gulped, struggling to keep the food down. "That's dark, dark stuff. To kill them and deny them passing on is of the darkest magic. And powerful, too."

"Does keeping them frozen in time serve a purpose?" Adwen asked.

Recovering slowly from the shock, some color returned to Kale's face. "Two things: First, the unicorns are the embodiment of pure magic and life. They spread those things with them everywhere they step in their lifetime. Upon death, they fade into the earth, giving rise to a tree. Those trees breathe more magic into the air, living long past a thousand years. The first unicorns to die at the hands of demons created a forest in the middle of the Elf-Wood. Magic is thick in the air there. You can see it congealing over you."

Kale fell quiet, so Alexander prompted him to continue: "And the second thing?"

Going from sad to sickened, Kale's red eyes flashed. "Their bodies can serve another purpose: inspiring despair. Their corpses can act as vile totem ornaments."

Although they were disturbed by the explanation, Adwen carried the conversation along. "There are these dark pillars. We broke one, and the sun was able to rise a little farther into the sky at dawn."

"Dark pillars? Is there black mist? Please tell me there is. If there isn't, then it's too late."

"There are miles of it. The mist is everywhere over the kingdom. It reaches the mountain passes to the north."

Kale was a little calmer. "Good. How did it break?"

"I forced my light to touch the surface, and it cracked before exploding. We only just got out of range before it blew."

Kale contemplated the descriptions. "Sounds like the Ereego Denagri."

Hearing demon words put a sour taste in Adwen's mouth. Only she among the Holy Hounds understood the dark spirit language. "Fingers of the Void."

"Yeah, and there'll be seven if I'm correct."

"There have been three or four sighted." Alexander said. "The one in the plains is really big, from what we heard."

"That doesn't surprise me. The ideal places for them are above magical pressure points in the earth. The plains are where the biggest of the temples stood; there were three and one for each light seal. These seals supported the Order of the Master Knights fortress and made it impossible to build the Fingers of the Void. Naturally, those temples marked the location for the biggest flows of magic in Dargadia."

Adwen connected the information with what they knew. "The last temple in Tanoaks fell a few months ago. That's when the Order fell. After that came the deaths of the unicorns and the first appearance of the pillars."

"So." Jack leaned forward, uncertain what answer he would get for his next question. "We just have to break down the Fingers of the Void and we win?"

Kale's gloomy expression darkened further. Almost angry at what was on his mind, he murmured, "Afraid not."

"Figured." Jack slumped back, disappointed.

"Who are we fighting?" Adwen's blue eyes shone with determination. "What is their name?"

"As I'm a hunted demon, it's best I don't speak it. They'd

find me." He snapped clawed fingertips. "And on top of that bit of bad news, there's something else." Holding up a hand, he opened his fingers, splaying them wide, wearing a bitter frown.

Oryn almost gasped, and Adwen felt nauseous.

Jack was aghast. "Are you kidding me? There are five?"

Putting the hand down, Kale nodded. "Yes, and then there is their leader. Adwen, remember Melanin? He's deader than death, so I can name him all I like, by the by."

She nodded. "Yes."

"You fought him. Recall how strong he was compared to you?"

The image in her memory of those white specs for eyes and the monstrous grin sent chills down her back. "A little stronger than me."

"He was a cripple; that demon lord was cut off from the Void by Darien's seal, making him weak and unable to hide anywhere outside his castle. We are pitted against five demon lords and the Overlord of the Void. He's also been called the Dark Heart."

Adwen shivered. "What can you tell us about them?"

"The Dark Heart is not his name. Titles and nicknames are safer to use. There is his second, The Weaver, who is more of a strategist. The Reaper is the one who stalks and hunts threats to them. That one is likely looking for you right now if we haven't already been found."

Seeing their reactions, Kale reassured them. "I can feel the ground here is outside of his bounds. We're safe. The Whisperer corrupts the living and drives some mad to further the demon lords' plans. The Tormenter likes to stay in the Void, feeding off the suffering, acting as the Dark Heart's entertainer. He rarely shows his face outside the dark plane. Then there is the Taskmaster. He's the one who sends demons out for special jobs. The Tormenter and the Taskmaster are the least of the five and not nearly as smart as the rest. The Taskmaster's a big tosser."

Alexander had more questions for their demon expert. "How strong are you? We can't sense your power at all. You're a dark iceberg to us."

The question distracted Kale, and he paused to stare. Then he shrugged, acting coy. "Well, I've never cared for boasting. I'm a bit shy."

Adwen answered for him. "He's as powerful as Sycan was."

Instantly, Kale's silly smile disappeared, and his face slackened. The whites of his eyes turned black around red irises, filled with a storm of emotions, staring vacantly at the table. He felt sick at hearing the name, let alone the comparison.

Adwen was apologetic, cupping a hand to her mouth. "I'm so sorry. I forgot. I'm sorry."

Swallowing the lump in his throat, Kale tried to recover from the statement's heavy toll. "That's alright. You didn't mean to."

The knight gave the werewolf a scrutinizing glare. "You were acquainted."

Briefly making eye contact, he could not hide the fact. "You might say that. We weren't friends. Met once or twice. He wasn't very good at introductions the first time around." A thought came to Kale, making him feel a little better, dispelling the black from his eyes. Forcing a smile, Kale looked at Adwen. "But he's gone now. I have you to thank for that."

"I didn't kill him."

Kale blanched. "You didn't? He's still ..."

"No! He's destroyed. I wasn't the one who killed him."

A big sigh of relief followed. "You had me going for a moment. Who do I thank then?"

Turning her head to the knight at her side, she beamed. "He killed him."

Oryn watched the creature look him over. Until now, Kale was wise enough to avoid meeting Oryn's gaze for long. The knight scowled, while Kale appeared pleasantly surprised.

"Wow," Kale murmured. "That's so perfect."

"What's perfect about that?"

"Adwen slays the artist, the Demon Maker, while you, her second in command, destroys his prized masterpiece. It's very fitting, isn't it?"

While Kale was somewhat distracted, Jack summoned an object. He used his telekinesis to launch it across the table right for Kale's face.

At the last second, the werewolf sensed the object flying at his forehead. He deftly caught it with one hand an inch from his brow, staring raptly at Jack unblinkingly. Kale took a moment to study the proud look on the police officer before examining the tennis ball.

Adwen groaned, embarrassed and exasperated, "Jack."

Kale's brow furrowed as he looked at the ball and back at Jack. "A tennis ball? How old are we? Twelve?"

At first, Oryn was irritated by Jack's prank, but then Jack nudged him with an elbow. Looking again, the knight was overcome by shock and suspicion. Alexander already was musing about Kale, but now was far more intrigued.

Befuddled by their reactions, Kale glanced around at them all. "What? Is it that surprising I caught it? My reaction time isn't that much faster than any of you lot."

Adwen groaned, "Kale."

"Hmm?"

Sighing, she was bewildered by Jack's trouble-making. "You caught it with your right hand."

Kale's eyes widened, and his smile slackened a moment, but he recovered right away. "So you've uncovered my secret. I'm ambidextrous. Well done, detective."

Jack's sly smile did not fade. "Adwen, is he ambidextrous?"

She gave Kale's cool expression a sad glance. As she had given her word, she was bound to tell them if he was lying. "He's not. He is right-handed."

Stealing a glance at his left hand and the piece of Adwen's heart, he knew he was caught. Kale rolled his eyes, puffing in defeat. "Alright, there are more important things to discuss than whether I'm left-handed, right-handed or use both equally. The worlds are ending. May we please get back to the bigger problems?"

While he was begging to change the subject, a mother and child in the restaurant walked by. The little girl tugged at her mother as they headed for the door, pointing at Kale eagerly. As soon as he heard the little voice, he froze, wishing he were invisible.

"Mommy! Mommy! He's a birdy! Mommy, look at the big birdy! Mommy? Mom!"

The mother saw a muscular man and felt uneasy, dragging her child out of the building faster. She ignored her daughter's unusual cries, assuming she was pointing out the window rather than at Kale.

Once the mother and daughter were gone, the Holy Hounds looked at Kale.

Forcing a toothy smile, he uttered weakly, "Kids."

Oryn was even more suspicious of the demon. "What do you really look like?"

"I'd like to know the same thing, Big Guy." Jack agreed, "What do you really look like under there?"

Avoiding the knight and staring blankly at the cop, Kale calmly replied, "That's going to have to wait for another conversation. That's rather private."

To get the discussion back on track, Adwen spoke up, "First things first: We need to take down more pillars."

"And with things the way they are," Kale said, "taking care of the demon lords will have to be played by ear. To avoid The Reaper, we will have to move quickly. Opening your portals near the pillars would work. You might be able to take them all out in a single day."

She bit her lip. The others became sullen.

The reaction at the table made Kale raise an eyebrow. "What's the problem?"

"I'm too weak to break the other pillars."

Kale made a befuddled expression. "You're plenty strong enough, sweetheart."

"A powerful demon named Impurus hit me with a dark seal."

He groaned, "Aw, bugger. What has it done to you?"

"It bound my strength in that world to the magic in Dargadia. While I'm in that world, I'm as weak as a human. I was weaker until the first pillar fell. Then I became a little stronger."

Raking both sets of claws through the thick, black hair on his scalp, he sighed. "That's some comfort. But if you don't have the strength to break the pillars, then no one can, and I'm out of ideas. There's just one thing left to do."

Alexander was curious. "What's that?"

"Take some yoga lessons, put your head between your legs and kiss your backside goodbye. The demon lords really thought this plan through to the last detail."

A clever look came over Adwen. "I have a pretty good idea. It just came to me."

They looked at her as Kale stared and expected a wondrous solution.

Her gaze sparkled at the werewolf. "You."

"Me?"

"You. You are going to break the pillars. I'll help."

After a long pause, Kale burst out loud in laughter. Other restaurant patrons glanced at him, uncomfortable with the disturbance. He slapped a hand on the table, shaking his head, tears in his eyes.

"That's a good one! I'm made of flesh, blood and darkness. I can't break the pillars."

She reached out to touch his left hand, and the golden piece glowed. His laughter abruptly ceased, and they locked eyes. The other warriors at the table and Kale began to see her plan.

As Adwen took her hand away, he lifted his gaze, contemplating the suggestion. A clever smile lit his face, and he chuckled, "Oh, that's good, sweetheart. That's very good."

Oryn disliked the term. "Her name is Adwen."

Politely, he nodded to the knight and went back to admiring his hand. "Adwen." Facing her, he was filled with excitement. "It can work, but the demon lords will come up with a counter-attack. And they're going to be very, very angry."

"Good. I already am."

Kale chuckled, flexing his claws, working the golden flesh in his hand. "When do you want to get started?"

"Right away. Let's find a place to open a portal."

He held up a finger. "Wait a tick." Kale gulped what was left of the little soda, slurping the bottom of the straw amid ice cubes. Placing it back on the tray with finality, he sighed. "Now I'm ready. Let's get to work."

Chapter 9
IDLE TEARS

Adwen's fiery portal opened by the riverside near the cave sanctuary. After they came through and it closed, the evil seal clutching Adwen activated. Her body shone as her strength ebbed and that of her warriors with it. When she became visible, her clothing had reverted to the form of simple cloth wrappings. Oryn supported her as the acute drop in strength made her stagger.

Kale stared, stunned. "You weren't kidding."

Taking a deep breath, she replied, "Nope, I wasn't."

With rushing water near their feet, Jack did not like being back in the dark. "You could have dropped us at the overlook, you know."

"There's an overlook?" Kale said. "Lovely!"

Adwen scoffed at Kale's comment before answering. "Uh, Jack? There are a lot of injured, tired and angry humans and gargoyles inside."

Jack alternated glances between her and the amused werewolf, both watching him think. "You know, that is an excellent point. How about he stays outside?"

Kale shrugged. "Suits me just fine. I'll wait by the falls and have a bath."

"No, he's coming inside, too."

Everyone cast her uneasy expressions.

"He is one of us now. Kale, you are going inside, but if things get out of control, you need to be ready to run. The Order of the Gargoyle is armed with weapons coated in gold. You're slightly resistant now, but they can still kill you."

He shook his head, chuckling. "I'm used to this. Don't worry about it."

"I want everyone – and I mean everyone – to be ready to protect Kale." Glancing at Oryn and Jack's disgruntled looks, she added, "Even if you don't want to. Remember, we need him for the pillars."

As much as the two hated to admit it, they would do their best.

"Okay, Kale, stay between us. Try not to talk too much."

He whined, "Aw, that's no fun."

"Just be careful. Let's go."

Leaving the dark bank for the equally dark cave, the roaring of the falls dulled. When it hushed considerably, Kale mused aloud, "Your Order of the Gargoyle has the perfect setup."

"How so?"

"No scent or presence from anyone or anything inside can reach outward. They'll never be found. Not to mention some magic here from a long time ago keeps it protected. It's perfect."

"They'll be glad to hear that. I'll let you tell them."

Kale laughed to himself, finally smelling humans and gargoyles, as well as their blood. It was a relief to be repulsed by it rather than enticed. Copper and mineral odors filled the air. Quiet whispers eventually reached their ears as they approached light from candles and lanterns.

Many who remained in this sanctuary congregated in a warm space. Low conversations and those redressing wounds looked up at seeing Adwen enter. Most got to their feet, and one rushed off. Just as their happy murmurs began, the rest of Adwen's company entered, and they saw Kale's red eyes in the gloom.

A knight shouted, drawing a silver-steel sword coated in gold. "Monster!" Others drew weapons, and some mages summoned energy in their hands preparing for a fight. "Tame One! What is the meaning of this? What have you brought into our refuge?"

Holding out her hands for calm, she was firm. The power in her voice helped soothe much of the tension. "Calm down! He is with us and is helping stop the demons. I would never put any of you in danger. His name is Kale."

While she calmed the humans, Kale smelled something. Fear in the room was thick, but a familiar hatred wafted over him; someone in this place knew him. He cautiously began to sniff to identify the individual before they could strike.

Jack and Alexander noticed. "Could you not do that?" Jack said. "You're making it worse. They'll think you want to eat them."

Not giving Jack so much as a glance, he continued the search. "Can't be helped."

One gargoyle asked, "What is this one you've brought? It smells like a werewolf."

Tensions rose again, forcing Adwen to work harder for calm. "He is bound to me. Leave him alone. Without him, we will lose this war. Now everyone, put your weapons away, please."

The human knight shuddered. "You've bound a werewolf to your cause? Against my own caution, I will trust you. You are the Heir of Darien."

Seeing them put their weapons and magic away set her and the warriors at ease. Adwen heaved a heavy sigh.

"Thank you. Where is the General?"

"He is atop the overlook discussing things with the Shield Captain and the Captain. I've sent someone to fetch them. It shall be a few moments, so you may wish to wait here." Despite trusting Adwen, the knight and the rest of those present watched the werewolf with scrutiny.

The chamber was crowded. With the Holy Hounds surrounding him, Kale nevertheless stood within reach of some of the angry, suspicious humans. Some wore deadly sneers. Sniffing more subtly, Kale kept searching for the source of the odor of hatred.

A tough female mage snapped at him. "Who are you looking at?"

He shrugged. "I don't know. What's your name?"

She spat on the ground, and some sneers turned to hard scowls.

Looking the other way, he sniffed again. A band of men in knight armor, though some were not knights, stared back. The familiar scent was someone among them. Studying the closest big knight, Kale cocked an eyebrow. "Have we met?"

After working his jaw, the human spoke with deadly calm. "Had we, one of us would be dead."

Wondering if it where this one, he leaned past Oryn and Alexander to sniff him. The knight and his comrades flinched. After sampling his scent, Kale determined he was not the one and shook his head. "Nah, you would have lived. You're not my favorite flavor."

Alexander restrained a laugh.

A young man in armor casually stepped around the knight. "We've met."

Swift as lighting, the young man in knight armor swung a jeweled silver-steel dagger for Kale's throat. Pulling back far enough to avoid death, Kale sniffed. He instantly picked up the scent of pained hatred.

Locking gazes with the young man, he raised his hands, sending the human flying backward into the wall. There the fighter slumped on the floor. Shouting erupted as Kale pounced, pinning the young man against the rocky surface. Everyone drew weapons, but Adwen's warriors kept them away. Kale never broke eye contact with the vengeful young man.

"You remember me, don't you, monster? I can see it your face!"

He was almost empathetic as he spoke gently. "I can never forget."

One knight yelled, "Tame One! Slay the monster! Slay it before it feeds!"

Her voice shook the air: "If Kale dies, we all die!"

The truth and gravity of the statement silenced the cave at once. The humans and gargoyles had no choice but to wait and see what would happen.

"Kale, please let him go."

Studying the human's mind and feelings, he softly replied, "I have to take care of this first."

Unafraid, the young man sneered: "That's right. Finish what you started with my father, filth." He spat on Kale.

The werewolf did not flinch, reading the pain and rage before him. Holding up the dagger the fighter had dropped, he held it before him.

Some murmured, stunned. "A werewolf touching silver-steel? Why is he not burned?"

Neither Kale nor the young man cared that he was unharmed by touching the blade. Holding it where they could both see it, he asked, "Where did you get this dagger?"

"From my father!"

"Tell me the truth. Where did your father get the dagger?"

He answered through clenched teeth. "From his father before him!"

Kale's gaze narrowed. "Don't you know better than to lie to a demon? Especially me. I'm made of lies. I'll ask again. If you can't tell the truth, I'll make you tell the truth whether you know it or not."

The human remained unafraid.

"Where did your father get this dagger?"

"From his ..."

The young man fell quiet, gasping as the werewolf's face came within inches of his. Blackness filled the whites of Kale's eyes. A thin current of dark mist flowed between their foreheads. As part of Kale's presence pierced the human's mind, the young man could not speak no matter how hard he tried. At last, the human felt afraid, his mouth opening and closing like a beached fish.

Kale's voice resonated, his true voice mingling with that of his living body. "Where did your father get the dagger?"

A moment passed, and the human tried to repeat what was said before. The more he tried to say it, the more he stammered and gasped for air. He had no choice but to let different words roll from his tongue and lips.

"From a nobleman. My father was a highwayman. We lived on the road." Telling the truth, including things he had not known, left the young man feeling defeated and as helpless as a child. Some of the young man's friends stood close by hardly believing their ears.

Kale frowned. "Brace yourself, kid. You're about to find out who your real friends are."

The young man's stare begged that there be no more questions, but it was no use; he was paralyzed.

"What happened on the night you met me?"

The human struggled to resist. Pursing his lips tightly, he tried to hold his mouth shut, letting no sounds come out. He could feel the thoughts and words forming, fighting his dire need to keep them in. It could not be held back for long, and his endurance broke under Kale's indomitable will.

Resisting the urge to cry as he spoke, his mouth told the story. "A rich couple went for an evening ride. They got lost near our hideout. My father spooked their horses to run, leaving them behind. When the man tried to resist, my father slit his throat." He started to sob.

"Continue the story."

"He grabbed the woman and tried to take her jewels off her neck and hands. Then you came. You told him to let her go. He laughed. So, you grabbed father's arm and broke it, letting her escape. She ran, and he pulled the dagger, but you broke his other arm. Then you started to eat him. I got the dagger, and I cut your side."

The young man paused for breath before Kale pulled away, relinquishing control. "Finish the story," he murmured.

Free of the touch from the demon, he remained despondent but continued speaking. "You looked at me, blood down your chin. You looked so sad. Before you ran you said you were sorry."

Silence filled the chamber.

Offering the gem-encrusted pommel to the human, he frowned the same way he had the night he took his father from him. "Do you still want this?"

Gazing long at the bright metal and precious stones, hatred for the demon ebbed. More pain and shame took its place for himself and for the father he lost four years ago. Smacking the dagger from Kale's open claws, it clattered away across the ground. No one would touch it.

"Leave me, beast!"

As Kale stood, some of the men walked off shaking their heads. Two remained, and he furtively glanced at them. "Your friend needs yah." Done with the encounter, he returned to Adwen, letting the humans tend to their own.

Adwen and her warriors took a moment to see how sullen Kale had become before observing the young man.

"You were in this world? Your body is from London, England."

Gazing vacantly at the ground, hands in his pockets, he quietly replied, "I was hoping to find something." Speaking even quieter, feeling the sting of old regrets, Kale added, "I only found heartache. Once I had ahold of his father, I couldn't let go. When he tried to fight, I couldn't stop. I was so hungry."

Jack was as disturbed as Adwen, but Alexander empathized. Yet none could comprehend Kale's experience. Oryn watched the young man, smelling the internal anguish. He knew such pain. Turning to give Kale an icy stare, his tone was cutting and cold, "You are a monster."

Adwen and Alexander were shocked but not surprised at his harsh statement. They waited, watching Kale.

The somber werewolf did not react right away. He seemed unfazed. Then he murmured, "I know I am. I came to terms with that fact years ago."

The Marine wanted to slug Oryn in the jaw but knew it was no use. Instead, he settled for glaring at the knight.

A cluster of onlookers by the next passage parted to let General Raglan through, followed by his brother and the one-winged gargoyle. His voice was the only sound in the dead quiet.

"Lady Adwen, it is good to see you back so soon. May we go to the ... overlook." He stared a long while unblinkingly at Kale. The sight of his glowing red eyes made the General freeze temporarily and lose his voice. When he was able to speak again, his words came slowly and methodically. "Lady Adwen? May we please go above? And I would prefer to not leave that unattended within the sanctuary."

The new situation broke Kale free from painful memories. While everyone else was silent, he scoffed. "That's a first. I've never been referred to as that before."

"Please," the General beckoned, perplexed. "We shall escort you there."

Adwen led her warriors behind the Order leaders.

On the way through chambers, more people caught glimpses of Kale. Those who got a better look flinched or recoiled, whispering to one another. When the group reached the overlook, they found the Order leaders, as well as Virgil and Tamis, were waiting. As soon as Tamis caught the scent of a werewolf, he snarled and raced toward them.

Thinking fast, Adwen used her power to stop him. "Tamis, no!"

The hound warrior's paws and claws skidded over stone. He came to a halt a few paces away, snarling at Kale, whose attention focused on the ring around Tamis's neck.

"Adwen, why is this fiend here? What is this about?"

"Calm down, and I will release you. Tamis, this is Kale. Kale, meet Tamis. He's the fourth of my warriors. As you can see, he's been through a lot."

Tamis growled, "Why is there a werewolf in the sanctuary?"

"He's bound to me! Calm down. We'll explain in the meeting. I'm letting you go now, so relax and return to the table."

Tamis's fur bristled from head to tail. Falling quiet, he returned to the table, keeping his distance from the werewolf. The way Kale's gaze followed made Tamis wary.

Adwen sat across from the Order of the Gargoyle. The other Holy Hounds stood around her, and Kale remained to the side. She waited as Virgil finished studying her new friend and remembered to start the meeting at last.

"Now begins the War Meeting between the Order of the Gargoyle and Lady Adwen. Lady Adwen, as the guest and superior, has first right to speak."

"Thank you, Virgil." She cleared her throat to draw the humans' and gargoyle's attention away from Kale. "I have found a way to destroy the pillars. As I am too weak in this world to break them alone, I found some help. Kale has agreed to the task. I've looked into his heart and found no darkness there. Also, I have bound him to me. Using the piece of myself I have placed in his hand, we shall destroy the pillars." She nodded politely to pass the right to speak.

"The table now turns to Sir Raglan, General of the Order. You now have the right to speak."

Many seconds passed before Raglan found the words. Glancing back and forth between Adwen and Kale, who was watching with great interest, he struggled to digest the news. He sighed and spoke. "To start, Lady Adwen, I am speechless."

"I understand. I would be, too."

"Also, I do not want to offend. I trust your judgment. However, I find myself rather uneasy looking at an alpha werewolf standing in the overlook. How did you come by a dark being without a dark heart?"

"I found him in the other world. He was protecting two human girls from demons."

The three leaders stole another look at Kale in time to see him shrug.

Raglan did not know what to make of him. "We have wounded combatants. A werewolf will not be able to resist his hunger long."

"I've taken care of that. One of his gifts for being bound to me is no longer needing human flesh and blood."

Dynic could not help but speak up. "That's not possible."

Kale could not help himself either. "Just had my first breakfast an hour ago."

"So, what sort of being is this alpha werewolf that does not have a dark heart or desire for human prey?"

Adwen wore a warm smile. "Kale is a rogue demon; he is not connected to the darkness. When he was made into what he is now, he retained the ability to feel as we do. His happening to be in possession of a werewolf body is inconsequential. What's more, he remains very powerful while I am weak, giving us the ability to fight back."

Taking another long moment, Raglan strummed his fingers, thinking. "This is very strange."

"I agree," Geoden said, watching Kale closely. "A rogue demon? Sounds fanciful. And yet, here he stands."

"Lady Adwen." Raglan appeared uncomfortable. "I have a very selfish request to make for the sake of our peace of mind: Is there anything this demon can do to prove good will toward the Order and those we lead?"

She was not offended but found it hard to think of anything. "Well, he's capable of it, but I don't know. Kale, have any ideas?"

His crimson gaze drifted over to Tamis, who was wrinkling his jaws at him. "Already have something in mind."

At this, Tamis snarled, "Don't let him touch me, Adwen! I'm through with demons touching me!"

Kale rolled his eyes. "Well that puts an end to that. Let me have a think."

Raglan raised a hand. "Hold a moment, demon. What was it that you intended?"

Nodding to Tamis, he replied, "That ring – I can read the runes. If I can take a close look, I might be able to help him. I may even be able to get it off, if we're lucky."

The General and his two subordinates nodded in approval.

Horrified, Tamis whimpered, "Adwen, no. Don't let them do this."

Turning to her friend, she soothed him. "Tamis, look at me." When he did, she stared deep into this frightened eyes. "It's okay. Trust me. But if you can't hold still, I will force you."

His tail wrapped about his leg, and his ears drooped while he began to cry. "No! No, no, no!"

"Tamis!" Alexander growled to him, getting his attention immediately. "It really is okay. You can trust him."

The giant rusty colored hound whined, "Sir Alex?"

"He's not like a demon at all. Just relax. He won't try to hurt you."

Tamis knew that any tampering with the ring would bring him pain. Hanging his head, he whimpered, "Alright. He may look."

Virgil announced, "This War Meeting is adjourned." As Kale approached Tamis, the ranger went to his friend's side to comfort him. "I'll remain here, my friend. I hope you find some resolve in that."

Kale knelt, scratching the wiry black hair on the side of his jaw, reading the marks. After a moment examining, he sighed bitterly, "Adwen was right; you've been through an awful lot of torture. They inscribed these after placing it on you. I'm afraid I'm going to have to touch it a little to read it better."

"Just do it," he whined, trying not to think about it.

"It will feel unpleasant." Putting his claw tips to the runes and walking them across the wicked symbols, they glowed into life.

Tamis yelped and quivered. "It feels like knives!"

"Going as fast as I can, kid. Just a bit more."

The hound cried and howled, shaking from the pain. Then it stopped as Kale finished his analysis. Tamis continued to shudder and whimper, dreading what was to come.

No one hated to see him go through this more than Adwen. "Well?"

Kale sighed, shaking his head at the demon device. "Well, we aren't lucky. I can't take it off. It's a good thing nobody has tried. This one is powered by his life force. It breaks, he dies. If it is removed, he dies. It can never come off."

Hopeful, the ranger rubbed Tamis's shoulders. "What can be done?"

"The runes have twisted him and his energy into knots. There are a lot of runes here, and they go in a sequence. By rearranging them into a different order, I can untangle his energy and undo most of what the ring does."

Sir Dynic nodded. "Do it then."

Kale shook his head at the knight. "It's his choice. He's the one who must go through it. This process will be more unpleasant than the average werewolf transformation."

The knights and those who had witnessed one shuddered.

Quaking with thoughts of all that happened while a prisoner of the demons, Tamis did not want to go through with it. He hung his head, crying while the ranger tried to sooth him. After the many terrible tortures in the castle dungeons, the horror of it made it more difficult to choose.

"It'll be quick," Kale murmured, "Say the word, and I will either change it or leave it."

Tamis became even more torn. He did not want to remain trapped in this shape forever or until death. But he knew what altering the ring entailed. Looking balefully into the werewolf's eyes, he saw something there. It briefly reassured him. Sick with fear, Tamis forced himself to whimper, "Change it."

Kale understood. "You're very brave."

At this, Tamis began to cry again while shaking, wishing he could die rather than go through with his choice. Anything had to be better than repeating this agony.

Kneeling beside the fear-wracked hound, Kale became deadly serious. "Everyone listen. Once I've started, no one can interrupt. Stopping me part way could kill him, or worse, leave him trapped forever in pain. No matter what, do not touch him. Ranger, you shall need to step back."

Virgil was determined. "I'm not bothered by transformations, Kale. I'll stay for his sake."

Reading the ranger, he replied, "This is for your protection. He is going to flail. Not even Adwen can hold him still."

At first, Virgil was alarmed. Then he sighed and stepped away to stand with the rest.

Kale whispered to Tamis, "Do you want them to look away?"

The hound nodded, eye's squeezed shut tight.

"He wants everyone but Adwen to avert their stares. Adwen must look for as long as she can to hold him still. It's not going to be pretty." To Tamis, he whispered again. "Let me know when you are ready."

His breaths came in rapid gasps until he was light-headed. Glancing sidelong into Kale's face, he gazed deep into the werewolf's eyes, not knowing what he would find. At seeing encouragement and true understanding, Tamis's breathing steadied a little. When he could not wait any longer, he finally whimpered.

"Do what you will."

Adwen held him rigid as a statue.

Then Kale moved, his hands like swifts, darting and swooping. His claws forced the runes to rise off the stone ring, dancing to and fro. As the runes floated, gradually drifting into a new alignment, Tamis howled as if he were being ripped apart. Despite Adwen's control over his body, he became harder and harder to restrain. Just as Kale made the runes set into the stone, he jumped back before she lost her hold on Tamis.

Tamis's legs shuddered about like the wings of a fly. Adwen knew she could no longer hold him when one of his legs spun and wrenched backward on itself, bones snapping. The shock caused her to let go, and his spine twisted, forcing his back end to turn the wrong way, making Tamis yowl in agony and horror. Limbs and ribs twisted and contorted in terrible directions under his fur. He gasped sporadically, unable to breathe through portions of the unraveling.

The knights and gargoyle looked away. Jack and Alexander flinched at each terrible cracking sound. Adwen tried her best not to cry, cupping both hands to her mouth. Virgil alone watched, forcing himself not to ever look away. For Tamis, Virgil would endure what he could of seeing him suffer.

Oryn could not stand by and watch the torment. Certain Kale had tricked them all, he lunged. His armored fists snatched the demon by the front of his jacket and pinned him high against the stone wall. Struggling to decide whether to let their only means of defeating the demons live, he sneered. Kale did nothing to resist. Suspended off the ground, he remained calm. His own face showed no emotion. Then the sounds of Tamis's horrible transformation ceased.

The angry knight saw the werewolf subtly glance over and heard awestruck voices. Daring to look away from Kale, Oryn was stunned by what he saw.

Tamis was getting to his pawed feet, having reclaimed his true form. The hound warrior stood tall, adorned in enchanted archer leathers. He looked at himself, studying his furry hands, flexing them, joyful at having them again. As a test, he summoned his golden magic bow, and it manifested in a small flash. Tamis breathed a deep, happy sigh, listening to his friends crowding around to share in the moment.

Oryn dropped Kale back to his feet tossed him a suspicious glance. Then as the knight went to join them, Kale put his hands in his pockets, coolly wandering over to the ledge. There he leaned one shoulder against the side of the overlook and gazed at the horizon above the mist.

Adwen saw him and wondered what to do, but Tamis noticed as well.

Ignoring the winking stars and lazy clouds, Kale's stare remained distant. He smelled Tamis approaching, and a hand the size of a dinner plate fell onto his shoulder. First looking at the large black clawed fingers, the werewolf looked up into Tamis's bright eyes. The hound's face showed gratitude and uncertainty.

Tamis's ears twitched as he tried to decide what to say. Sheepish, he growled softly, "I'd like to apologize for before."

Kale had already seen and smelled this warrior's true nature. He gave a warm smile. "You're a sweet kid."

Not knowing how to respond, he was even more unsure. "I am deeply grateful to you for this. Would you join me? I'd like you to be there when I show my friends what you've done."

The gesture forced Kale to chuckle. "You really are a sweet kid. There's not a bad bone in your body. It's alright. I'd like to stay here a while. Go on. I'm not going anywhere." After Tamis hesitated before leaving, Kale returned to studying the vast nothing in the distance.

Tamis passed Adwen, and she heard the General speak.

"Lady Adwen, we agree that what was done has laid to rest our concerns. Your werewolf is welcome here. However, while he is here, it is best that he remain in the overlook. Not everyone in the sanctuary can find the will to keep their weapons sheathed."

"I understand. Thank you, General Raglan."

He bowed on behalf of the Order and left with his brother and Geoden.

To her warriors, Adwen spoke less formally: "Could you guys go with Tamis and the General? I need to talk to Kale."

Jack and Alexander did not argue. They left for the caves, but Oryn lingered.

"What is it?" she asked.

He frowned. "You are weak in this world. Will you be safe alone with him?"

Adwen smiled. "He's bound to me, Oryn. I'm as safe as I am with you. I'll be down in a few minutes."

As no one was watching, the knight held her cheek in his hand, kissing her brow. He looked deep into her sweet gaze to show he was still worried. Tossing the werewolf another suspicious look, he did as she asked by leaving the overlook. Adwen watched her knight disappear in the passage before going to Kale.

He had found a better place to rest by sitting in the middle of the ledge. Elbows propped on his knees, Kale continued to look out at nothing, lost in a sea of thoughts and feelings. When she sat beside him, he did not respond. Wind created by the fearsome waterfall felt crisp. After a minute passed, Adwen knew he would not speak up first as he normally did.

"Are you okay?"

Feigning a smile, he glanced over to show that he was. "Yeah, I'm okay."

She shook her head, her tone sympathetic. "Do you insist on lying?"

His smile became bittersweet, sadness in his eyes. "Can you forgive a white lie?"

"What's bothering you?"

Kale looked away into the ocean of dark mist. "Memories."

"Do you want to talk about it?"

He fell silent. Then he sighed, sorrow in his voice. "It's all so complicated. And I don't know if I can."

"You can. I'm listening."

For a long moment, Kale watched how the wind from the waterfall rippled the haze back from the cliff. Fearful, his hands clasped, and he fidgeted. When he looked over again, the expression he wore showed how vulnerable and uncertain he felt.

"Can ... can you keep a secret?"

"Yes."

Anxiously, he added, "You promise?" Kale knew Adwen's promises were binding.

Becoming curious, she cocked her head. "Of course, I promise."

Oryn stood at the ready around the first bend in the passage from the overlook. He could not leave her completely alone. He was not certain to the extent of Kale's binding, leaving him guessing how much of a threat this insidious being could pose. The crashing waterfalls drowned out the conversation on the overlook, allowing Adwen the seclusion she had asked for. Oryn expected she would forgive him for not obeying completely.

"You're an idiot."

Oryn did not smell Jack approaching. Tossing an irritated scowl, Oryn remained by the wall, waiting for Adwen's meeting with Kale to end.

"She told you to go with us. Do you want to make her mad at you, too? I've had to tone it down since that weird breakfast. If she'd punish me for throwing a tennis ball, what do you think she'll do to you for trying to eavesdrop! She hates that."

"I'm not dropping eaves if I can't hear their voices. Stop pestering me."

Jack rolled his eyes. "Like that will make it any better."

"Have you been able to fiddle your way into the demon's thoughts yet?"

"No, I haven't."

Oryn was surprised. "Why not?"

"Kale's head is like a big, black vault. Also, each time I try, he does something creepy. Usually, that involves him picking at my mind a little."

"What do you mean by that?"

Jack shuddered. "He does it a little just to show me how easy it is for him. If I'm right, he could take anything he wanted from my mind. He chooses to make a point rather than make me pay for trying to invade his mental space."

The knight pondered this information.

"Do you want me to keep trying? I don't think I want to. Sooner or later, I'm going to make him mad."

"Such threats never put a stop to your antics in the past."

"Hah, very true, but that's physical pain. Mind pain and psychological stuff is not funny for me. Never going to forget when the Elf king reamed me. That hurt."

"If you do find yourself tapping into his thoughts, do not hesitate to share with me."

Taking a second to read Oryn's thoughts instead of asking why, he scoffed. "You think he's hiding something? Of course he's hiding something. A guy like that has to have a few skeletons in the closet."

"You forget," Oryn added, "this is not a man or an Elf king; this is a demon."

Adwen's eyes were as warm as her smile as she shook her head at Kale. "There's still hope."

"Hope?" Kale watched the darkness balefully. "Hope is treacherous for someone like me. Having no hope is better than letting it tear you apart from the inside."

A warmth in her chest made her eyes shine brighter in the dark. Watching his hands clasping, Kale's claws massaged at the gold piece, caressing it. Following the feeling in her heart, Adwen reached out.

He froze as she took his left hand. A moment later, Adwen had her lips pressed to the piece of her heart, eyes closed as she made a blessing. His breath caught in his chest, and he saw the gold flesh glow brightly. Kale gasped as the light faded and the simple spot was altered. The mark had the likeness of a tattoo. A tiny swirling line pointed from the back of his hand toward his wrist.

Adwen stood to leave.

Kale was confused, studying his hand. "What did you do?"

"It's a surprise. We'll be waiting when you're ready."

Rather than vainly try to guess, it felt more appropriate to be thankful. He went back to examining the mark.

As Adwen was walking away, she stopped and turned. "And Kale?"

He stared.

She said softly, "You're not a monster."

Truth in her enchanted voice hit his heart like an arrow. His bright red eyes became wide, filling with tears. Turning away quaking, he began to weep. Kale cried atop the overlook long after she left him there.

Adwen entered the passage wishing things were not so hard for Kale. As soon as she found Oryn leaning against the wall, she frowned. Her gaze became as hard as the stones.

Blue eyes bright in anger, she asked, "Did you listen to any of that conversation?"

He was honest. "I would not have remained here if I could. The falls were loud enough."

She could hear he was telling the truth. "You don't believe I'm safe near him, do you?"

"I am not in the mood for risks."

"You'll have to trust me more than you distrust him. He's going to have to carry me in these attacks on the pillars."

The knight disliked that idea more than leaving her alone with the demon.

"To fully activate the light in his piece of my heart, I need to touch him."

Oryn felt more uneasy. "Understood."

"No, I don't think you understand. Also, I want you to be careful how you talk to him. You and Jack are on thin ice."

"Bad or good, that being has dealt with worse things than lashings from Jack's tongue or mine."

Adwen's hard stare wilted into sadness. "Do you remember how you spoke to me when we first traveled together?"

Regret-filled memories flitted through his mind, and he was morose. "This is different."

She shook her head. "No, it's not. You need to cut it out. Please."

Oryn gazed into her deep blue eyes, and he understood that hearing his harsh words directed at Kale brought back horrible memories for her. It almost broke his heart. Pulling her close, they embraced, and he whispered. "For you, I will hold my tongue. Forgive me."

"I already did," She murmured. "Sooner or later, you'll have to ask him the same."

The thought put a bitter taste in his mouth, but he conceded, knowing she was probably right. She usually was.

"Perhaps."

Chapter 10
A HUNDRED SHIVERS

Tamis felt as though he were reborn now that he no longer was trapped in the form of a dog. Upon entering the largest chamber, a restored Tamis shocked the humans and gargoyles, who greeted him joyfully.

"Tamis! Brother, you're upright again!"

"How did the Tame One do it?" a mage asked. "How did she set you free?"

Tamis had not forgotten the look in Kale's eyes before rearranging the runes; he had smelled of empathy. "She could not. The ring can never be removed as long as I live. But I am much restored, and it is Kale who I have to thank."

"The demon?" Tamis' gargoyle translator was aghast. "It must be a trick! Or he has planted a lie in your mind."

This was expected. Tamis huffed and growled, "This demon can feel as we do. I've seen and smelled it myself. We have no reason to fear him."

Adwen came into the conversation. "He's telling the truth."

Everyone bowed when they realized she was near.

"As you were. Kale has the powers of a demon but has a heart like your own. Since he is bound to me, he cannot hide any treachery, even if it were in him. I can sense his intent at all times."

They began to believe but were hesitant.

"What is his current intent, Good Lady?" a fighter asked.

She raised an eyebrow at the fighter, making him look away in shame. "At the moment, to decide whether to feel hope or not."

The fighters, mages and gargoyles exchanged looks and murmurs.

"Most of you struggle to accept him, but I kindly ask that everyone respect him. Kale is preparing himself to destroy the pillar we failed to break. He is our only hope right now."

There were nods as one replied, "As you wish, Lady Adwen."

"Now, can anyone tell me where to find Colin and Remy? I've looked everywhere. Are they okay?"

Shield Captain Geoden entered from a nearby passage. "I sent the fastest of the clan to fly them to Jenkirk after your departure."

Adwen was anxious. "That's risky. What about flying demons?"

He chuckled. "Labrodin flies like a swiftlet eating insects. Not even the small demon fliers can keep up. He was commanded to be their guardian until further notice."

"Thank you, Shield Captain. It means a lot to me to know they're safe."

"Many feel reassured in the same way, Lady Adwen."

Elsewhere in the sanctuary caves, Alexander relaxed by a wall listening to conversations. Jack joined him.

"Hey, Big Dog."

"Hi, Bad Dog." The Marine carried on listening, while his head remained empty.

"Having a werewolf help fight; this is so weird."

"Compared to what?"

"That's a good point. Are you ready to do this again?"

Alexander corrected him. "This is going to be different."

"Good point, again. Speaking of different, I sense something weird about you. What happened during your night with the werewolf?"

"I told you already."

"Yeah, yeah. He tapped you on the shoulder. When was the last time you tried to hide something from me?"

Alexander shrugged. "Beats me."

"So, you admit you're not telling me the whole story?"

He groaned. "Leave it alone."

"I can't."

"Try harder. There's nothing to talk about."

Jack warned him half-jokingly. "All I have to do is poke your head and I can find out."

Alexander tossed an unimpressed sidelong glance. He knew Jack was not foolish enough to invade his mind and damage their friendship. "You aren't that stupid. You sense that this isn't a big enough issue to pry out of me. If you want to talk, talk about something else."

Nothing was said for a moment as Jack studied his companion's hushed mind. "You feel lighter, and there's more warmth about you. What happened in that rickety old office?"

The image of Emily at the bright window flitted through Alexander's mind. "None of your business. If it's any comfort to you, nothing wrong happened up there."

Then he saw Jack wearing a shocked look and his pupils dilating rapidly, obviously tapping into his thoughts. This irritated Alexander greatly. "Stay out of my head, Bad Dog. I mean it."

Closing off the connection, Jack had not anticipated this and became apologetic. "Okay, my bad. I'll shut up for a while."

Neither spoke again, waiting in silence for the next mission.

What Adwen told Tamis's friends trickled through the ranks until everyone was talking about the werewolf that would break the pillar. Wonder and disbelief filled hushed conversations. Whispers upon whispers compounded like rustling leaves. When the hiss of shushing came, they all fell silent in an instant.

Adwen and her warriors looked toward the passage, and Kale stood with his hands in his pockets. While the humans stared, she smiled and called, "Are you ready?"

Kale's blank expression became a clever grin full of wolf teeth. "Oh, yeah. I'm ready."

They raced with Adwen through the dead forest. Paws and boots made no sound on the soft, dusty soil. Oryn stayed close to her while keeping an eye on Kale. The knight would remain at her side until there was no choice but to leave her in the werewolf's care. The thought made him feel as if he had swallowed stones.

Kale kept up with the Holy Hounds. Using his demon vision, he peered through the dark as if it were dusk. No enemies were nearby, and this put him at ease. For now, the demon lords had their guard down. A sly smile came to his face at the thought. They would pay for their mistake.

Adwen's newest friend gave her great confidence. As they approached their target, the mist lifted a little. Green flickers and empty buildings lay before them. They stopped.

Remaining as a giant white dog, Adwen growled, "Kale, can you see anything worth worrying about?"

"I can't see through objects like real demons can, but I can smell them better than you lot." He took a big whiff. "A big horde in this place. Think I saw something flying. How would you like this done?"

"Divide and conquer."

"Sounds good."

"Remain undetected and take out any obstacles. Once we reach the main horde, it will be time to make an entrance."

Chuckling and smiling, the bones in Kale's face crunched, taking on more wolfish characteristics. "I love grand entrances." Seeing the looks of uncertainty from all except Adwen, he chuckled again. "Sorry, a little excited. May I go find a spot and put my other face on?"

Her tail wagged. "Go ahead."

He was thrilled. "Haven't needed to shapeshift in months. See yah in a tick."

When he dashed out of sight into the ghost town, Jack disliked having Kale out of their sight. "Um, Adwen? Is it okay if I'm uncomfortable with this plan?"

One ear folded back, and she wrinkled her jaws at him. "Be more worried about me. Tamis?"

He nodded his jaws. "Yes, Lady Adwen?"

"Watch our backs and don't shoot unless you have to. Just one of your arrows will blow our cover."

"Of course, as you command."

She sensed in her heart that Kale was ready. "Let's move. Keep your weapons out and your heads low."

As one, the Holy Hounds entered the alleys. She sniffed at each corner as Oryn peered out to check for demons. They went slowly, being sure to make no sound. After rounding several corners, the scent of demons grew powerful. Adwen crouched low, letting Oryn sidle to the edge and look.

A lone Wretch demon skulked in the open, sniffing with its

short snout for traces of human. None of the town's inhabitants remained, but the demon continued its hunt.

Careful not to be seen, the knight pulled back and growled to Adwen and the others, "Hold. A demon is in our path."

Jack growled back, brandishing the twin daggers. "How many?"

To be sure the fiend was alone, he stole another look. Seeing the street clear and the demon gone left Oryn uneasy, squeezing the hilt of his sword.

Adwen growled, "What's wrong?"

"The demon's vanished. We may have been detected."

She was reassuring and walked past Oryn into the open. "The coast is clear. Come on."

They followed her along the street. As they approached where the demon had stood, they saw a purple smear of its blood on the cobblestone. If this were Kale's doing, then he was swifter and deadlier than they had suspected. That was disturbing to Adwen's warriors but encouraging for her.

Continuing stealthily on the main street, many alleys lay on both sides. The air was tense, and they stopped to check every corner before moving forward. When Oryn checked around another dark turn, a Wretch saw his green eyes and charged. It was too late to hide, so the knight stepped out to face it.

As the demon bounded across the street, a black shape flitted past, too fast for Oryn's sight to catch. Before the demon could made a sound, its head was cleaved off, tumbling across the ground as its body fell limply to the stones. Oryn stood paralyzed, staring at the melting remains, and Adwen came to look as well. She gestured for the team to continue forward. Oryn scanned rooftops for demons – and the one killing them like insects – before rejoining her at the lead, leery from the incident.

The journey deeper into town remained tense for Oryn, Jack, Alexander and Tamis. They had not seen Kale – just purple smears and disintegrating monster corpses. The main street was long. Dark mist and dim floating green lights limited their view to a few yards. Suddenly, their sixth senses urged them to look skyward. Vast wings swooped low through the dark fog. A titanic Dred pierced the mist with clutching talons, long serpentine neck rearing to spit a glob of evil acid. As they saw it taking a breath, the four warriors stepped back, and Tamis raised his bow.

The huge black shape swooped from above a nearby rooftop. They caught a glimpse of jaws large enough to bite a pony in half ensnaring the flying demon's neck. Bright red eyes flashed at them before the black shape was gone again.

The Dred's wings trembled. It abruptly stopped flapping and crashed into the street before them, it's head rolling past.

Tamis lowered his bow and muttered, "That was swift."

The Marine agreed. "I'm glad he's on our side."

Jack uttered weakly, "Now you are reading my mind, Jarhead."

Oryn almost trembled at the sight of a downed Dred as Adwen skirted around it.

"We're close," she growled. "Get ready."

A few blocks farther into town, the humming from the pillar intensified – as did the stench of demons. Jack reached out with his mind to sense the nearest demons and found too many minds to tolerate. He was forced to block out the thoughts of the horde. When it came time to fight, he would endure the bombardment, but for the moment gave his telepathy a rest.

"Now what?" Jack whispered in the cramped alley.

Adwen's tail flicked in anticipation. "I'll give the signal, and we'll let Kale soften them up. Tamis, when there are fewer demons, I want you to start picking them off. Everyone else, provide cover for me and Tamis."

Jack had to know. "What's the signal?"

She closed her eyes, concentrating on making her golden heart shine. The glow from within her chest radiated out, making her white fur luminous as a star. At the same time a small glow appeared atop a distant roof overlooking the plaza. They saw Kale at last.

His gigantic silhouette among the glowing green wisps crouched low on the rooftop. He gripped the peak, careful not to damage the stressed structure with his immense weight. Red eyes the size of saucers glanced down at the glowing mark on one set of claws. Sensing Adwen's will, the thirteen-foot-tall beast leaped high into the air, past where the Holy Hounds could see through the mist.

Adwen let the light inside her fade before advancing into the open just as the monstrous werewolf dropped from the sky. When his form crashed upon the demon horde, the force pushed the mist back. Demons wailed and shrieked in shock. Purple ribbons splattered in all directions as Kale's claws ripped through the ranks, sending many flying in pieces. In seconds, the entire horde converged on the giant black creature.

Muscles rippled under thick layers of wolf fur and skin. The mane on his neck bristled, and gnashing jaws dripped with saliva. Thunderous growls and ravenous snarls echoed in the town over the din of demon cries. Each step he took was heavy, quaking the ground. He killed enemies in fours and fives, then roared when a Felon as large as a bull stabbed him with four long tendril spikes. Grabbing hold of the ropy appendages, the werewolf pulled the serrated points from his flesh. He began using its body to bash others into pasty smears, swinging and slamming the demon until it was almost dead. Finished using the monster as a giant bludgeon, Kale ripped off its head. The Felon liquefied instantly.

While the massive werewolf slaughtered the horde, Tamis picked off stragglers, letting his three friends move forward. Deafening roars and stomping shook the air and the earth. When only a few demons remained, Adwen bounded out to the werewolf's side. Oryn and the other warriors joined her but kept their distance.

Kale's head turned as Adwen approached, his heavy breaths vibrating the air until everyone could feel the force in their chests. He was covered in shallow red cuts and drenched in demon blood. Matted fur dripped everywhere as if spattered with paint. With the demons destroyed, the green floating lights drifted low, hovering around the pillar like fireflies. The werewolf and Adwen took a moment to be in awe.

The other four warriors were not comforted by the green lights' behavior. Jack tried to shoo some away to no avail, and Oryn growled at them.

A frightening snarl from the werewolf made them freeze. "Leave them alone!"

"What are they?" Tamis asked.

Kale's red eyes studied a few hovering by his filthy jaws. "I was one of them once. They are lost souls, the spirits of all who were sacrificed to build the pillar."

Adwen transformed into her elf-like form and said, "Let's set them free."

A heavy sigh escaped Kale's enormous lungs as he nodded.

Oryn remained with Jack, Alexander and Tamis, watching from a distance while Adwen and Kale approached the pillar. Oryn felt helpless letting her go anywhere alongside the dark beast. If Kale were to turn on her, there was nothing he could do.

At the base of the tall monolith, Kale stood to his full height, gazing into the fragment from the Void. When he felt Adwen grasp a sharp claw on his right hand, the gold mark on his left came to life. It felt warm as it glowed. He held it up and watched strong threads of light extend from the piece of her heart, swaying gracefully like vines in a gentle breeze. As he marveled, the runes on the pillar parted, and Kale froze.

In an instant, Kale saw the same face that had confronted Adwen in her first attack on this pillar. Examining the werewolf and Adwen with white specs for eyes, its expression turned from surprise to anger. Adwen stood firm, frowning. Kale peered closely at the face, then he howled in terror and thrust his claws and the light into the pillar. It shattered the mirror-like surface. Black stones exploded outward and rained down.

The blast pushed the four warriors back, and Oryn roared. He rushed through the raining debris to reach Adwen. As the dust settled, the frantic knight found a mountain of black stones. Gasping and panting, he feverishly dug with his hands. While he pushed and tossed large pieces aside, a thick, shadowy essence began to leak from under the stones like noxious gas.

As he paused wary of the strange substance, another explosion tossed him back. A shadow recoiled into the mound, sending much of it flying outward. Oryn shielded his face and then found the enormous werewolf rearing up from the resulting crater, shaking dust from his blood-matted fur. Their gazes met, and the knight tried to discern whether Kale was about to attack.

But once he heard Adwen coughing underneath the crouching beast, his heart leaped. Kale scooped her up with one massive clawed hand and passed her into Oryn's waiting arms. Oryn held her tightly as he strode away with her down to level ground.

Embracing him as he carried her, she chuckled, "That was a bigger explosion than the last one. Sorry we scared you."

Oryn squeezed her back, happy she was safe.

Shifting back into more human form, Kale's red jacket materialized on his shrinking body with his black slacks and boots. Rushing after them, he was urgent. "We have to leave! We have to go right now!"

Everyone stared with expressions of concern.

"We've been seen," he added breathlessly, giving off the scent of fear. "They know now. We have to get back to the sanctuary as soon as possible."

Chapter 11
LUCID NIGHTMARE

Kale burst out of the river, soaking wet and clean of battle filth. Trudging through the strong current, he shook off the excess water. Only then did he follow Adwen and her warriors into the sanctuary. He put his hands in his pockets and kept his eyes to the ground with an unfocused gaze. A weight was on his mind.

Adwen entered the first chamber to expectant humans and gargoyles. When she smiled back, they began to rejoice, saying hushed praises. Some gave nods as she passed, and a few were directed to Kale. Her gloomy friend took no notice. What he had seen in the pillar filled him with dread. For now, Adwen intended to focus on meeting with the Order on what was done and yet to come.

Kale again leaned by the side of the overlook ledge and stared out at the false night. He listened as the War Meeting began.

"Right to speak goes to Lady Adwen."

"Thank you, Virgil. The pillar is destroyed with all the demons in that town. Soon we will set out to attack the next closest location. I would like to pass my right to speak."

"Right to speak passes to General Sir Raglan."

The knight nodded to the ranger, then beamed at Adwen across the table. "You did it. You and your werewolf destroyed the pillar. Every member of the Order is grateful beyond description. Our wounded may be able to get medicines and supplies from that town."

"No."

Every face turned to Kale, standing off by the ledge.

Sir Raglan would be angry at the interruption if he did not think the creature was speaking for good reason. "Tell me, Kale. Why do you say no?"

Giving an uneasy sidelong glance, he replied, "We were seen. More importantly, I was seen helping Adwen. The demon lords have been lax, overconfident. But now they know there is a threat to their plan. They will intensify their search for human blood. Any scouts you send will never return."

Knowing he was right, Raglan, Dynic and Geoden were disturbed.

"If that is so, then it is time we left Dargadia. They will find this place."

Turning to face the table at last, Kale came a little closer, shaking his head. "They won't find this place. With the falls and the old magic shielding it the demons cannot find it. So they will starve you out. Forget that silly plan of sending small groups for food and supplies. Take everyone away together, and have them avoid the roads until they leave the mist. Follow the river's edge. That is the only way to get this many to safety."

Virgil raised an eyebrow. "Is that so? The terrain by the river is not the easiest to follow. Why the river?"

"Moving water," Kale replied. "A strong flow of water provides protection against evil spirits. Only a rare number of demons can get near running water without being weakened or debilitated. Even I'm somewhat affected. Energy given off by strong currents impacts their senses and their bodies. If strong enough, it threatens to push them through the veil back to the Void, so they avoid rivers. The life force of human beings is nigh impossible to detect from a distance when near a river."

At this, Virgil had to chuckle. "Very clever! Never considered such a thing. What say you, General?"

"A demon would know how to avoid demon detection. Lady Adwen has not refuted, thus he speaks the truth. How much time do we have to depart?"

"Less than a day," Kale said.

Sir Raglan gaped in surprise.

"The demons are now watching every town where they know your scouts scavenge goods," Kale said. "You can use that as a diversion, but only for the next 24 hours at most. They may send special hunters who can seek your order even by a large river current. Then anyone remaining will be trapped here. Light Spirits help you all if the Reaper comes. Avoid that monster and take what I say seriously."

"They would not extend their reach beyond the mist?" Raglan asked.

Kale shrugged. "Not likely. The mist gives the demons strength and protection, as well as easy access to different territories for spawning. They're investing their efforts in Dargadia. With Adwen here in their sphere of influence, they would see hunting outside the mist as a waste of resources – namely, their harvested human life force. They need to spend it frugally after so much was invested in the pillars."

Geoden frowned. "Humans were sacrificed to build the pillars?" He was disgusted.

"Many. Knowing that, you can see how angry they are now that two have been destroyed."

Sir Dynic nodded. "They will be seeking repayment and more souls to either fortify the remaining pillars or build another."

"That's right."

Adwen added, "By the time we get to the next pillar, everyone in the Order must be evacuated to Jenkirk as quickly as you can along the river. Virgil, I'm assuming you are their guide?"

"Of course, Good Lady."

"Perfect. We will be here a few more hours. When we set out, the demons will be hunting us more than the Order. That will buy some time for you to escape north. Don't waste it."

Sir Raglan became determined. "I intend to waste not one moment in ensuring the survival of the Order of the Gargoyle, Lady Adwen. It will be done; before a full day has passed, these caves will be empty. Thank you for your great efforts. Also, I am grateful to you, Kale."

He was taken aback at the kind gesture. "Well, then, you're very welcome, General."

The knight decided he liked the odd creature Adwen had found.

As soon as Sir Dynic announced the command to evacuate, every chamber came alive with motion. Not even the wounded remained still long in gathering supplies and a few small keepsakes they could carry. Through all that had happened to the fighters, mages and gargoyles, the command to leave the kingdom at once was accepted dutifully. With fervor, the new Order obeyed.

Adwen remained on the overlook until dawn. This morning remained bright a while longer than the day before. A little more life breathed into the land, restoring some of her strength. It fortified her golden heart and silvery spirit flesh. When the glow of her body dimmed and the sky became night again, she felt better.

Kale was pleased to see her stronger.

"Kale, do you know the best place to find another pillar?"

"The magic in Dargadia flows in a broad path from northwest to southeast. The strongest source is in the open plains, so that pillar would be the most heavily guarded and most difficult to destroy. But if destroyed, it would cost the demons more resources than they probably have."

Oryn frowned. "How high is the 'cost' to rebuild that particular pillar?"

Thinking about it made Kale sick. "Thousands of lives. Even if we could take it down, it would drive them to push for a very big harvest." He shook his head. "I'm not strong or fast enough to stop such a hunt. Adwen would have to be restored to full strength to fight that."

She agreed. "So we wait until later. Somehow, I'll break this seal and get my power back in this world. Then we can attack the big pillar."

"Even then, the advantage is theirs. If they have their elite posted there, and I don't doubt that, attacking under any circumstances cannot be taken lightly."

"Where do you suggest looking next?"

Kale pondered for a moment. "I think a good place to strike is the deep south. All the pillars will be more heavily guarded now, but the two we destroyed were in the north. Attacking the south might surprise them because they would not expect us to overextend."

She frowned. "I'm okay with that. No matter where we go, it's going to be dangerous. Do you think there is a pillar in Deleon?"

"That's a guarantee."

Taking a deep breath and letting it go, she decided. "Then we attack there, and after that we track down the princess. With the powerful allies she had, there's no doubt in my mind she escaped."

Oryn nodded. "Finding Toth and Balefire would add a great pair of allies to this war."

Kale chuckled. "Sounds good to me." His red eyes sparkled at a happy thought.

In the caves, Tamis found he was most useful in the supply store dispersing goods amongst the Order. Alongside Sir Dynic and Geoden, he helped fill sacks and anything that could hold medicinal herbs or rations. Placing the last roll of cloth for bindings into a sack, Tamis handed the bag to another fighter. He felt contentment seeing hope in the woman's eyes before she headed to the lower chambers.

General Raglan joined them. "Finished already?"

His brother smiled then cringed at the pain from the cuts on his cheek. "Of course. There was only so much left."

"I'll assign able-bodied fighters to assist the wounded. Any who struggle to walk will be given two comrades for the journey. All lanterns will be dispersed with small portions of oil. We'll let no one get lost in the dark."

Tamis nodded, growling softly. "If that is all that remains, the Order can depart soon."

Dynic beamed at the hound warrior. "We shall miss your company."

He thought about the meaning and nodded solemnly.

"Adwen shall depart soon." Geoden added. "Do not forget to bid us farewell, Sir Tamis."

"I would never forget such a thing."

The gargoyle chuckled. "General, shall we go and give instructions to the Order? They should be mustered in the main chamber by now."

"Yes, they've waited long enough. Until we meet again, Sir Tamis."

Feeling at a loss, the hound warrior growled softly. "Yes, sir." As they left the store chamber for the tunnel, Tamis lingered for a moment in the passage, listening to the percussive footfalls. His glowing gaze fixed upon the ground. Both long ears folded back at rising feelings of discontent. Even before the sky went dark, he was with the knights. Ever since the demon invasion, he spent every waking hour in their company. Then he remembered that most of his life had been spent caring for his ill mother. It seemed that there was no escaping that calling. He still missed her very much.

"Tamis?" Adwen was leading her warriors and Kale down from the overlook. Watching him turn to her, she smiled. "What are you doing by yourself? Come on. We're ready to leave."

The warrior found it difficult to express what he felt and hoped she would not be angry. "Forgive me, Tame One. I am confused. I am ready to depart, but ..."

"What is it?"

He hesitated to ask. "Might I go with them? With your blessing, I wish to help lead the Order to Jenkirk."

She was not surprised, but the other Holy Hounds were confounded.

"Your skill and your bow are needed." Oryn grimaced. "Without your strength, our task is more dangerous yet."

Tamis hung his head, ears low in shame. "Forgive me, Sir Oryn. I understand, but my heart aches to see them safely out of the dark."

"He's right; your bow is a powerful tool," Adwen said. "Then again, all the better to ensure that the Order survives the trip."

They looked at Adwen in astonishment that she would consider letting him go. She gave her youngest warrior a warm smile. "As much help as you would be, the Order is important. We'll manage."

Tamis was beside himself with joy. "Thank you, Tame One! Thank you."

"How many times do I have to ask you to call me Adwen?"

"I feel compelled to address you with respect as a leader."

She shook her head. "We're friends."

Tamis was stunned. Forgetting formality for a change, he bowed his head. "Adwen. Thank you, my dear friend. May the Light Spirits guide your feet."

Adwen beamed. "When the mission is complete, return to the sanctuary. You'll be able to follow the river safely on your own. Be careful out there, and we'll see you again soon."

Oryn saluted with a fist across his chest as they passed Tamis, and Tamis saluted back. Jack shook his head and chuckled.

"Behave yourself, buddy. Don't do anything I wouldn't do."

Tamis knew the list of things Jack wouldn't do was short.

Next in line was Alexander. "Stay sharp out there."

"Same to you, Sir Alex. Be safe."

Finally, Kale came by with his hands in his pockets. He paused to study Tamis's mind and smelled his nature, saying nothing. Tamis had not forgotten Kale's sad demeanor a few hours earlier. "I thank you again for what you've done for me, Sir Kale."

Hearing his name spoken with a knight's title touched him. Smiling, Kale almost laughed. "You're a good kid. Have to be one of the most innocent ones I've ever met."

The tall hound warrior cocked his head. "How would you know?"

Kale tapped his nose with a sharp claw. "You smell sweet. Even through all the torture and hardship, you've remained innocent. Don't ever let that change. Later, kid."

Watching the werewolf walk after the rest of Adwen's company, Tamis's tail wagged. "Until we meet again, Sir Kale. Thank you for everything."

An air of anticipation filled the chambers and passages. While Adwen led the way down her heart brimmed with the same energy. As much as she feared the unknown, determination propelled her. Walking into the cloud of conversation in the last chamber, the many eyes of the order fell on them and mouths closed.

She stopped to look at them, knowing this very well could be the last she saw their faces. When she began to walk through the ranks they parted, saluting as she passed. It became more difficult to refrain from crying. She tried to hide the tears and smiled, beaming at as many faces as she could, trying to commit them to memory.

Coming to General Raglan, Shield Captain Geoden and Captain Dynic, she stopped to bid them good-bye.

"I'm going to miss you all. If we win this war, I hope to see what amazing things your order will do in Dargadia."

General Raglan reassured her. "And you shall, Good Lady. In the end, you shall. Fare well and may the Light Spirits guide your feet."

"There will be much to build." Geoden beamed. "These cliffs will be made into grand halls of honor thanks to your actions. Fair winds and solid stones under you, Lady Adwen."

Adwen nodded, imagining what that would be like.

Captain Dynic sighed and shook his head. "You sound as if

you don't think you'll return and lead us into the new age. The future of Dargadia is in your hands."

She corrected him. "No, Captain; it's in yours."

At first, he was taken aback, but smiled and bowed. "Good Lady."

His brother and the gargoyle followed his lead and then the whole of the order bowed.

For the first time, Adwen felt encouraged by direct reverence. It emboldened her, granting more determination to face the dark outside. She spoke to them one final time, "Someday, somehow we all will meet again. I bless this order and ask the Light Spirits to guide you on in my absence. Until then, keep faith alive. Good-bye my friends."

Adwen took her companions through the tunnel and Kale stole a glance back at the General and his Order. Amongst the many faces he spied the young fighter. He could see the blood lust was gone from his heart. Then he locked eyes with Raglan.

The General gave a firm nod to the werewolf.

A warm smile flitted across Kale's face. Then he left them behind.

The small band of companions traveled far through the mist that choked the forests. For hours Kale aided in eluding danger by sensing where demons were likely to show themselves. On and on they ran, going eastward before turning southbound. They carried on until Adwen and the other Holy Hounds grew tired.

"This is as safe a place as any," Kale said as he brought them to a plot of deadwood where he sensed demon influence was weak. "Even with so much power, they can't control all of the land. We can rest here for a few hours and go unnoticed."

"Thank you, Kale," Adwen said, sounding exhausted. "Let's all get some rest." She let Oryn choose where to settle down, and she sat on the ground, littered with dry leaves. As Oryn lay back against a dead tree, Adwen leaned into his arms with her head on his chest armor.

Jack and Alexander exchanged looks. "Hey, Jarhead. Are you standing watch first?"

"Are you kidding? I could fall asleep in ten seconds if I sat down. You first."

Before the argument could start, Oryn snarled, "Jack stands first watch!"

They gave a small start before exchanging glances. Alexander shrugged and went to pick out a spot to sleep since the matter was settled.

Unusually tired, Jack rolled his eyes in irritation. He was getting hungry and reminded himself that all the animals in the kingdom were either dead or had fled. There was nothing to hunt. Remembering their very powerful asset, Jack waited to see what Kale would do. As he guessed, the werewolf settled on the edge of the clearing. Once he appeared comfortable by a dead oak, Jack picked a place to stand watch.

Sitting atop a fallen tree, he watched over everyone, especially Kale. While he used his telepathy to monitor their surroundings, Jack studied the demon in living flesh. The werewolf's eyes were closed as if asleep. Jack could sense the slumbering minds of everyone in his company but this one. Kale's mind remained locked tight. Was he sleeping or pretending?

Everyone looked tired except for Kale. Convinced that the werewolf was playing games, Jack contemplated whether to test that theory. As he began weighing the options, Kale's voice whispered amongst his own thoughts.

<I had a feeling you'd try to start something if I slept under your watch.>

Jack flinched then glowered, watching glowing red eyes open to lock with his. <And I had a feeling you were faking again. I didn't sense you probing my mind. What makes you think I was going to do anything?>

Kale's face remained stony and unreadable. <No need to probe a mind when surface thoughts percolate outward. You know that.>

<Why do you try to sleep? You don't need it.>

<You don't need to poke at others, so why do it?>

Jack raised an eyebrow. <Am I poking at you?>

He stared a moment, sniffing. Then the voice from Kale's mind became one of caution. <You're smart, cop, but you're not that smart. Stop taking blind shots at me and mind your own business. There's nothing in here you want.>

<I think there is, based on how tough your wall is.>

Kale stared blankly.

<What are you trying to hide in that thick head of yours?>

<I could ask the same of you, cop. What do you have rotting in the dark corner closet of your mind? If you want a bit of show and tell, you go first.>

Jack frowned. <Not on your life, demon.>

He scoffed. <See? That's the point. Mind your own business.>

<Yeah, but how are we supposed to trust you if everything about you is a secret or a lie?>

A sour look came over him, the glow of his eyes flashing dangerously. <Then don't.>

Jack realized he had hit a nerve. <How much of you is a lie, Kale? Is that even your name? Who are you really? Better yet, if demons like you are made from lost souls, then who were you before you were made a demon? What did you do to deserve being tossed into the Void?>

The whites of Kale's eyes turned black as pitch, while his face filled with bitter rage. Nevertheless, he stayed silent.

<What do you want? Do you want trust?>

Kale's tone was soft and deadly. <You don't want to play this game with me, cop.>

<Tell me what you're hiding. What are you afraid of?>

Suddenly, Jack felt a little of Kale's presence at last. It was ominous and tense. It gave the feeling of eyes watching from all around, making the hair on the back of his neck stand on end. Jack's spine tingled, and his mouth became dry and his skin clammy. Despite the demon's presence wrapping about him, Jack stared back in defiance. But when Kale let other voices speak in Jack's mind, he became rigid, eyes wide in shock.

<I can't do this.> Ashley's thoughts reverberated from more than a year ago, wracked with fear and pain. <I can't live like this. I just can't do it. This is impossible. I don't even know if I love you anymore.>

Jack snarled. <Stop it!>

Kale's demon stare was unmoving. <She almost left you more than once. Somehow, she stayed, and you don't know why. It's all the harder when she can't even make love to you without getting

hurt.>

"Shut up! Shut up! Shut up, sick monster!"

His loud shouting woke the others with a start, looking around for danger.

Letting the black color leave his eyes, Kale spoke aloud as well, relenting. "Here is where I am different, cop."

Adwen, Oryn and Alexander were befuddled, as Jack seethed. He wanted to use his daggers to kill the demon.

"I take no pleasure in knowing the pain of others. It is not fun. But you enjoy poking and prodding, don't you? I smelled it on you the first time we met. You see, I don't like that at all – never have and never will. That is how you are more a demon than I am."

Jack growled, summoning one dagger into his clenching fist. "Shut up."

"Jack!" Adwen shouted. "That's enough! Calm down."

Alexander went to his outranged friend's side. "Take it easy! Why would you try to mess with him? What's the matter with you? I'll stand watch, just put the weapon away."

Oryn wore a suspicious expression as he watched Jack dismiss the holy dagger snarling viciously. Knowing Jack, Oryn realized that the matter was far from settled.

When the angry Holy Hound stomped off to rest across the clearing away from Kale, the Marine sat atop the log and shook his head. At least he had gotten an hour or two of sleep for himself.

Adwen lay her head back onto Oryn's armor. Watching Jack slump by a tree facing away, she sensed his hurt and sighed. At the same time, the feelings in Kale's heart channeled through to her. As well practiced as Kale was at hiding his pain, she could feel it, and Jack's paled in comparison.

Sitting by himself, Jack continued to seethe, making his mahogany eyes shine. He tried to fall asleep. While anger made the attempt difficult already, holding up his most solid mental barrier kept him wide awake. More than sleep, he wanted to keep the demon from hearing his mind.

Unmeasured time passed. Jack could not sleep no matter how long he held his eyes closed. The sound of Ashley's voice in his head had reopened old wounds. Eventually, he became more and more sure that rest was impossible. Jack growled softly to himself clenching his teeth and fangs. He knew what he wanted to do to pass the time.

Keeping his eyes closed and holding the mental barrier firmly in place, Jack got as comfortable as he could. There was no telling how long this might take. One way to enter a mind was to touch the person physically. The other was more challenging – tapping into their thoughts through sleep. To create that kind of link, the target needed to be unconscious. Hopefully, Kale had drifted off and left a weak spot or two.

Maintaining his own defense, he reached out. Finding Adwen and Oryn asleep, the extent of his search stretched. Passing Alexander, who was none the wiser, Jack found Kale. That he could sense the werewolf this time was encouraging. Right away, several soft spots in the demon's psychic barrier became apparent. Kale stirred as Jack tested an opening, making the cop freeze, waiting for swift retribution. A few seconds passed, and Jack sensed it was a nightmare causing the werewolf discomfort, so he went back to inspecting the weak points.

Even after gentle prodding, there was no way to know which path went deep enough. Too much force was sure to wake Kale. Yet getting so close to penetrating the demon's elusive mind was too tantalizing for Jack to walk away from. Taking his chances, he tapped into the largest psychic fissure and let the dark inside envelope him.

Cutting himself off from the outside world, the interior of Kale's mind was much like others he had visited. Everything was empty at first. Random sounds from memories flitted by in fragments or whispers. Then Jack heard a loud series of sounds, like angry shouting. Drifting through the constellations of thoughts, he flew toward a steadily growing ball of light.

At the instant he entered the memory, Jack imagined his own body into the scene. Standing in an open street, there were dingy homes all around with barred windows and poorly kept yards. Paint peeled on the outside, revealing aged wood scorched by the sun. The suburb was very poor and quiet.

Behind him several gunshots made him whirl around. Three teens had gunned down an unarmed man. Jack watched his body fall backward onto the road. The man choked, quickly drowning in his own blood. A pit bull started barking and bolted out of a yard into the street. As the dog charged, the young man with the gun opened fire again. The animal yelped and flailed by the victim's feet, crying and whining horribly until another bullet ended it all.

Jack stared, horrified. Seconds later, the front door to the dog's home opened, and Kale vaulted over the chain-link fence. Frantic, he darted to the fallen man's side. While the teens stepped back, the werewolf ignored them and dropped to his knees.

Kale gazed unblinkingly at his friend's open eyes, staring at the cloudless sky. Reaching to touch the human's bloody chest, his claws got within inches, but he could not bring himself to touch the wounds.

The armed young man spat at him and cursed. "Was wondering if you'd show up. Gonna waste you, too."

Resisting tears, Kale asked softly, never looking way from his friend, "Why?"

The foolish human was appalled. "You asking why? You eat people, man! He was helping you! Getting a little payback today for my crew that you ate like a dog and a bunch of kittens! Gonna feed you a whole clip." Another magazine clicked into the grip on the pistol.

Kale's gaze fixed upon the silver rosary around the dead man's neck. Closing his clawed fingers around the pendant, it burned him. Smoke and steam escaped in tiny streams. His other hand found the dog's weeping side, as he touched both his friends one more time. Then, forgetting his tears, he asked, "Don't you know who I am?"

The humans were quiet. The one with the pistol waited to face him properly.

Kale tore the necklace from its owner, beads scattering around the pavement. Kale let the silver crucifix sear his balled fist. Getting up, he began to glare.

"Do you know why they call me the Reaper of Los Angeles?"

Two of the teens began to shudder, but their friend still stood boldly.

"I don't eat people."

Realizing that he was going to attack, the thug raised the pistol and took aim.

The whites of Kale's eyes turned black around his burning red stare. "I eat monsters."

The young man opened fire, and Kale roared as he lunged to pounce.

Then the world froze.

Jack stared at the dynamic scene frozen in place. It did not bother Jack; he had seen enough to know how this would end. Going closer, he inspected the man in the pool of blood. Right away, he could tell this was a good person. It was drawn into every detail of his face.

A sweeping chill came out of nowhere. It felt as if a door to a cold locker opened at his back. For a moment he was afraid. Jack turned to face the demon standing just behind.

He caught a glimpse of black metallic flesh. Then a spindly talon of a hand clutched his head like a fruit, his neck between two slender digits. He was lifted high to stare into big red eyes. Black feathery wings furled as the humanoid face sneered, showing pointed teeth. The demon hissed like a ravenous crocodile.

Jack wailed in terror, fighting to pull loose, kicking at the arm that suspended him. When he could not budge the giant fingers, he tried to sever the psychic connection. It was no use. The demon had ahold of him and would not let go.

The face of the demon was almost human in appearance. By the time Jack gave up the struggle, he noticed a long razor-sharp blade on the demon's forehead. It lanced forward like a horn, and the tip lowered, lining up with Jack's brow. The warrior's struggle renewed. He fought and writhed, helpless as the demon's sneer turned into a deadly snarl, and the blade came slowly closer.

When the tip touched Jack, and began to pierce his skin and then his skull, he screamed. The pain was immense. He squirmed like a worm on a hook as the demon's blade punctured deeper into his mind, burning like fire. Tears streamed down his cheeks as he wailed. Finished, the demon hissed and pulled back, then heaved Jack through a tear in the memory.

Jack sat bolt upright and gasped for breath. Sitting at the base of the tree where he had been lying, he feverishly felt his forehead for the bloody wound. There was none. Looking around to tell his friends what had happened, he blanched.

Everyone was gone. They had either left him behind, or he was blind to their presence. Everything was the same except for the absence of Adwen, Oryn, Alexander and even Kale. The discovery was as alarming as meeting Kale's true form.

"Adwen!" He shouted. The vast deadwood swallowed his

voice. "Oryn, Alex!"

<How dare you.>

Hearing Kale's angry voice in his head sent him reeling, looking everywhere.

<That was private!>

Jack bellowed, grasping his scalp and closing his eyes tight. "Get out of my head!"

There was a moment of silence before he spoke again. <And I thought you were smart. I'm not in your head, Jack. You are in mine.>

Suddenly the vast deadwood fell away into darkness, leaving a small island of dust, ash, dead trees and leaves. Jack panted and bolted for the edge. As he plunged into the dark, he passed through, only to emerge on the opposite side. Seeing himself vanish ahead as he came through made him groan in distress. He made another attempt to sever the link but failed. His head ached, making him gasp. Whatever had been done by the demon, it trapped him in this place.

Wandering into the middle of this imaginary forest prison, Jack finally saw a tall winged silhouette darker than the darkness. Two red eyes glowered at him. Jack growled and wished for his daggers. A shiver went down his spine when they did not appear. He was defenseless.

<My head, my rules. You had no right to come here.>

"Are you going to let me go?"

<Yeah, but I'm not finished with you yet.>

Jack tried to be defiant but still trembled.

<Why are you here?>

"Because you're hiding something."

The demon hissed in the dark. It sent more chills down Jack's spine. <Everyone has secrets. Even Adwen and the others keep some things to themselves. You are no different. This trespass was out of resentment! Do you even comprehend what you found?>

After taking a second to ponder the memory, he answered, "Regret."

<Ah, perhaps there was regret. What you found was fear.>

Angry at being held captive, Jack snarled, "Tell me your big secret! What are you hiding?"

The demon roared, making his imaginary world quake.

"Tell me!"

<No. You lost all right to that when you helped yourself to my mind. Since you helped yourself to my regrets, I think I'll have a look at some of yours."

Jack's head felt like it was being squeezed and reamed like a wet rag. His eyes rolled back, and he gagged at the extreme discomfort. When it ended, and Jack recovered, orbs of light like television screens floated all around. Each window glowed, illuminated with images of things he'd done. Some things he had forgotten; others he wished he could.

One showed him hitting Adwen, and he flinched at the sight. Another was of him stealing from a childhood friend. Among the worst were images of his father beating his mother as he watched, doing nothing. With every memory that followed, his heart sank. But then one memory window floated closer, held in the demon's huge hand. Pointed fingertips presented the image of Ashley sobbing, staring balefully.

Jack fell to his knees, gazing at her look of pure sorrow.

His voice was almost a whisper. <Your greatest regret.>

No matter how much it hurt, he could not look away.

<Say it.>

He never felt so weak in his whole life. "Going back. I thought I could live with her after all that had happened to me. I thought we could be happy again. I was wrong."

The memories floating around him flickered out one by one. The demon's ornate talons gently closed, dismissing the image of Ashley and retracted back into the dark.

Jack hung his head. His heart was incredibly heavy.

Observing the warrior in misery, Kale took pity on him. Perhaps he had gone too far.

<Not everything we believe or remember is necessarily true. You're not really a bad guy, are you?>

He felt his mind being tapped for a vast amount of memories again. Jack quivered, and he gasped when it ended. Then he looked up and saw more memories appearing.

They multiplied over and over, far beyond the count of the regrets. Thousands of glowing moving images surrounded the small patch of deadwood, pushing back at the darkness. As they continued to appear, they glowed around Kale's demon form, framing his tall body, broad shoulders and folded wings. Atop his long slender neck, his head coolly turned to admire the thousands of glowing spheres.

In awe, the warrior got to his feet. He examined a few to see what was drawn from his mind. There were many things. One showed him on his first day of school. He could not even remember it, and yet the memory was clear as crystal in the glowing orb. Another was of him on the first date with Ashley. Jack was confused.

"Are these happy memories?"

The demon did not reply. His wings furled and closed as he looked high overhead for something. He reached into a cloud of memories to gently pluck one out and brought it down to inspect it. Then he held it out for Jack.

At once, Jack knew what he was watching and was uncomfortable. It was himself at the age of seventeen in an all-out brawl with his father. Their fight went on for a long time, leaving many broken picture frames and keepsakes. His mother lay unconscious on the kitchen floor.

Jack became nauseous. "That's not a happy memory."

Continuing to hold the images before the warrior, Kale agreed. <It is important.>

The brutal fight ended outside when police arrived after a neighbor called. Jack was pulled off his father, who was on the lawn, beaten nearly to unconsciousness. The officer who grabbed Jack took him aside and listened when Jack said his mother needed help. As his father was handcuffed and taken away, Officer Evans went with him in the ambulance to the hospital.

<She stayed. Even when she didn't have to, she was with you to face this so that you would not be alone.>

Jack nodded, watching his younger self break down at the news from the doctor. His mother had died of a brain hemorrhage as she was brought into the emergency room.

"Why are you showing this to me?"

<These are the memories that make up who you are; they define you. This one is special. Without this, you would have become a career thief. You faced your father and fought for your mother.>

Jack's heart ached. "But she died!"

<I know, but you chose to live for her. And the cop who was there for you gave you a path to follow. She showed you a way to use the fire you still have.>

Jack took one more look at his seventeen-year-old self, clinging to Officer Evans, bereft and inconsolable in the hospital. Kale was right.

When the small galaxy of memories faded away and the dark was restored, the demon lowered his gaze. He rumbled to himself, trying to decide.

<I may have taken more than was fair in viewing your memories.>

Jack peered up into the silhouette's red eyes. They looked somber. Then the look was resolute.

<I have something to show you. It is not what you came to find, but I think you can grasp the meaning now.>

An invisible door opened wide at the edge of the imaginary prison. Blinding white light streamed through. Jack glanced between the giant demon and the opening. Taking a deep breath, he braced himself as he walked over the dead leaves until his body passed the threshold.

The blinding white faded into color, sound and motion. Across a busy, noisy street was a forest in a vast park. Honking horns and sirens filled his ears.

"Is this New York?"

Looking about to survey the surroundings, there was no sign of the real Kale, but he quickly recognized the Kale of a few years in the past. Seated on a wide bench, an open newspaper in his clawed hands, dark sunglasses hid his cherry red eyes. Jack went up close, observing his every move. He looked different, less worn. His body seemed far younger than normal.

Out the corner of his eye, he spotted a black shape on a nearby shop window. It nodded to the bench.

<If you like, have a seat. Try my shoes ... if you're daring.>

Looking between the demon's shadow and the demon's memory, curiosity overpowered apprehension. Turning to sit down into Kale's form on the bench, Jack merged himself into the memory and felt everything the rogue did moment by moment.

It was intense. The scent of human bodies all around made saliva pool in his mouth. Reading a newspaper was almost impossible. After getting through a single line or maybe two, a scent would threaten to drive him wild. Amid the smells of flesh and blood were the odors that Jack could barely comprehend. Was he smelling human souls? Then the tantalizing aromas of living prey broke his train of thought again.

Before it could overwhelm him, Jack all but jumped out of Kale's form. Backing away panting, the experience was nothing short of torture. Gazing in astonishment at the werewolf on the park bench, what amazed the Holy Hound was how calm and collected he appeared to be. The hunger had almost consumed Jack entirely.

Awestruck as Kale turned the paper and folded it to read another column, he shook his head. "How are you doing that? How can you even read out here with that drive to hunt?"

<Practice. Mostly I didn't. The paper is a distraction. By focusing on reading, I kept from getting too drawn into the urges. Once I became too hungry to read, it was a sign that I must watch myself and start hunting at night for easy prey.>

"Easy?"

<In the daytime I would sit and wait for the ones who are worse than thieves and thugs. The worst of the worst walk in the daytime like everyone else. With my sense of smell, they were easy to find if they happened to come by. Petty criminals are a complicated mess. I preferred to stalk the ones who smelled of terrible things. At all times, I waited for the strong scent of guilt.>

"Guilt. That has a smell?"

<Many different kinds. You smell of guilt more than the others in Adwen's entourage. Your guilt is fine and weak. The guilt I waited for was thick and stank of conceit – knowledge of guilt but without the emotions of it. Those are psychopaths.>

Kale's past-self stirred, sniffing. He coolly folded the paper and left it on the bench as he headed for the street. Putting his hands in his pockets, the werewolf crossed the busy road ignoring angry drivers stomping on their brakes and blaring their horns. Passing through the cars like a ghost, Jack followed Kale into Central Park.

The werewolf sniffed and sniffed after the scent, wiping away a little saliva at the corner of his mouth. The stronger the odor became, the harder it was to maintain control. Coming to a place where trees and bushes were thick, Kale moved more stealthily. The target was close. But when he found the human that gave off the terrible scent, his stomach churned.

Three boys with slingshots were in an opening. On the green grass was a dove with a bloody wing, flapping pathetically.

The boy that smelled so evil was no more than twelve, and Kale struggled to reign in his hunger. Even though this child was wicked, he could not allow himself to cross that line.

Two of the boys argued over what to do now that the bird was hurt. The nasty one insisted that he stomp on it to put it out of its misery. Before the child could make a move toward the wounded bird, they heard a rumbling growl.

Kale made the whites of his eyes turn black as he stepped out of the brush, baring sharp teeth. The boys scrambled away. It took all of Kale's willpower to resist the chase. Taking deep breaths, he gradually regained his hold over the powerful urges. With the scent of the evil boy dwindling, the commotion of the bird on the ground had his attention.

As Jack watched, the werewolf kneeled beside the dove, which calmed down. Kale scooped up the bird, which winced with pain but did not struggle. Its head bobbed, and it breathed rapidly, gazing up at the werewolf's torn expression.

The memory world shifted in a blur of colors and sounds. It reformed elsewhere in the park, where Kale sat on another park bench. The dove rested in his cupped hands. He stared at the snowy white creature as he pondered what to do with it. Releasing it would mean certain death. Keeping it would mean he would have to care for it.

Following a path through the park, a young woman passed Jack. She took pictures of the surroundings every few steps, deleting ones that turned out blurry. When the woman saw the man in the red jacket holding the dove, it was impossible to resist. Snapping a picture of the scene, a contented smile came over her. Checking the image for blurry edges, the man did not look the same. He was a solid shadow with red eyes, cradling the pure white bird. Her face blanched. She looked again at the bench, but found it empty.

"Did you know she was taking pictures of you?"

<I smelled her innocence a mile away.>

The memory blurred again and reformed in an abandoned apartment building. It rained outside. A cardboard box lined with newspaper and a clean rag held the bird with some seeds and fresh water. At night the glow from the city kept the room from being totally dark.

Jack gave a start when the door burst open and shut again as

Kale darted inside. He panted heavily as he leaned against the closed door, face covered in blood. It dripped from his beard onto his chest, mixed with the raindrops from outside. Sucking the last of the fluids from his teeth and swallowing, Kale went to a basin collecting rainwater on the fire escape. He washed himself before dumping the contents. Clean and the hunger dulled to a minor irritation, the box with the dove became his concern.

"Why'd you keep it?" Jack asked as he watched Kale cleaning the box lining.

<I don't know. Sometimes I wonder if it would have been better if I had killed it.>

Turning to give the shadow in the corner a questioning stare, the warrior was astonished that he would say such a thing.

The memory faded in and out many times. Colors shifted from light to dark and back again in the abandoned apartment. Day's moved in fast-forward. Kale's past-self traveled in a blur as he cared for the bird before leaving in the day and returning at night to do the same and rest in the corner.

Another morning came, returning to normal speed. The werewolf got up from the floor and checked on the dove in the cardboard box. It cooed, making him smile.

He turned to leave the apartment and heard wingbeats before the little creature landed on his shoulder. Rocking forward as it touched down, the dove trumpeted, clicking its beak. Kale stared in surprise. A happy look came over him. It was time to take his friend outside.

Everything faded out, and the memory returned to the vast green park. The sun was high, shrinking shadows into hiding, while Kale walked with the dove in his hands. It clipped affectionately at the tips of his claws with a gentle beak, flicking wings happily. Going to a vacant clearing surround by tall trees, he studied the cloudless sky then admired the sweet bird.

Having spotted the stranger in the red jacket on the way to the park, the young woman followed at a distance. She refrained from taking pictures and waited for the right opportunity. Realizing he was releasing the dove, her camera came up snapping shot after shot, capturing the moment that the eerie man tossed the little bird aloft. Strong wings clapped rapidly, lifting the dove ever higher over the treetops toward the sky.

Kale beamed at his little friend, glad to see him free. Then his expression collapsed into shock. A black mass plummeted for the dove against the burning sun. The falcon struck like a missile. Feathers flew, showering down like snowy petals.

Long after the birds fell out of sight amid the vegetation, Kale's horrified gaze remained while he stood rooted to the spot. The woman lowered her camera, almost in tears and thankful she had not captured the dove's final moment. She watched the stranger linger for a moment amid the green. Her empathetic stare followed him as he walked away, hands in his pockets and head hung low.

Once more, the memory transported Jack to where Kale sat on the bench on the side of the busy street. Sunglasses on and newspaper in hand, his senses dissected the aromas of many humans. There was only so much time before he grew too hungry again. The urges began to distract him from reading, ceaselessly clawing at his mind and insides. Among the scents of the natural and the spirit, a familiar innocence crossed his nose. Beside him, the young woman approached and stood by patiently waiting to be noticed.

He ignored her for a few seconds. Looking up at last, the hunger urged him to bite her throat, while he wondered why she had come. Obviously, she felt apprehensive about being so close. Her scent of fear was faint. Pretending not be afraid of him, she smiled meekly. Then she passed him an envelope.

Kale stared at it. Gently taking the unsealed envelope, he opened the flap and took out a high-definition photograph. The image of him releasing the dove in bright rays of sunshine warmed his heart. With a claw, he caressed the small white form against the trees.

Looking up at the girl again, Kale wore a thankful smile. She was so sweet; she was like the dove. Then the casual thought caused him to blanch. Fear gripped his insides with waves of chills. To the confusion of the girl – and the invisible observer Jack – the werewolf got up without a word. He set the photo and newspaper aside and walked away. He never looked back. Jack went to the bench. Looking down at the lovely photo of Kale and the dove, the cop watched it fade away with the memory.

The surroundings resumed the image of the deadwood. Jack frowned.

<What do you know of werewolves, Jack Towers?>

"Only what Adwen taught me. Mostly how to kill them."

<Werewolves are cursed things. Everything that the cursed thing cares for or strives for falls to waste and comes to nothing. By setting the human soul free from this body I took that curse onto myself. What happened to the dove was not coincidence. Neither was the death of my friend and his dog.>

Jack gave the giant winged demon a hard stare. "You're still cursed?"

The demon lowered his gaze. <The curse is attached to this body. It can never be broken.>

Jack was not convinced. "Hold on one minute. It can never be broken? What about the hunger and being burned by silver? Adwen's mark on you changed that. Wasn't that supposed to be impossible, too?"

Thinking on the concept, it seemed reasonable, but he shook his head in the deep darkness. <Changed, yes, but the curse will never be gone. Anything good I want I cannot obtain without taking lives as payment. >

"Why? You're bound to the servant of light. What isn't possible? Think about it."

The demon shuddered and hissed, glaring angrily, while the sanctum of his mind trembled in pain and anger. <It is not possible. It is not!>

"Why is that so hard to believe?"

More deafening hissing made the imaginary world quake. <Enough, Jack!>

The connection broke, and Jack woke with Adwen beside him. Holding a hand to his brow, she removed the branding Kale had placed on the warrior's mind. He turned to the sound of great snarls. While she and Alexander checked to see if he was alright, Oryn held the werewolf high pinned against a large dead oak.

"Jack, how do you feel? Your breathing was very shallow."

He shook off the dizziness, quickly recovered and tried to think. Locking eyes with her, Jack spoke with urgency, "Adwen! Is Kale still cursed?"

In Oryn's firm grasp, Kale's blank expression fractured into intense fear. Forgetting the knight who wanted him dead, his stared darted to the others.

Adwen was confounded. "What's going on?"

Sitting up higher, Jack asked again, "Is Kale cursed?"

The whites of Kale's eyes turned black in an instant, and he sneered, "Shut it, Jack."

To the werewolf, he replied, "You're scared. It's okay."

No longer patient enough to let the knight restrain him, Kale let a burst of dark energy surge outward. Oryn was forced to let go and stagger backward as Kale landed on his feet and shouted in outrage.

"Damn right I'm scared!"

"He's not cursed."

Everyone stared at her, none so stunned and silent as Kale.

She shook her head and gave him a sad, sidelong glance. "The curse is gone. As long as you are bound to me, it is no longer on you."

All eyes fell on him. His face showed quiet disbelief as he stood frozen like the dead trees. Red eyes shifted in thought. After a long moment of silence passed, he walked away.

Jack picked himself up to follow, but Adwen stopped him.

"Let him go. He's been through enough."

It was a struggle to obey, but Jack conceded. "Yes, he has."

Coming closer, Oryn growled, "What have you learned of the demon's mind?"

Adwen snarled, "Knock it off!"

Jack surprised them all when he ruefully replied, "Any time before now, I would tell you. Sorry, Cujo. This mouth is staying shut."

Kale wandered aimlessly. The dark mist felt like the inside of his mind. There was nowhere to go that was not depressing, dying or dead. The emptiness engulfed him, while the impossible circled around his mind.

Finally sitting against a boulder in an outcropping, He found that being away from the others was both better and worse. The thoughts were tormenting. Was he still cursed? He must be. The curse had no cure or escape beyond death.

Yet Adwen was the bane of all curses. A piece of her heart was on his hand. Looking at it, the design was even growing longer. Several more ornate floral lines scrolled up part of his forearm. If the curse was gone, then he had no more to fear. He was free. Her voice rang with truth, so it could not be a lie.

But his tortured mind ached, and he grasped his head with

sharp claws, baring wolf teeth in agony over the thought. He did not feel free of the curse. He could not be free. He could never be free. Tears of desolation ran down his face, while he swung between hope and fear. Even bearing Adwen's mark and hearing the truth, fear was still the greater.

Chapter 12
TASKS AND MASTERS

A few hours passed as the Marine stood the rest of his watch. Kale returned just as Adwen, Oryn and Jack awoke. They felt rested.

Adwen was rubbing her eyes and noticed Jack coming closer. When she looked at him he nodded to the quiet werewolf's back and wore a questioning expression. Realizing he wanted to know Kale's state, she sighed and thought the answer for her friend to read.

He heard her mind and nodded, frowning. Kale was okay, but could not believe he was free. It was just too hard.

The familiar hushed raspy voice spoke, and it was business as usual.

"Deleon is close. Adwen, once we get to the wall, how would you like to proceed?"

"That depends. Do you think they will be on the lookout for you?"

"It's likely, though there is a slim chance I may not be taken into consideration yet."

Oryn gave a suspicious glance. "I recall you claiming you were seen. No enemy would be so foolish as to not take you into account."

Kale gave a small dry laugh. "It's a feeling I get. Trust me."

The knight restrained himself from giving a bitter retort.

Adwen noticed and was thankful. "Then we can try the same thing as before: You enter first since you are so much harder to detect."

"Works for me."

"If there should be resistance due to your involvement," Oryn asked, "what would there be to prepare for?"

Kale pondered a moment and shrugged. "Too many possibilities to calculate that. If they are ready for me, then there would be a trap. It could be anything really."

Foreboding settled over the Holy Hounds, but Kale chuckled. "Come on. Don't let the unknown scare yah. No turning back anyhow."

Jack almost laughed. "Very true. Any chance they could sacrifice creepers to make a four-armed giant?"

Adwen and Oryn exchanged confused looks.

Kale was surprised. "Sure, however it's not likely. Where did you see a Demon Colossus?"

Jack and Alexander shifted a little, and the Marine answered, "In a trap."

"I'll be sure to let you know if I see them setting up something."

"It looks like it's that time again." Adwen smiled at her companions. "Let's move."

Their brisk sprint was silent in the stale air. Particle clouds rose in the wake of every footfall, merging with the dense, dark mist. Kale guided the run. The ground sloped higher, and the air became a little clearer. As the ominous haze lifted, the silhouette of the walls around Deleon loomed. For a moment they stood at its base studying the empty ramparts.

Adwen nodded to Kale, and he nodded in return, the whites of his eyes turning black. The wall was fifty feet high and the werewolf reached the vacant fortifications in a single leap before darting over the edge and out of sight. She waited with the others, giving him time to survey the area and make their foothold in the city. He made no sound. Adwen monitored Kale's state through their direct connection.

Sensing that he was ready, Adwen nodded to her warriors and began to scale the wall. They leaped most of the height and climbed the rest of the way. Dashing across the guard station, then dropping far down into a cramped alley, their ears were pricked for danger. The knight, the cop and the Marine summoned weapons, stalking with Adwen and sniffing for demons. The evil stench was everywhere.

Most buildings were ruins. Coming to a dark alley intersection, a dead Wretch lay melting on the ground. When they reached the dematerializing fiend, a deep breath in one of the alleys caught their attention. The warriors gave a start, raising weapons high, but Adwen smiled. She had known Kale was there.

The enormous werewolf crouched in the tight space with fresh demon blood on his claws.

"The pillar is in the lawn before the castle. There are an awful lot of demons in this city."

"Can you handle this?"

Dark mist began to radiate from his black fur, curdling and falling to the stone street like fog off dry ice. "Don't see why not. Ready when you are."

"Be careful."

Kale leaped overhead for the rooftops without making a sound. Adwen's bare feet padded along with her warriors' three sets of boots. As they advanced, the sounds of demon bodies splattering and falling were heard at random from unseen places.

Kale worked hard to keep the Holy Hounds hidden. Purple fluids stained the ruins, soaking the fur on his claws and arms. More of it splattered where he leaped, streaking down broken walls. Upon another roof covered in stone shingles, the sound of wings caught his ear, and he looked up in time to see talons.

On the ground, Adwen and the rest drew within view of the street leading to the castle. No sooner did they come into the open than a thunderous roar shattered the quiet. Black fur and scaly wings crashed beside them in a flurry. The titanic fight between Kale and the Dred lasted seconds, while the giant flying demon snapped and flapped, trying to spit in the werewolf's face and blind him. Monstrous wolf jaws caught the demon's serpentine neck, ripping it to pieces. The quivering corpse toppled aside and the werewolf got up and snarled as countless demons shrieked.

"Run!"

Hundreds of demon claws scrambled across walls, rooftops and over rubble toward the daring invaders. Hordes descended to meet swinging blades and Kale's brute force.

Jack was transfixed, making his daggers fly and killing demons the others could not reach. Alexander, using his ability to block out pain, ran alongside Oryn in leading the charge for the castle grounds. Both warriors protected Adwen, while the werewolf held waves of demons off at their backs.

Even more of the fiends began to pour down the hill from the site of the pillar. Adwen saw immediately that her warriors would be overwhelmed, and her heart called out, "Kale! We need you!"

He sensed her will through their connection. Giving a final immense swipe at the closest mob, he turned several into purple ribbons. Then he leaped, grabbing Adwen from amongst the warriors as he bounded toward the pillar. She clung to the thick fur on his neck as he ripped through the disorderly ranks. Snarling, gnashing and rampaging up the hill, he was sliced and bitten over and over. The path he carved through the demons gave Oryn and the others a way to fall back from the fiends in the city streets.

Two Felons stood at the dark monolith's base. Kale pounced on the first, plunging a hand through its middle as the second tried to whip him with bladed tendrils. Turning aside, Kale dodged the attack. The serrated tips sliced the dead demon instead, and Kale bit the limbs off in a split second. The fiend bellowed until large claws slashed its head off its stout body. Only then did it go quiet and collapse.

The warriors barely held back the tide of monsters as Adwen and her werewolf took control of the castle grounds. Purple and crimson splattered the three from head to toe. Jack and Alexander needed to transform to withstand the onslaught, while the knight retained his more human shape. This arrangement let the trio seamlessly fight as one. Nevertheless, their strength was waning.

Holding fast to the giant werewolf's mane, Adwen sensed how hurt and tired the others were becoming.

"Let's break it quickly!"

Giving a sidelong glance to the her, Kale nodded his monstrous muzzle and approached the pillar. He stood and planted his left palm against the cold surface. The marks that had grown up his forearm shone. The instant the light fractured the stone, a resounding crunch within alerted them both that it was time to get clear.

Every demon reared and backed away, giving the three warriors a much-needed reprieve. When the pillar exploded, the hordes wailed and fled. The earth trembled from the force. Oryn turned to see if Adwen was clear of the blast. Finding her safe atop the werewolf's shoulder put the knight a little at ease. Nevertheless, relying on

Kale for her protection remained disconcerting.

The warriors trudged up the rise of the sour earth. The giant beast let Adwen down with one big hand, and she rushed to meet Oryn, who dismissed his weapon to catch her in his arms. The blood that covered him was purged away wherever she touched. Letting him go, she turned to smile up at the towering werewolf.

"Thank you, Kale. Now we need you to track our missing friends from the castle. Our noses can't follow what yours can."

He was sniffing the air and distracted, but stopped when she spoke and nodded. "It shouldn't be a problem."

Continuing up the hill, they found the castle grounds littered with fallen pillars. Jack and Alexander reverted to their smaller forms, and Kale remained as he was, following close behind. Entering the withered royal garden, most of the ancient statues were destroyed. Larger ones stood with fragments missing – torn away during the demon invasion. Dry hedges were bare skeletons amongst the carved marble figures.

As the outline of castle Gailarien became discernable, Oryn grew warier. Kale had yet to shape-shift back, and the werewolf had yet to do anything at a whim or without deliberate cause. Although Kale's demeanor was confident, the knight sensed something was amiss. As suspicious as ever, Oryn scowled and went back to staring at the approaching castle's shadow.

Suddenly, Kale roared and lunged toward them. Oryn shielded Adwen, summoning his sword as Jack and Alexander whirled about in shock doing the same.

In the blink of an eye, the mighty werewolf grabbed the closest giant statue and slammed it down between himself and the warriors. As he did, a long black cord struck past him, cracking the side of the statue. Kale faced the dark hole in reality where the whip had flown from. He roared again, showing his fangs before the whip was joined by another. It whistled through the air to strike him. After barely dodging both, he roared, watching as the chaos portal widened to make way for its master.

An icy wind blasted outward. Darkness billowed like smoke to congeal into a thirty-foot being with insect-like wings made of mist. White specs for eyes locked onto the werewolf that dared to defy him. The mask-like face resembled that of a misshapen goat with many curved horns on his head like a crown. Pointed teeth gnashed within a horrible, ravenous sneer. Then the being with many mis-matched arms attacked again with the two whips.

They cracked and snapped at Kale, creating deep gouges in the dirt. The werewolf darted and raced about, snarling as he tried to attack the Demon Lord. Avoiding lash tips, he took a chance and leaped, summoning raw darkness in his claws to slash the fiend's face.

Adwen and the others passed the fallen statue in time to see Kale pounce. She gasped and her heart skipped a beat as one evil whip curled back in midair like a serpentine tongue. It ensnared Kale's throat and slammed him to the ground. The second returned to strike across his back, making him howl. Blood flew from the long cut left by the weapon from the Void.

"Kale!" she cried out.

Forgetting the werewolf, the demon lord looked over and hissed, furling misty wings in anger. He raised a whip high and sent it out to strike her down.

As Oryn shielded her, one of Kale's huge hands snapped up and caught the evil cord. The werewolf snarled, gnashing his teeth in defiance.

More enraged than before, the demon jerked back the whip, slitting Kale's palm open. The immensely powerful fiend whipped Kale again and again. Adwen wept and shouted for it to stop, feeling a fraction of what was dealt. Every strike rent flesh and bombarded Kale's mind with despair. Despite the merciless lashings, he tried to recover. It became harder with each strike. Unable to fight back, Kale turned up his jaws to the overbearing monster and roared.

Entertained by the show of defiance, the enormous demon chuckled. Then with both whips, the demon lord flung the werewolf up high and slammed him to the ground.

Kale fell quiet. When the dust settled, his body had shriveled into that of a man in a red jacket. Grievous weeping gashes covered his back. He lay a moment gasping for air, wheezing and wracked with agony. Despite being too weak to fight, Kale continued to resist. As he struggled to push himself up, terrible laughter echoed along with the cracking of whips.

"Break, break, break!" The demon lord jeered, "Break for me, little bird."

On hands and knees and searching for the strength to stand, Kale gazed at the dirt, caked in fresh blood. "When are you going to learn, Degah'lee?" Kale asked. "I'll never be yours."

"You are mine, my property. You are my creation!"

Standing at last, Kale planted his feet firmly and stared down the enormous demon. "But not from scratch. Only Melanin and the Dark Heart were ever any good at that. The rest of you lot are outright rubbish at making things. You stole me; I was never your property."

Degah'lee was persistent. "I made you. I own you. Break, break. Fall and become what you are meant to be; become my general. There will be no more pain. Give up hope, and the torment will end. Come to me, and you shall know only pleasure."

The others could see Kale's shoulders shuddering but could only hear weak laughter between intermittent coughing.

"That's all you got?" Kale asked. "You're crap at anything except giving others your dirty work. Leave the art of temptation to the Dark Heart and get lost. It's over, and this time I've got proof." He presented the golden marks, relishing the disgust on Degah'lee's face.

The demon sneered and hissed before shooting Adwen a deadly look. "Andredan, you've stained my pet!" It turned back to Kale. "Fall for me, little bird. Break away from hope. Leave her bondage and become free."

"No."

Cracking a whip over his head, Degah'lee was losing patience. "You will break. One way or another, you will be mine."

Kale wore a faint smile. "No, I won't, especially not now."

"Why? Tell me why. Make me laugh."

Taking a deep breath, Kale spoke with his true demon voice, "Ah'nay."

The demon lord's grin wilted and slackened as if he had heard the foulest word.

Kale spoke again with even more gladness and conviction, "Ah'nay... furak dut zoe!"

Glancing at the Holy Hounds as his unearthly face twisted into a hideous scowl, Degah'lee wailed and shrieked in outrage. He cracked his whips madly, many arms flailing, clutching at nothing, as the demon threw a massive tantrum.

All the while, Kale laughed weakly, coughing. "You understand that, don't you? See? I'll never be yours."

Seething, the demon calmed enough to resume the confrontation. Vengeance turned Degah'lee's already insidious voice even more deadly.

"But you will break. In time, you will fall and become true darkness. You won't fall for me, but you will fall. Even if you won't be mine, perhaps you'll replace Melanin!"

Kale growled, flashing sharp teeth.

"Five years," the demon said. "Five years in the living worlds was not enough? The torture of hope shattered and renewed, only to be shattered again, was not enough to break you?" The demon's many hands and arms formed a swirling black orb of darkness. "What about those five years on infinite repeat until at last you break!"

A terrified gasp escaped Kale as he blanched. The demon lord shot the swirling mass at the werewolf who stumbled in an attempt to flee. It struck, knocking him to the dirt, where he writhed and roared, trying to resist the horrible chaos spell. He could feel it overpowering him, and long years of misery spilled over, threatening to drown him. Before the spell could take hold, Adwen's soft hand touched Kale's shoulder, staving it off. Kale became quiet and breathed in rapid gasps. On hands and knees, he quivered, shocked at being saved and afraid of what might happen now that Adwen could not be shielded.

Oryn was at her side, while she stood over the quaking werewolf. Jack and Alexander joined them. They were defiant, but only she and the knight were unafraid.

"Adwen Andredan, pure-white Guardian, give him to me," the demon demanded. "Give me my property! Renounce him from your call, and you shall live."

She glared. "Weren't you just leaving, Degah'lee?"

This sparked the demon's rage anew. "You command me?! A tiny fly commands a spider to leave his web? How dare you?" An ocean breeze parted the mist around the castle, and weak sunlight nearly burned the wicked being away. Adwen's body shone like a star again, strength increasing with the life of the land. The demon shrieked. Like the recoiling shadows, Degah'lee was forced to hide behind the nearest statue. In the shade he slowly regenerated, glaring at the warriors, who had kept his prize. Rumbling and hissing, the demon realized he had lost this fight.

"My kin." He whispered dangerously, "My kin and I will revel in your destruction." Another tear in the world widened in his shadowy cover, letting the demon lord slip back into the Void.

Adwen's form stopped glowing, and her stern look softened as she turned to Kale. His quivering had lessened, but he was terribly weak and terrified.

"I'm sorry." She tried not to start crying. "I can't break the spell."

Kale's voice was meek. "But you kept it from becoming permanent. That makes a big difference to me." He wanted to cry as well but did not.

She held her hand to his shoulder. The many wounds from Degah'lee's whips were hidden beneath a layer of torn red leather. Thick blood trickled in streams down the sides of his jacket. Gazing long at the horrible mess, her heart sank. Adwen did not want him to endure any more torture.

Then he murmured softly. "You have to let go."

"I know."

He was quiet, but when he spoke again he was almost pleading. "Before you do, can you tell me something?"

"Yes."

Kale's weak voice cracked with notes of uncertainty. "You'll all be waiting when I get out?"

"I promise."

The thought of all of them still being here after it ended gave him enough courage to face this alone. His quivering all but ceased, and he was calm.

"You can let go now."

The instant Adwen withdrew her hand, Kale was ripped from the world, vanishing into a small black star devoid of light. It floated in place emitting wicked mist.

Oryn dismissed his sword as she lay her head against his chest for comfort. Studying the evil energy, the knight frowned. "How long shall he be gone?"

"I don't know. There's no way to tell."

Oryn sighed heavily in a mixture of disappointment and frustration. Remaining in one place too long would be risky.

"It doesn't matter how long it takes." She added. "We aren't leaving without him."

"No one here is suggesting that."

Adwen glanced at Jack. He wore a reassuring expression, and Alexander smiled in agreement.

Still frowning, Oryn asked, "Could this break him?"

She was resolute. "Never. Not in a million years."

This somehow perplexed him. "How can he withstand this?"

"Because he is who he is; there's nothing more to it than that."

Chapter 13
WHAT'S IN A NAME

The brief dawn cleansed the dark influence from the castle grounds. Degah'lee would not be able to reappear. Awaiting Kale's release, the Holy Hounds remained just inside the castle entrance. Everything was dark as night again, leaving them to sit in the stillness. Castle banners hung in tatters. Pottery and sculptures were defaced or broken.

Sitting by a wall with an arm around Adwen's shoulder, Oryn mulled over what had happened in the garden. A realization struck him, and he frowned.

"Kale was aware that Degah'lee was stalking him."

Jack and Alexander glanced over.

"He anticipated the demon's arrival; the werewolf expected it."

Quiet followed his words until Jack announced a second revelation. "If Kale knew, then that means she knew."

Their attention fell on Adwen's solemn expression as she gazed at the floor.

"Yes."

Oryn could not decide whether he felt betrayed. "Why did you say nothing of this?"

She refused to meet their eyes. "There was no time. If Degah'lee suspected that we knew, everything would have gone much worse."

Her answer helped the warriors accept the decision.

"Kale knew that if none of the higher-ranking demons came, then Degah'lee would come. He wanted to take Kale alive."

A grim look came over the knight. "Our tactics must

change."

"There has to be a way to fight back without hitting the pillars," Jack agreed. "If any of the demon lords shows up again, we're as good as dead."

She grimaced. "If any of the others had come besides Degah'lee, we wouldn't be here right now. If we're careful and lucky, the demons' hubris will give us some protection. He still wants Kale but needs to conceal his existence from the other demon lords. Having created a powerful rogue wouldn't make him popular among his counterparts."

Jack smiled. "No wonder Kale thought we would have a shot at one more pillar. He had a hunch Degah'lee was trying to cover up his existence. If the Dark Heart finds out that Degah'lee made Kale, then things could get sticky pretty quick."

Adwen knew he was correct. "For everyone." A tugging at her insides signaled the return of their dark companion. Her gaze lifted to the broken castle doors. "He's out."

After a few minutes, faint footfalls ascended the stone stairs. Then the strong scent of werewolf blood announced his arrival. He slowly walked beyond the threshold with hands in his pockets, paying no mind to their expressions. Plodding to a place not far from the others, he gingerly leaned against a wall and slowly slid to sit. Streaks of clotted blood painted the stones. Kale cringed, gritting his wolfish teeth with eyes closed. As the pain lessened, he rested his head against the wall and took a long sigh of relief. Suddenly a weak smile came over him.

He finally chuckled, and it hurt. "Did I ever mention that the Taskmaster was a tosser?"

Everyone kept staring, although the tension of the moment was shattered.

Alexander could not help but smile. "I think you did."

"Good. And he's a bloody sore loser, too." More painful chuckles escaped him, making him cringle. "So, where were we before that little spat? Can't remember."

Adwen refreshed his memory. "We were going to try to find our friends."

"Ah, now I remember." Kale paused before murmuring, "Give me a tick to sort myself."

She frowned, sensing he lacked the strength to get up. Empathizing with their werewolf friend, she turned to Oryn.

"Please heal him."

A sour expression came over the knight.

Kale put on a reassuring smile as he rested, eyes still closed. "He doesn't have to. I'll be alright."

Oryn detested the thought of touching the werewolf, but then he saw the looks from Jack and Alexander. The cop's eyes were burning at Oryn's hesitation, and the Marine wore a bitter frown. After shooting them a hard scowl, Oryn noticed Adwen gazing up at him. Her expression was not angry but sorrowful. She appeared on the brink of tears, and Oryn's heart sank when she turned from him and did not meet his gaze again.

Observing the injured creature, Oryn felt he had no choice. He strode to the wounded werewolf. Briefly, the knight considered this silent beast, mustering the will to lay his hands on him. Wanting the experience to be over with, he forced Kale to lean forward by pressing on the back of his neck.

The motion and the pain it caused broke down Kale's frail act. Immense agony ripped the placid smile away and forced him to cry out. He struggled to breathe, while his hands came out of their pockets to tremble and twitch, bracing against the stone floor for support.

Oryn paid no mind. Grabbing Kale's jacket collar, the knight pulled it down in a swift jerk. When Kale wailed and the wounds were revealed, the knight froze. They were far worse than he had thought. Each long slash reached bone. White slivers and fragments lay exposed. Blood wept between sliced folds of skin and flesh.

The knight could not look away. Any one of these deadly strikes would have killed any of the others. Just a single additional wound would have killed Kale. Judging by the seriousness of his condition, the werewolf had stood and walked into the castle by force of will. Glancing at the werewolf's quivering head, the truth was clear: Kale really was on their side.

The wounds were so grievous, it would take all Oryn's strength to repair. He dealt with the worst, repairing bone and sealing off bleeds. Healing magic arched from the knight's fingertips like green electricity. As the knight tired and could heal no more wounds, he left many lash marks partially restored. Oryn pulled the jacket up onto its owner's shoulders.

Kale uttered softly, head hung low in weakness, "Thank you."

Oryn realized that the werewolf could not get up. Taking hold of the front of the red leather jacket, the knight lifted Kale to his feet. The sudden motion caused the werewolf to yelp and wince. For a moment, Oryn stood toe to toe with him. Kale's red eyes remained downcast, concealing his suffering. As Oryn watched, he sensed that Kale was hiding something more than pain. Now a little more curious than suspicious, the knight stepped back and rejoined Adwen across the hall.

Kale's empty stare was soon replaced by discomfort. The pain was far less severe, allowing him to regain a casual demeanor. Settling the jacket more comfortably against torn skin, his friendly smile returned. "Well, who here is in the mood for some tracking?"

A few seconds passed before Adwen smiled, raising a hand. Alexander did as well, while Jack chuckled, shaking his head.

"That's what I like to see. So, where is this secret passage?"

Oryn gave a flat reply: "I know it."

"Perfect. Could you please lead the way?"

Not saying a word, he started down a long corridor deeper into the castle.

On their walk through the castle halls, the Marine stayed close to Kale in case he stumbled. The werewolf's footing never faltered. Entering the throne room and descending the stairs, Kale took deliberate steps to keep himself steady.

Scorch marks stained the stones over most of the chamber. The domed ceiling had been reduced to rubble scattered across the floor. Ahead, where the king's throne once stood, lay splintered fragments of the oaken great chair. It appeared to have been hewn into pieces by a sharp blade.

Jack's voice echoed off distant surfaces. "Can you smell anything interesting in here, Kale?"

"Everything smells interesting. But yes, I also smell many soul traces, too many to tell apart. I'm sure it will be easier to sort them in the passage we're seeking."

"Well, what does this throne room mostly smell like?"

Taking a big sniff, he replied, "Courage. It's everywhere. I smell traces of cowardice and corruption, but courage and honor almost drown them out."

For Adwen, seeing the once grand castle's heart in ruin left her feeling dismal. King Lorvan had died here along with many of his most loyal soldiers and citizens. She could recall how wondrous it was on the night of the masquerade ball. Now not even a spider occupied the chambers.

The knight was indifferent to what had become of the castle. It did not matter now. He brought them up the steps and past the decimated throne to the wall beyond it. The tapestry that had hung there was burned away, making it simpler to find the latch to the hidden entrance. Pressing a small stone, the knight opened a narrow gap and went inside. Shortly after everyone was through the entrance closed tight.

Jack said to himself, "That's not a very good place to hide the most secret escape passage."

Oryn glowered. "This is not the escape passage."

Near a turn in the cramped tunnel, the knight came to an unassuming section of wall. There he carefully ran armor clad fingers over stones. After a few seconds, his fingers found both hidden switches and pressed them in unison. A wider opening appeared as a section of wall slid aside. The air inside was stale and damp.

"This is the escape passage."

Jack mused, "Okay, this is a pretty good place for a secret passage."

The knight stepped aside to let Kale enter first.

The scents filled his senses. Touching one wall, he put his nose to it.

"What is it?" Adwen asked.

"More than a dozen people passed through." He continued to sniff, resampling as needed. "Three were noble. One among them was very different."

Oryn suggested, "Likely the princess."

"No, this one is male."

The Holy Hounds exchanged looks.

Kale smiled. "I would very much like to meet this one."

"With any luck, you'll get your chance. Let's keep going."

The passage bore them deep into the earth beneath the castle. Because the evil mist did not leech into the earth, the Holy Hounds could see better in the dark. None spoke in the confines; not even Jack said a word. They walked for an unknown amount of time down stone stairs carved into different layers of rock. As the stairs began to dwindle into a sloping floor, a scent passed under their sensitive noses. Kale smiled to himself, and the others began to sniff.

"Is that fresh air?" Alexander asked.

The werewolf held back a chuckle to avoid hurting himself. "All puns aside, that truly is a breath of fresh air. The exit must be close."

The passage leveled off as stronger drafts of fresh air swept through. The odors of the secret passage gave way to familiar aromas, belonging neither to the underground nor the barren wasteland. Around the final corner an exit appeared. Relentless currents of wind pushed through gaps between large boulders blocking the opening.

They waited as Kale went ahead to look through the biggest gap. He inspected the boulders before turning to the others. "One or two of your friends collapsed the exit to cut off any pursuit. Can I get a hand, please?"

The cop and the Marine stepped forward as the werewolf moved aside. Jack gave a confident glance to his blond companion.

"Shall we pick it apart or just save time?" Alexander asked Jack.

"Save time," Jack replied. "I want out of this gopher hole."

As Alexander transformed into a muscular yellow hound in thick plated armor, Jack closed his eyes to focus on the debris. Feeling with his mind through the nooks and crannies, he discovered many weak points. With as much strength as Jack could muster, he used his telekinesis to apply pressure on the targeted stones. Maintaining so many different motions stressed his ability.

"Ready, Big Dog?"

The yellow hound warrior rumbled, "Affirmative."

"Hit three quarters to the right, dead center on the big one. Hurry! My head hurts."

Alexander lowered his shoulder and charged the boulder. In a huge crash, he burst through, and smaller rocks rained down. Jack used his powers to clear remaining debris. Everyone strolled into the open and found Alexander staring out into the distance. As they came upon him, they began to stare as well. Warm expressions filled their faces.

The evil mist was thin, dissipating a short distance away. Beyond its reach was the Dargadian coast. The tunnel had taken them many miles west. Where the mist ended was healthy forest and growing things. Somehow, the woodlands along the sea were protected from the encroaching darkness. A true night hung over them, and the forest was teeming with wildlife.

Oryn could not help but marvel: "How is this possible?"

Adwen shook her head. "I have no idea, but it's a good sign."

Beside them, Kale spoke, sounding weaker than ever: "Hate to disappoint, but I need a lie-down."

"It's okay. It's time everyone had some real rest. Also, Bad Dog and Big Dog can go hunting for our dinner."

"I would point out that we have done enough work today, but I'm too hungry to argue," Jack said.

Alexander rolled his eyes. "How many should we try to bring back?"

"Two is perfect. First, let's pick a place to stay the night."

A grove of moss-covered trees served as the best place to rest. Jack and Alexander went hunting, and Adwen and Oryn sat by the trunk of a large tree. Kale rested across the clearing.

The knight's wounds were healing well, and pain was minimal. As he held her in his arms, Oryn's gaze wandered to the werewolf from time to time. Kale had not stirred since seating himself. A part of Oryn recognized that this werewolf was a genuine ally, but years of experience with demons and werewolves made it difficult to accept. Demons could not be good, could not feel compassion and could never be trusted. Most of all, Kale being a werewolf prevented Oryn from lowering his guard. Even after the display of grit and loyalty, old scars drove the knight to hold onto doubt like a shield.

To Adwen laying against his chest, Oryn whispered, "Is he asleep?"

"No. The pain is too much. It is keeping him awake."

Studying the way Kale showed no sign of overhearing, the knight frowned. "When faced with the Taskmaster, he risked everything to protect you."

"Us," she corrected. "And of course he did."

For a long while, Oryn was silent. Adwen could not take command of Kale's movements as she could her other warriors. Anything the werewolf did was of his own free will. Nevertheless, he was a powerful demon, and Oryn could not accept Kale as fully trustworthy.

Rustling sounds nearby signaled the return of Jack and Alexander. Deer musk wafted into the air with the scent of fresh blood just before they appeared carrying two does. The carcasses were fat and limp on the warrior's shoulders. While the Marine took his to Adwen and Oryn, Jack heard Adwen's thoughts and knew his prey was meant entirely for Kale.

As the large deer dropped to the ground beside Kale, he opened his eyes at last. After giving the carcass a glance, he looked up at Jack.

"Thank you."

Jack shrugged. "Can you eat that on your own?"

A wry smile found its way onto his face. "No problem. I apologize in advance for my poor table manners. It won't be pretty."

Jack arched an eyebrow. "So you think you look pretty right now?"

Kale was caught off guard and nearly laughed, but was too weak. "Shut your yap."

Chuckling, the warrior went to join the others in dividing up the first deer.

The fresh kill smelled delicious to the werewolf. It was a comfort to have a taste for anything except human flesh. However, in such a weakened state, finding the strength to feed was difficult. To do so, he needed to summon up something like the old hunger. To spur the primal instinct, Kale gazed at the body, breathing in the aroma of blood.

While the whites of his eyes turned black, the scent alone was not enough to arouse bloodlust. With sharp claws he swiped at the exposed deer's underbelly. The meek motion was just enough to open the dead thing's stomach, releasing entrails and pints of deep red blood. The instant the sights and smells struck him, his hunger awoke.

His breaths quickened, and his vision narrowed. The pain in his back spiked, while bones crunched and snapped with stretching sinews. While his body began to shift, everything turned to crimson. Involuntarily taking on much of his werewolf form, Kale rolled over onto the deer, sinking fangs and claws into lukewarm flesh.

The Holy Hounds were just beginning to eat when his heavy

panting and snarling drew their attention. They were disturbed by the way he ripped into the carcass. Taking ravenous bites with elongating jaws, he swallowed large portions whole. He blindly took chunks of bone as well. In minutes, the head of the deer was in his mouth, pulverized by a single chomp before it was swallowed.

For a time, Kale crouched low sniffing at the ground, shuddering. After regaining some sense, he reclined against the tree again. His form shriveled downward into his more human shape, and his breathing returned to normal.

Feeling stronger, Kale sighed, "That's much better."

Everyone tried to eat despite the grizzly event.

Jack, first to finish his share of the other deer, asked Kale, "Do you black out when you eat?"

"Most of the time. Why?"

"Just curious. You sure did wolf it down."

Alexander elbowed Jack hard and rolled his eyes.

Kale glanced at the patch of blood. There was nothing left.

"Apparently, I did. I need a nap after that."

Everyone else was almost fed, as Jack picked out his patch of turf for rest. "Not yet, Big Guy. We need to get better acquainted."

Kale had only just closed his eyes for sleep. They snapped open, casting Jack a perplexed look. "Haven't pried enough yet?"

Jack froze, feeling nervous. "I think we got off on the wrong foot. Normal people get past bad first impressions by getting to know each other." He hoped the explanation would keep Kale from doing anything unpleasant.

The werewolf smiled at last to show he was merely teasing. "Sure, why not."

Alexander chose his own sleeping spot, as Jack failed to hide his relief.

There was a moment of silence until Kale chided, "Well? What do you want to know?"

"How about the basics? What's one of your favorite activities?"

A pause preceded the werewolf's answer. "Dinner and a movie."

Even Adwen looked up.

Jack was thoroughly disturbed. "That's kind of dark."

Kale rolled his eyes. "You asked. So what about you?"

"Photography." A bittersweet twinge struck his heart. "Ashley and I always went out on hikes just to take pictures."

Kale smiled placidly. "That sounds nice."

The warrior smiled as well. "It is. Thanks."

"What about you, soldier?" Kale asked Alexander. "What's your favorite pastime?"

"Working on sports bikes. Not many things I can do hiding out."

"Ah, a gearhead."

"Thank you for not saying knuckle-dragger."

Kale grinned. "Grease monkey."

The way Alexander rolled his eyes illustrated how he felt about the term.

Jack decided he was not satisfied with Kale's answer. "Okay, I've got to know what you like that does not involve death somehow."

"Suit yourself." He pondered a long while. His expression became distant and thoughtful. "Names."

The friends exchanged glances.

"Names?"

Kale's cheery demeanor shifted to one of contemplation. "Part of my unique rogue nature is to know about people's names. Names become who we are, and sometimes we become them. They're important."

"How about an example? Try Jarhead here."

"Wait a minute. Leave me out of this!"

"It's too late for that."

As the burly warrior gave Kale an apprehensive look, the werewolf chuckled softly. "It's painless, I promise. Requires no touching or otherwise."

Groaning, Alexander conceded, "Just get it over with."

Kale nodded, and then is face became stony while the whites of his eyes turned black. Both red irises dilated with the cadence of a heartbeat. Whispers from a past he never lived chattered over one another in his mind. When the murmurs ceased, his friendly smile returned, and his gaze became normal.

Jack's curiosity grew. "So?"

Kale admired the name. "Alexander, your father was a history buff. He named you after the one man to conquer the ancient world: Alexander the Great."

The Marine almost laughed. "That's right."

"Me next!" Jack insisted.

The werewolf's eyes changed color again, this time dilating, fixed upon Jack. When they stopped, Kale puffed, starting to chuckle.

"What's funny?"

"Jack. You were named by your mother after the little man who climbed a giant beanstalk."

The warrior rolled his eyes. "Come on. Tell me something I don't know."

"She picked it because she craved green beans the whole time she was carrying yah."

While Alexander sniggered, his friend was confused. "Seriously? My mom always told me it was because she knew I would be short."

Kale shrugged. "It's the truth."

"Now Adwen," Jack suggested.

She had just finished eating and was sitting to rest, while Oryn continued to feed on his larger share. Her warm smile showed her approval.

The werewolf shook his head. "Which name?"

"Uh, why not all of them? How many does she have?"

"Two: There's her given name and her true name."

Jack and Alexander stared. "Do we have true names?"

Kale smiled. "Only the Light Spirits can know those names. Adwen is her true name, given to her by the Light Spirits. It means 'pure white.' As for the other name ..." He examined her with his altered gaze, listening to the voices from across time. An admiring expression came over him. "Shari. It was given by her mother. She was their first little princess."

Remembering good memories despite the sorrows, Adwen was thankful to know.

"So what else?" Kale asked. "Or is it my turn to ask something?"

"Hold on," Jack said, nodding toward Oryn. "What about him?"

Oryn was licking the last of the deer's blood from his lips. Having heard everything up to this point, he threw a glare at Jack and Kale.

Not so much as glancing at the knight, Kale shrugged. "What about him?"

"You just told us about all our names except his. Why leave him out?"

Adwen frowned looking between Oryn and the others.

Kale stared at Jack for a moment. After deliberating, the whites of his eyes turned pitch black again. His blank stare moved toward the knight but did not fall on him. Oryn continued to scowl. A few seconds passed before the blackness left and Kale faced Jack.

"Oryn," he began coolly. "There is a tiny pale green bird native to Dargadia, unless the demons drove them to extinction. It is called the Oryn. They say it has a song so beautiful that all other songbirds fall quiet to listen. It was his mother who chose it."

A vicious snarl from the knight caused all but Kale to stare.

Seething with rage, Oryn glared. It took every ounce of self-restraint to stop himself from tearing the creature apart with his hands. The strain made his face blush several shades of red and purple. To stop himself from killing the wounded beast, he stormed off into the night.

Adwen watched him leave. He would be alright and return as soon as he was ready. All the same, it was hard to let him go.

Alexander and Jack were confounded at the outburst. But before the shortest warrior could speak, he remembered why Oryn hated werewolves and demons so much. He felt as if he were the size of a thimble.

Kale gazed vacantly at the ground and whispered softly to himself, "Oh, bugger."

Sighing loudly, Jack admitted his shame. "I screwed up big on this one. Guess I better go and try to talk him down."

Adwen's frown deepened. "That would be foolish."

"I've done it before." Jack was about to get to his feet when Kale stood up. He remained weak, but he felt strong enough to move.

Alexander was aghast. "Where do you think you're going?"

Wearing a wry smile, Kale replied, "Jack may have a very big mouth, but the blame is on me this time."

They watched him start into the forest with his hands in his pockets. Jack tried to talk him out of it: "Me going is dumb enough, but he won't kill me. He just might lose it if you show up."

Kale kept walking despite the warning. "I'll be fine."

"Adwen? Aren't you going to say anything?"

Kale froze and waited for her word on the matter.

Her heart was heavy, but the way things needed to be was clear. Looking somberly after him, she murmured, "Be careful."

In return, Kale gave a sidelong glance and a nod.

Nearly a mile away in a small meadow, Oryn paced to and fro. He growled with jaw clenched and fists balled tight. His boots flattened the grass, leaving a path for the fuming march to continue. No nocturnal animals in the area dared to linger. The only sounds were seething snarls and low growling.

Oryn put a momentary halt to the private rampage and stood still to think. The demon dared to speak of his family. Oryn wished to silence the thing for good. The treacherous fiend had no right to ever speak of him or his past. If it did so again, the knight was unsure what he would do. Jack and Alexander seemed to be accepting the monster as a friend. Adwen would not suffer the demon's presence if it were a danger to any of them. However, befriending this rogue demon was not necessary. For Oryn, it was not even a possibility.

Movement caused the knight's emerald glare to burn bright in the dark. Once he realized it was Kale, his blood boiled, and he turned rigid. In silence, Oryn waited to see what the werewolf intended now that they were alone.

Kale walked through the waist-high grass without taking his eyes off the enraged warrior. His expression was blank. He stopped about ten feet away. At this safe distance, Kale studied the knight. There was so much rage, so much pain underneath.

A long silence lasted between them while they stared at each other. Oryn tried to detect anything about the werewolf that would tell of intent. There was nothing to glean from that almost lifeless stare. It was frustrating. Was the demon waiting for something?

Gaining nothing from locking gazes, Oryn growled, "Why are you here?"

Kale replied, "I need to give you a message."

Wondering why Adwen would not come herself to speak with him, his glare intensified. Perhaps it was from Jack.

"Who from, pray tell?"

He fell quiet again. His unreadable face shared no answers. Then he spoke softly.

"During my time in the Void, before I was bound to this body, I had one friend."

Oryn's blood ran cold. A message from the Void? Nothing good could come from this. The scowl he wore soured like the feeling in his stomach.

"Just one. Before he was discovered and locked away, he asked that if I ever got out and if I ever found you, I would tell you something for him."

Angry and uneasy, Oryn sneered, "Who?"

Kale was quiet for a moment. "Kai."

In an instant, the knight felt weak. Then he was enraged. Oryn erupted with a bloodthirsty snarl as he lunged. Rapidly transforming, his giant hands snatched Kale around the middle and squeezed. Claws dug into the werewolf, adding to the pain of the injuries from the previous battle. The pressure squeezed the air from his lungs. Tears from physical agony blinded him.

"Do not say that name to me, demon! You have no right! Am I clear?"

He heard, but could not speak yet from the lack of air.

"Am I clear?!"

Using the little breath available, Kale wheezed, "Crystal."

In a flash, Oryn threw him to the ground, and even more pain radiated from his back. There he writhed, waiting for the horrible sensations to ease. As the pain ebbed, the sound of Oryn walking away forced him to raise his head. The Holy Hound shrank into his more human form as he left.

Kale called weakly, "Wait."

The knight stopped, though he did not know why he bothered. Was it morbid curiosity?

"Won't you at least hear the message?"

Oryn's jaw clenched. He wrestled with an overwhelming mess of feelings and thoughts. Unable to think of any other response, the knight snapped, "Say it so that I may forget it."

Kale could not see his face but sensed the turmoil and sighed ruefully. Then he worked hard to find his feet. When he was standing, he spoke again.

"He said, he forgives what yah did. And that he'll always love his brother."

At the fringe where the meadow melded with the forest, Oryn stood frozen. A chill coursed through him, and the next breeze threatened to topple him over. His brother forgives him? The last he looked at him, his dying eyes were filled with fear and betrayal. The memory of his twin's bloody head on the ground plunged Oryn's heart into wrenching grief. Growling in bitter resentment of himself, Oryn stalked away.

Kale waited until Oryn was out of sight, then frowned. He shook his head and made his way back to the tiny camp.

Chapter 14
FRIENDS LIKE THESE

"Oryn isn't stupid," Alexander said. "He won't kill Kale."

"Sure, Jarhead, but he has his moments."

There was silence for a time. It had not been long since Kale went in search of the angry knight. While Alexander was calm, Jack worried. When he spoke anew, his question was directed at Adwen.

"You can sense if Kale is safe or not, right?"

She seemed distant. "Yes, and he is okay."

The news was reassuring. "When is he coming back? I've never seen Oryn rage like that. I'm not putting anything past him until the big guy gets back."

A course murmur came through the trees. "The big guy is back, so you may put anything you like past him."

Kale's arrival brought the cop some needed relief. He would have felt responsible for any harm done. Seeing no sign of injury lifted the weight off his shoulders.

"I'm glad to see your scruffy mug. Did you find him?"

He went to his resting spot in the clearing. "Oh, I found him. He was in a right bad mood for sure."

Jack exchanged glances with Alexander. "Did you talk to him?"

"We had a rather short chat. There was no consoling that one."

"You are lucky he didn't take your head off."

An entertained smile came over Kale as he sat scratching his throat with sharp claws. "That thought had crossed my mind."

"I thought you were going to do something to bring him around. Where is he?"

"Relax. Your knight friend will be back once he sorts himself out." With that, Kale closed his eyes to rest.

Jack sighed as he realized it was best to be quiet. As much as he wanted more answers, it was better to let the werewolf sleep. With nothing to say or do, he shared another bewildered look with Alexander.

Minutes passed in the hushed meadow. Wind rustled leaves over their heads, veiling the cloudless starry sky. Just when Jack felt like going to sleep, the sound of someone approaching grabbed his attention. Kale slept, but everyone else turned to watch Oryn approach.

Saying nothing, the knight went to Adwen. He settled beside her and pulled her close. She returned the half embrace beneath their tree. His heart was heavy. She could feel it as her ear pressed against his chest. Even through his armor, the sound carried a somber cadence. To ease some of the pain, Adwen leaned into him to share warmth as they went to sleep.

The cop and the Marine frowned. Standing watch would be left to them. They needed the least amount of rest among the weary team.

The sun woke them. A true dawn bloomed beyond the mountains over the sea of shadowy mist. Sunlight stirred the waking forest, and birds flitted in the boughs above. Kale was first to rise, ready for travel.

Adwen woke and saw him taking in the daylight. Then she stole a look at the knight holding her in his sleep. With a gentle nudge, she brought him too. He flashed a faint smile and stretched awake. The werewolf stood in the corner of his vision, and the knight avoided looking at him. Oryn wanted as little to do with Kale as possible. Had the message been a lie? Of the things the demon said, what was true and what was false? Oryn concluded that these questions were better left unanswered. Knowing would change nothing and bring only heartache.

Breathing in the crisp morning air, Kale sighed. "Everyone ready to get this show on the road?"

"You are feeling better?" Alexander asked.

"Thank you for noticing. I'll be at my best by the end of the day. Come along then."

They resumed their search, astonished at the strange conditions along the coast. With nowhere else to go, large numbers of animals and magical creatures filled the forest along the shoreline. A herd of deer darted out of sight at their passing. Sprites, pixies and a multitude of other beings watched from thin, leafy branches.

The band followed Kale as he sniffed. The scents of the souls who traveled this way were faint. Although, three were strong and one of them still tantalized his curiosity. Animals and magical creatures of all shapes and sizes skirted out of his way. They murmured amongst themselves at the werewolf leading the Holy Hounds. Then he whispered to himself, making the frightened things flinch.

"I wonder ..."

"You wonder, what?" Jack asked.

"Ah, it's nothing."

"Know if we are getting close?"

"No way to tell. You could ask them." He glanced at some animals and fairies, prompting the little things to duck into hiding.

Jack chuckled at the small creatures. "I don't think so. They've been through enough without me irritating them."

Alexander rolled his eyes.

"I saw that, Jarhead."

Suddenly Kale gasped in awe and surprise. "Wow. Now this is very intriguing."

No one could disagree. Enormous trees leaned in dramatic angles, their roots in the air interlocking like fingers. The earth was churned, leaving mounds and deep trenches. Parts of the root barricades were ripped apart as if by sharp claws. Ice shards that would not thaw stuck out of dirt and bark alike. The amazing scenery continued on an uneven path as far as they could see.

"Looks like your friends were chased."

Adwen and her warriors remained silent. They followed Kale through the twisting mess hoping to find a sign that their friends had survived. Over and under broken barricades, their search took them toward the shore. Where the forest gave way to a grassy slope, they saw the remains of a fishing town.

Before any of them started toward the burnt Dargadian port, Kale cleared his throat for their attention. Then he nodded at the sheer cliff nearby. To their astonishment, a series of icy sheets created a stairway reaching the surf. Hundreds of feet below, everything lay under a dense veil of mist.

"Seems to me they intended to catch a ship," Kale said. "The princess and the others went this way to try to escape the hordes waiting in that mess."

Adwen became desperate to know what had happened and dashed along the steps. Kale and the rest of the Holy Hounds followed. Descending into the fog, their chilled feet found shifting sand. They caught up to her as she stopped somewhere deep in the dim vapor. She sensed something. Her eyes wandered, scanning the blank air. There were only the warriors and the werewolf, but she did not end her search.

Oryn, Jack and Alexander stood by to see what was wrong as Kale crept past. He sniffed. Making his way along the trail, he came to the edge of the breaking waves. His gaze intensified. Taking a final sniff at the surf, he pointed out into the water.

"The trail ends just out there in the waves."

Alexander was disturbed. "Did they drown?"

Thinking about what he could read, he shook his head. "Nah, they vanished. It's impossible to tell where to. One of them didn't make it that far, though."

Their faces tensed and Jack grimaced. "Who didn't make it?"

Pondering the question, Kale turned to face them. Suspicion engulfed him as he studied the seemingly empty fog. "He's still here."

The others tensed and joined Adwen in scanning the area. Whoever or whatever was here was beyond their senses to detect. However, Adwen and Kale felt the presence drawing near.

Their gazes fell on a growing light source in the mist as a figure manifested. The male shape was adorned in what appeared to be ethereal robes, rippling slowly like that of a ghost. Drifting closer, pale blue light glinted from one side of the being, which appeared crystalline, while the other side of him was dark. Red flames lapped along the smooth ebony skin and phantasmal robes.

Everyone gazed at the powerful entity, and Adwen alone found the will to speak.

"Balefire."

The face of the being frowned, glowing red and blue eyes were dismal. Then he forced his visage to resume the familiar once-human mage. Standing on the sand before them, Balefire's form continued to glow in hot and cool hues. His eyes never left Adwen's. When he spoke at last, his voice echoed, filled with sorrow.

"Where were you?"

A chill coursed through Adwen as she suddenly felt sick. She cringed as her expression became pained, gazing back at what remained of Balefire.

"Why weren't you here?" He began to glare bitterly. "Where were you when we needed you most?"

Adwen's three warriors growled. Just as Oryn stepped between her and the immensely powerful Guardian made of fire and ice, Jack was going to tell the entity off.

However, Kale spoke first: "That's not fair asking her that." Glaring past his friends at the Guardian, he was unafraid when the intense stare turned on him. "It's not right to put her on the spot for something that's not her fault just because you feel cheated."

Out of rage, Balefire lost hold of his human shape. Flames blazed along with crackling ice flesh. In an instant, he vanished and reappeared before Kale, leaning in face to face until the intense temperatures chilled and seared the werewolf's nose and cheeks.

This had no effect on Kale, who never stopped glaring back.

A second passed as they each dared the other to make a move. Then the Guardian looked beyond the demon. Flames and ice shards settled down. Balefire's expression shifted from one of anger to one of surprise and empathy. Studying the dark oddity, he frowned.

"You would know what is unfair, wouldn't you?"

Kale felt discomfort but hid it well. "Could talk about it all day. Where would that get us?"

A pause followed as Balefire calmed, conceding. "Nowhere." Able to regain his human shape, he faced Adwen again feeling ashamed. "Forgive me. I was wrong to ask such a thing. Had the Light Spirits commanded it, you would have come. If you had been here for the attack, you likely would have perished as well."

Alexander took a step closer, confounded by the Arch Mage's transformation. "What happened to you?"

Sorrow returned to Balefire's resonating voice. "They cornered us. The king's advisor could not use his powers to shield us any longer so far from the forest. None of the other mages or royal guards could hold them off. To protect them and the princess, I made the waves turn to ice. The demon spawn disliked being near the waters. My fire could slow them down but not forever. I held them at bay to give Moira time to open a portal." Thinking of her brought a bitter-sweet look to him. "She found a way for her portal to go to somewhere instead of from. When they had gone, the demon Impurus came."

The companions cringed.

"If you know of him, then you know what that abomination is capable of. When he breathed evil flames at me, I used all my power to resist. It was no use. I felt my body being destroyed, but ..."

Adwen continued for him. "You did not die."

"There was an explosion as the last of me burned away. I can only recall a little because my essence was cast over this expanse of shoreline. Lesser demons were destroyed as a result, and Impurus had to retreat. My consciousness was fractured. It took time to gather myself enough to be coherent or even manifest myself. Then I did everything within my power to shield as much land as I could." Sweeping one hand aside, he commanded the fog to dissipate in a rush of wind. Blue sky unfurled overhead, and the sun shone bright.

Jack almost laughed. "It was you who parted the clouds over the castle at dawn!"

The Guardian wanted to smile. He could not. His heart remained heavy, so he simply nodded.

Oryn approached with determination. "Then you can fight with us."

Shaking his head, Balefire put the matter to rest. "Have you any idea how much of my strength and concentration are required to protect this sliver of land?"

The knight was taken aback.

"Sending a gale from the sea to the castle was a great risk. This haven nearly collapsed as a result. I cannot leave and can do no more than I already am."

"We understand," Adwen reassured their ally. "You've awakened as a new Guardian of Dargadia. This is your purpose."

His frown deepened.

"Now the Light Spirits speak to you the same way they speak to me," she added. "Do you have any guidance for us? Do you know where the princess was taken?"

Looking across the sea at nothing, Balefire answered, "To the island continent of Eskrana. The winds whisper to me often that the princess and the rest of the company survive."

This was encouraging for the Holy Hounds and the were-wolf.

Adwen shook her head in bewilderment. "We need to find them and meet with the princess. Darkness has destroyed all of the portals in this region, so we will have to wait until dawn to use the Gray Blade."

At last, Balefire flashed a wisp of a smile. "One is still intact." He a pointed to the rocks before the beach cliffs. This news brought Adwen great relief and helped the Guardian maintain his warm expression. "You may set out as soon as you wish. Once you have finished with business there, go to the desert in the far southeast."

"Why?"

"I only know that you are needed there."

She did not like the sound of that. "Then we'll go to the desert. Thank you, Balefire, for everything."

He nodded. "And the same to you." As they were walking away, Balefire watched Kale, who pretended not to notice. Before they went far, he called out.

"Adwen?"

They all paused, while she looked back at the Guardian's sad face.

"Could you do one thing for me? Please, tell Moira I'm sorry."

She was unsure of the request. "What for? If we succeed, you can tell her yourself when she returns."

A solemn moment passed until he let go of the human form and became the entity of fire and ice. Then he dissipated into the air and was gone.

In silence the small company continued to the cliff. Oryn followed at Adwen's side sensing she was troubled. They approached the entrance, which lay open as the hidden door had crumbled away. Inside, Oryn spoke with a hushed tone.

"What is it that you fear?"

"The desert. It's only just occurred to me how bad things might be in the other kingdoms."

"You anticipate Eskrana is not well?"

"I hope I'm wrong."

At the end of the long tunnel, the altar shimmered as a magical mass appeared. A light portal manifested and glowed brightly in the shadows.

"Be ready for anything," she warned.

Everyone silently agreed and followed. They passed through the portal to the other side, where wind whipped in mighty gusts. Beside them, the once wonderful water fountain was cracked and dry. That was the least of their concerns.

The capital city had become a ruin. No humans or griffons were in sight. It smelled as if none had frequented the streets for some time. Buildings had crumbled with untended roofs collapsing. Adwen wished this discovery had come as a shock, but it did not. The mighty Eskrani nation had fallen.

Setting aside despair, Adwen turned to Kale. "Are you able to detect any of those who escaped with the princess?"

Studying the ruined city, he shook his head. "Not a thing. I'll let you know once I pick up on it."

"Let's start by searching the palace," she said. "This city seems empty, but that doesn't mean it will stay empty. Keep alert."

Walking along the winding streets, they picked up many scents but none belonging to humans or griffons. Oryn carefully examined the signs in the surroundings. Homes smelled abandoned, most showing no indications of a fight. Whatever had happened, the weather washed any evidence away. As they neared the palace, Jack noticed what the knight already had.

"Does anyone else see something weird? There aren't any bodies. Where are the dead?"

The Marine muttered, "I don't think I want to know."

Adwen calmly addressed the werewolf: "Are you picking up anything yet?"

It was a moment before he answered. The jumble of physical and ethereal scents overwhelmed him. "Oh, yeah. I smell plenty. Nothing of your friends, though."

"What can you tell us?"

"There was a slaughter. I can smell death. It leaves a mark like footprints, and it's everywhere."

Jack willed himself to ask, "Where did the bodies go?"

"They were taken. From what I'm smelling, it was done by

survivors.”

"Cannibalism?" Jack suggested.

After giving Jack a harsh look, Kale realized the cop was serious. "For burial."

Jack was sheepish. "Sorry."

Alexander rolled his eyes.

A new scent surprised Kale. "Ah, I've got a hit."

Adwen sniffed. "Me too. Some of them were here."

At a brisker pace, the company followed the scent up the hill to the royal palace. Guard stations stood vacant, and the courtyard in shambles. Wild plants grew out of control. Vines covered everything in radiant indigo blooms. A sweet aroma from the flowers stifled everyone's senses. By the time they entered the palace, they could smell nothing but the blooms. None of the Holy Hounds made a sound, in case enemies lurked nearby.

Alexander sneezed, warranting stern glares from his friends.

Jack elbowed the Marine's ribs. "Nice going, Jarhead."

Adwen rolled her eyes. "It doesn't seem like he's announced our presence to anyone."

The knight remained vigilant, studying every detail. Jungle plants, including the overbearing flowery vines, covered walls and pillars, and even sealed some doors shut. Something about these vines roused his suspicion. Noticing a flower nearby slowly open in a flourish of deep indigo, he frowned.

"What is your command at this juncture?" he asked Adwen.

She watched a few more of the flowers blooming. "We split up."

The others gawked, and Oryn stared back at Adwen.

Rolling her eyes, she added, "Oryn and I will search the central chambers and the dungeon. Jack, look through the west wing. Alexander, you take the east. Kale, search the northern chambers. We will meet here afterward. Let's move."

When they parted, Oryn glared after the werewolf.

Adwen saw and chided. "Are you sure you wouldn't rather go search with him instead?"

The thought disturbed the knight. Recognizing her teasing smile, he shook his head. "I detest leaving him unwatched, but it would irk me more if you were unprotected."

Adwen and Oryn's search of the main chambers was fruitless. Vines grew everywhere. Unable to smell or see anything of interest, they moved on to the dungeon. Part way down, the vines ceased to reach any farther. Entering the dank cave where wind whistled through an opening for griffon riders, few things were left behind.

They exchanged suspicious glances and began walking along the dungeon searching every barred cage. Some were locked, but all were empty. Not only were their no occupants, dead or alive, but even the meager accommodations were gone. The buckets, chains and everything else was missing.

Pondering to herself, Adwen frowned.

Oryn watched as she stared in contemplation at the bare prison cells.

"We've seen enough," she said. "Let's go wait for the others."

"Indeed."

In the palace's west wing, Jack sliced away more vines to open another door. Attempting to turn the handle, he discovered that the mechanism had rusted. Groaning, he resorted to lowering his shoulder into the wood, bashing it open with a crash. Jack brushed slivers and dust off himself as he entered, looking about.

It was clearly a library. Books bound in leather and scrolls sat on dusty shelves. The vines from the main corridors had reached under the door, spreading to the walls here as well. He was about to leave and search another room but stopped. His instincts held him there, scanning the walls and shelves. Unlike every other room he had explored, the library's vines did not cover everything. Taking note of the details, Jack headed back to tell the others what he had discovered.

Alexander cut through dense, flowery vines to open several doors. Some were old supply stores. Finding only more vines growing up walls, he moved onto the next room. The Marine expected to find something other than empty chambers covered in pungent flora. Everything had been empty, and the search became monotonous.

Slashing vines to open the door to another room, he swore

under his breath. "This better be good." With the thick vines removed, the door opened easily.

Light shone through the tall window from one side of the chamber. No vines grew here, leaving everything in the royal bedchamber untouched. Alexander slowly stepped inside and never took his eyes from the bed, covered in fine silks. Standing by one of the jungle-wood posts, he gazed at the pair of remains lying atop the bed. They had been dead a very long time. Silks were discolored from decomposition around the dry corpses.

Now wishing he had found nothing, the Marine bowed his head to the brave king and his queen one final time.

Adwen waited for the others to return to their rendezvous location. Arms folded, she stared vacantly, lost in thought. It was impossible to believe that all the Eskrani were dead. On top of that, there was the fact that the princess and the others from Dargadia had been here somewhere. She could only speculate their whereabouts.

Sensing movement, she and Oryn glanced to see Jack returning. He looked determined.

The knight greeted him with a question: "Did you find anything of note?"

He shrugged. "You could say that. To tell the truth, it's what I didn't find that is interesting."

"Same with our search," Adwen said. "The dungeon was empty. All the supplies are gone. Nothing is left."

"Besides the vines, you mean."

"Yes. They're everywhere but the dungeon."

Jack smiled. "And the bookshelves."

They gave the cop befuddled expressions.

His smile turned sly as Alexander also returned.

"What did you find, Jarhead? Nothing at all?"

To everyone's surprise, he replied with a dark look. "I found the king and queen."

Their brief shock passed, and they were dismal.

His friend gently prompted, "Anything else?"

Alexander shook his head. The four stood in silence for a time. Then Adwen shook her head ruefully.

"That can't be all there is in the palace. Kale hasn't come

back yet, and he should be here by now. We need to know if he's found more than we have."

Oryn grimaced. What had the demon gotten himself into while unsupervised?

Even more flowers dotted the walls in the north wing of the Eskrani Palace. It smelled so strongly of nectar that Kale could almost taste it. Foregoing his natural senses, he searched with his shadowy powers. The distraction of the flower scents made progress slow. Pausing at each door, rather than opening it, he let a little of his shadow slip through the cracks. This allowed him to get a glimpse inside without disturbing the vines.

These vines were more lively than other jungle plants. They seemed to be watching. Wherever he went, they opened and followed his movements. He avoided cutting them down; he sensed that doing so would be a mistake.

Stopping by another door, Kale extended his shadow sense inside. Retracting it again, he was about to move on but froze, studying the door. Everything within seemed normal, yet something told him otherwise. Touching the handle, wrapped in a cord of vines, he sensed very old magic. It was older than this palace. A power he did not recognize called soundlessly.

He paused, holding the knob and wondering whether there was some danger. It was impossible to tell. The magic calling him was not commanding or pleading; it simply called. Suspicious and curious, Kale chose to enter.

Using a little of his shadow to pry back at the vines, he opened the door to peer inside. It was a large chamber with empty troughs along walls that once held oil for lighting. Big open sills let wind from the sea blow in the scents of salt and brine. The breeze pushed back at the flower scents, and Kale could detect the smell of magic. It was neither good nor bad; it was neutral in nature. The call grew stronger, and he could not resist.

Kale slipped past the vine-entwined door. Immediately, a tall frame atop three stairs grabbed his attention. A long cloth draped over the towering thing that beckoned. He took cautious steps to the mysterious object and methodical steps up the stairs until he stood before the tall, narrow frame.

There he hesitated. The call was not so strong anymore, but he knew he was here for a reason. For good or ill, there would be no leaving this room without seeing what was under the cloth. Heaving a sigh, he became determined and yanked the drapery down. A breeze billowed the sheet as it fell to the floor. His eyes widened at the sight of the golden lion head atop the metal frame of the ancient mirror.

Frightened, Kale knew mirrors with magic could be dangerous, whether good or evil. He stared into the glass at his reflection in anticipation. Before him, the magic of the mirror altered his image. He stared, waiting for the colors to stop swirling. When they did, it confused him. This was no longer his reflection at all. When Kale recognized the image, he could not breathe. A gyre of shock, fear and awe held him transfixed.

He fell to his knees before the glass, staring longingly. Beginning to shudder he glanced down to see if he had changed, but the mirror had done nothing to him. It merely showed a different reflection. Studying the image, wondering what was happening, he extended a shaky set of claws toward the glass. Firm footfalls came beside him, and a low rumbling growl followed.

Kale had not noticed Oryn enter the room because he was so captivated. Retracting the hand, he did not try to touch the mirror again. Instead he stared, unable to turn away.

"What is this?" Kale asked the knight. "Is this a trick?"

The knight sneered beside the golden object. "This is the Mirror of Truth. It only shows the viewer their true self, no more and no less."

A weak smile flickered on Kale's face.

Oryn glowered. "What do you see?"

Breathless, he muttered with a real smile, "I see me."

Oryn disliked the evasive answer. "We are waiting for your report." Giving the mirror a bitter glance, Oryn departed to wait with the others.

Before he could leave, Kale called out, still entranced by the image. "What do you see when you look in it?"

The question was innocent, but it stopped Oryn in his tracks. A terrible memory resurfaced and he reburied it as swift as he could. Angry that the demon had stirred another painful memory, the knight stormed out with no intention of ever returning there again.

A few minutes after Oryn had gone in search for Kale, Adwen led Jack and Alexander after their trail. Many of the flowers were blooming in the halls to the north, making it difficult to track Oryn's and Kale's scents. Fortunately, she knew the lay of the palace from previous visits.

"I'm still surprised that you let him look for Kale alone."

"Jack, take it easy. I know what I'm doing."

Alexander gave a sidelong look. "Are you doing something?"

She rolled her eyes as they walked. "Did anyone notice Oryn volunteered to find him? If I thought for a second he would hurt Kale, I would have stopped him. Not long ago, you didn't trust Kale, but now you don't trust me and Oryn?"

The two exchanged looks.

"We trust you, but we know Cujo's habits."

"Which he can control. Believe me: I know what I'm doing."

Again, the friends glanced at each other in befuddlement.

Hearing footfalls prompted them to stop before Oryn rounded the corner from another corridor. His brisk march made him seem surly. This worried Jack and Alexander, but Adwen shook her head.

"You found him, I take it?"

Resisting the urge to snarl, the knight replied, "I did."

As Oryn continued to march past, Kale followed from around the same corner. His demeanor was serene, lost in thought with his hands in his pockets. Thinking of the mirror made him feel light-hearted. Now there was something good to remember. For that, he was very grateful.

Suddenly, an ice-cold chill ran up his back, replacing happiness with alarm. He froze in place and realized a second too late that he was under attack. The tiles underfoot and on the mosaic walls exploded. Plaster, dust and stone fragments flew in all directions. Kale roared in surprise as he was ensnared by thick, hard roots that pinned his arms to his sides and wrapped around his legs.

Jack and Alexander raced in to mount a rescue. Oryn summoned his sword an instant after the blast, while Adwen shouted in dismay. They ran after the others to help, then realized this was a familiar scene. One of the pillars consumed by vines stirred.

Close to where Kale was enveloped in a crushing ball of roots, the pillar uncoiled. Vines forming a façade of a column retracted, revealing the attacker; a blond male Elf emerged. The lacy plants formed a cape and mantle about his shoulders. A patch over his left eye bore a rare crimson flower with a cluster of moss. With a stern face, the powerful Elf reached out with one hand, directing the roots that ensnared Kale to constrict further.

"Toth, no!" Adwen shouted.

The Elf hesitated and looked at Adwen in surprise.

"Adwen? Oryn? How long have you been here?"

Jack kept slashing at the plants around Kale, but Alexander stopped cutting at the roots to stare. "Toth?"

Adwen remained urgent. "Let him go!"

An appalled look came over their friend. "This abomination is with you?"

"He's bound to me!"

This news left Toth speechless, and he stared.

"Please, let him go."

Such a request from anyone else would have gone ignored. Gazing at Adwen, he pondered. "This is against my better judgment, but I trust you."

With a wave of his hand, the mass of roots expelled the werewolf. Kale landed on his hands and knees, gasping for breath. The roots withdrew back into the ground. Bloody holes all over Kale closed. Clothing and flesh mended as if never harmed. Once healed, Kale scoffed to himself.

"That stung a bit."

Toth glared as the red-eyed stranger picked himself up and took notice of him at last.

The werewolf began to stare, amused. He chuckled, intrigued at meeting an Elf. "Hello."

Stepping between them, Adwen smiled. "This is Kale. Kale, this is my good friend, Toth."

Toth said nothing and never looked away from the werewolf.

Kale, however, wore a clever grin. "Toth, huh? Can I call you Toady?"

Beginning to scowl, he replied, "You most certainly may not. Call me Fedius. My friends call me Toth." Then he gave Adwen a welcoming glance.

Kale shrugged innocently. "Suit yourself."

"Where is everyone who came with you?"

"Hiding. I've been keeping them hidden."

"That's good to hear. Let's go somewhere safe so we can talk."

Toth paused to stare down the suspiciously amused were-wolf.

Her tone became one of annoyance: "Toth."

His eye returned to her glinting with disquiet. He did not like the idea of a demon visiting the sanctuary.

Adwen reassured their old friend: "Trust me."

Toth led them to a wall covered with intertwined plants, concealing two towering metal doors. Before going any farther, Toth glanced at Kale and warned, "The way is sealed with magic as well."

Before Adwen could say anything, Kale merrily replied, "Don't worry. I won't have any trouble following you lot past the barrier."

Alarmed, Toth threw the demon another deadly glare. The flower growing on his eyepatch blossomed, revealing poisonous barbs that could fly. They aimed directly at the Kale's face.

The threatening gesture filled Kale with apprehension, but the show of force impressed him. He could not help but gawk.

"Toth, calm down," Adwen said. "He's not a danger to us or the others. Let's focus on the tasks before us."

The Elf scowled at the demon. "I am focused, Adwen. I've grown much since we last met."

The poison dart blossom closed, and his attention returned to the wall. "We will speak more of this in the sanctuary. I warn you: I cannot vouch for his safety."

Toth raised a hand and commanded the plants to part.

As the sound of rustling plants and groaning door joints grew louder, Jack leaned close to Kale. "Hey, Big Guy?"

He wore a curious look. "Yeah?"

"You know, I was just thinking: Now is probably not a good time for you to talk ... at all."

It was difficult for Kale to resist laughing. "Are you, of all people, telling me to shut up?"

Agreeing that this was unprecedented, Jack nodded. "Yeah."

Kale laughed, shoulders shuddering as he shook his head.

Oryn gave them an irritated glance.

Once Toth had opened the doors, the group passed beyond the threshold into what was once the entrance to a Light Guardian's lair. Toth resealed the entrance, shutting out the brilliant daylight. The Elf waited a moment for many flowers on the walls to open. They emitted light like candle flames. The blue tint of their glow illuminated the way.

Much of the cave had collapsed over the past few years, filling much of the cavern gorge and creating a safer path. Flora adapted to darkness wove through crevices all around and overhead, supporting the cave walls and ceiling. This created a haven like an emerald chapel.

Adwen whispered, "Toth, this is beautiful."

"Thank you." Her compliment made him smile, but then he frowned.

Though she noticed his abrupt change in mood, it did not seem the time to ask why.

From around a bend, they saw stronger lights and heard voices. The scent of flowers dwindled, and the Holy Hounds could use their sense of smell again. Along with the scents of humans, there were sugary fruits and crisp greens.

A blond woman marched toward them carrying a sword. A few guards and mages followed her ready to fight. But the closer they came, the more the woman's aggressive gait turned to a swift and expectant walk. Seeing that it was Toth accompanied by familiar faces, she sheathed the blade.

"Adwen! Sir Oryn!"

"Eyrie!" The princess pounced upon Adwen and embraced her tightly.

"I knew you would find us." Releasing her hold, she stepped back to greet Toth. "I thought you said you sensed a demon was wandering in the palace?"

Jack and Alexander casually glanced at Kale, who deftly summoned a pair of sunglasses to conceal his eyes. In the gloom of the sanctuary, no human would notice him.

Toth was reassuring. "There was, but Adwen has made it clear there is no danger. It seems our refuge remains safe. We should take them elsewhere to talk."

"Of course. Please come this way, Adwen."

The princess's guards escorted the band through their mystical encampment. On closer inspection, the enchanting appeal of the cave was offset by dreary circumstances. Several men and women were gravely ill, some in agony. The rest looked malnourished but focused on helping the sick. Even the princess showed symptoms of hardship but refused to let it weaken her resolve. Her strides were confident as she led them to a private part of the sanctuary.

They arrived at a wall of dense vines and roots that blocked the way. At Princess Eyrie's command, the guards took their leave, just as Toth made the plants part like a living curtain. Inside, they saw even more floral lights and a collection of chairs taken from the abandoned palace. The plants closed the entry behind them, and everyone took a seat to begin the meeting.

The princess sat beside Toth in silence for a while, beaming at Adwen. When she spoke at last, she was almost breathless. "I cannot begin to describe how good it is to see you again."

"I feel the same."

For a moment there was a flicker of apprehension in her stare. It was quickly masked by stalwart determination. "There are many things to discuss. Please tell us what has become of Dargadia."

For the sake of the princess, Adwen shut away all emotion before speaking. Her tone and manner were cool and controlled.

"A small territory of the coast is preserved, but the rest of the kingdom is enveloped in black mist. Along with it, the sky is cursed; it is always night except for a moment at dawn and sunset when the sun is almost visible on the horizon."

Princess Eyrie blanched, while Toth clenched his teeth in disgust. Seeing the princess's reaction led Adwen to refrain from providing too many details. The woman's hope dangled by a thread.

There was silence until the princess found the will to speak again. "I see." Then her gaze wandered across the faces of her companions. "I had thought Tamis might be among you. Where is he?" She dreaded the answer and waited in suspense.

"He is alive. I've sent him to lead the last of the new Order to Jenkirk."

"A new Order?"

"The people who chose to stay in Dargadia to resist the demons; they are the last of the mages, knights and gargoyles who escaped the fortress and other parts of the kingdom. They are the Order of the Gargoyle."

"There were those who chose to stay?" A faint smile appeared.

Toth gave the princess a searching glance during the silence that followed. She struggled to speak. Struggling to ask the next question, the princess could not move her tongue.

Adwen and the others watched in surprise as Toth's hand touched the arm of the princess's chair. Princess Eyrie grasped his hand and clung to his warm fingers as she fought overwhelming feelings that held her mute.

Finally, she spoke again: "Tell me, what has become of the king?"

Unable to say it aloud, Adwen frowned and shook her head. Tears turned the girl's bright eyes glassy. She had sensed the loss all along. Grasping Toth's hand helped. Now was not the time for mourning. Bottling up the immense emotions, the princess turned firm.

"Who is responsible for this? Melanin is destroyed. If not him, then who is to blame?"

"A reliable source has revealed to me that Melanin was originally one of seven," Adwen said.

Princess Eyrie looked as if she had been slapped, as did Toth.

"To conquer Dargadia, these demons placed a series of black monoliths throughout the kingdom. As far as we know, these pillars curse the sky into perpetual night. We think they tap into the magic deep within the earth to do so. Three have been destroyed, and four remain."

At the last statement, Toth and the princess were visibly relieved.

"What will you do now?"

Adwen could not hide the uncertainty. "We need to find a new way to defeat the demons and break the black structures. The enemy expects us now. Assaulting them outright is too risky. After we finish here, our next destination is the desert. I anticipate learning how to defeat the demons once we finish helping the survivors of the Kingdoms of Day."

"Something has happened in the desert as well?"

She frowned. "I suspect the worst."

Princess Eyrie nodded grimly. "Indeed." Since the start of their meeting, she had hardly noticed the stranger in red sitting between Jack and Alexander. With hands in his pockets and dark lenses over his eyes, he seemed different from Adwen's warriors. Clearly this was a new ally.

"And who is your new companion? I've never seen him before."

Toth grimaced in silence.

"Princess Eyrie, I would like to introduce Kale. Kale, Princess Eyrie."

He bowed his head to the curious young woman.

Smiling kindly, she was intrigued. "May I see your face more clearly?"

Kale made a discreet glance to Adwen, who gave a nod.

The princess found it odd he would look to Adwen for approval. Her gaze turned back to Kale, who raised a hand toward the sunglasses. Just as the princess realized his fingers had long claws, the dark lenses vanished in a flourish of black mist at his touch. Then his cherry-red eyes locked with hers, and she felt a chill. Becoming rigid, Princess Eyrie's breath caught in her chest as she felt it tighten.

Kale studied her. Even now, he could see she was brave and determined. He waited to see what she would do after seeing a demon in a werewolf body sitting before her.

This was the last thing Princess Eyrie expected. First, fear struck her, then fear paired with confusion. Was this a demon? It clearly was. But unlike any demon she has ever seen, a subtle sadness lingered in the depths of his crimson eyes. No demon could comprehend such an emotion. And he was a member of Adwen's company.

Battling reproach, she mustered the will to speak to him. Fear made her voice fragile. "Tell me, what kind of demon must you be to fight against your own kind?"

His raspy voice remained low and soft: "It's complicated."

"I cannot begin to imagine."

Doubtful of the demon, Toth spoke in cold tones, "Might I ask, what is it that you have done to help fight the darkness?"

A faint smile came over Kale, and he was casual. "Ah, a bit of this and that."

Jack puffed while Alexander shook his head smiling. Oryn seemed indifferent, so Adwen explained, "Kale has destroyed two of the three monoliths we've assaulted."

The princess and Toth did double takes at the friendly demon.

"It wouldn't have been possible without him," Adwen said. "In fact, we would be dead."

The other three Holy Hounds nodded to the princess. Toth saw that they spoke the truth, as Princess Eyrie continued to gaze at Kale. From what she could determine, this entity had cunning because it was not easy for most demons to hide their nature from her skilled sight.

The princess could not help but ask another question: "Why do you fight the darkness?"

The words she chose were deep. Kale could tell she meant more than just the armies from the Void. Taking a little liberty in tapping into her mind, he was frugal in his search – out of respect. Once he uncovered the meaning behind her question, he sat forward in his chair, admiring this remarkable woman. Keeping his voice low, he replied, "For the same reasons you do, Your Highness."

Hearing truth in those words made her gasp. Tears threatened to rise in her eyes.

Giving Princess Eyrie a searching glance, not even Toth knew her personal reasons for fighting the darkness. There was never reason to ask until now, if only to know the demon's motives. Perhaps the monster was trying to undermine them. Toth looked to Adwen, who would never allow such foul deceit. Immediately, his suspicion of Kale dissipated.

The princess took a breath to regain her composure. Important matters still needed attention.

"What shall you and your companions do here, Tame One?"

"We will help with what we can. I noticed your people are struggling."

"We are. We have just enough food to prevent starvation, but not enough to thrive. Foraging the jungle has been disastrous; there are so many poisonous things. Some have died, while other lives hang by a thread. Even hunting is a deadly endeavor."

Adwen and Oryn exchanged glances. "We can help with the sick or afflicted. Jack and Alexander can help as well."

The gesture comforted the princess, but she remained despondent. "I am grateful. Any assistance is priceless at this point, but we need more than what you can provide. You cannot stay here long."

It was true, and Adwen frowned.

"We need to unite with the last of the Eskrani people."

Adwen was taken aback, as were the others. "There are survivors?"

"They've been seen riding griffons deep in the jungle. We doubt they've seen us. If they have, they avoid contact, perhaps fearing we are demons in disguise. If we unite with them and gain their knowledge of the land, there is no doubt that we will be able to carry on."

Toth added, "There are obstacles to an alliance. We do not believe any of the survivors speak our tongue, so even if we find them, there are no means to negotiate. Tracking them will be impossible, as they do not leave a trail."

Perplexed, Kale asked Toth, "What are you on about? You of all people should be able to find them easily."

The Elf's one eye darted to the demon and glared.

Princess Eyrie was confused. "What do you mean? He has no better means to find them than anyone else."

Kale took a deep sniff. "Your scent – you don't smell like an ordinary Elf."

Sneering and wishing Kale would remain silent, Oryn said, "Toth is half Elf."

The werewolf corrected, "He's royal,"

At this, Princess Eyrie gasped.

"His soul is that of an immortal Elf of royal blood. That bloodline doesn't dissipate."

Toth clenched his jaw in fury at the announcement of his secret.

Kale understood why Toth was angry, but finding the survivors of this land was more important. "Does the jungle even recognize your authority?"

A tense silence followed as Toth glared. Then bitterly he answered, "It acknowledges me but will not bow to me. My authority is only in Dargadia and the lands surrounding it."

"Why did you not tell me this?" Princess Eyrie asked, in awe as well as wounded that he would keep such a secret.

Toth's gaze left the befuddled demon and found that neither Adwen nor the others appeared to be surprised. Staring at the heir of Darien, he was unsure how to feel. How long had she known and kept it from him?

Adwen returned focus to the meeting: "How close to the city were these sightings of the griffon riders?"

Toth could not return the princess's intensely somber gaze. His tone turned melancholy. "A couple of leagues east. There was nothing more than glimpses."

The princess's heart ached, and she let go of Toth's hand to clasp her own on her lap. A long silence fell on their meeting. Adwen and her warriors waited to see if either of their friends and allies would speak again. Both appeared lost in thought.

Then Adwen smiled. "I have an idea."

Hope sparked to life in the faces of the princess and the Elf prince.

Toth was the more eager between them. "You do?"

Shaking her head, she admitted, "You won't like it, but it will work."

He was ready to try anything. "How I like it or not makes little difference. Say it, and it shall be done."

Adwen turned to her company. "Kale?"

"Yeah?"

"Would you be able to track a griffon's trail?"

Toth understood what she intended, and a bitter taste flooded his mouth.

The werewolf thought it over, then nodded. "Sure. Not going to be as easy as tracking this lot, but it can be done."

"Perfect." Turning her attention back to Toth, she pretended not to notice his scowl. "When can you set out?"

His one eye remained fixed on the grinning beast. Nauseated at the thought of relying on a fiend, Toth began to stare down Adwen instead. "If this demon can find the last of the Eskrani, what is your solution for communicating with them?"

Kale spoke up, still smiling: "As you put it, I'm a demon. I can speak to them."

While her frustrated friend glared daringly at the powerful werewolf, Adwen elaborated: "Demons can speak any language of the living. He can translate as needed. Kale is the perfect solution to this task of finding and contacting the Eskrani."

Before Toth could reply, Princess Eyrie swiftly answered, "Agreed."

Everyone stared at her, but none as Toth did. Her eagerness to utilize the demon was unsettling.

"I trust your word, Lady Adwen. I also have faith in this strange new friend."

The sincerity touched Kale. It was no wonder Toth was in love with this mortal woman.

Pleased that her plan had been accepted, Adwen nodded. "It's settled. While Kale leads Toth and any guards he needs to find the griffon riders, the rest of us will help with anything else we can. How soon can you set out?"

Seeing no alternative, Toth threw Kale a far deadlier look. "Within the hour. We'll not need guards."

At this, Kale scoffed to himself. Toth's glare intensified, and the poison dart flower on his eyepatch reopened. The princess touched his arm. Making the lethal flower close before looking her way, he almost forgot the demon when he saw her expression. Though trying to appear strong, Princess Eyrie felt feeble. "Be quick in finding them. Then return to me with haste."

A twinge struck his heart. Seldom did she ever say simple things. The pained look in her stare tore his insides to pieces.

With a sad smile, he replied, "As you wish, Your Highness."

Sensing that she had not lost his affection was more comforting to her than anything else in the world.

Princess Eyrie and Adwen stood, and the others followed their lead. The wall of vines parted, allowing them to leave the private chamber amid the sound of rustling leaves. Approaching the encampment, several knights, guards and mages waited for word from their meeting.

Adwen stopped to convene with the others. "Oryn, I need you to be ready to tend to the wounded. Spend your strength wisely."

He nodded firmly. "As you command."

"Jack, Alex? You two need to go hunting."

They exchanged hesitant looks before Jack raised an eyebrow. "Come again?"

"The poisons in the jungle can't hurt us. Try to bring back as much game as you can carry. These people are starving."

"Sure thing." At that moment, Jack caught a glimpse of Adwen's thoughts. "Uh ... is there something else in the jungle besides poisonous plants and creepy crawlies? Something big?"

She was in no mood to debate and growled. Her blue eyes shone brightly in the gloom.

Jack gave in. "Okay, let's go hunting, Jarhead." They set out immediately.

Finally, Adwen addressed the rogue. "Kale?"

He had been lost in thought and was caught off guard. "Yeah?"

Glancing at Toth a moment, she crossed her arms and gave a questioning look. "This is very important. Keep focused at least until you make it back. Now is not the time to get distracted – by anything."

Understanding that she knew what was on his mind, he felt caught. Sighing ruefully, the werewolf shook his head. "You've got it. We'll come back soon. Are you ready to go, Your Highness?"

Toth detested that the demon had exposed his secret to Princess Eyrie. "I am prepared to get this over with quickly. Lead the way, if you please."

Kale could not help but smile. "Suit yourself."

Toth decided he would never turn his back on Kale. As they too headed for the cave entrance, the princess stood by Adwen and felt more hopeful.

"Please tell me, where did you find this one, Lady Adwen?"

She considered her answer. "I found him lost and alone."

Both Princess Eyrie and Oryn turned to stare.

"Despite that, he was slaying demons to protect humans." Adwen smiled at the princess's stunned reaction. "That was before I took his hunger away."

Finding herself gazing after the red jacket dwindling in the dark, she remarked, "What a will he must possess."

Adwen smiled. "And more." Facing Oryn, who seemed to be struggling to decipher what was said, she asked, "Are you ready?"

It seemed the riddle of the rogue demon was doomed to be unsolved. "I am."

"Then let's get to work."

Chapter 15
QUALITY OF MERCY

The interior of Toth's emerald subterranean sanctuary was peaceful. The brightest of the glowing plants grew among the sick beds. Poisons were the main source of misery. Some struck at the ability to breathe, and others produced symptoms as serious yet far fouler.

Sweet smelling plants filtered the air around the bed of a man who was afflicted by snake venom that decayed the flesh. Medicines for pain no long had any effect. Immobile, the guardsman waited to die. Too sick to move and in too much pain for sleep, a fever plagued him. Cold chills swept across his body, making him tremble and sweat.

Nearby, another injured refugee uttered, "It's you."

"Lie still."

Hearing the woman on the next bed speak lifted him a bit from his delirium. She had been unconscious for days after being struck by a strange creature. With foggy vision, he watched a dark-clad figure kneel beside his neighbor. Green light radiated from a hand that reached toward the site of her injury. Bright threads like tiny lightning bolts lit the cavern.

The man in elaborate plated armor spoke again as he ceased his work. "You now have enough strength to recover on your own."

"Bless you," she whispered, exhausted by days of fighting poison and blood loss.

The figure in black stood and started toward the guardsman. Once the warrior knelt beside his bed, he recognized the visitor.

Astounded, he weakly exclaimed, "Sir Oryn?"

If the knight were affected by the pungent odor of rotting

flesh, he did not show it. "I remember your face," Oryn frowned. "You were among the king's guardsmen."

While Oryn inspected the necrotic infection, the man smiled. It had spread far after reaching his veins. Even now, he could feel tissues inside dying. Patches of dead skin were visible over his entire body.

"Is the Tame One with you, sir?"

Frowning at the severity of the man's condition, he shushed. "Save your strength. She is here. Be silent."

Oryn held armored hands over the man, and the same pale green light appeared. Warm arcs of magic in the form of lightning coursed into flesh and bone. He had never known the general was capable of using magic. The guardsman feebly remarked on the phenomenon: "You are a mage? Of all the things about you, this is most surprising."

This healing took all Oryn's concentration, and he became irritated. "I warned you to be silent. Let me work."

But he smiled. "I am dying, sir."

Oryn glanced at the serene look in the guardsman's eyes. Clearly, he was accepting death. Nevertheless, Oryn resumed pouring magic into this plagued body.

"The Tame One needs you at your best," he told Oryn. "I suggest you not waste your power."

As the man admired the general, warmth from the green lightning breathed feeling into tissues long dead. He noticed that Oryn was growing tired. Waiting patiently, the man remained in awe of the return of feeling to his flesh. Parts of him began to awake from decay. Blood flowed into reopening veins. Strength filled his once weak heart.

Oryn was nearly faint. After expending all the energy he dared, he considered the amazed guardsman's eyes. "I've done all I can. There will be extensive scarring. Keep the sores clean, and the infection will not return."

"Why do this? I am a soldier, sir. Why expend your strength on me when more important matters call on you? What of the other wounded?"

Oryn wore a stony look to mask physical weakness. "They are tended to. My magic was not spent thoughtlessly."

Unable to think of more to say, the only words that came

were simple: "Th-thank you, sir."

"We are all valuable. Even a soldier's life is greater than any sum of gold. Do not waste what has been given."

"Never, sir. I would shame myself."

Without another word Oryn turned to go.

At a distance, Adwen and Princess Eyrie saw him choosing a place to rest and recover. While he had tended to the wounded and as he settled down, the two collected rations. Among the plants gifted to Toth by the jungle were prickly fruits and meaty melons. With even more of Adwen's power restored since the fall of the third pillar, she used her strength to help the refugees. The basket that the princess carried began to fill, and Adwen's basket strained to contain the amount she could carry.

For a time, they hardly spoke. Conversation consisted of which pieces to pick and which had yet to ripen. But as they noticed Oryn leaving the infirmary, the princess felt a weight lift from her shoulders.

"He healed them? All of them?"

"Yes."

Then a twinge of regret struck her heart. "If only the others had been able to hold on a little longer."

"It's probably not a comfort, but if there had been any more, Oryn would not have had enough strength," Adwen said.

The princess was shocked. "Wasn't he stronger the last you were in this world?"

Adwen grew sullen and withdrew, returning to picking melons. It was almost time to unload the basket before it could give out.

The princess mused then frowned. "You've been weakened."

The basket's groaning alerted Adwen that it could not hold more. She could relate to the strain and pressure it held. "I've been linked to the fate of the magic in this world. Breaking the pillars has restored some of my power, but not enough. If we were to attack another pillar, there is no chance of succeeding. The demons would cut us down; even Kale wouldn't survive."

A firm expression came over Princess Eyrie. "It was Impurus, wasn't it?"

Adwen stared. "You've met him?" She was surprised that Impurus had allowed Princess Eyrie to escape.

The princess shook her head. "I only know of him from the few who escaped the fall of the fortress and Plexus. For something like this to happen to you, I could think of no other cause."

"He's not a true demon, Princess."

"What do you mean?"

"He's an abomination; a melding of darkness from the Void and a human being. What's more, I know who he used to be: It's Jacques."

The young woman almost dropped her bundle of produce. "A former knight." Then she was thoughtful and wore a grim look. "Father and I never liked that man. We were relieved when you banished him."

"I regret letting him live. Then again, there was no way to know what he would become."

"Indeed, you could not have known. Come. This is the way to the food store."

They said no more as they left the jungle garden. They shared some of what they gathered with people they passed and took what remained in the alcove used for storage. Several women in the alcove sorted out what was overripe or rotten. Shelves salvaged from the palace stood in aisles and against stone walls, supported by roots. Two helped Adwen unload her basket and sort the contents.

"Thank you," Adwen told the sorters. "The Eskrani sure make strong baskets."

While the princess handed her basket to a worker, she called out beyond the shelves. "Moira, how are losses today?"

A young woman's face popped up beyond a shelf beside them. "I'm here, Your Highness!"

Princess Eyrie gave a small start then chortled. "You frightened me."

"Apologies, my lady. Lady Adwen? It is good to see you!"

Seeing the tired face of Moira reminded Adwen of the encounter with Balefire at the beach. "It's good to see you, too! You look like you're doing well."

"The princess has recently given me the responsibility of keeping this store. I would much rather be sorting, but she insists."

Moira came around the shelves carrying a quill and parchment. As she reported on the state of the rations, Adwen restrained a gasp. A bulge shaped like the melons pressed against the waistline of the mage's dress.

"There are forty-three red melons; seven of those are starting to bruise. We've learned to keep the green and yellow fruits separate. They rot one another. Losses have been offset greatly; only four had to be discarded since yesterday, Your Highness."

"Very good news, Moira. I knew you were perfect for this. Be sure to find the most suitable place to store meats. Sir Jack and Sir Alexander will return soon, and I have no doubt they will succeed in their hunt."

"It is already done, my lady. Men are hanging cords in the cool, dry part of the store."

The princess shook her head. "Again, you amaze. Carry on, Moira."

She dipped her head. "Your Highness."

Leaving the food storage with Princess Eyrie, Adwen listened as she spoke.

"It was not easy to convince her to take on less straining duties," the princess informed. "That woman is more tenacious than any beast of burden. We mustn't allow her to push herself too hard for the child's sake."

Adwen failed to hide a twinge of uncertainty. "Yes, Princess. Take good care of them both."

Eyrie heard the apprehension in Adwen's voice and stopped where no one could overhear. "What is it, Adwen?"

Glancing back to where Moira tended to the supplies, it seemed appropriate to confide in the princess. "That is Balefire's child."

Princess Eyrie frowned bitterly. "I'm sure you've seen that he is not here among us any longer."

Gazing long at the princess, she replied, "I've seen him."

She was instantly aghast. "His spirit lingers! The poor soul."

"He's not dead; he has become a Guardian."

This news stunned Princess Eyrie into silent awe.

"He asked that I tell Moira he's sorry. You can understand the implications."

"That would not be a good message to give. I suspect that the work I've provided is what keeps her in such good spirits. I've also held her many nights when she wakes in tears. Please do not deliver Balefire's message."

"I won't. As soon as I saw her, I knew this needed to be handled differently. I have promised Balefire that I would speak with her."

"And what will you say?"

"Don't worry. I'll be tactful."

A guard shouted from the entrance, alerting others in the sanctuary. "Tame One! Princess Eyrie! Fedius Toth has returned!"

They exchanged startled looks and dashed toward the entrance. A small crowd gathered but parted when a man shouted to make way. On the other side of the barricade of clamoring mages, knights and guards, Toth faced them all. Kale stood just behind wearing sunglasses and with his claws hidden in his pockets. He went almost completely overlooked by the unwitting humans.

Princess Eyrie raised her voice, waving a hand. "Quiet! Hush, everyone!" When they fell silent, she continued: "I share your need to hear news of the search for assistance. Please, be calm. It is difficult for me to ask, but please return to your tasks. Do not forget that we rely on one another to survive. News will be given at dusk, as normal. I will personally share the news. Now please return to your charges, everyone."

Hesitantly and sheepishly, the desperate men and women heeded her command. As they dispersed, there was a tense air about the emerald sanctuary. Once the people had stepped out of earshot, the princess chose to hold a meeting at the doors.

"We'll keep this brief so as not to aggravate them further," Princess Eyrie said, looking to Toth and Kale. "How fared your quest?"

The Elf prince and the werewolf exchanged grim glances.

"Did you not find them?"

Kale chuckled. "Oh, we found them quick enough. They're alive and well living in the jungle canopy a few miles north."

Smelling griffon dander on Kale was reassuring for Adwen, but the griffon's absence was confusing. "So where are they now?"

Toth sighed, shaking his head. "One afforded a return flight to the palace. The winged beast brought us back in gratitude for going to the trouble of finding them. However, they made it clear they cannot help us. No matter how we pressed for answers, they would not say why. My guess is that they are struggling, and fear charity would be too taxing. But Kale suspects otherwise." To the werewolf, he nodded, "Tell them what you told me."

"They were very tight-lipped, those survivors," Kale began thoughtfully. "It had little to do with me. I would have noticed if I had been what put them off. I did notice an unusual odor. It was a bird's scent, but not a normal one. It wasn't griffon either. The only reason they gave was that their people are forbidden to leave the jungle. If they do, their protection will be forfeit."

Adwen was bemused. "Interesting."

"I agree. From what I could pluck from their thoughts, their protection came at a price. Got a glimpse of a memory from the slaughter of their people – it's a nasty picture, I'll be the first to tell yah."

"What can you tell?"

"Something infected the biggest of the griffon breeds. It spread quickly, and they went mad. It looked like a curse created in the Void. The infection was a lot like the one used on the gargoyles in Mortigad, making them like demons. Unlike that place, the sun still shines here. Before the sunlight could destroy the corrupted things, they decimated the kingdom."

"Do you think the curse might be still around?"

He shook his head. "Once the things die, it disappears. The infected turn into meat pudding like regular demons do. Nothing is left after a few hours. Any thoughts, Adwen?"

"I have one," She responded, frowning. "But it doesn't make any sense."

They all looked to her as Kale shrugged. "Well, let's have it then."

She was about to explain but smelled Jack and Alexander. The huge doors steadily opened to let them in. Afternoon light shone from the palace corridor.

"You're back!" Adwen was relieved. "You need to hear this."

The two friends stood at the open doors wearing confounded expressions. Then Alexander elbowed Jack's arm, prodding him to speak. Even more at a loss for words, the warrior eventually found his tongue again. "Uh, Adwen? Everyone? We have visitors."

The company shared a moment of pleasant surprise.

"Well?" Adwen replied. "If they're here to help, introduce us."

Slowly turning to the opening, Jack called to someone. "Did

you hear that? You can come in now."

Expecting Eskrani warriors, they were terrified by the sight of black and brown feathers, red-orange eyes and razor-sharp beaks. Hands with yellow talons held bone spears. Beautiful armor carved from rare wood as hard as steel adorned their human torsos. Heavily beaded jewelry hung from their arms, legs and shoulders, marking the high ranks of the three harpies that entered the sanctuary. The tallest stood six feet high. His harsh eyes surveyed their faces carefully. Once he saw Adwen he furled his wings, trilling. Pointing his long spear carved from a giant bone, he shouted, "Have you been cleansed?"

Everyone tensed, and Toth's dart flower bloomed, preparing for an attack.

The question took Adwen by surprise. "What?"

Fanning broad wings, the harpy male's angry voice called again: "The darkness that was in you! Has it been cleansed?"

The last time she had seen harpies, she was infected by a demon sliver. It had caused her to slaughter one of their kind needlessly.

She nodded hurriedly. "Yes, I've been cleansed. I am myself now."

Calming down, the harpy folded his wings and planted the butt of his spear to the floor. The clack of bone on stone expressed finality on the matter.

"Very well." He looked to all their faces once more, appraising the gathering. "I have words for the leaders in this place." Then his piercing stare fell on Adwen. "I have also been given words for you."

The shock of speaking with harpies subsided. Adwen, Toth and Princess Eyrie exchanged looks, wondering what the others thought.

Taking a brave step forward, the princess addressed the visitors: "All of the leaders are present. This is Fedius Toth, and I am Princess Eyrie, daughter of King Lorvan. If you are here to help in any way, you are welcome. Might we have your name?"

An awkward silence followed, as the harpies stood still and said nothing.

"Have we unknowingly offended you?"

Finally, the lead harpy spoke. "My name is beyond your

tongues to speak, and it will not be shared. The names of a messengers are meaningless, as they are but vessels for breath. I will only say what is permitted and necessary, nothing more or less."

They were taken aback yet again.

Then the harpy inclined his head proudly. "Yet your greeting is well received. It rang with the sound of sincerity. That shall be reported when I return."

Relief filled the tired woman. "Please, share your message."

Satisfied, the harpy clicked his beak and began: "Greetings and welcome to the land of the jungle and the clouds of stone."

No one ceased to be surprised and they continued to listen, enraptured.

"Stay in the palace atop the cloud of stone and earth. No humans from afar are permitted entry into the jungle. If this rule is accepted and obeyed, all visitors in this place will be given fresh prey daily. It will be gifted only as it is caught. No request for more than their share will be heeded. Should the one rule be broken, protection will be provided still, yet no prey will be gifted. Until the day we are fed upon by shadow or you return to the green lands, this treaty shall stand by the might of the harpy."

He briskly tapped the butt of the spear once more, signaling the end of the message. The small gathering exchanged glances and pondered.

Adwen carefully asked, "May we ask questions for further clarity?"

The harpy's reply was flat, as he was not surprised. "I have been permitted the answering of many questions."

"Why are we banned from the jungle, while the griffon riders may live there?"

"They are of this land, and it knows them as they know it."

She stared, confused.

An expression came over the harpy at her silence that could have been either irritation or amusement. "The jungle is not open to you and your other humans. Have you seen how it rejects you and your people?"

A chill swept over her.

"Naïve humans wandering the hungry jungle do not see where the venom, claw or fang flies. If your people think they can brave the jungle, then we will not stop you or help you in surviving its bite. Admit that it is not your place, and we will agree and hunt in its branches and boughs on your behalf. We cannot waste precious daylight hunting in search of medicine for every poison your flightless kind happen to find."

The princess stared, astounded that this was being offered.

"Do you admit that the jungle is no place for you or your human visitors?" the harpy pressed.

"Yes, we will not go into the jungle anymore."

Toth spoke at last: "What of me? I am not human, and neither are some of my friends. What of us and this treaty?"

The question pleased the harpy. "You are good at sight of mind. While humans are not permitted in the jungle, this does not concern you or these friends." His piercing eagle eyes fell on Kale for a few seconds before going back to Toth. "The jungle knows you. While it does not obey you, it welcomes you. Only the humans here are bound by this rule. Go wherever you please, child of the trees."

Toth nodded in thanks to the messenger.

Still stunned by this treaty from the harpies, Adwen was suspicious. "I am curious: Why are you helping humans? You are protecting the Eskrani, and now you're offering protection here, too? What's your purpose?"

The leader's gaze drilled into Adwen, while the two harpies behind him shuffled nervously. The big harpy began to trumpet, wings flicking and shuffling. The raptor's laughter calmed his comrades.

"You think us human? The harpy are too strong and proud for deception. What we want we take. What is not ours to take, we leave to its own."

"But why are you helping the Eskrani people and the griffons? Your kind has always attacked them."

This changed the air about them in an instant. The three harpies turned cold as stone. Glaring long and hard at Adwen, the proud creature sounded as confused as angry. "This cannot be true, and yet I see and hear no lies. What are these attacks you speak of? Tell us in detail."

"What sort of details?"

All three of the bird men stared raptly. "Those who attacked – their height, armor and weapons. Describe all you can recall."

Joining Adwen, Oryn locked eyes with the lead harpy with

equal intensity.

"They were the height of the average human. They had no armor, only loin cloths. The weapons they used were spears or bone daggers."

A lasting silence came as the harpy weighed Oryn's report. Both escorting harpies became uncertain and waited for their leader's response. This information clearly troubled him.

When the harpy spoke again, his tone turned from proud to sober. "This will be made known and the details shared upon my return to the flock. Thereafter another message will be delivered; I anticipate it shall be a message of regret. Our young have broken the rules."

Jack raised one eyebrow out of suspicion. "How about you tell us what rules they broke?"

"Those who you describe are fledglings, and those who have passed the first test. Humans would call it a coming-of-age trial. They are tested for the honor of becoming true harpy. If they pass and survive, they have the right to undergo the trial of the Harpy Guard."

"And you would be one of these Harpy Guards?"

Giving Jack a scrutinizing look, he replied, "We are among the Harpy Guard. We are among the truly loyal, the most cunning, the strongest and the fleet." To Adwen, he finally showed a glimmer of hesitation in his burning avian stare. "The fledglings you described have broken the rules. All who break the rules can never be Harpy Guard. More grave is that they have broken the promise; harpies are not to hunt humans for any purpose other than survival. This trial has rules: With a bone dagger of their own making, and a feather from their chest tied to the hilt, they are commanded to go out and return with blood staining the tip of the dagger."

Jack shrugged. "That's all?"

The harpy grew angry again at the thought of a breach of obedience and trust. "Those who return with more or less have failed. If the feather on the dagger is stained, so is their honor for they have taken more than what is their own. Another mark of a true harpy is courage and restraint – discipline. Obedience to the flock is placed above all else. These young are commanded to bring blood but never permitted to take life."

Oryn took in the winged warrior's words and could hear an apology by the manner he spoke. The knight asked, "What will be done with the offenders? Will there be justice for their crimes?"

The harpy was silent for a moment, contemplating his words. "I am not permitted to make promises. I may only deliver messages given or inform on what is known. I am a messenger; I am but breath."

"What is likely to be done with the ones responsible?"

The three harpies stood like stone for a time. When the lead harpy answered, Jack listened carefully.

"Nothing."

The answer shocked Jack, so the cop continued to be suspicious. "Nothing? If obedience is most important to your kind, then they've committed a capital crime."

This made the harpies uncomfortable, and their feathers fluffed and flattened unevenly. "Any who break this series of rules face public plucking, breaking or death by the jungle's vengeance."

"Plucking?"

"We, the Harpy Guard, rip the feathers from their wings. If commanded, we then break their bloody wings. Should they be allowed to live, they would be unable to fly and would be bound to servitude to the whole flock. For young to come to the cloud of stone for blood means they thought humans easier prey than the creatures of the jungle. Not only were they disobedient, they were foolish and lazy. Any of these you killed are considered punished."

Jack studied the harpy, listening to his voice and mind. Suddenly he found the truth. "They're all dead!"

In shock and outrage, the harpies flapped wings and trilled.

"I knew your sight and hearing were keen, but now we see your sight of mind is keener!" The lead harpy shouted. "Such deceit!"

"What happened to those harpies?" Jack pressed.

Adwen snapped, "Jack! That's enough."

He recoiled.

The wings of the raptor men folded, although the shock of Jack rooting out information without permission had agitated them. Their leader pointed the elegant spear at him and grilled her. "Has he stolen our thoughts on your command, or has this one been disobedient? What is this treachery?"

"Jack has a bad habit of doing things without asking."

Her short companion growled under his breath, "Thanks for

throwing me under the bus."

Shrieking and slamming the butt of the spear down, the harpy demanded, "Shall his disobedience be punished?"

"Absolutely. You have my word."

Jack was aghast. "Hey!"

At this outburst, Alexander elbowed his friend's ribs, while Kale shook his head, chuckling.

"Keep this Jack under control," the harpy said. "His offense shall go overlooked, as you have promised to make him pay. All that has been exchanged here will be reported upon our return."

"Thank you." Adwen was relieved, but what Jack had uncovered troubled her. "I don't mean to offend you, but what happened to those harpies? Has something happened to your flock?"

Tense quiet filled the air, while the three gazed back with unreadable expressions. When Adwen sensed that they would not answer, she asked another question: "You mentioned a promise; one that those fledglings broke. Was it to the Eskrani people?"

They held their stony silence.

"Why are your kind helping humans?" She grew more curious. "Why won't you answer?"

The harpy addressed only her last question: "I am but breath, sent to deliver a message and say only what is necessary. Anything more said or done is treachery to the flock."

This perplexed Adwen greatly. "How are we supposed to be allies if we cannot help you?"

The two harpy escorts began to chortle softly between each other and blink curiously. Their leader held his ambiguous posture.

"Isn't that why you were sent here? To be our allies?"

As the two harpies started to babble louder, the leader slammed his spear down for quiet. The bird men stood at attention. Everyone observed the stalwart harpy as he contemplated.

Jack kept to himself what was running through the bird man's thoughts. It was fascinating, and Adwen's words were getting through.

Softening a little, the harpy spoke again. This time he all but cooed. "It has been too long for my kind. The humans of this land were once our allies. Their memory proved too short, and they broke all promises. A day came when they saw us as no different from the prey or predators of the jungle. We left them to their own, and they left the trees for the clouds of stone. Our promises lay broken like the nest they built.

"One other made a promise to the harpy. That promise is whole and stands like the Harpy Guard, strong and true. Darien and the Light who sent him keep their promises."

"Your kind has an alliance with Darien?"

Admiring her glowing blue eyes, the harpy grew softer still. The prideful posture dissipated as he spoke. "He came at a time when our kind faced extinction. Long ago, a sickness of shadow took almost all our mothers. They were few and became fewer. Harpy fought against their own kind, driven into madness by darkness. Darien ended the sickness. In return, the Harpy pledged loyalty. Darien asked the flock to never hunt humans and to keep them from extinction should they ever be in need. We harpy gladly and proudly keep his promise."

Princess Eyrie mused aloud, "You say that like you were there."

Those fiery eyes and their warm admiration turned to the princess. They were tired.

"You were there, weren't you?"

Adwen and the others were baffled. "How long do your kind live?"

As it was not necessary to share this information, the harpy hesitated, but chose to tell: "I have lived to see the birth and death of many a human king and the sprouting and growth of many a tree. Like the jungle, our kind are strong and slow to grow, but last far longer than most."

She pitied the humbled being, as he clearly felt somber for some unknown reason. "When you leave to go back to your flock, tell them I promise to help any way that I can."

All three harpies' eyes widened in hopeful surprise. "When we return to the flock, your message of promise will be shared. Before we take flight, we must give our message meant for you, Adwen Andredan: Should you need us for any reason, call. We will answer."

She beamed. "It's good to be allies with you."

The bird being appeared to smile by the way his eyes glinted. Pleased, the proud creature shuffled his wings. "We must go. There is a hunt calling in the wind."

"We'll see you again soon, I hope."

Even the escorts seemed to beam. "If the jungle permits it,

you shall," the lead harpy said. "May the wind be fair in your flight, Warrior of Light."

The raptor men briefly bowed then sprang out the gap between the sanctuary doors. Bright sunlight masked their departure amid wing beats that sent gusts rustling their robes and hair.

Whispers filled the air. Several Dargadian refugees gathered at a distance during the strange meeting. Everyone stood in a dumbfounded stillness. That stillness broke at the sound of Jack clearing his throat.

"Uh, I have a question."

Adwen and Alexander gave him hesitant looks.

"Did anyone else know they could talk?"

The two exchanged glances before gazing out the opening again.

Having gotten his answer, he muttered, "Someone needs to write that down."

Some of his friends nodded in agreement.

Shortly after the harpies' departure, Oryn resumed his rest. Sleep was vital because they needed to leave in the morning. All the meat Jack and Alexander had gathered went to the hungry survivors.

Princess Eyrie pleaded with Jack, while Adwen listened with arms folded.

She urged them, "You must go and find Sir Oryn something of sustenance. What of your journey to the east? Surely, he will need his strength if there is great danger there."

Jack shook his head. "The animals here are hard to find and catch. Check this out." He rolled back a sleeve, revealing puncture wounds. The wound oozed, and the surrounding flesh had turned purple.

She gasped. "I thought you were immune to poisons!"

Jack straightened his sleeve, rolling his eyes. "Adwen is completely immune, but the rest of us must fight it off. In a few hours, this will be gone; you should have seen it a while ago. Alex has three bites."

To be reassuring, the Marine shrugged. "I'm fine, Your Highness."

"It's hard hunting in that jungle, even for us. I'm shocked

anyone here is alive after what we went through just to catch a wild pig."

Adwen corrected him: "That was a male Tapir."

"It sounded and tasted like pork to me."

Princess Eyrie frowned. "Forgive me, Sir Jack. Your strength is just as precious as Sir Oryn's. Save what you can."

"Don't worry about it. You can trust those harpies. When Adwen mentioned being allies, they couldn't stop thinking about it. I'll bet they can hunt better than a pair of clumsy Holy Hounds."

The young woman felt consoled. "You are anything but clumsy, Sir Jack."

Adwen chuckled. "He's many things, but not that."

Alexander scoffed at the compliment, while Jack gave a mocking glare. "Very original material, missy." A sudden idea came to him, and he looked around. "Has anyone seen the big guy? He pulled a disappearing act after the harpies left. And where is Toth?"

Adwen and Princess Eyrie exchanged looks.

"What?"

The princess cast a distant expression. "I last saw Toth go into the meeting place alone and close himself in. He has not come out."

Turning to Adwen, Jack grew wary. "Where's Kale?"

She wore a firm expression. "That's his business, not yours, Jack."

He raised a curious eyebrow.

"Don't bother him. Not now."

It was clear that she was firm on the matter. "Alright, alright. I'll leave him alone."

Knowing Jack would heed the warning came as a comfort. "The two of you should get some sleep. We leave at dawn. I'll wake you when it's time."

The warriors nodded. Giving the princess a polite bow, both departed for the evening. Adwen did the same and turned to go, but the princess called to her.

"Will you not rest as well?"

For the princess, Adwen put on a reassuring face. "I'll be strong enough."

Adwen still had a promise to try to keep. There was no assurance that the opportunity to fulfill it would come again. She found

Moira in the storeroom. The others were out preparing the meat that Jack and Alexander had brought. Adwen watched Moira tend to her duties for a while before announcing herself.

"Good evening, Moira."

"Oh! Lady Adwen! If you have need of the storeroom, I can leave and complete my duties afterward."

"I came to talk to you. By the way, shouldn't you be getting some rest by now?"

Moira turned sheepish and blushed. "Counting fruit and vegetables is hardly stressful work, my lady. I appreciate your concern. What could you possibly wish to speak with me about?"

Studying her eyes for a moment, Adwen saw that the pain in her heart lay just beneath the surface. "How are you feeling?"

"Quite well, so long as I lift nothing heavy. The princess has done well in charging the others with forbidding me from that activity."

"You work hard. It shows. This store is very clean and orderly."

"You flatter me. Though I wish to do more, I love my work." Her happy guise wavered for a moment. "Did you wish to speak with me of anything else?"

Adwen was quiet for a long time. "Yes. In the morning my warriors and I will be leaving. I do not know if we will be coming back. There is something I need you to do for me."

At the thought of Adwen never returning, a chill ran down Moira's spine. "What can I possibly do that is important?"

"Should we succeed and save Dargadia, I need you to return to the beach by the cliffs."

Moira's face drained of color. She muttered, "I don't think I can do that, Lady Adwen. Why do you ask this of me?"

"When we were searching for you all, I left something behind there. I need you to find it for me."

The prospect of going to that place brought back horrible memories. "What will I seek there, my lady?"

Adwen remained vague. Moira's heart could not yet bear more. "You'll know when you've found it. Just promise me you will do this."

Trying not to cry, Moira nodded fervently. "As you wish, Lady Adwen. I will do as you ask."

"Thank you, Moira. And don't work much longer tonight. Go get some well-earned rest. In case I do not see you in the morning, farewell, Moira."

"May the Light guide your feet, Lady Adwen."

Moira watched, trembling as Darien's Heir departed. Once she was alone, she crumpled to her knees dropping her paper and quill. Aching sobs shook her under the candlelight. Cupping hands to her eyes, she trembled and whispered, "Oh, Balefire, why did you leave me?"

The wall of vines around the meeting place was too dense for sound to penetrate, even if Toth had not cast an enchantment. Since the Elf entered, they remained woven tight. Jack waited in the shadows at a distance and watched the vines like a hawk. Arms folded, he leaned by a boulder and tried to sense inside with his mind. There was some occasional movement, but something was interfering with his abilities. It did not matter. The wall would part eventually. Hushed comings and goings were rare in this part of the sanctuary.

When the vines finally parted, Jack was the only witness. Through the green he saw Toth, and Kale was with him. A sly smile came over Jack. He could hear what they said now that the enchantment was gone.

Kale had his claws in his pockets and looked somber. He moved to leave, but Toth grasped his shoulder. Turning back to look at the Elf prince, the werewolf was silent.

Toth's face showed great concern as he softly pleaded, "You cannot give up."

Kale whispered, "There's nothing to give up on."

The words made Toth flinch then frown. Kale ended their conversation by withdrawing from Toth's weak grip. The werewolf strode away. Coming to the corner, he only just sensed Jack before he stepped out. The warrior approached smiling, and the glint in Jack's eyes was not encouraging.

The bold Holy Hound blocked the way and restrained a grin. Anticipating questions, Kale tensed, and anger made the whites around his crimson eyes turn black. His tones were dangerously low. "You look like you want to talk about something."

"Yes, I do. But not with you." He gestured to Toth sitting in one of the chairs.

Kale glanced back. As the black faded from his eyes, he moved past and warned, "Go easy on him."

While he strolled away, Jack called out, "Couldn't help but notice, Big Guy: You and Toth are pretty chummy since you got back."

There was no response. Jack chuckled anyway.

Fedius Toth sat heavily in one of the chairs among the hanging vines. Reclining, one hand supported his weary head. Footsteps and rustling caught his ear. Looking up, he found Jack standing beside him. This came as a small surprise.

"Sir Jack, what can I do for you? I was not expecting you." He politely gestured to a chair, inviting the warrior to join him.

Jack sat across from the tired looking Elf. "So, you came here to meet someone? I thought you came to your vines to hide."

Toth's kind look disintegrated into bitterness.

However, Jack continued to smile. "My mistake."

Toth found some patience before replying, "I came to this place for careful thought."

"That's good to know. Here's a new thought you need to have: Stop being an idiot."

Toth's patience began to erode. "I hope you did not come just to insult me, Sir Jack."

Roots and vines underfoot took hold of the legs on Jack's chair. The threatening way the plants squeezed made it crack. Jack pretended not to notice the threat. "If you weren't expecting me, were you expecting Princess Eyrie to find you?"

The chair's legs started to snap and fracture.

Toth began to seethe. "She and I are none of your concern. What is it you want?"

Knowing he had Toth's attention, he replied, "I'm going to say something, and you can stop me any time I miss the mark. She's on your mind all the time. Everything you do, you think of her before you do it. But something's in the way, and it's you. No matter how much you love each other, the differences are too big. You stay only because you know that the hell of not being with her would be much worse. So, you think: Maybe, just maybe, it would be best if you found a way to make yourself disappear. If she moved on without you, it would be better that way. Then at least she could be happy."

The Elf froze, as did the plants engulfing Jack's chair.

"Am I close?"

Regaining a little sense, Toth was unsure whether to cry or to let the vines crush the chair. Perhaps Adwen would not protest if he were to teach Jack some manners.

"I had thought I would know if you were stealing into my mind, Sir Jack. I've sensed nothing. Tell me, have you taken from my mind against my will?" He wished to unleash his anger on the Holy Hound.

Jack's smile never wavered. "Don't need to."

At first, Toth felt further insulted, but then he saw Jack's smile more clearly. It was not mocking; it was understanding. Swelling anger ebbed. Then he saw the ring on Jack's left hand. The gold shone by the light of the blooms around them.

While the plants on the chair receded, Toth sighed heavily, frowning. "This is the first I've ever felt anything in common with you, Sir Jack; this of all things."

"Funny how that works."

"Not funny enough for laughter, I'm afraid. So how am I being the fool when the two of us share the same plight – loving a mortal human while we ourselves are not?"

"For starters, you're only thinking about yourself."

This struck a nerve. Toth's entourage of flora rustled in anger. "That is not true."

"Yes, it is. Do you know how I know you are?"

The deadly, one-eyed glare returned as Toth awaited the answer.

"You haven't told her anything. She had no idea what you were going through."

"I'd rather not share my sorrow with her. I chose to spare her that."

"That's not an option anymore. And that brings me to the biggest reason you are an idiot, or a fool, as Oryn says. You think whether to stay in this relationship is your decision alone to make."

The statement befuddled Toth.

"What you have with the princess isn't just yours; love is shared. Hiding these feelings is as much a betrayal as it is for you to think you can break it off without consulting her. This love belongs to her, too."

"My sadness is something I would never wish on her."

"Wouldn't you want to know if she were hurting?"

Toth was shocked. "Of course I would."

"How would you feel if she didn't come to you about it? What would you think if the one you loved refused to come to you for comfort?"

Suddenly feeling ashamed, his gaze was downcast. "I see. It's not the pain I've withheld; I've kept my heart from her. I truly have been a fool."

"Glad we finally agree on that."

"Tell me, what am I to do? I am at an impasse."

Jack chuckled and shrugged. "Why are you asking me? There aren't any clear-cut answers with this."

"How does it work – loving someone so different from yourself?"

"I only know what works for me and Ashley. We make the most of what we can. We spend time together. There are things we do to make each other's life better. Being there for her is the most important thing to me. I know that's what I need."

"Yes, but how is it faring?"

Jack's smile finally melted. Toth read the pain in his face.

"It's not easy."

"Clearly."

"But my situation is different. As an Elf, you are way closer to being human, and that makes things easier."

"What do you mean?"

Thinking of the answer made Jack feel sick. "Trust me. You don't have it that bad."

He nodded solemnly. "I shall."

Jack found it difficult to shake off the haunting memories. "My only advice is to never think this love can end just on your terms. And if you really want to end this, talk to her. If you need to leave her, she needs to let you go also. It's the only way."

The words gave stability to his uncertain mind. "Thank you, Sir Jack, for calling me out as an idiot." A weak smile showed itself at last.

It was proudly returned. "Any time, pal. I need to get some sleep."

"Of course."

"And one more thing: You might want to get rid of this chair. The next person who sits in it is going to get a surprise when it falls apart."

Fedius Toth chuckled a little.

Chapter 16
THE PAIN BE MINE

In the final hours of night, Adwen woke Alexander first. She then went to wake Jack and Oryn for their dawn departure. As the refugees slept, Adwen spoke with Kale while they awaited the rest of her company at the sanctuary doors. She finished speaking with him, and the werewolf's red eyes spotted the warriors approaching from deeper in the sanctuary. His expression was like stone. Silently, he stepped outside, and Adwen turned to welcome the others.

"I hope you all got plenty of sleep. How are you feeling?"

Jack and Alexander exchanged casual glances. "We're solid."

Oryn's answer was confident: "I am well rested. I have enough strength to continue."

Hearing a tone she recognized in the knight's voice, Adwen knew he was still quite weak. He was too stubborn to let his condition interfere with their quests. She took note but did not mention it. "Excellent."

"Adwen? Oryn?" Toth called as he and Princess Eyrie strode to the Holy Hounds. "Did you think to depart without saying farewell?"

Adwen's expression became apologetic. "I know how tired you both are. I did not want to wake you just for this."

"Nonsense!" Eyrie replied. "It is our responsibility to see you off. That is the least we can do."

The gesture pleased the Holy Hounds.

Adwen smiled. "Thank you. Now we are going to the palace roof."

Eyrie was taken aback. "Oh! I'm not certain we can follow so far as that."

Toth smiled. "We shall observe your departure from below. Lead the way."

Outside the sanctuary doors, the air was crisp. Wind blew through the halls near the small atrium garden. From the overgrown plot, they saw Kale standing silhouetted atop the palace. He gazed out at the glowing seam where the sky and sea collided. Creamy light seeped outward to splash the dark blue heavens into day.

While Toth observed the lofty scene, the princess spoke to Adwen: "I know we cannot make any undue requests, but don't stay away too long."

Adwen's smile held a twinge of regret. "I can't promise anything, but I don't intend to be gone long this time."

Princess Eyrie's eyes turned moist, and she lunged to embrace Adwen. The tone in her whisper sounded cautiously hopeful: "Please come back to us soon."

Adwen held her gently until the princess pulled away to stand by Toth. Looking at the pair filled Adwen's heart with warmth. "It's almost time."

Toth nodded. "May the Light Spirits guide your feet."

Adwen leapt to join Kale atop the roof. Oryn and Alexander followed.

Jack lingered a moment, smiling slyly at Toth. <Don't be an idiot while I'm gone.>

At first Toth was surprised, but then his own smile widened. <Of course.>

Chuckling to himself, Jack left the ground for the ancient stone shingles above.

The small company gathered atop the palace in silence. The sun began to rise, while powerful gusts tugged fervently at their hair and garments. As the sun bloomed over the horizon, Adwen's form shone, and she summoned the Gray Blade.

Kale sensed eyes on him. Looking to the ground, his gaze met Toth's. Seeing a hopeful expression there, the werewolf gave a subtle nod. This seemed to reassure the Elf prince.

In a mighty roar, blue fire on Adwen's sword shot out and burst in midair. A wreath hovered, showing a sand dune surrounded by many more. She and her four companions jumped through, and the portal snapped shut behind them.

Toth and Princess Eyrie shared the moment of watching

them vanish. Surely, their friends would return.

The travelers traded the humid gales of sunrise in Eskrana for the dry wind of the sandy wasteland. Farther east and now under a mid-morning sun, they set foot on shifting sands. Blue flames at their backs extinguished, along with Adwen's sword, and their door to the jungle region vanished.

Kale stared out at the desolate landscape in a mixture of awe and hesitation. Jack noticed right away as Adwen pointed out the walls surrounding the Lorisan stronghold in the distance.

"Sorry guys," Adwen apologized. "Looks like I was a mile off. I was in a hurry to open a portal and get through while we had the chance."

Kale hardly heard a word. The shadowy dunes captivated him.

"Hey, Big Guy?" Jack asked him. "You alright?"

"I'm fine. It's just that this place feels familiar."

"Been here before?"

"Nah, don't worry about it." He forced a chuckle. "The desert isn't so bad, though. It's kind of beautiful."

The walk to the city walls gave the company a chance to ponder and collect themselves. The solace of the windy dunes was hypnotic. Solid earth formed underfoot the closer they got to the city. When the gates were in sight, Adwen began to worry; the fortress was silent. No travelers or merchants with goods were passing in or out through the gates.

She murmured, "No." Then she bolted. The others chased her inside and looked around. Human smells were faint.

Turning to Kale, she asked, "What do you sense?"

He remained calm, studying the place with suspicion. "No one is here. It's like everyone up and left."

"Spread out," she told her warriors. "Look for clues to what caused them to leave."

They all scattered except Oryn, who stayed by Adwen's side. Jack and Alexander took to the rooftops, while Kale explored on the ground. The Holy Hounds ran, but the werewolf strolled coolly along empty streets. He took great care in reading his surroundings. It reminded him of hunts at night near playgrounds – a place intended for life to thrive was perverted into a forsaken hole. Empty playgrounds had been perfect for finding easy meals, but they also had made Kale uncomfortable. This silent city gave Kale the same feeling. Though he had never been to this place before, it felt wrong.

The sun rose a little higher as they regrouped near the gates. Alexander, Jack and Kale waited for Adwen and Oryn, who had gone as far as the palace.

Adwen saw their dismal looks but asked the others anyway, "Did you guys find anything?"

The Marine shrugged, and Jack reported, "Nothing. It's just like the Eskrani nation."

Kale interjected, "Not quite." Drawing eager stares, he added, "These people weren't killed and chased out. They left. Perhaps because the wells are dry."

The Holy Hounds were shocked, and Adwen became urgent.

"All of them?"

"I only looked down three, but yeah. It looks like a drought created this ghost town."

Adwen was thoughtful and then turned, alarmed. "The lake!"

In a flash, she shifted into a giant white hound and raced out into the desert. The others caught up quickly. Several miles away from the city, they reached the shores of Ula Lake. Sand dunes gave way to stable ground. Shrubs clung to earth battered by unceasing winds. Stopping at last, Adwen changed back into her woman form and gazed in astonishment at a muddy lake bed. The water was gone, save for undrinkable muck and slime. The shriveled lake reeked. Everyone stared in silence.

Kale spoke after pondering the scene: "Where's the next nearest city?"

Adwen looked at him, wondering what he had in mind.

"The people weren't killed; they left. They went somewhere."

"Can you track them?"

He shrugged. "No point really. If they went to another city for water, it would be faster to look there than to comb the desert."

"Good point. The Bebidin have enchanted walls. They might still have water."

As their walk brought the Bebidin guard towers within view, their keen vision saw figures moving about. With hope restored, their pace quickened. But as the gates became easier to see, they were met with a very unusual sight: A pair of towering Minotaurs stood guard. When Adwen and her company approached, the Minotaurs blocked their path and brandished long gold-plated spears.

Adwen and her warriors recognized the weapons made by Zsu blacksmiths. She had not gotten a good look at the figures atop the walls, but she smelled no humans. Prepared for resistance, she took a diplomatic approach: "I am Adwen Andredan. I am here to speak with the leader of this city. Please let us pass."

The Minotaurs snorted, and their ears perked at hearing her name. "We have special orders to allow you passage into the city."

She was relieved, but hesitated when they did not step aside. "Is there a condition that I'm not aware of?"

The beastly guards shared uncertain glances. "You must enter as prisoners."

Jack scoffed, and Oryn growled, eyes lit with rage.

While Kale smiled and thought to himself, Adwen made her decision. "Alright, we'll go as your prisoners. Please take us inside."

One of the Minotaurs gave a bovine bellow to city wall attendants. The bronze gates slowly parted, and the guards took positions in front and behind the company. Adwen stole a glance at Jack to see what he could read from the Minotaurs' thoughts.

Jack appeared amused at the situation. She felt better about the intent of these Minotaurs. Even if they could not hurt her, it was reassuring to sense that they meant no harm.

The guards led them through the gates, which closed behind them to the cruel desert. As they left the shadow of the wall, a sea of smells told them many individuals lived here, but few were human. Minotaurs of different genders and ages wandered about. Among them were even more impish creatures. These beings had rough skin like shark scales and patches of tender flesh like that of a toad. Their ears came to hard, sharp points, and their eyes were reptilian. Dressed in all manner of clothing, these sandy colored beings stood at barely three feet in height. Most of the guards atop the wall were these creatures, bearing telescopes and crossbows. They whispered among themselves and watched intently when the prisoners passed.

Reaching streets deeper in the city, their arrival finally caught the attention of humans. They were filthy, hungry, thirsty and angry. Emaciated men and women shouted and sobbed at the Holy Hounds in their foreign tongue. Some spat, earning Oryn's deadly snarls of warning.

Disturbed by this greeting, Adwen turned to Kale. "What are they saying?"

He gave the humans stern looks, and his red eyes made some hesitate. Frowning, the werewolf replied, "They're cursing you."

"I know, but why? What are they saying exactly?"

"They aren't saying why. What they are saying, I prefer not to translate."

She swallowed a knot in her throat. "Thank you."

The shameful parade continued to the palace at the heart of the city. Closer to the royal grounds, even more humans gathered. An angry mob shouted curses and venomous cries, swarming to block the way. Adwen and her friends braced for more hostility, while the Minotaur guards tried to clear a path.

Gradually the humans began to encircle the warriors. Soon ravenous shouts came from all sides. No matter how their Minotaur escorts and the approaching palace guard Minotaurs bellowed, the people would not back off. Out of the masses, someone lobbed a rotten egg. It struck Adwen. The putrid contents and broken shell sullied her garments. A moment later, her magic dissipated the filth, but she was startled.

Oryn summoned his sword and Jack his daggers, while Alexander bared sharp fangs. They snarled, but the humans started to draw their own weapons. A wave of cold rage filled the air. It made the air heavy and hard to breathe. Everyone fell quiet. Adwen and the others stole a look at the source.

Kale's body emanated dark energy. Face set in a cold glare, the whites of his burning red eyes were like onyx. Black mist poured from his shoulders as his presence extended out in all directions, enveloping the crowd. Low rumbling like thunder came from him. Studying the horror-stricken humans, Kale's rage silenced theirs, making many step back. Reaching into their minds, he snarled, unleashing a terrifying vision.

At once, the masses screamed and scattered, fleeing the dark presence. As the last of them disappeared, the Minotaur guards stared at Kale with uncertainty.

Withdrawing his demon presence, his eyes returned to normal. Hands back in his pockets, Kale frowned and puffed incredulously, muttering under his breath. "Tossers."

A guard snorted, pointing a golden spear tip. "What is this among you? Why do you harbor a demon?"

Kale glanced at the Minotaur in mild curiosity, smelling his fear. The guard flinched, snorting as he took a step back. Other Minotaurs stepped forward, ready to fight.

Adwen quickly called out, "He serves the Light."

The Minotaurs paused. The highest ranking among them stepped forward, unafraid. His tone was hard as stone. "No show of force can be made beyond this point. Any perceived threat will be considered an attack. Do away with your weapons." Glaring at Kale, he added, "And keep powers restrained."

Kale said nothing as he stared back, studying the bold bull humanoid.

It took a nod of reassurance from Adwen to get her warriors to dismiss their blades. When they obeyed, their procession resumed.

No humans were found within the palace. The fabled thousand guard statues stood in their stations, but not one of the statues was without damage. All had scratches and gouges in their carved bodies, and many had missing limbs. The faces of the giant enchanted guardians did not rise to observe Adwen's arrival. Their bronze eyes were downcast, as if in mourning.

The short sandy creatures with rough complexions milled about. Those who saw Adwen and her companions stopped only briefly before continuing onward. None of the Holy Hounds had smelled anything like these imps before, but to Adwen they seemed familiar.

Deep in the heart of the grand palace, they entered a vast chamber. Red banners hung amid the green and pearl of jade and marble walls. The throne room glowed with natural light filtered in through many skylights. Sunshine cast hard shadows on the hulking figure seated at the back on lavish pillows. A Minotaur with a scar across his nose watched their approach, as did a young man at his side wearing common robes. This young man was in far better condition than any other humans from the city.

The armed guards brought them before their leader, then

stopped and bowed their large, horned heads.

"We have brought the one named Adwen and those who follower her. What is your wish, Grand Chief?"

They watched as the Grand Chief studied the prisoners. At last, he commanded, "Leave us."

The guards were taken aback. One stole a glance at Kale, apprehensive of leaving such a being with their leader. But their superior insisted with a grunt that echoed in the throne chamber. It made the pair of Minotaur escorts obey. They bowed and withdrew toward the hall. The sound of their shod hooves clicking filled the air. When the doors closed, the Minotaur clothed in silk spoke using firm tones.

"I've been expecting your arrival, Adwen Andredan."

She still felt confused. "What's going on here? Why are we prisoners?"

"Did you see the people? The humans?"

She frowned. "Yes."

"They are angry. The humans curse your name and the Light Spirits. It is their belief that they have been abandoned to die. When evil came and you did not, they lost all hope."

This news weighed heavily on her.

Oryn snarled bitterly, "Fools."

The Grand Chief snorted, flicking his bull ears. "You judge them too easily. They are taken by fear and hunger. Few can resist the drives of a body desperate for survival."

The knight still glared.

"You have seen my kind living in this city," the Grand Chief said. "It was foretold to the children of the sand long ago that they would come to inherit this place and no longer need to wander like the wind." He grunted bitterly. "The previous Grand Chief believed that the Minotaurs were destined to conquer the humans to fulfill the prophecy. He was proved wrong when he fell to a human and his bones were taken by the desert. Such is the price for foolish pride." The Grand Chief stared at Oryn who was defiant as ever. "I know it was you who brought him low."

The companions tensed, and the knight growled, "If you want vengeance, then try and claim it."

A hush came over them. The Grand Chief finally replied, "There is no reason for vengeance. He was wrong and deserving of his fate to feed the sand. Do not be too taken by outrage at being prisoners. I have no choice, if the fragile peace here is to last."

Adwen and her friends relaxed as they began to understand the situation.

"The humans here hate you, and my kind do not follow the Light Spirits. Many cling to the old ways and worship the wind and sand. Should they think I've abandoned the desert for the Light, there would be civil unrest, possibly even war. Now is not the time. For now, you must be called prisoners to be guests."

"You follow the Light Spirits?"

"Yes."

Kale sniffed the air and began to wear a clever smile. "You smell interesting."

The others looked to him curiously, and the Minotaur snorted in indignation.

Jack eyed the Grand Chief with growing interest. "What is it, Big Guy?"

Adwen tried to shush them. "That's enough."

The Minotaur stood until the tips of his horns almost reached a banner overhead. "This secret, too, must be kept."

A brilliant light enveloped the huge Minotaur. When it dimmed, it revealed his true form. A second set of smaller horns grew beneath the others. The four curving protrusions glinted golden in the sunshine. His fur and hair were snow white, while his eyes blazed like fire. Silvery glowing symbols flickered in and out across his body beneath the silks. The young man at his side stood in awe but did not seem surprised.

Everyone except Kale was astonished to be face to face with yet another Guardian.

Flicking ears beneath heavy, golden horns, he added, "This makes it clear where my allegiance lies."

Adwen recovered from the shock and nodded. "We understand. You have my word that none of us will interfere with what you are doing."

"Of that, I have no doubt." The Guardian took on his original form, disguising himself once more as a Minotaur. He sat on the cushions ready to resume their meeting. "My name is Gargeth."

Everyone had become far less suspicious.

"What's been happening here?" A bad feeling came over Adwen, and she remembered. "Where is King Isban? What happened to King Loggias? Can you tell us anything about Queen Xenorithia and the Zsu?"

The eyes of the young man grew dark with despair, as the Minotaur released a long breath out his ringed nose. Adwen began to realize that the worst had happened.

"Some time ago, the river that fills Ula Lake grew weak, then ceased. When a few days passed and the river did not flow, the three rulers held a moot. In their moot, the king of the Lorisans was eager, certain that the problem would be easily remedied. The queen of the Zsu, keen of mind, sensed that this could be more than a dry river and a shrinking lake. It was her desire to learn more first or wait for you to arrive. King Isban concluded that if this were meant for them to face alone, then you would not come and that their hands would be forced. After the moot, the Lorisan king gathered many soldiers and beasts. Riding his three-headed creature, they set out. None returned.

"At the disappearance of King Loggias, the mighty queen's suspicions were confirmed. Taking all her army, the moth riders, spearmen, archers and her fearsome Sandshark, she set out. Hundreds were with her. None were seen again."

This news horrified Adwen and her friends. The queen's Sandshark alone was a force to be reckoned with. Her army had the most power among the desert nations. For them to be wiped out was inconceivable.

The Guardian's story was not finished. "King Isban Leshano waited. Many came seeking refuge. His city alone had an underground wellspring. He watched the ever-shrinking lake, knowing the burden of so many on their spring would have consequences. When the wells showed the first signs of going dry, he knew it was time to attempt what King Loggias and Queen Xenorithia had failed: He must find a way to restore the river. No men went with him. Some were too terrified, and those who volunteered to join him he dismissed to spare their lives. He took the thousand stone guards. With the immortal giants, he departed. Days passed. Then the living statues returned, marred and broken and without their king."

A heavy silence fell over them in the palace chamber.

Sick from what she had just learned, Adwen swallowed a lump in her throat. "Do you know what's doing this?"

Before Gargeth could answer, another voice rose from behind the long banner behind him. The sound made the Minotaur all but roll his eyes.

"I know exactly what killed the kings and queen, Tame One." He cackled deviously and emerged from around the draping crimson cloth, arms folded. It was one of the sandy, scaly beings. It eyed Adwen, smiling toothily. He was a little taller than the others they had seen.

Staring at this imp, Adwen gasped, "Chief? Is that you?"

His sly smile widened. "Welcome back, Lady Adwen. It has been years."

The warriors gave Adwen confounded looks, and she asked, "What has happened to you and the other goblins?"

Oryn, Jack and Alexander finally realized these desert beings were once the goblin tribe that joined in the battle against Melanin. In disbelief, they sniffed, trying to comprehend how this was the same species as before.

He saw their perplexed expressions. "Aiding you came with its benefits and costs. As promised by the crystal, we have grown stronger – at the price of no longer being goblins."

Gargeth added, "They are now the first of their kind: Sand Imps."

The Chief cackled and gave the Minotaur a calculating glance. "You say that like we are such devils, my friend."

He snorted indignantly. "Fairy kind are neither good nor bad. Though your kind is good, you have distinct flaws."

Jack gave the imp a hesitant look. "What kind of flaws?"

"They are given to mischief."

The Sand Imp Chief did not protest but reassured them when they appeared concerned: "We are bound to the pact with the light in the crystal. Our allegiance is unbreakable. Though we love our games and funny tricks, we take our duties seriously."

Adwen was still staring, and he realized why. He tilted his head, chuckling. "Do you so miss my primitive speech patterns? I can speak that way again if it entertains you?"

She smiled, shaking her head. "I never had a problem with it."

The imp lost his deviousness for a moment, beaming like a cat pleased to be petted. "You are sweet, Lady." The slitted pupils widened in satisfaction.

Gargeth snorted. "Get on with sharing what you've learned, Imp Chief."

Though the Chief of the Sand Imps still smiled, he lost much of his fun-loving posture. Incapable of appearing wholly serious, his smile was grim in the deadpan look he gave.

"After the death of King Isban, humans of different nations began to fight amongst themselves. Gargeth and his kind came and took leadership with help from me and my kind. After some order was established, we made plans to finish the humans' quest to restore the river. I sent five scouts. They swam in the sand to the Ebony Range. One returned; the others had been killed swiftly. My scout reported that the river is dammed by an enormous piece of rock. It was not fallen, but cut and dropped in place. He only caught a glimpse of the monster, but what he described is enough to leave us little doubt."

"What killed your scouts, Chief?" Adwen asked.

His tone turned darker than his look. "A Boneworm."

The Holy Hounds knew nothing of this creature but could tell by the Imp's tone that it was dreadful.

He raised an eyebrow. "Do you know what a Boneworm is, Lady Adwen?"

"I've studied about a lot of creatures, but I've never heard of it."

The chief's look was unblinking. "They are unique to this desert and far rarer than the Sandsharks. Where they come from is conjecture at best, but it is agreed they are not born or hatched, but formed. They are something like an elemental. Most think they manifest out of a conjoining of magic, wind, sand, bone and blood."

Adwen did not like where this was going. "What do you think?"

"They are evil, a manifestation of darkness conceived out of the desert. They are made of bones swallowed by sand and stained by bloodshed, an embodiment of impurity and rage. Can you imagine how many bones are buried in this desert, Lady Adwen? Can you?"

"I can't imagine."

"Creatures great and small die and are lost under the dunes. It is those bones that form the body of the worm. Sand stained in blood makes up its flesh. It is unknown whether it possesses a heart. I do not think these things manifest of their own accord; it is my belief they are made."

Adwen and Oryn shared ominous glances and she frowned.

She asked, "You think this thing was sent to guard the dam?"

The Imp Chief nodded. "Precisely. It cannot be coincidence that a Boneworm suddenly forms at the same place where the river happens to be blocked. Likewise, a Boneworm could not have created the dam. They cannot carve stone; they pierce or impale with bone and ensnare with tentacles of bloody sand. There is no doubt that whoever summoned the worm is also responsible for the dam."

Kale called to the Imp, "Alright, how do we kill it?"

His snake-like eyes locked with Kale's. "How does one kill a force of magic and nature? How do you kill a storm?"

Their gazes held for an intense moment.

Then the imp's smile became sly. "You might be able to kill it. You are like a storm yourself." Kale's scowl made the Imp chuckle. "Does it not take a storm to kill a storm? Just be careful not to let it blow you out as well."

The werewolf asked, "What makes you think I'm a storm?"

"I'm an Imp, but not blind, Rogue Demon."

Kale gave a dry laugh.

Gargeth spoke up to prevent the Sand Imp from stirring conflict. "We have arranged a means for you all to leave unseen."

Adwen nodded to them. "Thank you, so much, both of you. We would like to go as soon as we can."

The Imp Chief sniggered. "We thought you might say that. Guards!"

At the sound of the shrill call, the chamber doors burst open, and the guards entered the throne room with several additional Minotaurs. They leveled their spears at Adwen and her companions.

Pointing with an accusing finger, the Sand Imp called out at the top of his raspy voice: "Take these prisoners to the dungeon immediately! They will stand before the council for judgment tomorrow!"

The warriors were led out at spear tip without resistance or word of protest.

When they were gone and no one else was around to hear, the Imp cackled: "That was fun! We'll have to do this again some time! The guards really seem to think they are prisoners!"

Gargeth sighed. "Your nature is taxing to me."

Taking a sweeping bow, the Sand Imp Chief grinned. "It will always be a pleasure."

One by one, the captives were placed in dry, dusty cells and locked behind steel bars. When the Minotaur brought Kale to a cell, a glance from the werewolf made the guard snort and flinch. Kale chuckled before he stepped into the cell, allowing the door to close and lock tight. The guards were relieved that the cooperative demon was locked up. After the incident with the mob, they wanted nothing to do with this creature.

They prisoners waited, listening for sounds made of other inmates. Their own cells were clean, while the scents from others were dreadful. Minutes passed after the guards disappeared.

Gripping the bars, Jack peered around to get a bearing on their surroundings. "This place looks nice. Bet the property value is great. What do you think, Big Dog?"

"Shut up, Jack," Alexander replied.

Jack's chuckles echoed down the corridor to the other cells, where Adwen, Oryn and Alexander rolled their eyes.

Kale leaned in a corner. "I doubt they will keep us long."

Adwen agreed, "He's right."

A stone rattled in the wall behind Adwen, and she hushed. Dust fell around the jiggling stone, and more stones at the backs of all their cells started wiggling and withdrawing. Whispers and raspy giggles echoed through the gaps. Small scaly hands moved more stones, opening the way to a tunnel behind the wall. Mischievous hushed cackles filled the air, as a few Sand Imps beckoned the warriors to follow them into the dark.

"Come on, come on. Let's go."

They waded into the small army of Imps and exchanged abashed expressions. Right away, the little creatures began rebuilding the wall, and a few others ushered them through the dark tunnel. It twisted and wound about before straightening. The sound of the Imps' rapid little footsteps drowned out the sound of the Holy Hounds' steps. At the end of the secret passage, they found a few more Imps waiting by a dead end.

When they arrived, the small team manipulated the sand. As they dug at it, the grains moved like water and flowed aside and created an opening. Fresh desert air gasped into the Imps' tunnel. The group emerged from a dune beyond the city walls.

One of the Imp guides waved up at the high wall. An Imp above at a guard post waved back then vanished.

Adwen was grateful. "Thank you so much for your help."

The same imp giggled. "Thank us later, and we can thank you if you come back alive."

Their admiration of the Imps collapsed at hearing his statement.

"Be on your guard," the Imp added. "There may be more than a Boneworm to worry about." With that, he and the others returned to the tunnel, closing the magical exit.

Adwen turned to face her friends, who appeared ready for battle. She took a deep breath. "Let's get moving. I don't want a fight in the dark."

They could not agree more. With that, Adwen transformed into her large dog shape for the journey.

As they ran, the White Sea Desert grew hotter and brighter. Their course led north to the lake, then veered northwest along the dry riverbed. By the time their destination was in sight, it was late afternoon. Evening would descend sooner than they had hoped.

Hot red light from the dying sun stained the sky like blood when they arrived. The mouth of the riverbed lay a few miles away, empty and dry. At last, Adwen and the others stopped. She reverted to her woman form and looked around.

While Jack glanced around trying to sense this Boneworm, he failed to hide the fear in his cracking voice. "Hey, Big Guy? Have you come up with any ideas on how to kill this thing?"

Kale gave the desolate landscape a suspicious glare. "Not really." When he received four uncertain glances, he shrugged. "I know a lot, but this is not in my area. I've heard of Boneworms, but never heard of anybody killing one."

Alexander was unsettled. "No one's ever killed one before?"

Pausing to think, Kale's face showed a hint of fear. He shook his head. "No."

Jack groaned, "Crap."

Adwen pressed onward, studying the river's source. "We don't have a choice but to try. Kale, is there anything you can tell us that the Chief didn't know?"

"Yeah, and nothing good." He elaborated as they walked, wary of their surroundings. "Jack and I won't be able to sense it by thoughts; it has none. This thing is held together by dark magic. It has no mind, heart or life force – like the undead. Even golems have life force, but not this thing. Instinct will be our only warning when it comes."

"It's like a spell?"

Kale nodded. "Yeah."

She felt reassured. "Then it has a weakness. We have to find it."

He smiled to himself. She was right.

Oryn remained silent, secretly regretting he had spent so much of his energy saving lives in Eskrana. Only Adwen was weaker than himself currently. He felt he would be useless in the coming battle. Adwen picked up on the uncertain feelings as they walked together. Giving the knight a searching glance, she announced their orders: "When the Boneworm shows up, I want Kale to take the lead. Jack and Alex, provide backup however you can. Oryn will stay back with me as protection."

"Whatever you say," Jack replied.

"Roger that."

Oryn nodded. "As you command."

Right away, Adwen sensed that Oryn's assignment made him more confident.

Out in the emptiness, the wind whipped small flurries of sand around the dry riverbed. The sun's dying light cast hard shadows among washes of crimson, tangerine and gold. Black rocks jutted skyward ahead as high as mountains. They seemed to go on forever like a monstrous wound on the earth. Oryn thought he saw movement in the corner of his vision. He studied the tops of the black stones with great scrutiny.

The others took notice and paused. No one liked the look he wore.

"What is it?" Adwen asked.

He grimaced. "It was nothing."

Everyone doubted it was nothing but carried onward. Jack and Kale were on the highest level of alertness. They stretched their mental abilities to their maximum. Their expressions were distant. An abrupt pang of alarm suddenly hit the two. Just when Adwen,

Oryn and Alexander began to sense danger, they exchanged startled glances. The knight and Marine summoned their weapons, and the cop tackled Oryn and Adwen and pushed them aside. The werewolf did the same for Alexander just in time to dodge an explosion of intense heat hitting the ground. Purple flames furled outward and streaked through the dune, carving a path of burnt sand and smoky glass.

Broad wings burst open above as a flying demon abomination laughed maniacally. It landed on another sand dune. The warriors leaped to their feet, baring fangs and raising sharp golden weapons. Jack summoned his daggers and joined Alexander in standing between the enemy and their friends.

Grinning, Impurus shouted, "I see you are all still living! What a wonderful turn of events." Seeing Kale at last, he paused. Confusion played across his twisted face. Then his insidious grin returned. "A rogue? What fun! Which of those fools let you out of the pit?"

The whites of Kale's eyes turned black, as he glared at the winged monster. "Who's this clown?"

Adwen balled her fists and scowled. "His demon name is Impurus, but his real name is Jacques."

The abomination's temper flared, and he summoned his wicked sword. Pointing it, he bellowed, "I am no longer a weak pathetic human! I have a new name, and it is Impurus!"

After getting a good look at this villain, Kale was unimpressed. He smiled and scoffed.

Impurus curtailed his rage enough to get back to business. "So, Adwen, you've brought a weak little rogue to fight?" He grinned. Rogues were always weak, a wisp in comparison to even a Wretch. "Have you not heard of my new pet?" Stabbing his demon blade into the ground, a wave of evil power pulsed outward. A low rumble resounded from the desert.

"He shall feast on your flesh and bones."

A whale-sized shape erupted from the sand and grew skyward like a wriggling tower. Tendrils made of brown sand waved like hair on a colossal caterpillar. Bones bleached white by the sun made up its body. Ribs of small and massive species aligned in rows, forming the Boneworm's mouth. The jawless maw opened like a spiked pit, jutting forward and outward in a wide, horrific yawn. A shrieking wail sounded across the wasteland.

The Holy Hounds bared their fangs at Impurus, as the other monstrosity slithered toward them in the sun's dying light. Before long, the Boneworm would be in range to strike.

Rage brimmed within Kale. He wanted to attack both enemies but could not fight the two at once. If he had to choose, he wanted to unleash his full wrath on Impurus. Black mist began to fall from his shoulders like a mantle of pure night.

Adwen knew what he wanted to do. "No!"

Everyone paused – including the angry werewolf.

Staring at him, she commanded, "The Boneworm."

She was right. That thing could not be allowed to get close to the Holy Hounds. Kale needed to find a way to kill the worm as soon as possible, before they could shift their attack to Impurus.

Surprising and intriguing to Impurus, the rogue demon tossed him a deadly sneer before racing toward the Boneworm. Curiosity and confidence led Impurus to hold back and watch.

Bounding toward the Boneworm, Kale leaped. His rage toward Impurus helped him transform rapidly. Landing as a gigantic beast with thick black fur, he roared for the attention of the nightmare made of sand, blood and bone. It reared, shrieking again, while he stared it down.

"Hmm." Impurus studied the rogue demon. This one was stronger than he seemed.

The Holy Hounds tensed, watching Impurus slowly turn back toward them. A sick mad grin all but parted his head in half. Jack and Alexander held their ground.

Unfurling broad sinuous wings, the abomination laughed.

The two friends exchanged hard looks. The cop received a nod, and they started walking toward Impurus. Growling, both shifted into their true hound forms, but they knew they were no match for the giant demon.

When the pair of warriors stopped several yards away, Impurus could not resist: "What is ever the matter, Jack? Nothing clever to say?"

He growled. "Not really." In the blink of an eye, he sent both daggers whizzing through the air.

Even faster, Impurus batted both away like flies with his sword. Folding his broad wings, he laughed mercilessly as the warrior

caught the blades. "You're so weak that I'll get to make you pay for what you did to my wing."

Alexander snarled and lunged for the smiling fiend, as Jack stood firm and sent his daggers flying again. The yellow hound in thick armor slammed his blade against the edge of Impurus's sword, only to be thrown back. Impurus again swatted away the flying daggers. The instant the demon fended off Jack's blades, Alexander rebounded to strike.

Kale's werewolf body was big and powerful enough to fling a human like a doll, but the Boneworm dwarfed him. Using his unique senses, he smelled so many soul traces on the worm that even he could not tell them apart. It saw him and reared, sand tendrils waving wildly. Kale wondered what held it together. Was it the soul energy?

His thinking came to an abrupt halt. Despite the Boneworm's immensity, it lunged like a cobra, spiked mouth gaping wide. Kale narrowly darted aside. The ground rumbled from the monster's explosive impact, forming a cloud of dust. More angry wailing filled the air as it realized it had missed.

There was no time to waste. He needed to find a way to kill it fast.

The head swung upward from the fresh crater as Kale leaped into its body. He dug claws into the creature, crushing sunbaked bones and Minotaur horns. To his horror, the skulls forming the head of the worm turned toward him. Those were its eyes. Kale snarled at the sea of eyeless pits gazing blankly.

Wind rushed through his fur, whistling in his ears, as the worm swung to slam him against the ground. He ran up the worm's body and leaped from above its head, but some of its tendrils ensnared his limbs. The instant he realized he was caught, he braced for the brutal impact of the worm slamming to the ground.

Everything went dark and silent. Immense pressure tore the air from his lungs. He could not move. The worm began to rise, and Kale barely clung to consciousness, as well as the bones covering the worm's skin. Another wailing cry resonated, announcing that the creature was not pleased that Kale was still alive.

Bloodied and sore, the crushing impact would have pulverized any mortal creature – perhaps even the Holy Hounds. Kale's broken bones throughout his body fused during the moment it took for the worm to raise its head high into the night sky. The instant that Kale's blood had dried on his pitch-black coat, the werewolf roared and swiped his sharp claws at the tendrils ensnaring him. The sand broke apart, as several bones in the tendrils shattered, setting him free. The worm was already rearing to slam him again.

Scrambling across the worm's back, he ran through a forest of waving sand tentacles. The sound of another mighty crash came. For the few seconds that the worm was idle, Kale stopped to claw at its body. Each swing pulverized bones. Sand poured out like blood for a few seconds until the surface resealed itself. Kale kept slashing the same spot regardless. After he had flayed the patch of bone carapace several times, the bones stopped surfacing to reseal the skin. The blood-stained sand started to pour anew and showed no sign of stopping.

Hearing the enraged groan of the worm brought Kale some satisfaction. His guess was correct: The bones were what held the titanic monster together. By the corner of his eye he caught a glimpse of the head rearing back and taking aim. His moment of jubilation gave way to frustration. He would need to rip this thing apart piece by piece and leave no bone untouched. More than he feared the worm or losing Adwen and the others, he feared what killing this monster might do to him.

While the Boneworm lunged, Kale broke off attack. He leaped out of harm's way, struggling between the desire to save his friends and his fear of the cost to kill the Boneworm.

Jack's daggers swirled through the air like live boomerangs, flying at Impurus wherever an opening appeared. The constant bombardment gave Alexander a fighting chance. The daggers deprived Impurus the time he needed to breathe demon flames. All the fiend's attention focused on fighting toe to toe with the Holy Hounds.

Alexander never relented. The demonic being batted him away once more, scratching his thick armor, but he rebounded immediately. Growling and snarling, Alexander's duel continued as he sought an opportunity to subdue the fiend. Alexander was close enough to see the glint in the monster's eyes; his instincts told him the Holy Hounds would lose this fight.

The twin daggers came in for Impurus's flanks in unison as the hulking yellow hound was swatted back yet again. Sensing Jack's flying blades, the monster laughed and swung his sword wide, striking both daggers at once. They spun away just as Alexander made a desperate swing. The demon's wings burst open and flapped at Alexander. Dark power poured into the move, sending the warrior aloft. Alexander flew skyward, propelled with such force that his body arced miles from the battleground.

Watching helplessly as his friend was blown away, Jack recalled his daggers. The impact of the grips colliding with his padded palms felt reassuring. It was the only comfort after being left alone to fight. Jack growled, wrinkling his black and white muzzle.

Impurus heaved a satisfied sigh. "Now, where were we, Jack? Ah, yes, repaying a favor."

The warrior lunged, daggers out, but Impurus leaped and landed behind him. Jack barely blocked the demonic sword. His blades shrieked like nails on a chalkboard while they pressed against the evil weapon. The opposing edges sparked where they touched, resisting each other.

Jack saw Impurus taking a deep breath. Using telekinesis, he left his daggers to hold the sword back and dove out of the way. A split second later, red fire torched the sand into pitch and glass. The blessed weapons returned to him in time to deflect a fearsome sword strike from the laughing fiend. Maniacal guffaws filled Jack's ears.

The blow pushed the warrior until he slid across the ground, barely keeping balance. A whoosh of wind followed the sudden disappearance of Impurus. Detecting the monster with his mind, Jack looked up and sent the daggers flying for the ascending villain.

His efforts counted for worse than nothing. Impurus swatted them away, leaving Jack defenseless. Again, the abomination took a deep breath while staring down at the hound warrior.

Jack whined, fangs bared. There was nowhere to run. The daggers were returning to his aid but would not come soon enough. He glared as Impurus began to swoop and expel intense purple flames across his tongue. Jack's instincts took over. He reached out with his mind.

Opening his arms wide, Jack roared. Without letting go of his control of the daggers, he focused all his remaining mental power at the sand. Straining mind and body at once, he howled. Blood trickled from a nostril. A ton of white sand flew upward at Jack's command. Millions of tiny grains gathered as a solid cloud, blocking the demon's way.

As the flames struck the sand barrier, it turned hot orange, then yellow and white. Then it exploded. A shower of glittering glass and ash burst outward as Jack's daggers returned to his hands. The smoking cloud that replaced the sand descended, then parted. Jack raised his daggers to block the black, jagged sword.

His eyes followed the demonic blade as it cleaved off his right hand and sliced through the flesh above his collarbone. Searing pain shot up his forearm and neck. The smell of his own blood was a shock. A nauseating chill struck his stomach. Unable to concentrate, Jack stumbled, reeling from the blow. Another swing came, hitting his side. His armor absorbed the damage, but he was sent tumbling, dazed and in shock.

Impurus kicked the warrior's severed hand after him, laughing louder than ever. Adwen felt sick with fear and anger, while Oryn seethed. He tightened the grip on his large sword.

Fanning evil wings, Impurus turned, grinning sadistically. "So, Conrad, it is down to us. It is time for our rematch. It is a shame you won't even be able to put up a fight like your little friend just did."

Oryn's emerald eyes shone, fangs bared as he growled.

"You're angry! That's perfect!" Impurus lunged with a flap of his wings and a flourish of his blade.

The knight took a lunging step forward, transforming as he did. Pure determination drove his movements at the demon's charge.

Salivating with maddening glee, Impurus swung his sword with all his might.

Oryn put all his power into blocking. Using magic to encase his blade, he raised the weapon. But to his horror, the barrier broke the moment the demon struck. The Rose Thorne blade flew from Oryn's hand, as a second swift strike landed across Oryn's chest. His armor held, but he was whisked off his feet and thrown afar. Oryn tumbled down a dune, disarmed.

Adwen stood before Impurus, afraid but unwavering.

He cocked his head, brandishing the wicked sword.

She scowled.

"If you won't humor me by running for your life, won't you

at least do me the courtesy of screaming? I know you want to."

As an act of defiance, she spat at him. Adwen would do nothing for his amusement.

Impurus's rage sparked again. "Have it your way, little beast!" He plunged his sword through her.

Kale scrambled all over the Boneworm, crushing sections of carapace at each opportunity. Tendrils that tried to grab him fell to his claws. His mind remained full of doubt. To kill the Boneworm meant tapping into his true demon potential. He needed to use that power now, but it was the last thing he wanted to do. There had to be another way.

Then he felt something, and time seemed to stand still. Jack, Alexander and Oryn felt the same thing, but he felt it in far greater magnitude. Adwen had been pierced by Impurus's sword.

Kale smelled blood and felt hot pain in his guts; this blood was fresh. It was his own. A grievous wound appeared in his middle. In shock and feeling his strength ebb, more tendrils ensnared him. The Boneworm arched its head and lunged once more. Massive uneven rib bones drove through the giant werewolf.

Kale felt nothing. As the worm raised him high to drop him into its mouth, red color washed over his vision. His mind felt like it was humming. A hot sensation filled his heart. Impurus – he had hurt Adwen. That demon had hurt his friends. He hated Impurus.

The darkest part of his being unlocked. Every ounce of his power quickened, barely within his control. Completely awoken, darkness like thick smoke exploded from his body. Kale's demon presence invaded the entire Boneworm, filling it, consuming it inside and out. As soon as he occupied every bone in its corrupted body, his roar rang out along with his true demon voice, shrill and resonating.

All but the biggest bones shattered. Tons of sand burst out like water through a ruptured dam. The darkness surrounding Kale extended beyond the reach of his physical body. It moved like living smoke, swirling about him as a thunderhead, gathering huge bones ripped from the worm that was no more. As he set his sights on Impurus, the bones flew with him.

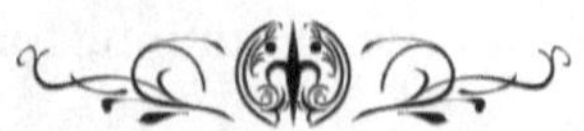

Impurus held his sword through Adwen's middle. He heard the cry from the werewolf but thought nothing of it. With a flick of his wrist, the sword swung, tossing her limp body aside. The fiend chuckled then fluttered to land nearby.

Adwen lay prone, staring unblinkingly into his merciless face. He straddled over her with talon-like feet. Wings open in the excitement of having her at his mercy, Impurus raised the sword pommel up, ready to drive the tip into her heart.

"Any last words?" he asked her.

She choked on some of her own silvery blood, but managed to scowl. She coughed out, "Good-bye, Jacques."

Confused by her tone, he was enraged. He raised the sword high.

First something flew by just over his head, ripping the sword out of his grip. It had barely left his hands when another object hit his side. In a split second, Impurus watched in dumbfounded amazement as a large rib bone encased in demonic energy disarmed him and a second tore through his flesh. Purple blood exploded on impact. He glanced behind. What he saw made him realize that he still possessed enough human essence to feel fear.

That rogue. It was impossible to sense his strength, but now it was visible. The giant beast, surrounded by a thick cloud of darkness, came leaping down toward Impurus. This rogue's strength was far beyond his own. While Kale came for him, the darkness aimed the many bones. For an instant, Impurus thought the cloud took the form of a winged demon.

The fiend moved as fast as his wounded body allowed. His wings beat with desperation, propelling him as far and as swiftly as he could. Rib bones coated in darkness struck the ground around him like ebony and ivory catapults. Sand erupted all around.

The last two bones hit their mark, tearing Impurus's wings to shreds. He tumbled through the sand and far down a dune. Bleeding from tattered stumps on his back and the gaping hole in his flank, the demon scrambled backward on the ground as he tried to open a portal out of this place. The powerful rogue landed on huge paws and leaped straight for Impurus, who had focused just enough energy to manage the feat. A black pool opened, and he fell into it and out of the living worlds.

Kale pounced with claws outstretched, but landed too late to reach Impurus. The portal to the Void vanished, and he skidded far, roaring ravenously. With the target lost, his dark energy began to subside. More control over his actions returned, as the red vision diminished. The wound gushed red blood.

Adwen lay alone and bleeding just as badly. Oryn arrived, rushing to her side after racing back from the distance Impurus had thrown him. He changed back to his smaller shape and cradled Adwen's cheek. The knight bordered on panic. Fear threatened to make him feral.

Though she grew weaker, she forced a smile for him. "It's bad, but I can make it." Agony forced her into cringing fits, while more silver fluids poured out.

On the next dune Jack fought to pick himself up. Having reverted to his human shape, he crawled through the sand. Blearily following the scent of blood, he happened across something that was equally pleasant and disturbing: his severed hand. He snatched it up and pressed it back in place. Sand coated the exposed joint and ligaments. When he pressed it firmly to where it belonged, the granules intensified the pain many times over. He bellowed and roared in anguish, while more blood pushed out tiny stone impurities.

Alexander bolted to the sound of his wailing. Still in hound form, he panted, frightened that he might be too late. It seemed he was by the look of his friend knelt on the ground. The bleeding would not stop from either of Jack's horrible wounds.

He whined. "Where's Adwen!"

Catching his breath while shuddering, Jack muttered through clenched teeth, "Cujo's with her. Don't worry about us. Find Kale." Another bout of tremors wracked him into silence.

Alexander spotted the giant werewolf loping toward the mouth of the river. Darkness radiated from him and trailed in his wake. Giving Jack a final glance, Alexander did as his friend had asked.

Kale maintained his precarious altered state. It would not last much longer. The blood loss made everything increasingly difficult. He was beginning to feel pain again. It was a sure indicator that the power he needed was diminishing rapidly. A manlike presence came alongside, and he recognized the mind and scent of Alexander.

The warrior smelled werewolf blood before he saw it. A fount of red fell like water from the gargantuan beast. Alexander barked for Kale's attention: "Kale, where are you going?"

Werewolf jaws big enough to bite him in half turned to face him in a flash, snarling. Both froze in place gazing at each other. The Marine did not know what to make of the look in his large carnivorous stare. The tone was angry, but Alexander sensed pain and desperation.

"We still have a job to do!"

Glancing at the dam at the river's mouth, the yellow hound's ears flattened. Then he nodded in acknowledgment.

Kale growled deeply and raced ahead. At reaching the crude dam, he summoned the unearthly strength to leap. He sailed upward and landed atop a ledge. His ears picked up the sound of wind howling through the black rocks, as well as the sloshing of deep waters. The mist stopped coursing from his body, but he snarled, fighting to make it return. It did, and he faced the cleaved stone forming the dam.

More darkness fell from his form as he approached. With incredible force, Kale drove both sets of claws into the stone. After anchoring himself, he summoned all his power, roaring from the strain. Black mist rushed into the crevices, drilling into the rock. Dark energy traced fissures through the stone. A cracking sound followed.

Kale fell quiet, the last of the dark power spent. Feeling weak, he pulled his claws free to limp away. The altered state was gone, leaving him to face the pain. It was overwhelming.

Even more cracking came, as the water pressure became too much for the fatally fractured dam. It burst in gushing torrents. The power of the flow began to wear at the ledge where he stood. More cracks appeared under the wounded werewolf. Resisting the disabling weakness, he jumped free of the black rocks.

Kale sailed far through the air. When he hit the ground, he landed on his feet but stumbled and collapsed. His body shriveled to its more human form just as Alexander arrived.

The yellow Holy Hound knelt low, nose close to Kale's face. The Marine watched him for a moment. It was unclear if he should be moved. When Kale smiled and spoke, Alexander was encouraged, but only a little.

Kale tried to chuckle but did not have the strength. "Hey, Yankee. Don't worry about me. Check on the others. I'll be fine."

"You can't even move."

The smile flickered before he murmured, "Just help me up. I can walk."

Alexander stared for a moment. "You're such a liar."

Kale's reassuring smile disappeared. His red eyes were forlorn.

Using big hands, Alexander carefully scooped Kale up and started back to where the others were waiting.

Kale whispered, "Thank you."

"No problem."

Placing Blame

Vast pillars stretched upward out of sight in the darkness. Spherical cages of black metal floated like chandeliers. Spikes jutted inward at glowing green orbs emitting soft sounds like sobs of great suffering. The cries of the damned went unanswered. The torturous cages were so great in number that they formed a nebulous cloud. Theirs was the only light in this temple of the Void.

Impurus's feet, soaked with his blood, slapped against the cold black stone floor below the cages. The shredded membranes of his wings dragged, leaving a trail of purple smears. Pointed teeth clenched in a ravenous scowl, the monster walked to the end of the grand hall. Pain from the wounds enflamed his rage. When he came to the sweeping Altar of Shadow, he knelt out of formality, as well as succumbing to his injuries. His body wanted to buckle into a ball, yet he took a knee instead.

He bowed his head. Then he sneered, venom in his words. "You said I would be powerful. You promised me the death of the creatures of light."

The hall was silent, and the altar remained still.

Rage and anguish brought on almost violent tremors. He shook, eyes burning bright as he raised his head and spat, "I want their heads! I want what is rightfully mine! Give me more power!"

A flawless hand of dark energy materialized on the loftiest tier of the altar. The giant hand pressed its forefinger and thumb together, then snapped. The sound echoed over and over in the impossibly vast space. A black shadow appeared on one side of the altar near the top tier. A whip streaked through the air and cracked, striking Impurus across the face.

He bellowed in pain and surprise. The cut nearly removed

the side of his jaw. Demon flesh hung as an oozing flap, quivering pitifully like his tattered wings. Recovering from the shock, Impurus glared sidelong, bracing for more lashings.

At last, a smooth voice replied, sounding almost sweet: "You have been given those things. Clearly, it is you who has failed to hold your end of the bargain; the death of the child from the Gray Kingdom for power beyond your comprehension. By the look of you, it is your own incompetence that is to blame."

The hand snapped again. The lash flew. It ripped a piece of purple flesh from Impurus's broad chest, making the servant of darkness howl in agony. His face twisted into a vengeful sneer. "You broke your end of our bargain! You! You told me I would be all powerful!"

Another snap of the giant hand, and yet another lash strike carved a piece of flesh from the other side of his chest. This rendered Impurus silent.

The voice from the deepest shadows crooned, "I said no such thing. You were promised power beyond your comprehension. It is the measure of your own comprehension that limits you. Being a fool will not help in this endeavor."

Mad with pain and anger, Impurus shouted at the top of his voice. Spit flew from his lips. "How is it possible for me to be bested by a rogue?"

The hand was about to snap again, but paused.

"A rogue?"

Impurus screamed, having lost almost all sense. "A rogue!"

A broad shadow formed beyond the giant hand. It and four other figures materialized to join the entity brandishing the cruel whip. The tall collection of shadows stared with white specks for eyes, drilling into the bloody servant. Impurus's form was the size of a kitten in comparison to their dreadful visage. A little more detail was visible as they revealed their mask-like faces. Their appearances were like that of various deadly creatures from the living worlds compiled into one. Wings, hands, claws, stingers, fangs and tentacles gave each demon lord unique forms, matching each of their terrible natures.

Degah'lee toyed with his whip at his station on the huge altar, savoring the suffering he had inflicted. It would not be long before he was given the order to use it again.

The giant among giant demons gazed down from the deepest

shadows. "What was the rogue's name? Give it to me."

Becoming hesitant for a change, Impurus stuttered, "I-I don't know it."

The giant-handed entity snapped. Degah'lee lashed him again.

When more howls of misery ceased, the sinister being with a sweet voice asked another question: "Did the rogue do this to you?"

Sneering, he replied, "Yes ... after ripping my Boneworm apart like a toy!"

A deep rumbling filled the air. Everything became still in the wake of the wrath that emanated from the largest entity atop the altar. Each demon lord froze, eyeing one another while their master studied each of them in turn.

As the rumbling ended, Impurus was bold enough to grin. "Which one of you fools let him out? Who's to blame for this? It's certainly not me."

A tense hush fell over them. Then the overlord snapped yet again, and Degah'lee was glad to oblige. This time, Impurus crumpled to the floor. His face pressed down into the stones, while the pain became more than he could bear.

None of the demon lords was foolish enough to glance at their leader. Only they had the power to create demons from damned souls. The overlord would either find the one responsible or simply choose a scapegoat at random. Silence on the altar grew thick. Even the lords were unsure what would be done in answer to this revelation of a rogue demon.

When their leader spoke at last, the demon lord covered in venomous barbs and dripping blades flinched.

"Nephalos."

"Yes, my master."

"You are my Weaver of schemes, are you not? So too are you responsible for keeping watch over our domains. Tell me, what is the state of our holds in Dargadia?"

Summoning an orb made of darkness, Nephalos clutched the edges with many mismatched spider-like appendages. Visions of territories with pillars blinked into sight. At first, they saw the monoliths untouched and intact. But then images of those that had fallen came into view, and all the demon lords wailed in outrage.

Their master hissed softy, and the lords fell silent.

After a few seconds, their leader crooned softly, "Nephalos?"

"Yes, my master?"

One of the overlord's smooth hands snatched a cluster of Nephalos' insectoid appendages and ripped them off. Black fluids sprayed from the wounds as the being screamed and writhed. Dega-h'lee and the others smiled to themselves in amusement.

The overlord turned to the Reaper among his court. "Kahli'nah?"

"Yes, my master?" the demon lord answered with tentacles waving in anticipation. He was rarely summoned for a hunt and relished the opportunity.

"Where is the daughter of the Gray Kingdom and this unknown rogue?"

Kahli'nah grinned. "At once, my master." The demon lord held up a pair of spindly hands, summoning an orb of pale colors to peer into the worlds. Before the scrying ritual could form the slightest image, the orb burst and dissipated.

All the demons were shocked and hissed in unison.

"They cannot be scryed, my master. Something hides them from our sight."

Lifting his head from the ground, Impurus glowered. "The rogue."

They looked to the pitiful mess at their feet and listened.

"I underestimated him because he can conceal his power. His presence cannot be sensed except by mortal means."

The lords exchanged glances before turning to the overlord. Deep in contemplation, the entity said nothing.

Kahli'nah could not resist the challenge this hunt posed. "Mortal means are not beyond my skill. They shall be found."

"No."

The Reaper paused in his plotting.

"If they are not to be found swiftly, then there are better ways to move."

"But, my master, I can find them swiftly."

Once the overlord's gaze locked with the Reaper's there was tension, but their master made no move to exact punishment.

"We are not all powerful in the living worlds yet. Lest you forget, we must account for that orderly element of time."

They sneered in frustration.

"Waste not one second. In the proper moment, those who stand against us shall fall into our hands. There is no need to hunt what will willingly walk into our grasp. Nephalos?"

The bleeding stopped, and the appendages were growing back. "Yes, my master?"

"Degah'lee?"

"Yes, master?"

"I have work for you both. Weave new plans to intertwine with what is already in place. Account for the rogue's involvement with the light child."

"How shall you wish it done, master?" Nephalos asked.

"The plans are already in motion. They cannot be stopped. I sense that the truth may be uncovered by these pawns very soon. Set the stage. Make those puppets dance for me."

They both replied, "Yes, my master."

"Tetalong."

The Whisperer's many tongues wriggled in monstrous mouths. "Yes, my master?"

"Continue your work. Cultivate the desirables and inform me once they are ready."

The demon lord bowed and vanished.

"Degah'lee?"

"Yes, master?"

"Use your power. Root out the name given to the rogue by the black lake from whence he was made. If it is spoken, I want that knowledge. Find it for me."

For once, Degah'lee was pleased that the rogue could not be scryed. With a single look at him or by learning his name, the overlord would instantly identify his maker. Prepared to disobey, Degah'lee bowed deeply. "Yes, my master. It shall be done."

Glancing at another lord, draped in a mantle of disease, the overlord sighed, "Loflamel."

Cackling, the demon lord answered, "Yes, my master?"

"I want entertainment; bring more before my feet. I long for sweet music of misery."

"At once, my master!" The entity happily vanished to collect a troop from among the damned.

Alone by the Overlord, Kali'nah was left without work once again. Angry, the shadow being glared at the brutalized abomination

Impurus.

"Master?"

"Yes, my Reaper?"

"What would you prefer I do? This insect is useless. Shall I dispose of him?"

Impurus snarled in indignation.

"No. Have him repaired in the lake. Set him loose once it is done. His work is not finished. There is much more Impurus must do for my pleasure."

Disappointed at being given a menial chore, Kali'nah hissed, then bowed and vanished in a swirl of shadows. Impurus vanished with him.

Alone on the altar pinnacle, the darkest shadow reveled.

"I am hate. I am seduction and despair. I am Umbradonus."

Chapter 17
-If

The battle had begun at sunset and ended before night had fallen. The Holy Hounds followed the newly freed river's flow. Oryn and Alexander remained as hound warriors to carry Adwen and Kale. Their wounds still bled but much more slowly.

Jack's bleeding also had eased, but the dark sword made healing very difficult. Where Impurus had struck him was sore. It hurt to breathe, indicating the likelihood of a broken rib or two. If not for his armor, he would have been cut in half. Jack's entire side felt excruciating – his likely broken ribs, the deep slice above his shoulder, and the severed hand he held in place with his other hand. He still couldn't feel the severed hand and feared it would not reattach. Every step hurt, as did each breath of crisp arid air. Yet he plodded alongside the ten-foot brown hound carrying Adwen and the eight-foot yellow hound bearing the unconscious werewolf.

Jack stepped on shifting sand and wobbled. The sudden effort to keep balanced began a domino effect, irritating each injury in his body. Gasping, Jack crumpled to his knees. A canine yelp escaped him from the jarring sensation. There he bent over quivering.

The others stopped, and Alexander whined, "Hey, Bad Dog. We must keep moving. Do you need to be carried?"

"No, Big Dog," he murmured trying not to breathe too deeply. "I just need a minute."

Oryn wanted to keep moving more than any of them but chose to grant their companion a brief reprieve. He desperately wanted to get Adwen to the palace. Looking at her unconscious in his armor-plated arms, he felt grateful to the werewolf for rescuing her yet again. The knight had not seen how or when, but the demon was able to drive off Impurus. With this, he could convince himself to trust Kale a little more.

Ready to get on his feet again, Jack braced himself for the pain of standing. But he froze when something strange caught his attention. A small mound of sand rose up beside him and meandered about the feet of the others. He and his companions watched two more join it. The mounts erupted, and Sand Imps sprang out wearing goggles. Their leader removed his goggles to examine the abashed warriors. The little creature looked relieved to see them.

"We have a message from the palace: Follow the river; do not leave its banks."

Oryn growled angrily, "We have no time for games. The palace is not near the lake!"

But the imp insisted, "This is a mission, not a game. You must trust us. Follow the river as far as the lake. It is better this way."

The enormous hound's jaws wrinkled in a dangerous snarl.

Unafraid, the imp became irritated. "Do you want a place to keep her and your friends safe and warm?"

Oryn stopped snarling.

"Then do them a favor and trust an imp."

As quick as they appeared, the Sand Imp readjusted his goggles, and the three dove into the sand. The warriors exchanged uncertain glances.

They walked throughout the night. They took breaks for Jack to rest whenever his injuries hobbled him. As they continued toward the lake, Jack's mind grew numb to his agony, and his strength waned.

At dawn they approached within view of the lake as they climbed over another sand dune. At the bottom of the lake bed, the water level rose steadily. Light danced on the ripples like winking stars. No one marveled at the success of their mission. Instead, the warriors pressed forward. Desert plants clung to life through the recent drought. Hardy trees and vegetation formed a tiny forest. Once they passed through part of the lake's wilted surroundings, they stumbled upon a stretch of beach. Humans were there – hundreds.

Peoples from the three desert kingdoms mingled as they gathered water from the rising lake. They used ropes to reach down muddy slicks with big jugs. In teams, the humans cycled jugs down, filled them and pulled them up. They loaded the containers onto carts, drawn by emaciated oxen or horses.

The warriors watched the scene for a moment before the humans spotted them. Shouts rang out. Many men and women gathered close to watch as a few ran toward the tall beasts.

Oryn and Alexander prepared for the worst. Jack struggled to force his exhausted mind to attune to those of the humans. It was impossible to interpret language by telepathy, but sensing their emotional state would indicate their intent. The armed men drew closer, and Jack sensed uncertainty and fear despite their fearsome expressions.

The hardened humans halted a few yards away, gritting their teeth, brandishing dull weapons. Their intense stares wandered over the large dog-like creatures wearing armor and holding unconscious companions. The biggest among them was far larger than any Minotaur and bared his teeth, green eyes glowing. The injured man on his feet between them wore similar armor. As they waited for the inhuman creatures to attack, nothing happened. The inaction brought confusion.

At last, one of the men saw Adwen's face lulling in the crook of the colossal beast's arms. Jack felt relief at sensing the recognition as the man began to tell the others. The men quickly understood that these strange beings were responsible for restoring the river. Gritty expressions turned to pleasant surprise. The men put away their weapons and beckoned the Holy Hounds, urging them to follow.

Oryn and Alexander gave Jack suspicious looks.

"They recognize us. And they're happy."

Ceasing his snarling, the knight trusted Jack.

Right away the humans told others who these strangers were and what they had done. Most watched quietly. Many of the people who had been in the mob in Bebidin were gathered here and now gazed at the warriors in shame. The men brought a cart for water jugs that was full and offered a ride for the Holy Hounds. Oryn placed Adwen's limp form on the cart before climbing on. His transformation made some onlookers gasp.

The men hesitated to accept Kale's body, but Alexander threw a firm look with ears pinned back. They conceded and placed the werewolf on the cart. Alexander helped Jack onto the cart, transformed and joined them. The driver pulled on the oxen's reins and shouted for it to go.

No one spoke. Occasional jostling of the cart made Jack wince. Their weary gazes never locked. What thoughts came to mind stayed private.

Oryn, sitting beside Adwen, had a mixture of feelings. Seeing her alive brought relief, but the large sword wound in her middle filled him with anger and regret; he could not protect her. If not for the rogue demon, she would be gone.

As the cart approached the city gates, the knight looked at Kale for more than a passing glance. It was then that he saw Kale's wound in detail. His expression grew stern as he studied the familiar hole. As far as he knew, Impurus had not stabbed the werewolf. So how did Kale receive a blow identical to Adwen's? The answer took the knight to a bitter conclusion, and he scowled.

Entering the gates and passing through the mostly empty city, the cart eventually reached the palace. What appeared to be all the Minotaur guards and the Grand Chief waited to receive the warriors. He looked pleased.

As soon as the cart stopped by the horned assembly, Oryn took Adwen into his arms. He shot Kale a venomous look. It felt good to move her further from that creature. The knight climbed down first, and Alexander helped Jack do the same. Two Minotaurs offered to carry Adwen, but Oryn did not let them take her. Alexander lifted Kale. Bringing him to the edge, he offered him to the burly guards. The instant they recognized the werewolf, they flinched, snorting in fear. This reaction angered the Marine.

"What is your malfunction? He killed the Boneworm!"

Confused looks came over them.

Then a booming voice belonging to the captain rang out, "Carry him, you cowards! You owe that one your lives!"

Hesitantly, one of the Minotaurs took Kale. Only then was Alexander free to climb down and follow his friends into the palace.

It was still morning. The sun rose higher, filling the rooms with light. Alexander and the Minotaur carrying Kale marched along the corridors. Some of the ancient statues raised their heads a little to watch. Others only followed with their eyes.

They entered a chamber, where Adwen lay on a soft bed.

Jack sat on another nearby, while healers attended to his wounds. The Marine motioned for the guard to take Kale to the third sickbed across the room.

Oryn snarled, catching everyone unawares. The knight's green gaze burned as he scowled. Alexander returned the look. To the Minotaur, he firmly instructed, "Put him on the bed. Thank you for your help."

A terrible rumbling growl carried on even after the guard left.

When the bull-man departed, Alexander rounded on Oryn snarling, "Do you have a major malfunction?"

"I don't want that thing near her!"

The men and women attending Jack were nervous with all the snarling and growling. But then Jack barked, making them recoil, "Are you kidding, Cujo? What's your problem now?"

Too frightened to continue, the healers scurried out and left the quarreling creatures alone.

Watching them leave, Jack snapped, "That's your fault too, I hope you know. Have an issue with Kale? Spit it out."

Oryn stood by Adwen's bedside and pointed accusingly at Kale.

"That monster is no willing servant. His wound is hers; what harm is done to her is done to him in turn. Their lives are tied as one."

Alexander glowered. "What's your point?"

Bitterly, Oryn sneered, "I had thought his loyalty honorable for a brief time. But now I see that loyalty on his part is but a ruse. He came to her aide only because he had no choice. If she dies, then so does he!"

Forgetting his own pain, Jack was aghast and outraged. "Are you serious? Cujo, you are being a complete moron! How is that any different from us? How does that make him any different from me?"

Jack was right, but the knight still glared.

"We all felt her pain when that happened, right? That's probably how he knew she needed help. Kale is one of us. Or is this whole thing just jealousy that he can share more of her burden and saved her when you couldn't?"

Alexander thought that would have sent the knight's temper over the edge. It did not. Oryn maintained a stern glare with Jack. Perhaps his suspicions were faulty, or perhaps not. Either way, Kale was a demon given to deceit.

With a firm tone, he called, "Alexander."

The Marine frowned, wondering what Oryn wanted.

"You and I have hunting to do," the knight commanded firmly. "Once my strength is restored, I will return to heal her. You shall find what you and Jack need." Then he turned on his heel and marched out into the halls.

As much as Alexander did not want to go with him, he knew it was necessary. He looked at Jack.

Jack nodded. "I'll keep an eye on them."

That was a welcome statement. It released him to join Oryn for a hunt.

The healers had not fled far. They returned and applied numbing herbs and bandages to Jack's wounds. A cloth sling cradled his arm, and a tight bandage bound his hand in place. He thought he could feel a little in the fingertips. Jack lay down and closed his eyes.

Adwen's bed stood in the brightest place and Kale's in the darkest. The light helped Adwen a little. At the least, the daylight stopped the loss of silvery blood. When her bleeding ceased, so did Kale's. Both were in a bad state, yet stable. Oryn and Alexander hunted all day and into the evening. Large prey was scarce.

Late in the evening, pain woke Jack. His salves had worn off. He eased his eyes open and watched light from a tiny candle dance on the pale walls. A servant apparently left it on a table. Sensing movement beyond the candle flame, Jack turned his head. They were no longer alone in the room.

Three women entered the chamber. At first, Jack thought they were servants, but their clothing style was not of the desert cultures. A redhead, a blonde and a black-haired woman in pure white robes approached the beds. How they had gotten past the Minotaur guards was beyond Jack.

The redhead stood at the head of Kale's bed, while the blonde knelt low beside him. As Jack watched, the strange blonde leaned in close, giving the unconscious werewolf a gentle kiss on the cheek. She then stroked his head before standing again.

The black-haired woman in robes stood by Adwen. She touched his unconscious leader lightly on her brow, smiling.

Jack was about to sit up, but all three women looked at him in unison with pleasant expressions. The mysterious black-haired woman elegantly placed a finger to her lips in the gesture meaning to say nothing. Then all three vanished.

After the women, spirits or whatever they were had vanished into thin air, Jack knew he needed to check on Adwen. There would be no going back to sleep with this pain and the strange visitation, so he sat next to her bed.

Adwen awoke. Opening her eyes, she saw Jack sitting in a chair beside her. She could have sworn there was a hand on her forehead a moment before. Adwen could barely move.

"How are you feeling?" Jack asked.

A faint smile flickered on her face. "Like a train wreck. Where is Oryn? Where is Kale?"

"Cujo took Alexander to get food so he can heal you himself. The big guy is asleep over there."

She was glad to hear. "Good. Is the river flowing?"

"Yes. And the people are a lot less hostile."

"That's not surprising."

"The imps arranged for us to meet a crowd by the lake so they would know it was us who got the river flowing. I think I like these imps better now than when they were goblins."

Her eyes glinted. "Me too." Sudden pain made her cringe and hold her breath.

"Do you want me to get the healers?"

Recovering, she reassured him, "No, it's alright; only a twinge."

"You know that Kale's hurt?"

A somber light appeared in her now distant stare. "Yes."

"He's tied to you big-time. Is that a failsafe?"

Looking over, she replied, "No. It is because my heart is physically connected with him. All of you are bound to my heart, but his link is more direct."

Jack frowned. "I saw him when he killed the worm. He didn't need to fight Impurus; he had that bastard running scared like he'd seen the bogeyman."

Adwen's expression was blank.

"Something happened to him out there," Jack stated with finality. "If he could have done that in the fights before, he would have.

That means this battle was different. I know you know what I'm talking about."

Her gaze drifted back to the ceiling, dancing with candlelight. She refused to answer.

He felt more concerned. "I like the big guy, but I'm worried about him."

The truth of his words got through, and she returned his look. "Please, Adwen, tell me something, anything."

She became stern. "You cannot speak a word of this."

"That's a deal. I'm not breaking this promise."

She knew he would not. "He gave in a little."

"What do you mean?"

"When Degah'lee attacked us at the castle, he was trying to make Kale his servant, as he had intended from the start. He failed when he created Kale because his heart has too much light. For him to become a real demon, his heart must break and turn dark; his darkness must become greater than his light.

"The darkness Degah'lee has infused into him is immense, but it still isn't enough to break Kale. Now the one way for him to fall is if he gives in. When Impurus hurt me, Kale realized what happened to all of us and snapped. For a moment, he hated Impurus for it. That was how he was able to temporarily become like a true demon."

Jack swore under his breath.

"But once the reason for the hatred was gone, the darkness started to subside. While in that state, he had to use all his power to resist the darkness. He cannot allow it to control him."

The warrior did not like where this was going. "Or what?"

"While in that state, if he kills anything or anyone harboring even a shred of humanity, then some of his own will die. This has happened to him before. I sense it in his heart as a horrible aching regret. He thinks of it again and again to remind himself not to allow it to repeat."

Jack frowned, recalling the memory he had stumbled upon during his intrusion into Kale's mind – the look in his eyes when he lunged for those teens was horrible. His face was different back then – he was very young. Jack knew that the humans in that memory did not live long after killing Kale's only friend.

Jack grew more worried. "Is there anything you can do?"

"I already have. My heart bound to him gives a little more control and ability to resist, but not much. Beyond that, this struggle is his burden to bear."

"Can I do anything for him?"

"You're already doing that. Be his friend."

Jack was bemused.

"It is hard on him, but having more to care about and feeling cared for helps," she explained. "The darkness makes these feelings bittersweet. Nothing can feel truly good. Fears and doubts try to poison them. All we've done to counter this has helped so much already."

Jack scoffed. "Oryn isn't helping much."

Adwen sighed. "I know."

"I understand why Oryn acts this way after what happened to him as a kid, but it's going to put him and Kale at odds."

Then she wore a tiny smile. "Don't worry. Kale and Oryn are no threat to each other."

Glancing sidelong at Kale, Jack replied, "There's no way I'm telling Cujo any of this. He's aching for a reason to get rid of Kale."

Adwen reassured the warrior: "Oryn will come around eventually."

Jack turned sarcastic. "Really?"

"He will. I promise."

He smiled, shaking his head. "I don't think that's your promise to keep."

"No. Oryn will keep it for me."

"So, if Kale does turn darker, how will we know?"

Her smile faded. "We all will know if it happens. Your promise to say nothing about this includes Alex."

"Why?"

"It would change the way he looks at Kale, and Kale senses how others perceive him. What happened in the desert scared him. It still does. He's terrified. He doesn't want to lose friends, especially not to fear. Never let him know you are aware of this. Should he realize you know, then he is likely to distance himself. Acting as if the darkness is not there is his only tool."

Jack nodded. "Pretending to be normal to feel normal."

"I'm very tired," she said.

"Me too. Let's get some rest."

"Jack?"

"Yeah?"

She beamed at him. "Thank you for being a good friend for Kale."

He shrugged and instantly regretted it as his wound ached. Then he added, smiling, "What can I say? I like having the British hairball running with us."

She could not agree more.

Tingling warmth woke Kale. Strength flooded his body as soon as it began. Dull soreness gave way under the push of warm energy. Opening his eyes, he saw barely any light from the weak glow of dawn outside. He smelled that he was not alone and rolled his head to look.

Kale could tell Jack had been here but was no longer. Across the room, Adwen lay asleep with Oryn at her side. Pale green magic flowed from his fingertips, healing the wound in her abdomen. The knight's magic simultaneously healed Kale's wound. Looking down at the bloody hole in his own middle, he watched the flesh continue to mend. He felt strong enough to stand and got onto his feet. Like a ghost, Kale left the room to walk the halls.

Oryn heard something and turned toward the chamber entry. He glimpsed the werewolf's red jacket and boot heels as they disappeared. It seemed that healing her also healed Kale's echo wound. Thinking briefly on Jack's words, Oryn wondered if he had been jealous. No, but perhaps Jack was right about one thing: He was wrong to suspect Kale based on the conditions of his link to Adwen. Either way, he would continue to watch this rogue demon closely.

In walking the silent halls, Kale found some solace. After the battle with the Boneworm, he wished to stay away from the Holy Hounds. He did not want to be seen in his current state. It had felt horrible and wonderful and painful and awesome. Though he could not understand how it happened, Kale knew he had been like a demon, a real one. The thought made his heart sick.

The memory of the first time he had come close to becoming a true demon made him sicker. Once it had started, he lost control. He decided long ago to never allow it to happen again. Yet it did. Darkness took him. He had let it happen. That idea made Kale sickest of all. He stopped for a moment, realizing he was letting despair get the better.

Taking a deep breath, Kale relaxed, pushing the dark feelings back. Just as he did, he glimpsed a mirror. His reflection broke his meditative rest, and he was apprehensive. Going closer, he inspected his face. Finding everything the same as before, relief melted the tension. All the same, Kale still studied the face that did not truly belong to him. A blank, sad expression looked back. Red glowing irises shone with sorrow. How much further could he go? How long could he resist without falling to the darkness inside?

A presence appeared in a nearby doorway. The expression in the reflection turned harsh. Smelling Minotaur and magic, Kale knew it was the Grand Chief before he turned to look. He gave the Guardian a bitter stare for spying.

Gargeth pretended not to notice the hostility. "It is good to see you well this morning."

Kale did not stop glaring.

"I know what it is you fear."

He made a harsh scoff. "Is that so?"

"I know what it is you fear better than even you do."

Realizing the Guardian spoke the truth, Kale's resentment crumbled, and he felt weak. "What do you want from me?"

After a silent moment, the Grand Chief replied, "When Adwen is well enough, I need to speak with her and have all of you meet with me."

When the big beast turned his horns to leave, Kale's fear got the better of him.

"It's not about me, is it?"

Gargeth paused. Glancing back, the Minotaur shook his head. Kale gasped with relief, hanging his head.

While Gargeth continued away, Kale looked to the mirror. The intense emotions had made the whites of his eyes turn black. Those weren't werewolf eyes; they were demon eyes. Seeing them made him ache. Kale's clawed fists clenched. He could barely stand the sight. Anger compounded on itself until he started to shudder, tears swelling. Kale growled at the demon that was himself. In a fit of emotions, he raised a fist to destroy the reflection.

But the instant before he could swing, he froze. His eyes filled with tears from all the pain in his heart. Seeing his own tender misery stalled the urge to strike. Restraining a sob, Kale turned away. A few deep breaths helped. Growing steady, he relaxed and opened his fists. Drying his eyes, Kale surprised himself by giving the mirror a final look. It appeared as if he had never been crying. With a guise of calm, it was time to find the others.

Oryn had just finished mending Adwen's wound when she awoke.

Seeing him, she smiled. "Hi."

The knight was pleased to have healed her. As she sat upright, Jack and Alexander returned. The short warrior took off the last of his bandages, along with the sling. Well-fed and healed, he worked his hand to test it.

Adwen called to him, "How's the hand?"

He scoffed. "I can feel it, for one. And it doesn't hurt either. Can't wait to use it on that waste of space called Impurus."

"Glad to hear."

Just before the warrior could ask for Kale's whereabouts, the werewolf entered with hands in his pockets. Everyone except Oryn smiled.

Jack greeted him warmly, clapping a hand on his shoulder. "Hey, Big Guy! It's good to have you back."

Kale stared a moment, filled with happiness at the honesty behind the gesture, but said nothing.

Jack was surprised by the reaction as Kale was beaming, apparently lost in thought. "Uh, did you have something to say?"

The werewolf recollected himself. "Yeah, I got a message. The Grand Chief wants a word with Adwen and us. It must be important."

Oryn gave Adwen a searching look, and she reassured him, "I'm much better now. We shouldn't keep the Grand Chief waiting."

When the Holy Hounds entered the throne room, the guards closed the doors. Bright daylight filtered down the skylight, and Gargeth sat on his throne of many cushions. He nodded to Adwen and her warriors.

"Everyone here is grateful for your efforts," he told them. "Unrest is quelled for now, and survival in the desert is possible again for these people and my kin."

The leader of the Sand Imps emerged through a hidden door, chuckling. "And my scouts have searched the area where the battle took place. All remnants of the Boneworm are to be purified so that it cannot reform - at least, not from those bones. You did good work, mighty storm."

Kale huffed indignantly.

To keep the imp quiet, Gargeth resumed speaking: "Lady Adwen, you need a way to continue this fight against the demons. For that, you must make a journey far north."

"I'm grateful for your assistance. What are you suggesting?"

He paused before saying, "The Dragon Mother."

The Holy Hounds were confused and concerned, but Kale smiled and laughed.

"Of course!" Kale became excited. "That's perfect. Why didn't I think of that?"

"Find the Dragon Mother. Gain her favor, and she can help you."

Adwen hesitated. "I don't mean to be rude, but why do we want help from an ancient dragon?"

Gargeth smiled at Kale. "Would you like to explain?"

"Yeah." He was excited. "When this world was born, the first being made was a dragon. She was sent to fly and breathe into the barren earth. Her first breath struck in the heart of what is Dargadia. That is why magic is strongest there.

"Out of the ashes sprang magic, manifesting into more forms. The first were the firebirds and unicorns. The unicorns were most important. It was those children of the Dragon Mother's fire that sowed life. They are considered sacred even to the dragons. Any of their kin found to have hunted or killed one were exiled or worse. Most get their wings ripped off."

Adwen did not like the sound of how fearsome they were, but liked the idea of getting help. "So, she might be able to break this binding on me? Or help Dargadia with fire?"

Kale shrugged, grinning. "It's worth a shot."

She looked to Gargeth for reassurance.

"I have told you all that I may," the Grand Chief said. "These things are for you to decide."

She sighed. "We need help. If we don't get all the help we can, then there isn't much we can do."

Kale interjected, "Wait a tick."

They looked to him expectantly.

A clever smile came over the werewolf. "I know someone. They would probably love to lend a hand."

Jack gave him a look.

"No pun intended, I assure you."

Kale sparked Adwen's curiosity: "Where can we find this person?"

"In the other world, in a city."

They waited quietly as Adwen weighed the options. Should they proceed straight for the mountains or make a detour for a potential ally? She felt compelled to seek this new ally.

Becoming certain, Adwen nodded. "We'll find your friend. After that, we can go to the mountains together."

Gargeth was pleased.

The leader of the Sand Imps called for her attention. "There is a world gate you may use."

"Really? That's great!"

"My imps stumbled upon it in a hidden chamber under the palace. It seems the tunnel door mechanism was broken. I had them repair it just in case."

"Thank you so much, Chief."

The Sand Imp cackled mischievously. "No problem."

Chapter 18
THE CORNER

The portal opened atop a forest-covered mountain. Passing into the non-magical world severed Adwen's connection with Dargadia and the influence of the evil binding. Power surged within her heart, and her body shimmered. Light robes and cloth became armor. Her warriors felt their own strength restored to normal. She and three of her warriors transformed their attire into clothing to better blend into this world.

Kale waited for her to finish manifesting a blouse and jeans before saying anything. "Everyone ready?"

"Where do we need to go?"

Sniffing the air, he chuckled in amusement. "That portal must have been made just for this occasion. We're here."

Alexander shrugged. "Where's here?"

"Where you can meet an old acquaintance of mine." Turning to Oryn, he added, "You might take a liking to him."

The knight scowled. This did not dampen Kale's spirits.

A nearby hiking trail led down the mountain to a vast city surrounding the island of trees. An odd feeling nagged at Jack and Alexander. Suspicions intensified when they reached the trailhead and started along a roadside. Noticing familiar landmarks, Jack stopped. Alexander also froze.

"Hold on for one pea-picking minute, Big Guy!" Jack told Kale.

Adwen, Oryn and Kale looked back.

While the Marine stared at the werewolf in astonishment, the cop wore an accusing expression. "Can I ask one question?"

Confused, Kale's brow furrowed. "Sure."

"Care to explain why we are looking for your friend in San Francisco?"

"Because he lives here."

"What's the matter?" Adwen asked, failing to understand the issue.

Jack and Alexander exchanged looks. "How long ago were you here with this acquaintance?"

Kale was uncertain. "I thought there was only one question."

"Alexander, Ashley and I have lived in San Francisco for a little over two years."

It was the werewolf's turn to be perplexed. "Oh." Then he chuckled and shrugged. "Funny, that." Smiling and chuckling, he continued to lead them into the city.

"Where is this person and what's his name?" Jack asked.

"He goes by Vaughn. Probably not his real name. You'll have to wait and see where that clever blighter stays. I'm sure it'll be a big surprise for you, beastie cop."

If Jack had not grown to like Kale, he would be irate at evasiveness. As for this Vaughn character, the two warriors wondered what he was more than who he was. Perhaps Vaughn was a spirit who kept him company when not out hunting for the dregs of society. Whoever or whatever Vaughn was, Kale seemed thrilled to introduce him.

The companions walked many blocks into the city. Late in the afternoon, they entered a dreary district. Tension in the air alluded to harsh living. Despite the danger to humans, pedestrians wandered freely among the many bars and small businesses. Shadows flooded the city, and sunshine made rooftops glow in the sunset.

Jack grumbled, "Couldn't we have just taken a cab? I have cash."

Kale smiled. "Any cab that stops within four blocks of here is watched. I want our visit to be a surprise, so I chose a route that skirted surveillance." He stopped on the sloping sidewalk atop a steep stairway into a basement-like suite. It was as dark as night at the bottom.

"This is the place."

Adwen spied a faded sign with no light to illuminate it. "The Corner. Is this a private club?"

This got a chuckled from Kale. "The most private in the

city."

As they joined him, Oryn caught the scent before anyone else and snarled, "Vampires!"

Everyone gave the knight startled glances and stared at Kale for an explanation.

He was nonchalant. "What?" The werewolf shrugged. "Did you expect a killer rabbit?" Chuckling at the poor joke, Kale descended the steps.

Adwen and her friends exchanged disturbed expressions. When the men ended up staring at her in unison, she shrugged. "Why are you all looking at me?"

Alexander replied, "Did you know about his friend being a vampire?"

The answer was honest and her tone befuddled: "Not a clue. Can't say I'm surprised. Let's see how this turns out."

Kale waited for them at the door. His gaze traveled across its surface studying familiar imperfections. This was the one place he knew as a home. No matter how cold the metal door was to the touch, it always felt warm and welcoming to him. When the others reached the bottom of the stairs, Kale held out a hand to stop them. Adwen and her warriors wore questioning looks.

"Wait a tick," Kale told them. "Charlie watches the door. He's a jumpy bugger, but he's sweet; wouldn't hurt a fly. You lot would give him a heart attack."

Jack disliked vampires in general and knew their hearts did not beat. "No pun intended?"

Still in good spirits, Kale chuckled. "Sorry, that was intentional." Ready to see familiar faces at last, he knocked three times on the peep hatch.

A moment later a voice shouted from the other side. "Who the hell is that? We aren't open yet, you sorry leeches!"

The Holy Hounds were not expecting an abrasive response. Once they saw Kale's reaction, they determined that he didn't either. Kale froze holding his breath. That was not Charlie. He pounded on the door harder, eager for an explanation.

More shouting followed. "I said, get lost, leeches! We aren't open yet!" Then the peep door slid open, and a set of angry black eyes peered out. "Don't make me say it again or ..." The moment the vampire saw Kale, the brash façade crumbled, and the undead man whimpered like a startled child. He snapped the peep hatch shut, and the Holy Hounds heard the clicking of many locks, sealing the visitors out.

As soon as Kale glimpsed the vampire, a deep anger began to build. The whites of his eyes turned black. A thunderous rumbling sound made the air tremble. Darkness fell from his shoulders like mist to the ground. It filled the bottom of the stairway as he glared at the heavily locked door. They quietly watched Kale brim with bridled fury.

Adwen calmly asked, "What do you need?"

The depth of his anger let his demon voice be heard. It reverberated like several voices at once. Despite terrible emotions, his tone was low and controlled.

"I apologize for the scene I am about to make. No light, please. There might still be friends inside."

She nodded. "You got it."

His form turned black. His red eyes shone, leaving trails of red glow in the air like neon as he moved to the door. Curdling dark fog congealed, engulfing the door frame. It seeped into cracks. Pressure made the metal groan, while Kale's darkness pried.

The edges of the steel door crumpled inward as if it were tinfoil. The force sent the thick slab flipping end over end. Kale's shadow flooded the hallway as he entered. His deep demon rumble echoed in the gloomy rooms.

In the bar beyond the empty frisking station, the fog that was Kale's presence billowed. Five vampires stood around the bar, keeping silent, watching as he entered. Black light fixtures buzzed and winked overhead. The vampires' shaking hands clung to handguns with silver bullets. Two more vampires watched from behind the counter, smiling – a male and a female who were thankful for Kale's return.

Standing at the threshold between the hall and the bar, Kale surveyed the opponents. He saw and felt everything. No one could hide. Then he roared. The sound spurred the armed vampires into action. Guns fired from all sides. The undead were swift, and their aim was good.

Kale used his darkness to fling up tables. Bullets riddled the solid oak undersides before he sent them flying at the shooters. Two were smashed to the walls, impaled on table legs and reduced to dust piles. The other three dodged just in time to keep from being crushed. There weren't many bullets left, making the undead desperate.

One ran for cover by a disc jockey booth. The undead man turned and aimed again for the red-eyed shadow. One of his cohorts had run out of ammunition and took a swipe at Kale's face. Faster than a blink, the werewolf snatched up a chair and shoved the legs through the other vampire as if he were made of wet paper.

Kale headed for the other vampire standing frozen with fear, but the one by the DJ booth fired two more rounds. They whizzed past their target.

Two burning red eyes turned on him. The darkness of the enraged werewolf started to flow more like water than smoke. Before the vampire knew what was happening, Kale grabbed him and shoved him against a wall. There was a loud crunch as the rogue reached into the wall through where the undead man's heart would be. Grasping a two-by-four inside the wall, he ripped a piece off and pulled it through the vampire's chest, leaving it there. The creature turned to dust.

Kale stalked back to the bar, where the last of them cringed, paralyzed by terror. Resigned to his fate, the cowardly creature shivered under the werewolf's demonic gaze. Kale bore down, pinning the vampire to the counter, gripping his throat. Retracting his presence into flesh, Kale let the black lights cast purple hues on the vampire. His demon voice rang with anger.

"Where is Charlie?"

The female vampire behind the counter called out, "Kale."

He glanced up at her unblinkingly.

"They killed Charlie."

Kale's crimson eyes widened in shock. Mind numbing pain and rage made his hands shake and squeeze. Then he bellowed. The unearthly sound shook the foundation of the building. All his anger focused on the culprit in his grasp. With deadly claws, Kale speared his hand through the vampire's middle. He clawed viciously as he took the hand out, making the fiend scream. Red and black fluids dripped to the floor. Kale wanted the vermin to suffer.

Adwen called to him as she and her warriors entered the bar. "Don't kill him, Kale. We need him for finding Vaughn."

The resonating voice came from Kale again, still cool and

controlled. "There is no need to remind me, Adwen. I intend to do both; two birds, one stone."

Jack disliked vampires intensely, but the sound of Kale's tone made the warrior begin to pity the undead. He had seen Kale furious, but never this enraged. Jack grimaced as Kale formed a familiar blade on his forehead like a horn. Grasping the vampire's head with shadow-drenched claws, Kale thrust his face forward. He plunged the blade into the vampire's brow between the eyes. He sneered into the fiend's black gaze as the psychic blade made his victim cry out, shaking violently.

"It hurts, doesn't it? Your kind can barely stand truth. Now, I have a few questions."

The vampire froze under Kale's gaze like the man from the overlook caves. He was paralyzed and unable to resist.

"Where is Vaughn?"

The vampire shook violently. Kale held his head in place despite its body's convulsions. Pain showed in the vampire's face as if he might explode from the strain.

A loud gasp preceded a frantic answer. "Vaughn was taken away! He is gone!"

Kale frowned. "Tell me: Who has Vaughn?"

"Men in black! Masked men in black with guns!"

Growling, Kale glared into the pleading stare of the vampire, wracked with agony.

"One more question."

Terror made the vampire's eyes bulge.

"Where are the masked men in black?"

Shaking more violently than ever, the vampire could not speak. Suddenly, the creature froze and turned to dust on the counter and bar stools. Adwen, Jack and Alexander stared in shock.

Oryn sneered, "Why did you kill him before he could speak?"

Kale's voice returned to normal, and the darkness withdrew. Anger lost, his expression was dismal. He swept the dust off the counter and stool. Taking a seat, Kale laced his fingers to think.

The knight did not appreciate the silence. "What is your explanation? We need answers!"

Kale murmured at the wood counter, "That was not intentional. If he were human, we would already have our answers; they have enough light to produce truths. Vampires have some, but not enough. The stress of trying to ream truth out of an undead is enough to kill them. They normally last until question three or four before they expire."

A moment passed, and the Holy Hounds found themselves staring at the pair of vampires behind the counter. Both looked terrified now that they knew what these visitors were.

Kale noticed. "Garret. Leena. It's alright. They're with me."

Adwen stepped forward smiling kindly. "I'm glad at least some of Kale's friends are okay."

The lady vampire frowned. "Charlie was my brother."

Garret held her shoulder. "Vaughn was taken two weeks ago. These people smelled human, but they didn't seem normal."

At this, Kale scoffed. "If they were normal, they wouldn't have been able to take Vaughn."

"Why are you looking for Vaughn?" Garret asked.

Adwen answered, "We're fighting a war, and we were hoping Kale's friend would be interested in joining us." An interesting idea came to her. More hopeful than before, she asked, "Do either of you remember how it happened when they took him?"

Leena gave a firm nod. "I remember everything perfectly."

"Jack?"

He read Adwen's thoughts and did not like what was there. "Seriously? I'd rather not."

Curious, Kale turned to see what was going on. "What are you lot on about?"

While Jack looked as though he had sucked on a lemon, Adwen explained, "If Jack looks at those memories, we might learn something important."

That glimmer of hope made Kale turn to Jack expectantly.

The cop stared, wishing Adwen would reconsider. To see the memories would require touching the vampire. Jack felt very uncomfortable just being in the same room. After the treks in Mortigad and encounters in this world, he had grown to loathe the creatures. But Kale's cautiously hopeful expression twisted the warrior's heartstrings. Taking account how much this meant to his friend, Jack figured these vampires did not look too bad compared to most.

Scratching the itch at the back of his neck, Jack grumbled, "Fine. You win. I'll do it. Leena, let me have a look in your head. Try to bite me, and you'll regret it."

She huffed incredulously. "I'm no blood-crazed leech. You don't even smell good enough to lick."

Raising an eyebrow, he was abashed. "You don't say?" Jack cautiously joined the undead behind the counter and stopped. A second ago he was willing, but now the creatures were so close and watching intently. The sight of the vampires made the hair on the back of his neck stand on end. A growl rumbled in Jack's throat. How he detested the undead.

Barking in frustration, Jack turned to his werewolf friend. "Can't you do it?"

"Yeah, but that would mean using this." He pointed to his forehead, reminding Jack of the blade horn. "Demons can pull memories from dark feelings, but not in detail. For me to get at them would kill her. Even then, I might not find what you could. Mortal psychic abilities have a gentler touch."

The warrior grimaced, studying the passive vampire woman.

"Please, Jack," Kale added. "This isn't asking too much, I don't think."

The warrior still hesitated, and Leena rolled her black eyes in irritation. "For heaven's sake, stop acting like a child."

He shot her a disgusted look.

Garret was nervous after Leena's provocation, but the lady vampire showed no fear. "If you think I'm a threat, then kill me and get it over with. I have nothing to lose."

Again, Garret gave his companion a questioning glance.

Instead of being offended, Jack was impressed. There was a subtle urge to smile, but he hid the feeling. If his new assessments of Leena were correct, they had a lot more in common than anticipated.

Far less disgusted, Jack inched closer, still cautious out of habit. "We always have something to lose, lady. Always."

Leena's expression was as cold and unmoving as stone.

"Now hold still. I've never looked through undead minds before."

She scoffed and smiled. "This should be a happy skip through the park then."

"Just close your eyes and relax."

When Leena complied, Jack lightly touched hands to her temples. The skin was cool. Though it was not clammy, it made him uncomfortable. Jack briskly set his reservations aside and focused on the task of retrieving deep memories. Entering Leena's mind, his physical eyes remained open and unseeing. All became dark.

Jack watched the memory unfold as if through Leena's eyes. Her/his hands cleaned spilled blood on the counter with a rag and bleach water. Garret attended to messy tables, where ravenous patrons had left more splatters. It was dawn, so all the customers were gone. Leena/Jack looked over to talk to Garret, but something made a strange noise at the entrance. Her/his hearing was sharp. It sounded like many feet and metal clicking. An object the size of a soda can was tossed into the bar.

She/he and Garret looked at it an instant before the bright explosion. The flash-bang grenade tossed a few chairs aside. This was not a normal suppressive weapon; something like sunlight burned the vampires and knocked them off their feet. Both screamed and hissed. Charring covered wherever the light struck their skin. Garret took refuge in the DJ booth, and Leena/Jack ducked behind the bar.

The burns on her/his hands had embers that still glowed red hot and smoked. It hurt so badly that she/he felt paralyzed. The intruders flooded into the room, and she/he glimpsed them passing the bar and heading for the back rooms. Leena/Jack gasped; they were after Vaughn in his personal quarters.

There were eight. The gear was mostly Kevlar, and their weapons were unrecognizable but very advanced. One by one they filed into a stairway. Leena/Jack knew there would be one chance to fight. When the last of the intruders reached the doorway to the back, she/he swooped along the floor without a sound. Like a vengeful phantom, her/his hands grew talons that latched onto a militant and lifted him into the air. Clutching the human from behind, she/he brought him high to a dark shadow in the corner of the ceiling. The man tried to reach for weapons on his tactical gear belt.

Leena/Jack would not allow that. Careful to keep him alive a little longer, she/he held the man's head back to bite the jugular vein. Discovering a Kevlar collar in the way, it was obvious that these humans knew what they were dealing with. Angrily taking the human by the wrist to stop him from grabbing a weapon, Leena/Jack tore away the collar and sunk long fangs into tender skin and flesh. A wave of knowledge surged into her/his mind with the flow of hot blood. The more the man's life was drained, the more clear and coherent the information.

This was a soldier for a private contractor on an assignment. He came with seven others. Their training was brutal and highly unconventional. Their weapons were unfamiliar, and some made them feel strange; some became ill. He came with the others from an underground facility with a corporate façade at the surface. A logo filled his/her mind clearer than all the rest. She/he knew where the base was located.

Lost amid feeding, Leena/Jack barely noticed the armed humans return from the hallway. She/he dropped the lifeless corpse and prepared to pounce, but another solar flash grenade exploded. She/he shrieked and fell between two tables. Feeding on the human had restored her/his body, but the second blast came without the protection of the counter. Leena/Jack lay barely alive, quivering and unable to move. She/he watched helplessly as the men carried a wriggling body bag through the bar and out the front passage. Two more recovered the body of their comrade and followed.

When they were gone, a haunting quiet she/he had never known fell over the room. A few seconds passed, and a blonde young vampire with short hair came to her side. He looked shaken but unharmed. Seeing him safe made Leena/Jack momentarily forget the burns.

Having witnessed enough, Jack withdrew from the vampire's memories.

As soon as Jack was cognizant again, he removed his hands from Leena and glared at her. Eyes glowing brightly in frustration, he growled, "Would you have told us anything if I had not read your mind?"

Kale grew suspicious, glancing between his opposing friends. "What?"

Completely disgusted, Jack snapped, "She knows exactly where the kidnappers came from!"

Garret grimaced at her, and Oryn and Alexander snarled. Adwen gave the vampire an unimpressed look.

Not surprised at all, Kale sounded disappointed. "Leena."

Ignoring the others, the lady vampire addressed Kale: "I had planned to get Vaughn back on my own." She glared at a remaining pile of dust on the counter. "But then they came." With a swift sweep of her hand, the dust dissipated and drifted away.

Adwen pitied the vampire. "We are going to get him."

Leena put on a firm expression. "I'm coming with you."

Talking to her as if she were a sister, Kale wore a stern expression. "You're staying here."

She hissed and snapped, "I'm going! I'll bring Vaughn back! Where were you? Gallivanting with the Holy Hounds trying to play hero again? Did you have fun out squashing baddies?"

"I almost died, Leena."

She went silent. If it were possible, the tone of her skin would have become paler.

"This is out of your league," Kale told her. "I almost didn't come back. The lords are involved."

She swore bitterly under her breath, as did Garret.

"Listen to me just this once," Kale pleaded. "Stay and help Garret with the bar. Get this place up and running. It's what Vaughn would want, and there's no promising that any of us are coming back. Understand?"

Leena sighed and hung her head as a sign of acceptance.

"We'll clean this mess up," Garret assured him. "After the ruckus you made, the whole underground will know you're back and that this place is safe again. It'll be busy in no time."

Jack cut in: "Not if I can help it."

Everyone turned to him. He was examining wine bottles lining the shelves.

"O-positive female, age 22 ... O-positive male, age 45 ... You expect us to let a vampire bar keep running? You serve human blood!" He snatched a full bottle and threw it.

"No!" Leena and Garret lunged to stop him.

Kale was quicker and caught the bottle. While Kale had the attention of the Holy Hounds, he brandished the glass container full of dark fluids. "This is not what it seems."

Adwen spoke for the others, though she believed him. "What's going on here?"

"It's donated." He set the bottle on the bar with a loud thud. "Every drop."

Jack was incredulous. "You're pulling my leg."

"I'm not. Vaughn started this place over a century ago. That blood was donated. Ever heard of donating to save lives? This is a whole new spin."

Garret explained further: "We help keep leeches off the streets, especially the weak ones. Everyone pays in cash. This way, they are encouraged to have a human life as best they can."

Oryn sneered, "Far too small a treat for such a price. It is far easier for vampires to hunt for prey, especially in this naïve world."

At this, Leena scoffed, folding her arms proudly. "Not when our supply is the most addictive in the region. We purchase donated blood from special partners. Blood given willingly is so addictive and nourishing that once they have a taste, most vampires don't crave stolen blood. It's the nastiest of the leeches that still hunt in this city – unless they are broke."

Jack was starting to believe this strange explanation. "You keep saying that. Why do you call other vampires leeches?"

"Most of us are. A leech is a vampire who is a slave to the thirst and lets it rule them. Some vampires have a strong enough will to function regardless of thirst. I am one of these elites. Garret is, as well, and so was Charlie."

"And Vaughn?"

Kale answered, "Vaughn is on a whole other level. He's a legend in the underground, as well as other circles."

Garret wore a rare smile. "He has been known to go years without tasting blood and not grow any weaker."

The explanation mollified Jack somewhat. "Intriguing. Cujo, you know anything about this?"

Even more suspicious of the undead than Jack, the knight shook his head. "No, and I doubt the Order knew of such things."

Garret and Leena gawked at the green-eyed warrior in a mixture of curiosity and reproach. "You are from the Order? In the other world?"

He sneered, "What would you know of it?"

The vampires exchanged entertained looks. "You really must meet Vaughn. The two of you will have a lot to talk about."

Seeing the knight's skepticism, Kale chuckled. "I told you. Just wait till we find him. Speaking of which, we best get going."

Garret raised a hand. "Wait a moment! There are some

things you need to take." He ran so fast, he appeared only as a blurred streak from the back of the bar to the hallway. A moment later, he walked back at a more human pace. In his arms rested a long, oblong bundle wrapped in layers of soft cloth. He presented it to Kale gingerly.

The werewolf was shocked, then relieved. "Good. The bloody buggers didn't get at them."

"Not a chance," Garret said, appearing proud of his resourcefulness. "Return those to Vaughn safely. I hope he is not in need of both when you find him."

Darkness consumed the bundle, making it vanish from Kale's hands for a later date. "Thank you for remembering. The two of you will do fine running this place."

Leena smiled. "Just need to fix the door, then find a new watchman and an enforcer. You interested in starting up again? Vaughn kept your room just like you left it."

He raised an eyebrow. "Almost empty?"

She could not help but laugh a little. "Yes, but without dust."

The idea was tempting. "I'll think about it."

Adwen called to him and the rest, "We need to go."

"With any luck, I'll see you lot again soon," Kale told the vampires.

Leena urged, "With Vaughn?"

"With Vaughn. Stay out of trouble, little waif. You, too, dirty cup-licker."

Garret sighed. "Still won't let that one go. See you when I see you, mangy beast."

Good-byes exchanged, Kale joined Adwen and her warriors, and they left The Corner behind.

Chapter 19
BETWEEN TWO EVILS

In an adjacent alley, Adwen used the Gray Blade to open a fiery portal according to Jack's directions. Passing through, they left the dark narrows and emerged on the open rooftop of a large factory. A strong wind blew at their backs as the opening in reality closed. Adwen and the other Holy Hounds reshaped their common clothing back to armor. Jack and Alexander summoned their weapons.

Kale looked far out over the sea of city lights. A familiar aroma of smog brought back memories, some he wished to forget.

Sensing the abrupt change in mood, Adwen turned to check on him. "Are you alright?"

"Yeah, it's nothing. Never thought I'd see this place again." Jack chuckled to himself.

"What are you on about?" Kale asked the cop.

"Well, it's kind of funny that a hardcore rogue demon like you would shack up in the City of the Angels is all."

Alexander should have seen this coming. "Shut up, Jack."

"I'm just saying."

Kale sighed but not at the weak joke. "It has some irony in it."

"Jack, how close are we?" Adwen asked.

"Very close. Should we use the rooftops or stay low?"

She pondered the risks. "It probably doesn't matter. Let's get within two blocks and decide how to go from there. Until then, the rooftops."

They followed Jack's lead. He took them far southeast into the wind. The air was dry and smelled of smoke and noxious chemicals.

Eventually Jack called to the others, "Adwen, we're close! That's the building."

"Let's stop and look it over."

Everyone gathered at the edge of a rooftop several stories high to study the complex. It stood in the middle of a wide-open lot packed with parked vehicles. The building was also too tall to jump from the ground to the roof without being spotted. In silence, each appraised the situation.

"Oryn, what are your thoughts?"

"It is too quiet here even for night hours. I see no guard patrols."

Alexander frowned. "I have a bad feeling about this place."

His friends quietly agreed. There was an aura about the facility that gave them all the creeps. Even Kale felt uneasy.

"Kale, what do you sense?" Adwen asked.

His brow furrowed in concentration. "I see and sense no demons, but there's something here. Whatever it is, it's bad."

Jack shrugged. "That's not news to us, Big Guy."

He gave him a grim glance. "I sense a very evil presence. I'm getting a few impressions. This feels like witchcraft."

She was worried by his indecision. "You sound unsure."

"I am. I sense witchcraft, but there's no dark magic."

Oryn scowled. "If humans in this world are performing dark rituals without the use of magic, it must be dealt with regardless."

Jack growled, "No arguments from me, Cujo."

The knight looked to Adwen. The way she gazed at the facility worried him. "What is it?"

Adwen had noticed a sign by the fence. The name Nu Advance Industries meant nothing, but the logo itself resonated in her mind. It was familiar – a red ring with a line through the center, like a calligraphy depiction of a cat's eye. Though she could not recall where or when, she had seen it before. The symbol chilled her to the core.

"Adwen?"

Though she snapped out of it, dread remained. "Everyone be ready. Don't forget we are dealing with the unknown here."

They put on hardened faces.

Adwen's blue eyes shone brilliantly. "I prefer to enter quietly. Kale, we need your experience and senses. Find us a way inside."

The white of his eyes turned black. His presence stretched thin, reaching out. In moments, the smoky haze from Kale's body wrapped around the building to feel for weaknesses.

Kale's demon voice resonated: "There are many points of entry. No movement or signs of life above the ground floor. Lots of cameras outside. They are active."

"Where do you suggest?"

A moment passed. "Second floor, side windows. One is broken. A camera blind spot will let us through. Best not to mess with the electricity. That might tip them off."

Alexander grimaced. "I thought you said there was no one inside?"

Jack explained, "There's a huge underground complex."

The Marine did not like that prospect. "Do we have an extraction method if we get cornered?"

Pulling the darkness back into his body, Kale replied with a normal voice, "Yeah. Me."

Adwen chimed in, "Me too. I can get us all out with a portal. If that doesn't work, Kale can tear the place apart."

Feeling a little better, Alexander nodded. "Roger that."

"Okay, let's move. Kale, take the lead for now. Guide us in."

The company dropped from their four-story perch. They landed nimbly on pavement and skirted around the property. They leaped the fence, making a beeline for the broken window on the second floor. The warrior's boots crunched pieces of glass as they entered a large office space full of cubicles.

Light's suddenly flickered on, making them tense. Adwen and Kale were first to relax.

"There are no security cams in here," Kale said. "It's just motion-sensor lights."

It became apparent something had transpired in this huge office. Loose paper littered the carpet by most of the cubicles. Chairs were overturned. A few mugs of coffee had fallen, leaving brown stains in the short taupe carpet.

Jack tested one drying puddle nearby. "It's still wet. I think whatever happened here took place less than a day ago, possibly this morning."

Adwen found a small blood smear on a partition wall. It was not enough to be life threatening. "This was a struggle. Does anyone smell anything besides humans?"

No one detected anything else.

"Who attacked these people and why?"

Kale approached a chair by a computer monitor. He turned it on and waited for the screen to load. Pure blue appeared with a lone cursor.

Everyone frowned when Kale stated what was evident: "This computer is wiped clean."

Adwen exchanged looks with Jack, as they came to the same conclusion: "This looks like a house cleaning, disposal of evidence," the cop deduced aloud. "The workers were attacked from within."

Kale said what was on everyone's mind: "This must be a trap."

"We have to search for Vaughn." Adwen frowned. "Let's assume we're expected."

Lights in the hallways and stairwells turned on at their passing. Kale maintained the lead with Adwen at his heels. Jack watched everyone's backs. On the ground floor, the same ransacked and abandoned scenes awaited them. Offices lay in shambles, doors ajar. At the end of the long hall they came upon a door into the smelting factory beside an elevator.

"Kale?"

"Already checking." He extended his presence to feel the elevator shaft for traps or sensors. Finding nothing, his eyes returned to normal, and he frowned. "It's safe."

"You seem worried by that."

"This is too easy. Not only that, but the dark presence becomes stronger down the shaft. Something or someone is still here. And there's something else."

"What?"

A cold chill coursed through the werewolf. "I sense a darkness I recognize. I can barely pick it up, as it has not been here in years, but ... I don't know. It's subtle and makes me sick to my stomach."

Oryn frowned. "I am experiencing the same effect."

Adwen picked up on a familiar scent, but it was too thin to identify. "Do you two smell something familiar, too?"

Jack and Alexander exchanged looks. "A little. Seems to be bugging Kale and Oryn more."

Kale could not accept the convenience of the elevator. "There's another way down – a supply lift in the factory. I saw it in a corner. Shall we use that instead?"

As much as the idea made Adwen leery, her heart urged her to take the more frightening route. "This elevator."

"I can break it open," Kale offered.

Adwen stopped him. "Allow me. No point in making more noise than necessary. Be ready."

Touching the retina scan panel by the stainless-steel doors, the energy from her body woke the circuits. The powers of light she carried gave the elevator life and rudimentary consciousness. They saw the lens focus in and out, locking onto her face.

"Please, open. We need to go down."

A beep of acknowledgement came in reply. Three green lights blinked, and the doors parted to let them in.

As they entered and the doors closed behind them, Jack whispered, "I know this isn't a good time, but I just have to say that is awesome."

Adwen murmured nervously, "Thanks, Jack."

Descent into the bowels of the factory was quiet and ominous. The evil presence Kale had noticed thickened. It made the warriors hyper aware of every sound. When the soft tone of the elevator chimed, their hearts skipped a beat. An innocent sound had become an omen of unknown horrors. Pristine metal doors parted.

A wash of dark presence swept into the tiny compartment. The air appeared clear and clean, but they felt it. This unseen energy pressed on them. No one said a word. Adwen stepped out and sensed that Kale was the most frightened among the warriors.

That familiar scent was a little stronger. It made the werewolf feel small and helpless. Adwen's abrupt whisper made Kale flinch.

"There are security cameras down here," she told them. "If this place is as big as I think it is, we need to find the security room. Can you help me?"

He thought about it, then nodded nervously. "Yeah." This time, when Kale reached out with his presence, he felt resistance because the air was already thick with another darkness. Moving his energy through it was like swimming in mud.

The three warriors realized Kale's hands were trembling.

Oryn frowned as they waited for the search to end. Curious,

he growled, "Is there something you know that we do not?"

Kale's demon voice was low and rushed: "Why would you ask that?"

The frown intensified. "You shake with fear."

He was not going to answer but found himself speaking. Balancing concentration between searching the halls and being in conversation was taxing.

"It's this smell."

Everyone listened as he went on. Adwen pitied him and what this place was doing.

"I know this smell. It fills minds with despair, terror and death. Visions flash before my eyes, images of suffering. The presence here is overpowering. It resists my movement. Whatever the source, it might be stronger than I am."

The news made Jack and Alexander consider retreat. Oryn became more alert, and Adwen shuddered.

Sensing a room with its lights on, Kale's head snapped up in surprise. "Found it." He was relieved to be able to retract himself from the dense evil in the air.

"Take us there," Adwen commanded. "I can try to use the cameras to look for Vaughn."

Sensitive motion sensors flicked on lights in the halls at their approach, then dimmed in their wake. It gave them the sense that they were being tracked. The security room was deep inside the complex. Rounding a corner, they saw the soft glow from monitors spilling onto the corridor floor. The security center beckoned with pale blue light.

The companions filed into the large room. LED screens covered the wall. Squares were illuminated or dark in a random pattern. Tiny lights blinked at a control desk. Adwen approached, and her friends gathered around to watch.

Leaning over the controls, Adwen found them simpler than anticipated. A few monitors were for computer work, and the rest were for camera views. She began flicking from one view to another, cycling through. The first dozen showed hallways, which were dark and empty. Then she discovered the laboratory and factory cameras. Manufacturing machines for weapons and firearms lay still. Laboratories contained upright tanks holding strange shapes. Zooming the camera on the tanks, she and the others gasped in shock. Parts of demons floated inside, apparently suspended in preservation fluids that kept them from melting away.

"No way..." Adwen whispered to herself.

Jack urged her, "Keep going."

She flicked from camera to camera. Eventually, one showed a large cylindrical tank with a human shape inside.

Kale blurted out in horror, "Vaughn!"

"That lab is two levels down, in what they call the red quadrant. There are maps at hallway junctions giving directions. Let's get there now."

Alexander pointed at one of the screens above a second control console. "What's that?"

The computer desktop screen had one icon: A red grinning smiley face with devil horns floated over the title of the file labeled "Play me."

As Adwen cautiously approached to consider it, Kale scowled. "I knew this was a trap. Think carefully before you touch that."

"I am." Sitting in the plush desk chair, she rolled closer and grasped the mouse. Hovering the cursor over the icon, it began to animate soundless wicked laughter. Tiny ha ha's flashed in and out by the toothy mouth. She hesitated.

Then Oryn growled softly, "Do it."

Her delicate clawed finger double clicked. The screen blinked and froze before turning black. She leaped out of the chair as all the monitors turned black. The companions drew weapons. Blue flames on her sword illuminated the room. Kale growled dangerously. Still fearful, he bared his carnivorous teeth at the screens, flickering back to life.

The program Adwen had launched united the monitors as one. The wall of screens showed a figure sitting in a desk chair. Facing them, the pale man with wine-red hair and white irises smiled, showing shark-like teeth. The image of Sycan cocked his head a little.

"Greetings and salutations."

Everyone but Kale took a step back. He roared in a mixture of horror and rage. That scent throughout this place was Sycan's. Seeing his face brought it all back to Kale. The memories were torture.

The monster in human shaped chuckled. "If you're watching this, then Melanin is dead ... and so am I." He grinned. "Adwen, I hope it's you watching this. And that you've brought your precious knight along. Hello, Conrad."

Oryn growled louder.

"After our little game in the Mirror of Lies, I got to thinking: You might figure out that my business actually exists. Well, if you're seeing this, it doesn't anymore. My master work is complete."

Adwen growled, sapphire eyes flashing with blue fire like her sword.

"Humor me a moment before I get to that. I have a few things to share in my lovely little video. First, you likely noticed the weapons factory." He put a mockingly contemplative finger to his chin. "Oh, I wonder where the bullet that killed you on the border of Mortigad and Dargadia was made." He dropped the innocent wondering expression to grin devilishly.

The grip on her sword slackened, and she almost dropped it.

"That was a prototype. I needed to test a few theories and eliminate you, as well. The bullet was one of a kind – successful forging of demon steel in the non-magical world. It was no small feat. In the end, you resurfaced a year later, and I ordered the mass production of demon steel. I had realized it would be far more difficult to get rid of you than I had first thought. Demon steel would make my magnum opus more powerful, even if it meant a longer process was involved.

"Now, pay attention, kiddies. I have a small history lesson for you. In a far-off land, there once was a kingdom called Wallachia. A man ruled it, and his name was Mircea."

Adwen gasped. "That's what he called himself in the mirror!"

"Sound familiar?" Sycan taunted. "I hope so."

Fighting the urge to smash the screens showing the evil face, Jack grumbled, "This guy loves the sound of his own voice."

The recording Sycan left behind went on: "The king had a few sons. No one knew that I had taken the king of Wallachia and sealed him away for years. While he lay in sleep, I took his place." He sighed contentedly. "With his face, voice and name, I seduced a woman, and 'King Mircea' had another child; this son grew to be a strapping young lad. He was half human and did his other half proud. That rascal of mine, Mircea the Younger, earned the title Mircea the Dragon. What a good boy he was. So much death and destruction.

"As good as he was; it was his son who was the real apple of my eye. He was perfected by his father's instrumental beatings and years of torture by Ottoman enemies. My grandson, Vladislav the Third, painted the land with blood; he was a warlord beyond human reckoning. Know his other name, by any chance?"

Adwen had a guess but did not want to say. Oryn knew from the many books he had read. Among them, Kale knew even more. The darkness of the Void knew this name, and it was planted into his well of knowledge.

"Vlad the Impaler. I did love my time in this world more than the magical lands. So much fun to be had! My grandson will be reborn into a body that will let him rein over this world forever as a king of death. No one knows where my grandson's bones were buried. What if I told you I had them?"

They growled in defiance of the vile message.

"If you're lucky, he will still be here, asleep. Would you kindly go and wish my little boy a happy birthday? He has lots of friends with him, but you are the perfect guests." Sycan laughed maniacally. Catching his breath between fits of laughter, the whites of his eyes turned black. "And one more thing: I have a gift, Adwen. It should get you in the mood for the party. Enjoy the lovely slideshow!"

A storm of laughter broke out. The demonic energy from Sycan made the footage flicker with images of his true, hideous form under the human exterior. Thin pale skin stretched over red and blue veins. Bulging flesh with bloody, back-rolling eyes flashed across the screens.

The video cut away from Sycan. Slide images of documents and photos of individual people appeared across the wall of monitors. The company logo stamp was in the upper corner of each one.

Subject Daddy: father of subject Princess, see file for subject Ghost; Status: eliminated.

Photos of her father crucified on a pine tree in a quiet wooded camp site were held to the file with a paperclip. Similarly, there were others.

Subject Mommy: mother of subject Princess, see file for subject Ghost; Status: eliminated. Subject Boy: brother to subject Princess, see file for subject Ghost; Status: eliminated. Subject Girl: sister to subject Princess, see file for subject Ghost; Status: eliminated.

Even more files of other blood relatives with photos attested to their murders.

The endless loop of gory files did not stop. Blue tongues of fire licked the air from Adwen's shoulders, and she lobbed a ball of holy fire at the console. Plastic, metal and wires melted into smoky puddles on impact.

Oryn took a step forward. "What are your orders?"

Adwen's fury made her body glow hot. Light shone through her skin. As she turned to face her warriors, blue fire licked from her glowing eyes and radiated from her breath. The air danced with the blazing heat where she stood.

"Jack, go with Oryn. Find Vaughn. Bring him to the control room. Alex, watch Kale's back while he helps guide me. I'm going to find and destroy Vlad."

Everyone but Kale nodded. Shaking his head, he said, "That's not a good idea. Vlad was created to destroy you. Sycan knows you wouldn't be able to resist this bait."

Adwen stalked past him for the door. "I'm going. Watch the cameras. Warn me of any movement other than ours."

He did not give up trying to change her mind: "I know exactly what you're feel, Adwen. Don't play into his plan! We need to grab Vaughn and get out of this place!"

She shouted back from somewhere down the hall, "Just do it, Kale!"

The stubborn response made him swear, "Aw, bugger it all."

Oryn could not help but agree with Kale's sentiments. It was clear she would not listen to reason. Unfortunately, Sycan had ensured that through his abominable message from beyond oblivion. The knight took a moment to look where the monster had been and then at the werewolf, leaning heavily over the console, hanging his head. For once, Oryn saw how different Kale was from their enemies.

"Cujo?"

"We move now," Oryn announced. "Keep alert along our path."

The knight led Jack down another hall. Alexander remained with Kale. Seconds dragged by, but Kale did not raise his head. Stepping alongside, Alexander saw that the whites of his eyes were dark. Kale looked terrified. If this were a soldier from his platoon, he would slap sense into him. Being of few words, Alexander chose them wisely.

"Sycan's dead. He's never coming back."

This caught Kale by surprise. His frightened demon gaze turned to the warrior. The video had left him a quivering mess. Thankfully, this new friend knew what to say to choke the fear.

Regaining control, his eyes returned to normal. "Thanks, Yank."

The warrior nodded. Kale went to work. Deadly claws tapped computer keys. Five monitors untouched by Adwen's fire flicked back on.

"Question for you, Yankee: Are you computer-savvy?"

"A little. I'm a better mechanic than a tech."

"Do me a favor," Kale asked as he started scanning camera views. A few were blank, showing nothing but a room name. "Get that other console running. Try to find more files."

"You think there's something useful?"

He gave a grim look. "There has to be. Do your best. I'll look in a few ticks. Need to deal with Adwen for now."

"Roger that."

Jack and Oryn ran. Motion-activated lights traced their path. Anxious after what they had learned in the security center, Jack growled, "Have you ever seen her this mad before?"

The knight grimaced. "Only once."

"How do we stop her? You know Kale was right about needing to get out of here."

Thinking back to that fateful day when Jack was shot by the witch Nadeen, a steely expression came over him. "There is no stopping her when she is like this."

Jack did not like the answer. "Nothing?"

"Nothing. Fire will pour out of her like breath. She will try to burn everything opposing her."

"What if the big guy was right? What if Vlad was made to kill her?"

Frustrated, he snapped, "That is why we are running, fool! Move faster!"

Leaping down stairways, the duo reached the D3 Level, where Vaughn was sighted. Racing through several corridors, they arrived at a thick steel door. Oryn used brute force to smash it, bending it almost in half and out of their way. Once inside, they paused as the lights flickered on. There were dozens of vampires in tanks. Green liquid held them suspended. Jack and the knight exchanged glances, and there was an unspoken agreement to split up. There were almost fifty tanks holding humanoid specimens.

Jack struggled to recall what Vaughn looked like. "What was he wearing, Cujo? I remember his hair was short and black."

Oryn's memory served him well. "A long dress-coat. There was a yoke broach around his neck with a thin scarf."

"Found him!" Jack shouted.

In a flash, the knight joined Jack to examine the vampire, imprisoned in a dormant state. Oryn recognized the clothing from the footage right away. Now that they had a better look, they found that this vampire was different. Vaughn's features were male but so smooth that he was beautiful in an almost feminine way.

Oryn gasped, "He was a half-elf!"

"You mean is, Cujo. He's right here."

"This used to be a half-elf. That is past now that he is un-dead. How do we open this without causing harm?"

Jack shrugged. "I don't see a latch or a door. How about this?"

The warrior gave a fierce kick to the base of the glass column. It ruptured under the crushing blow, and there was far more pressure than anticipated. A rush of foul chemicals washed over their feet, making them step back. As soon as they recoiled, they saw that Vaughn was going to fall forward.

Despite their distrust of vampires, both warriors caught him by the arms. Surprised at themselves, Jack and Oryn felt the suspension fluids settle on the floor. They held still as Vaughn began to move. The warriors suddenly realized the vampire's head was resting on both their shoulders, dangerously close to their necks. They waited to see what would happen as Vaughn slowly awoke.

The vampire made a groggy groan. He weakly lifted his head to see who was holding him. Finding the shortest warrior's face, Vaughn saw the light in his eyes. The stranger was neither human nor intending harm. That was a comfort.

Jack was startled to be holding a very powerful vampire, and far leerier after seeing his eyes. They were unusual even for a vampire.

Oryn noted Jack's expression and braced himself when

Vaughn looked his way. When the knight saw those strange eyes, he was uneasy for a moment. That feeling vanished, and he was in awe. This vampire had the eyes of a newly bitten man; a thin fiery ring at the edge of the irises. Though Vaughn's eyes were black like a true vampire, the orange and gold rings remained. Oryn breathlessly muttered the name from the ancient stories.

"Evrox."

Vaughn's brow furrowed in confusion. His smooth voice was deep. "Do I know you?"

This was the legendary Evrox, and Oryn was slack-jawed.

Jack did not know what was happening and did not care. "Focus, Cujo. We have to move fast, remember?"

The knight recomposed himself. They needed to stop Adwen. If they were too late, then it was vital that they join her to defeat Vlad. With or without Kale's assistance, she would find Sycan's spawn eventually.

Adwen stalked the halls in her true form. Blue flames bathed her. The ceiling over her scorched, and her feet left sizzling paw prints. Tiny blue flames trailed behind, flickering in the gloom. Blinding rage continued to burn, keeping her inner fire stoked. Her one desire was the destruction of Sycan's evil creation.

Unable to track the sinister presence any farther, her burning gaze turned to a nearby security camera. It was high in a corner over a small intercom. A ravenous snarl wrinkled her muzzle. Her power reached into the security system, rapidly flooding it.

Flicking from camera to camera, Kale continued to search for Vlad. He was becoming ever more suspicious of the blank screens. Their cameras had been cut off. Sycan's spawn was likely waiting for Adwen in one of those locations.

Alexander asked nervously from the other console, "Find anything?"

"Maybe. How about you?"

The Marine growled in exasperation, "There's nothing here. The computer is empty except for the dirtbag's message."

Kale pondered, glancing at the computer monitor. "Perhaps

it is empty."

Suddenly all the electrical systems in the room came to life. Even equipment that was turned off switched on. They braced for an attack. All the screens, including Alexander's, showed Adwen standing in a hall. She snarled at them through the distant lens.

Recovering from the surprise, Kale frowned. "Aw, bugger. She hasn't cooled off at all."

They could not hear her, but they saw her roar. One monitor kept showing her, while the rest blinked with flickering mismatched letters: "Where Is Vlad?"

Sighing heavily, Kale pressed the button that allowed him to speak through the intercom at her location. "I don't know. I've looked through all the cameras. I can't see anything."

Two screens burst in a flash of sparks, and a few machines whined, making Kale and Alexander flinch. The three surviving monitors flashed big letters in more mismatched fonts: "DO NOT LIE TO ME."

Frustrated by the fright she gave them, Kale spoke into the microphone with a firm tone. "Calm yourself! I did not lie, and I was not finished answering you. Four cameras are inactive. He's most likely in that place."

The word "WHERE" multiplied endlessly before them.

Kale shared an uneasy look with the Marine. As the werewolf leaned forward and pressed the button to speak, Alexander groaned miserably. Things were getting worse by the minute.

"The feeds are tagged for Room 667. It's on Level B6. You're on B2. You do the math."

Kale raked a set of sharp claws through his hair in frustration when she took off running out of the camera's view. Adwen's power over the systems disappeared with her.

"This is going to be a nightmare," Kale muttered bitterly. "Best be ready for Jack and Oryn when they bring Vaughn. We need to get after her."

Alexander gasped, pointing at his monitor. "Look at this!"

Kale rushed to Alexander's console and took over the mouse and keyboard. Several document icons appeared after Adwen's power left the computers. Kale opened them all. His clicks flooded the screen with various documents. Most were lists of materials and long-winded manifestos, written by Sycan under the name Mircea. What caught Kale's attention was a series of blueprints.

Alexander could barely make heads or tails of the exploded-view illustrations. Several notes were typed on them explaining specifics. Just as the warrior began to recognize a humanoid shape, he heard Kale mutter in horror.

"Bloody hell." The whites of his eyes turned black, red pupils dilating wildly at the information in disbelief. "We can't wait. Let's get Adwen out of here now!"

"For what reason can you not wait?" Oryn asked as he entered, supporting Vaughn by his shoulders. The knight glared at Kale in demand of an answer. Jack was just behind in the hall listening.

As happy as Kale was to see Vaughn, the urgency did not leave: "Vlad is about to kill Adwen!"

Sick with anger and impatience, Adwen melted her way through the steel floor from Level B5 down to Level B6. Like a flame on a welder's torch, her form burned through layers of metal until it glowed, softened and belched her downward. Level B6 was much larger, and the drop was fifty feet. She landed nimbly, and metal flooring sizzled and warped under her heat. Molten steel dripped around the rampaging Holy Hound as she stood, clutching her sword.

Just ahead stood enormous closed doors marked B667 with black paint. There were no other markings, but the evil presence felt thicker than ever. She stalked to the door intending to melt her way through. As she drew near, warning lights illuminated blood red, and she paused to growl.

A buzzer sounded continuously as the door began to rise. Adwen's fire roared as she watched and waited. A puddle of melted steel lay around her by the time the way stood open. The buzzer silenced, and the lights died. With a thud, the doors locked in their open position, allowing her into a dark space.

The stench of rotting flesh wafted into her face. The extreme heat of her body repelled most of the scent of death, but not all the particles vaporized before reaching her nose. When she entered, defiant of the omen, lights hundreds of feet above her began to turn on.

Adwen prowled through what appeared to be a forest of metal rods rising from the floor. There was plenty of room to move between them. Too enraged for curiosity, she prowled through the posts in search of the powerful evil entity. There seemed to be nothing but a maze of these metal rods.

Just when she thought she sensed someone watching, something small fell over her. It collided with the flames and vaporized with a sharp hiss, causing her to stop dead. Then there was another and another. Tiny masses were dropping onto her from above. Growling dangerously with her fire flicking hungrily, she gradually raised her gaze. It was not Vlad, as she had anticipated. What she saw horrified her.

The corpse of a young man in a lab coat was impaled through the heart twenty feet above on one of the steel rods. Blood dripped from his mouth. Foggy eyes stared just past her. Surrounding him, many more human bodies were mounted on spikes like a collection of insects as far as she could see. The company employees were still dressed in their work attire. Sticky red layers of blood caked the posts in trails running to the floor.

Adwen roared, her fire rising in a fit of outrage. Feminine laughter caught her attention from a high catwalk. She growled, ready for a fight.

"This took a lot of work, you know?" the distant voice complained. "The ritual is finished, so you can take them down if you want."

Watching Adwen among the hundreds of rotting corpses, a woman with a white mask that covered half her face leaned lazily on a guard rail. A large platoon of armed men in black Kevlar stood with her. Their faces were blank, while hers showed passive interest. Red hair in a tight pixy cut feathered at the edges of her smooth cheekbones and brow. Her left eye was the color of chocolate, but the eye behind the half mask was snow white with no pupil or iris.

Adwen rumbled like thunder, "Where is Vlad?"

The woman frowned, confounded. "Hmm? Are you trying to speak? If you were, I did not understand a word."

One of the men beside her murmured, his face stony and expressionless.

"What was that?" Hearing the militant whisper again, she smiled slyly and turned to Adwen. "Oh, you want Vlad. As a matter of fact, he's all around us."

The reply frustrated Adwen even more.

"Do you see these men? They are his many puppets. They used to be controlled by Guillot, but you know what happened to him. Now they belong to Vlad. I have waited a long time to thank you."

Adwen's ears flattened in disgust.

The woman was entertained. "You killed Nadeen. Sycan told me how badly that witch wanted to come to this world. There would have been quite an awkward conflict – I was his favorite; she was not. I know so because Sycan entrusted me with his prized creation: a new body for his cherished grandson."

Having heard enough, Adwen snarled and leaped, bounding off a few posts. Jumping high to reach the wicked humans, she collided with a thin net of wire, holding her below it. Her blue fire melted the net a little but not enough to get through, and she fell. Landing amongst the bloody metal landscape, a ravenous gleam lit in Adwen's gaze.

A thoughtful smile came over the woman on the catwalk. "Oh, good. That's never been tested. If it had failed, these puppets would have shot you down. I don't have to tell you what their bullets are made of. Sycan's instructions were very specific: Leave you to Vlad as a test for his new body."

From the broad entrance Kale's voice called out, "Adwen! We have Vaughn. Let's get out of here!"

She did not move. Though her deadly staring match with the evil woman wavered, Adwen did not trust that this wicked human would remain passive. Vlad's new body was nowhere to be seen. She refused to leave before it was destroyed.

At the entrance, Kale faced the others. "Stay back and protect Vaughn."

The vampire was semiconscious in Oryn's grasp, and the knight frowned. "I'm not leaving her to this fight alone."

Kale stopped him from trying to pass the burden to Alexander. "It won't do any good."

The knight, the cop and the Marine stared back in silence. "Why not?"

"You've seen how strong I am. Vlad is stronger by a long shot."

The three warriors knew he was telling the truth.

"Sit tight. If a fight starts, stay out of it. Wait for Adwen. I'll get her out of this, I promise."

As much as Oryn hated waiting in the wings, he and the others gave him looks of acceptance. Kale bolted into the overwhelming cloud of deathly stench. The paw prints in melted metal were still hot and smoking. Not only did it stink in here, but his demon sense told him what was overhead. He refused to look at the impaled humans.

He spotted Adwen and her blue fire on the far side of the huge room. When he reached her, the heat of the blaze forced him to stay back; even bound to her, Adwen's holy fire was deadly. Kale was about to call to her, but the woman on the balcony spoke. The sound instantly made him angry. His eyes changed as he snarled.

"So it was you; you're the rogue all the fuss is about."

Kale's bellow shook the air, "Diana!"

Diana gave a dry, unimpressed laugh. "Time for a little payback."

"Is that so?"

The woman flipped off the half mask. Down the right side of her face, three deep scars showed where claws had raked her flesh. The eye was made of snow white glass, replacing the one that was destroyed. Bone and muscle remained permanently disfigured under brutal scarification.

"A little piece of you for the piece of me you took," Diana hissed at Kale.

"Not a day goes by that I don't look back and wish I had taken it all."

Putting the mask back on, her tone was cold: "If you were smart, you would have. Sycan told me about you after you did this. He told me to give you a message if we met again."

Kale gave a deep rumbling growl.

"No child deserves hell ... or do they?" she asked.

"Those kids didn't. But you deserve worse."

She smiled. "Worse than hell? I'm only a pawn, and so are you. Now, I leave you to meet Vlad. Please try to survive. I have a few more creations to test." Diana beckoned the soulless drones to escort her out.

Adwen would not allow it. With a fearsome swing of her sword she lobbed a large ball of blue flames. The bright mass roared through the air.

Diana heard it coming, and her first instinct was to look and see if the demon-steel netting would hold. When the wires melted, she sneered in frustrated at the failed invention. With the help of the men controlled by Vlad, the foul woman dove out of harm's way. In a burst of holy fire and twisted metal, the catwalk collapsed behind them. A few soldiers went up in flames with it.

Angry at Adwen and the destroyed netting that was difficult to make, she hissed venomously to the surviving drones. "Get me out of here!"

Adwen roared in outrage as the woman disappeared down a tunnel.

"Adwen!" Kale shouted.

She stopped to look back, snarling.

He took a step closer, and the blaze forced him to shield his face. "Vlad is coming. We need to leave."

The sound of hydraulics stole their attention. Among the poles, a steel block began to rise out of the floor. It gradually came up to a smooth stop at seven feet high. The sides were smooth, exposing a thin line down the front. Adwen and Kale stared, sensing a presence converging and condensing on the cube.

The presence vanished, and the heaviness they had felt in this complex lifted. Everything felt light and cold, even near Adwen and her fire. More hydraulics parted two panels on the front of the cube, and Kale braced himself as Adwen took a step forward.

More desperate than ever, he snapped at her, "You can't kill him, Adwen!"

"Why not?"

"He's made of demon-steel!"

"What?!"

A metallic thud echoed. A figure like a human-sized doll dangled from its elbows, where two swords held it suspended. The robotic construct was mostly geometric, but bones of a skeleton were cast into the structure. Where perfect, smooth angles ended, raw black steel encased bone like dried wax. Ribs resembled a nightmarish cage around inner systems for the body's basic functions. The head tilted on one shoulder as if dead. The skull and jaw, cast in evil metal, were set seamlessly into more hard edges and polished surfaces.

Small purple lights began to glow in the empty sockets. The head, wearing a permanently attached crown, lifted to look at them.

Rough crackling laughter emitted from audio devices inside like radio static.

Adwen started to gnash her jaws, the fire roaring and rising.

Shrinking away from the surging heat, Kale held both hands up to shield himself. "There's nothing you can do. Please, Adwen!"

"Stay out of this!"

A bigger blast of heat made him growl in pain. He had no choice but to watch as she raced toward the abominable conjoining of witchcraft and technology.

Steel poles turned orange, warped and toppled in her passing. Adwen summoned up all the power she had to make her fire hot enough to melt even demon steel. Each step on the ground left molten impressions with deep claw gouges.

Currents of purple electricity flashed along Vlad's arms. The two swords came free, dropping him to his feet with a dull thud. The sword hilts, gleaming with evil energy, then flew to the mechanical talons that were his hands.

More static laughter crackled as Adwen roared, swinging the Gray Blade to cut the robotic shell apart. The Gray Blade came down with incredible force, only to be blocked by Vlad's dual swords. Blue fire and purple electric currents swirled as they collided. Adwen pushed hard, the fire turning his body red hot and melting the ground where he stood. She drove him back and through the metal container as if it were made of butter. No matter how hot she made her fire or how hard she pressed against the swords, Vlad did not falter.

The fact that he was not harmed by this much heat confounded Adwen. She kicked Vlad in the chest, sending him sliding back on molten metal, and she pounced. He sidestepped the attempt. When she fluidly turned to swing her sword, Vlad laughed, and their battle truly began.

The fiery Holy Hound exchanged clanging volleys with the evil entity. Together, they wove between steel posts that melted and toppled over. Rotting and bleeding corpses began to combust. The overpowering stink of decay was eclipsed by that of burning human flesh and smoke. Each driving step in the battle shifted on the liquefying metal floor as if it were mud. Adwen continued to blaze until her body was like a star, shinning bright white, burning everything.

Even the raw, unbridled power flowing from her was not

enough to slow down Vlad. Though the demon-steel body glowed red hot, it would not reach a melting point. Their duel carried on in stalemate, and Adwen's energy laid waste to the underground battlefield. She slashed and swung the holy sword again and again. Vlad deflected every effort and reposed, forcing her to do the same.

The other Holy Hounds watched from the entry in disbelief. They had never seen her pushed this far. What mystified them was the sight of the metal body standing against that power unflinchingly.

The intense heat forced Kale to retreat father. His piece of her heart protected him somewhat, but not completely. He could not intervene if she kept this up. Baring his teeth, Kale prepared himself. At any moment the battle would turn. Based on the notes in the schematics left by Sycan and Diana, he knew Vlad would not fall to her, no matter how hard she tried.

Amid another bout of clanging blades Adwen swung to cleave Vlad's head from the vile construction. Vlad did not dodge. Instead, he moved to slice across her middle. She had thrown all her strength into decapitating the demon-steel monster. She could not take back the choice.

Her ivory blade struck red hot demon metal. There it stopped. Adwen's blue eyes widened in horror. Vlad's twin blades found her spirit flesh where her armor did not protect her. Silver blood hot as the fires over them spilled to the ground just before a merciless kick caught her under the chin. The white Holy Hound flew backward end over end across the vast chamber. Her blue flames wavered.

Kale gasped, buckling over. The warriors outside the door felt the blow, as well.

Alarmed, Oryn turned feral in the distress. He roared and lunged for the door. Jack held him back. While the knight transformed and summoned his sword, Jack used his mind to hold him. Lifting the enormous brown creature inches off the ground took all of Jack's strength and concentration. Oryn's thrashing and roaring made it almost impossible.

"Knock it off, Oryn! Get a hold of yourself. There's nothing you can do. Give Kale time."

Adwen bled badly, her body cooling until the fluids shone like a watery mirror. Watching with wrinkled jaws as Vlad approached, she held her blade high, pointing it vainly at the nightmare.

Her stance received more static chuckles. Then the fiend spoke with a voice that sounded like a demonic recording: "Your defiance is appreciated, daughter of the Gray Kingdom. It is most amusing."

Her gaze flickered from Vlad to beyond him and returned. Noticing this, he stopped to look behind him.

A half-melted container was flying straight for him. The diversion gave Adwen an instant to roll out of the way. The block of solid steel crashed into Vlad, sliding across the floor, and did not stop until it smashed into a wall. There it stayed.

The giant werewolf resisted the laceration across his stomach, panting from the pain and the effort of throwing the heavy block.

He growled at Adwen, "Go now!"

Bitterly, she admitted defeat. The white hound creature dismissed her fire. Cradling the grievous wound, Adwen dashed toward the door, where the others waited.

When the block pinning Vlad against the wall shifted, a sickening screech echoed. Orange steel cooled to black, and a figure stepped out from behind the hunk of metal. Glowing purple lights for eyes locked with Kale's. Anger made electrical currents dance on his shoulders and crown.

Crouching low, the werewolf rumbled. Vlad held the swords out at his sides. His stride displayed his confidence in his power. Four small holes opened in the machine's upper back, letting out fine mesh connected to intricate orb nodes. At first, the four limp pieces draped behind Vlad like weighted nets. Then a surge of purple electricity made the mesh glow and rise, furling outward. Flat mesh and nodes mimicked moth wings, crackling with energy that made Vlad float off the ground.

Kale snarled at the display.

"More defiance is good. Give me the taste of fear."

Vlad swooped through the air like a bolt of lightning, crackling with energy and laughter.

Grabbing a bent pole with ashen remains, Kale ripped it loose and swung fast. He caught the flying figure, sending Vlad twirling away. The robotic entity recovered and flew back, Kale swung a second time. Ready for the pole, Vlad sliced the end off and kept coming.

Kale was also ready. He swatted with open claws, throwing

Vlad into a far wall with a loud clanging thud. New pain made him snarl. Vlad's swords had cut deeply into the bones of his hand. While he growled at the weeping injuries, a shrill audio scream of rage pierced his ears announcing Vlad's return. The demonic robot flew circles around Kale with its blades swinging. Purple streams of light arced over Vlad as he slashed repeatedly from all sides.

The coarse electric racket sounded like a swarm of insects as the flurry of sword strikes tore at Kale's flesh. Ribbons of red blood flew. Crimson misted the air, and Kale roared, summoning his darkness to resist. Black fog poured from Kale to blunt some of the vicious strikes. Desperate to evade Vlad, he leaped and bounded, slashing with claws to swat the buzzing nightmare.

His efforts were futile. Vlad began to stab, making Kale howl. Bloody springs swelled, soaking and matting black fur. Kale managed to deliver a strong backhand, knocking Vlad far across the room. Instead of swooping back, the monster stowed a sword and grasped a broken pole. Before Kale could react, Vlad hurled the pole like a javelin, impaling Kale. He had no chance to remove it or prepare for Vlad's next move.

The steel-encased demon grabbed the long rod. The buzzing became deafening from the power required to lift Kale high by the pole. The mechanized fiend slung him off the rod, sending him rolling far across the floor over a mess of melted metal and burnt bodies.

Oryn had begun healing Adwen the instant she had reached the hallway. Both took on more human shapes as he worked his green magic. When the knight finished, he embraced her tightly, and she returned it gladly.

Alexander guarded the unconscious Vaughn, while Jack watched the battle between Kale and Vlad. Kale was doing better than Adwen, but still badly. Once Jack saw the two-ton werewolf impaled and thrown across the giant chamber, he flinched and turned to the others.

"Kale's in trouble!"

Everyone faced Jack with frantic looks. Adwen broke free from Oryn's arms to go to the doorway.

Vlad landed, folding wicked wings, and stalked to Kale, who staggered backward on all fours.

Adwen summoned the Gray Blade again.

"Wait!" Jack protested. "What are you doing?"

She was determined to help their friend. "I'll only have one shot. I have to take it now, while he's far away from Kale."

Blue flames licked the white sword, building into a small inferno. When it was ready, Adwen swung the blade and sent the most powerful blaze she could muster at Vlad. She and the warriors watched it roar toward the unwary monster.

A bright flash like an exploding star filled the chamber. It blew out Kale's fog, rippling his matted coat. He held his eyes shut to avoid being blinded. When the blast died down, Kale looked around. Blue fire had consumed everything where Vlad had been a moment before. Then he heard heavy footfalls and saw a red-hot figure with purple lights for eyes.

Vlad survived the greatest of Adwen's powers unscathed. This came as no surprise, but there was an effect. Kale squinted, examining the monstrosity's metal skin. Vlad's entire body was etched with runes. They glowed like embers before dimming out as the demon-steel body cooled.

Realizing the secret to the indestructible enemy, Kale growled. As Vlad strode closer, the werewolf began to tremble and snarl. Maintaining some distance, they moved ever farther to the other end of the chamber. Fear radiated from Kale, enticing the robotic demon. Vlad fed off it, as if it were honey to a hungry bee.

As Kale quivered, backing in amongst equipment, pipes and tanks, the fiend followed. The monstrous werewolf backed himself against the wall between two yellow tanks the size of school buses. Cornered, he shivered under Vlad's sadistic stare.

The radio voice rasped at the werewolf, "All rogues can feel fear. Fear makes you weak."

As Vlad reached for the twin swords at his hips, Kale ended his act. The instant the scent of pure terror vanished, Vlad realized his mistake, but it was too late.

Kale pierced the sides of both nitrogen tanks with his claws and pulled, tearing them open. Pressurized gas exploded, shaking the compound. The watching Holy Hounds winced at the harsh concussive sounds. They could not see through the cloud.

Shifting into his more human shape after being blown against the wall, Kale's agony turned excruciating. Hugging his bloody, blistered stumps, they immediately began to heal as he panted loudly. As the air cleared, he could see the tanks and pipes around them were thrown aside by the blast like paper. Nearly on top of him stood Vlad, held motionless in a shallow pool of liquid nitrogen. Fine frost covered his metal body, which was frozen with both arms up when he tried to shield himself from the blast.

Not waiting to see how long Vlad would remain frozen, Kale darted around the frigid pool and debris. He raced through the cloud of vapor and dust to find the open doorway. When the filthy, blood-ied werewolf emerged, the Holy Hounds were stunned that Vlad was not in pursuit. Alexander watched Kale, who panted and cradled his hands and sides.

"Did you kill him?" Alexander asked.

Kale shook his head. "Nah, I only slowed him down. Make a portal, Adwen and get us out of here right quick."

She slashed the sword at the air. A blue wreath of flame opened wide to take them far away from the subterranean deathtrap. Dark cityscape lay on the other side, lights winking in the night. Alexander collected Vaughn, Jack supported Kale, and Adwen and Oryn watched their backs on the way through.

Chapter 20
OUR DOUBTS ARE TRAITORS

The portal closed behind cutting off the enemy's pursuit. Atop a roof, the small company heaved sighs of relief. Jack helped Kale recline against a ventilation box, while Alexander smiled at the familiar cityscape.

"After that, I'm happy to be back in San Francisco." He gently set Vaughn down by a short wall. "Kale, how did you stop Vlad?"

Trembling from gouges, cuts and frostbite, the werewolf smiled. "A little liquid nitrogen goes a long way."

Jack chuckled. "You, my friend, are a genius."

Kale puffed incredulously. "Does a genius rupture tanks full of the stuff with his bare hands? Call me a genius when I figure out how to kill him."

Adwen stood nearby listening to the banter and feeling ashamed. The knight reassuringly placed a hand on her shoulder. It helped a little. Smiling, she nodded to the werewolf, and Oryn went to work healing Kale's wounds. Damage from everything but Vlad's swords mended quickly on their own.

Forgetting the warriors around him, Kale glanced at Adwen's somber stare. "You know, you're as crazy as I am when you're mad." He smiled.

The sign of forgiveness took some weight from her shoulders. His joke even made her quietly laugh.

By the time Oryn finished, the werewolf's hands had regenerated. Picking himself up, Kale summoned the bundle that Garret had given him in The Corner. Setting it by Vaughn, he unfolded the cloth. A bottle and another long object in a thin cloth lay before them. Kale grabbed the ornate black wine bottle and flipped open the gold mechanical stopper. While the Holy Hounds picked up the scent of human blood, Kale smelled a pure sweet aroma.

The smell caused Vaughn to stir. Kale helped him drink a few drops, then closed it tight. The vampire gasped, invigorated. Fully revitalized, Vaughn gently took the bottle, smiling at the way it caught the faint light.

"Is this a dream? Waking to those visions ... I feel as if I might still be sleeping. Kale?"

The werewolf chuckled. "It's good to see you, too."

Vaughn beamed. "I am awake, and you are truly here." He glanced around at the strange faces. "Who are these friends of yours?"

Helping him to his feet, Kale introduced them: "Vaughn, I'd like you to meet Adwen, Jack, Alexander and Sir Oryn. They are the Holy Hounds."

Intrigue filled the vampire as he inclined his head, studying them closely. "Ah, fitting company for you, boy."

Kale rolled his eyes and scoffed. "Don't call me that in front of them."

Vaughn chuckled softly in his deep, smooth voice. "Adwen, Heir of Darien Andredan, it would be an honor if you would accompany us to my place of business. It is far more appropriate for rest and discussion than a windy roof."

She nodded. "It would be my pleasure."

Vaughn stood before the threshold to The Corner. He stared at the place where the door was missing, silently irate. Slowly turning to give Kale a raised eyebrow, he muttered to the sheepish werewolf, "I see you've been here already – before you found me elsewhere."

Kale chuckled, scratching the back of his head at an invisible itch.

"Your manner speaks fathoms."

Trading shame for a more somber expression, Kale replied, "What can I say? Leeches wreaking havoc make my blood boil."

Understanding, Vaughn frowned. "I see."

The ancient vampire prepared for worse news than a broken door as he entered. In the bar, Leena and Garret worked hard to clean up the mess. A few hours had passed, and they were still collecting broken furniture and the dust of dead leeches. When they sensed movement in the hall both turned, their faces transfiguring into fearsome ghouls. Hands turned into deadly talons. Both hissed to warn off potential leeches.

Soft laughter came in response. "Do not worry. I do not thirst."

Only one voice ever spoke those words in the bar. The vampires took on more human appearances and switched from guarded to glad in an instant.

The sight of their smiling leader almost brought Leena to bloody tears. "Vaughn! That brute brought you back!"

Kale was incredulous. "Who are you calling a brute?"

While Adwen and the rest joined them, Vaughn paused to survey the look of the place. "This is not as I left it. Leena?"

"Yes, sir?"

"Leave Garret to clean for now. Look into procuring the stocks we were unable to obtain during my absence."

Garret frowned. "Easier said than done. Charlie is gone."

Deep sorrow filled Vaughn's ember and steel gaze. "Ah. There shall have to be a service provided for his ashes."

Leena scowled. "The leeches threw them in the gutter."

To her, he nodded kindly. "His most prized possessions then. Do not let the wanton leeches ruin his memory. I will not allow them to poison what good Charlie gave us in his undeath."

Cooling her rage for the first time, she looked away while trying not to cry. "Yes, sir."

"Leena, if you please. Do the best you are able without Charlie's abilities. We shall need to procure another who is trustworthy and able to perform his duties."

"Gladly, sir. I'll get right to work." She left to make a few calls to those who would answer in the late hours.

Vaughn went to a large round table, gesturing for everyone to join him. "Please, honor me by sitting, Lady Adwen."

"So you've heard of me?" she asked.

A pleased smile warmed the beautiful vampire's pale complexion. "Stories and rumors that leaked from the other world. I'm certain you know how distorted they can become with conjecture and fabrication." He said this to Oryn, who could not stop staring.

Kale chuckled in amusement. "I think someone wants to talk to you."

"Sir Oryn Conrad, is it?"

The green-eyed warrior frowned, confused. "You know of me?"

"As I said, rumors and stories are often riddled with false-hoods and lies. At the least, I've heard your name whispered by fear-ful fiends. They say Sir Oryn is a knight whose rage toward inhuman beings is rivaled only by his skill with a blade. Others say that the knight was dead and rotting in an unmarked grave, lost while on a deadly hunt. The wildest of the rumors was that the Heir of Darien walked into the fortress and handpicked you from the ranks to serve as second in command. And that you gladly kneeled and accepted her favor with honor for the Order."

Oryn's frown deepened.

"Is there any truth to these stories?" Vaughn's expression showed how little credit he gave to the rumors from the mouths of wayward fiends.

The knight finally replied, "As much truth as one would dare add salt to a meal."

An amused look came over Vaughn as he studied the knight. "You were of high rank, were you not? The look of your posture and manner betrays you. Captain, perhaps?"

"And General."

Intrigue vanished from Vaughn, and he saddened. Recover-ing from the moment of lament, the vampire forced a weak smile. "As was I."

No one was more shocked than Oryn. "There has never been any mention of this."

"Of course not. I was only ever remembered in Dargadia as Evrox. But my true name? Even I have forgotten it. Too many years have gone by without hearing it said. Any record of my name was scrubbed from the Order; it was smeared from the hall of honor be-yond recognition. A whole swath of history was burned to keep my prideful mistake from dishonoring the Order."

"What history was lost?"

"A war – one I led against the forces of Mortigad in the east. I built Fort Wight. It was my greatest outpost." Sighing heavily, he shook his head. "But it seems the undead are not the issue; not anymore. Nor are leeches. We must discuss the circumstances of my rescue."

Adwen leaned forward in her seat. "What did they want with you?"

Vaughn grimaced. "Experimentation, samples and such. Those humans wanted to find the secret of my nature – a vampire immune to the burn of daylight. It was their goal to unlock the riddle and reproduce it for their purposes."

Jack felt sick to his stomach. "Did they figure out how to make day-walkers?"

A sincere smile came over Vaughn. "No, they could not. Neither could they reproduce the abilities of other vampires. It seems that each vampire's ability emerges spontaneously upon becoming undead. They were unable to discover anything useful."

"How do you know all of this?" Jack asked.

"What happens to humans who are careless around vampires?"

The warrior pointed to his own neck and rolled his eyes.

"I drained the human leading the vampire research in the blink of an eye. That poor excuse for a human died before his mind registered the feel of my bite. It was that incident that forced them to drain me into hibernation and cancel their vampire experiments."

Adwen turned harsh. "They were trying to make vampire soldiers? What else were they doing down there?"

"Through the fragmented memories I drank, I could only learn so much. By his blood I saw many floors without windows, filled with machines and laboratories for other dark experiments. The bulk of what this man knew had to do with his own branch of research: vampirism. However, he did hear whispers about other departments. The soldiers who frequented the halls frightened him."

Kale explained, "They have resurrected Vlad the Impaler."

The information made Vaughn's gaze dart to his, grim and intense.

"He's been made a demon and has possession of those soldiers, as well as a body made of demon-steel. It's covered in protective runes to make him immune to Adwen or any holy powers."

Vaughn became even more intense. "Who is behind this?"

Kale hesitated before answering, "Sycan."

The vampire's beautiful face transformed into a monstrous

visage, raking talons clenching. He stood and hissed in anger, gnashing long snake-like fangs.

Despite the reaction, Kale remained calm. "Sycan's dead. He left a message for Adwen to find, along with a pet witch. She continues his work."

Somewhat reassured by Sycan's death, Vaughn ceased hissed and retracted his fangs and talons. As the ghoulish face displayed relief, his face shifted back to human. He leaned back in his chair as his shock dissipated. Jack and Alexander were unsettled by the display of rage.

"My apologies for the outburst. It will not happen again."

Oryn was unfazed. "You knew that wretched beast?"

Vaughn frowned deeply. "We only met once, but I had more than enough cause to revel in his undoing. If he is behind this, I need not tell anyone here how terrible this is. Like the leaders of darkness, he spun his webs wide enough to ensnare worlds. This can only mark the beginning of more sorrows."

"There are already more sorrows," Adwen added.

The vampire stared.

"The Order of the Master Knights is gone. Dargadia is trapped in an endless night, and I have been bound to the fate of the magic in the earth there. While on the other side, I am the weakest of us."

Heavy regret came over Vaughn. "Then all of the temples have fallen to ruin."

"Yes."

"It seems my departure did not prevent their collapse. I was present when the temple in the east fell. After that, I was in the Grand Temple of Light in the heart of Dargadia as it fell. So I left that world and vowed never to return. It was my fault for the loss of those holy places."

Adwen shook her head. "You are not to blame. This was always meant to happen."

Her kind words did not sway Vaughn. "All things that happen were meant to happen, good lady. Our faults are still our own, even if they are foreseen. It does not excuse the mistake."

She frowned. "We came to find you to see if you would like to help us."

Vaughn was speechless.

"Things are getting more complicated," she told him. "We need all the help we can get. If you really are to blame for anything, helping us could only redeem you."

Vaughn beamed.

Smiling at the look on his old friend, Kale gently nudged him with an elbow. "This is the part where you accept the offer."

"I ... must apologize. Words escape me. It would be the highest honor to serve the Light with my blade once more."

The genuine gratitude warmed Adwen's heart.

"What would you ask of me, good lady? For your service, I would break my vow of exile from Dargadia."

"That won't be necessary. With Vlad and this witch, we are spread thin. The magical world needs us badly, and it looks like this world is in great danger."

Bowing his head in agreement and respect, Vaughn continued to admire her. "Say no more, Lady Adwen. The witch shall be tracked down, as will the demon in his shell."

She shook her head. "Stay away from Vlad if you can. Avoid taking him on alone. I need you to find information. If Vlad and Diana the techno-witch are trying to make supernatural soldiers, I want to know how many, where they are and how to stop them."

Vaughn frowned in confusion, "Diana the techno witch?"

Kale explained, "Remember what I said about my leaving Los Angeles? Turns out she was a witch from the start. She has no magic. It's what threw me off the scent the first time."

Vaughn nodded. "I shall use the utmost care then."

Jack called for their attention: "Excuse me, but what's the story with this witch and Los Angeles?"

The vampire and werewolf exchanged dark glances before Kale answered, "I tracked down a black-market ring selling children as play things. No need for me to say what kind of play things."

All the Holy Hounds were disgusted.

Jack's stomach wrenched with anger. "Why isn't she dead, Big Guy?"

Kale sighed with bitter regret. "My own code of ethics: no women, no children. Cut-off age for feeding on bad ones was sixteen. I refused to break my own rules. Had I realized what she really was, the rules would not have applied."

As much as the warrior admired the werewolf's intentions,

part of him wished that Kale had broken those rules just once. Jack bit his tongue, recalling how hard things were for him with the hunger for human flesh.

Vaughn interrupted the gloom with a firm word: "Had you not spared the woman, no matter how wicked, I might not have extended my hand to you in the first place."

Kale felt a little better. "Thanks."

"Now then," Vaugh said, "I would like to take care of a few details in my business before setting out."

"Of course," Adwen agreed. "We need to get moving, too. They're a few steps ahead of us. It's time to move faster."

"Indeed. May the Light Spirits guide your feet, Lady Adwen."

"Same to you, Vaughn. Or should I call you Evrox?"

He chuckled. "No, just Vaughn, good lady."

When everyone stood to go, Kale had an idea. "Adwen?"

They looked at his begging expression. Sensing his heart's desire, she frowned. "I told you I can only do that once."

The werewolf sighed, and Vaughn grew curious.

"Whatever is the matter?" the vampire asked.

"It's nothing," Kale muttered.

But Adwen smiled. "You can, though."

"Say what?"

She nodded. "You can lend him a piece, but it would set you back a little. Is it worth it?"

Grateful and certain, Kale beamed at Vaughn. "Absolutely worth it."

More confused than before, the vampire watched Kale draw back a sleeve on his jacket. Vaughn saw the marks of golden flesh catching the black light. It was then that he understood he was about to be given a part of that impossible gift.

To Kale's surprise, the swirling markings had spread beyond his elbow. To find a piece to share, he had to remove the jacket. The large exposed scar on his chest contrasted with the brilliant metallic markings. Garret stopped cleaning to watch from across of the bar as the werewolf chose a section to offer the vampire.

Before Kale could begin, Vaughn tried to refuse: "You need whatever gift this is more than I do. Keep what you've earned. You deserve it."

But Kale was firm: "So do you."

Vaughn frowned. With no interest in hesitating, Kale dug two claws deep into his skin around a fragment of golden flesh. It was rooted deeper than expected, so he dug deeper, drawing thin streams of blood. He snarled at the pain but did not let it distract him. Gripping a piece grown from Adwen's heart, his claws pulled and pried at it like a loose tooth. The effort paid off when the piece was in his claws and the wound rapidly closed. Satisfied, Kale turned to present it.

Garret saw how it shone and was frightened. "Sir, don't!"

"It is alright," Vaughn reassured his companion. "I will not be harmed." He approached Kale, giving a stern look. "I accept this on one condition."

"Sure."

"Don't waste what time you've been blessed with."

Kale froze. Uncertainty came over him. Vaughn's gaze was stony and unmoving in the seriousness of the terms. His strange, haunting eyes spoke to Kale in a way that only he could understand.

Swallowing a lump in his throat, he nodded. "Alright. I promise."

At this, Vaughn inclined his head and gave Kale a scrutinizing look.

Kale smiled and scoffed. "I promise."

"Good. Waste is unbefitting of one of your caliber."

Kale presented the small piece of golden flesh. "In turn, don't waste this."

"These are terms I agree with completely." Nodding in thanks, Vaughn gently accepted the warm, metallic mass.

As it left Kale's claws the piece of heart shone then glowed with light, making Garret duck behind the bar. It was barely brighter than a candle. The light vanished and reappeared as a ring around Vaughn's middle finger. A smooth blue gem sat in the golden band.

Vaughn took a moment to admire it. "Adwen, I may not comprehend this gift, but I do not take it lightly. Thank you."

Jack smiled. "For a vampire, you're not half bad. If the big guy says you deserve it then that's good enough for me."

Alexander nodded. Oryn kept to himself that sharing the piece with Evrox was pleasing to him as well.

Adwen beckoned her friends. "We had better go. Until we

meet again, Vaughn. Be careful in your search."

He bowed deeply. "It is an honor to serve the Light, Lady Adwen."

Chapter 21
First to Fly

Leaving the world of machines for the world of magic, the fiery portal closed at their backs. Adwen staggered from the sudden loss of strength. Oryn held her steady as she adjusted.

"Thank you."

The knight smiled and nodded.

Cedars and pines towered around them in a valley at early dawn. High mountains surrounding the little valley cut them off from any recognizable landmarks.

"Where are we?" Jack asked.

"In the mountains far north of Dargadia."

"Should we stop by Jenkirk? I miss our pup, Tamis."

She shook her head. "Absolutely not. I'm sure it's chaotic, but the new Order must deal with that on its own. We have a bigger job to do."

The warrior frowned and fidgeted. Noticing at last, Kale laughed hysterically at Jack.

"What's so funny, wolf-man?"

Pointing a claw at the warrior, he sniggered through sharp teeth. "You're scared of meeting the dragons."

Jack scowled, folding his arms. "I am not."

Alexander cut in: "You are. When you cross your arms, you're lying."

"What?"

"Ashley told me awhile back, and you just now crossed your arms."

Oryn snapped, "Enough!"

"He's right, guys," Adwen agreed. "Stop fooling around."

The argument ended, but Kale could not stop sniggering. Adwen led the way north shaking her head and smiling.

Dawn brought brilliant daylight to the windy passes. Birds flew, and eagle calls sounded from lofty updrafts. After a few hours of silence, the banter returned. Oryn wished they would be quiet, but he tolerated the petty games so long as they left him alone.

"My turn," Alexander stated as he began to sniff and ponder. "I smell with my little nose, something that rhymes with hat."

Sniffing the air, Jack pondered. "Good one." He sniffed a second time. "Is it animal or plant?"

"Not giving any hints since you cheated last round. You read my mind."

"I did not!"

Kale joined the game. "It's a rat."

They stared at the grinning werewolf with his hands in his pockets.

Alexander admitted, "That's right."

"You're good," Jack told Kale. "Now it's your turn to pick something."

"Alright, mate. I smell with my little nose, something that rhymes with dumb."

The warriors exchanged skeptical looks.

Jack was suspicious. "Are you really playing?"

"What do you think? Guess already."

Alexander sniffed then sighed. "Plant, animal or mineral?"

Kale stared with a sly expression.

Rolling his eyes, Jack groaned, "Okay, I'll bite. Plum."

"Come off it, mate. Do you smell fruit trees out here? Guess again."

"Crumb?"

"Nah-ah."

The Marine raised an eyebrow. "Is it bum?"

Kale chuckled, "No."

"Is it scum?"

"Try again, losers."

Jack scowled.

He sighed, still smiling. "Give up yet?"

For a long moment, Jack glared, trying to figure out the answer. Coming up with nothing, he growled, "Fine, I give up, Big

Guy."

"How about you, Yankee?"

"Sure, I give up." Alexander replied.

Kale heaved a satisfied sigh. "I smell boredom."

While Alexander frowned, Jack was affronted. "I knew it!"

"You're as bad as he is," Alexander admonished.

Shaking his head, the werewolf corrected the Marine: "No, I'm worse."

Even Adwen found herself giggling. The knight rolled his eyes in annoyance.

"That's the last time I try to play with you," Jack groaned.

"Aw, don't be a wet blanket. Would you like me to change your nappy?"

Jack smiled at the casual insults. "Vaughn sure put you in a good mood."

A warm expression came over Kale. "It might come as a surprise, but he's like a father to me. Vaughn's a good one."

"You two have a lot of history?"

"Only a year or so. He found me at my worst, picked me up and dusted me off. No telling where I'd be without him. Garret, Leena and Charlie were similar cases, but they came long before I did."

"Glad we could rescue him," Jack said with a smile.

Kale beamed at the short warrior. "So am I – more than you'll ever know."

Alexander interrupted the moment: "I smell something."

"Seriously, Jarhead?" Jack rolled his eyes. "The game ended as soon as Big Guy broke the rules and killed the mood."

An instant later, everyone picked up a strange scent. A powerful source of magic was speeding their way. Trees along the mountain pass miles away swayed and rocked as something big rushed down the slopes. The rumbling underfoot made everyone tense. Oryn put himself between Adwen and whatever or whoever was headed toward them. Whatever it was, it had dark matted fur and bright glowing eyes that shone like suns. A thunderous bark echoed to them from a beast the size of a small shack.

"Hold where you are!"

Seconds later, a giant beast with carved oak armor slid to a stop before them, claws scrapping into the earth. It resembled the

Woar Dog breed from Dargadia, and it wore the breed's helm on its head – a long spike mimicking a unicorn horn inlaid with golden swirling designs. The rest of the fearsome beast's armor glinted with the same lustrous runes. Adwen and her warriors recognized this being as one of the new Guardians. His body radiated magic.

"Adwen, the Tame One, so it is you. I thought I smelled werewolf on the wind." Then the Guardian spotted Kale. He snarled, lowering his helm with the spike pointed for the werewolf's heart.

But Adwen blocked the Guardian's path. "Wait! He's not like the others. Kale serves me and the Light."

The Guardian was stunned and suspicious. "Serves the Light? Let me see this one for myself." He approached and began to sniff Kale, gazing deep into his eyes.

Adwen stepped aside. She knew Kale would be accepted. As the armored Guardian inspected the dark stranger, suspicion gave way to curiosity. Then intrigue made the creature cock his head. Kale was unafraid, waiting for this Guardian to come to a decision. Long ears pricked as the beast cocked his head to the other side.

"You are not like the others. I see the truth. Does that frighten you, boy?"

Kale frowned. "Not really, no."

Wagging his short tail, the Guardian laughed.

Adwen greeted the creature: "I'm grateful that you came to us. We need to find the Dragon Mother. Can you tell us where to find her?"

Confused, Jack asked Adwen, "Were you planning on running into a random dragon to ask directions?"

Alexander rolled his eyes. "Shut up, Jack."

To their surprise, the Guardian nodded. "Though I have never been there, I know where the grand dragon can be found."

Adwen was relieved and pleased. "Where and how far is it?"

"I can do better that tell you; I can take you there."

"Thank you so much! We need to hurry."

Lowering his shoulders, the Guardian offered to carry her. "Of course, there is never time to lose."

She climbed onto the thick armor, sitting behind the broad piece that rose up past the creature's neck. Taking hold of the edge of the armor plate, Adwen was ready to ride. "Let's move, Keeper of the Strays."

Eager to run again, the Guardian darted through the forest, and the others followed.

Their pace was as swift as a falcon. While the warriors and Kale ran with Adwen astride the Guardian, trees bent and flexed out of the way. When groves grew too dense, the trunks magically warped to let the Guardian through and resumed their normal shape after he had passed. Groaning wood echoed in their ears, and leaves and needles fell at random. The Holy Hounds marveled at first then grew accustom to the Guardian's abilities. Nevertheless, the journey was unforgettable.

Green valleys faded into rugged rocky canyons. Forests dwindled into groves in the ascent to higher elevations. Slopes became thicker with snow the farther they raced, and biting cold wind rasped at their faces. Throughout the day, the trek took them deeper into the mountains than they had ever been.

Sunset was upon them when their pace began to slow. The Guardian did not tire, and neither did Kale, but the warriors were exhausted. The lack of their usual strength made the journey arduous. Eventually the giant creature carrying Adwen slowed to a plodding gate along a broad path covered in snow and ice.

Coming upon a cavernous opening, the travelers came to a halt. The tired Holy Hounds gazed into the deep shadows unable to smell what lay inside. The Guardian crouched to let Adwen off at the snowy sloping entrance to the tunnel.

"Here is the way to the grand dragon. I know she is here, but I do not know how far inside you must go."

"Thank you so much for your help. Did Tamis and the new Order reach Jenkirk safely?"

He nodded. "They reached the valley without incident. I spoke briefly with your youngest warrior. He is well and was preparing to set out on his own back to the hidden cliff sanctuary. This Order of the Gargoyle has strong leaders."

Adwen smiled. "It does."

"Will you need my services after your meeting with the Dragon Mother?"

She shook her head. "We will be fine. I won't keep you any longer from your service at the border."

A grim look appeared in the Guardian's glowing eyes. "I must inform you that something is amiss. For some time, demons assailed the northern border. Of late, the assaults have ceased."

Oryn and Alexander exchanged glances.

"Since the darkness fell over Dargadia, they pushed at the borders, but not now. This troubles me greatly."

"Thank you for letting us know. We'll take that into account."

The Guardian bowed. "I take my leave, Tame One. Good luck, and may the Light Spirits be with you."

"Same to you."

As the Guardian in oak armor raced away, they turned to the looming tunnel. The path was steep, and deep snow spilled far inside, forming a treacherous slope. Climbing out would prove difficult even -with their strength.

Giving her friends a shrug, she clasped her hands eagerly. "Well, looks like there's just one way to go. Everyone ready?"

Oryn gave a firm nod. Alexander and Kale wore amused expressions, glancing at Jack between them.

The short warrior grew frustrated. "I said I'm not scared! Back off already."

They could smell the faint scent of fear and shook their heads.

Adwen rolled her eyes. "Ready enough, I guess. Let's move."

Oryn stayed by Adwen to help her descend the slippery slope. Snow crunched, spilled and crumbled with every step. With an arm around her shoulder, the knight braced her by his side.

Jack started to follow but whipped around to glare at Alexander. Pointing an accusing finger, he snarled, "I hear that thought, Jarhead. Don't even think about it."

"Calm down. It was only a thought. I'm not going to do anything."

Scowling, Jack hesitantly started trudging down.

Kale shared another sly smile with the Marine, having had the same idea. Because Jack could not perceive Kale's thoughts, the werewolf could not resist this opportunity. Aiming a hand for the unaware warrior, he flicked a claw at the air. Jack felt a gentle push in the small of his back. He flung his arms like a windmill, trying to maintain balance. It was no use. With a high-pitched yelp, he tumbled and slid down into the dark.

Jack sped past Oryn and Adwen. They watched in surprise as Jack careened by them shouting in fright and outrage. She and the knight exchanged bemused looks before continuing.

Alexander chuckled. "I've been wanting to take him down like that for years."

"I can tell. Shall we follow?"

The Marine gave a nonchalant shrug.

By the time everyone found the bottom, Jack was sitting on a rock, surly.

Adwen approached first. "Are you okay?"

Kale answered for him, "Looked like a lovely ride, mate. Want another go?"

"Ha-ha. Very mature."

The knight raised an eyebrow. "It would have been better to wait for the rocky slope before pushing him."

Adwen threw Oryn an incredulous nudge. "Oryn!"

He fell silent, but smiled at the mental image.

"Don't give them anymore ideas." She shook her head. "Now that you guys have had your fun, we are here. This is a dragon's lair."

Kale agreed. "And we aren't invited. We're trespassing."

Playtime ended, and their mood turned serious.

"Good to know." Adwen sniffed the air. "I smell them, but it's faint. Let's continue with caution."

The vast tunnel's darkness lay before them. The way was rocky but grew less steep and then leveled off. Wind howled in the now distant exit, diminishing while dripping sounds replaced it. Nimble footing allowed the companions to hop along uneven ground and avoid tiny pools of water. Limestone formed smooth rippling walls and undulating ceilings lined with stalactites. The collection of jutting stones was so high that their night vision could barely perceive them. Along the path, small objects scattered among the rocks crunched underfoot.

Jack picked up one after stepping on it. The smooth fragment reminded him of a very dry fingernail clipping.

"What the hell are these? They're everywhere."

Kale didn't need to look to know what he was talking about. "You really want to know?"

"Yes, I do."

"Dragon whelp scales. They shed them when the adult scales start to grow."

"Oh." It was the size of a measuring spoon. He dropped the broken scale and declined to ask where the baby dragons had gone.

Far inside the depths, Alexander began to feel somewhat claustrophobic. The scent of dragon thickened until they could taste it in the air, and the silence made everyone leery. When the tunnel narrowed into a subterranean canyon, no one knew what to expect. No dragon could fit through this space, but the smell was stronger than ever.

As Adwen led the way, she studied the walls of sheer rock on both sides. The damp cave passage ended before the canyon, where layers of different stone appeared in colorful ribbons. The farther they walked, the more the stripes of different rock seemed to mingle – to the point of swirling.

The strange rock perplexed Adwen. "Does anybody know anything about geology?"

Jack and Alexander nodded.

"A little," the marine shrugged. "But we aren't experts."

"I do," Kale replied.

They gave him questioning looks, and the werewolf shrugged.

"The mind of the man I was placed in is a college graduate. He was into music and earth science. What do you want to know?"

"Take a look at this." Adwen pointed at the strange way the layers of earth intermingled. "Is that unusual to you?"

Staring at it, Kale puffed. "That's not natural. Looks like magic to me. The shale, sandstone and limestone would have been deposited in parallel layers. This ruddy mess is ridiculous."

Tired and still irked by the prank, Jack leaned back against the opposite wall. Cold, dark stone supported him as he listened. Heaving a sigh, the warrior laid his head back against the cool surface. The image of an enormous scaly eye lid opening filled his mind.

His eyes were wide open, but he could see only the psychic vision. Terror paralyzed him.

"Guys?"

They turned and found him leaning back, staring up at nothing. Jack's face was drained of color. Mouth turning dry, he wet his lips nervously.

"Jack?" Adwen grew concerned. "Are you alright?"

The vision of the huge reptilian eye staring and dilating made his voice hoarse.

"They know we're here now."

Control returned to his limbs, and Jack leaped away from the wall just as the cave system began to rumble. He joined the others in bracing against the intense tremors. When they braced for a run, the layers of earth moved like water. A river of rock closed off their single escape route. Layers of earth swirled all around and closed in overhead, forming a constantly rippling bubble of sandstone and shale. In the darkness of the magical trap, the ground underfoot remained solid.

The warriors gathered around Adwen, watching how the stone barrier flowed. Loud grinding sounds drowned out their fearsome growls. She was as tense as her friends as they waited to see what would happen.

The dome of swirling earth parted from the top like a falling curtain. Ribbons of multicolored flames streamed through the air. When the earthy barrier vanished, they found themselves atop an endlessly tall pillar. Stable ground was far from reach inside the unveiled epic cave. Solid bronze shelves lined with soft metals were fitted into the walls like swallow nests, creating the appearance of a hive. Roaring and trumpeting dragons looked out from the countless nests, welded with their fire.

The warriors tensed as Jack marveled. "There are thousands."

A female voice rattled the air and vibrated in their chests, "Indeed, there are."

She was so vast that no one recognized her form at first. Moving at last, wings uncountable meters wide opened as the Dragon Mother woke from her slumber. Raw magic flowed in veins visible through the skin on the velvety membranes. Pale glowing rainbows of raw energy coursed through every scale. She appeared like a constellation in the near blackness of the lair. Her eyes were like two novae swirling with light when they opened to stare at the tiny pedestal. Smoke glowing with magic curdled from closed jaws.

Everyone gasped once they saw her clearly.

Thunderous chuckles caused stones to tumble from the

sides of the tiny island pillar.

Wishing to show no fear in the face of this being, Adwen stepped forward. "You are the Dragon Mother?"

For a moment, the dragon that appeared to be made of night sky studied her. Then her jaws loomed closer to inspect them all. The dragon was vast enough to swallow Castle Gailarien whole. She studied them for a moment. Another set of booming chuckles sent blasts of air that threatened to blow them away.

Adwen asked, "Why are you laughing?"

"You cannot comprehend my reasons, Child of the Gray Kingdom. None of you can."

Adwen said nothing, while the being with power beyond imagining chuckled again. Oryn moved to stand at her side against the breaths. Kale came forward.

"Then you know why we are here," the werewolf responded with caution.

The Dragon Mother's attention fell on him, but he stood firm despite the sudden end to the dragon's amusement. Much more serious than before, the creature answered, "I fathom the unfathomable. I see truth. Whatever the Light Spirits bid, I know, I understand. Yes, I know why you all have come."

Oryn glared up in defiance. "Then why do you laugh at us? Do you find our need amusing?"

Kale became urgent: "Watch yourself."

The knight ignored the warning but fell quiet.

The dragon watched the knight and mused for a moment. "You hold me accountable for the actions of the fallen among my brood. How vain. Shall I hold Keegan Jagger Conrad accountable for the crimes you have committed, Sir Oryn Reynard Conrad?"

Anger toward the creature vanished, and the knight found himself trying not to tremble.

"I see truth. I see your hearts as open testaments to your past, present and future." Eyes the size of small lakes fell again on Kale. She stared at him in silence.

Adwen humbly addressed her with a pleading expression: "The worlds are in danger. We need your help. The new Guardian of the White Sea Desert told us to find you and ask for aid."

Turning her attention on the woman in white with silver and gold hair, the dragon stared.

The quiet response made Adwen nervous. "The demons must be stopped. Won't you help us?"

The dragon seemed curious. "What would you ask of me?"

This felt like a test. "No more than you are willing to offer – no more and no less. Anything is welcome. Even a word of guidance is something."

Pleasure caused the swirling magic in the dragon's eyes to glow bright and churn. More shimmering smoke curdled and billowed from her jaws in a cascade.

"Please, help us."

At last, the Dragon Mother answered and sounded amused: "The Light Spirits made you well. Though not perfect, they crafted you for your purpose. You ask for help. I shall give it to you."

"What will you do?"

"What is needed and what is permitted. Do you wish to sever the dark tether that binds your strength to the navel of this earth?"

Adwen was breathless. "Yes."

"Then you must retrieve an artifact – the only item I have ever been commanded to forge. Find the Soul Focus."

Kale was confused. "What is the Soul Focus? I've never heard of it?"

The first dragon gave him a sly glance. "Why is that, I wonder?"

While he was busy pondering the riddle, Adwen repeated the question: "What is it?"

"The Soul Focus was made for you. It is forged from one of my scales with my fire and tempered with my blood."

Oryn scowled. "A black scale for Adwen?"

The others winced when he challenged the creature again, but this being was not susceptible to petty insults.

"You trust your sight too much, dear knight. You look at me and see darkness, a cut of night sky." To the cave around them she whispered, "Messengers, come to me with your light."

Hundreds of the fiery ribbons streaked toward their mother. When they were close, the companions saw that they were odd wingless dragons that floated by magic alone. They flew like scaly eels with thick manes, antlers, eagle talons and lion tails. Bright as comets, the messengers of the mother swarmed. They circled her head, neck and body, illuminating what the deep gloom concealed. Leagues of veins pulsating with magic fed many more miles of golden flesh and scales. Light danced on undulating metallic skin, lancing off in brilliant bursts as the glowing dragons flew past.

Everyone stood in awe at the sight.

"You, child of the Grey Kingdom, and I are alike. We were forged. Find the Soul Focus. It will break the bonds on your powers. It shall also unlock your full potential, harnessing your power enough to fulfill your purpose. With it you shall become all that you were intended to be."

"Where is it?"

She rumbled in anger, causing the messengers to scatter and disperse. Appearing again to be a piece of the cosmos, the dragon replied, "Stolen. It was taken by those that my children refer to as Mountain Fleas."

Dragons throughout this colony of bronze shelves lined with silver and gold bellowed, roared and hissed.

"You call them Dwarves."

"They have it?"

"It is the one thing they have been able to steal from my lair. They knew it was here; one of the tiny rock mites witnessed its forging."

Alexander asked, "How did they get it?"

"A small band took it from under my talons."

At this, Oryn scowled. "You let them take it then. Why? If we could not enter this place undetected, then you surely knew that they had come."

The grand dragon let more shimmering smoke roll from her jaws.

"Clever, knight. Yes, I saw them come and saw them go, while all others were unaware. There was one other who witnessed the crime. That name, I will not say."

Kale frowned. "Will not or cannot?"

Giving a discreet glance, she said nothing.

Oryn grimaced. "You allowed them to steal it. Why?"

"Obedience. I was commanded to let them take it. Had I been permitted, I would have gladly fed them to the brood of my brood. Everything is as it should be. The Light Spirits have cursed them for their added transgression. My children hate them for stealing the gold that lines their nests. It angers me, but I despise them for their pride. The Dwarves refused to take part in the first great battle for this world. Instead, their people chose to continue a fruitless war over petty pebbles."

Adwen was determined. "We'll get the Soul Focus."

Pleased with her, the Dragon Mother's eyes swirled with more light.

Adwen looked to her friends. Everyone was ready to go. Adwen nodded to the vast eyes hovering in the gloom. "We are ready."

"Once the focus is obtained, return the way you came. I shall ensure your escape. Take heed, for most of their kind are in turmoil. Their throne is contested and rightfully so. Their king is the foulest yet to bear their crown in eons."

Chapter 22

MADNESS IN GREAT ONES

An orb of stone again encapsulated them. Grinding sounds filled their ears as the powerful dragon sent them speeding toward Dwarven territories. Adwen let her body glow to light their journey. Earthen colors swirled past, but the ground remained solid, allowing them to stand or sit as they pleased. No one spoke for some time.

"Man."

Everyone glanced at Jack, wondering why he broke the silence.

With an uncomfortable expression, he shook his head. "She's way too big."

The others frowned, but were in no mood to tell him off.

"I still can't wrap my head around how big she is. I bet she could fit snug in the Grand Canyon."

Kale stood with claws in his pockets, deep in contemplation. "Probably."

Likewise, Adwen's gaze was distant. She had heard the phrase twice – first from Vlad and then from the Dragon Mother. Her heart ached to know.

"What is the Gray Kingdom?"

Alexander, Jack and Oryn turned to her and pondered.

"Where Darien came from," Kale answered.

She and the other Holy Hounds faced him. A grim look filled his eyes.

"It's where this war began. To be correct, it was where the darkness started a war with everything else. There are two worlds of the living: one of magic and one almost devoid of it. There are two realms of the spirit: one of chaos and the other of peace.

367

"The Dark Heart knew if they were to conquer all planes of existence, then they must eliminate all threats. Darien's kind were the only ones who could destroy them. The irony was that the light beings were peaceful. Only when one of them showed interest in combat did the Dark Heart finally act. The darkness was desperate to prevent others from becoming like Darien, the Prince of the Gray Kingdom.

"Darkness flooded the endless realm. The Guardian spirit race was exterminated. Countless souls were taken, as well. If it weren't for Darien's parents, hope would have died there. They sacrificed themselves to make a place for souls to seek refuge. Their two bodies came together and grew into the Great White Oak."

The others were enraptured. Even Oryn remained quiet and did not doubt the story.

"At the treetop, there was a way for Darien to escape. On the other side he found one of the living worlds. Slaying the demons that followed into the magical realm, he saved the lives of an Elf prince and his fellows who were on a hunt. But Darien was a spirit not meant to exist outside his own realm. After the short battle, he fell and began to fade. The Elf prince gave him life and a living form. The darkness forever knew him afterward as the Neverborn."

Turning to face Adwen, Kale's expression was like stone, and his eyes were sad.

"Somehow, you will have to go there and put an end to this imbalance of light and dark, to finish the war."

She felt fearful of what that journey would entail.

"If you cannot, then this fight will continue for too long and they will win," the werewolf cautioned the Holy Hounds.

Jack saw how frightened this made her. "How do you get to the Gray Kingdom?"

Kale wore a grim stare. "Die."

Jack's face flushed pale.

"But that would mean losing all physical things including weapons," Kale informed them. "Somehow, she must enter her domain with weapon in hand. All of you must join her in the final battle."

"What about you, Big Guy?" Jack asked.

Kale scoffed with a bitter-sweet smile. "I don't think I can go with you. If or when she wins, all shadow will be purged there. I would disappear."

His friends were taken aback.

Kale scoffed again and looked away. "It's for the best."

Jack scowled but held his tongue.

"Adwen must be the Heir of Darien, return with the Gray Blade and fight." Kale proudly added, "I will join you there if it is necessary. Whatever it takes."

The knight listened while gazing out at nothing. "Whatever it takes."

Sighing heavily, Adwen changed the subject. "Let's deal with the problem we currently have: Dwarves. Oryn, do you know anything about them?"

"I know a little of their language but nothing else of use."

"Kale?"

"Never met one, but I heard they are short, hairy and smelly."

Alexander furrowed his brow in irritation. "Have you heard anything helpful?"

"They are stubborn," Kale replied. "They live in a large network of chambers and halls they carve in the depths of mountains. Did I mention they smell bad?"

Jack rolled his eyes. "Yes, you did."

"How accurate are the stories from the other world?" Adwen asked, anticipating another flippant answer.

"Close enough. One thing to note is that their politics are brutal. Don't cross a Dwarf if you can help it. They hold a grudge for the rest of their long lives and tend to pass it on to the next generation. Likewise, favors are honored just as long, if not indefinitely."

She shrugged and nodded. "That's pretty close to the stories."

Jack smiled. "Dwarves sound charming."

Kale turned to him, aghast. "You mean you're not a Dwarf? All this time, and you didn't think to tell me! Cheeky bugger."

A sour frown pulled at Jack's face, while the others tried not to smile. "Low hanging fruit, Big Guy. I thought you were better than that."

Chuckling, Kale grinned, showing rows of sharp teeth. "Didn't want to miss the chance."

Alexander sniggered.

"Think that's funny, Big Dog? Wait until we get back home. A storm's coming your way, blondie."

"Roger that, but it won't matter. I can think back to these moments, and I'll still be laughing."

Jack could not help but chuckle as well. He knew it was true. Before he could add a quip, the front of the stone barrier opened. The side of the small space fell back, unveiling an unfinished corridor. Tools and rubble lay about, and the workers were nowhere in sight. The stone bubble let them out at the dead end and remained in place. The smooth convex shape would remain for them to be whisked back to the Dragon Mother.

Walking amid the unfinished construction, they sniffed. Tiny crystals glowed in strategic places, illuminating narrow paths. They shone in bronze lantern contraptions the size of coffee pots. A musky odor from sweat mixed with dirt and dust permeated the area.

Adwen led the way past vacant work sites segmented by scaffolds. "You were right; they smell."

"Doesn't help that this lot are heavy laborers. Water is a critical commodity, so baths are not an everyday thing."

Reaching vast polished halls with high vaulting ceilings and broad pillars, Adwen stopped.

"Kale, it might be best if you stayed back for this one. We can handle things from here. I doubt these people will care that I'm the Heir of Darien, so I can't vouch for you."

Kale chuckled. "That might even get you in a bit of trouble. Like I said, Dwarves hold big grudges. Darien warned them that refusing to help would bring misfortune. They likely blame him for every bit of bad luck."

"Great."

"You'll do fine. I'll scout out the tunnels here and be ready for when you're on the way back. I have a feeling a hasty retreat might be in order. Need to be prepared."

"Excellent. Do not to be seen."

His eyes glinted. "I won't be." Dark mist engulfed him as he prowled away and disappeared in the shadows.

Adwen led her warriors the other way into a soft breeze that brought faint smells of musk and hot metal. The halls were vast and long. No matter how far she took them, the scents in the air remained subtle. After several hours walking in the yellow ambience of crystals embedded in the walls, they still found no one. It became ever clearer that the Dwarves' scents were carried great distances from deep underground.

The passages and chambers were empty, and Oryn finally mused aloud, "It seems they were expanding and have yet to use these places."

Jack added, "They haven't been in these areas in a long while. There are a lot of reasons for construction to be put on hold, Cujo. What do you think?"

The knight pondered. "Perhaps it is due to what the dragon told. If their king's rule is being challenged, then many efforts would cease – some indefinitely."

"The big lizard doesn't like the dwarf king very much," Jack mused aloud. "Do you think it's just dragon bias?"

Adwen answered, "She is bound to tell us the truth or nothing at all. If the Dragon Mother says this current king is bad, then he's definitely rotten."

Alexander grimaced. "Roger that."

"What's the plan?" Jack asked, uncertain about dealing with the Dwarves. "Are we staying covert to look for the Soul Focus?"

Adwen continued to lead the way, staring straight ahead. "We are supposed to be walking this way until we find something."

Jack almost laughed. "Okay, so we're winging it."

Taking a moment to give him a smile, she laughed softly. "Yes, we're winging it."

Scents of smoke and blood drifted to their noses, striking the conversation from their minds. Roaring war cries echoed from a passage. Surprised by the suddenness, the Holy Hounds waited to observe. A small battalion of cloaked figures wearing metal masks burst from a doorway and sprinted down another passage. Just as they vanished, a flood of armed warriors charged into the vast hall waving steel swords and spears. An army continued to pour into the chamber, bellowing at the top of their lungs.

When the tide of angry Dwarves spotted the Holy Hounds, Adwen stood her ground, and Oryn looked for an escape. Soldiers charged from all passageways. Adwen knew there was no escape, and her warriors joined her in waiting as they were surrounded.

Oryn, Jack and Alexander prepared to resist, but Adwen growled. They froze.

"Don't fight them. Don't let them see what we are."

The knight liked this plan the least. He detested playing coy.

But when the swords and spears came within inches, he held his composure. No one so much as snarled at the soldiers, who gnashed teeth behind thick beards. The chamber was a sea of shouting Dwarves with hip lanterns and sharp blades.

Jack frowned, and Alexander wore a hard expression. Adwen remained indifferent to the aggressive display. She noticed a pair of armored figures wading through the ranks. A loud bellow reined the din into silence just before they reached the ring of swords and spears pointing at the intruders.

A heavily clad Dwarf with a vicious spiked hammer studied their captives with glowing eyes. His face showed equal amounts of disbelief and anger. Beside him, the second militant sneered. When the leader pointed at Oryn and spoke in broken Elvish, the knight was barely able to understand.

"How dare you trespass on our land? Who are you, and where are you from?"

Oryn glared and said nothing. This made the Dwarf turn shades of red and purple in outrage. Waving the hammer over his head, he bellowed in Dwarf language, "Take them to the palace!"

No one resisted as the army marched them to the hidden city. Hundreds of boots pounded on the way deeper into the mountain. Bigger and brighter sun crystals speckled the walls. After traveling several miles, they arrived. In the colossal chamber, a brilliant light shone like the sun. A netted ball of many crystals hung high over the city, filling the streets with daylight. Everything was like a hive around the powerful glow with golden beams filtering outward. It made the Dwarven city resemble a giant paper lantern.

The companions had no time to gawk as their captors forced them to continue. Down broad stairs they marched to the heart of the underground civilization. They passed levels of workshops, common housing and markets. Few Dwarves were in the streets. Those that saw the army hid. Men, women and children remained out of sight.

Down a darker passage they reached a broad cavernous chamber. Their fearsome parade moved steadily to an expanse between stout pillars where an empty throne waited. Behind the throne, a mosaic mural of mighty Dwarven kings glowed with inlaid gold and crystals. The ranks filed outward until Adwen and her friends were at the front, behind the two commanders.

A few yards from the steps, the greater of the pair gave a brief shout. The ranks halted and stood quietly. Then the two ascended to the throne, and the first sat. The younger one stood by his side. The king focused a cruel gaze at the strange captives. With a rough, booming voice, the Dwarf king shouted, "I am King Norin, son of Borin. You all are found guilty of trespassing in my domain! Who are you and where do you hail from?"

The question appeared to be directed at Oryn, but the knight maintained his cold demeanor. No one spoke.

"What manner of Elf are you? Speak! I know you are no mute."

As the Holy Hounds refused to answer, Jack's jaw clenched as he heard a whisper of the king's thoughts.

The heavily armored king swept a hand through the air, instructing a soldier forward. A Dwarf approached the Holy Hounds from behind. Without hesitation, the soldier drew a knife. Grasping Adwen by her hair, he held the blade to her throat. The warriors didn't move. Even Adwen held her defiant glare with the king.

Though angry, the king was amused.

"Elves cherish their women. Yet you show no fear of me taking her head. Tell me how you found Steel Crag Mountain when every entry is under heavy guard. Speak."

The soldier pressed his knife against Adwen's neck and gripped her hair more roughly. Still, the knight, the cop and the Marine stood unflinching.

King Norin sneered, "You're running out of chances. Where are you from?"

The Dwarf standing beside the king showed confusion at their refusal to speak. Growing angrier, the king's voice sounded like a low growl.

"Why have you come?"

Adwen and her warriors remained silent. Fury showed in the redness of King Norrin's complexion. Flicking a finger at Adwen, he commanded the soldier to do away with her. The instant she felt the knife move, Adwen countered with blinding speed. She flipped the soldier over her shoulder and onto his back. A loud thud of armor against marble echoed in the stillness.

For a few seconds, all was quiet. The army and the two Dwarves at the throne stared aghast. How the Elf woman had flung a Dwarf in full battle gear as if he were a doll was beyond their comprehension. Some Dwarves were slack jawed. Their king's eyes grew wide in shock before he gritted his teeth and stood.

In angry Dwarvish, the king shouted at the top of his voice creating a din of echoes: "How dare you show defiance in my presence? Take the Leaf-ears and keep them under lock and key!"

A small battalion marched forward and encircled them.

Amid the ruckus of boots and armor, the king pointed at Oryn. "We will speak later."

While the soldiers marched the intruders out, the fearsome glare of the Dwarf king never turned away until they were gone.

Keys mated with matching locks in the prison, securing the Holy Hounds behind steel bars in cramped cells intended for Dwarf occupants. Once the soldiers locked all the cells, the soldiers departed for other duties. Adwen listened to the fading footfalls.

When quiet replaced the subtle beats, Jack called to them, "Alright, they're gone."

Oryn growled resentfully as he bent the bars open to free himself, "They had better be."

Adwen struggled to bend her cell's bars, so the knight assisted, while the others freed themselves.

"Thank you," she told Oryn. "Everyone, bend the bars back to normal. Let's keep them guessing. If the cells are still locked and we're gone, they won't know what's going on."

Jack grinned. "I like the way you think." He and Alexander gladly did as instructed.

Once the prison bars were no longer bent, they gathered around.

"We evade detection for as long as possible," she instructed them.

The knight frowned and nodded. "The treasury should be the first place to search, but it certainly will be guarded."

Sensing other ideas in Oryn's head, Jack scoffed. "You just want a chance to take out the king."

He glared at the warrior for revealing his plan.

Adwen shook her head. "We leave the king out of this, if we are able. Killing him while we are here would be a relief but not for long. That would bring too much chaos. It might even start a war with the surviving Dargadians in Jenkirk."

The knight knew she was right, and Jack patted Oryn's shoulder. "Sorry, Cujo. No assassinations today."

Alexander mused, "What about whoever is contesting the king?"

"We'll see," Adwen shrugged. "I don't think finding them will be easy, though."

With that, they turned to go. Jack spread his psychic senses far to keep a look out. Smelling Dwarves was tricky in a network of tunnels with unpredictable airflow, so they relied on their friend's talents.

Jack could not help but remark, "Anyone else think it's weird the prison is empty?"

Alexander grimaced. "No. With a king like that, it would surprise me to find anyone alive."

Everyone frowned.

Jack suddenly growled, and they froze. "Wait!"

Adwen growled back, "Where are they?"

Studying a blank wall across the way, he was confused. "There."

Adwen trusted him. "How many?"

"Three. No, eight. Twelve. They are on the other side of the wall."

Before anyone had a chance to reply, a small blast knocked four large blocks of stone from the wall, sending dust and dirt flying. After a moment, the dust settled, revealing a tunnel. A dozen metal-masked Dwarves in black cloaks and armor emerged and locked gazes with the Holy Hounds. For a few tense seconds, Adwen's company studied the surprised figures.

A few spoke to one another. Then one beckoned them to follow.

Adwen's warriors hesitated, but she accepted. Joining the strangers in the tunnel, she looked back and called quietly, "Come on! The king's soldiers would have heard the blast. Let's move!"

Exchanging glances, they obeyed.

The mysterious Dwarves took them through a labyrinth of passages, secret doors and tunnels that led to false dead ends. Eventually, the Dwarves brought them to a safe house filled with black banners decorated with a gold anvil and red flames. There were two doors out, as well as the secret passage that closed behind them.

Once the door closed, the Dwarven company removed their hoods and polished steel masks. None attempted to speak with Adwen or the others. They exchanged whispers, studying the visitors with interest and hesitation. After a moment, Oryn stepped toward them, and their murmuring ceased.

"Why have you brought us here?" the knight asked.

Some of their faces hinted at understanding, but they struggled to interpret the words.

Another voice came from a door at the top of a stairway: "There are a few reasons you are here, Outlander."

Adwen and her friends recognized the armored Dwarf who had stood by the king's side, and they flinched. The Dwarf walked down the stairs into the brighter parts of the room. He removed his helm, watching how they studied his face.

His eyes were sharp, alert and calculating. Calmly appraising the small group of interlopers, he eventually burst out in merry laughter. "My father is such a pig!"

Oryn sneered, untrusting of the prince, "What is so amusing?"

Stifling the laughter, the Dwarf shook his head, smiling. "He's such a damned fool. He would never suspect that the leader among you is actually the woman."

Adwen and Jack shared surprised smiles. They sensed that this Dwarf was a good guy.

"Please tell me your names. I'd prefer if we were better acquainted after the nasty performance I had to play."

"My name is Adwen."

"I am Quin. You seem more than worthy of your name, if I do say so myself."

She smiled, beaming at the prince. "The same can be said of you and yours."

Prince Quin chuckled.

Jack was curious. "Where are we?"

"A safe place," Quin answered. "It's better that you only know that for now. Might I have your name as well, warrior?"

"It's Jack."

"Glad to make your acquaintance. How you all found this city is astonishing. The place where our army found you is a dead end with no exit. Topside is miles away. How did you come to be in this happy kingdom of ours?"

Jack puffed. "We didn't dig, if that's what you're thinking."

Quin had been thinking that, and Jack's statement got a beaming smile of amusement.

"That is the only explanation that is close to rational. Don't tell me you were part of a magical experiment that landed you in one of the worst places in this world. There are far better places to land. How in blazes did you get here?"

They did not answer.

The prince sighed. "What was done to free you was no small thing. That escape plan was intended to be used only if one of us were discovered – and fortunate enough to be imprisoned rather than executed. I've taken a large risk in bringing you here and an even larger one in showing my face."

Adwen considered his reasoning. "Why did you free us?"

"A feeling."

Jack raised an eyebrow. "A feeling?"

"Call it instinct, if you like. Instincts are a part of how I am still alive."

Oryn interjected, "What makes you so certain that your father does not suspect you?"

A cold glint flashed in Prince Quin's eyes. "Do I seem dead to you? If he so much as suspects anyone, they die. You saw his hammer?"

Adwen frowned. "Yes."

"I had to clean it after it was used on my brothers and my sister. They died solely on suspicion. No one wants to undo my father and his followers more than I do. Please, do me a service by extending a little more trust. To rescue you from that blasted dungeon, I've expended months of sweat, blood and lives of preparation. Tell me more of yourselves."

The truth of his answer tugged at Adwen's heart. "We came from Dargadia."

Abashed, Prince Quin's deadly expression turned into disbelief. "You're not dropping pebbles on my head, are you? You are a very long way from home. Whatever for? Not for the scenery, I'm sure."

"We're here for a relic. It appears to be made of gold. I need it."

Puffing incredulously, he shook his head. "We're Dwarves, good lady. We have an awful lot of gold here."

She hesitated to clarify. "It was forged by a giant dragon."

A chill ran through the prince. "Ah, that one. What do you want with it?"

"Demons have overrun Dargadia. I need it to fight them."

Confusion swirled in Prince Quin's mind, and he blinked hard. Thinking on all that he had learned, his conclusions were staggering. "You slay demons? And you need the one thing ever known to be forged by a dragon other than their gaudy nests?"

"It was made for me."

Realization dawned on him, and he blanched. Then he swore under his breath. "You're from the bloodline of the Light Warrior, Darien. If that trinket is indeed meant for you, no wonder we are cursed." To the other Dwarves in the room, he spoke their own language: "They are here for King Degrin's Heirloom."

Anxious banter erupted among the resistance leaders. One urged the prince, "Please, do not consider this! It is a folly! Think of the lives that it will cost! The whole city could be forfeit!"

But Prince Quin turned twice as fierce as the king. "I'll not take part in the crimes of my forefathers! If that damns me, so be it!"

The prince's outburst put an end to the frantic chattering, and they stared in fear.

He added calmly, but with no less intensity: "This could end the curse. Understand the gravity of that. She is the Heir of Darien Andredan. I will give back what was stolen."

A Dwarf Noble, who knew he could not talk Quin out of this, asked, "And what if the curse is not broken or if they fail?"

"Then the suffering of this city will end sooner than planned."

After a solemn pause, the gathering conceded. "As you wish, Your Highness."

Prince Quin turned to their guests. "I apologize. A few of my comrades spoke out of line." Becoming cautiously hopeful, he asked Adwen, "If you obtain the artifact, will that end our curse?"

She knew the truth and was glad to share it: "Yes."

Relief made his expression soften. "If you agree to take it far away from this place, I will tell you everything I know."

"I will take it worlds away from your city."

"It is a bargain then."

Hardly believing this was happening, the prince felt as if he might be dreaming. He launched into the story of the heirloom.

"When King Degrin was still a prince, he took a band into uncharted regions. They witnessed the making of a treasure like no other by the powers of a dragon as large as the sky. When it finished, it slumbered, and Prince Degrin stole the treasure from under the beast's claws. The impossible feat earned the favor of his father the king, as well as the people. They later made him king, even though he was third youngest among his brothers.

"King Degrin's rule was prosperous many a year, but he took ill by some sickness that none could cure. Before he died, he ordered that the relic should be entombed with him. After King Degrin was sealed in his rightful place in the necropolis, the curse began.

A grim look came over him. "Dwarves, good lady, revere our dead, especially our kings and queens. Our family lineage is like the rock we stand on. Their glory is ours beyond death. We have known no greater nightmare than our own ancestors' reanimated bodies hunting us down with the weapons and shields we buried them with. No matter how many times you cut them down, they get back up again and again and again, endlessly. Thousands of soldiers died in the fight to seal the passages where we used to lay down our dead."

Jack did not like the sound of this. "Used to?"

Frowning bitterly, the prince explained: "We've had no choice but to cremate them and grind their bones to dust. There is a tunnel dug for disposal of the ashes and bone meal into the depths. As far as we know, this is the one way to prevent our dead from haunting us. Rumor has it that even the wastes can reassemble into invincible fighters."

Adwen frowned. "I see why your friends were upset. Letting us into the necropolis would mean breaking through one of the barriers."

He nodded. "And risk letting them out."

Adwen weighed the options and glanced at the solemn resistance fighters. It was evident by their expressions that they expected to die very soon. To Prince Quin, she tried to be reassuring: "We will need to move fast, and the place we enter carefully chosen. Is there any way our entering and taking the relic would be beneficial to your cause?"

A small chuckled came in reply. "If you mean to kill the king, there is no need. We among the resistance know that the king is dying. My brothers led the cause before me. One of them slipped him a rare poison with no known antidote. It acts slowly – two to three years until it is fatal. Only now is he showing physical symptoms. His days are numbered less than a year now. If he learns what is happening, then may the Light help us all.

Then an idea struck him. "Perhaps your task can further benefit us. Most of my father's supporters dwell close to one of the sealed doors. Also, our resistance could claim some credit for the ending of the curse."

Adwen nodded. "It wouldn't be a lie."

The prince was pleased. "That is a little sugar in bitter water for our peace of mind. Should we survive this day, we will have the best chances we've ever had."

"Then let's put this to an end," she replied. "We're ready when you are."

"That is best. I've lingered too long. I must be back where the king expects me and play my dreaded role."

Quin issued a few commands to his compatriots. A few stepped forward to lead the travelers out of the safe house.

Before leaving through the secret passage, Adwen smiled at the prince. "You are nothing like your father."

Quin softened further than they or even the other Dwarves had ever seen him. "That is the most wonderful thing anyone has ever said to me. I wish you the best, Lady Adwen. We are all depending on your hasty success."

Oryn posed a final question, one that had been troubling him for much of this meeting: "Prince Quin, the king trusts you. Why?"

All color flushed from Quin's face, and Jack's expression turned sad. Forcing a kind smile, Prince Quin answered, "Through great effort and even greater sacrifice. Fare you well and take care. The accursed necropolis awaits you."

Bowing to Adwen, the prince stood and placed the helm back on his head. Quin's pace up the stairway showed no sign of weakness, though his heart was heavy. When he was gone, the resistance fighters donned masks and ushered the adventurers out.

On their way through the narrow passages, Oryn turned to Jack and growled: "I saw your face. What did you witness in his mind?"

For a moment, Jack considered not telling the knight. "His sister was killed by the king when Quin's brothers were being sentenced simply because she cried out for mercy. Then the king tested Quin by handing him the hammer. Quin had to execute his own brothers and pretend nothing but hatred for them, or else he would have been executed, too."

Oryn understood and felt great pity for the cunning son of a monster.

Chapter 23
THUNDER, LIGHTING AND RAIN

The Dwarves left the Holy Hounds at the doors to the cata-combs. The guides intended to be far away when the seal was broken. Fleeing the presence of Adwen and her warriors, the Dwarves vanished. Towering bronze doors bore stout symbols and skull shapes. As they approached, Jack whistled in awe of the sight.

"Would be nice to have the big guy right now. He could open this no problem."

Adwen gently touched the entrance to inspect it. "This is not locked. The seal must be inside."

Oryn and Alexander went to work pushing the heavy doors, and Jack joined in. Their combined strength parted the way, and a gasp of stale air whistled through the crack. When it was open enough, Adwen slipped inside. The others followed and discovered the sealed passage. An arch over the reinforced wall was engraved with Dwarven runes.

Adwen murmured, "Oryn, can you read that?"

Frowning, he admitted, "A little. What I can ascertain makes the rest somewhat clear."

Jack hesitated, then asked, "What's your best guess?"

"Here resides the cursed city of the dead. Any who open the way shall join them."

Jack wore a distressed look. "Nice. Very to the point."

Adwen cautioned her friends, "They can't kill us, but that doesn't mean this will be easy." She shivered.

Oryn nodded, then transformed. The colossal hound warrior in black and gold armor went to the barrier summoning his sword. While the rest watched, he bared his fangs and struck the blade into the rocks, creating a weak spot. Making magic cover one set of claws, Oryn withdrew the sword and snarled, delivering a mighty punch to the weakened wall. Green light burst over him, and the rocks exploded inward and rained down from overhead.

Wind rushed out from the concussive force. Dust shrouded them, and a faint glow from sun crystals made the air dance. Smells of mold and mummified bodies engulfed their senses. Out of the gloom and warm light, bright red eyes appeared. Angry groans rose higher, as the numbers of figures multiplied exponentially. Eventually the dust cleared. As it did, the vengeful dead saw the intruders and raised swords, axes, hammers and shields, and roared terrible battle cries. The sight and sound sent a chill through Adwen.

Seconds later, the dead army of Dwarves charged as if they were alive. Oryn roared and swung his sword, sending the first wave flying backward. Adwen ran to his side and let him lift her onto his shoulders. Jack and Alexander transformed, leaping into the fray, while Oryn carved a path through the ranks. Pushing into the necropolis, the dead behind them flooded outward into the city like fire ants.

Fighting against a river of raging corpses, the Holy Hounds never ceased striking and slashing with their weapons. No matter how many Adwen's warriors cut down, more replaced them, and those struck down rose again.

By the time they reached the first cavernous chamber of the necropolis, Jack gave up using his daggers. Instead, he used brute strength and telekinesis to throw the dead attackers out of the way. Casting them aside with his mind was challenging. Inanimate objects were simple, but objects that moved and squirmed loosened themselves from his grasp.

Alexander centered himself and became ignorant to pain. Heavy armor made him the best equipped in this fight. He helped protect both Oryn and Jack. The yellow hound warrior was as unstoppable as the soulless opponents.

Once they had fought their way into the rows of open crypts and mausoleums, they did not know where to go. The sea of dead was endless, and no signs indicated where the royal crypts lay.

Jack barked up to Adwen, "Where is it, Adwen? Where is the ..."

He yelped and howled as a wave of dead fighters dragged him down. The black and white Holy Hound disappeared under the army.

Adwen tried to sense the Soul Focus, while Alexander charged to rescue his friend. The masses that swallowed Jack were ancient warriors, far superior to the rest of the dead. They started to overwhelm the yellow Holy Hound and then went for Oryn. The most powerful among the revered dead hacked at the giant warrior, forcing him to kneel as they started climbing his body. Oryn roared, slashing madly to keep them from reaching Adwen.

A feeling stirred in Adwen's heart. The power of the Soul Focus called to her from deeper in the city of the dead. Stealing a frantic glance at Alexander and Jack, she knew what she had to do. Turning to Oryn, she felt guilt about her next move, but it was necessary.

In his big back-pinned ear, Adwen whispered, "I'm sorry, Oryn."

Just as he turned his head to look, she transformed into a large white dog. Adwen leaped from his shoulders and bounded across the combatants like a nimble cattle herder.

Alarmed, he howled, "Adwen!"

The dead were about to bring him low. The knight fought with even more ferocity, casting bodies off in all directions.

Adwen's paws pounded helms and broad shoulder armor as she raced. The tugging force on her heart led Adwen farther, and it grew stronger. Ahead, a well shaft to a lower level caught her attention. She darted for it and leaped over the dead. Her white form sailed down into the dark away from the chaos of the main chamber.

The fall was long, and wind rippled the soft white coat on her body. Solid ground appeared, and she landed in a smooth obsidian hall. All was still and quiet here. Tiny sunstone shards emitted enough light to cast faint shadows on the floor. The black rock in contrast gave the effect of walking in a starry night. Gold-leaf inlaid designs on the walls seemed to float in the air in rigid Dwarven runes. Down the passage, the guiding force pulled at Adwen more strongly. As she turned to gaze at a royal crypt, it continued its soundless call. The heavy door made of volcanic glass stood ajar. Thin beams of light filtered through the narrow opening.

She transformed out of her creature shape and crept toward the opening. Adwen's bare feet padded on cold rock, and her fingers gripped the edge of the door. With some effort, she moved it aside, and it glided open. The resting place for the ancient king held many coffers overflowing with gems and coins. Golden ornaments on shelves surrounded the sarcophagus at the center. As she looked upon it, the feeling called stronger than ever.

Standing beside the carved stone coffin, Adwen gazed upon the remains of King Degrin. Lavish silks clothed the mummified figure with a sword lying on his chest. The shining crown atop his head drew Adwen's attention. It was gold encrusted with priceless jewels. The center piece seemed different. The flat disk shape was not the Dwarven style. This part of the crown was smooth. Intricate engravings wreathed the ornament. While she cautiously reached for it, she saw what appeared to be damage on one side.

As Adwen was about to touch it, the king's shriveled hand lunged to stop her. His eyes opened wide, burning red with angry light. Out of fright and determination she snatched the crown and leaped away. Examining it feverishly for a moment, she gasped as the dead king started to rise and wail in anger.

Adwen tried to separate the Soul Focus from the crown. Soft metal snapped apart immediately. When the vengeful dead king saw her toss the useless crown away, he sneered, reaching toward her, "The treasure is mine! It belongs to me!"

The focus began to shine brightly in Adwen's hands, and she glared at him. "This was never yours, greedy spirit."

"No!"

In a flash, the focus flew from her hands into her chest. An explosion shook the mountain above and below. Blinding white light blazed throughout the necropolis, and a rush of wind howled. The burst of energy demolished the remaining seals, blowing the doors open wide. As quickly as it had blazed, the light vanished. All became still.

The dead had fallen and lay unmoving. They littered the ground like autumn leaves. Oryn, Jack and Alexander pushed corpses aside so they could stand and shifted into their more human shapes. Incredible strength filled their bodies. When a white light appeared from a distant hole in the ground, they saw Adwen approaching and smiled.

The light softened around Adwen before fading away. More powerful than ever, she felt relief when she spotted her warriors. Rapidly vanishing and reappearing in several flashes of light, Adwen reached them in seconds across the vast space, beaming.

Jack wanted to laugh, and Alexander felt as relieved as she did.

The knight was content to smile. "What is your command?"

Blue light swirled in her eyes. "We leave."

In a flash, the Gray Blade manifested in her grasp. Adwen swung it through the air and opened a flame portal to the unfinished Dwarven tunnels. Everyone leaped through, glad to leave the sea of corpses. The portal closed behind them, cutting off the sights and smells of the lifeless place.

Once in the gloomy hall far from the city, they were forced to stop, uncertain of their way. Many passages appeared the same. Adwen used her link to Kale for help navigating back to the stone orb.

Subduing his dislike of being underground, the Marine frowned. "Are we close?"

Adwen's expression went from distant into pleased. "We are. It's this way."

"You! Stop!"

They turned at once and saw a band of Dwarf scouts charging. The king had sent them to investigate how the strangers had first entered the mountain, but now they drew their crossbows. Oryn growled, baring sharp fangs.

Adwen scowled at the militants. Instead of fighting, she darted away with the warriors at her heels. The scouts could not hope to keep up. Nevertheless, they tried. The tunnels were their home; they knew them by heart. This passage was a dead end, giving the Dwarves great confidence. Weapons ready, the scouts continued the chase.

As the Dwarves arrived in the unrefined corridors, the shadows came alive. The small band gasped and froze when the sunstones vanished and an ominous presence came over them. It was difficult to breathe; the air was heavy. Not even their hip lanterns could dispel the dark. The hair on the backs of their necks stood, their eyes searching vainly.

The scouts remained stalwart until they heard faint wailing that chilled their blood. Their greatest fears began to manifest before their eyes. Ancestors long since dead with glowing red eyes charged from the end of the tunnel. Unearthly battle cries broke their courage at the sight of an invincible army of dead. Crying out in horror, the soldiers turned and fled. They did not dare to look back.

As soon as the Dwarves escaped his presence, Kale withdrew. Like water flowing down a drain, the dark energy siphoned back into his flesh. When it was gone, the many sun crystals illuminated the tunnels once more.

Smiling, Kale stood by his friends with claws in his jacket pockets. "Hairy, cheeky buggers."

Adwen smiled as well. "You were right; they were."

His raspy chuckles echoed off the hewn rock walls.

After another long, noisy journey underground inside the stone orb, it opened and folded back into the stone pillar. The nebulous eyes of the Dragon Mother gazed at the Holy Hounds. When she spoke, her tone was pleased.

"You have completed the task in good time and set that part of the world on a better path. Well done, Golden Child."

Adwen bowed, smiling, but when she looked again at the dragon, she was troubled. "There's something else."

Feigning surprise, the dragon remained pleased. "Oh? What is the matter?"

Holding a hand over her heart, she replied, "It's about the focus. It's broken."

Her friends were alarmed. The dragon tilted her head to one side. Her vast gaze seemed amused. "Indeed, it is. How inconvenient. I can see the Soul Focus wreathed around your heart. A piece is missing."

"Where is it?"

The Dragon Mother laughed softly, and the sound pulsed in the air. "Where? Who can say? Not I. You shall need it. The focus, as it is now, makes you mighty indeed. You no longer wear armor; the fire you attain through anger can now be called upon at will. But without the whole Soul Focus, your power is incomplete. Seek the knowledge of its whereabouts."

Kale had been in a quandary. Unable to standby any longer, he wanted answers. "You must know where it is. Are you not allowed to tell us?"

When the dragon looked at him, cool mirth dissipated. Serious as life and death, the creature stared.

"That knowledge is forbidden," she murmured.

At that reply, Kale clenched his jaw tight and flushed pale.

With the werewolf suddenly silenced, Adwen spoke again: "What do we need to do?"

Glowing magic mist curdled from the Dragon Mother's nostrils and between her gargantuan teeth. "Rest assured, Child of the Gray Kingdom, it will be found in due course. But I have something of great importance to tell you. Listen well, all of you.

"An army is mustering to swallow the land of sin. The power to open the black door will come after the sapphire shatters. To find the knowledge, open the black door. For now, it is beyond sight. You shall know the end is near when the demon called Cygnus dies and is no more. Then a sacrifice must be made in blood and tears, or else there is no future for the Gray Kingdom or any other. Heed these words, children. Never forget them."

Many dragons bugled in approval and reveled in her wisdom from the Light Spirits. The roaring and whooping echoed into the distance until they faded into whispers.

With the great dragon quiet, Jack turned to Kale. "I don't understand most of that. What do you think, Big Guy? Have you ever heard of a demon named Cygnus?"

He shrugged, "Can't say I've heard of that one."

Oryn became determined. "If it means ending this war, the fiend will be slain."

Adwen added, "But first things first; we need to take care of everything else."

No one disagreed. Then the dragon spoke anew, and they fell quiet.

"The path from here shall take you to Dargadia. It is time for my part in restoring balance."

"What are you going to do?" Adwen asked.

The great dragon beamed. "What dragons do – fly and breathe flame."

At this, Kale was thrilled. "Are you really? You're going to breathe into Dargadia again?"

The look she gave was full of warmth. "Yes, child, that I am."

Kale made an ecstatic fist pump in celebration.

"Understand, my fire contains magic, not light; it is no substitute for Adwen's powers."

She nodded. "We understand."

"Where the Fingers of the Void have been cut will dispel the fog. I shall clear the Fields of Despair and release the fallen innocents from the cursed limbo. Keep to your stone sanctuary in the north until the rains come. Then you will know it is done." To Kale, she added, "You will know what comes next. Be ready, child."

His red eyes glinted happily. "I will be."

The swirling galaxies in her eyes glowed at him with pleasure.

"Then we should go now." Adwen smiled at the creature. "It will be time soon."

"Yes. I have a final word."

They stared, enraptured. To their surprise, they saw the dragon do something none thought possible: She tilted her head and wore a pleasant smile.

"Good luck." Having bid them farewell, she roared, "Children, to me! We fly!"

Adwen summoned her sword to take them back to the overlook sanctuary as they watched the dragons swarm. The multitudes took wing, while the Dragon Mother raised her head high. They swarmed and encircled her like a cyclone as she used her magic to open an exit through the mountain top. Stone rippled in waves to make way for the gigantic dragon. Her body began to float upward as if weightless through the passage.

As she continued to rise, Adwen led her warriors through her portal. It closed at their heels. Turning around, they saw the blue flames vanish. The black mist enshrouding Dargadia greeted them atop the overlook. Adwen started toward the sanctuary entrance with Oryn at her side.

Jack called to her, "So, we just wait here?"

Stopping to look back, she smiled and nodded. "We will use this time to rest. Then we'll see if Vaughn has any information for us."

The sound of rapid movement in the tunnel caught everyone's attention. A rusty colored hound warrior came running.

"Lady Adwen! Sir Oryn, Jack and Alexander!" Tamis was glad to see them. He looked at Kale and was calmer but no less happy. "And Kale, it is good to see you all."

The werewolf chuckled.

Adwen quickly went to hug the youngest of her warriors. "Tamis, you made it safe! How was the mission?"

He growled softly as they released one another: "Kale's guidance served us well. Staying to the river was harsh, but no attacks came. Everyone made it to Jenkirk without losses."

She was afraid to inquire but asked, "How are the boys?"

"Remy is well, but Colin has taken ill from weakness."

The news was better than she had feared. "Thank you for telling me the truth."

Tamis cocked his head. "Colin will recover. He was improving before my departure."

This was encouraging. "Good."

"If you would like to catch me up on what has happened, we can go below," Tamis offered. "I've brought two deer from beyond the mist for everyone to share."

Jack walked with a skip in his step to the tunnel. "You're a lifesaver! I'm starved!"

Kale made no move to follow, so Tamis called to him: "Are you not joining us? You must know you are welcome."

Smiling, he shook his head. "It's nothing like that." Giving the black mist a sidelong glance, he added, "I want to be here when the fireworks start. I have to see this with my own eyes."

Adwen smiled. "Call us when it does."

"Count on it. Then again, you might not need me to."

The Holy Hounds left to talk and share a meal, leaving the werewolf to wait for the Dragon Mother's fire. When they were out of earshot, he went to the ledge and smiled to himself.

"Such a sweet kid."

In the black hours, Kale sat alone. He let his feet hang off the ledge over the shrouded landscape. The clear space between the fog and the stars stretched to the horizon beyond. It felt familiar. It was neither calm nor turbulent. Constant tension suspended in the heavenly purgatory.

He wondered: Did the stagnant air in this magical world sense or feel anything? It spoke to the Guardian by the sea, but he was not here to explain what that meant. A soft breeze began from the north, breaking across the face of the cliffs. True clouds began to roll in until the sky and the earth looked like mirror reflections. Kale's existential pondering ceased when he recognized the signs; it was almost time.

He squeezed his left hand with Adwen's golden marks as he smiled in anticipation. She would sense this and know what it meant. He enjoyed the calm while it lasted.

Adwen's bare feet and the boots and paws of her company reached his ears. Not taking his eyes off the clouds and mist, he called, "You're just in time. It won't last long, and it may never happen again."

To this, the Marine replied, "No wonder you're excited."

The werewolf chuckled. "Are you kidding, Yankee? What you're about to see has only happened once before at the dawn of this world. Before any creatures touched this earth, the first dragon flew and breathed her fire." A distant serene look came over him, and he added: "We're going to see this land reborn. It's going to be our job to deliver it."

Jack was overwhelmed by the analogy. "That's a big delivery."

Kale laughed to himself. A short quiet passed among them. Then he pointed at a rippling in the clouds above. "Watch there."

Resonant, pulsating sounds banished silence from Dargadia. The slow beating of unseen wings sounded like a gargantuan heartbeat echoing off the cliffs. Ripples in the clouds traveled from the north. The force reached the mist, causing it to undulate as the middle of the sky began to churn violently.

An intense golden glow appeared in the sky's misshapen vortex, and it erupted in a pillar of fire miles wide that pierced the mist. The light grew brighter than a sun. Like a nuclear explosion, the fire engulfed most everything. The column of fire began to travel across the land like a tornado, and many waves of rainbow colors trailed in its wake. Pure magic radiated the air, randomly creating odd shapes that looked like living things flying or walking in the heavens.

The massive shock from the fire striking the earth reached the overlook. Dust fell from crevices and small ledges, as it shook everything violently, then dissipated. The roaring pillar of fire rumbled in their ears. For several minutes, the golden column trailed by pale colors and shapes swept across the land. The observers marveled at the mist's retreat. When the task was done, the last tongues of flame fell like a curtain and vanished on the ground.

A sound like thunder reached the ledge. The wing beats faded, as the Mother Dragon flew off. After a momentary silence, a crackling boom sounded, and raindrops started to fall. The ensuing sprinkle became a deluge with roaring thunder and flashes of lightning.

Everyone stood in awe. The spectacle left the companions speechless and with hopeful faces.

"I love the smell of rain," Adwen sighed contentedly.

Kale stared into the storm with a dreamy look. "Same."

She fitted her arms around Oryn, as he wrapped his about her shoulders. They shared the brief happy moment.

"Let's get some sleep," she advised. "After the storm ends I'll open a portal."

The two continued to embrace as they left the overlook for the sanctuary. Jack and Alexander took a little longer to watch the rain before going as well. Kale did not move from the cliff ledge. Distracted, he did not notice Tamis approaching. By the time he did, the hound warrior was beside him.

"Might I join you awhile?"

Entranced by the rainstorm, he replied, "Please yourself. I won't stop you."

Tamis sat close to the werewolf and watched the weather.

"They told me all you've done for them – Adwen and the others."

For the first time, Kale's focus on the rain wavered. He wore a wry smile.

"Jack spoke very highly of you, as did Alexander."

"And Adwen?"

Tamis smiled as much as his canine face could allow. "That goes without saying."

To this Kale gave a genuine chuckle, "Of course."

"But Sir Oryn hardly said a word."

Kale made no comment.

"He mostly listened to the others as they spoke."

"I'd be surprised if he said a word of praise about me."

Tamis's huge amber eyes turned to stare. "I sense he distrusts you."

Kale muttered, "Shocking."

"But ... he respects you."

To this, Kale said nothing.

"He did not say it, but I sense it. I think he wants to trust you."

Finally, Kale faced the hound warrior. "Why are you telling me this?"

Tamis's ears flattened in discomfort. "I'm not entirely certain. I suppose, because you're one of us. You're a friend. Doesn't that mean I should tell you these things?"

Kale forgot the rain. Tamis's pure-hearted intentions left Kale in more awe than the sight of the Dragon Mother's fire.

Taken aback at how Kale stared, Tamis whimpered, "Did I say something wrong?"

Turning his gaze back to the storm, the werewolf muttered, "Nah, you're alright."

They sat awhile longer. Sounds of wind and water were like music. The waterfall beside them crashed, occasionally joined by rumbling thunder.

"I won't keep you, Sir Kale." Tamis stood to leave for sleep like the others.

"Just Kale, kid. I don't need an honorific."

Tamis did not correct himself. "See you again when I wake, friend."

Smiling, he murmured softly, "Later, kid."

Even after the warrior was gone, Kale did not feel as if he were alone. Was this what it was like to belong? Kale sighed. He did not know.

A sudden pang made him look far out into the storm. Unblinking, he got to his feet, staring past curtains of rain. Realization dawned on him, and he gasped, the whites of his eyes turning black. Lightning streaked over the falls, as he leaped out into the windy downpour.

Muddy slicks flowed down barren hills with no grass to hold the soil. Many cloven hooves stamped the ground, and a frightened cry erupted as one of the white creatures fell bleeding. The rest of the unicorns gathered close together, recoiling from the Wretches and Creepers encroaching. There was no path of escape. The large herd churned in circles, hemmed in from all sides by demons. Silvery wet bodies rippled under the lightning like a school of fish.

A Wretch lunged, and the unicorns screamed like elk. As it leaped, huge claws slashed the demon into ribbons of purple ooze. The giant werewolf bared his fangs at the rest of the monsters, stunned at his arrival. Under a brilliant flash of lightning, the demons broke ranks. Their circle around the herd collapsed, as they shrieked and charged for the meddling rogue demon. The fiends leaped like angry cats. Their bodies flew through the sheets of rain.

Bloody black claws rent them apart. The enormous wolf creature slashed the attackers and dodged their strikes. None could touch him. He steadily tore the horde to pieces. Purple muck diluted in deep muddy footprints.

When the demons' roaring and hissing ceased, Kale checked to make sure none were left. As he glanced around, he saw no enemies. He froze and stared in confusion. To his disbelief, the herd of unicorns had not fled. Hundreds stood still. All faced him, big doe eyes unblinking. For the longest moment, he stood in the downpour watching the pure white creatures, and they watched him. None flinched, staring as if mesmerized.

The cleansing storm reached its peak. Howling wind and driving rain whipped at the reviving earth, feeding muddy streams. Kale raced back the way he had come, his claws leaving deep gouges, which the mudflows quickly washed away. A new kind of thrill made his heart race. As he ran, the vigor flooded his body until he felt the sensation of flying. The unicorn herd ran with him.

Slowing somewhat, he let the unicorns at the front of the heard come alongside. His glowing red eyes studied the elegant limber creatures. They seemed to shine. The whole herd followed him through the night. Their presence filled his heart with a joy that no word he knew could do justice.

Chapter 24
THE REST IS SILENCE

The unlit chambers in the cliff sanctuary were quiet. Adwen slumbered in Oryn's arms, and he held her close. Their dreamless sleep carried on uninterrupted for many hours. Finally, they stirred at the sound of Jack's voice. The air smelled oddly sweet.

"Hey, Adwen. Oryn, wake up. Wake up."

She gave a groggy, quizzical expression. The knight scowled. Jack and Alexander stood over them, thrilled looks on their faces.

"Come look outside," Jack whispered. "You've got to see this."

Suddenly wide awake, Adwen exchanged a glance with Oryn, now also very curious. The two warriors lead the way to the overlook. It was filled with bright golden sunshine from the blazing sunset. Where the false sky had weakened on the horizon, the sun shone through, casting hard shadows between fiery splashes of light. Going to the ledge together, they marveled and took a moment to bask in the glow.

"The sun feels so warm," Adwen sighed. Then she gasped and stared at the ground far below.

When Oryn looked down, he became rigid and breathless. He gave up trying to count the number of unicorns meandering about the foothills beneath the cliffs. Even more of the creatures continued to arrive and join the gathering. They drank from the clean river and ate at the green grass their magic made sprout. Everywhere the unicorns tread, green things sprung to life.

Adwen smiled. "When did they get here?"

Alexander shrugged. "I have no idea. It started while we were sleeping."

Jack added, "It must have been during the storm." Jack looked over to Kale, who sat exactly where they had left him hours earlier. The cop was going to ask for confirmation but stopped himself. He chuckled and asked, "Hey, Big Guy?"

Kale pretended to ignore Jack. He smiled placidly and watched the unicorns play and graze.

"You're sopping wet," Jack pointed out.

Everyone turned to Kale. Oryn became dumbstruck and glanced back to the white creatures. "He led them here?"

Adwen beamed at Kale. "Yes, he did."

The knight could hardly wrap his mind around the concept. These pure beings followed the rogue demon through the dark to this place. No matter how powerful, he could not have corralled so many by force. Adwen and the others began to watch the unicorns again, but Oryn's stare was distant. Unicorns are attracted to one thing: purity.

Furtively stealing another look at Kale, the knight pondered: Perhaps something pure in this dark entity is what made him different. Is that mysterious trait the reason for him being unlike other demons? Was it Kale's loyalty that was so pure to the unicorns? Thanks to these innocent beasts, Oryn knew what to watch for to confirm this theory.

Forgetting the white creatures for a moment, Jack glance around. "Hey? Does anyone know where that pup Tamis got to?"

Kale pointed down over the edge with a sharp claw. "The kid couldn't wait."

The companions peered over for a better look and smiled. The young hound warrior sat on a rock among the herd. Soft snowy noses nuzzled Tamis from all around. Try as he might, he could not acknowledge so many at once. They continued to beg for Tamis's touch, which he was glad to oblige.

The scene charmed Kale. "Those sweet things will eat him up while we're gone."

"I don't think he'll object," Adwen chuckled. Then she shouted, "Tamis!"

Surprised, the young warrior raised his nose to the shrouded sky and saw them watching. "Tame One! What is your command?"

"We're just leaving now. Take care of them while we're gone."

Pleased to be given these charges, he barked back, "As you command, Tame One! Nothing will harm them in your absence. Light Spirits watch over you!"

"Same to you. Be safe." To the rest at her side, she murmured, "Let's go."

Adwen summoned the white sword. She swung it, slinging flames off the end to open a portal. The ring of fire revealed a high building rooftop awash in afternoon light. Everyone stepped through to the other side into the bright California sunshine.

As the portal closed, they sensed a presence nearby. Adwen smiled and dismissed the weapon. Kale chuckled at Vaughn, leaning against the roof access door.

"Did you know we were coming?" she asked the vampire.

Standing with folded arms, and a sword in its scabbard at his hip, the ancient warrior replied coolly: "The rumors say the Heir of Darien has uncommon timing. They seem to be true. I didn't expect you; I happened to be here enjoying the view of the city. The sun is warm today."

Jack was thrown off guard by the statement. "You like the sun?"

Vaughn inclined his head, eyeing the warrior. "Is it so strange to you that a day-walker might enjoy the sunshine?" His expression was one of amusement.

Uncomfortable, Jack shrugged. "I guess not."

The vampire quietly laughed. "Shall we take this meeting to my study?"

Adwen nodded. "Of course."

Vaughn opened the roof access door. In silence, the companions followed him below. At the bottom level they turned from the hall and walked farther from the bar. Deep inside the basement, Vaughn let them into his personal office and living space. It was well lit, but when everyone came inside he flipped a second light switch. A set of brighter bulbs glowed, warming the Holy Hounds. Adwen almost laughed.

"Those are full-spectrum lights," she remarked.

"Yes." Vaughn smiled. "They keep out the leeches when the bar is open. Of course, they are off much of the time for Leena and Garret's safety. Everyone, please take a seat." While they claimed chairs throughout the office, Vaughn sat behind his desk with precise posture and waited for the others to get comfortable. "There is much to discuss, Lady Adwen. How fares the battle on the other side?"

"Better. I'm no longer bound to Dargadia's magic; in fact, I'm stronger than before. And unicorns have returned."

"Excellent."

"In that world, our next objective is to take down the key pillar. With it gone, the sky can heal, and the unicorns will be able to restore the land. Sunlight will destroy the remaining pillars."

Vaughn nodded. "And the dead unicorns will grow new magic-breathing trees. Dargadia will be rich with pure magic."

She agreed with a smile then changed the topic: "How have things been here? I sense that you've already discovered something."

The demeanor of their host turned from cool to intense. "That I have. I've found a second base of operations. It is, as far as I know, still functioning."

Oryn eyed him suspiciously. "How did you come by this information so quickly?"

Staring at the fellow knight, he replied, "You would rather not know those details."

Oryn frowned, guessing that human blood was necessary.

"There are a few things of note regarding this base: First, it is also a manufacturing facility. Second, it is heavily defended. Third, it is a repurposed series of silver mines in the Calico Mountains."

Kale fidgeted and frowned.

At this, Vaughn wore a faint smile. "These mines were not chosen for obtaining the ore, my friend. The location is purely for isolation and secrecy."

Adwen leaned forward in her seat. "But they would be seen at some point. How are they doing mass production without the landowner finding out?"

He laced his fingers as an ice-cold expression came over him. "Unfortunately, the owner of the property was one of my sources. That man lost his soul years ago."

Jack growled, "You know there's going to be an investigation if someone like that is attacked. Is he dead?"

"Of course he is."

"I hope it was worth it."

"It was, Jack," Vaughn reassured him. "And, regarding your concerns of police involvement, they won't know for some time. Everyone involved has been made into thralls, slave puppets to the will of another. When the one who took their souls is slain, they will recover and have no memory or fall into a permanent vegetative state. Some police are in this thrall network but not enough to render the departments toothless."

The news sent a shiver down the warrior's spine. "The chief of my old department is hooked up to life support. Doctors say he'll never come out of it. He was behind a conspiracy to kill me, but no one could figure out a motive."

"Then you understand this situation," Vaughn told Jack. "I'm certain Vlad is the master of the thralls. Extinguish him, and they will either be freed or left soulless husks for hospital beds."

Eager to formulate a plan, Oryn asked, "What knowledge do you have for entering and navigating the base?"

"Partial, but enough. A few years ago, heavy construction was finished under the mountains utilizing preexisting tunnels. Tunnels close to the surface are a maze with dead ends designed to entrap intruders. Beyond the first level, a more organized framework begins. Unfortunately, my information extends only as far as the second level. The base is much deeper. Those who work in those sectors do not leave. I was unable to obtain their knowledge."

Adwen was leery. "What risk is there that your investigation drew attention?"

"Minimal; thralls like these are unlike those that follow the witch. Vlad does not see through them as with the soldiers. That raises another issue: All the militants defending the base are his puppets. The instant one sees intruders, he will know, and all of them will know. There are no cameras because they are not necessary."

Kale grimaced. "Our plan must account for them seeing us coming."

Vaughn nodded. "Yes, and that they are equipped with demon-steel ammunition."

The Holy Hounds were alarmed.

Alexander scowled. "We're fast, but dodging bullets isn't easy."

Jack agreed. "It'll be impossible to avoid being hit."

"One round to the head or the heart will be instant death," Adwen added grimly. "This is bad. We can't assault that base."

"None of you lot, at least," Kale corrected.

Oryn and Adwen exchanged looks after glancing at the smiling werewolf.

Vaughn began to smile, as well. A clever glint appeared in his fiery stare.

Adwen was confused. "Demon-steel hurts you, too."

He tilted his head. "Yeah, it can. But I'm resilient to it. Same goes for Vaughn."

Everyone stole a look at the vampire.

"Tell you what," Kale offered, "Vaughn and I can deal with the soldier puppets. While we clear a path, it will also serve as a diversion, letting the rest of you lot deal with stragglers."

Vaughn added, "Not all of them are fully equipped. Destroying generators will cut the lights, as well as shut down the facility. They are in the lower complex levels. This will render most of the thralls blind. I trust everyone here can see in the dark?"

The Holy Hounds smiled.

"Good. Lady Adwen, how close must you be to destroy the generators?"

"It depends on how complicated the network is. My energy traces through the currents of electricity. I can blow them as soon as I find a live wire."

"That is better than I'd hoped," the vampire replied. "There are several generators. Each supplies power to different sections. Aside from shutting down this facility, what is your ultimate goal here?"

She replied in earnest: "To destroy anything having to do with Vlad. If I can, I would like to bury that place. If we're lucky, we could find out more about that demon-steel machine he's in – maybe find a weakness."

"There is a chance that Vlad himself will be there. Are you prepared for that risk?"

"Yes, I am."

The knight gave Adwen an uncertain look but held his tongue. He knew she was not capable of defeating the metal monster. None of them were.

Vaughn wanted to be sure Adwen and her friends were aware of the challenges. Staring raptly, he went on: "Once you follow us inside, your power will be sensed. There is no way to know how soon. The situation can change in the blink of an eye. Knowing that this is the result of Sycan's work, we should assume they have always expected you to attack eventually. Anticipate the worst and pray for the mercy of the Light Spirits that we survive."

The shine in Adwen's eyes flared like candle flames. "I'm not afraid."

"When do you wish for the assault to commence?"

"Immediately."

Vaughn was quiet for a moment, then smiled. "I could not agree more. Please excuse me while I advise my charges before setting out."

She nodded and waited as he stood behind his desk. Going to the door, he turned off the full-spectrum lights. Only then did he open the door and call for the other vampires.

"Leena. Garret."

Both came silently into the hall and greeted him with confounded looks.

"What is the matter? Why did you wake us at this hour?" Then Leena saw Adwen and the rest of the guests inside. She and Garret felt a surge of dread.

Vaughn's voice brought their attention back to him: "We are about to set out. I'm leaving the second lights off for you."

Garret pretended to be calm. "How long with you be out, Sir?"

"A few hours, perhaps. If all goes well, we should return before opening hours."

They said nothing and stared with black eyes. Their faces showed signs of unease.

At this response, Vaughn put on a clever smile and inclined his head. "If I don't return, what is to happen here?"

The mock expression he gave almost made them smile.

Garret finally sighed and answered, "Business as usual, sir."

Lowering his head to look at them plainly, he replied, "Very good. Return to sleep now. The Heir of Darien will bring me back by the time you wake for your duties." As they turned to go, he closed the door with a soft click. Facing the guests, he smiled. "I received the same looks when I went to gather information. Since my abduction, they've been worried for my safety."

Everyone began to stand as Kale replied with a shrug, "Can you blame them?"

Vaughn flashed a casual frown, tilting his head. "I suppose not. Lady Adwen, the best location from which to assault the mines is at the peak. It is a blind spot in their security measures. Can you open your portal there?"

"Yes. Are you ready?"

The undead knight gave a small nod and a bow. "Indeed, good lady. Please, if you would be so kind."

Adwen summoned the Gray Blade and slashed at the air by the antique desk. A ring of blue fire created a window to a colorful barren mountaintop. Leaving the cool gloom of the vampire's office, everyone walked through and found themselves under the blaring afternoon sun once more.

When the portal vanished, powerful gusts whipped at their backs. On all sides were sloping gradients of red, brown and ashen earth. The terrain looked like paint spilled in nonsensical patterns. Sunlight made the wastes glow and the air radiate.

Stepping to the front, Vaughn looked around to get his bearings. Eventually, he pointed down the east slope in the growing shadows. "There is an entrance that way and another four miles north of it. Which one has your favor, Lady Adwen?"

The warriors watched as she calmed her mind and listened to her instincts. Nothing about the north entrance drew her attention, but the east captured her interest right away.

"This one," Adwen advised.

Vaughn nodded and resumed the lead. Minutes of hiking on uneven rocky slopes felt eerie. Outside in the sun was peaceful, and yet their hearts were steeled for what horrors might await underground. Coming to a crude hole large enough to walk through, their nerves hardened. Smells of humans filled their noses at the threshold to the old mine.

The vampire's smooth deep voice echoed softly inside as he stopped: "From here until the elevator, there are sensor traps. Follow my steps exactly to avoid detection."

While filing into the dusty passage, they kept their steps restricted to that of their guide. He brought them steadily deeper into the maze. After a few minutes, a red glow from a flood light appeared. Around the next turn stood a stainless-steel elevator. Only Vaughn's form did not reflect on the doors in the bloody gloom.

"We've come to the precipice. From this point forward, we

cannot go unnoticed. Any unusual activity will alert the thralls guarding the levels below."

Alexander continued to do his best to shrug off the claustrophobia. "How many levels did you say there were again?"

"I do not know the number."

"Outstanding."

"Lady Adwen, how do you advise we proceed?" Vaughn asked.

"If there's no hiding, then I'll control the elevator to take the two of you down first. Once I receive a signal from Kale through our link, the rest of us will follow."

The werewolf smiled. "Sounds good to me."

"Let me know when the way behind you is clear. We will destroy generators and equipment as we find them. Hopefully, hitting the power consistently will keep you guys covered."

Vaughn added, "There are no guarantees it shall proceed that way. At the worst, the shadows will provide fallback cover."

Kale tossed him a questioning glance. "Did you forget about me?"

He smiled. "Of course not. You can provide excellent cover, but the more darkness the better."

Adwen took a deep breath. "Okay, is everybody ready?"

The three Holy Hounds answered by summoning weapons and donning stern expressions. Kale and Vaughn gave firm nods.

Satisfied, Adwen approached the shiny metal doors. Her hand pressed against the cool surface, and her energy tapped into the machine's electronics. The magic made the elevator come alive, and the yellow light by the buttons blinked. The contraption began to raise the compartment from the depths. When it arrived, a soft tone chimed, and the doors parted to present a clean well-lit booth.

Side by side, Kale and Vaughn entered. The doors closed, and the mechanisms of the elevator shaft hummed. Wheels and cables gradually lowered them into the mountain.

The calm air inside the elevator was deceptive. The werewolf and the vampire gazed at the blurred reflection that Kale cast.

Glancing at the place where his own reflection was missing, Vaughn pondered, "The odds are good that we can procure secrets regarding Vlad. If he has a weakness, we very well may discover it within the hour."

Becoming suspicious, Kale muttered, "You sound very confident."

"I am." Then Vaughn sounded grim. "There is a fact that I specifically neglected to mention in front of your friends."

Kale wore an appalled look. "Why would you do something like that?"

Slowly turning to look at him, he replied, "Because I did not wish to discuss this with you in front of them; the witch is here."

The whites of Kale's eyes turned black. Every muscle in his powerful body tensed. Looking away, Kale growled deeply.

Still calm, Vaughn's tone was stern. "You cannot afford to kill her, boy."

Growling louder, he gave a deadly reply: "Who's going to stop me?"

Vaughn did not answer. Kale felt unease through numbing rage. He glanced over to find the vampire wearing a solemn expression. The look gave him pause.

"You must not kill her," the vampire said.

Astonished, he muttered, "What are you on about?"

"You hate her."

He scowled. "What of it?"

Vaughn fell quiet for a moment. "No one wishes you to repeat what happened in the streets of Los Angeles two years ago ..."

His face slackened, and his heart skipped a beat. The darkness left his eyes, as they began to fill with fear.

"... when you hated those boys as you killed them."

Horror gripped Kale's heart. What they had done made him hate them, but it did not matter. What happened when he hated Impurus made his blood run cold – it was the hate. It was breaking him. How could he have been such a fool not to realize? It was too late now. There was no going back, no hope. The hatred would eventually consume him. It was only a matter of time. If only he had not come to this place.

Then Vaughn spoke again in a cool tone. He faced the blank metal doors and inclined his head. "I will kill her."

Kale whirled toward the vampire, who drew his Elf-crafted sword to inspect the sharpness. Pretending to be ignorant of Kale's reaction, he flicked the razor-sharp edge careful not to cut himself.

"I will drink her blood. Interrogating the witch is pointless.

Draining her will yield all her secrets. That is more effective, don't you think?"

Kale quivered and nearly wept with relief. "Thank you."

Head held high, Vaughn nonchalantly glanced at Kale. "Whatever for?" Then he beamed.

Beginning to smile with glassy eyes, several weak laughs escaped his dry throat. Turning again to the dull reflection, his fear subsided.

"I've wondered for a while what it must be like to fight alongside you," Vaughn told him.

Still smiling, Kale wanted to laugh again. "Funny, that. I've thought the same thing."

Vaughn made low, soft chuckles. "It has been ages since I've held my sword against an enemy."

"Any chance you've gotten rusty?"

The vampire gave the werewolf a fiery glance and smiled.

While the elevator descended, black boots pounded on carved out mountain rock. In the upper level of the base, the elevator doors were soon covered in red laser sights. Tiny dots on steel wandered like a swarm of silent insects, clustering tightly at the seam between the sliding doors. The dead eyes of the soldier thralls set firmly on their target and waited.

Soft humming increased in the elevator shaft. When all went quiet, an ominous tone sounded before the doors slid open. Darkness filled the booth as if the air were solid. When the doors parted fully, the thralls opened fire. Demon-steel bullets flew into the elevator, punching through the back. Ricochet music resounded in the shaft, and the shadow-filled compartment. Despite the lack of effect, the thralls continued to shoot, intent on shredding the hidden occupants.

Sheltered on opposite sides of the elevator doors, Kale's bright glowing eyes fixed upon Vaughn. The vampire looked back, waiting for the time to move and held his sword gracefully at the ready.

Reaching out with his presence, Kale detected that the magazines in the rifles were depleting. When a few rounds remained, but before they could begin reloading, he nodded to his partner. Vaughn nodded back. The vampire began to whirl the Elf-steel sword and the holes in the blade caught the air. A high pitch shriek grew louder and louder. He and Kale were slightly irritated by it but hoped the thralls would be far less resilient.

In the hall, the evil power that controlled the human puppets wavered. The thralls' vision swam as the sound pierced their ears. Control over them was not broken, but it weakened. The puppets acted as if intoxicated. Their once-focused firepower turned sporadic. Bullets struck wildly off target in the hall outside.

Kale grinned, and Vaughn chuckled as he continued to make the sword sing. Then gunfire tapered off, and the thralls started to reach for full magazines. Sensing them fumbling, Kale gave another nod. The vampire knight nodded back again to show he was prepared.

Taking a deep breath, Kale roared. His darkness flooded the hall, enveloping the thralls and lights. The werewolf crouched low and darted out, while Vaughn did an acrobatic flip and began to follow upside-down along the ceiling. Kale's claws eviscerated thralls in gory fashion, dropping them to the floor. His partner in the assault decapitated the rest. Heads plopped and rolled as the soulless bodies toppled and twitched.

Despite the front lines falling so easily, reinforcements waited around the corner. Kale maintained his shadow cloud and Vaughn the disorienting cry from the slayer's sword. Kale's demon presence expanded, filling far more halls and rooms. There was no sign of Vlad's aura, and Kale was encouraged. The thralls would make an easy slaughter with their controller so far away.

When Adwen and the others arrived at the bottom in the bullet-riddled elevator, the smell of human blood was stifling. The hall was such a mess that the sight made Jack grimace.

"They were perfect for this purpose," Oryn said of Kale and Vaughn.

"I won't argue with that," Adwen grimly replied.

The lights around them suddenly hummed, grew blindingly bright and exploded. Glass and metal showered corpses and pools of blood. A resounding boom echoed in a distant chamber. Even the lights inside the elevator died. Everyone froze, then turned to Adwen.

She took her hand from the wall where she had tapped into a live wire.

Alexander shifted uncomfortably. "Now the only easy way out is your portal."

Her expression was stern. "Only us and our friends will leave this place. Let's move."

The chambers in the topmost level were for ventilation. Adwen burned the machines into piles of slag. Reaching a lit stairway, she pressed a hand to the rock wall. Yet another distant generator exploded, shaking the ground underfoot, followed by a second explosion that killed the lights. After destroying the pair of generators, she led her party to the second level.

Passages were larger and filled with many more corpses. They could smell some of Kale's blood as well, but not enough to be of concern. Taking a moment to examine the series of doors and hallways, she came to a decision.

"Split up. Destroy everything. Regroup here after all rooms are cleared."

Oryn, Jack and Alexander darted for different doorways, as Adwen claimed her own path. They smashed computers, devastated metallurgy equipment and the weakest of spare demon-steel parts. Throughout the destructive spree, thunderous roars echoed from deeper in the mountain where Kale and Vaughn continued to fight.

On the way to the third level Adwen overloaded the next set of generators. Then the Holy Hounds split up to carry on their destruction of the facility. They found manufacturing lines for unknown devices in huge rooms. The equipment made of steel and copper was easy to cut using holy blades. The knight, the cop and the Marine worked hard and fast to leave nothing intact.

Adwen rushed into yet another manufacturing chamber. She summoned more blue fire, but then she smelled rotting flesh and gasped in shock. The fire on her shoulders flickered out. Her warriors joined her and stared when they saw that she was dumbstruck. They too gawked at the contents of this dead manufacturing line.

The largest room yet lay before them filled with stations on both sides that filed down to the opposite wall. Hundreds of platforms faced open booths meant to hold man-sized machines. The booths were empty; clips and couplings lay open without a contraption to hold. The vacant steel mounts were ominous, yet the platforms demanded attention with the reek of decomposing humans. Black-clad bodies sat on their knees with their backs, heads and arms strapped to an inclined plate that held them still. In the open-armed poses, they appeared to kneel in reverence to whatever had been in the steel mounts.

Adwen crept close to one body. It was one of the soldier thralls, but as she peeked around to see its face, what she found made her quiver in horror.

Vice grips held ribs open like a bloody mouth, with the diaphragm hanging out like a tongue. Blood lay in a pool under foot, and a trickling trail led to the missing contraption.

That was the moment she and her warriors recognized the style of the empty box: It was like Vlad's from the other facility. All the platforms and empty receptacles were identical. As a realization set in, Adwen felt weak and she dropped her sword. It clanged on the stone floor by her feet. She continued to stare at the vast number of ritualistic stations.

The knight came to inspect the first sacrifice himself. Standing over the desecrated human, his sharp eye saw what was missing, and he frowned.

"Their hearts are gone."

Jack and Alexander felt sick, but Adwen did not move.

"These people have been dead for at least two days."

The short warrior growled, gritting his teeth and small fangs. "Let's get this over with. Adwen?"

Snapping out of the fearful daze, she picked up her flaming sword and found determination. Adwen was grimly resolute as she moved to the aisle. She lifted the ivory blade and pointed it at the end of the abominable chamber. Flames poured out like a river. Swaths bathed flesh, bones and metal, and filled the room with black smoke. In silence, they watched everything melt and burn.

Adwen was silent. Then a sudden pang in her chest made the flow of fire cease. Her eyes became wide, and her sword arm quivered. Seeing her reaction, the others braced for the unknown.

Tears swelled in her eyes. Then she whispered, her voice weak with terror, "Kale, no."

Just as they realized what she had said, Adwen dismissed the sword and disappeared into the hall in a streak of light. They scrambled after her but could not keep up. She moved so quickly that they were left far behind.

A pair of generators exploded, throwing a few of the thralls across the room and taking out half the lights. This gave Vaughn time to sprint along the ceiling without being shot and for Kale to pounce, slashing viciously. Even more thralls filed inside. Bullets flew, clipping the werewolf in the red jacket and tossing clouds of blood into the air. Vaughn was a more difficult target, weaving around rocky protrusions overhead. While darting about, he twirled the blade, making it shriek. It disrupted the minds of the thralls and freed Kale from their trained firepower.

Focusing the darkness around his body, Kale lunged, laying waste to the arriving ranks until the onslaught forced him to duck behind large equipment for cover. Panting and bleeding all over, the pain was not enough to slow him down.

Vaughn spotted a large ventilation shaft running alongside him. It fed through the wall into the next room, from where the soldiers had been coming. Raising his head to look at Kale, hunkered beneath him, he made his decision quickly and carefully.

"Kale."

The werewolf looked up. Darkness shrouded all but his red glowing eyes.

"I'm pressing forward," the vampire advised. "Their aggression has betrayed them. I believe our prey is in the next chamber. Keep these pawns busy, while I end this."

Darkness masked Kale's pleased smile, but his eyes showed it better as he nodded. Vaughn saluted with the blade then carved a hole in the duct. Sheathing his sword, he slipped into the vent and sped through like a snake. He reached a grille that fed fresh air into a large cavern filled with elaborate machinery. The equipment's noise covered Vaughn's movement. He saw more thralls waiting to be deployed. They stood like silent dominos waiting to fall.

Taking advantage of the din, Vaughn extended his long claws. The pale nails were sharp as surgical knives. Gently piercing the aluminum of the air duct, he held it in place as he carved a large smooth circle with his other hand. Freeing a metal disk, the stealthy vampire slunk out to crouch low on the ceiling and survey the scene.

Twenty thralls stood in formation facing the hall where Kale still fought. His attention came to a figure standing over an active computer station. A woman with very short red hair worked the keyboard. He could barely make out a half mask on the side of her face.

Recognizing the features from fuzzy recollections, Vaughn knew who this woman was.

No longer creeping upside-down like a ghoul, Vaughn retracted his claws and stood from the ceiling rock. Coolly, he stalked toward the foul woman and hung above her. Observing the manner with which she worked, the commotion in other parts of the base was a mere irritation. None of the thralls guarded her. There was no sign of tricks or traps. Apparently, they never considered a vampire might join Adwen's ranks.

As soon as the rest of the thralls marched into the passage, Vaughn let his smooth human face fade. Cheek and jaw bones became broad and curved like a cat's. Long fangs stretched inside his mouth, yielding a sensation of both pleasure and pain. When the last thrall left the room, he descended like a nimble spider, landing behind her without a sound.

Suddenly snatching the woman's wrists, Vaughn held her arms outstretched, sinking his fangs deep into the pulsing artery on her neck. The instant he took a deep draw of blood, images flashed in his mind. None were clear. He was taken aback at the emptiness of this human's memories. Then one image came into focus: the face of the witch taking off the mask.

A loud pop made his ears ring, and some unknown force pushed him back several feet. Stunned, he found himself standing at the computer, now covered in blood. The woman lay in pieces on the floor. Black strands tumbled past a wig flung askew, and her half mask lay beside the lifeless and unscarred face. It was a decoy.

Feeling weak, he examined himself. Tiny wells of red sprung up across his chest and middle. Some shiny fragments stuck out of him, making his flesh burn and smoke. The decoy had been armed with an explosive filled with pure silver shrapnel. A panel on the side of a machine fell with a loud clang, revealing the witch. She stood in the machine's gutted interior. Sauntering out with a crossbow, she stopped to stare and was amused.

"A vampire? I didn't see this coming."

Smiling, she took aim with the silver-armed weapon. Stunned and too weak to resist or flee, Vaughn stared. As she pulled the trigger, he raised an open hand as if to stop it. While the shot flew, the gem on the ring Kale had given him suddenly burst into a million pieces. A surge of warmth flooded his body. Fangs withered. Features turned smooth. The fiery rings in his eyes vanished, and his irises regained their amber color. A subtle thumping in his chest brought tears to his widening eyes.

The witch's bolt struck his heart, and the thumping ceased. He toppled back and landed flat on the ground. There he stayed.

Diana strolled over to reclaim the mask from the growing pool of blood on the floor. Her shoes clicked, and the echoes rebounded off the walls and humming machinery. Picking up the damaged item spattered in red, she proudly placed it back on the disfigured side of her face. She then casually checked the quiver and reloaded the crossbow. Before the witch could return to hide in the hollowed-out machine a deafening roar erupted nearby.

Crimson spilled out of the hall as the werewolf emerged. With the surviving thralls behind him, he glanced around for Vaughn. Before he could call his name, a sick sensation filled him. A limp figure lay in the middle of the room dressed like Vaughn and riddled with bloody holes.

Time began to move at a snail's pace. Kale's heart quivered, his face turning pale. The darkness around Kale began to writhe like the feeling in his chest. He waited through the ticking seconds for Vaughn to get up. Thralls charged in from the hallway raising guns, and disbelief turned into fear.

Bullets bit into Kale's flesh again and again. The pain was nothing compared to the indescribable sensation mounting inside his heart. No word could hold a candle to what threatened to tear him apart. Claws quivered. Tears swelled. He could not move. His body stood frozen and shook as if cold. Realization set in, and tears streamed. Kale gritted his fangs against the pain but could not look away from Vaughn.

More demon steel bullets punched through Kale, encased in his shadow. He could barely feel the wounds. The physical trauma began to dull. Anger started to swell. Trapped in fear, pain and rage, he felt defenseless and alone. He tried to push back at the anger, but the whizzing bullets and the terrible sight denied him control. The darkness in and around him grew.

Diana smiled at the look of anguish on his face. "Oh! I see now."

In a flash, Kale finally looked at her, and the black cloud about him roiled like smoky hydra heads. It took all his will to keep

the shadows contained. He felt control slipping now that he was looking at her. A snarling sob escaped him, and the shadow condensed
and expanded rapidly. Frightened of himself and enraged by the
witch, his demon presence melded with his will. He wished desperately to destroy.

Despite great efforts, the shadow swallowed the remaining
thralls. Kale gasped for air past the lump in his throat, and the darkness ripped the guns from their hands. Ravenous slashes appeared
across the human puppets. Kevlar, flesh and sinew ripped and tore
under the strikes of many invisible talons. Kale's presence lacerated
the thralls over and over in a struggle to quench his desires.

It did not work. The more his anger manifested violently
against the soldiers, the stronger the darkness became. His control
eroded faster, making him even more frustrated and afraid.

Finally, Diana pointed the loaded crossbow at the tortured
werewolf and fired.

Fear and rage reached a fever pitch, making his shadow expand like an explosion. The silver bolt flew into the darkness surrounding Kale. On its path for his head, the pure silver instantly tar-
nished, turning ruddy black and brown. Before it could strike him
between the eyes, the bolt collided with a surging force. The ruined
bolt corroded into useless particles.

The witch softly gasped in dismay, "Oh."

Kale's darkness filled the room completely and lifted the
witch into the air. He roared. The sound shook the mountain to its
roots as he fought his rage. He wanted the witch to die. He hated her
with every fiber of his being.

Adwen darted into the darkness that was Kale and saw the
levitating witch and a growing cyclone of blood. Sensing what was in
his heart, Adwen called out at the top of her voice: "Kale! Kale, no!"

Deaf to her in the moment, he pressed in on Diana with all
his might. The woman's flesh and bones burst in a gory spray, leaving
nothing but the mask behind. He roared in ravenous triumph – and
in defeat and despair.

Chapter 25
GENTLY INTO THE NIGHT

Kale roared again, unable to stem the tide of darkness surging inside. It swelled, lifting all the blood into the air against his control and swirling it in a crimson hurricane. Barely aware of anything beyond anguish and fear, he knew darkness was consuming him. He could feel it eating him alive. His heart cried out for merciful death.

Adwen's warriors arrived at the entrance to the cavern but did not dare enter the storm of blood and shadows. They stared in horror at the black figure in the center of the vortex.

Blue fire shielded Adwen from the darkness and flying filth, turning it to dust as the storm flew around. Afraid for her friend, she called out again, refusing to give in.

"Kale!"

This time he could hear her voice. Something inside his heart refused to die, and the darkness ceased to spread. With returning senses came more awareness and control. Everything felt cold and empty. Lowering his gaze back to the prone figure on the ground, he wanted to see if he was wrong, if this was not so.

Suddenly, the storm of blood froze suspended like a cloud. Then Kale's power cast every particle against the walls and dropped the unrecognizable thrall remains with a series of wet slaps to the floor. Stillness followed. Only Adwen, Kale and Vaughn were untouched by the contents of the red room.

Cautiously entering to join Adwen, the warriors watched the black figure. Adwen stared at their friend with tears in her eyes.

Able to move at last, Kale took methodical step. The shadows about him withered. His jacket was gone. A red band of cloth wrapped around the top of his right arm, furling and fluttering as he walked in a nonexistent breeze. Black linen wrapped about his waist seamlessly transformed into a smoky loincloth over equally dark breeches and boots. Each step became more numbing the closer he approached Vaughn's body. Stopping just short of his friend's head and shoulders, Kale stared, clawed hands quivering. Dropping to his knees, a plume of darkness furled and dissipated under Kale like dust. Gazing balefully at Vaughn's half-cast dilated eyes, Kale took a shaky breath, trying not to cry.

The soft sound of sobs alerted the warriors that Kale had not turned against them yet. They followed Adwen when she went closer. Surrounding the two, no one uttered a sound.

Kale begged in shaky whispers, and his voice resonated as if many spoke the words at once: "I'm sorry. I'm sorry."

Vaughn's face showed no reaction to his plea.

Struggling with disbelief, Kale spoke aloud. His demon voice was not gone. Kale realized it would never be gone again. It made the tears roll, falling to his lap.

"Please, say something, anything."

Oryn frowned. He had witnessed this reaction to loss many times as a knight. Alexander had as well in war. The Marine exchanged a look with Jack. Both moved closer and began crouching to inspect Vaughn for themselves.

As Jack's and Alexander's hands reached for Vaughn, Kale became terrified. If they touched him, it would mean he really was gone. They would make it real. He shuddered uncontrollably, gritting his fangs.

Then he cringed and shouted in demon tongue, "Krefnan!"

The warriors saw a flash of long smoky feathers, batting both away from Vaughn's body. Alexander's back crushed the computer station, and Jack was sent sliding across the floor. Oryn flinched and growled, while Adwen covered her mouth in shock.

Horrified at what he had done, Kale became rigid. Then, squeezing his eyes shut, he grasped the dark cloth on his knees and twisted the unearthly material. Bowing his head lower in shame and sorrow, his echoing voice cracked: "Please, don't touch him."

Jack sat up to stare aghast, and the Marine did the same from the wrecked workstation. Neither was harmed. Warier than before, they took care to avoid provoking Kale.

Adwen wished to ease the suffering. Gently, she called to

him, "Kale."

He heard and refused to respond.

"Kale, look at me."

His heart ached to be reassured. He forced himself to glance at her.

The whites of his eyes were permanently blackened. At the center of his pupils were soft pinpricks of pale light. Adwen was not afraid. She looked into his heart, and what was there still put a sweet smile on her face.

Her lack of fear and or hesitation to accept him blinded him with tears. Quickly looking away, the soft weeping resumed.

"We can't stay. Do you want to carry him?"

Getting control of his sobs, Kale whispered, "Yeah."

She watched for a moment, then summoned the Gray Blade and cast blue fire into the air nearby. The ball of flame formed a ring and a portal within. An empty office beckoned. The warriors watched patiently as Kale lifted Vaughn. His black claws moved carefully, as if he feared the remains might crumble. Cradling the welcome burden, Kale's look became distant, and his expression turned stony and un-feeling. They walked through the portal together out of the crimson-bathed chamber into the sanctuary of Vaughn's office.

Once they escaped the nightmarish scene, Adwen glanced back at Kale, as did her warriors. He looked like a graveyard statue the way he avoided anyone's gaze. She was going to speak, but the door to the office burst open.

Leena screamed, "Vaughn!"

The vampire rushed for the motionless form mad with grief. But as soon as she came close, she saw Kale. In an instant, her face took its true ghoul form with long fangs and large black eyes. She leaped back, hissing and raising long claws to defend herself.

Kale gave no response. His vacant stare remained far off.

Garret came from the bar to investigate. "Leena, are you al-right?" He found her crouched near the door and saw the Holy Hounds beside the desk. When he saw Vaughn, his face slackened, but once he took a good look at the one holding him, he flinched and stared. It was not clear if they were in danger.

Adwen broke the tense quiet with a soft tone, "Garret."

The hesitant vampire stared at her instead of the entity hold-ing his master's remains.

"You're safe."

His heart believed her, yet instincts told him to be wary. Leena began to calm, as well, and her more human appearance returned. While the fear ebbed, anger rose, making her sneer.

Through clenched fangs, she spat, "What have you done?"

Again, Kale appeared unmoved.

She screamed, "What have you done?"

Garret hissed at her, "That's enough, Leena! Get a hold of yourself."

Red tears trickled from her black eyes. "What did you do to him, you great death shadow?"

Having had enough, Garret lost his normally calm guise. Suddenly a powerful vampire, he hissed and roared at her, "Control yourself or leave the room, Leena! You know Kale would never harm Vaughn!"

She felt Kale was to blame but knew Garret was right.

Kale gently laid Vaughn on an old chaise lounge.

Garret continued dealing with Leena in a far less vehement manner: "He made his wishes perfectly clear – everything is business as usual. The leeches will arrive in a few hours. It is best they don't suspect anything has changed. Now is not the time to allow rumors. We can hold ceremonies for him after work."

Noticing Kale coming closer, Garret fell silent and stepped aside. Without a word or a look, Kale walked quietly into the hall. His powers made the door softly close behind him with a light click.

Jack and Alexander exchanged somber glances, as Garret heaved a stress-filled sigh, putting a hand to his head. Smoothing his hair back, he knew he must address their guests. It was much easier now without Kale in the room.

"Please, Lady Adwen, forgive Leena and me for the outbursts. This is ... difficult."

"It's difficult for all of us," she replied.

He grimaced and nodded, glancing furtively at the closed door. "Of course. You are all welcome to stay for a time. However, you've brought the smell of human blood with you; it is potent. The leeches may be enticed to seek it out."

Jack grimaced. "All of us but her can't help it after what happened."

"What did happen?"

Jack shook his head. "You don't want to know."

Raising her head, Leena wore a firm look. "I want to know."

"Leena," Garret chided.

"No, I need to know." She took brisk strides to the figure on the antique recliner. But when she got close, Oryn stepped in her way.

He stood over her with eyes alight, growling. Leena was undeterred.

"I know what you think of us, slayer. Vampires live damnable false lives, stealing from the living, and everything we do is filthy. I might very well live forever. I refuse to spend the rest of my undeath not knowing what happened."

After considering her motives, Oryn allowed her to pass. Not wanting to violate Vaughn's body further out of respect, she did not bite. The lady vampire dabbed at a splotch of blood. As soon as she put it to her tongue, she shuddered. Garret jumped to brace her as she crumpled to her knees. The look in her dark eyes worried him.

"Leena, you should not have done that."

"He's human," she said.

Everyone else in the room nearly gasped.

"What did you say?" Garret asked.

Leena wanted to cry. "The ring – it let him become mortal. He felt his heart beat just before the end."

It was Garret's turn to fight back tears. His were happy ones. "He got his one wish then. Thank the Light Spirits for that." Turning to Adwen, he was breathless. "Thank you, kind lady."

Adwen answered sadly, "It was Kale. Remember?"

Feeling ashamed, he nodded. "Yes, good lady. I remember."

While the vampires shared a brief silence, Jack took the moment to admire the room that once belonged to Vaughn. The office was highly organized. Quickly, he realized it was a private library. Knick-knacks from foreign travels sat as random memento bookends. One wall was dedicated to encyclopedias. The rest were novels, many rare and some new.

Turning to the old desk, Jack was not surprised to find how tidy it was. If not for that, he might not have taken interest in a folded paper lying in the center.

"Garret? Leena? Did either of you leave this note?"

"What note?" Garret asked. "We haven't been in here since

you left."

Picking it up and taking a sniff, Jack found only Vaughn's vampire scent. As soon as he opened it he stopped reading and instead passed it to the undead hosts.

Garret reached for it, but Leena snatched it. She opened it and began to read. Suddenly unable to get beyond the first few lines, the lady vampire averted her gaze. She shoved the paper into Garret's hand as she scurried to a corner to cry. Wrapping her arms about herself, mournful beastly sounds emanated from the shadows.

Looking at the contents himself, Garret was shocked then wore a grim frown.

Adwen grew concerned. "What is it?"

He stole a glance at Vaughn beside him. "His Will."

The Holy Hounds exchanged curious reactions.

"Could you read it aloud, please?"

He nodded.

"I go by the name of Vaughn Epherghast. I am leaving this as a final testament to my will. Should anyone find this, then that is evidence I am no more. If I am no more, then I can only hope that my final actions in this life were a success. Success in such an instance would mean that the witch called Diana is dead and that my dear friend is still alive.

"If whoever is reading this knew me or was my ally, I must apologize. I kept secrets from you. It was for everyone's betterment. My closest friends would have done everything within their power to stop me. That could not be allowed. After days of pursuing leads, I devoted many hours to consider our enemy. I weighed their actions and goals against our role as a threat to their ends. Therein, I was able to imagine the chess board. It was clear to me that a trap would be laid and that it would not be for the Lady Adwen, but for someone else.

"If he is not present or refuses to read this letter, tell him I'm sorry and ask him to not be cross with me. I am sure, if I am indeed gone, he will need to know why. That word 'why' has always eaten at him, so please tell him not to let it. In the chance that I have failed to take the life of the witch, please forgive me. Know that I tried. I pray your heart keeps the light burning strong despite the dark. Never let it go out. I trust Lady Adwen to do right by you, no matter the outcome.

"That being said, I assign my possessions thus: Dear Garret, I leave to you The Corner."

The vampire paused a moment in shock, then continued to read.

"You are strong. You will only grow stronger. That is a good thing. I trust that everything will be business as usual, since it was you who coined the term for me. Use your best judgment and skills to find another hand or two to add to the family. They are out there somewhere in the city. Show the wayward ones worthy of such a home that they are not alone. Good luck, and Light guide you.

"Dear Leena, I leave to you all the contents and possessions within my office."

She gasped. Turning to stare and no longer crying, her eyes widened in surprise.

"I know how you've pined for my books. Also, I have enjoyed our little game of you trying to sneak inside and read them when I am out. I always knew. You had but to ask, and I would have allowed it, but the game was fun. It would have been a pity to spoil it. Thank you for never asking. Light be merciful to you always."

At this she trembled and began to sob anew.

"Kale, my dearest friend, I have made this choice for your sake. I understand it is a terribly bittersweet gift. It will have caused you the greatest of pains. I've stopped you from dying before, and now I hope I have stopped you again. Though I may be gone, my wish is that a part of me will never leave your side. That is why I desire you to carry my blade. Take it, please. Do not let your fear or sorrow spoil the time you've been given. You know what it is that I am talking about, and it is not about time spent with my sword. Despite this loss you've suffered, I beg of you, do not allow this chance to pass you by. It would render all you've endured a waste."

Night loomed over the city sprawl. An amber horizon choked on the tide of deep navy-blue filling with stars. Sirens wailed in distant places, howling like crazed wolves.

Kale stood atop the short wall by the roof's edge feeling the wind. Looking out at the basin full of lights, his companion was the nudging breeze. If he were a leaf or sheet of paper, it would blow him off the side and eventually dash him to the ground. The thought was tempting – to be plunged to earth and never stand again. Rose petals have the pleasure of being free to fall, float and then land and rot where they lie, he thought. How beautiful a life is when it can end? He wished he could take a dive now, float like a leaf, then let the earth devour him.

What a tragedy that death is so difficult to obtain now. Even death of his body would not be enough. He needed something more. If only Adwen would grant his wish. Sensing her ascending the stairwell to the roof, Kale waited. The staring match with the city continued uninterrupted, even when she emerged by the half-open door.

Adwen knew the state of his heart, feeling things she understood well. It would be difficult to free his mind from this melancholy. After pondering, she approached. The concrete roof was cold under her bare feet, like Kale's aching heart. Watching a little longer, she waited to see if he would acknowledge her presence.

Sensing he would not, Adwen's voice was low and soft: "Could you come back below? There are things we all need to discuss."

Kale's compound demon voice was hushed and somber: "I don't feel like talking."

"We found things in that place. It's important. We need you with us."

"No, you don't," he murmured. "Not anymore."

The dismal responses made Adwen frown. "I brought something for you."

He could care less but humored the offer enough to reply, "What?" A sound of metal on metal chinked. It perked his curiosity enough to steal a glance. Adwen held out the Screaming Sword in its sheath for him to take.

His face flinched, and his heart skipped a beat. Then Kale scowled. "You have no right to give that to me."

"I'm not. Vaughn did."

Dazed, the anger caved in as he stared in dismay.

"He left a will for us to find. He gave this to you."

It felt as though a hand wrapped around his heart and squeezed. Resisting tears, Kale quivered and kept looking away.

Adwen sighed. He would not accept it from her at this moment. She magically dismissed the sword for another time. Watching him become steady, Adwen asked softly, "What do you need?"

"To die."

She was not surprised, but the answer made her frown.

"Please. I can't go on like this – not like this."

"You know I won't do that."

He knew she would refuse but could not accept the answer. "I beg you: End this."

Adwen stood firm and did not grace the plea with a reply.

Kale sighed. He knew better than to hope she might fulfill the request.

"Well ... if you won't, I know someone who would like to try."

His gaze turned again, this time at the open door beyond Adwen's shoulder. She whirled around and became furious. Oryn stood at the threshold listening. In silent rage, Adwen watched the knight begin to approach. As soon as he took a few paces, she took control of his movements. She froze him in place and stormed to him growling deeply.

He was not alarmed by her anger. His expression remained calm as she stood before him glaring. Oryn waited as she looked inside his heart to see if he was indeed a threat to Kale. Watching Adwen's face gradually relax and the growling cease, the hold over his movements diminished.

Adwen considered what she had seen. Carefully weighing both warriors' hearts, she came to a decision. Without a word, Adwen gave Oryn a stern look as a warning against crossing her again. An almost placid expression was his form of acceptance.

Adwen glanced at Kale's turned back before going into the dark stairwell. She left the knight to speak with the rogue demon.

Sensing her gone, Kale waited. With any luck, he would feel the bite of a golden sword.

Oryn stepped closer, enough to be able to make out Kale's face. For a long time, he watched. It was plain that Kale was no longer playing coy. The acts and smiles were gone, and he was as readable as an open book.

Almost a minute passed, and Kale grew agitated. "What do you want?"

He took a moment to reply, "To understand."

A pained scowl came over Kale. "A bit late for that."

"Tell me, why do you wish for death?"

Gradually, the scowl withered into a deeply sullen look. "I hate ... everything that I am."

Oryn was almost taken aback at the honesty.

"I'm tired of always hurting and being afraid. This thing that I am is a lie – all of it. I despise everything that the darkness is, but it is inside of me, as well. I simply don't belong. If this half-existence continues, there are only two outcomes for me: either I remain as I am, suffering in this tortured limbo, or eventually break and become one of them."

The knight listened patiently.

"I don't want to turn," Kale continued. "I don't want to lose myself; my identity is all I have left that's mine. Most of all, I never want to be against all the things in life that matter. The one way to put an end to this downward spiral is to cease to exist. I need oblivion. Is that so much to ask?"

Becoming stern, the knight wore a firm frown. "What do you really want?"

The question was grating, and Kale growled, "I thought I made it clear I don't want to exist anymore."

"That cannot be the truth, or else you would have been begging for death for the duration of our travels. There is something you want more. What is it?"

Kale trembled.

Oryn smelled tears long before Kale turned to face him. Shuddering, trails of tears ran down his miserable face.

Weakly, he uttered, "Happiness."

Showing no reaction, the knight listened.

"I want what was promised to me. I was promised joy." Turning away, the trembling ended, and Kale choked on a sob. "Now I see that the only joy for me is seeing my own end. It would bring me joy to know all of this was about to be over. Nothingness is the only of peace I can find."

"So, you've given up hope."

Kale glowered. "I never had hope to begin with."

"That is the first lie in the duration of this meeting."

At this, Kale shot the knight an angry glance. Tears still gathered in his eyes.

"Why do you lie?"

Kale looked away.

Frustrated at being ignored, the knight persisted: "If happiness is what you want, then you are being a great fool."

Anguish and rage swelled inside, manifesting as two broad shadows at Kale's back. He rumbled deeply and shot Oryn a fierce look. His stare was pained and full of vengeance.

Oryn was unafraid. "If you harbor nothing but hatred and fear for who or what you are, then there can be no room for hope or happiness."

Kale anger suddenly vanished. The shadows on his back faded away, and he stared, unable to make a sound. His expression turned into shocked revelation.

With a firm tone, the knight continued: "I've made no effort to conceal that I despise what you are. It is clear now that the feeling is mutual. It is a pittance, but I can make an assurance: If the time should come to put you down, and if Adwen hesitates, I will step in."

A bittersweet wave of warmth flooded Kale's body. The knight held no malice toward him, and the promise was not of wrath, but of mercy. A weak smile flickered across his face. "That's sweet."

Oryn frowned.

Still wearing a faint smile, he addressed the irate knight: "I do not mock you. Truly, I am grateful. I appreciate the gesture. But you should know, if ... when the time comes, only she will be able to kill me."

Kale struggled to smile despite the sorrowful truth. Seeing a glimmer of pity hidden in the knight's eyes, he turned away to gaze at the city. For a little longer, Oryn watched Kale. Finished with what he had come to do, the knight started back to the office.

"Lithus," Kale muttered.

The knight paused at the doorway and looked back in confusion.

Kale murmured somberly, "Vaughn's real name was Lithus. He forbade me to remind him of it – too many sad memories. Please tell Garret and Leena. They'd want to know."

Understanding Kale did not want to see the fear the vampires harbored for him, the knight refused. "Tell them yourself." With that, he departed to avoid further requests.

Again, Kale felt alone. But somehow, he felt less so.

Adwen sat in an office chair with eyes downcast, reading the feelings flowing through Kale's heart on the rooftop. Jack watched but did not pry into her mind. She sat still since returning from the failed attempt to collect Kale. Whatever she was up to, the cop trusted her judgment.

Alexander returned to his seat after using a linen sheet that Garret had delivered to cover Vaughn. With the grim chore finished, the Marine solemnly reclaimed his chair under a wall of books. His look was distant, like Adwen's. Neither of the warriors was in the mood for banter to pass the time.

When the door opened, Adwen did not bat an eye, but both Jack and Alexander quickly looked expecting Kale. The two frowned when Oryn entered. The knight was unreadable. He coolly joined Adwen, sitting beside her in another chair.

Alexander returned his gaze to the floor.

Jack immediately tapped into Oryn's thoughts and instantly frowned. The cop decided it was time to break the silence. Angry at the audacity of the knight, Jack gave a dry scoff. "You actually thought you could bring him down here."

Oryn offered no reaction. This did not ease Jack's aggravation. Before he could think of a remark, the door opened again, grabbing his attention.

Avoiding everyone's gaze, Kale entered and locked the door behind him. He strode to sit in the darkest corner beside the foot of the chaise lounge, now covered in a plain sheet. The warriors' stares were a nagging discomfort.

He slouched back. "Let's get this over with."

Adwen nodded and began the meeting. "While you fought the thralls, the rest of us destroyed the machinery. We found several manufacturing rooms and eventually something like a programming line." She hesitated to go into detail.

Kale's voice remained low, but the sound reverberated. "And?"

"There were stations with thrall sacrifices. The machines that they were linked to are missing."

He sighed heavily. Finally looking at her, he said, "Puppets – made of demon-steel, aren't they?"

"It looks that way," Adwen replied.

"The thralls sacrificed to new machines would make them

easy for Vlad to control."

Adwen felt sick to her stomach. "We have no way of tracking them."

For a long moment, Kale thought to himself in silence. Then, gazing down at one of his hands, he made a pale blurry orb manifest in his claws. In the center, moving shapes became clearer. To the astonishment of the Holy Hounds, Kale was able to scry the missing machines. The sight was beyond disturbing: an army of flying robots modeled after their master. On electric wings, they hovered over rocks and sand. As the image blurred and faded, Kale frowned and let the orb disappear.

"They are protected. We can't know where they are."

The ability impressed Jack. "How did you do that?"

Kale's black and red eyes with white centers locked with his and stared blankly.

Clearing his throat, the warrior became apologetic: "Never mind. Forget I asked."

Leaving Jack alone, Kale addressed Adwen: "They can only be located by waiting for them to make the next move."

Oryn disliked the news: "Until what time?"

"When they begin to do what they were made for."

A chill coursed through the warriors.

"There's no way to know when that will happen," Kale added.

Adwen agreed: "There's no choice but for Kale to keep an eye on them. We can deal with the pillars now. I would like to see the biggest of them come down."

"There's a problem with that," Kale informed as he scryed the unicorns in the palm of his hand. The white creatures romped and grazed in hills of green.

"What do you mean?" she asked him.

"They cannot go unprotected." He dismissed the orb again. "The demon lords do not know our movements. For some reason, they are unable to track us."

This intrigued the knight. "How have you come to such a conclusion?"

"We've not been visited by them since Degah'lee," Kale explained. "If they could find us, they would have sent their best to finish us off without hesitation. But if I can scry the unicorns, so can they. I can't find where they are due to the ancient protections over the cliffs, but they will be looking for them. The demons won't make their move right away. If you attack one of the pillars, it would create the perfect opportunity to eliminate the unicorns."

Adwen did not like their predicament.

"You cannot be in two places at once," Kale emphasized.

She nodded. "Thank you. I need to think about this."

"There is a little time left but not much. That pillar must come down soon, and we must preserve the unicorns. The Dragon Mother is unlikely to breathe fire for us a second time if we allow the innocent ones to die. They are sacred."

Adwen gravely agreed. "Their protection is the highest priority. When we go back to the overlook and get Tamis up to speed, I'll make a decision."

Kale nodded. Then he gave a sidelong glance at the shape under the linen cloth. For a long time, he stared.

Adwen concluded the discussion with a gentle tone: "Thank you, Kale."

Eventually, he stood and strode across the room past the warriors of light. As quietly as he had entered, he left and closed the door again.

The hallway was almost totally dark. As he came around a corner on the way to his old quarters, a shadow along the wall recoiled and hissed as it fled. The illusion projected by the leech fell away in the undead's frantic retreat to the bar. Garret's angry voice, telling off the fiend for creeping away from the bar, was deafening.

Kale was indifferent to the encounter. He opened the old wooden door to the dismal room with a plain mattress on the floor. Someone had finally placed a fitted sheet on it. That could only have been Leena. As he was slipping into the near-empty space, Garret appeared. He laid a hand on Kale's bare shoulder. Kale did not move or turn to look at the vampire.

"Here, take it." The sound of paper came, and Garret's hand held out folded parchment.

Kale gave no reaction.

Garret insisted, "You need to read this."

No matter how much Kale wanted to refuse, he took the letter. Then he felt the hand leave his shoulder, and there was nothing else to hinder him. He disappeared into the dark room and closed door with a gentle click.

By the darkest hour before dawn, the last of the bar patrons had finished their drinks and left. Garret and Leena worked hard to close up and bolt the entrance tight as soon as the leeches were gone. Cleaning could wait, as more important matters needed attention.

On the way to retrieve Adwen and her warriors for the ceremony, they stopped to knock on Kale's door. They rapped pale knuckles against old wood again and again. When no answer came, the vampires had no choice but to move on. They needed to complete the ceremony before daylight so that the vampires could safely attend on the rooftop.

In Kale's dark room, hushed sobs went unheard. The letter now stained with tears lay open beside Kale on the mattress. He crouched in a corner grasping his head with sharp claws, knees up tight to his chest as his body convulsed with ragged sobbing fits. It felt as if he could cry forever after reading the letter. There were answers and closure but no freedom from grief. The emotions ripped at his heart like cold hooks.

Adwen led the somber procession to the rooftop. Oryn carried Vaughn, now wrapped tightly within the snowy linen. In the open air, the knight laid the bundle in a wide space. Dawn was due in minutes.

The three warriors stood behind Adwen, as the pair of vampires waited on the shadowed west side of the access door. Seconds of silence passed. The hushed moment allowed the tiny gathering to steep their minds with wandering thoughts. When not thinking of the situation, some checked the progression of sunrise. It was about to break; a peach and magenta glow grew, announcing the sun's arrival.

Leena heard a sound at the stairs. Light footsteps caught her ear, and she looked. Then Garret looked, as well, and they both watched Kale emerge. He showed no sign of having sobbed heavily. The rogue never looked at the vampires or at the warriors as he strode past.

Jack and Alexander exchanged abashed glances and watched him stand beside the knight behind Adwen. Neither she nor Oryn reacted. As soon as the sun cast its golden rays on the Holy Hounds, it danced like golden threads and fire on Adwen. While the light flowed about her body, she summoned flames from her heart. Like a flower, it fluttered in her hand in the wind.

Adwen approached Vaughn's remains and placed the holy fire on the linen wrappings. As she stepped back, her heart guided the flames. Black smoke began to rise. Her fire engulfed the bundle, turning the surface to pitch and embers. The fire was hot and fierce. The body quickly turned to ashes.

Kale stood among the warriors of light, determined to no longer let precious moments like this pass him by.

Chapter 26
DIRGE

By the time the sun had risen above the horizon, a mound of ash lay before the small assembly. A little blue flame remained at the heart of it where embers still smoldered.

Adwen knelt low and reached into the pile. What she pulled free glowed hot, as the fire had not yet gone out. Turning to her friends, she opened her hands to reveal two small hot lumps. She made the fire diminish, and the masses cooled into a pair of stones – one pearly white and the other glistening black. The vampires were more puzzled than the Holy Hounds.

"They are diamonds, easier to keep than ashes," Adwen explained. Going to stand before Garret and Leena in the shelter of the shadows, Adwen asked, "Which will you keep?"

Garret stared in astonishment, and Leena worried, asking, "What will happen to the other?"

"I will take it back to Dargadia. Then we will decide where it is most appropriate to keep the stone."

The pair exchanged glances before Garret decided. "The black stone would not be out of place with us, Lady Adwen."

Careful not to touch her skin and be burned, he plucked the black diamond from Adwen's fingertips.

"Thank you, Lady Adwen," Leena uttered frowning. "This will be easier to protect. And none of the leeches will know what it is. An urn would give us away. If they think Vaughn is gone for good, there is no telling what trouble they'd cause."

Jack frowned. "Won't they ask questions when they don't see him after a while?"

Leena scoffed. "Vaughn rarely showed his face to them. We

might go a hundred years without them knowing."

This was reassuring, and Jack shrugged. "That works."

At this, Garret was quizzical: "Are you agreeing with our work for a change?"

Jack looked uncomfortable. "To an extent. I've had time to think about it. You help keep those leeches from wanting to hunt. So long as your method of getting stock doesn't change, I won't have a problem with you guys in my city."

Leena was taken aback. "Your city?"

Garret shushed her to end the conflict before it could begin. "If all ends well, you are welcome to visit any time – during afterhours of course."

Jack doubted he would ever visit The Corner for entertainment. "Thank you."

The vampire wore a pleased smile. Then his dark eyes turned to Kale, the only one who continued to gaze at the pile of ashes. The unnatural strip of red cloth fluttered from his arm by his back.

Without hesitation Garret called out, "And you are welcome anytime, day or night."

Kale did not respond or move. This surprised no one.

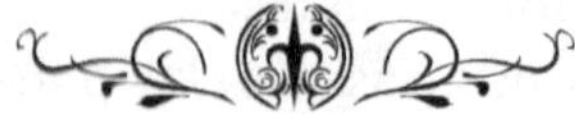

Under the false night, the unicorns grazed and rested on fresh grass, which was wet with dew. In the overlook, there rose soft lofty tones. Tamis sat by the ledge watching over the white creatures. To pass the hours, he magically summoned his old pan pipe to try and perform a song he felt the urge to play.

It was nearly impossible. He could not take human shape, and his current form struggled with the simple task of playing a clear note. Beastly jaws and lips resisted his efforts, but Tamis was determined; he intended to play, even if just a few notes. His long ears folded back in frustration as he tried again and again to get a proper sound.

After over an hour of trying, he hit a sublime tone that rang in the overlook. It pleased him so much his tail swatted across the rocks. Ready to continue practicing, a sudden surge of blue fire by a wall stole his attention. Upon seeing Adwen, followed by his other friends, he jumped up and dismissed the instrument for later.

Tamis greeted them warmly: "Tame One, Sir Oryn." When he saw their dismal expressions, his excitement dwindled. "Jack, Alexander?" At seeing Kale, he stared for a moment and did not call to him. Judging by the downcast gaze, it was clear Kale wanted no interaction. By the time the fiery portal vanished, Tamis became very concerned. Ears pricked and alert, his attention returned to Adwen.

With a low whimper, he said, "It is good to see you all safely returned."

Still somber, Adwen nodded. "Thank you. It is good to see you safe, too."

Fearful of the answer, he whined, "Has something happened?"

After a brief pause, she answered, "We lost a friend."

The hound warrior's ears flinched. Giving Kale another glance, he noticed that his appearance was somewhat altered, including his garments.

"Is there anything I can do?"

Adwen shook her head, then mustered some determination to press onward. "We need to talk – all of us. It is time to tear down the key pillar."

A chill swept through Tamis. "I see."

Wordlessly, she led the five companions into the sanctuary caves inside the cliffs and entered a dark chamber. The Order of the Gargoyle had taken all the sanctuary's candles. Their eyesight did not need much light, but Adwen made her body glow to brush back the gloom. Sitting on one of the many chairs left behind, she waited for the others to settle in. Oryn sat on her right. Kale took his place at her left, and Jack, Alexander and Tamis completed the circle. Adwen's light cast her companions' shadows on hewn rock walls as she surveyed their faces. All but Kale met her gaze, as his remained low.

Suspense weighed on everyone even when Adwen spoke: "They were ahead of us again. That means the demon lords are still ahead of us now. They tried to kill Kale, and they failed."

His eyes closed in a solemn frown.

"This can only mean they consider him a threat," she continued. "In the other world, as we speak, there is a demon-steel army on the move. Before they strike their first target, I propose we push back; we need to attack the largest pillar. It would heal the sky and cause a domino effect that would begin to restore Dargadia. The demons need lots of magic and human blood to rebuild the pillars. With no large populations in Dargadia, it will be difficult to replace the largest of them."

Oryn spoke with a tone of caution: "I sense the enemy will foresee this move." Then, to everyone's surprise, he asked Kale, "What is your council on this matter?"

In an echoing whisper all could hear, he agreed, "Yeah, they will."

Tamis flinched at the demonic voice. Kale sensed his reaction but pretended to not notice.

"I have my doubts that they will ever send the Reaper," Kale added. "However, there are others who are equally dangerous. Their most powerful will be guarding the pillars."

Adwen was worried. "And are the unicorns safe?"

"If any demons are searching for them, I cannot sense it," Kale answered.

The knight frowned. "Does this mean they are not seeking them out?"

Raising his gaze a little, Kale answered flatly, "No."

Alexander pondered aloud: "The biggest threats to them I can see are Adwen, Kale and the unicorns. The softest target is obviously those animals."

Jack also turned to Kale for advice: "What do you think will happen when the pillar falls? What might those demons do?"

"I'm not worried about after; during is the more worrisome question."

Everyone tensed.

"If they know we will try to take it down, and I believe they do, then they already have a plan for an immediate counterattack."

Adwen pondered, "Is there some other way to strike in which the odds would be more in our favor?"

"Any other move will have the same degree of risk, but with less reward," Kale cautioned his friends. "We cannot hunt the metal army while Dargadia's life force hangs by a thread. Taking that pillar down is the only reasonable choice."

"And that is why they know we will make that move," Adwen added.

Kale nodded.

Oryn turned to her. "Then a plan is needed."

"Yes. The priority is still the unicorns."

Kale grimly reminded Adwen, "You have to destroy the pillar. And you cannot be in two places at once."

"I know. That's why I want you to protect the unicorns."

The warriors were aghast. Even Kale raised his eyes to gaze in disbelief.

"You, the unicorns and I are the keys to undoing their plans in this world," Adwen explained. "As you put it, there will be the same level of risk no matter what move we make. I choose you to safeguard the herd."

Breathless, he muttered, "You risk yourself."

Staring into him, Adwen replied, "None of us can afford to hold back."

Kale's face flushed pale and he returned his gaze to the floor.

As much as this plan worried Oryn, he admitted, "This appears to be the only course." Looking to the other three, he asked, "Are there any who disagree with this decision?"

Jack spoke first: "I don't see any point in arguing. This won't be the first time we've waltzed into a trap or two. Might as well continue the trend."

Alexander shook his head ruefully. "You know, Adwen, they will be focusing on you the entire time."

"I do."

Sighing heavily, the Marine replied, "Roger that. I've got no issue. Ready to move out when you are."

Their attention passed to Tamis, who had remained silent for the entire meeting. His gaze rested on Kale. Hearing and seeing what had changed in him was terrifying. Realizing that the others were waiting on him, the hound warrior deliberated. Looking around at everyone, his soft growl hummed in the stone chamber.

"I think it is time to destroy the great black pillar," Tamis agreed. "After all that has happened, I'm not afraid to fight them. I'm not afraid of dying."

Jack wore a bittersweet smile. "Nobody here is afraid of death, Tamis."

The Marine and the knight nodded in agreement.

Yet, Tamis admitted, "I am a little frightened, but I don't know of what."

Adwen smiled. "The unknown."

"I suppose that is it." Long ears pricked alert atop his head, his jaws lowered intensely. "I am ready to use my bow, Tame One. Name the hour."

"Alright, then. We leave in a few minutes. I want to destroy the pillar while the sun is still shining."

Glancing at Kale, Adwen became sad. Kale sensed her will, and fear gripped his heart.

The group returned to the ledge and watched the snow-white creatures afield. The pure bodies crowned with fine spiral horns dotted the land. Tension from the meeting lingered. Dread clung at their shoulders. Each warrior searched inside for doubts to kill them quickly. This was sure to be their most dangerous battle yet.

Kale stood at the ledge staring balefully at the herd. His body was still as stone, while his heart trembled. When Adwen approached, he hesitated to acknowledge her. As he finally did, the trembling weakened. Kale felt her using the bond to coax him. Stubbornly, he refused.

In a low voice the others could not hear, she whispered urgently, "Please."

Insurmountable fear clutched at his insides. Kale swiftly looked away in shame. She could not sway him. Adwen's expression flashed with fear.

Kale heard the familiar sound of metal chinking. Looking back, he saw Adwen offering the sheathed sword once more. His claws gingerly reached and clasped the black scabbard. Holding it at his side, he resumed watching the unicorns. The sight of the gentle beings helped combat feelings of entrapment.

Facing the warriors, Adwen raised her enchanted voice enough to drown the roar of the waterfall: "It is time. Are you all prepared?"

Four battle-hardened faces nodded with steely stares. Adwen summoned the Gray Blade and launched blue flames to open a portal. It roared and yawned wide. Dark wastes of sand, ash and dust awaited. A calm fell over Adwen in their march. The choice was made and their die cast; come what may, there was no turning back.

The instant they vanished and the portal disappeared, Kale wept in disgrace.

The five warriors stood still in the emptiness. These were once green hills in the heart of Dargadia. All that remained were distant temple ruins. A thin sliver of pure darkness stood silhouetted by countless wayward souls. No wind blew. The air was thick and stale, and it hummed with the power given off by the pillar. They watched for signs of enemy forces. Adwen's intense stare held fast on the ancient stones. Nothing moved as everyone surveyed the potential battlefield.

Jack's thoughts wandered back to the meeting and the moments afterward. Wary, the warrior turned to give Adwen a stern look. She did not seem to notice.

Trying to tap into her mind a little, he growled, "What's wrong with Kale?"

A fleeting thought only stated the obvious: Kale was frightened. Adwen said nothing.

Oryn, Alexander and Tamis became curious also. The recent interactions were odd, to say the least.

Determined to get an answer, Jack grilled her: "What did you say to him before we left?"

All he could pluck from her mind was that she had asked him for something and that he had refused. Her evasiveness made Jack leery. She was hiding something – something that made her nervous. The others knew nothing of her thoughts but could smell Adwen's dread.

Instead of answering, she frowned and whispered, "They know we're here."

Their attention snapped to the rubble several miles away. Jack suddenly cared less about the matter of Kale's behavior. They could feel it now: unseen eyes watched.

Adwen's tone was resolute and harsh: "We push through. No matter what, do not stop. As soon as you do, they will overwhelm us. If that happens, I will go on ahead without you."

The declaration made Oryn look at her, hoping she might reconsider. Jack grimaced. Alexander frowned. If they were pinned down, failure would be inevitable.

Tamis summoned the golden bow, fitting two clawed fingers on the string. The taut resistance was satisfying, and he felt prepared for battle.

Swiftly transforming, blue fire cloaked Adwen's body to serve as armor. It made her and the Gray Blade shine brightly. Jack and Alexander followed suit, transforming and summoning their weapons. Oryn grew massive among them, towering at ten feet tall with pearly fangs bared in a tight snarl. His sword the Rose Thorne appeared in his fierce clutches.

"Ready?" Adwen asked.

The four rumbled dangerously in affirmation.

Growling deeply, the White Holy Hound bathed in blue fire gnashed her fangs and barked. At once, they raced forward in formation, leaving dust clouds in their wake.

Trembling, Kale stood by the back wall of the overlook. Cradled in his claws, a pale orb showed Adwen and her warriors charging. He hoped beyond hope that they could succeed without him. However, he sensed that they did not stand a chance. Kale quaked, staring unblinking at the images scryed with his powers.

A flood of low fog swept from the ruins to cover the barren fields and rocks. As the Holy Hounds reached the mist, horrible wailing shrieks filled the air. Dark purple jaws and claws erupted from the ground on all sides and underfoot. A seemingly endless horde spawned from the earth.

A flood of tall Wretches and scrambling Creepers lunged and snapped. As swiftly as they came the holy blades and arrows reduced their forms to filthy slime. The warriors followed Adwen in carving a path through the ranks. Oryn's huge sword and Tamis's deft aim helped keep back those that Jack and Alexander could not reach.

Adwen's fire kept the weakest away and allowed her to run unhindered. Light from the spectral flames scorched any weak monster that dared to come close. Thousands of the fiends continued to swell out of the desecrated ground.

Then to Jack's and Alexander's horror, the lesser demons began to wail, scream and explode.

Jack barked in alarm, "They're summoning the colossus!"

Oryn braced for what might appear, as did Tamis, but Adwen did not react. She continued to lead the way.

Purple spray in the doldrums turned to black, and many giants began to rise. An army of titanic four-armed demons stood clutching evil spears. They kept appearing all around, then began lobbing wicked shafts. The enormous spears exploded in the ground and stuck fast, impeding the warriors' charge. Deadly volleys launched from every side forced Adwen and her warriors to run in a serpentine path.

Adwen leaped with sword raised at the giants in her way just as a spear clipped Oryn's shoulder. He stumbled, and a second spear plunged through the armor on his leg. It pinned him to the earth. Unable to move, the pain made him roar and howl.

No matter how badly Adwen wanted to go to his rescue, she dared not. She barked to the others, "Leave me! Stay with him!"

They obeyed without hesitation and turned to defend their comrade.

In a blinding flash of light, Adwen avoided being impaled by multiple spears and reappeared on a giant's shoulder. She decapitated it, then shot tongues of flame to blind the others. They bellowed in outrage, as she raced into the vast ruins.

Beyond the first columns, no enemies were to be seen, and she ran faster. Adwen bounded off fallen rubble and over crumbling walls. As she darted through an opening, a black shadow slammed into her. Raising her sword just in time, she careened through the air and held off the blade of a terribly powerful demon. The side of its face was smooth like an onyx egg. The whole side of its body was smooth with little definition, while the other half was covered in deadly angular points. A wicked purple light for an eye burned at her from over a segmented grin.

Then she sensed more movement. A second demon, resembling a mirror image of the first, lunged to cut her down. Adwen swiftly performed her blink. In a flash of light, she vanished out of harm's way.

The demon twin's sword struck empty ground. Purple lightning set off an explosion, leaving a crater in the settling dust. The first twin leaped over. In a burst of darkness, the demon vanished and reappeared at Adwen's side.

Alarmed that they could move as she did, Adwen barely had time to block before the other twin blinked in close, manifesting just behind her. In another flash, she dodged being cut in half. She stopped to stare as they slowly turned to gaze in wicked glee. Though they were separate, their bisected faces tilted in unison as if they were one. They laughed at her fear.

One began to blink to her side, and she swiftly twirled to stand behind it. As she tried to swing the Gray Blade, the second twin appeared beside her to block the blow. While she was stalled by the twin, the first turned, swinging his blade.

With all her strength, Adwen flipped upward. Landing behind the twirling twin, she tried to attack. Despite the valiant effort, the second darted to block again. Adwen's blade sparked and screeched against evil metal. The offensive twin turned again, forcing Adwen to leap out of range.

They came at her again, and Adwen snarled with ears pinned back. She intensified the blue fire for more protection. Bracing herself, she knew retreat was no longer possible.

Rapid flashes of light and dark pulsed in the ruins, while the combatants vanished and reappeared sporadically. Adwen took them closer to the pillar whenever possible, but each time they grew stronger and faster. They fed off its energy. The perfect timing of their attacks and parries forced her to focus on evasion. There were no openings to retaliate.

Among piles of large stone slabs, her enemies grew stronger. Vaulting over the stones to dart behind cover, she slid and dove to avoid direct attack. Blinking to the other side of a large stone, one of the demons blinked, appearing by her side. Before she could react, their sword swung fast. It caught her chest, and her blue fire barely saved her from death. The power behind the blow smashed her body through solid marble in an explosion of dust and stone. Adwen flew limply through the air unconscious. The Gray Blade fell from her hand, landing among the stones.

The shadowy sibling blinked into the air over Adwen as she was falling. Sword overturned in its grasp, the demon prepared to plunge the tip through her heart.

A bright blast of gold struck the demon in the head and then in the chest. The two well-placed shots from Tamis's bow knocked the demon out of the air. It was stunned and flew backward among the piles of rubble. Adwen fell hard onto a slab unharmed.

Tamis leaped from the wall he had scaled. From a formidable distance, his arrows found their marks, and now he could see a second demon like the first approaching to finish what the other had started. He fired another arrow as he sailed down to earth.

The demon was ready. It blocked with the sword, ricocheting the condensed light with ease to explode a nearby boulder. At seeing this, Tamis's heart skipped a beat. No demon had ever survived a direct hit from his bow, and this one could also deflect it. He bounded off more crumbling walls, racing to Adwen's rescue and firing repeatedly to stall the demon. The fiend continued to stalk toward Adwen's defenseless form.

Desperately, Tamis fired shot after shot. Nothing stopped this monstrous shadow. Leaping down from the final wall, the warrior darted across the ground as fast as he could. Tamis's jaws wrinkled in a fierce snarl. He panted heavily from the effort to reach her in time.

Adwen was just beginning to stir, and the demon raised its sword, ready to either deflect another arrow or to plunge it into her chest. Just as her eyes opened and recognized the nightmare bearing over her, Adwen felt something hit her side. She tumbled off the slab to the dirt, as the sword came knifing down.

Tamis slid sideways across the slab, arrow aimed for the demon's face. As he fired the arrow it lanced off the sword. Disbelief filled his eyes.

Raising her head at the sound of the ricochet, Adwen watched in horror. The demon drove the sword through Tamis's armor with no resistance and into the stone. She wailed as some of the pain passed to her, immediately grieving with a baleful howl.

The demon bellowed in triumph, pulsing purple lightning through the blade. The force extinguished what little life remained in the warrior and shattered the stone. Spider web fissures splayed under his body. As the dark sword was pulled free, red blood flooded its sides. The demon collar around Tamis' neck crumbled, and his body became human, turning pale. Wide eyes became half-cast, dilated and foggy.

Kale cried out in anguish, and the orb shattered like glass in his hands. Grasping his head and weeping, he screamed an unnatural wailing cry. Succumbing at last, more tears fell. Staring at the ground, he muttered weakly, "I'm sorry. I'm sorry."

Dropping his arms to his sides, he dashed to the ledge and stared desperately at the unicorns. The thousands of white bodies stood or lounged about, unaware of the tragedy that was unfolding. Tears nearly blinding him, Kale raised a set of claws at the massive unwary herd.

Darkness cloaked his body. The red and white of his eyes shone, while the powers he called upon swelled and bent to his will. A black mass swirled before his fingers as a sound like thunder rumbled from its depths.

Restraining another sob, he whimpered again, "I'm sorry."

He unleashed the energy upon the herd. Thousands of screams filled his ears, making the tears fall faster. The cries reminded him of children.

Forgetting Tamis's desecrated remains, the demon stalked Adwen. She crawled backward, unarmed. She sensed where her sword lay, but it was too far to reach. Even if she summoned it to her hand, it would not arrive in time. The demon was too fast. She ran out of room to withdraw, and the demon began to raise its sword again. Adwen growled in defiance from the ground.

In the blink of an eye, as the demon raised its sword, a hole appeared over her. Out of the pitch-black portal, a terrible shriek broke the quiet, making the demon pause. In confusion, it watched as a black shape like a giant bird flew from the center.

Talons forward, it struck the demon's chest and knocked it to the ground. As the portal vanished, the shape that had struck the demon rode upon the fiend as it slid between the stones. The astonished demon twin swung the sword, making the attacker retreat. The figure cloaked in darkness leaped up high, landing on a nearby stone. As the smoky energy settled, the figure of a man with claws and red and white eyes became clear. The red strip of cloth fluttered from Kale's right upper arm as he glared, challenging the demon to a fight.

Hissing angrily, the fiend could not refuse – not after being insulted.

Adwen summoned her holy sword, and it flew to her hand. Stealing a sidelong glance at the figure on the fractured stone, blue fire burned brighter around her. She sensed the wounded demon twin was returning to the fray. Her jaws wrinkled as she bared her teeth and began to growl.

While Kale battled one fiend, the twin stood up from behind

a wall shrieking in outrage. It charged, raising its sword. Adwen watched as it came at her, while its wounds dealt by Tamis tried to mend. When their swords clashed, she sensed the enemy was weakened, though only a little. Gnashing fangs in the monster's half face, their duel resumed in a flurry of blink dodges and dancing blades.

The white Holy Hound led and pushed, trading off many fearsome strikes and vicious parries. She and the demon disappeared and reappeared behind or beside each other, swinging swords of light and darkness. Like lightning, the battle moved about the ruins. They were an even match and dealt equal blows, drawing silver and purple to spatter the stones and dust.

In Kale's fight with the second half, the demon blinked rapidly, appearing to strike or stab from all sides. No matter what it tried, the rogue was too fast and even more perceptive. Through the darkness, he knew where the villain would manifest. Fully cloaked in black smoky energy like armor, Kale dodged or swatted away the blade with sharp claws. Cuts dealt to Adwen appeared on his body, but he was not weakened.

Enraged by this rogue's impenetrable defense, the demon shrieked in its vile language, "Fight me!"

On the fiend's next swing, the sword sliced through the darkness surrounding Kale, and the blackness dissipated revealing nothing. He was gone. Then the demon heard whistling air and claws raked across its back, making the demon scream and whirl around. Kale was already on the monster's other side. He swung again, leaving more black bleeding gashes across its sword arm.

Blinking in a flash of blackness, the demon put some distance between itself and Kale. The effort counted for nothing, as Kale was already there. More deep wounds appeared when powerful claws carved demon flesh like a rake through mud.

Adwen and the twin flitted from place to place in flashes of black and white. Their swords cut the air, occasionally finding each other's flesh. They pursued each other to and fro, hissing and snarling. Eventually their fight came to the pillar's foundation. Wayward souls descended around the duel, turning everything green. The demon grew strong this close to the pillar, healing rapidly, while Adwen's endurance withered in turn. Even more silver blood dripped across her sides, back and legs. A cut across her face wept a curtain of silver as she snarled. She let her foe back her closer to the demon monolith.

Ready to finish her, the demon twin advanced with confidence. It swung the black sword hard, forcing Adwen to block. The strength behind the attack made Adwen's injured legs buckle. Again, the demon swung down with a punishing blow.

She blocked the strike and barely stayed on her feet. The demon moved even closer, and her fangs clenched at the strain of resisting.

To end it, the demon twin exchanged several parries with Adwen and put on a spurt of blinding speed to run her through. She roared in pain at the demon's sneer as they came face to face in a deadly embrace. Enraged, the demon hissed.

Growling and cringing, Adwen grabbed the demon's spiky shoulder. With a firm grip, she held the Gray Blade tightly where she had plunged it into the monster's torso. Demon flesh turned gray like ashen embers. It withered away where the sword touched. She cleaved the demon's side. Then she brought the blade back and rent it in half. In her grasp the fiend began to fade into shimmering flecks.

When the demon was gone, she pulled the demon-steel sword from the fleshy part of her flank. Dropping the wretched thing, she tried to stymie the flow of silver blood. Adwen faced the monolith and the clouds of many lost souls waiting for release.

While Adwen moved to complete the mission, Kale whittled down the remaining demon twin. It shrieked and bellowed as Kale continuously ripped it apart. Defiant to the end, the fiend swung blindly to catch Kale at least once. As the demon became too weak to swing the sword, it dropped to its knees.

Prowling around from behind, Kale gave the demon the coldest of looks. Standing over it, the bond with Adwen let him know she was about to destroy the pillar. He summoned Vaughn's blade to his side. Ceremoniously drawing it from the sheath the razor-sharp edge sang a clear tone. The fiend watched as Kale used a claw cloaked in shadow to etch a rune into the core of the blade.

The demon was shocked, then became bitter and sly.

The sword emitted a sound like a gasp for air and a sigh, as pale white mist began to emanate from it. The golden marks on Kale's hand and arm reached to his shoulder. They began to glow as Adwen stirred her own power. The light from the shining marks flowed into the Elfish blade. It was not as potent as the holy weapons, but it could finish this monster.

Grinning up at Kale, the demon hissed with glee, "Do you hate me?"

Gazing blankly, he answered with cold indifference, "No. You are nothing to me."

The fiend turned resentful.

While Adwen's heart poured light into the pillar through her hand, the same surge of energy imbued Vaughn's sword. The white mist turned bright like sunshine. He stabbed the demon through the chest, taking the vengeful look from its face. Then he swiftly cut the head from its shoulders. It toppled over, then burst into nothingness.

A rumbling shook the earth, and Adwen knew it was time to flee. Tremors rattled the ground as cracks spread throughout the black pillar. This monolith was vast, and its explosion would be just as immense. Dismissing the Gray Blade, she bounded away at top speed. Kale joined her side, letting the dark mist dissipate at last.

Adwen scooped up Tamis's body without slowing. The rumbling of the ground intensified. At the outskirts of the ruins they found Oryn, Jack and Alexander alive but severely wounded. The demon colossus that remained began to flee the falling pillar or else be extinguished with it. The warriors were free to run with Adwen and Kale.

Moments after they reached the plains, a blast shook the air. They paused and looked back. A concussive force swept out from where the pillar collapsed, sending a wall of dust flying. They shielded their faces from the particles and braced against the shock wave.

As quickly as the explosion came, it ended. A hush fell over the land. The warriors shifted into their more human shapes. They tried to avoid breathing in the dust as it settled. Darkness began to ebb, and everyone saw the edges of the false night receding. As the sky brightened and the air cleared, the weary warriors exchanged glances. When the three looked at Adwen in her hound form with a human cradled in her arms, their hearts quivered.

Jack flinched and stared in disbelief. "Tamis?"

The dust cleared enough for their senses to pick up the strong smell of human blood. Standing apart from them, Kale turned away. He could not watch.

Oryn went to Adwen, while Jack and Alexander stood by. The somber look Adwen wore made hoping otherwise difficult. After the knight checked for a pulse, he withdrew his hand and gave the fellow warriors a grim frown.

The Marine became stone-faced, while Jack swore profusely and snarled. Getting a grip on himself, the cop muttered bitterly, "Poor kid."

Adwen gently laid him down on the cool ground. She shifted into her woman form, closed his half-cast eyes and touched the short rusty brown hair on his head. A few tears fell as she did.

"What should we do now?" Jack asked.

He didn't intend to be answered, but Adwen softly replied, "We say good-bye."

Oryn stood in silence. Farewells to the dead were not his strong suit after having lost so many brothers in arms.

Before anyone could move, Adwen gasped and started to smile. She looked up and beamed at a figure walking toward them. Oryn, Jack and Alexander stared in shock. When Kale finally looked up, his heart skipped a beat. Tears filled his eyes as his insides contorted into knots.

Tamis, appearing as his youthful human self, walked to them leaving no footprints in the dust. The rising sunlight shone through him, casting no shadow. Adwen smiled at the brave warrior.

Joining them around his body, Tamis glanced at himself for a moment. Then he smiled proudly. "It was an honor, Tame One. I'd do it a second time if I could."

She wanted to cry but laughed instead. "I wouldn't allow that."

Tamis chuckled. Then he shook his head at Jack and Alexander. "Neither of you are to blame. I was about to seek Adwen, even if you had not sent me."

It was Jack's turn to try not to weep. Alexander placed a comforting hand on his friend's shoulder, and it helped a little.

Facing Oryn, the lingering spirit of Tamis gave a knight's salute. The knight proudly returned the gesture.

Lastly, the warrior looked to Kale, who shuddered under his gaze. Wracked with remorse, Kale shivered and choked on small tearful sobs. Then he felt the warm touch of a hand on his shoulder. He could not help but glance up just enough to face Tamis. There was not an ounce of anger or regret.

The young warrior's spirit beamed. "I see you."

Kale gasped, eyes wide.

"Nothing of this was your fault," Tamis added.

Self-resentment and self-doubt stabbed at his heart, as he wished it were true. A loud sob escaped Kale, and he hung his head. Clawed hands balled into tight fists. Kale pleaded again, "I'm sorry. I'm sorry!"

As he looked up to profess his shame, the smiling human ghost faded away. The young warrior's spirit was gone. Kale drew a ragged gasp as he tried to stop the flow of tears. The others watched as he took deeper and deeper breaths to regain control.

Adwen spoke softly: "It's the truth: None of this was your fault."

He snapped angrily with a cracking resonate voice, "How do you know that?"

Her reply was simple: "Because it was meant to be this way."

Hearing the ring of truth almost made the tears return with full force. Looking back at the group, he added, "If I'd been here sooner ..."

Adwen cut him off: "The result would have been the same. There was nothing you could do to prevent this. Stop blaming yourself."

Kale made no reply, but the bitter look showed how much he disagreed.

Oryn became wary. "Why are you here?"

At hearing the question, Jack was alarmed. "Why are you here, Big Guy, and how did you get here so fast?"

He said nothing and heaved a shuddering sigh. Sorrow filled his gaze.

Jack verged on panic. "Big Guy? Where are the unicorns?"

Lowering his gaze somberly, Kale clenched his jaw and fists.

If he had left the unicorns to the demons, Oryn considered whether it was time to kill Kale.

A black ball like a pearl appeared in the palm of Kale's hand. The mysterious smooth gem did not reflect any light. Grunting in frustration at himself, he tossed the black bead far out into the wastes. As Kale turned his back on it and the warriors, an enormous dark mass engulfed a hillside. A sound like thunder rumbled. Then loud whinnying met their ears, and the cloud vanished. Thousands of unicorns raced down the dusty hills. Green sprigs and blossoms sprung up wherever they tread.

In amazement and relief, the three warriors watched the creatures run. A moment passed, and Oryn turned to stare at Kale suspiciously. Jack heard the knight's thoughts and whipped around.

Abashed, Jack blurted out, "You could have done that before we left?"

Alexander turned and stared wide-eyed.

Adwen lowered her gaze and murmured, "Yes."

Jack looked between her and Kale and remained confused about how to feel. "Why didn't he?"

When she did not say, Oryn frowned at the rogue and answered, "Because he fears his own power."

Kale shivered. He neither faced them nor denied the accusation. This made Jack sigh as he realized it was true.

Alexander stared at Kale's turned back. "You shouldn't be afraid of yourself. There's no reason to be."

Oryn explained further: "He also hates these powers. They disgust him. Having them reminds him of the fine line that separates what he is from the true demons."

Kale spat bitterly under his breath, "Shut up."

Adwen stepped in. "That's enough, Oryn. Leave him alone."

Jack frowned and crossed his arms indignantly. "Alone? I'm pretty sure that hasn't helped much lately."

She gave him a deadly look. "Trust me, Jack. He needs to sort this out himself. Back off."

The warrior grudgingly held his tongue.

To Kale, Adwen called softly, "Come on. Let's get Tamis back to the overlook so we can take care of him the right way. He deserves at least that much."

Kale muttered bitterly under his breath, "He deserved better than this."

A sad frown came over Adwen.

Oryn had less sympathy. "Tamis made it clear that he chose his own end."

Pain made Kale clench his fists tighter. Shuddering, he muttered, "He didn't deserve death. More than any one, he deserved happiness."

Despite injuries, the knight took a few steps closer wearing a harsh frown. "Tamis died a hero's death. He was a warrior."

Anguish exploded within Kale, and he whirled around to wail, "He was innocent!"

The knight did not bat an eye. Kale blanched, and his blood ran cold. As he stared in horror at Jack and Alexander, his heart felt weak.

Coming to their senses, both warriors realized they had automatically summoned their blades to their hands. In shock at themselves, they watched Kale's face go blank and his stare distant. Every muscle slackened in defeat. Jack dismissed the daggers and Alexander the short sword, but the damage was done. Helplessly, the two watched Kale turn to walk away.

Adwen tossed the pair a betrayed look and moved to go after him down the hill. "Kale!"

He considered ignoring the call but forced himself to stop.

She stood just behind sensing what was in his heart. "We aren't leaving without you. We'll be right here when you're ready."

Kale continued trudging down the hillside, now covered by fresh shoots of grass.

As Adwen returned, Oryn looked at the others and realized what had set Kale off. The knight glowered. "Fools."

Alexander was ashamed, but Jack far more so. He could not understand why he drew his daggers. As the knight came closer, he asked, "Why didn't you summon your sword?"

Oryn sneered, "Because I'm not afraid of him."

Jack swallowed a knot in his throat. The knight was right; they were fools.

For Kale, every step was jarring. His mind felt like the desert: empty, vast and lonely. It was cold despite the light spreading through to heal the sky. Following his feet in a daze, he walked farther and farther from the others. The sick, numb sensation would not leave after seeing them draw their weapons at him.

A part of Kale wished to cry. He could not. The cold disoriented feeling held fast. As his boots found a small boulder, it was as good a place as any to stop. Kale sat staring out into space. Again he wished to weep, scream, roar or anything to dispel the state he found himself in. This feeling was obscure and hollow. It felt like death.

Yet he could do nothing; he could not move. His mind became blank, while the wind whistled in his ears. The unicorns scattered, breaking off into smaller herds to venture about. Many remained to romp and graze where they had been released. Kale did not notice that they were steadily drawing near.

A hush came. Even the wind fell quiet. The cold inside Kale faltered at the sight of graceful cloven hooves as white as snow drawing close. A single unicorn approached and stared at his face, while hundreds of others gathered around. Deep glassy eyes glistened by the sunlight as the false-night spell dissipated.

On the verge of finally weeping, Kale shivered in shame and lowered his gaze. These creatures were so pure. The innocent ones were pristine. He was their opposite. It was beyond his right even to touch a unicorn.

A sudden feeling of warmth shot through him from his forehead. Frozen in place by surprise, Kale dared not move. The unicorn had lowered its horn. The ivory spiral subtly pressed against the side of the invisible blade reaching from Kale's brow. The creature greeted him as one would their own by crossing horns gently.

Tears swelled in Kale's wide trembling stare. Still, he did not dare to move for fear of frightening the innocent ones. Slowly and gradually, the herd began to move. They started to circle the stone as a gyre of silvery white bodies. Beams of sunlight cut through the black sky and glanced off their horns like ripples in a stream. The sound of hundreds of hooves plodding intensified until it mimicked the song of ocean waves.

Moments into the graceful stampede, the roar of their hoof beats gave way to silence. As they continued to race, Kale found the will to raise his head and look up. When he locked gazes with the unicorn, he saw no fear. The discovery left him breathless. A soft sound echoed like a whisper in the air. Through the herd's combined magic, they spoke to him without words. His ears heard, his heart understood, and his mind could scarcely comprehend.

Tears trickled down when he closed his eyes to listen to their song. Warmth flooded him in waves. The creatures comforted and consoled. They imparted their wisdom, and for that time, there was no suffering.

Chapter 27
CONFRONTED WITH AN OPPONENT

Adwen and her three remaining warriors basked together, allowing the sunlight to mend their wounds and ease their aches. A few stray unicorns passed, trailing carpets of green. The new growth took hold fast in the rich dust and ash.

Jack was unable to think of anything but the look on Kale's face when he saw the two warriors summon the daggers and sword. Glancing at Adwen, resting her eyes as she sat, Jack asked, "When is he coming back?"

"He won't be much longer."

Wishing she would be more precise, Jack ran a hand through his short hair. His attention wandered to the knight. Oryn chose to stand and wait rather than recline and rest. A short distance away, the knight watched whatever Kale was doing in the valley. Tapping into his mind yielded almost nothing; it was blank. Yet whatever he was watching clearly intrigued him.

Oryn studied the strange formation of the herd and how it circled. He was certain it was Kale sitting on the rock in their midst. For a moment, the figure did not look the same. But as soon as Oryn blinked, only Kale sat on the stone before a bowing unicorn. The animals then dispersed. By the time the final snow-white beast departed, the knight decided that what he had seen had been a trick of the light.

Oryn turned back and sat among the warriors at last. He noticed how Jack was watching curiously, apparently spying on his mind. This irritated him, but he decided he was too tired to tell off Jack.

"Kale will be along soon," Oryn replied.

Jack and Alexander both felt some relief, but Adwen knew more: Some peace had settled in Kale's heart – a parting gift from the unicorns.

Minutes passed before their strange friend walked up the knoll, now covered in new grass. The red cloth at his arm flowed gently by his side despite the powerful breeze. His gaze was reserved. The Holy Hounds stood at his arrival.

Before Adwen or even Jack could say a word, Alexander spoke: "We are glad you're back."

He stared. Kale sensed their feelings. The Marine and the cop smelled of regret – the kind after an argument where ill-chosen words were exchanged. To settle the issue, he softly spoke and his resonant tones were almost melodic: "There's work to do. I'm ready."

Oryn noticed the change to Kale's demon voice. It was smoother. The unicorns may have affected his nature. Facing Adwen, the knight was direct: "What is your command?"

"We're taking Tamis back to the overlook."

Only Kale had the nerve to give the bloody remains a glance.

"Afterward, we will hunt on the coast. There's no telling how long before Vlad makes his move."

Unable to take his gaze from the human body, Kale murmured, "I have theories."

"Good. We'll discuss them right after our strength is restored." Summoning her sword, she burned open a portal to the overlook, where sunlight was starting to break through.

The remains of the young warrior were laid on a windy corner of the overlook. Adwen determined that dawn was the best time to perform the last rites. While she and her warriors were far off in the southwest hunting game, Kale stood at the ledge once more.

With his gaze firmly set on the horizon, he pondered many things: himself, his new nature, the unicorns and the things they had told him. Then he pondered Vlad, the phantasm in an indestructible shell of demon-steel. While the sun battled with the cursed sky, his mind swam in visions of light and dark colliding.

At sunset the wreath of blue fire appeared, announcing the return of the Holy Hounds. Looking back at them, Kale saw that the four had been fully restored. He waited for the portal to vanish before addressing business. His haunting voice resonated smoothly and powerfully over the roar of the falls: "Ready to talk?"

Adwen nodded. "Yes."

They entered the sanctuary chambers. Adwen's light filled the room with a soft glow, and they took seats. When she spoke, it was with renewed determination.

"I'll get straight to the point: I sense Vlad will resurface very soon. Kale, have you checked on his army recently?"

Effortlessly, he summoned a pale orb. It showed the robotic soldiers. This time they were somewhere in darkness. There were strange noises, as if they were digging.

He frowned. "I still cannot pinpoint their location."

"Check frequently. Let me know as soon as there is a change."

Dismissing the orb, he nodded. "Of course."

Becoming troubled, she continued: "We were successful in taking the tower without losing the unicorns. What is the risk that the demons will try to erect more pillars?"

"Depends," Kale answered. "It would require a lot of life blood. What bothers me is that they haven't been fighting very hard to keep Dargadia to themselves."

Jack scoffed, rubbing at places where wounds had barely healed. "Seems to me they are putting up a fight."

Kale acknowledged the point. "Given, but even the guardian in the north noted how demon assaults at the borders had stopped. Dargadia appears no longer to be the focus of their efforts."

Grimly, the knight added: "Then there is likely a new target. One would think Jenkirk, but I have doubts."

Alexander agreed, "If they really wanted that city, I get the feeling the guardian would have had a harder time keeping the demons back."

Sighing anxiously, Jack combed his hair back with his fingers. "I don't know about that, but the lack of resistance right now has me nervous."

"As it should." Kale wore a hardened expression. "If they are not here, then they are someplace else. That the Reaper did not appear at the battle tells me one of two things: Either he's busy with other things or the demon lords are confident that they've already won."

Adwen growled about the situation. "Pride – it's why you're still alive, too. Looks like Degah'lee is still keeping his mouth shut and shielding you to protect himself."

Kale nodded.

"Who knows how much longer that will benefit us?"

"Impossible to say," Kale added darkly. "The tosser is not a complete idiot. Still, with the unicorns returned to this world, and the greatest pillar destroyed, the rest will crumble on their own. If you lot were them, what would your next move be and why?"

Jack pursed his lips tightly. "If I were them, I would already be onto the next move before the pillars were threatened. Then I'd want to settle the score."

"What is the move, then?" Kale asked. When they replied only with bewildered looks, he helped the conversation along: "What is their end game? What do they want?"

Oryn replied, "Everything to be consumed by darkness from the Void."

He nodded. "Yeah, and how can they do that?"

"The black pillars work pretty well, so long as Adwen isn't around," Jack shook his head. "I'm convinced they will make more."

"They're going to try bloody hard to do it," Kale warned. "I can promise you that."

Alexander grew curious: "What do they need to make them? Just human blood?"

A glint appeared in Kale's gaze. The Marine was close to the crux of the conversation.

"No, Yankee. Human blood is the most potent ingredient, but there are other very important things required to summon the Fingers of the Void. One of the most crucial is magic."

Adwen's face slackened, as she began to understand. The knowledge terrified her.

Oryn smelled her fear. "These pillars were a taxing step for the demons to take. If they are not showing themselves since the greatest has fallen, then what was the goal? Why erect them?"

Kale answered the knight's question with yet another: "What did those pillars do?"

The three warriors exchanged perplexed looks. They never pondered this before.

Jack suggested, "They turned the sky to night and made demons stronger."

"Those things were favorable side effects," Kale admitted.

"But what did the pillars do?"

Adwen knew the answer: "They drain magic from the earth."

"That's right."

Jack was aghast. "Those things are like oil pumps. They pull magic out of the ground?"

"Think about it," Kale urged. "Was the magic in the air tainted? Could you smell it?"

Alexander admitted, "We couldn't smell any at all."

Oryn began to understand, as well, and growled under his breath. Jack sensed some of the knight's thoughts. They alarmed him.

"For months those things syphoned magic out of Dargadia," Jack mused. "They must have an incredible amount stored up. Do they have enough to build those pillars wherever they want?"

"Not just anywhere. It would need to be heavily populated, yet secluded."

"Sounds an awful lot like Jenkirk," Alexander remarked.

Kale corrected him: "Yeah, but there's already magic there. Remember: They want to take over all the worlds, all of creation. If they harvested that much magic, where could they put it to the most use? Where would they need it so badly?"

Jack realized the answer but immediately became dismissive. "That's not possible. How can they take magic from Dargadia and transfer it to the other side?"

"They can." Kale insisted. "They do it all the time in small amounts – such small amounts that you can't even smell it."

The knight grimaced. "Then with enough magic accrued, there remains the demand for blood. How will they take it, and from where?"

"Wherever and whenever they attack," Kale answered.

Jack felt sick to his stomach. "Where?"

"We already know where they are going to attack." Adwen wore a bitter frown.

They stared at her expectantly.

"The Dragon Mother told us: An army is mustering to swallow the land of sin."

Jack was dumbfounded. "Sin City?"

Alexander frowned. "Vegas?"

Kale nodded. "The mines where the demon-steel army was

made were five hundred miles southwest of there. It's been a few days. I think the assault is hours away at most. Knowing them, the attack will begin at night."

Adwen's eyes blazed. "The timing of the days there is not too different. If you are right, the battle will begin shortly. We need to go."

Wary of the danger, Oryn stated the obvious: "Vlad will undoubtedly be present. No matter your power, he can defeat you."

Before she could reply, Kale spoke: "I can kill Vlad."

The Holy Hounds stared in surprise at the declaration. Kale's expression showed no doubt.

Leery, Jack asked, "How?"

Eerie dark eyes locked with the warrior's, and the resonate demon voice answered, "I'll make you a deal: I'll tell you – after he's dead."

Jack was taken aback. "Don't get me wrong. I trust you, but he's indestructible. His body is demon-steel reinforced with runes."

"And?"

Seeing no change to Kale's opinion, Jack shrugged. "That's it."

Adwen was anxious. "We should go. I want to be there when it starts and not after." She got to her feet and summoned the flaming sword. As the others stood, she muttered, "It has to be Las Vegas."

"It is," Kale assured her.

Surrounded by her loyal friends, Adwen felt prepared for this night. With a flick of her wrist, the sword arched through the air, scratching a hole through time and space. Blue tongues of fire opened the way to a brilliant desert sunset. She strode through to the other side, and the others followed.

Atop a luxurious hotel resort, the wind whipped relentlessly. It was nearly sunset but still hot and arid like the blazing orange sun in the distance. Adwen marched to the edge and surveyed the city. Nothing escaped her gaze, but there was only a normal chaotic metropolis. Though there were no enemies, her heart and instincts knew otherwise. Kale was right; they were coming.

A freeway on the cusp where the city and the desert met pulsed with cars, trucks and cargo rigs. Headlights flickered to life in the dimming twilight. As the masses sped on their way, the sunset seemed ordinary. The fiery glow steadily faded, and they paid no mind. Some drivers headed for dates or work shifts. Others were homeward bound pondering bills or dinner options.

When the signs of the cataclysm began, only the most alert people took notice. The handful of witnesses glimpsed the ground collapsing on either side of the freeway for miles. Suddenly an explosion in their path collapsed the road in the deep trenches. Drivers slammed on their brakes, some screamed and many cars collided trying to avoid falling into the new ravine. Traffic piled up, as the unlucky travelers tumbled into the pit.

The same phenomenon struck the four other major motorways into and out of the desert city. A deep trench encircled Las Vegas, severing access to the outside world. In the moment that the tunnels dug by the drone army were detonated and collapsed, more underground explosions went off at the airport. Essential landing and takeoff strips were devastated, while onlookers gasped in dismay.

As hundreds of drones with luminous wings emerged from the craters, people froze in disbelief. Some witnesses tried to record the event with digital devices. But when the things flew for the windows of the airport, most regained sense and fled. The last to flee before the drones came through the glass were the first to die.

Adwen and the others barely heard the dull thuds of explosives. The concussive bursts reached their sharp senses from miles away. Fully alert, their attention went to the closest source – the airport. As they watched, neon green lights in the likeness of fireflies rose to scatter about the city. The swarm rapidly spread to the streets for the harvest.

She growled as silvery blue fire erupted on her head and shoulders. "Oryn, Jack, Alexander: for this fight, stay in your true forms. Let no one see your human faces. The four of us will have to spread out and hunt down as many as we can. Kale, you know what to do."

He glared at the monstrosities and replied, "I'll send Vlad a special invitation."

Transforming into her pure white form cloaked in holy flames, she glanced back at him. "We're counting on you."

He heard something else from the piece of her heart, which had spread to his shoulder: "We believe in you."

The three warriors looked back at him, as well. It was true.

With even more resolve, Kale transformed. A cloud of darkness radiated from him as he turned black and grew. Hunkering low, the giant werewolf's body poured out dark energy as smoky mist. Over him was a mixture of coarse fur and iridescent raven feathers that fluttered in the wind. His deep breaths seemed to seethe with each draw of his vast lungs.

Adwen nodded to their friend. A burst of shadows came, and Kale was gone over the side of the building to draw out their enemy. The others transformed, baring fangs and sharp golden blades.

Before leaping into action, Adwen growled, "If you cannot kill the drones, disable them. But if nothing else, keep as many busy as you can to buy Kale time."

The three nodded and rumbled in affirmation.

"Be careful out there." As a wordless dismissal, Adwen dove over the side.

Oryn ran in another direction to leap off. Jack and Alexander did the same. They sailed downward to the streets. Each warrior raced for the sound of human screams and chaos.

At street level, drones pinned helpless humans using unyielding clamp vices. Scorpion-like tails armed with thick hypodermic needles uncoiled from their backs. Once their prey was struck with the steel stinger, it took only seconds to drain every pint of blood. Desiccated bodies littered the city exponentially, as humans were helpless against them.

City police and others with weapons tried to shoot the mechanical abominations. It was no use. Bullets glanced off haphazardly, leaving only scratches. These petty attempts went ignored. The drones carried on sucking the life from victims, storing the precious fluids in internal flasks under thick armor.

When a drone moved to pounce on another human on a sidewalk, police emptied their magazines. Nothing worked, and they were forced to watch the civilian die a swift, gruesome death. The sight caused them to curse under their breaths. When the thing turned to face them and discarded the corpse, the officers began to panic.

Then a creature, as tall as a man, with black and white fur

leaped in, and the officers were dumbfounded. The creature wielded golden daggers that spun in the air on their own as if controlled by a ghost. They whirled around the mesh wings of the evil automatons. Thin wires snapped under the blades, and the thing was rendered flightless. It wailed with an angry static voice.

The drone charged the anthropomorphic creature in fantastic armor. In a blur, the creature dodged and struck the drone again. Snarling, slicing and clawing, he continued to search for weak points in the metal thing's design. The drone uncoiled its stinger and lunged for the creature. Snarling, the beast caught the syringe end with both hands. An instant later, it swung the man-shaped machine over and slammed it to the ground. Despite the punishing blow, it remained fully functional.

Jack hung onto the ropy probe tail, using the time it took the thing to stand to look for weaknesses. While he was busy, a loud pop reached his ears before something punched through his neck. It stung and surprised him. Looking back at the small band of police officers, the one responsible looked even more frightened.

Irritated, he growled as he used his telekinetic talents to prevent further interruptions. The men and women gasped in fright as their guns ejected cartridges and magazines. Metal fragments hit the pavement at their feet. Some officers fled right away, while the rest stood rooted by fear.

No sooner did Jack disarm the bystanders than the android puppet turned to lunge.

Alexander faced a drone in an all-out brawl after cutting off its wings. His blade could not cut the demon-steel frame. They threw each other into cars and buildings, smashing the surroundings to pieces. Bystanders fled, but many stayed to capture the scene with cameras. But when a second drone arrived, they ran for their lives. More screams filled the night.

The warrior became numb to pain as he heard the second abomination arrive. In desperation, he tried to find a way to finish the drone that was consuming all his attention. Its stinger was fast and difficult to avoid. When the thing thought it had him, the tail tip struck out like lightning.

Instinctively, he swung the short sword. The ringing of metal chimed as he sliced off the needle at the tails' first joint. Human blood leaked from the severed end of the deadly tail, making the drone shriek. As the thing charged again, Alexander aimed the golden sword for a glowing seam in the chest plate. It gave off the odor of dried human blood. Metal on metal screamed in Alexander's ears as he plunged the blade through the hair-thin gap. The sword penetrated to the back of the interior cavity.

A wailing static cry came from the mechanical nightmare, and it writhed. The light inside burst, and steam blasted from every seam. The contraption fell limp. Alexander realized he had pierced the sacrificial human heart. Thrilled, the yellow Holy Hound raised his jaws high and howled to his friends what he had learned.

Oryn fought three at once. No matter how many times he swatted them away, they came back unfazed. Two still possessed the power of flight, making the battle daunting.

Then he heard the howl.

Armed with the knowledge, the knight in the form of a giant hound prepared the next charge. One drone flew for his face like a ravenous wasp. This time, he took aim for the fine seam barely visible down the chest plate. Indeed, there was the scent of dried human blood with a reddish glow. He roared, then knifed the tip of the six-foot sword through thin gap. The sword pierced its chest. The thing shuddered violently, then expired. Snarling at the hunk of worthless scrap on the end of his blade, Oryn swung. The machine came free and crashed through a distant window just before the other two moved to pounce.

Adwen stormed the streets bathed in dense flames. Blazing like a white and blue star, she hunted Vlad's puppets. The heat from her fire cracked pavement in seconds. Car windows shattered, and paint and enamel cracked and flaked.

Drones flew to her like mosquitoes to a bright light. As they flew in close, their frames turned red then white hot. By the time they reached her, their bodies were soft like flesh. With ease, she was able to carve them to slag.

Adwen heard Alexander's howl. They were doing well to

have found a weakness so quickly. She did not need it, however. As the snow white Holy Hound demolished all enemies who dared to approach, she sensed Kale's progress. His battle would begin soon.

A drone finished draining another human and dropped the dead weight with a pathetic thump. More targets for harvest screamed and ran to their cars, unaware that all roads were cut off. Those who knew panicked and sought hideaways in hope of surviving the night. None could hide from the drones' thermal sensors.

As the drone slowly turned, a massive heat signature appeared in the periphery of its sensors. What it glimpsed through normal vision was a black smoking mass with a big red eye. Pale white light shone in the depths of the dark pupil.

Too fast for the drone to detect movement, something ripped the wings from its back. Its tail ripped out, along with the bottom of the reservoir and one leg. Before the drone toppled over, enormous jaws with dragon-like teeth clamped onto its torso. The black creature raced away with the drone clenched in its jaws.

The drone's sensors watched trees and city lights streak past with blazing heat signatures. They rocketed up the side of a building. The dark creature tossed the broken yet functional drone onto the rooftop. Leaking red, it rolled to a stop beside ventilation machinery. The automaton twitched as it turned its head trying to right itself. Without wings and a missing leg, there was no fight left in it. The drone made static growls as it stared at Kale.

Reverting to his smaller form, the red cloth fluttered wildly from Kale's arm. His expression was calm. Going close, his clawed fingers clutched the side of the drone's head and lifted it to eye level. He gazed deep into the robotic lens and sensed Vlad through this broken puppet.

"You know where to find me."

Steel alloy screeched as Kale's dark powers split the chest of the drone wide. The human heart ripped free and flew swiftly into his hand. While Vlad could still see, Kale squeezed, reducing the pulsating flesh to a burst of red mist. The drone died instantly.

Wails from the city streets floated on the wind. Night had fallen completely with indifferent stars twinkling in the sky. Dry gusts swept over the tower of cement and glass. Long before Kale saw

Vlad, he sensed the monster's presence as its floated up along the building's side. Kale watched with a cold expression as the lord over the steel fireflies loomed into view.

Landing gently on the ledge, Vlad stared at the challenger. A long silence followed until the evil entity greeted him: "What is your name, rogue?"

Kale said nothing.

"You challenge me, and yet you will not do me the honor of sharing your name? I see. When we last met, I underestimated you. Your skill and wit in battle are impressive."

At last, Vlad saw what had changed since their first encounter. It had been hard to see through the drone's perspective. The villain became astonished and was left in awe.

The radio-static voice sounded captivated: "You are powerful."

Again, Kale made no effort to respond.

"None can sense your presence, yet in your eyes I see the tip of the iceberg," Vlad said, making a humble bow. "Come to me and become my lord. Dethrone the Dark Heart, and you will have my will as your own. You shall rule all the worlds, and I will be your eternal servant, my liege."

Kale finally spoke, and his resonate voice was cold: "I'm not interested in ruling."

Glancing up from his bow, Vlad's glowing eyes flickered in surprise. "Destroy, then?"

Kale could see that the monster was truly seduced. Nevertheless, it changed nothing. With passive disgust, he replied, "Just you."

At first, Vlad was taken aback. Then he sneered and stood tall. "As you wish. No matter how great your dark power, being a rogue is your weakness. Such an abysmal waste." The embittered specter drew both laser-sharpened swords from his back.

Black fog solidified in Kale's left hand, and the blade from his late mentor manifested there. Pale mist rippled along the edge of the ancient steel. More dark fog cloaked his body, leaving only his luminous eyes and glinting golden marks visible. The red cloth at his arm fluttered more rapidly. All the while, his expression remained resolute.

Vlad was amused. From their first meeting, it was clear the rogue was right-handed. The metallic fiend tilted his head to one side.

"You keep your strong arm free. Interesting choice. Why is that, I wonder?" Vlad did not expect an answer. "I know you to be a worthy opponent, rogue. Fight me. Show me your magnificent power."

Kale growled.

The menacing metal king flew forward and cried out, "I want to see it!"

Their forms collided in a blast of black mist and wicked lightning. Locked in deadly combat, the combatants careened over the side of the tower. Vlad roared in excitement, swinging both swords only to be deflected by Elf-steel shrouded in pale energy. Dark fog trailed behind them as green currents of electricity arced from Vlad's wings. In the descent, Kale fended off two demon-steel swords at once. The challenge caused the metal monster's eyes to burn with a terrible thrill.

In a burst of unearthly speed, Kale beat back the swords and kicked up at the skull cast in evil steel. With Vlad off his guard for an instant, Kale slashed his darkness-tipped claws across one mechanical arm. The power of the attack knocked the fiend back through the air. Vlad laughed outloud.

As the monster corrected his flight path, the ground rushed up to meet them in the blink of an eye. Vlad flew in at full speed, but Kale deflected and slashed again with claws dripping with black fog. Hitting the other arm, Vlad was thrown into the second floor of the building, shattering glass to sparkling slivers.

Kale turned at the last second to land on his feet. The pavement crunched and cracked as he slid backward, maintaining balance through the shallow trench dug by his impact. His gaze never left the broken windows where two pinpricks of light stared out between luminous gossamer wings.

Vlad flew into the neon and fluorescent night. He dove low, eager to draw out more of Kale's potential. With no fear of death, Vlad felt only greed to witness the glory of this rogue demon's power. The monster brandished both swords as he swooped downward like a javelin.

Rather than deflect or defend, Kale dodged at the last moment, avoiding a strike by a hair's breadth. He swatted as the villain passed, striking the back of the steel-cast skull crowned with spikes. The impact flipped Vlad end over end, forcing him to land. Turning to face each other on the evacuated street, they stared each other down.

Perplexed, Vlad mused, "You're holding back."

Kale scowled behind the thick darkness that shrouded his visage.

The thought of it annoyed the demonic phantasm. "I know you are clever, but toying with me is quite foolish, rogue. Are you cleverer than I perceive, or is it merely that you toy with me out of spite? Will you fight or will you allow me to destroy you?"

He whispered back, "I'll let you be the judge."

Vlad sneered. "You deny me your name and now deny me witness to your full power. How rude. If I must, then I shall do my best to make you show me."

An instant later, they were face to face. Vlad pushed the limits of his mechanical body, and his speed was immense. The ravenous fiend slammed into Kale. Together they smashed into the foundation of the damaged tower. Once inside, their combined energy caused lightbulbs to explode in showers of sparks. Wiring inside walls sparked fires that spread wildly. In moments, fire and smoke stifled the air.

As strong as Kale was, his body needed air. In a flourish of black mist, he dodged another swinging blade, then another. He ducked low under the twin swords to claw at Vlad's leg. It knocked the monster off balance but not enough to stall him long. A heartbeat later, the fiend kicked Kale, sending him crashing upward and out of the burning building.

About to pursue him, the mechanical fiend sensed something strange. Glancing at the place where Kale clawed him, a faint mark shimmered. Surprised, the villain examined both arms where other claw strikes had landed. The same demon rune glinted in the blaze, and he began to laugh mercilessly. Vlad reveled in the dancing shadows of the burning structure before launching himself after the foolhardy rogue.

Waiting atop another tall building, Kale watched Vlad fly toward him. A cut on his side wept red-hot blood. He hardly felt the sting. The metal menace perched nearby to gloat.

Chuckling, Vlad indicated the growing collection of runes made by Kale's hand. "Is this what you're up to, rogue? Runes? Sealing runes? Is that all you can think to do to me? With all the strength you possess, you try to defeat me by binding me permanently to this body?" He laughed. "Thank you for making this my permanent form. I never had any intention of leaving it. Now I can never die! No one can kill the king of death!"

Kale frowned, bracing himself.

"Fight me! The king demands it!"

Kale made no attempt to dodge the next blow. Vlad's swords cut into him, unhindered by the black veil. Fresh blood flew with each slash. His enemy's movements were faster than ever. Cuts welled up crimson streams. Amid the bombardment, Vlad left a narrow opening. Kale took it and slashed with his claws at Vlad's core, leaving another mark.

As entertained as he was irate, Vlad grew tired of the lack of resistance. When the next seal shimmered on his body, he hissed, "Enough!"

One of the swords caught Kale's right wrist. He clenched his fangs tightly as his hand fell away. Blood spurted from the wound, spattering the rooftop. More swinging blades slashed his chest and midsection, cleaving pieces of flesh. Kale did not cry out or resist.

Vlad lost patience. "If you will not fight, then I will not waste my time on a false demon such as you."

Kale crumpled to one knee, straining to keep the blood from leaving his body. Dark fluids and energy swirled about him in a tempest of red and black.

The ancient evil spirit stowed one sword and gripped the werewolf by the throat. Staring into his eyes, Vlad tried to steal a glimpse of the power he knew was deep inside. Unable to see it, the anger turned to rage. Vlad used all his strength to throw the fleshy body skyward.

As Kale was cast hundreds of feet up into the air, Vlad flew up to end the fight before Kale's body fell to the ground. One well-placed sword to the heart would kill even this rogue. Ready to send the pitiful excuse for a demon back to the Void, Vlad raised his blade skyward as Kale fell back toward the monster. About to strike, Vlad muttered, "What a waste."

To Vlad's surprise, Kale whirled around and batted Vlad's dark blade aside with the Elfish sword. As he swung, the darkness in his body rapidly mended his flesh. In an instant, black and red swirled and congealed to restore his lost hand. Witnessing Kale's vast power stunned the greedy villain. In awe, Vlad stared as Kale pulled him close.

In a fraction of a second, Kale's shadowed claws struck the center of Vlad's chest. His claws scribbled a series of complicated runes into a single design. Just as the monster realized what was happening, Kale unlocked the set of powerful runes, causing them to shine brightly. The white glow blazed and stung Vlad as it engulfed his metal frame.

Frantic, Vlad screamed and back-handed Kale hard to break free. Kale easily blocked the swing but let Vlad fall. Unleashing a fraction of the power he had concealed for the duration of the fight, Kale emitted darkness in the form of two broad shadows on his back. They caught the wind and floated him downward like a feather. He watched Vlad as he descended. Sparks arced all over the mechanical body that had become a prison.

Kale landed gently on a roof surrounded by flashing lights and smoke. Vlad landed hard several yards away. The rogue dismissed the Elf sword with a flourish of shadow. It was no longer needed.

The robotic shell harboring the entity sparked and twitched. Vlad gazed in disbelief at the large rune. It bound his dark heart to Kale's, forcing Vlad to feel as he does without relent. Never had such a rune been written by dark hands. This was beyond Vlad's ability to foresee, and the shock of it left him speechless. He raised his fidgeting, twitching head to try to stare at Kale, who was now closing his eyes as if to sleep on his feet. A strange sensation fluctuated within Vlad, and it burned.

With a cry of pure vengeance, he lunged and shrieked, "How dare you!"

As the monster flew at Kale on sputtering wings, Kale murmured, "Can you guess what awoke me from darkness?"

Vlad roared and swung the sword for Kale's throat. The razor-sharp edge came inches from striking, but some force stayed his hand. No matter how hard he tried, Vlad could not harm Kale. The burning grew, and the failure to slay Kale made the phantasm bellow miserably.

Slowly raising his eyes to stare back, Kale looked somber. "It was mercy that woke me."

Unable to comprehend the feeling, Vlad felt it tear him apart from within. He shrieked as his body began to shudder more violently. Smoke issued from joints. Wires snapped, and the evil metal began to tarnish.

"I pity you." Kale had tears in his eyes as he spoke softly. "In your past life, you never understood. In this tainted afterlife, you can never understand."

Vlad's joints began to fail. Falling to one quivering knee, he screamed louder. Smoke issued from every inch of him.

"What you call weakness is what is killing you now. I have a heart that can feel. I know mercy, compassion, courage and hope. Then there is the one thing greater than them all."

The surging sensations Vlad could not comprehend nor tolerate began to warp the frame of his body. Shaking violently as if electrocuted, he continued to shriek at the burning.

Mustering up the warmth that filled his heart, Kale allowed a flood of bittersweet emotions to overflow.

"And it will always be greater than death."

Black smoke wafted off Vlad, and components exploded in all directions.

"Ah'nay."

Unable to harbor such emotions, Vlad's ghost within the shell was extinguished. As the entity perished, the core of the mechanical body ruptured and split wide open. The head cracked and rolled backward, hanging pathetically from the shoulders. Joints locked in place, bent from the stress of containing such an incompatible essence. The heat of the metal monster's demise charred the pavement.

Kale approached the fallen figure, which still held a sword in its skeletal hand. Prying it free, Kale planted one boot in the demolished frame and pulled. He took the blade for himself as the demonsteel contraption decomposed into inert debris.

In the streets, the instant Vlad was no more, the hearts within all the drone bodies burst simultaneously. The machines crumpled to the ground and plummeted from the sky.

The Holy Hounds took a moment to marvel. Oryn heard the small explosion atop the building above him. Looking up, he saw curtains of smoke from an unearthly flame engulfing the roof. The fire cast a vast silhouette across the rising plumes. There stood a figure with vast wings that appeared to be wearing a crown-like halo. They pulled a sword from an outstretched arm, kicking its holder to the ground.

Gusts of wind surged in from nowhere, catching Oryn off guard. Brilliant spotlights beamed down from helicopters. While the knight hound had been watching the figure, another helicopter hovered toward the rooftop, blowing the smoke and unveiling Kale, who was standing over what could only be a defeated Vlad.

Oryn was about to howl that the battle was won but snarled at many strikes of metal to his armor. A few bullets grazed his neck and ears, as sharpshooters in the aircraft opened fire. The warrior shielded his head with the sword, then roared out a call for retreat.

Kale heard Oryn's ominous roar as the helicopter nearest him hovered closer to the rooftop. Still shrouded in darkness, he eyed the gunman at the side door. They were about to open fire when his powers reached the pilot. Nightmare visions caused the human to panic. Kale made the pilot see a legion of demons coming to claim their souls. Wildly turning the aircraft, the human franticly directed the helicopter back the way it had come and far away from the city. The crew barely hung on amid their companion's breakdown.

Jack and Alexander were first to reach Adwen, who was beset by three more military aircraft with heavy firepower. While they shot at her, the fire from her heart surged. Bullets melted in midflight. Some evaporated, but most struck like raindrops before dripping to the fractured pavement. The heat was intense. For the warriors, it was no different than stepping into a sauna. Her holy energy sheltered them from the downpour of fiery hail.

Oryn joined them through an alley to dodge more gunfire. Finding refuge in Adwen's pale blue fire, they waited for Kale. More helicopters circled, preparing to open fire. Many muzzles of guns flashed in the night behind blinding spotlights. Gusts from the helicopter rotors fanned the edges of her blue fire.

A blood-chilling roar pierced the ruckus of the helicopters. A few gunmen paused to look as black wings glided closer against the wind. Red and white eyes burned at them. It looked like a stealth aircraft, but the soldiers knew better. The closer it came, the more dread they felt. A few of them radioed the sighting, but not soon enough.

To all the pilots, their worst nightmares became real. Fears from childhood appeared in the sky on every side. Rows of teeth, venomous wriggling things and ominous shadows played in their vision, sending them into horrified fits. At once, the flight patterns broke. Like a flock of spooked pigeons, the squadron retreated. As the humans and their airborne assault departed, the broad wings folded and vanished.

Adwen dismissed her blaze in time for Kale to land nimbly beside them. His darkness faded away, and he strode closer.

His sonorous voice announced, "It's done."

She nodded and growled, "Then it is time for us to go."

Swinging the fiery blade, the white Holy Hound opened a portal. The armored creatures walked through, and the dark being followed close behind. The portal closed in a flourish of pale blue fire in the middle of the devastated street.

Chapter 28
BEYOND THE BLACK DOOR

"I've always wondered why I'm not like other demons," Kale admitted. "What makes me different? The unicorns got me thinking of other questions: Is it that demons cannot or should not feel what I can feel?"

Jack shrugged. "And?"

"The answer is yes."

Adwen and her warriors were intrigued, as they sat in the overlook.

"The things they cannot feel are incompatible with what they are," Kale elaborated. "Virtues are light. By binding Vlad to me and forcing these things into him, I introduced light. He could not comprehend it – like a computer program given a paradox. The light eclipsed Vlad. It made him disappear."

Impressed, Jack chuckled and gave a slow clap. "You're a mad genius, Big Guy. That had to hurt – from what you described."

Kale remained stoic. "It did. Light is like fire. It burned him alive."

Adwen smiled softly. "You purged him."

Looking up, the realization sank in. He, a demon, had purged another with his own light.

"What does that mean? Darkness cannot harbor light."

"All living things are made of both," Adwen explained. "To create demons, light is ripped from them, and they can no longer hold it. You remain whole. This makes you not truly dark and allows you to hold light."

Kale knew she was correct, but questions persisted in his mind.

Jack spoke with much less enthusiasm: "At any rate, the demon lords didn't count on us slaying Vlad. I'll bet my right hand they are livid."

Kale murmured, "Understatement of the ages."

"Where do we go from here?" Alexander asked. "They are never going to give up."

Oryn added grimly, "They will aim for Adwen's destruction." The warriors frowned.

A fierce glint appeared in Kale's eyes. "They'll have to try bloody hard."

Adwen remained calm. "In the meantime, it's almost dawn."

Jack and Alexander gave solemn nods. Oryn growled softly. When she turned to Kale, he heaved a sad sigh. Then he nodded as well.

The company of five filed out of the dark chamber after Adwen. In the open overlook, Jack used his telekinetic abilities to float Tamis's remains to the center of the ledge. The body drifted across the rocks and settled before them. They watched the night slowly fade.

Dawn quietly shed bright rays over the cliffs and spilled onto the plains. As the first golden rays touched the verdant hills, Adwen summoned a small blossom of blue fire. Setting it gently on the fallen warrior's chest, she stepped back to let it spread. The ghostly dancing tongues covered the body, consuming everything. Wind from the falls carried ashes and embers out, scattering them far and wide. In the hushed ceremony, every face was thoughtful.

Jack had enjoyed the young warrior's company. Tamis's wit showed itself in the most unexpected times. Nothing ever went to his head.

Alexander wondered: If things had been different, he would have been proud to have a son like this young man. That would never happen now, but it was an honor to have known him.

Oryn found Tamis's naïve nature troublesome on occasion, but he never thought less of him for it.

Adwen remembered first meeting Tamis. He was kind and sincere. When she and Toth were lost out in the cold, he let them inside for the night. It was long ago, but it seemed like yesterday. Faint tears dampened her lashes.

All the while, Kale thought back to when Tamis looked at

him before he had altered the runes on the dark ring. It was that instant when Tamis suddenly extended trust. The brave, pure heart being gone from this world surely would make it a lesser place. Kale shed no tears; not this time. It was as if they were dried up.

As the last of Tamis turned black and gray to be whisked away by turbulent gusts, Adwen abruptly stopped crying. An eerie sensation crawled down her spine. Just when the others noticed her unease, she took a step forward staring out into the plains.

Oryn instantly grew tense. "What is it?"

Kale sensed it, as well. Sorrow gave way to terror.

Determined, she replied, "I'm not sure. Let's move. Come on."

While she and the three leaped over the ledge, Kale hesitated. He forced himself to follow and make sure they would be safe.

They ran many leagues to the west, passing countless saplings that grew in the fields where the unicorns had lain. Magic wafted about the leaves of the tiny sprigs. Just beyond the young mystic woodland, the travelers came to the top of a hill and stopped. A chill washed over them at the sight of the anomaly in the valley basin. Kale joined them and cringed.

A black oval mass of darkness hovered. Where it hung close to the earth, nothing grew. Light bent as the menacing shape consumed all color, turning the surrounding a dismal gray. No scent or sound emanated from the mysterious vortex.

Kale took a few frightened steps backward. His skin turned clammy, and beads of sweat formed on his brow.

"What is that?" Alexander pondered.

Jack grimaced. "Don't know, Big Dog. Looks like a portal."

A golden light flashed in Adwen's eyes, and she understood. She became resolute. "I know what it is."

Kale flinched, sensing her will. It felt as if he had swallowed live snakes.

Gazing long at the nothingness, Adwen explained: "It's the Black Door, the one from the Dragon Mother's message. It's open now."

The knight sneered in disgust.

Jack did not like the look in her eyes. "And what are we supposed to do with it? We aren't going in there, are we?"

Adwen turned to look at Kale. She was gentle yet firm: "You have to go; it's the only way."

On the verge of either vomiting or running away, he shivered.

The two friends were concerned. "Big Guy, are you alright?"

Weakly, he gasped, "No."

The knight glared. Adwen's expression hardened.

Desperate, Kale pleaded, "No."

The refusal and surrender to fear angered Oryn to the point of growling.

Jack would not tolerate the knight's behavior and snapped, "Cut it out, Cujo! Adwen, what is going on?"

Frowning, Adwen shook her head. "I'm sorry, Kale. I can't keep hiding all your secrets."

He became far more terrified of what she might utter next. Eyes wide, he could do nothing to stop her.

"The missing piece of the Soul Focus needs to be found. Without it, we cannot win. A long time ago, the Dwarves were manipulated into stealing it and tampering with it to make a crown. They lost the piece that broke off. Since then, the piece was hidden by our enemies. To make sure no one could learn its location, the knowledge was sealed away. Only the Dark Heart knows where to find it. There is one way left for us to go: We need to break into the Vault of Forbidden Knowledge."

Jack shrugged. "Then if Kale is too afraid to go, how about we go find it ourselves?"

"It's pointless to go without him," Adwen warned. "We can go in, but we would never be able to open a way out. My portals only work within the living worlds. Spirit-world portals are very different. Even if we found the vault, we couldn't open it. If we did somehow open the vault, none of us can take the knowledge." Giving Kale a stern glance, she added, "Only Kale can do those things."

Unable to look at their faces, Kale whimpered, "Please, Adwen. Please stop."

Alexander was astonished. "He's gotten that powerful?"

Knowing what she was going to divulge made Kale cover his ears in distress, cringing.

"It's nothing to do with how powerful he's become. It's because he's become a Demon Lord."

Kale felt the instant fear that took root in Jack and Alexander as they stared. Fear and loneliness squeezed Kale's heart tight like talons, making him moan. The pained wail echoed over the hills for miles.

Oryn was the least surprised. He had guessed as much. Having had enough of the rogue's cowardice, the knight snarled and lunged, summoning his sword. "Enough of this."

Jack yelped. "Oryn, don't!"

At hearing the warrior's cry of warning, the mind-numbing feelings vanished, and Kale swiftly turned around.

The knight sneered, swinging the long blade for the were-wolf's vulnerable neck. But to Oryn's surprise, the rogue made no move to defend himself or retaliate. He only stared. At the last instant, Oryn stayed his sword from cleaving Kale's head off. His intent was not to slay Kale but to snap him out of this melancholy stupor. It worked, although not as predicted.

While the edge of the shining blade held steady by his neck, Kale stood paralyzed. His stare was wide. The last of the color completely drained from his face as if he'd seen a ghost. He looked vulnerable, frightened and betrayed.

Oryn stared more suspiciously. Something in that expression was odd. For many drawn-out seconds, they locked eyes, frozen in the tense moment. No matter how long the knight studied that pitiful look, he could not understand why it was strange.

It was difficult for Kale to snap out of the fear that gripped him. He mustered what will he possessed to regain control. Frustration formed tears in his now angry glare. Brushing the sword tip away, he turned his back, unable to look at any of them any longer.

Adwen spoke again, continuing to explain: "Only a Demon Lord can enter the vault, absorb the knowledge and then open a pathway out of that world. Kale, you're always asking why, but you're so afraid to find the answers. This is why – all of this around you. If it weren't for who and what you are, we never would have made it this far."

Defeated, Kale whispered dejectedly, "Why me? What did I do wrong?"

Her confident voice soothed, "It was never about deserving anything, Kale. You are this way, because it was the only way."

"But why me? Why not somebody else?"

"You are the only one capable."

A shaking sigh dragged from his lungs. "It's not fair."

"I know. That's why I won't make you go alone."

The warriors flinched then turned to stare.

Kale gasped and turned around. "You can't. No. None of you can go there."

The somber glimmer in her eyes showed she would not be swayed.

"I know your heart," she consoled. "You can't go alone. Either I join you in that place, or if I must, I will walk through and wait for you on the other side."

Seeing no way out of this made Kale groan.

Oryn scowled at the reluctant demon, then announced his feelings on the matter: "I won't allow you to enter on your own regardless of his choice. Where you lead, I follow."

At this, Kale choked and gasped. He couldn't breathe.

Jack shook his head, and Alexander rubbed at the back of his neck in thought. Both exchanged looks, shrugging.

"Looks like we're all going in with you, Big Guy," Jack told Kale.

Kale felt so sick he could hardly stand it. He squeezed his eyes shut, trembling. A moment later, he felt her hand touch his arm as she spoke.

"We're with you. You're not alone."

On the brink of tears, Kale's breaths became short and ragged. The spark of hope she gave him was a painful gift he could not refuse. Adwen sensed his heart conceding at last.

"Tell us what to do," she told him. "Once inside, how do we help?"

Shaking his head weakly, he answered, "Yah don't."

The others were confused. Stealing a sidelong glance at the portal, Kale struggled to swallow the lump in his throat.

"In that place, there is no light, no hope. You, Adwen, have no power there. Time is meaningless in the dark. We'll be gone as if we don't exist. When – if – we make it out, either a few minutes will have passed, or maybe a hundred years. By entering, you risk everything."

She was not afraid. "We risk everything by not trying."

Steadying himself, he nodded. "I know."

"What else?"

"You all saw what those monsters did to Tamis for torture. If any of us are caught, you can expect worse than that for eternity."

"How do we avoid being caught?" she asked.

"By being careful and really bloody lucky."

She smiled. "I trust you."

Taken aback, he stared.

"Tell us how to improve our luck."

Completely given into his fate, Kale replied, "You lot will need to stay close to me and do exactly as I say. One wrong move, and it's over."

Adwen nodded. "Got it."

Her lack of fear left him stunned. "You're bloody crazy."

"So I've been told."

"Just so you lot know, I will have limited authority there. I'm not really one of them. No clubhouse perks, you could say. I can't manipulate the maze."

Jack became straight faced. "Come again? What maze?"

"You ever see the Escher's drawing of the Endless Stair? It's like that – all of it."

For a second the warrior contemplated backing out of this venture. "Okay."

Kale whispered weakly, "We'd better go before I change my mind."

The companions faced the valley basin and the Black Door. Their feet marched slowly toward the source of all fears. Kale reached out his presence to shroud himself and his friends. The potent spirit vapor made it difficult to breathe. As they drew near, the world around them turned to night.

Their guide tucked emotions away to avoid drawing attention from the denizens within. Detecting the discomfort Kale's presence caused, he advised, "Now's the time to turn back if you need to. Once inside, you'll all need to stay in my shadow, or else they'll smell you and track us down. Last chance."

Alexander wore a stony look. "Lead the way."

That none of them turned back weighed heavily on Kale. His echoing voice answered with a dismal tone, "As you wish."

The world around them turned dark. A high-pitched ringing

filled their ears as if they had all gone deaf. Their breath came out as fog in the sudden surge of cold. No sight or sounds could be heard. The darkness was complete.

After a moment in the emptiness, something glowed in the distance. The pale glow drew closer and grew steadily. It moved more swiftly the nearer it came until it rushed at them at an alarming speed. Colors surrounded them and formed the shape of an ominous hallway like that of a villainous cathedral. Green wisps of lost souls were held in cages like giant lanterns. Wicked spikes jutted inward at the wisps to draw light and faint cries of pain.

Now that they had arrived, Kale stood still gazing vacantly down the hall. He wished never to return to this place. Now he was here, and the nightmare was real. It left him dazed.

Adwen's hand cupped his shoulder. Glancing at her, all he could see was the outline of her form and the brilliant shine of her blue eyes. Those of the others glowed brilliantly as well.

The sight reminded him: "One more thing: If I tell you to close your eyes, do so immediately. Don't open them until I say."

Oryn scowled. "Why?"

"There's no true light here. I can disguise our bodies, but not the light in your eyes. If anything sees it, we'll be detected. Please, trust me."

The knight huffed but made no argument. Neither did anyone else.

"Alright then," Kale murmured, bracing himself for the mission. "Here goes."

He led them through cavernous halls of astounding height. They turned into several small corridors passing familiar facets. Walking along for an immeasurable distance, the Holy Hounds became disoriented. They tried to recall the turns they had taken but could not. It was a confounding mess in their minds.

Disliking the sense of being lost, Jack whispered nervously, "Didn't we come this way already?"

Kale was calm. "You can't trust your eyes. None of this is here. It's like a nightmare. Only difference is that it's real."

"That makes no sense," Jack groaned.

"I know. Imagine if you could will the world into the form you wished it to take. This is the demon lords' vision made manifest. We are in their world, a lot like when you visited my mind. Problem is that our living bodies are along for the trip. Lose them, and you'll never leave."

As nervous as before, the warrior shivered. "We'll be careful then."

Alexander liked this place less and less. "Roger that."

Kale hissed, "Quiet!" Taking a second to listen, he urged, "Close your eyes. Close them tight!"

Everyone obeyed without question. Gathered close together in Kale's dark essence, they listened as a demon drew near around an impossible corner. Swelling his energy wide, he rumbled dangerously at the very strong demon.

A fiend with many arms and eyes stalked closer, confused by the massive size of the stranger. The demon could not sense how strong Kale was. In fact, he could not sense him at all, aside from sight and smell. Growing out deadly claws, it strode over, gloating in vile harsh words of how it would feast on him and defile the remains. But as it came near, it froze at the sight of Kale's eyes. Stopping dead in its tracks, the evil creature turned feverishly apologetic. It bowed and begged for forgiveness it knew it would not receive. Kale snarled, and his friends listened as the demon gasped and yelped. The sound of fluids spilling across stone came just before his calm voice.

"You lot can look now."

The huge demon lay in pieces. It dripped down in places like filthy rain. As they passed the gore and left it behind, the knight was on guard.

"Will this not arouse suspicion?"

"No," Kale replied sadly. "This sort of thing happens all the time here."

Jack found that disturbing. "Really?"

Kale knew the question was rhetorical, but answered anyway: "The weakest stick to what is considered the bottom. The smarter ones learn to navigate the maze. This is the final tier – where the lords stay."

Adwen added, "And the vault."

"Yeah, among other things."

Entering the next cavernous corridor, they stepped into a passage twisted in a spiral. Adwen and her warriors stayed closer to Kale while their sense of balance, and perception of up or down, began to blur. Walking along the contorted floor became dizzying.

Stairs took them sideways. Random cries echoed from nowhere. No one could decide if they were screams of pain or ecstasy.

Upon reaching a more neutral plane, the blond warrior huffed. "I'm out of breath. I need to rest."

Glancing back, a grim look came over Kale. "Can't stop. There's no point."

Everyone stared in silence.

"The paths are constantly in motion. What's more, the longer you lot are here, the weaker you become. Time may be meaningless in the Void, but your strength is like sand in an hourglass. Let's not waste it."

Jack groaned. "Now you tell me."

Kale spat, "You wanted to come in here. Did I need to tell you all of the reasons why not to?"

The warrior was apologetic. "Guess not. Sorry, Big Guy."

Kale's mood simmered down. "It's alright. Just keep close and keep chit-chat to a minimum. There could be eavesdroppers."

Even Jack decided to remain tight-lipped. Without the luxury of conversation, the search became more disorienting for the Holy Hounds. The forces of darkness wore steadily on their minds and bodies. How long they continued was immeasurable. Long was short, narrow was wide, and gravity appeared to be null.

Adwen cringed as they came to another turn and wobbled. Oryn braced her, and Kale turned to see what the matter was and grew worried.

"What's wrong?" Oryn asked, keeping his voice low.

Jack and Alexander gathered in close just as she cupped a hand to her mouth and wretched. Shivering, she gasped and regained some control. The brightness of her eyes flickered.

"I don't feel so good. Is anyone else cold?"

The knight looked to Kale for answers.

He was visibly tense. "She's more susceptible than the rest of you. The little bit of darkness within you three gives some resistance, but Adwen has none; she is pure light."

Oryn sneered, "Can we not move faster?"

Kale glared. "I warned you. No, we cannot go faster. How often must I repeat myself? Time and distance are meaningless. Travel in the Void is based on sensing exits and entry ways. They are always changing. Help her as best you can. We must keep moving."

Adwen became ever more unsteady. Jack helped the knight support her along stairs that never seemed to end. They weaved upward and backward, intersecting others like a Jacob's ladder. She began to have cold sweats and shiver. They all sensed Adwen rapidly deteriorating. When a much darker corridor with towering columns manifested, the path vanished at their heels.

Kale froze. The Holy Hounds felt his energy quiver. He couldn't move. Adwen raised her head after stymieing another urge to vomit. Sweat beaded all over her skin, and she whispered, "What's wrong?"

"We have to pass through here."

Alexander grew uneasy. "And?"

"This is a place where we shouldn't be. The exit is past the altars."

They did not understand.

"The demon lords' throne room."

It was Jack's turn to gulp.

Kale whispered, struggling to control emotions, "Don't look at anything except the floors and walls. Keep your fear in check. We can't let them smell it. No one uninvited is supposed to come in here. Come along now."

The vastness of the dark space made them feel small. For a while, they took brisk strides with light feet. Strange noises began to catch the attention of the Holy Hounds. As he followed keen demon senses, Adwen buckled and gasped in pain. Oryn helped her to sit against a pillar as her legs gave out. She squirmed, covering her mouth so as not to scream or purge whatever wanted to come up from her stomach. Before the knight turned to demand Kale to do something, he saw him duck behind another pillar. The blanched expression he wore made it clear he sensed something terrible.

Alexander growled nervously, "What's that noise?"

As the knight tried to comfort Adwen with what little healing magic he could spare, Jack became disturbed. "That sounds like a lot of people moaning. Big Guy? We're close, aren't we?"

He uttered weakly, "Yeah."

"What are we hearing?"

Looking was not necessary. Kale could remember glimpses from before being released into the living worlds. "People. They're dancing."

Everyone looked at him – including Adwen, who felt temporarily relief thanks to Oryn.

Kale continued to describe what was happening nearby: "Thousands of people – men and women – dancing naked. They sold their souls for beauty in life. Now they belong to the Torture Master as entertainment for the Dark Heart. Their bodies slowly decay to spite them as they are forced to dance. Those poor souls will never be allowed to rest or to stop dancing while their beautiful forms rot."

Oryn sneered, "They asked for what they received."

Kale frowned. "They made a mistake. Even if they deserve some punishment, it doesn't make the sight any less awful. Adwen, can you move?"

She nodded as she felt a little better.

"Come on then. Keep your heads down. The next exit is ahead."

Their fleet scurrying was soundless. As they passed several more columns, Adwen's body lurched and buckled violently. She vomited copious amounts of silvery blood, tainted with green. The fluids splashed, spattering her feet and Oryn's boots.

Everyone flinched and froze, staring wide-eyed at her and the shimmering silver blood, which turned green on contact with the floor. Everything in the Void was poison to Adwen.

Kale smelled the intense fear from his friends as she became sick. Alarmed that they may have been detected, he used his energy to tug them along. Toting the group using his shadow was jarring and hard on Adwen. They were all grateful when they exited the grand sanctum and he no longer need to whisk them across the floor with his powers.

Kale approached Adwen and came to a decision: "That tears it. We're leaving. She can't take much more of this."

The warriors wished they could argue but could not.

Adwen mustered her strength and replied, "No, we're not. We can't leave yet. The vault must be close."

He frowned, shaking his head. "I've told you: This place doesn't work like that."

A terrible sensation came over Kale. Whirling around, a towering black silhouette stood over them in the surreal passage. White pinprick eyes stared down from a head crowned with spikes and tentacles. The mask-like face tilted curiously to one side.

Kahli'nah studied the odd demon with eyes like his own, perplexed that this stranger's power could not be sensed. The Reaper soundlessly summoned his brethren to see for themselves. Kale and his friends cringed when the rest of the demon lords appeared. The company was surrounded by towering figures with grotesque forms. Beings with many spikes, tentacles, barbs, arms, and mouths with wicked fangs gathered to stare.

Huddled in Kale's merciful shadow, the company stood still. While the Holy Hounds held their heads low, only Kale was visible to the demon lords.

A shadow far darker than the rest rose from the floor. Taller than the others, the overlord gazed down at the cloud of dark essence where red and white eyes stared out. Kale had carefully tucked away his fear, but there was no point. The overlord was no fool.

Umbradonus casually raised an elegant hand. With a flick of his wrist, the malevolent entity cast the disguise away, revealing the werewolf and the pack of huddled Holy Hounds.

The lords hissed in unison. Degah'lee froze in shock.

At first, the overlord was silent. Though he saw that Adwen and her kind had stepped foolishly into their domain, his attention never wavered from the werewolf with white in his eyes. An instant later, the Dark Heart saw the rogue beyond the flesh and knew his name.

Eyes widening in astonishment, the greatest shadow sneered, "Cygnus!"

Kale flinched.

Umbradonus turned to the demon lord with whips and bellowed, "Degah'lee!"

Shrieking in alarm, the Taskmaster cracked the lashes as his master flew into a violent rage. The Holy Hounds braced themselves, while the titanic fiend took on many shapes and none. When Umbradonus pounced at Degah'lee and was joined by three of the lords, chaos erupted. The world trembled and began to contort as its masters went wild.

While the other shadow kings assailed the fool among them, the Reaper, Kahli'nah, laughed with glee. He leaped at Kale and his friends summoning sickles with many mismatched hands. Kale reacted without thinking. His presence swelled about him, and he threw a solid wall of darkness at the enormous fiend. It struck hard, sending the Reaper flying backward, roaring in pain and surprise.

Kale hollered to his companions, "Run!"

To escape the battle and the enraged Kahli'nah, the company fled through an odd gap that appeared in the walls. The knight carried Adwen just behind Kale, with Jack and Alexander at their heels. They raced down through stairways and holes their presence created. The powerful rogue took them along paths he was certain would elude the monsters.

Rooms and halls twisted, bent and warped in awful shapes, while the gargantuan battle continued somewhere in the Void. The floor, walls and ceiling caved in at random, giving way to gaping black holes to unknown reaches. While stairs started to crumble and explode, Kale sensed the Reaper charging from behind.

Jack and Alexander yelped, sensing the danger. They leaped up a crumbling floor that turned into a wall. They were forced to climb. Oryn reached the top with Adwen, and Alexander was just behind when the Reaper arrived. Kahli'nah's giant hand pinned Jack to the wall, and the fiend laughed at Jack's horror.

The warrior summoned his daggers. Stabbing one into the wall for a hold, he sliced the hand with the other. It carved away dark flesh but only annoyed the demon lord. The darkness of the Void healed Kahli'nah faster than Jack could cut. As the shadow raised a sickle high, Kale slid down with claws raking stones and sending sparks. Stopping at Jack's side, he unleashed a mighty blast, striking the Reaper in the face.

Stunned, the fiend lost hold of his prey and fell through a massive hole. Kale grabbed hold of Jack's armor and lobbed him up to the ledge with the others. He leaped to join them, helping the startled warrior to his feet. Echoing roars shook the world as the unseen brawl carried on. Broad passages started to collapse and explode. Stones flew across their path, forcing them to jump, duck and weave.

In the knight's arms, Adwen barely clung to consciousness. Green and silver wept from her ears, eyes, nose and mouth, choking her. She could hardly breathe and the Void's obstacles enraged Oryn. When they sensed the Reaper returning, he barked, "Jack!"

The warrior kept running, but looked to the knight and read his mind. Seeing recognition in Jack's face, Oryn tossed Adwen. Using his telekinetic powers, Jack directed her fall into his arms. Holding Adwen tightly, he let the knight carve their path of escape.

Leaping around with all his strength and speed, Oryn mustered magic to cover his armored hands. Taking vicious swipes, he swept the way clear of debris, allowing them a straight path.

Kale held the lead, desperately searching for a way out. Finally, on a distant wall, his sight caught a rare glimmer like a star. He realized it was in fact a seam leaking true light from the living worlds. Desperate to escape this mad world, he roared and commanded the pinpoint of light to become a threshold.

It obeyed. A portal as large as a doorway opened wide, shining bright white and gold. The forces of the Void pressed in on the edges, fighting to close it. Kale's willpower sustained the portal. He was almost there with Alexander hot on his heels.

As Oryn worked hard shielding Jack and Adwen, Kahli'nah barreled down the exploding hall. The greedy fiend was thrilled by the hunt and just as furious at being foiled by a rogue. Nevertheless, the deadly demon crashed through debris as if it were snowflakes.

The warriors drew close to the exit with the monster just behind them. Then the entire side of the fragmenting hall collapsed. Degah'lee, assailed by Umbradonus, crashed through from another part of the chaotic realm. Their enormous bodies came down on top of Kahli'nah, dragging the Reaper down into another plane. A hurricane of large debris blasted outward.

Before anyone knew what was happening, a piece of rubble struck Oryn.

Adwen's heart shuddered, and she looked up from Jack's shoulder. As she did, she screamed at the top of her lungs, "Oryn!"

Kale heard and spun around. He saw Oryn unconscious, falling toward a black hole. In the blink of an eye, Kale bolted from the exit. As he passed the others, he used his powers to cast them through the air toward the bright light. Just before they escaped, Kale dove down after Oryn into the dark nothingness.

Adwen, Jack and Alexander passed through the portal. With a dull thud, they landed and rolled over green grass. Immediately looking up, they saw the black portal vanish. Adwen sat upright with eyes wide, gazing at where the Black Door had been.

Jack quickly checked her for injuries. "Adwen, are you alright?"

The bright sunshine had not moved since the second they

entered. It was as if they had been inside for a moment. The light healed her rapidly, while she stared long at the now empty valley.

"Adwen?" Jack repeated.

On the brink of tears, she murmured, "I can't sense them."

Chapter 29
EXCEEDS ALL THE WORLD'S LOVE

What sounded like rippling water echoed in Oryn's ears. He began to stir, catching his own scent, as well as the thick odor of werewolf. It was pungent, filling his nose on every draw of breath. It stank; it recalled the night as a child when he had slain his first werewolf and it had fallen onto him. The nightmarish memory attached to that scent awoke him.

The knight's waking mind was foggy, but as he opened his eyes he found the side of his face rested in a carpet of black fur and feathers. Sounds of a vast body breaching water snapped him out of the daze. Just as the dripping sounds stopped, Oryn realized he was lying on the forehead of the rogue's werewolf form.

Flying into a disgusted fit, he snarled and flung himself to the ground. Finding his feet, he bellowed, summoning his sword, and panted from the shock as he raised it at the giant beast. Kale said nothing. In a surge of mist, he transformed into his lesser form. He calmly watched as Oryn glared.

Regaining enough sense to find words, he snapped, "You are Cygnus."

Kale gave no response beyond the subdued look.

The knight seethed. "Answer me! Are you or are you not the demon named Cygnus?"

"This is not the time or place for this."

Oryn shouted, red in the face, "I don't care!"

Finally, the rogue frowned. "Fine." With a sorrowful voice, he answered, "I am."

The knight's eyes flashed, as he clenched his jaw. "You lied. You lied to us and to Adwen."

"No."

The denial surprised Oryn.

"I only lied to myself. She's known all along."

The knight's green glowing eyes widened. Suddenly feeling weak, the knight lowered his weapon. Adwen had kept this from him – from all of them. Feeling frustrated and betrayed, the knight glowered. "Why did she not trust us with this?"

He shook his head sadder than ever. "It's not that. She did it for me. Adwen wanted to let me pretend for a little longer, just for a while."

"Pretend? Pretend to be Kale?"

Glancing sidelong at the false water, he replied, "When I was dipped into the Heart of the Void and made into a demon, the darkness named me Cygnus. It is what I am. When I awoke as a rogue, I named myself Kale. It was my first act of defiance to the dark that had done this to me."

Oryn wanted to take pity on the creature but resisted out of anger. Becoming fearful, he demanded, "Where is Adwen? Where are the others?"

Kale reassured him, "They made it out. They're safe."

The knight gasped with relief, silently thanking the Light Spirits. With a little less anger clouding his thoughts, Oryn asked, "Where are we?"

Indicating the substance that moved like water, he frowned. "Do you see that?"

Oryn could and did not like the look of it.

"That is the Black Lake."

Oryn froze.

"We're in the Heart of the Void."

Despair threatened to take root. The knight nearly dropped his sword.

"We need to get moving," Kale warned.

Oryn brought his sword high, pointing at Kale's heart. The werewolf gave the same solemn stare in return for the threatening gesture.

The knight seethed with renewed anger. "You have to die. The end is near when the demon called Cygnus dies and is no more. That was what the Dragon Mother foretold."

"I know ... and I want to die."

Though the declaration was not new, it remained astounding to Oryn.

"There are few things I want more," Kale continued. "Right now, there are more important things to worry about. I must get you out of here. That's not going to happen if we stay in one place too long."

Kale's loyalty left Oryn speechless.

"Your strength in the Void won't last," he warned the knight. "Do you still want to try to slay me here and now, or are you going to let me do my job?"

There was no choice. Oryn dismissed the weapon and dropped his arm limply at his side. Mustering some determination, he asked, "Am I going to die here?"

A long pause followed. "I don't know. You're the strongest of her lot. There's a chance you could last."

Oryn was not reassured. Grimly, the knight stated his desire, "I want to leave this place."

"As you wish."

False light shone from countless green soul orbs. While they walked through the emptiness, the ground they tread upon was invisible. A nebula of damned souls hung suspended above and below. The endless space and vast number of lost souls made Oryn feel a mixture of awe and pity.

"There are so many of them."

Kale tried not to pay attention to the wisps flickering in the blackness. "I know. This is the place where the damned come. Some are gathered for decoration in the highest levels."

Aware that Oryn had stopped following, Kale looked back. Having been struck with a realization, Oryn began to search the endless numbers of identical looking souls. He was overwhelmed but refused to ponder the infinitely slim odds of finding a specific individual.

"Can they speak?" he asked, struggling to decide where to begin.

What the knight was doing began to irritate Kale. "They are all deaf, dumb and blind. Do not touch them."

In defiance, Oryn reached for one. Gauntlet fingertips were

inches away when dark energy burned him. A loud crack like lightning snapped, making the knight yelp and reel backward. His hand felt tender within the armor.

Kale glowered. "What do you think you're doing?"

Checking for injuries, the knight flexed his fingers. The painful surprise left him angry. "You know exactly what I'm doing."

Kale dismissively lied, "No, I'm afraid I don't."

Oryn stomped off to examine other souls by the sound of the faint whispers inside. After checking a few, he saw no discernible differences. "Stop playing coy and help me find him. Where is he?"

A cold glare came over the now angry rogue. "Gone."

"What do you mean gone?"

"He's not here. You'll never find him."

"How do you know that?" Oryn continued a fevered search.

"They have a special place to torment rogues."

The knight froze. He felt his heart skip a few beats. Color drained from his face as he hoped he had misheard Kale.

"What did you say?"

"You heard me."

Oryn's breaths became heavy and rapid. In a fit of rage and anguish, he bellowed, "No! You lie!" Oryn summoned his sword. "Where's Kai? Where is my brother?"

The show of force disappointed the rogue deeply. "Even if I could, I wouldn't. I told you: He's gone."

"Why won't you tell me?"

"Only the Dark Heart knows where captured rogues are kept." Seeing the hopes dashed and the knight's shoulders slacken, he added bitterly, "And for once, I'm glad."

The response left Oryn confounded.

"If you did find him, would you recognize him? What would you say? What would you do? Probably cut his head off all over again."

Oryn flinched and gasped, gripping his sword far tighter.

The rogue scoffed. "I see: You'd consider it. Lovely. Can't say I'm shocked. All the better you'll never see him. If he saw you raise a sword to him again ... it would break his heart."

All anger vanished from Oryn. The image of the boy's frightened and betrayed expression flashed before his eyes. If faced with his twin brother now, would he attempt to put him down even out of mercy? He was uncertain. With that thought, Oryn hung his head in defeat. Kale was right: It was agonizing, but he chose never to look for his brother again and spare them both the pain.

Still angry, Kale spat, "Put that away before something sees it."

Though dazed, Oryn heeded the warning. He bid the weapon to vanish. His heart still pounded. The idea of hurting his twin again was a crushing blow.

Kale calmed a little. "He was my friend, my only friend. I couldn't save him, but I can do your brother one last favor by saving you." Huffing indignantly, the guide beckoned, "Come along then. The first level is just ahead. Keep your wits sharp."

They walked through a dark portal to a different plane of the Void. The lost souls vanished, leaving empty darkness. Oryn could only see within a few yards. If Kale went too far ahead, the knight would lose sight of him completely.

Walking slowly, the rogue studied the surroundings. Only his eyes could see the hints to navigate this lesser maze.

"This is one of the planes of torment. From here, there are ways to reach any other level. Stay close."

The lack of response did not bode well. Looking back, Kale saw a swirling portal where he was certain Oryn had been. The knight was gone.

He grumbled aloud, "Aw, bugger it all."

Oryn tried to keep up with Kale, but no matter how fast he walked, then ran, the rogue pulled farther away.

"Stop! Stop, blast you!"

It was no use. He was alone in the deep darkness. Irate and afraid, the warrior roared at the top of his lungs. There was no echo as the vast space devoured the cry.

Oryn quietly glowered. He started to wonder if this was a betrayal when a sound reached his ears. Metal plates chinked, and the sweaty scent of human wafted in. Faint noises came from everywhere at once. A sudden whoosh alerted Oryn and he reacted fast enough to avoid having his head cleaved off by a sword.

Snarling, he dodged and dodged again. A man in werewolf slayer armor assailed him. False light rippled across the detailed visor, crafted into the shape of a snarling canine's face.

Aggravated, Oryn snarled and shouted, "Stay your hand, fool! I am your ally!"

The sword swings became swifter, displaying a keenly focused bloodlust. Oryn grew certain this knight would not heed him. To knock some sense into the foolish human, he backhanded the attacker, sending him to the ground.

The armor clanged heavily, but the attacker did not drop the sword. When he began to get up, the helm came loose and tumbled off. The human knight seethed through gritted teeth. Raising his weapon, he turned to sneer.

Astonishment gripped Oryn. The knight stood a little over six feet in height and had short brown hair with bangs. His features were long and lean, and his skin was pale. The attacker's eyes were a clear, deep emerald green. When the shadow of Oryn's own past spoke, he stared in disbelief.

"Answer for yourself," the shadow Oryn snapped.

Taken aback, Oryn remained tongue-tied.

"Why did you betray the Order and forsake your honor?" his former self demanded.

He was afraid but snapped back, "I have my honor. I serve the Heir of Darien. Put down your sword."

The former Oryn stalked steadily closer. "The Order fell because of you."

Aghast, he spat, "What?!"

"Had you not been polluted by that dog, you'd still be a real man."

Snarling, Oryn ranted back at his old self, "She is no animal, you blind fool! She is the heir!"

Seeing that his old self would attack again, Oryn pounced, pinning the human Oryn to the ground. His past-self raged and struggled to get free.

Enraged, Oryn shouted in the face of his former self in a desperate bid to make him see reason: "It is you who is without honor! Your hatred will destroy all you hold dear! Let go of your sword and see the truth of what you are! You are the real monster! I am no longer you!"

The former Oryn stopped fighting. His face wore the deadliest of icy glares. He sneered, "I am you."

A chill swept through Oryn.

"You are me. You will always be me, foolish dog. By pairing yourself to an animal, you spit on the bloodline of your forefathers. In allowing your body to leave humanity, all honor is forfeit. I am the only true Sir Oryn Reynard Conrad, and the proof is that you cannot deny it."

Oryn found he could not rebuke the shadow. The human Oryn raised their father's sword again to attack, and this time, the Holy Hound could not find the will to move out of the way.

Dark claws covered his face from behind, and another arm wrapped around his middle. Oryn barked and roared in surprise. He struggled with all his might to break free of whomever had grabbed him.

Kale held Oryn fast, covering his eyes, just in time. Doing so froze the lethal apparition. The shadowy counterfeit stood locked in mid-swing of his sword. With the knight's eyes covered, the doppelganger faded away. Kale glared at the vanishing figure as the real version frantically struggled to get loose. Oryn snarled and raged with fear and pain. No matter what he did, the claws would not let him go. Then he heard Kale's voice and recognized the werewolf scent.

"Keep your eyes closed," Kale instructed. "It's only a shadow. They have as much power as you give them. If you let it, it can kill you."

The knight shivered, as understanding set in. He was rattled.

"It's gone. I'm going to let you go now."

The instant Kale released him, Oryn snarled and jumped back growling. The rogue studied the knight's eyes deeply. After glimpsing what had tormented the warrior, his own bitterness diminished. Clearly, Oryn despised many things, but nothing so much as himself.

Shaken, the knight demanded, "What was that?"

Kale gently answered, "A manifestation. It was a shadow to plague you with your deepest pains and fears. There will be more."

He was alarmed. "Can you stop them?"

"I don't know."

The answer left Oryn feeling helpless.

Kale warned, "Should this happen again, close your eyes."

"What?"

"Close your eyes and cover your ears if you can. It takes away their power."

Oryn doubted this advice. "How will I know the difference between an illusion and an enemy?"

Kale frowned. "I'll be with you to help determine that. If you lose me, that may be an indication you've fallen into another illusion."

Oryn hung his head; his eyes were wide in horror. He stood on dry grass and dead leaves. Blinking in astonishment, he looked around at a dreary forest. He sensed this was southeast Dargadia. It was nearly sunset in the woodlands. Evening songbirds trilled in the boughs.

He growled deeply at this new manifestation. Then there was a voice; it was Adwen.

Oryn bolted through the trees swift as the wind. Ahead he saw the pinnacle of a manor emerging. It confounded him until he found the edge of a clearing, where three travelers and a pair of horses stood. Recognizing the scene, Oryn could hardly breathe.

He heard his old self issue a command: "The manor must be searched. The princess is likely to be found within."

Frightened, Adwen refused. "No, she's not. The princess isn't here. I can tell."

"What do you base this assumption on?"

"My instincts! I know she isn't here."

"Your instincts? How can you be so sure?"

She fell quiet.

Oryn knew what was going to happen. He tried to run in to stop it, but unseen forces weighed him down, making every movement laborious.

"You're sending me inside of that by myself? I don't think so."

Oryn watched his past-self dismount and snap, "Why not?"

Struggle as he might, he gained no ground.

His old self sneered, "You wouldn't do this, even for the princess?"

"That's not fair! Why don't you go inside? Are you scared?"

The past Oryn's movements were smooth and quick. Adwen was caught completely off guard when he pulled the knife from his boot.

Oryn became frantic and verged on turning feral with desperation. He roared, trying to reach her in time. Adwen's eyes went wide, as the knife flew for her upper chest. The silver-steel blade slid through linen, pierced her skin and cut into red flesh. She screamed.

Crazed with grief and rage, Oryn howled before Kale's claws covered his face again. The anguish made him thrash and roar. Kale stared in shock at the scene, now frozen in time. This was a true memory. The fact left Kale speechless. Oryn really had done this to Adwen.

The knight stopped fighting. Instead, he clutched at the hand that held him, quivering like a leaf. He fought to restrain tears and wished death upon himself. Oryn wanted terrible, bloody, painful death to take him. It was all he deserved.

Sighing heavily at the dissolved illusion, Kale murmured, "It's gone." He let go, and Oryn stood shuddering and gazing out at nothing.

In a daze, the knight muttered weakly, "I couldn't stop it."

Kale frowned. Growling angrily, he took hold of the knight by the wrist. Oryn gasped and snarled. Startled, he stared at the rogue's piercing gaze. He could not understand what was happening and watched Kale search the emptiness.

Angry, Kale muttered, "Let's see them try to take you from my grip."

Oryn's mind was numb. Could the demon keep these tormenting traps from whisking him away again? Nothing was clear. Oryn resigned to whatever fate had in store.

Determined, Kale tugged him along. "Come on."

After several paces, a jarring pang struck Oryn, making him cringe. No illusions emerged. Nevertheless, it took a small toll on his body and spirit. Kale was moderately pleased.

"Thought so. This realm can go bugger off. We'll be onto the others soon. Bear through it."

More pangs struck at random. They stung like a swarm of wasps until Oryn's whole body ached. Each step became painful, as the feeling of planting a foot caused him to wince in anticipation of the merciless stings. If the darkness could not torture with visions, then it would use more physical means.

Kale's resolve held fast in search of an escape. Finding a rare alcove among the dimensions, he darted through the elusive portal. When they stopped at last, Oryn sensed no change in the surroundings. Weary from the bombardment, he waited for another horrible rush of pain. Once Kale knew they were safe, he let go of the knight.

The instant he did, Oryn panicked and latched onto Kale's wrist. His grip was like a vice. Eyes wide, Oryn wore a pleading expression. Kale pitied the knight clinging to him as if he were life itself.

Softly, Kale whispered, "We've left that plane of the Void. You can let go."

After hesitating, Oryn methodically released. With more calm, there was sanity and sense enough to ask questions.

"Where are we now?"

"An in-between, limbo. This is a small pocket among dimensions like the eye of a hurricane. There is true emptiness here. We're safe."

"How do we proceed?"

"Like a hurricane, everything here turns and moves. For now, there are no doorways to this empty hole. A door will open. I intend to wait for the best opportunity. With any luck, a door to the highest levels will appear."

"Can anything get in?"

Kale scoffed. "Not likely. Even if something did, they'd be really sorry right quick."

Convinced enough to relax, Oryn swayed and sat heavily on the nonexistent ground. He was exhausted. Eventually, he broke the silence.

"I deserve this place."

The statement distracted Kale from looking for doorways. His attention turned to Oryn, who appeared to be giving up.

"Don't even start. That's exactly what the darkness wants."

The knight hung his head. "You saw for yourself. You've seen who I am. It is true."

Kale growled and huffed indignantly. "Back there? All I saw was deception."

Oryn whined and growled as he finally looked up. "You've seen what I've done. It was no lie. I lived it, and I can never forget it. I deserve the Void."

Wanting to grab the knight by the neck, Kale restrained himself. When he spoke, it was with a fiery determination: "Few deserve the horrors of the Void. I've preyed upon and fed upon those monsters and tasted their sour, bitter flesh. You are nothing like them."

The knight stared.

"The Void is a pit for the dregs. Evil things with no mercy, no hope, no love are bound for this black well of false wishes. To believe for even a moment that you are meant for such a place, you've got to be bloody mad."

Oryn wanted to believe him. "I've done atrocities. I've condemned innocents."

Kale frowned. "I smell that. I've smelled it since our first encounter. The scent of your soul is such a complicated mess of light and dark that I've been unable to make sense of it up until now. But I know now what the primary scent of your nature is: redemption."

The rogue's words killed the fears instilled by the dark.

"You were right when you confronted the shadow imposter," Kale explained. "You are no longer the same. You've transformed. The Void belongs to those who do evil and refuse to change. You don't deserve this. Not by a long shot. So, will you stop being a bloody fool by buying into these packs of lies?"

Oryn saw that he had been quite the fool. He turned away and stared off vacantly.

Kale sighed out of relief and stress. Whatever door came, he refused to consider any of the tormenting dimensions. Several showed themselves, and he quietly let them pass. Torment, it seemed, wanted to take them on. Those doors were everywhere.

Finally, a very different door opened.

Oryn sensed Kale shift his weight. "What is it?"

The rogue demon lord became tense. "A door we have no choice but to take."

Oryn quickly picked himself up.

"It is one of the highest realms," Kale explained. "This is the dimension of war. The most powerful demons fight among themselves in a free-for-all. Only if they become powerful enough can they find the doors to the realm of the demon lords."

"They become demon lords?"

"They are allowed the privilege of stalking their domain. There are no illusions there. If we are lucky, we will come across a vacant space with a door straight to the top."

Oryn frowned. "Doubtful."

Kale agreed. "Indeed, it is doubtful. Go ahead and draw your sword. I hope you won't need it."

With a flash, the Rose Thorne appeared in the knight's hand. The holy metal repelled the darkness, creating a white-hot glow like Adwen's.

Kale took a moment to admire the shine. It was comforting. "Come along before we miss it."

They passed through and stopped on the other side of the invisible portal. While Oryn kept alert, Kale glared at the numerous blinking rips in the plane. Enemies could come from all sides. For the moment, there were none.

"This place won't stay empty long. Let's move."

They bolted. Distant roars from other realms echoed. Loud hissing with mingled guttural cries shook the air. Sounds of blood-letting carried on, while they flew from one dimension of war into another. When the roaring bellows grew louder, Kale stopped dead and extended an arm to keep the knight back. Many sets of red eyes shone from the shadows. Waves of brawling fiends of varied sizes and shapes emerged. They began to forget their battles and stare hungrily at the newcomers, especially Sir Oryn and his shining sword. They fixated on it like moths on a flame.

The knight tensed, ready to fight.

Kale sensed this. "Save what's left of your strength for the uppermost level. I'll exterminate these insects myself."

Darkness shrouded Kale from head to toe, as the red strip of cloth fluttered wildly from his arm. The demon-steel sword appeared in his right hand, and the ghostly Elf blade glowed in his left. The golden marks from Adwen's heart radiated to his chest, empowering the silvery sword. As Kale stalked the horde, broad smoky wings unfurled, shielding the knight. Vengefully, he rumbled and hissed to goad them to fight.

Some fiends recognized his eyes as those of a lord, but all desired to reach and destroy the light. Like lemmings before a cliff, the monsters rushed forward heedlessly.

The rogue demon lord flapped his wings and flew up to dive down like a falcon. He struck like a meteor, throwing some aside and crushing many others. The dark and light swords danced before eerie eyes and smoky wings that continuously flapped and furled. Like kite shields they blocked or bashed enemies away.

Oryn marveled. Foes that strayed to pursue him were pounced upon and stabbed before the winged warrior flew back into the fray. The knight kept his sword ready. To allow his dark guardian more room to fight, Oryn stepped farther from the fringe. A chill ran down the knight's spine. Spinning around, he saw a single towering figure stroll out from the gloom. Kale was preoccupied, so he deduced that this one must fall by his own hand. But as the wicked toothy skull face became clear, Oryn saw something that made him turn rigid. His heart pounded like mad.

Stalking out of the dark was the shadow of Sir Vigo Odette. The demon created from the lost soul of his teacher rumbled. On his back were many weapons. Handles and pommels stuck up in a broad fan behind his head, crowned with wispy pale hair and many upward raking spikes. Razor-sharp teeth glinted in the lipless grin, as the familiar fiend stared.

During battle, Kale was nearly finished culling the enemies. A few remained when he sensed something terrible. As he leaped high and hung in the air on gigantic wings, he saw the demon with an armory of weapons on its back. It was powerful but within Oryn's skill and strength to slay. Kale was not worried until he saw that the knight was motionless. Oryn's sword lowered before the enemy. The knight's face was full of fear.

Desperation made Kale roar, and he plummeted to the ground. His dark energy and swords shredded the rest of the challengers. Straight away, he flapped his wings and darted through the air, urgent to reach Oryn in time.

The towering demon summoned a spear and pitched it straight for the rigid knight.

Kale's black wings beat harder, and he thrust himself into Oryn. The impact knocked Oryn out of the spear's path. Kale raised both his swords, but the dark spear shattered both blades. He instantly moved his wings to try to catch the spear before it impaled his chest.

Oryn looked up in time to see the spear strike Kale and his furling wings. The two swords broke as the impact launched the rogue demon backward. The knight gasped as the darkness enshrouding Kale dissipated. His wings vanished. Kale lay on his side trembling, gazing at the spear piercing his heart. Using all his dark strength, he struggled to pull it free.

No longer dazed, Oryn sneered, raising his sword into a proper stance. The shade tilted his wicked head, intrigued by the knight. Drawing a long Claymore from his back, Dark Sir Vigo stepped forward to answer the challenge.

Oryn roared, transformed and snarled, bashing into the living nightmare with all his might. The monster fought back with all the skill of Sir Vigo, but Oryn had learned far more after traveling the worlds. With every strike, he saw flashes of the once-great man's face. It filled Oryn with sorrow but only fueled the desire to defeat this abomination that insulted the memory of his wise teacher.

Kale slowly drew the spear out, letting it fall with a dull clang. He poured his energy into preventing his blood from gushing out of the wound. His heart was his most vulnerable place – his greatest strength and greatest weakness. If it stopped, his body would die. Kale fought hard to stay alive but slipped farther and farther.

Roars resounded with clanging metal. Oryn relished battles, but this was unlike any other. More than anything, he wished for it to end. Knowing time was running short for Kale, the knight called forth all his might and speed.

The shade slammed the claymore down like a hammer but missed and struck the ground.

Oryn made a swift sweeping sidestep then slashed, making the revenant shadow bellow. An instant later, the Holy Hound struck from behind. He moved faster and faster until he was nearly a blur. Many steps and strikes took him in a tight circle around and around, drawing black blood with angry cries. Oryn's onslaught was like a cyclone that rivaled even Jack's talents.

Swinging the sword one more time, Oryn roared and ran to Kale's side. As he darted off and reverted to more human form, Sir Vigo's shadow fell to the ground and became still. A second later, he collapsed in a heaping pile of sliced demon flesh. Steam issued from the refuse as it liquefied.

Dismissing his weapon and standing over the rogue, Oryn stared. Black energy like smoke swirled in the wound to keep the blood contained. Droplets slipped past and spilled. The knight, watched to see if the rogue was powerful enough to save himself. When large spurts of blood splashed between them, he and Kale knew the answer to the unspoken question.

Feeling faint, Kale continued to resist. He feebly looked up at Oryn. The knight's green eyes were full of concern. It was a comfort – one that brought a weak smile to his now deathly pale complexion. He forced a laugh, feeling his life slipping away.

"It's just a scratch." Then he began to lose breath.

In denial of this outcome, Oryn leaped into action. He crouched low and pressed both hands to the wound. He sneered with the effort and focus it took. Healing magic surged from him into the werewolf's body until Oryn felt dizzy. Despite the drastic siphoning of his own strength, the knight would not take back the decision.

Kale swiftly became aware. Oryn's energy was plummeting like a stone. The werewolf yelped in dismay. All but the last of the warrior's strength was spent. Desperate to stop him, Kale swatted the knight back, shouting, "What do you think you're doing?"

As weak as a mortal human, the warrior stumbled but remained on his feet. He snapped as Kale picked himself. "I saved your life."

Kale was alarmed and angry. "At the likely cost of your own! How do you expect to last when you've made yourself so weak? You're bloody crazy!"

Oryn stepped forward. "If you die and I have no one to guide me, my fate is sealed."

The statement left Kale abashed. Looking as if the knight had said something very naïve, he scoffed and shrugged. "I'm a demon, mate. Where would I go?"

Now the knight understood: Kale was a demon lord. Though his body would have expired, his existence would have continued. The loyal shadow would have survived beyond death to guide him out of the Void.

Oryn was stalwart in his choice and frowned. "This argument is pointless."

Kale read his feelings by the stony expression. "Yeah, it is."

They gave each other hard looks until a twinkling in the dark caught Kale's attention. Oryn recognized the reaction. Still irate, the rogue demon lord sighed, working his jaw. He gave the knight a harsh sidelong glance.

"You might be lucky. A door just appeared. It goes all the way to the top."

The knight's stern expression stayed.

"Come on."

As they were about to press on, Kale collected the fragments of the old Elf sword. Leaving it lost to this place was unthinkable.

Then they stepped through the invisible tear and passed out of the plane of war.

Through the hidden portal, a gloomy cavernous hall opened. Stone walls with arched vaulted ceilings glowed green by the false light of damned souls. Everything was eerily calm. It seemed quiet among the lords had been restored. They cautiously surveyed the hall with firm glares.

Oryn did not trust the silence. "Are they not searching for us?"

"I doubt it. As far as the lords know, all our lot escaped. They also figure this world would kill any who didn't escape."

It made sense, but the knight decided to keep a watchful eye. Kale refrained from casting his shadow over Oryn. If stalking demons showed themselves, they would be killed before any alarm sounded. Their ears stayed pricked for threats on the way through the wicked temple maze.

Something about what Kale said nagged at the knight. As Oryn pondered the rogue's words, he followed closely. Recalling every detail of their wild flight, one thing was certain: Kale had been standing by the pale portal when he had fallen. Rounding another distorted corner, they found the way clear. So were the truth and the lie.

Glaring at the rogue demon lord, Oryn asked with a tone of suspicion, "You fell during the crumbling of the passage when I did?"

Kale ignored the question, busy navigating the shifting labyrinth. Oryn was more curious than angry.

"You lied when you claimed you fell with me into the Black Lake. Why?"

Kale growled in irritation as he focused on keeping alert. Already he had avoided several pesky scavengers without bothering to tell Oryn.

"What are you on about?" he asked the knight.

"I know you lied. Tell me why."

Huffing, Kale turned to the insistent warrior. "You want to get into semantics at a time like this?"

Oryn stood firm and wore a hard look. Kale returned it. After seeing something in the knight's eyes, he considered how to answer.

"Tell you what: If we both get out of here, we'll see how far you're willing to listen. That's the deal. Take it or leave it."

Carefully appraising the vague offer, it satisfied Oryn for now. "I'll hold you to your word."

Kale scoffed. "I'll be shocked if you hold your end of the bargain. Come on then. We've lingered too long."

Briefly scanning for threats, Kale led them into another cavernous corridor. Upon entering the zone, they saw an enormous arch set into the wall. As the door of locks and chains over heavy devices loomed, the two trespassers gawked. Many tons of demon-steel formed a seamless door as dark as the Black Lake. They stood under the arch in grim awe.

"Is this what we came for?" Oryn asked.

Staring long at the vault seal, Kale grew more cautious. "Yeah, it is." A hard decision had to be made. "If we go in, there's no telling how long it will take or what dangers are inside. You could die before we find the piece of hidden knowledge."

Oryn already had considered that possibility. "Not retrieving what we suffered to find would be a greater waste."

Kale grimaced.

The knight was firm: "As you often say in such instances: We have a job to do."

Sighing heavily, Kale agreed, "Alright then."

Darkness shrouded Kale once more. He raised a clawed hand high at the vast seal and bellowed, causing the chains to rattle and the locks to shiver. His energy seeped into the metal door. The steel links, locks and plates warped then rippled like water. Infinitely fine details softened, melting into a single undulating portal of pure shadow.

With the way opened, Kale asked, "Are you sure you want to go inside?"

Oryn was unafraid. "Lead on."

"Suit yourself."

Kale walked into the vertical pool of black water followed by the bold knight. The substance was identical to that of the Black Lake. It forced them to hold their breaths. Oryn's skin started to burn as if he were submerged in acid. Before it could do too much harm, the barrier ended, and they stood within the Vault of Forbidden Knowledge.

"You alright?"

The knight felt even weaker but would not admit the fact. "Stop concerning yourself with me and get to your task."

It was easier said than done. They stood by the arch among an infinite constellation of pale white wisps. Like a giant brain, flashes of energy flitted all around in a constant dance. Clouds of these flickers extended above, below and beyond their view, like the realm of lost souls.

Knowing to ignore appearances, Kale pondered deeply. They walked quietly among the pieces of stolen knowledge. When the door was some distance away, they stopped. Kale closed his eyes, raised his hand and reached out to the contents of the vault. His power touched the fabric of the senseless reality. At his bidding, the orbs of pale white flashed. In an instant, the wisps were gone. The vault began to transform. It became a gigantic library with infinite columns of bookshelves on either side. A cozy fire crackled in a vast hearth illuminating a lonely study desk. In the center of the oaken tabletop rested a condensed white crystal ball. It sparkled and shone.

When Kale opened his eyes, he was pleasantly surprised.

Oryn noticed. "How did you know to do this?"

Kale felt very clever. "The Void is like a dreamscape. The vault itself is neutral territory. I commanded it take the form that pleased me most. Not only that, but the one thing we want presented itself in the open." Pointing to the orb on the table, he added, "The only piece of knowledge not in the form of a book is what we are looking for."

The knight turned impatient. "What are you waiting for?"

Kale smiled. "Good question."

Facing the table and the warm fireside, it was time to collect their spoils. Their boots strode over warm chamber floors in Kale's welcoming bastion. As he approached the table and reached for the orb, he hesitated. He looked over both shoulders. Oryn sensed Kale's hesitation.

"What is it?"

After stretching his presence far and wide in search of other visitors, he found nothing for miles. "Just jumpy. This might take a moment."

Kale reached to grab the orb, and intense energy danced. The knowledge was locked securely. Realizing this, he pressed both hands to the orb. With much more effort, he latched onto the knowledge, surging his dark essence around it and urging the contents to merge with him. The seal resisted but began to crack.

Oryn watched, intrigued by how Kale's black essence arched around the orb in ribbons. They danced with the pale object in a ballet of black and white streams. The sight was intensely beautiful, and he wished Adwen could have been here to witness this. Just as the orb collapsed under Kale's iron will, an ice-cold surge washed over him.

It confused Oryn. The fire was so warm a moment ago. Then he found he could not move. Then he could not breathe, but he did not grow faint. The gigantic library blurred at the edges and stretched. He saw something fall before him. To his shock, he gazed at his own body lying face down on the floor.

A cold force tugged at him like a kite. It drew him backward farther away from his body, and from Kale and the dancing black and white energy.

The instant Kale absorbed the knowledge, he heard two things. First, he heard the gasp of someone who had just passed on. It made him sick to his stomach. Then he heard a body fall to the floor. By the time he heard the second noise, he whipped around in a flurry of swirling light and dark. The knight's body collapsed as the wisp of his soul was plucked by Degah'lee. The demon lord grinned, reaching to catch Sir Oryn's stolen soul. It drifted closer at his bidding.

Blinded by fear, rage and desperation, Kale roared and reached for the knight's soul.

The Taskmaster's grin grew ever wider. The mighty soul rested in the palm of his twisted clutches when the unthinkable happened. A much larger black talon snatched the soul from his grasp. Stunned, the demon lord shrieked as the dark essence within Kale formed the arm that took what he had just claimed for himself.

Billowing, congealing darkness surged from Kale's body. As he pulled the titanic talon back, his presence continuously grew and became a solid mass. Black wings became real. Vast feathers longer than wall tapestries stretched out, fading from black to silver and to white at the tips. They furled around, shielding the retracting arm in time to block Degah'lee's deadly whips.

Over and over the demon's cords cracked against monochromatic feathers, which continued to grow. The demon lord paid no heed to the fact that Kale's form was growing far larger than his own.

Blind with rage, the wrathful shadow summoned many more whips into the rest of his misshapen appendages. The lack of effect fed into the mad tantrum.

Oryn had just glimpsed the fiend as he landed in his clutches. He was barely aware that another force had whisked him away. Now in complete darkness, he was terrified and confused. Two giant eyes opened in the dark. A moment later, he calmed, recognizing them as Kale's. They looked very sad. With limited vision, the knight saw that Kale was not only colossal, but very different in appearance. After a moment, several spindly talons enclosed, cutting off his sight. From within the rogue demon lord's hand, sounds echoed beyond comprehension.

Certain the knight's soul was intact, Kale's heart ached. He enclosed the precious light safely in one hand and shuddered. Waves of sorrow wracked him at his failure to prevent this crime. Kale hissed past pointy teeth in humanoid jaws. With it he sent a wave of energy at Degah'lee, whose whips had yet to cause harm.

A dense wall of darkness flew at the Taskmaster. When it hit, every whip was ripped from his hands and tossed away. Stunned at being so easily disarmed, the monster froze. Not even Umbradonus could do this. Nevertheless, the fiend stood his ground, bent on getting back what should be his. When the pair of wings began to part, he sneered at the rogue.

Glaring from between gigantic wings, Kale hissed again.

A force pushed at the demon lord like howling wind. It rocked him, pressing in as if to blow him away. Shadowy robes and nightmarish gossamer fluttered in the fierce gale. When the surge ended, Degah'lee roared angrily.

Kale was unimpressed. Opening his wings wide, holding them high, he showed his true appearance and nature. The Taskmaster's expression tensed. The kneeling mighty being's form had the signs of both noble and fearsome animals from creation.

Though his body was like man, it was twisted by darkness. Skin rippled like iridescent dragon scales made of molten steel. Hands and feet were intricate talons with exaggerated angles and exposed tendons. His form was long with birdlike bone extensions tipped with blades that glinted in the gloom. Atop a long slender neck was a crown of black feathers under sweeping antlers. The horns arched over his brow and above his head, forming a thorny halo. A

single horn from his brow formed a shining blade, aimed at the evil demon lord of tasks.

The rogue demon lord scowled, clenching pointed dragon teeth. His kind human lips quivered as he growled in anger.

Despite the drastic mismatch, Degah'lee demanded Oryn's soul: "Give it back! Give it back to me! Give me back what is mine!"

Kale rumbled and responded softly, "No."

The demon lord screamed, "I took it, and it is my own to do with as I please!"

Cupping the soul in his hand, the rogue refused. "You have no right, just as you never had a right to me. He is not yours, and he never will be."

Degah'lee shrieked, flailing in a wild fit. "Give it! Give it to me now!"

Kale growled. The force shook the imagined world of towering bookshelves. It made the fiend become even more crazed.

"Begone," Kale whispered. "Go back to the lake where you belong."

"You dare command me? A rogue has no authority in the darkness! Be silent and give back what is mine!"

Broad wings of black and white furled. "Begone."

Another surge of unearthly wind howled far stronger than the first. It blew, tugging at the raging demon lord. Robes, insectoid wings and arms flailed in the roaring wake. The force began to overpower Degah'lee. The monster bellowed in defiance.

Continuing to unleash his power, the rogue spoke again: "You never had a right to anything, least of all my soul. That was your greatest mistake. You made me into what your master feared most."

Beginning to lose grip, the demon lord struggled to remain grounded. His strength started to fail.

The rogue hissed, "I am twilight. I am endurance and unending faith in the night. And I will never be one of you."

Degah'lee wailed in outraged defeat.

"Begone!"

Another surge escalated the wind beyond what the demon lord could withstand. It lifted the fiend high. The incredible force slammed the shadow to the false walls of the vault. Staring down at the rogue, he was helpless, as the power of the flawed creation turned on him. It pressed harder and harder as if to squash him like a bug.

Pieces of the demon lord tore free and disintegrated.

When the surging gale ended, Degah'lee fell to the floor, scowling and twitching. Only one arm remained, and it had been shredded. The horns of his crown were broken. His robes were stripped away, revealing a bulbous mass of a body like a squirming grub. His pustular thorax wept in places from the punishing assault.

Kale hissed again.

Flinching, the demon lord transformed himself into black mist and flew off. The shadow retreated to escape more harm.

Kale allowed the wounded fiend to retreat. The angry scowl on his metallic face wilted into a frown. He looked down, peering at the contents of his left talon, the one covered in Adwen's golden markings. The tiny soul was no larger than a raindrop compared to him. Below where he knelt, Oryn's body lay unmoving and without breath.

He wished to cry. Tears of black water formed in his eyes, but he resisted. One spatter of the substance might extinguish the little light. Glancing between the shining soul and the lifeless body, Kale knew he had to try. Perhaps he could stitch this one back where it belonged.

Kale cupped monstrous talons and raking claws, lowering the soul down. Taking another fearful look at the fragile light, he cautiously pressed it through the armor and into flesh. While he pressed, he grew frightened as it resisted, but after Kale pressed a little longer, warm light shone. Glowing threads from the soul flared to anchor themselves. Expectantly, he retracted his talons to watch as Oryn's soul entered fully and vanished.

The knight was still without breath. Touching the warrior with ginger claws, he silently urged him to come to life. A loud gasp broke the silence. Violent coughing followed, and Kale heaved a sigh of relief.

Shivering and struggling to breathe, Oryn coughed between deep gasps. As his mind became more alert, he recalled something like a dream. Then he heard a loud hiss and looked up. An enormous demon crouched over him with even larger wings, unfurled like clouds.

He gasped and froze, eyes wide. Then the warrior realized its massive claws hovered over him. The span of the talons was several meters. Each long claw was curved and came to deadly points. Startled, Oryn gasped again and yelped, struggling to crawl away. In his weakness, he only moved a few feet before tiring. He panted heavily, gazing up at the hovering talons and the giant figure with an elegant antler crown.

A moment passed, and the demon did not move. This confused Oryn's already confounded mind. After studying the dark entity a little longer, the rest of the knight's faculties returned. Then he recognized those sad red eyes with specks of white at their centers. The feathers upon his head mimicked the outline of what was normally the werewolf's long, thick, unkempt hair. Even the face seemed familiar, though Oryn could not place it. All the while, the black steel angel watched in silence.

Kale felt dismal now that he was fully exposed. He would never be seen as anything other than this afterward – a winged nightmare. A soft rustling filled the library as his wings folded tight. Withdrawing his talon now that Oryn was alright, he willed his form to diminish. Steely demon flesh, feathers and horns became mist. The resulting nimbus shriveled to the height of a man.

In seconds the human form of the werewolf stood over the fallen knight, gaze downcast at floorboards. While the warrior stared, Kale waited patiently for whatever rebuke was in store. He could see the knight grimacing. Without a doubt, harsh words were being prepared.

For Oryn, it was very hard to move. A harsh frown formed on his face when he was able to get up on one elbow only. Looking to Kale, who seemed very melancholy, Oryn acted on his first impulse.

To Kale's confusion, the knight reached out. It took a moment to understand that Oryn was asking for help getting to his feet. Not a shred of distain or reproach could be seen. Dumbfounded, Kale extended his hand.

They grasped each other by the wrist and worked together to hoist him from the floor. But as soon as Oryn was upright, he collapsed and fell hard into Kale, who caught him. The knight was very tired and ashamed of his weakness.

Kale was in shock. Oryn trusted him.

Unable to move, the warrior's mind, body and soul were weary. He could hardly speak as he murmured, "May we please leave this place?"

At first Kale wanted to weep. If they tried to go through the vault door or any evil barrier, the knight would not survive. But then a glint of light high above caught his attention. A warm smile came over him. Where he had crushed the Taskmaster into submission with unthinkable power, the barrier between worlds was worn thin. A doorway to the living worlds awaited them.

Still smiling, Kale answered. "Yeah, we can leave." He chuckled a little. "Degah'lee was kind enough to give us a door before he buggered off."

Oryn could not understand but found it funny, as well. He tried to laugh, but only weak huffs came out.

Kale rumbled at the rip between worlds, willing it into a large oval of white light from beyond the veil. Mustering smoky wings to his back, he clutched the warrior and took flight. With a few short wing beats, they flew into the pale glow back to the other side.

Chapter 30
THE CONFLAGRATION

A black breach in the magical world dilated open. Out of the lightless hole, broad wings glided. They left the Black Door, and it closed with a thundering boom. The earth was dark under the stars, and solid ground was not far below. Drifting onward, Kale's wings lowered them steadily to a rocky outcropping. Their feet found stones and grassy soil at last, christening their escape from the Void.

Oryn gladly accepted assistance in sitting by a boulder. Reclined against the cool surface, he watched with heavy eyes as Kale sat on another mossy stone. Looking up at the cloudless night, a happy smile came over Kale. The knight looked, as well.

"They look lovelier than before, don't they?"

"Yes." To Oryn, they seemed like the most precious jewels woven into black silk.

Still admiring the sky, Kale's thoughts turned toward the practical: "I don't recognize any of this landscape. Do you?"

At a glance, it was alien. "I've never been to this place," Oryn replied. "Where is King's Peak?"

Kale sighed and nodded northwest. "I can barely see it, but it's there."

"We must be deep in the uncharted lands east of the cliffs. Can you make a portal to take us to the overlook?"

Frowning, Kale shook his head regretfully. "I can, but it would do more harm than good. You're not strong enough to use my portals. It would be like jumping into the Black Lake. With the state you're in, that's a death sentence."

"Pity."

Kale scoffed, "Yeah."

"Flight then?"

Kale smiled, shaking his head again. "Wouldn't that be a grand way to get back to the others? Unfortunately, I can only fly where no light shines. I can glide but not much more."

"Even more's the pity."

Kale was about to agree, but a chill swept across them both. The werewolf growled.

Oryn scowled. How could he have been foolish enough to think for a second they were safe. "What are they sending?"

Still growling, Kale replied, "It's a horde – a big one. Looks like the Taskmaster was still sore about losing us."

"You should have killed him."

"A lot of ruddy good that would have done. Kill him, and he instantly respawns from the Black Lake whole. Maiming that bloody tosser was the best option. We can't stay here. Let's find out how much distance the sore loser bought for them to chase us."

Roaring, the rogue transformed in billowing mist into the feathered werewolf. Gentle claws swiftly collected the helpless knight on his way down the side of the mountain. The beast raced with blinding speed. Wind streamed dark essence and loose feathers in an evanescent trail. Eventually the fastest of the fiends caught up.

Oryn never saw them, but he heard and smelled the demons. Pressed to thick fur on the werewolf's chest, he listened as Kale ripped them to shreds. Under the protection of the being that was neither of night nor of day, Oryn thought perhaps Kale was death itself. This would come as no surprise. Not even the Dark Heart had dared to attack him outright.

Raking claws through more purple flesh, the titanic werewolf bounded over the earth. Through tall trees over the hills, his path wove like a needle in a loom. A flood of dark creatures covered the land, spawning from every shadow. Small fiends evaporated on contact with the black mist. Bigger ones foolish enough to try to pounce or swing blades from mounts died just as quickly.

Taking harsher terrain, Kale forced the monsters to climb and leap over ground that was easy for him to run across. It slowed their enemies considerably. But as the giant werewolf leaped over a cliff up to a grassy knoll, his path was cut off. A second horde extended as far as he could see. The fiends came from everywhere.

When Kale paused to snarl, Oryn stole a glance. Somehow

the sight did not shake his confidence, or perhaps he was just too weak and exhausted to care. Kale set him down on the green atop the hillcrest and stood to his full height. A giant, he towered over the trees. He began to gather his power to punish them all. The moment before the seemingly endless horde reached them, Kale looked down at the knight by his feet.

The warrior watched with half-cast green eyes. As Kale glanced at him, the knight gave a kind smile. While mustering his power, the sight did something to Kale. He could think of no words to describe it. The dark energy was cold, but the sensation that rose alongside it was different. Feeling as if he could do anything, Kale faced the horde and roared.

Darkness cloaked him and formed vast wings outstretched in a threatening display. More energy expanded out in waves like raging wind. A protective sphere formed over the knight, while all else was gradually blown away. Not even Degah'lee received the full force of Kale's power. Dark wind flowed from the rogue, sweeping fiends off the ground and shaking trees. Demons of all shapes and sizes were lifted off their feet and obliterated by the deadly force. The immense power of the rogue demon lord blotted out the sky, as he unleashed himself. When they were gone, his black storm withdrew, renewing the beauty of the quiet night.

Kale's power granted mercy enough to the trees to keep their leaves. Birds and other animals were unharmed in their roosts and dens. Seeing his desires granted made the victory all the sweeter. Checking on the knight again, he found him safe.

Oryn was grateful to the oddity towering above him. Kale held tight to the sensation swelling within his heart. It was unlike anything he had ever known.

The knight took a breath to thank him, but it became trapped in his lungs. He stared as the golden markings running the length of the werewolf's left arm started to glow. Kale soon noticed. The glow bloomed brighter as the last few marks encircled where his heart resided. Pure light radiated, dancing in the night on the moonlit hilltop.

Breathless, Oryn asked, "What is happening?" As he spoke, a pale flame hissed to life on the back of Kale's hand. It made the beast yelp in painful surprise, and Oryn gasped.

It burned. The fire grew before their eyes, and Kale howled

in horror and agony. He swiped to try and douse it but only aided in its spread. In a flash, white and blue tongues of fire burst along the rest of the design. Kale moaned and howled miserably, crumpling to the ground. The holy fire engulfed him, taking his breath away, while it raced down his throat. It choked the life from the feathered beast.

The knight strained to reach Kale but found he had not even the strength to crawl. Oryn watched because there was nothing else he could do. In disbelief, he tried to wake up from the nightmare. Could this be a tormenting trap? Were they still in the Void and was all this a vision set to assail his mind?

Monstrous werewolf jaws fell to the ground nearby. The eyes had gone dark. The creature did not stir, while the white fire danced on his form. Oryn waited, expecting Kale to rise, shake off the flames and be alright.

Defiant of what his eyes showed him, Oryn called out weakly, "Kale?"

A sickening crunch met his ears, as the skull of the beast caved in and cinders flew. More tongues of fire broke through. Smaller flames hollowed out the eyes and nose, turning all to ash with each passing second. The morbid sight forced Oryn to look away, clenching his jaw tight. It was almost more than he could bear. Rolling away as the fire continued to feed, the knight gazed somberly up at the stars. They were still beautiful.

Death was no stranger for Oryn. To him it was a fickle acquaintance. When Adwen had been dead in his arms, his heart felt broken, but with this loss there was only nothing. It was as if he himself died and was filled with emptiness. Past, present and future were no longer divided; they ceased to be.

A sense of being cheated started to come over him, as he lay prone on the grass. He could not help but question. Staring vacantly at the heavens he murmured softly, "Why did you have to die?"

The world gave no reply.

Unsatisfied, Oryn posed another question and yet feared the answer.

"Why, Adwen? Why did you do this?"

Looking to see the state of the burning beast, he found a smoldering hill of ash. Too weary to lament anymore, Oryn closed his eyes. He hoped this nightmare would be gone once he opened them again.

When Oryn opened his eyes, the sky was hazy navy with faded cream stretching from the east. Stars had faded and gone to sleep as he began to wake. For Oryn, it felt as if he only just closed his eyes a moment before. Hours had passed, while he slept an empty sleep. Turning his head on grass damp with dew, the knight looked to see if anything had changed. The sight of shriveled cold ashes made his heart sink. It had not been an illusion at all.

He picked himself up now that he possessed the strength. His gaze hovered over the large gray mound, and he despaired. Oryn understood that this was what Kale had wanted, but the knight could not help but object. As he went to stand over the remains, the sky began to brighten. Oryn stayed to pay respect where it was due. The fire came too soon for dawn to allow a proper funeral. Again, he felt they both had been cheated. Oryn wore a solemn frown as he waited for the sun.

Golden rays spilled over the hills and trees. The morning was still. Few animals made calls to disturb the crisp air. As the warm light cast on the knight's face, he sighed. It was over. He turned to begin the journey back to Dargadia alone.

Oryn walked steadily down the sloping hillside. Then a sound permeated the air. It was like breath in his ears from all around. Surprise at the anomaly made him stop in his tracks.

Then he heard a gasp for air come from behind. He spun round to stare in shock looking for the source. The rise of the hill masked the pile of ash, but he saw a form emerge in the shape of a man. As the figure fell out of sight coughing, Oryn took brisk strides back the way he had come. Keeping his distance, he stood like a statue, while the one who crawled from the ashes breathed more clearly. A breeze brought a scent, and it was unknown to him, but it was distinctly that of a Holy Hound.

The one born from the ash and dust picked himself up. The sun was so bright he had to shield his eyes a moment. At seeing his hands, the figure held them out and marveled at their shape. Breathing deeply, he basked in the light of day. It was so warm.

"So that's what it feels like," the strange warrior murmured.

Oryn could see this was not Kale, though the hair was much the same length and just as unkempt. Its shade was brown. His attire was enchanted garments in the shape of black armored mage robes, accented by many white and gold swirling runes.

The figure sensed he was being watched and slowly turned to look back. As the new warrior faced Oryn, the knight could see features far better. His body was lean and tall, and his face was like looking in a mirror. It startled the knight to look into those eyes. They made Oryn feel weak enough to collapse.

Those amber gold eyes stared with uncertainty, waiting.

The knight became short of breath. He darted closer and stopped abruptly before the warrior, who looked so much like himself. Afraid this was a dream, he did not dare blink. Oryn desperately wanted this to be real. With all his heart, he wished this was not a dream.

Seeing the knight could recognize him, Kai smiled. "Told you your brother still loved yah."

Oryn gasped and embraced his twin. The knight could scarcely breathe. Overwhelming emotions choked him, welling up in his chest until it hurt. He refused to let go for fear this twin might vanish. But he was real. Kai felt real in his arms. He could smell him and hear him.

Kai froze when his brother latched onto him in a frantic hug. The suddenness was startling. Never did he think he would have the chance to feel loved by his twin ever again. Relieved to have this wish among others granted, the wayward warrior returned the embrace. He wanted to cry from the indescribable joy.

In that moment, Oryn was so full of happiness he could weep. Then the gravity of Kai's words set in. He became alarmed and forcefully ended the embrace to grab his twin by the shoulders, staring into his face. It felt as if he were going mad in trying to understand what was happening.

How hard Oryn clutched his shoulders and the expression of total confusion made Kai worry. His brother seemed to be trying to wrap his mind around something. After a moment, he checked to see if the knight's mind had broken.

"Are you alright?"

The sound of the British accent caused Oryn to gulp and blanch.

It was then that Kai could see Oryn was starting to understand. Already, Oryn looked as if he were punishing himself.

Recalling how to speak, Oryn asked, "The whole time?"

Kai knew what this would do to him. As gently as possible, he replied and nodded, "Yeah, I was Kale."

Oryn dropped his gaze in shame, quivering as he squeezed Kai harder. It was the one thing preventing him from falling on his face.

Urgent to keep Oryn from pushing himself too far, Kai grabbed the knight's shoulder and braced his neck to make him look up again. "Hey, hey, don't start that now. That's enough of that. It's alright."

The knight still felt weak as he locked eyes with Kai. Was he forgiving him?

"I'm so sorry," Oryn began. "Forgive ..."

Kai cut him off: "Don't start that. It's okay now. We're okay."

Sweet relief lifted a terrible weight from Oryn's shoulders. "It's really you."

Kai smiled, and his eagle eyes shone like the new dawn. Chuckling, a glad smile returned. "That's right. Well, we can't stay out here forever. I still have to get you back to your girl. What do you say?"

The thought of seeing Adwen lifted his lofty spirits even higher. It made him so happy he laughed a little as he nodded.

Cuffing his twin on the shoulder and messing his hair, Kai encouraged Oryn to be at ease. "Come on, then! We've got a long way to go. Let's find out who's still the slowest."

Oryn playfully batted the hand away. A clever glint in his expression spoke fathoms.

Taking a few bounding steps down the hillside, Kai called out, "Come on."

Oryn began to glare. Concern made Kai pause. He was off guard as his green-eyed twin suddenly bolted and sped past chuckling. Amused, Kai laughed before racing after him. "Cheater!"

Oryn cherished every second. As Kai came alongside to run with him, he saw that the feeling was shared. They ran like the wind across the land heading back to the overlook, where the others were surely waiting. All the time the two could spend together the better, until they were able to share it with their friends.

The knight could hardly wait to see Adwen again. Oryn wanted to hold her in his arms and tell her she had given him everything; Adwen had given him everything he could ever want and more.

Chapter 31
A DAY NOT WASTED

Since being flung free of the dangers of the Void, Adwen hardly spoke. When they returned to the overlook sanctuary, she went to the ledge and never left. She was cut off from the two who were left behind. It felt as if they were dead. Adwen sat in the sunshine by the falls to wait. The warm light provided some comfort.

In the days that passed, the saplings of the enchanted trees grew like weeds. Animals migrated from the coast, and birds flew near the cliffs. Jack and Alexander checked on her periodically. The warriors were worried, though they turned to tasks for comfort instead of the sun. At Adwen's blessing, the warriors went on a hunt. They were successful, but she ate nothing. Jack had Alexander help with drying the meat. If or when Oryn and Kale returned, they would need it. Each feared this wait could last forever.

Late one evening after Jack checked on Adwen, she lay on the cool stones staring somberly out at the world. The stars were especially beautiful. A warmth stirred in her heart as the tiny lights seemed more wondrous. She did not understand why at first. Then she did, and her eyes shone, filling with happy tears. It was their hearts she felt, filling with awe at the night.

The following morning, Jack and Alexander trekked up to the ledge to check on her before going for a morning run.

"We need to make her try to eat something," the Marine advised. "It's been five days."

Those five days since their own escape were taxing on Jack even without battles. "I doubt the two of us can force-feed her. When she's ready, she'll have a bite. Just give her time."

Conceding, Alexander frowned and averted Jack's gaze. The

two friends went to where she sat. As usual, Adwen gazed over the fields and flourishing forests. Jack and his friend stopped a few paces short. She did not acknowledge them.

"We're going out for a run. If you want something to eat, there's plenty in the storeroom."

As was normal since their escape from the Void, Adwen did not speak. However, before Jack turned away, he sensed something different. He could not stop himself from touching her mind. The instant he recognized patient anticipation, his mood took a rapid turn for the better.

Jack tossed Alexander an excited glance. He was shocked then beamed happily.

He asked Adwen, "How long?"

She smiled while watching the wind in the trees. "By the end of the day."

The warrior wanted to whoop with jubilation. Facing the Marine, he admitted, "Sorry, Jarhead. You can go for a run, but I'm staying. There's no way I'm going to miss this."

Alexander was insulted. "You think I want to miss seeing them get back?"

To Adwen, the friendly argument was like music to her ears after such a long silence.

Jack struggled to stop himself from pestering Adwen for updates. Jack periodically paced when not leaning beside the ledge. Alexander stood by her at parade rest with arms neatly folded in the small of his back. Hours passed, and they wondered from where they would come. Suddenly, from over a tree-covered hill there was movement.

Adwen laughed a little.

Jack darted to their side, and Alexander joined him in straining their enhanced vision. The instant they saw two giant beasts bounding, they howled with excitement at the tops of their lungs. At hearing Oryn answer in kind, they began to laugh.

Adwen was unable to wait any longer. She shoved herself over the ledge into a long, controlled fall. Wind whipped her hair and mystical garments, whistling in her ears while she grinned. Landing and bounding forward, she raced to meet them. Jack and Alexander followed.

The large brown Holy Hound with black magical markings transformed into the knight and sprinted toward her. She yelped with excitement and joy just before blinking through the air and flinging herself into his arms. She sobbed, thankful to have him returned. She laughed and wept, pressing her cheek to his neck; her feet dangled over the grass.

Oryn sighed deeply, smelling her skin and soft silvery hair. The knight had all his heart's desires with him now. After a moment, he looked up to see the others joining them. Their faces were the happiest he could recall.

"Cujo! You are the luckiest dog in the universe."

The Marine took Oryn by the hand as he released Adwen to stand. They nodded to one another in a nonverbal greeting. Their eyes glowed brightly.

Then everyone hushed. Adwen smiled at the brown Holy Hound with white magical markings under black, white and gold garments. She and Oryn had warm looks. Jack and Alexander were perplexed by this stranger. The new warrior beast was as large as Oryn when transformed. His eyes shone with a clever glint.

Jack tried to read the mind of this Holy Hound. When he was rebuffed by a strong barrier he grew suspicious. "Adwen, Oryn? Who is this?"

Alexander sniffed and growled, "Who are you?"

Tossing the knight a sly glance, the Holy Hound rapidly reverted to elf-like form and shrugged. The face was identical to that of the knight, but the eyes remained like a raptor's.

Kai grinned, "Just an acquaintance."

Jack and Alexander yelped and screamed. Adwen giggled as Oryn rolled his eyes.

Pointing in flabbergasted horror, Jack shouted, "Why are there two of you? That's not right!"

Kai was mockingly impressed. "Oh! He can count."

Alexander stood by slack-jawed, leaving the confusion for Jack to sort out.

Then the warrior turned fearful. "Oryn, where's Kale? Where is the big guy?"

Raising an eyebrow to his twin, the knight passed the question: "Is this not your question to answer?"

Jack and Alexander's attention darted back to the yellow-eyed warrior.

Kai shrugged passively. "Kale won't be coming back. I hope that's alright with you."

The voice was like Oryn's, but the accent was distinct. It was unmistakable.

The cop's jaw fell open. "Kale?"

In matter-of-fact tone, Kai corrected him. "Well, not anymore."

"What?" The reply did not make sense to Jack or Alexander.

Adwen gladly stepped forward. "His name is Kai."

The confounded duo looked at her speechless.

"He's Oryn's brother."

The two were stunned. The knight turned to her, uncertain. "How long had you known?"

Kai puffed incredulously at her. "Aw, you're no fun at all. I was going to make them guess."

"Stop teasing them," Adwen chided.

Oryn was becoming impatient. "Adwen?"

She turned to him and grew apologetic. "When I first looked in his heart, I was suspicious. But when we had our private talk in the overlook while the Order was still there, he told me."

The knight was wounded and gave Kai a betrayed stare.

His brother protested, "Oh, please don't start that again."

"You told her. I assumed she knew from the start."

This killed the merry mood, so Kai shrugged. "Can you blame me?"

"Yes."

Adwen was appalled. "Oryn!"

The knight sighed, resigning to being disappointed.

Kai pleaded, "I did try."

He could not deny it. "I know."

Their banter halted when Jack raised his hands. "Woah, woah. Hold everything for one minute. I need to get something straight here." Going to stand before Kai, the short warrior stared into his bright golden yellow eyes and tried to search his mind. Again, he was unable to get through. Jack took a deep breath to clear his own head. "Do you mean that the whole time, the entire time, you were

Kale?"

Kai smiled sheepishly, "More or less."

Jack took a moment to think, then shot an accusing look at the knight. "You must feel really great about yourself right now."

Oryn scowled.

With that established for the cop, he moved on to the next question. "Are you really Oryn's dead brother, the one who died when he was ten?"

Alexander was unable to stay silent any longer. "He had a brother?"

Kai gave a dry laugh. "Yeah, and I'm not shocked it wasn't common knowledge. It was a rather sensitive topic." He stared blankly at Oryn.

Becoming uncomfortable, the knight looked away and cleared his throat.

Kai went on to add, "Sensitive enough to crush someone."

Oryn cleared his throat more loudly and gave a stern look. Finding Kai smiling rather than glaring, the knight could not stay angry long. He softened.

Alexander's stare flitted back and forth between the twins. So much bewildering news made him dizzy. "How? When? Where did this start? I'm confused."

Jack returned to his side, massaging his own temples. "It's okay, Jarhead. We'll get through this one together."

Kai interjected, "You lot forgot 'who' and 'what' in that line of questioning."

To this, Jack turned to glare indignantly. "Don't even start, Big Guy." He froze and was astonished. "Can I get away with still calling you that?"

After thinking it over, Kai replied, "I don't see why not."

Alexander slowly raised a finger to point. "You really were Kale!"

Everyone took pity on the Marine.

Jack sighed, patting his friend's shoulder. "It's okay, Jarhead."

Adwen beamed at her friends. "It's good that we at least got the two of you back."

In that instant, Oryn looked at Kai, who wore an impish smirk.

The two bewildered warriors exchanged glances, as Adwen realized why the twins were sharing smiles.

"Stop teasing, Kai," she told him. "That's not funny."

"We think it's quite funny."

"You know where the piece of the focus is," she replied.

He chuckled, entertained by their great surprise. "Of course, I do."

The reunited Holy Hounds sat together on the bright overlook. Kai was bemused by Jack and Alexander because the two warriors kept staring blankly. Oryn was quietly annoyed. After a minute of gawking, Adwen sighed and decided to postpone an important meeting.

"Fine," she told them. "Get it out of your systems. Ask him questions, and make it quick."

Jack was faster than his friend: "How did you get to be a Holy Hound?"

This question made Kai chuckle a little. "Well, Adwen's heart piece did the trick. Let's just leave it at that."

The cop whistled. "Wow."

Alexander took his turn before Jack could skip him: "Did you always know you were Kai?"

"Sort of. I started trying to sleep for the first time a few years ago. Some memories came up that got me wondering. Eventually more and more things fit together. Thanks to Adwen, I was finally able to recall my name."

She beamed at him. "You're very welcome."

Curious, Jack asked, "What is your weapon?"

"Don't have one, I'm afraid."

Adwen corrected Kai, "Yes, you do."

Confounded, he insisted, "No, I'm fairly certain I do not."

Still beaming, she replied, "Think again."

Kai became intrigued, then had a thought. He summoned the broken sword. The halves of the blade lay in his hands shining in the afternoon sun. As the Elf-steel caught the light, the two pieces glowed and vanished in a blinding flash.

A magnificent double-edged sword made of silver and gold manifested in his hands. One side had a row of angled holes, just as the original weapon. Elegant designs ran the length of the exaggerated fuller in the center. The one-handed sword he had been given took his breath away.

"You had better name it," Adwen insisted, enjoying his pleasant surprise.

Right away, he decided: "Horizon – made of both Dawn and Dusk."

Jack was perplexed. "What?"

Kai had a clever look when he dismissed his gift. "Maybe you'll see in the next battle. Any more questions?"

The Marine was next: "Did you ever search for your brother?"

This line of questioning caught him off guard. He shared a brief look with Oryn and admitted, "Yeah, I did. In hindsight, I shouldn't have. I found a portal to this world, and things went south in a hurry. That adventure was a bloody disaster. I was nearly gutted, then hunted by knights for weeks."

"Why did you give up the search?" Alexander asked.

Kai looked to his brother. "Rumors."

Oryn understood and wore a bitter frown.

"I heard the knights talking," Kai explained. "They said Oryn was dead. I gave up after that."

"How did you travel between worlds without magic?"

A cold chill flooded Kai's body, and he frowned. "I'd rather not talk about that today."

Everyone shared glances.

"Next question, please."

To lighten the mood, Jack decided to be a pest: "Which of you two is older?"

Kai quickly screwed up his face and puffed incredulously. "I'm not answering that! Next question."

"Was Adwen the only one who knew you were really Kai?" Jack asked.

Chuckling, he answered, "No." Instantly sensing an icy glare from his brother, Kai grew nervous. "Not exactly. Next question."

Oryn glowered with a deadly tone, "Who else knew?"

Kai muttered through his teeth, "Aw, bugger."

"Who knew?"

Giving sheepishly furtive glances to the angry knight, the warrior gulped. "Vaughn knew. He knew everything."

"That comes as no surprise," the knight glowered. "Who else knew?"

"Um ... Balefire. He figured it out pretty quickly."

Oryn became more impatient with his rascally twin. "Of course. He's a Guardian. Who else knew?"

Kai could see he was running out of time to sway Oryn away from this question. "Um, let me think."

"Kai, who else?"

The new Holy Hound strained a coarse cough into a balled fist, averting Oryn's gaze. "Agh-k-toth-hm."

Oryn's scowl hardened. "I beg your pardon?"

At long last, Kai gave up the fight. "Toth. Toth knows."

This made the knight bare his teeth angrily. "You told him."

"I bloody did not!"

"I know you told him," Oryn insisted.

Adwen stepped in to tame Oryn's temper: "You know he's telling the truth, so calm down."

The knight shot a harsh look that made Adwen flinch and declared, "You and I will speak of this matter in private later."

Feeling shock and guilt, Adwen bit her lip.

Again, Kai protested, "I told only Adwen, so get over yourself. Toth figured it out himself."

"How?" Oryn persisted.

Weary of his brother's questions, Kai's shoulders sagged. "He's a bloody Elf king. All he had to do was touch me, and he saw me."

"Saw you?"

Both were calming down, and Kai felt a mixture of relief and nostalgia.

"His hand brushed against mine while we were in the jungle. He was able to see me for me under all ... all that ruddy mess. It was like he could see what the Mirror of Truth could see."

The others noticed how melancholy Kai became and fell silent. After snapping out of the mixture of happiness and gloom, Kai was impatient: "I only told Adwen and Vaughn anything, so just come off it. Any more questions?" He muttered to himself, "Cheeky buggers."

Jack and Alexander shared amused expressions, and Oryn

seemed satisfied with this interrogation. Adwen took advantage of the quiet. "I have one more. Where is the shard from the soul focus hidden?"

Liking the change of topic, Kai wore a sly smile. "In a secluded castle off the northern coast."

Oryn frowned. "There is no castle to the north, aside from Castle Sax. It is rubble and does not lie on the coast. What castle?"

Kai knew his brother would love this piece of history: "It is an enchanted ruin that predates Dargadia as a kingdom. The first humans in this world built it."

This sparked Adwen's curiosity too: "Did the first humans in this world come from the other one?"

"Yes and no. Some were already here before the great breach. But that's neither here nor there. When the sea began to erode the earth, the castle was fortified with magic to sustain it upon the rocks. Unfortunately, the sea kept eroding the land. Eventually the castle became secluded on an island. It was abandoned and eventually forgotten."

Alexander added, "The demons didn't forget."

"Umbradonus, the Dark Heart, was the only demon to remember after sealing the knowledge in the vault."

The Holy Hounds exchanged grim looks. Oryn voiced their thoughts: "Then we do not have the upper hand."

Kai replied regretfully, "No, we don't. The upper hand we have is the Light Spirits. Still, we must be the ones to move forward. If my guess is correct, Umbradonus already knows what was taken from the Vault of Forbidden Knowledge."

Jack groaned, "Great."

Alexander seconded the motion: "Outstanding."

Adwen leaned toward Kai. "What are your suggestions?"

The warrior rubbed at the back of his neck, trying to think. "Well, Kale was able to spot runes and hiding demons, but that's out now. At best, I can help distract any bugger assigned to guard duty."

"Hey, Big Guy?"

"Yeah?"

"Aside from being psychic, what else can you do?"

A clever smile slowly spread on Kai's face making his yellow eyes glow. "Magic."

"What kind?"

"The fun kind."

Oryn sighed heavily. "He means his abilities are as appealing as they are effective."

Kai chuckled. "Glad you finally admitted it. Are you envious?"

The knight gave a deadpan glare.

"Sorry, brother. I was quite the spoiled little show-off as a child."

The knight agreed. "Understated."

"Come on, now," Kai reassured his brother. "Healing is far more useful. Song magic is powerful and rare, too. And you've found interesting ways to use your small protective barriers."

Oryn scowled, insulted. "My barriers are capable of being far larger now."

Intrigued, Jack interrupted: "You can make barriers?"

"In a manner, yeah." Kai paused when he saw Adwen growing impatient with the wandering conversation. "I can handle whatever they throw at me."

She raised an eyebrow, "Even Impurus?"

Kai scoffed. "Oh, yeah, especially that one."

"Good to hear," she told him. "Oryn, what are your thoughts?"

The others fell quiet, as the knight pondered: "The danger is very high. This place has been in use by the overlord for innumerable years. Whether they are aware that we intend to strike it is irrelevant. The location of the hidden piece would not be left unguarded. It is my judgment that this will be as dangerous as our venture into the Void."

Kai was grim. "I agree."

"Again, we have a gambit set before us – it is all or nothing," Oryn concluded.

Adwen appreciated the council from the twins – Kai's wealth of knowledge and Oryn's tactical advice.

"Unfortunately, there is no way to know what's ahead of us," Adwen cautioned her warriors. "I expect that Impurus will be there because we haven't seen him since the desert."

Oryn growled, "That is likely."

His brother chuckled. "Good. I look forward to having a go at that blighter."

She brushed stray strands of hair from her eyes. Looking up at them, she decided.

"There's no point in setting out today. Oryn, you need food and rest. Everyone needs to eat and get plenty of sleep. We will continue planning tomorrow morning."

Before Adwen could declare the meeting on hold, Kai spoke up: "One minute, if you please."

"What?"

Kai began to smile, and Oryn pressed his lips together tightly, bracing for whatever his brother might say. Adwen and the others sensed they were at the new Holy Hound's mercy.

"I have a question I'd like to ask."

Jack wore an impatient scowl. "What?"

"I'd just like everyone's approval on a style change."

Kai magically willed his hair to be a perfect match to Oryn's short cut with bangs. Adwen went wide-eyed, silently horrified. Jack and Alexander cringed, shielding their eyes.

"No!" Jack cried. "Don't do that! Having just one of him is bad enough. An Oryn who's a troll is crossing the line!"

"Put a halt on that!" the Marine added.

Oryn maintained a distant scowl, averting his eyes from his brother. Then he turned to look at Kai, who was grinning back. The twin chuckled to spite the glare Oryn gave.

Then Oryn's stern expression twitched. He softened, then broke into a fit of laughter. Loud mirthful laughter filled the overlook – to the astonishment of everyone but Kai. Adwen mused at the knight with happy tears in his eyes. Never had she heard him laugh like this.

Jack and Alexander were dumbstruck.

"Bad Dog," Alexander asked Jack, "have you ever heard him laugh before?"

Jack shook his head. "No, Big Dog. This is a first. It scares me a little."

Regardless of the varied reactions, Oryn could not stop laughing.

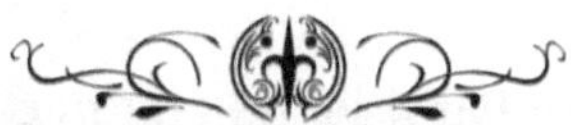

Those who were hungry ate their fill. Afterward, Adwen and Oryn went alone to bask in the sunset. The knight laid his head on her lap to sleep, soothed by the warmth and the sensation of her fingers combing his scalp. Into twilight, they dozed as the stars came out, replacing the fiery sky with a deep ocean of twinkling lights. As the first of the four moons rose full, the knight awoke. Adwen sensed he was discontented. It saddened her as she watched him sit up. He stared at the moonlit landscape, and she waited for the knight to speak.

"All that time, and you never told me Kale was my brother. Why?"

Adwen lamented, "I couldn't."

"Why did you not trust me?"

"I do trust you, Oryn. It wasn't about you."

Taken aback, he found the will to look her in the eye. Her bright sapphire gaze was sad.

"He told me on condition that I never to tell anyone, including you."

Falling quiet, she hoped he could forgive her.

Unable to be angry, his gaze turned away to the hills and trees cast in moonlight.

"And you keep your promises. I understand. In the end, it was for the best."

Relief eased the tightness in her shoulders.

Knowing he had upset her with his questioning, the knight pulled her close. Adwen gladly accepted the warm embrace. Opening her eyes again, her smile vanished. With a firm look, she muttered, "Kai, what are you doing?"

Both turned and cast deadpan stares to the warrior, who was leaning back by the ledge. Unfolding his arms, he shrugged.

"Making sure my brother doesn't berate you for doing the right thing. I'm glad he saw reason."

As Oryn growled indignantly, she asked, "Why aren't you asleep with the others?"

Shrugging again and strolling over, Kai admitted, "We couldn't sleep." He knelt between the two frowning faces, wrapping his arms around their shoulders. "Tell me how you two met? I've been dying to know."

The knight looked as if he had bit into a lemon. "Do not answer, Adwen."

"At a royal masquerade ball," she replied nonchalantly. "I

was invited by the princess, and the king invited Oryn."

This answer surprised Kai. "That's better than anticipated. That's quite lovely."

Then she added indignantly, "He tried to cut my head off."

Kai was nonplussed, but eventually found his tongue and apologized: "Sorry I asked." He smartly cuffed his growling twin on the shoulder. Then Adwen and Oryn realized what had been said. They looked back in unison. Jack and Alexander stood side by side observing. The cop waved innocently hoping for no reprimand.

Giving up entirely, Adwen beckoned the pair. "Whatever. Get over here, you two."

Kai stood by the couple, while the two joined them in admiring the lights in the newborn forest. Tiny fireflies and fairies flitted through the boughs. A warm summer breeze combatted the cool gusts from the roaring waterfall. As the wind buffeted the companions, they were silent for a time, enjoying one another's presence. They lingered through the darkest hours of night just to share the next sunrise.

Chapter 32
AFRAID OF THE CLOCKS

With regret, Adwen ended their silence in the early dawn.
"We have no choice."

Her friends said nothing.

"We must try before they find another way to consume everything."

Kai added grimly, "They likely already have another plan."

"The overlord must be destroyed," she continued. "Kai, what will happen if the Dark Heart is slain?"

"There can never be another overlord. That is a fact. There will always be demon lords, but without a true overlord, they will only every fight among themselves. The shadows plot against one another endlessly. Killing Umbradonus would scar the Void forever."

Jack frowned. "It would be better to destroy the Void."

"The Void is a part of the balance," Kai explained. "It will always be - so long as light and dark exist in the hearts of the living. That cannot be undone."

Oryn got to his feet and helped Adwen stand.

She addressed them again wearing a firm expression: "Is everyone ready?"

The twins nodded, as did Jack, and Alexander coolly answered, "Hoorah."

Adwen's heart swelled at their willingness to fight at her side. "Alright, let's go."

She summoned the Gray Blade and used it to open a burning wreath of pale blue flames. After they walked through, and the portal closed at their heels, relentless wind lashed them. They stood on shelves of old lava flows that overlooked the sea. Smells of salty brine wafted off the rocky waters far below. Roaring waves crashed on porous stone.

Kai pointed over the deep blue at a faint shape. "That is the castle."

They mused, but none so much as Oryn. How far the land receded was astonishing. Surely, the castle was built many ages ago.

Adwen tilted her head curiously. "What is it called?"

"It has had a few names," Kai explained. "Castle Grayside, Stonevale Keep, and the Outcast Palace after the island formed. The most popular, I think, roughly translates to Moonset Bastion. The Elves helped build it when the races befriended one another. The alliance wavered off and on through the eras."

Adwen mused. "That castle would have the most wonderful view of the moons at night."

"And the stars, which the Elves loved dearly," Kai added.

"Do you know where the Elves went?" she asked.

A clever glow filled Kai's eyes. "That is not meant to be shared."

She smiled. "Is that staying in your own Vault of Forbidden Knowledge?"

Kai chuckled.

"Once we get there, we must stay alert. I want all weapons ready before I make a portal."

Everyone summoned blades: Alexander, his short Feather Blade; Jack, the daggers Heart and Soul; Oryn, the Rose Thorne; and Kai, Horizon. Adwen raised the Gray Blade and opened a gateway to the distant castle's gates. Her deep blue eyes glowed at the cold stones on the other side.

"Jack, Alexander," she instructed, "cover our backs. Oryn, you're with me. Kai, you know what to do."

The warrior mage smiled, eagle eyes aglow.

Adwen marched to the ring of fire with her ready warriors. They stepped past the threshold and crossed leagues of water at once. With the mainland now far to their backs, the Holy Hounds stood at the gates to Moonset Bastion. Tall towers and spires were interconnected in an elegant series of fine arches and flying buttresses. Pale marble inlaid with gold glinted in the rays of light that broke through the overcast sky. The castle was silent except for the wind and crashing waves.

Right away, Adwen and the rest sensed evil forces standing guard.

She growled, clutching her fiery sword. "I sense Impurus."

Jack could not help but snarl.

Kai was direct: "Can you detect the fragment?"

"Not yet. Would they move it from here and hide it elsewhere?"

He reassured her: "They cannot touch it. The moving of the fragment to this place was through great pains and by manipulating mortals. It cannot be moved unassisted."

"Good. Let's go get it."

Fire cloaked her body then blanketed the ground at their feet. As she walked, the circle of flame followed to provide some protection. It burned hot, though it left her warriors untouched. Passing under another arch, her fire growled, as did the four warriors. Jack and Alexander watched for threats, as the twins guarded their flanks. On their way through the courtyard and barren garden, they sensed observers.

As they walked farther along a winding path between high walls, Alexander and Kai sensed danger. Both looked up and snarled.

"Harpies!" Jack shouted.

Dodging wicked spears made of demon-steel, the Holy Hounds snarled at the surprise attack. Adwen intensified her blaze to scorch the stones around them. Tongues of white blue fire crept up the walls.

The knight was outraged. "They betrayed us!"

Jack was first to fell one of the flying attackers, cleaving a wing from its back. It landed nearby in the fire. While it began to burn, the bird-man stood to fight, ignorant of the pain. The ancient harpy warrior was black as tar, and his eyes deep red and purple. Dark essence trickled from his beak like saliva, as the feathered being tried to attack.

Seeing the signs, Kai snarled at the grisly discovery. "They've been corrupted. They are like the gargoyles of Mortigad."

The others paused to stare while dodging vicious volleys.

Kai warned his friends, "They've been force-fed the waters from the Black Lake!"

Adwen pitied the creature as her fire devoured him. "Can they be cured?"

Kai showed a pained scowl. "Only through death."

The immortal abominations needed to be put down. With great remorse, she issued orders: "Kill them all if you can, but our mission has not changed. Let's move!"

Oryn and Kai used green and yellow barriers to shield incoming spears and arrows. Adwen and Jack used fire and daggers to take enemies out of the air. Those that fell nearby were left for Alexander to cull. Whirling blades clipped wings, sending the creatures to feed the blaze. Her sword shot balls of explosive fire, consuming the merciless attackers. Feathered bodies rained from above with wicked projectiles. No matter how many fell, more took their place.

Reaching enormous bronze doors, Oryn bashed his shoulder into them. They opened wide, while Kai continued to block incoming arrows and spears. It had become a downpour of black metal that tested even his talents.

Adwen barked to her friends, "Both of you, step back."

Jack and Alexander gladly moved away, letting Kai hold his ground. Adwen stood beside him, as Oryn joined his brother in creating a second magical barrier. Between them, she raised her sword, mustering some of her strength. Flames on the sword roared as she pierced the gap between the green and yellow walls of magic.

Then Adwen roared, eyes blazing. A long tongue of fire erupted from the white sword and furled outward like a living whip. At her will, the river of white blue fire waved about. It swayed, writhing in the air, defying the strong winds. The fiery lash consumed hundreds of corrupted harpies. When she dismissed the flames, ashes swirled in the gales like snow.

Hearing loud bird trills, Adwen and the others knew more were on the way. "I can't spend any more time here."

Jack and Alexander stepped up.

"You've done enough," Jack urged his friends. "Go get the piece of the focus. Jarhead and I can handle them from here."

The brothers relinquished their barriers to join her in heading deeper into Moonset Bastion. Wind wailed along the halls from lofty windows, shattered by many a raging squall. Overpowering smells of burnt feathers and flesh were everywhere, while ashes blew into the keep. Gray flecks steadily dusted stone floors, swirling around passage corners as small gray hurricanes.

When they burst into a main hall, Kai sensed a mind and

stopped. He grabbed Adwen and his brother, pulling them back.

A pillar of purple fire poured down from the arch overhead. Its heat forced them back, growling. When the billowing tongues of fire vanished, they heard wingbeats. Then came guttural laughter. Impurus flew to the middle of the room and landed heavily, displaying his renewed body. Spikes grew down his arms and along a whip-like prehensile tail. He laughed at the three Holy Hounds confident in his increased strength.

Snarling, Adwen stormed into the room with the twins. "It's over, Jacques! Leave, and you'll live."

He found the gesture of mercy funny: "You are much stronger now, but so am I, Heir of the Neverborn." Then he blinked, confounded to see Oryn and the one who looked so much like him. "What sorcery or trickery are you attempting here? Where is the rogue demon hiding? Did he finally turn on you?"

Kai wore the same calculating expression as his sibling. "I didn't turn on her, unruly whelp."

Realizing the truth, the abomination's jaw dropped. "Impossible!" In an instant, he roared with laughter. "Brothers? All the better to slay you one at a time. This shall be a day to remember!"

Impurus leaped up, flapping wings of bony membrane. He drew his breath before unleashing another plume of demon fire. Laughing maniacally, the monster relished seeing Adwen and Oryn fleeing from his fiery assault. Scorch marks streaked the stone floor, and the rogue reborn was gone. Grinning, Impurus hovered, sneering at the knight and his leader. Heat and smoke radiated on his breath.

"This will be easy."

"You're right, blighter."

Startled to hear the voice from above and behind, Impurus whirled around shrieking. Kai stood on a current of wind made solid under his feet by a yellow barrier. With Horizon, he sliced, leaving a gash across the fiend's cheek. Watching the monster reel backward summoning a wicked sword, Kai's amusement grew. "This is going to be easy."

Impurus screamed in fright and rage before breathing a fireball. The warrior leaped and twirled over the deadly flame, landing nimbly on another wind current. It turned solid wherever he chose to tread. Running through the air as fast as Impurus could fly, Kai slashed again and again.

Adwen and Oryn stuck around long enough to see that Kai could hold his own. Impressed and no longer concerned, she led the knight into the halls just as Kai chased Impurus through a grand window. The mage warrior raced after the winged abomination higher and farther from the castle. Impurus found himself at a loss against such magic. Deciding it was no different than facing a flying opponent, he prepared to turn and fight.

Kai dodged another ball of fire, forcing him to turn. With such strong wind, there were limitless places for him to go. From the wild air over the open waves, the warrior pounced.

Their swords clashed. Metal on metal sang high notes in their ears. Impurus wore a tight scowl, and Kai flashed a relaxed smile. Effortlessly, he walked on air, deflecting blows and delivering deadly counterstrikes. The warrior moved in close and tried to deliver a fatal blow.

Impurus was just fast enough to save himself from being impaled. Dodging the shining blade, the monster grabbed Kai's sword arm and slammed the pommel of his own blade into the warrior's forehead. Kai gasped, and his eyes rolled back, head lolling. Horizon vanished. The air he stood upon stopped glowing yellow, and he toppled backward into a freefall to the raging sea.

The abomination crowed in triumph. With a mighty bellow, Impurus thrust his wings and dove after the limp warrior. He beat his wings faster into the steep dive, then tucked them to his sides. Wind whistled in his pointed teeth.

Headfirst, Kai plummeted. His hair and regal warrior robes whipped about him.

Taking a deep breath, Impurus exhaled a huge pillar of flame.

Sensing the moment had come, under the cover of the purple fire, Kai flipped. Landing hard on a gale, the warrior raised both hands, creating a powerful barrier.

Impurus was confounded to see his fire rebound. The instant he realized he was flying through his own flames, he hit something harder than steel at full speed. The collision broke a horn on his head as he bounced. Stunned, he floated for a moment amid his dying flames. Both wings fidgeted pathetically.

Kai leaped skyward, twirling. Rising high to meet the vulnerable opponent, he whirled to gut Impurus, summoning his shining sword. Coming to his senses just in time, the monster shrieked as he blocked the holy blade. But he was not ready for the repose.

Horizon shone like a brilliant sunrise down the middle to the pommel. In the blink of an eye, Kai grabbed something from the weapon then swung it.

Impurus moved one hand to block the blow and lost three fingers to the second sword as a wailing cry stung his ears. He fluttered his wings, regaining control enough to back away. Purple blood caught on the wind like string.

Kai watched while standing on the wind with both halves of his weapon. Dawn's smooth sides reflected the waves far below, while the breeze whistled along Dusk's fine holes, making it sing. An angry roar came from the monster.

"How dare you! I'll make you suffer! You will know true torment when I'm finished with you!"

The warrior passively stared and whispered on the breeze, "I already do."

This reply made Impurus screw up his face in astonishment.

"But, you are free to try." Kai pointed Dawn at the confounded fiend. "Little fly."

The abomination roared and flew up to meet the warrior head on. Kai could not help but smile.

More ash swirled in the keep as Adwen and Oryn ran. They both sensed the fragment. Its call reached a feverish pitch at the doors to a royal ballroom. When they entered the vast atrium of stone and broken glass, they stopped. Far on the other side rested a tiny wooden box. Light shone from under the lid.

They hardly took another step when dark beings revealed themselves. Two bloody marks manifested on the floor near the little chest. Out of the substance rose armored winged figures in the same form as Impurus. Their tails flicked, and their wings quivered. They brandished spears and kite shields. Adwen glared, and Oryn snarled, baring sharp fangs.

The Holy Hounds and the Shadow Vanguard sized each other up before charging. Adwen's fire erupted like a flood, cloaking the floor. It licked the walls hungrily. The ballroom became a furnace. Heat made the air dance in their clash with the demons.

Oryn pounced, narrowly avoiding a spear, and bashed against a shield. Adwen defended herself from several thrusts from the other demon, swinging at the raised shield, while the monster hovered. Lobbing blue fire at the fiend, she watched in frustration as it dodged.

Diving downward, the winged fiend held up its shield, aligning the spear through a grove on the top. Adwen was forced to be defensive. She barked angrily and tumbled away to avoid being smashed. The demon's shield protected it from the flames, and it sprung back upward. While the monster flew higher, she blinked in a flash to reappear at its side, swinging her sword.

It swatted the blade aside with the spear and swung its shield back, forcing her to recoil. Again, it bombarded her while repelling the blue flames.

Across the room, the knight transformed into his towering hound form, striking and slashing with superior reach. Like his opponent, he possessed a shield. He used magic to block spear jabs and refused to surrender ground, standing in the protective flames.

Irritated and impatient, the demon cursed aloud before rising high and diving at the knight. The fiend put all its heft into the assault. Oryn caught the full weight of the bash while deflecting the spear. The impact pushed him back against a wall. Despite the hit, the warrior remained standing.

As the knight fought his adversary, Adwen began blinking about. She stayed in the periphery of the demon's limited vision, which was hindered by the thick helm on its head. She moved faster and faster, making swift strikes to overwhelm the monster. Keeping the fiend guessing, Adwen made it whirl back and forth.

Once she was ready, she blinked again and reappeared directly overhead. Shocked and furious, the demon raised its spear and shield high. Adwen roared.

The flames beneath the demon swelled. In that moment, it realized its error, but the fire already had swallowed its wings. The flames surged upward, washing over the fiend's body. The monster was defiant to the end and thrust the spear to strike her out of the air. She pounced, deflecting the weapon, then counterstruck with her sword. Adwen knifed the blade past the demon's shield and pierced the armor, which was weakened by the blaze. They came down with a loud clang. The fire burned hotter, leaving nothing of the monster except a charred stain.

As Oryn continued his duel, he caught sight of Adwen's victory. When she turned to come to his aid, he barked, "No! The fragment!"

She nodded and bolted for the pedestal. Fire had burned away the chest and melted the metal fittings. In a pile of cinders and ash, the golden piece sat. It glinted like a beacon by the stone wall.

While Adwen claimed the artifact, Oryn prepared to restrain his enemy from pursuing her. He watched the demon, anticipating that it would forget him and fly after Adwen. It did not.

Seeing the confounded look Oryn wore, the demon gave a low ominous laugh. The fiend grinned, hovering between him and Adwen. The flying demon kept the knight from stopping her from reaching the pedestal.

Horror gripped his heart. Long ears folded back in distress. He lunged, only to be bashed backward. Oryn howled at the top of his lungs, "Adwen, don't!"

She already had grabbed the golden fragment. Amid a burst of bright light, she could not hear Oryn's warning. Adwen gasped as the piece fused with her heart and the rest of the Soul Focus. The immense energy held her immobilized. Her body glowed bright white. A black watery portal swirled open on the wall. The focus was almost whole within her, as the Reaper leaned through the darkness. Kahli'nah grinned, tentacles waving in delight. The demon lord lobbed a dark basin full of fluid drawn from the Black Lake.

Adwen raised her sword. The container shattered and the liquid contents flew in all directions. Fire evaporated much of the ooze. A glob splattered across her face and covered her eyes.

Oryn heard her scream and felt the pain on his face, as well. The fire cloaking the floor dissipated, as her powers were rendered useless without her sight. Oryn fought harder, barking and slashing with all his might. No matter what he did, the demon would not let him pass.

The energy within Adwen swirled out of control. Light fluttered across her skin. She wailed and winced, trying to wipe the burning liquid away. Hearing cruel laughter, instincts urged her to leap aside. The Reaper's sickles sliced the air, missing Adwen. The demon hissed in irritation and took aim to try again.

Tumbling across the floor helplessly, Adwen called out,

"Oryn!"

The beastly warrior roared and shrank to his more human shape. He rushed forward, but the flying demon landed in his way with shield and spear raised. Smashing into the metal plate with all his might, he made the monster slide back on his heels, snarling.

Unable to get past, the knight hollered in desperation, "Adwen!"

She heard him and knew the demon lord was over her. No rescue was coming. Blindly, raising a hand toward his voice, she hesitated. Tears and watery darkness ran down her face at the painful indecision. There was no time left.

A bright white orb shot along her arm and out her hand as the black sickles and scythes swept for her. The light flew like a shooting star as Adwen's body turned to stone. Evil blades struck and stopped, ringing as they hit the unbreakable form. Kahli'nah saw the light leaving her and wailed in outrage.

Oryn pushed against the demon, gritting his teeth, determined to make it move. He sensed something happening to Adwen, as the demon lord bellowed. Before he could look, the flying demon in his way burst like an overripe fruit. There was a flash of blinding white light. Demon flesh flew in all directions, and its armor turned to scrap.

Finally, something hit Oryn like a giant's fist.

Impurus panted. His purple blood flew away like ribbons as it caught on the wind. Kai wore a few scratches from the demon's blade, but his opponent was much worse for wear. Their blood mingled in the air over the ocean mixing with brine and rising fog. He stalked the demon, ready to end the one-sided duel.

A burning sensation ran down Kai's face, making him flinch and pause.

The exhausted abomination was encouraged by Kai's expression but was no longer foolish enough to take it as a sign of weakness. This warrior was as cunning and deceptive in battle as any demon. Instead, Impurus watched with satisfaction, as Kai's face turned pale in horror.

An explosion reached their ears, and they looked in time to see huge rubble and dust burst from the side of the castle. With his enhanced vision, Kai saw Oryn falling amid the stones. He was not conscious.

"No!"

Impurus thought this was the moment to catch the warrior unawares. He heaved his mighty wings to lunge. Kai knew his every thought and move. He dismissed both halves of Horizon. Without looking back, he created a barrier. After Impurus crashed into it and fell, Kai let the barrier vanish. He transformed and bounded on the wind straight for his twin, who was falling faster toward the choppy waves.

Jack and Alexander fought the tainted harpies even as they felt searing pain on their faces. There were too many left to turn their backs for even a second. But the explosion shook the whole castle, making the two exchange looks. The ground shuddered again and did not stop. Dust fell, mixing with cyclones of ash and feathers. Pebbles rained from crevices, as everything shook. The friends knew they needed to flee, but the harpies were too numerous.

"Help me close it!" Jack shouted.

Alexander nodded and assisted in slamming the doors shut. A few stray arrows came through but missed the Holy Hounds. Three winged figures crashed through already broken glass, entering the castle. They landed in the hall not far away with spears in hand. At first, the bewildered warriors prepared for another fight, but they hesitated.

Kai ran faster. While he bounded, he saw the castle and the earth it rested on begin to rise. Rocks rained from the base of Moonset Bastion, as it rose higher. Oryn continued to fall. To catch up at last, Kai leaped with all his might. He dove after his brother through the air, gusts whipping mercilessly. The warrior mage wrapped his arms around Oryn and landed on a strong zephyr.

Now that he had his brother and sensed he was alive, his attention turned to the castle. The structure was beginning to fly. Kai growled. He needed to try to rescue the others, but carrying Oryn would make that impossible.

A shrill bird call caught his attention, making him look up.

Overhead, a second flock of harpies emerged from the clouds. They attacked the dark ones. Kai could see these bird warriors were not tainted. He ran to meet them with Oryn over one shoulder.

When Oryn was struck, his world turned dark. Then every-thing turned blinding white. Blinking blearily, he found himself stand-ing in a meadow. Honeysuckle vines clung to oaks and the silvery bark of weeping birch. The sun shone brightly over the forest be-tween pure white clouds. Songbirds chirped in the distance. Some-how, the knight was instantly calm.

Footsteps in the tall grass caught his ear, and he found Adwen walking from the tree line to meet him. It was a relief to see her safe. Going close, Adwen smiled weakly. Her eyes were glazed with tears that wanted to overflow.

"Are you hurt?" he asked.

Adwen took a deep breath, as many things she sensed were distractions. Detecting the others were safe, her focus returned. Gaz-ing longingly at the knight, a sorrowful look killed her sweet smile. Oryn disliked the silence.

"Are you harmed?" he asked again.

She struggled to find the words. "I'm okay." This relaxed him and it made it easier for her to continue. "But you're not."

The knight was confused. Then he examined himself and the place where they stood. "This is a dream."

"One that I control," she reassured. "It will last only for a while, so we can speak."

Oryn disliked this information. "What has happened?"

"I had to keep the Reaper from killing me. It was the only thing I could do."

Impatient from worry, he snapped, "Tell me!"

Adwen flinched, looking away. The knight instantly regretted the outburst and frowned.

She mournfully admitted, "I left my body behind."

Horror washed the color from Oryn's face, and his eyes wid-ened. Adwen could not look at him.

"I sent my heart away from my body. You are carrying me."

Letting the information set in, the knight grew determined. Holding her shoulders, he tried to reassure her: "I swear to you that you will be returned. I will restore you to your body."

Adwen still could not look at him. "I don't want to lose you."

"You will not lose me." Suddenly, he was more concerned. "What do you mean?"

She forced herself to look at him, but could not speak. Tears trickled down her cheeks. It pained him to see her cry.

"Please, Adwen, tell me what is wrong."

"If you cannot put me back soon enough, you will die when you do."

Oryn swallowed a growing lump in his throat.

"My power with the focus is too strong for a body of flesh to hold. Even a fortified warrior with rapid healing cannot take it for too long. My strength can carry you as far as necessary, but if I stay for too long ... you'll die." Her face screwed up as she wept. "I'm sorry."

He wrapped her in his arms despite his shock at the news. She cried, and he wished to make it stop. After pondering the worst, a kind thought came to mind. Softly, he murmured in her ear, "Should that come to pass, do not weep for me. I will wait for you. I will be on the other side waiting. No matter how long it takes, I will wait. Then we will be together forever."

The naïve promise made her smile. "No, you won't."

Her words shocked him.

"It is a place of peace," she explained. "All who go there eventually forget. To be free of the living worlds, the land of peace washes away memories, leaving only feelings. Your heart will keep loving, but when you see me again, you won't know me."

To this, there was nothing he could say.

"I will be less than a ghost to you."

Oryn held her tighter, thinking of how to change this fate. It seemed set in stone already.

"I'm going to let you wake up now. The castle has flown away with my body inside."

Holding her cheek with one hand, he made her look up at him. Frightened, but resolute, the knight spoke softly: "Then I will go there. You will be restored swiftly. I swear to you and the Light Spirits you will be restored. And I promise to you that I will never leave or forget you."

She smiled, still crying. "You can't make that promise."

He grew firm: "Yet I have."

Adwen made the dream fade. The last thing Oryn saw was her glowing blue eyes and the tears falling like diamonds in the sunshine.

Kai sat with Jack and Alexander on a windswept ledge by a cave. The sun shone brilliantly, healing their wounds. None spoke for a time, and the mage continued to watch Oryn, who was lying beside him. The knight remained unconscious since the fall. What troubled Kai more than Adwen's absence was the golden mass that attached itself to his brother.

On Oryn's throat, a shiny ball of golden flesh wrapped sinews and strings around and through his tissue like a cancerous lump. Kai kept a close watch over the patches of purple, blue and yellow. As minutes passed, the bruising worsened.

Sensing Jack's mind tapping on his like a door, Kai glanced over.

The warrior was afraid. <Is that what I think it is, Big Guy?>

Kai nodded.

Jack frowned. He too noticed the ominous bruising. <Can he make it?>

<I don't know. Please don't ask again.>

Alexander was aware of the exchange. "You two don't have to keep me out of the conversation. I can see you're talking."

Kai apologized for both of them. "Sorry, Yank."

The Marine instinctively knew what the psychic conversation was about. "How much time does he have?"

Kai replied calmly despite rising tension and nerves, "I'm going to tell you what I told Jack: I don't know, and please don't ask again."

He took pity on the warrior. "Roger that."

Kai saw Oryn open his eyes at last. They were bloodshot, yet alert.

"Oryn, do you know what's happened?"

Getting to his feet, the knight's neck felt uncomfortable. When he reached to rub the soreness, he discovered where Adwen's heart had latched. It did not bother him as much as he thought it would. She would be safe there.

The knight nodded. "Yes. We must reach Adwen's body,

post haste. Where has the castle gone?"

Kai nodded to the northeast. "I've been keeping an eye on it."

The four warriors looked out to sea over a stretch of jungle. Only Kai could still see it from so many leagues away.

Oryn was firm. "We need griffons."

His brother rejected the plan. "We can't get them, but have other help. The harpies have brought us to their aerie."

"All the better. I wish to speak with them."

Kai escorted Oryn and the others inside. The walls of the cave were dry and the ground smooth from hundreds of years' worth of warriors passing through. Glowing plants grew in gourd pots on shelves. When they approached the inner chamber, the sounds of many raptors chattering filled their ears.

The sanctum of the harpy aerie was well lit by natural skylights. Rainwater dripped down into clear ponds with aquatic plants and rare fish. There were shelves and stalagmite perches for thousands of occupants, but only a few hundred remained. The harpy chatter died off at the arrival of the Holy Hounds. Red eyes followed their progress to the high center perch, where the only hen sat.

The grand female harpy had the head, shoulders and breast of a woman, while the rest of her was a proud bird of prey. She wore beaded decorations made by the males. They hung from her neck, veiling her bare chest. Rusty brown flowing hair draped past shoulders and down her feathery back. The leader of the last true harpies watched the Holy Hounds closely as they approached.

Kai nodded politely to their host. "We are able to seek audience with you now, Great Harpy."

The ancient being nodded. Her voice was almost musical with powerful magic: "Of that, I am glad." Looking at Oryn and the shape that gently destroyed his flesh, she grew grave. "Can she hear us, warrior who speaks on behalf of the Heir?"

Oryn heard Adwen's voice as if she were beside him.

"I can hear and see everything around us."

It confused Oryn because the others did not appear to have heard. The harpy patiently waited for an answer.

Finally, the knight nodded. "She can hear us well."

This relieved some of the bird woman's tension. "Very good. We will help you reach the castle. It travels farther from our coast.

There is a single thing in return we require."

"Name it."

The stare from the harpy woman burned. "Kill the tainted mothers of the lost flock."

Oryn grimaced, and Kai wore an uncomfortable look.

She took notice and spoke before they could interject: "They are the ones making the castle fly. The fallen harpy hens reside in the dungeons, where they spin magical songs and lay black eggs."

Some of the bird soldiers made low, guttural sounds of anger.

The twins exchanged hard glances, and the knight spoke plainly: "Restoring Adwen is of the most importance. There is no greater need than this."

She frowned. "I understand, but I do not think you know the risks of leaving the hens to brood."

Kai corrected her assumption: "I know quite well what the risks are. The dark harpies are contagious."

Oryn, Jack and Alexander were horrified.

"Left to their own devices, the darkness would have them infect the world."

The harpy nodded gravely. "Yes, they would. Slay the mothers. Destroy them, and you destroy the nest that shields them from the sun. The last of the fallen will wither in the light."

Oryn heard Adwen's voice in his ears: "She's right. We have to try."

Everyone else saw the heart on his throat blink with soft light.

He relayed what he saw fit to say: "Adwen is willing, but we make no promises." The knight sensed Adwen's frustration at his denying a promise to the harpies.

Kai detected the conflict and cleared the air: "However, we will make every effort to do what you ask. That is what we can promise."

The grand female smiled. "The word of the Heir and her chosen warriors is good. It is surely in the favor of the Light Spirits, the Maker, Master of Creation. My warriors will take you now, but they cannot fight for long against the Lost Flock. Be swift. They will await your call above the clouds, where the fallen cannot fly."

The four nodded, and Adwen's heart flickered in approval.

While a team of armored harpies with protective masks glided down, the youthful harpy hen began to sing a melody. The magic in her song caused etchings on the armor to shimmer with many colors. The wooden plates became harder than steel, then she nodded.

"Go, and Light be with you."

Beneath a sea of clouds, Moonset Bastion soared for miles over turbulent waves. Dark Harpies perched along flying buttresses like vultures. Black essence dripped from their beaks and wept from multicolored eyes. The darkness imbued in their flesh knew a second assault was inevitable. It made the creatures sit patiently clutching spears and bows.

By noon, the true harpy warriors caught up with the flying fortress. They skimmed the tops of clouds under the protection of the sun. When the scout rose above to report, he trilled.

The others returned the sharp call. Four of the beings carried the warriors by their armor. In a tight formation, they swooped after the scout. They sped through cloud cover, picking up speed until the wind pressed on their faces like rejecting hands.

A familiar Harpy Guard came alongside clutching a spear. He called to the companions, "Be ready. Entering the stone nest will not be a gentle landing."

None of the warriors minded.

"Do what you must to protect your kin," Kai replied.

The bird creature nodded, then trilled to the formation. They trilled in reply and donned primitive face shields made of fused broken glass. The instant the flock appeared above the castle spires, the dark harpies screamed and took flight. Arrows darted upward with the rabid calls.

Taking tight turns in a sweeping spiral, the flock carried the warriors downward. When the fallen flew up to intercept, the flock split into two formations. One group whisked the Holy Hounds aside, as the larger formation played the role of decoy. They lured the fallen ones into giving chase.

The warriors braced themselves, drawing weapons as their carriers swooped alongside large windows. A formation of fallen ones dove at them. The harpies sounded a sharp warning call before tossing their loads into the castle. Oryn, Kai, Jack and Alexander crashed through windows, landing nimbly in the hall. Outside, the harpies and the fallen flock collided.

Kai could not look, but the others stole a glance. Fallen ones that got close enough vomited black filth in the faces of the harpies. The puke broke one harpy's visor loose, allowing the vile substance into its eyes. He writhed in agony before the black essence consumed him. In seconds, he became one of the fallen. He turned on his brethren summoning evil weaponry.

Kai barked, "Move it!"

Oryn roared in outrage before bolting to seek Adwen's body. Kai led Jack and Alexander to slay the brooding harpy hens.

Using their combined psychic abilities, Kai and Jack searched for the dungeon. With telekinesis, the dark-haired warrior sensed the flow of the structure. Soon they found the stairs downward. They darted into the dark, where black filth coated the walls and steps, and quickly detected tainted minds. Then the three moved more carefully into the enemy's den.

Kai whispered, "This is going to be very dangerous. Their songs can bewitch. Alexander, use your ability to fight without thought. Let your mind sink into itself. Jack, I'm going to teach you a little trick. It's the only way we are going to survive."

Jack was unsure whether to be excited or uneasy.

Oryn sprinted to the ballroom, where Adwen's body was left behind. Sounds from a terrible aerial battle outside spurred him faster. Their harpy allies could not last long in a headlong assault.

"Don't worry about them."

Hearing Adwen's voice surprised him after such a long silence.

"Their leader did not cheat us," Adwen reassured her knight. "She sent her best. They know what they are doing. Trust them."

It was easier said than done after seeing what the fallen could do. Oryn feared the small flock could be turned against them.

"Trust them," she repeated more firmly. When she spoke again, her tone was urgent. "Demon ahead!"

Oryn gritted his teeth and fangs, growling, "I smell them."

When the knight reached the hall before the ballroom, he skidded to an abrupt stop. The sight of a hulking monstrosity made him snarl and grip the Rose Thorn with both hands. This would not be an easy enemy to defeat.

A heavy-set demon covered in rough scaled armor crouched like a tank blocking the closed bronze doors. Red eyes shone behind a thick horned helm, giving the many armed fiend the guise of a wicked beetle.

While sneering, he murmured to her, "I may need your help."

"Oryn, I can't."

Surprised, he did not like her fearful tone. The knight snapped back as the fiend charged, "Can't or won't?"

Adwen couldn't respond to this new dilemma.

Oryn transformed, as the thundering fiend bore down on him raising four swords. With a swing of his own blade, he deflected two sword blows, then two others with a barrier-cloaked hand. The fiend kept marching forward. Despite Oryn's efforts to leap aside, he was tackled by the heavy juggernaut and bowled over.

Hypnotic voices sang in harmony from four harpy hens.

Jack struggled with the rapid-fire instructions from Kai on how to project images into the minds of others. He caught on, though Oryn's twin was far more skilled.

<Are you sure about this?>

<You have enough power to do this. I'll project at the two on my side, and you handle the pair on yours.>

<This is crazy. I can barely do it to you, and I can't even get Jarhead to hear me in his head. How am I supposed to project images and sounds into their two minds at once?>

<There's no time. The harpies and Oryn are counting on us. So, what's it going to be?>

Jack scowled.

Alexander disliked the look of things.

Kai spoke to the Marine with his mind: <We move on your mark. Once you're confident you're deaf and numb, charge ahead. Jack and I will bring them down. You finish them off. If you've got it, thumbs up.>

The Marine frowned and raised two fingers in a rude British gesture.

Kai would have laughed any other time. <Close enough.

Whenever you're ready, Yank.>

Roger that, he bitterly thought to the eagle-eyed Holy Hound.

Unaware of the stalkers, the tainted harpy matrons danced as they sang. Black ooze wet their lips and drooled down chins and necks. Among them, several fallen soldiers stood guard. Dozens of glistening eggs sat on the floor, oozing from the darkness within the hens that had laid them.

A loud snarl made the bird beings turn and stare. As soon as they saw the heavily armored Holy Hound, the guards swooped and the matrons sang louder. Their harmony became a threatening acapella meant to frighten and disable Alexander.

The powerful warrior could not hear them. He fought several bird men at once, while the matrons sang even louder. They could no longer hear over their own voices, as Jack and Alexander made their move.

Flanking the wretched bird women, the warriors focused hard on showing the one image they could imagine would frighten the creatures most. Kai was first to manipulate his targets. Before their blackened eyes, the bird women saw the ceiling crumble away and the sun come blazing through. It was blindingly brilliant. Right away the pair flailed and screamed, losing focus on their songs.

Jack tried his hardest, but he was able only to make his two targets see the ceiling crumbling. It was enough to make them falter in their pitch and stare.

All four were distracted. Jack sent his daggers flying, and Kai bounded on weak gusts from their wings. They barely supported his weight, but he was fast enough to run up them like a downward escalator. At once, Kai slashed alongside the twin daggers.

A hen lost its head and another a wing. Kai gutted one and maimed another. Alexander finished off the guards a second later and plowed through the eggs to slay the mothers. All three worked to catch the confounded creatures as they flailed. A moment later, blades silenced them for good.

As quiet returned to the desecrated dungeon, Jack and Alexander heaved sighs of relief that the plan had worked. Kai, on the other hand, was wary. Confused, Alexander asked, "They were singing to keep this place flying. Why doesn't it feel like we're falling yet?"

That was the same thought what bothered Kai.

Jack mused, "Where is that humming coming from?"

Frantic, Kai yelped, "Jack, no!"

It was too late. The warrior swayed. His grip on the daggers loosened, and they dropped to the ground by his feet. Alexander joined Kai in watching in horror as Jack awkwardly tilted his head, making a ravenous growl. He gazed at them baring teeth, and his eyes turned black under the spell of the remaining tainted harpies.

The yellow hound whined to his friend, "Jack? Bad Dog? Can you hear me? This is not funny, little buddy."

Kai growled grimly, "I'm afraid he's quite serious."

Transforming into hound form, Jack salivated profusely with wrinkled jaws. A moment later, his telekinetic powers took hold of all the black weapons scattered about the dungeon. The sharp shafts and blades floated upward and aimed at his astonished companions.

In a split second, Kai gave Alexander instruction: <I'll stall him a moment. You'll be on your own for a bit.>

The big yellow Holy Hound yelped in reply, "What?"

Jack roared, sending a storm of dark weaponry flying in for the kill. Tossing up a bubble barrier, Kai shielded them both and sent an image into Jack's mind. For a few seconds, his enslaved mind saw Oryn come from nowhere to cut him down.

The dreamlike vision made him snarl in anger. He withdrew the collection of weapons to form a bladed shield too thick to see through. Before Alexander could argue, Kai darted off using telepathy to track the remaining harpies.

He barked after him, "Wait!" Then Jack's agitated growling brought his attention back, and he cursed under his breath.

Kai knew sense of smell was useless. Black filth drowned out all other odors. He considered staying to hold his friend off indefinitely, but time was working against everyone. Not one second could go to waste, and Alexander was not as well suited for finding the harpies.

As Kai grew anxious, he detected a pair of hazy minds filled with primitive dark thoughts. Using the link like radar, Kai raced against the clock. A pair of wicked harpies perched on a steel chandelier in an old guardsmen feast hall. One sang to Jack, while the other kept the castle in the sky. The instant Kai found them, he launched a psychic bombardment. They screamed and flapped.

The ground quaked, as the bird women flailed and Kai pounced.

Oryn struggled to dodge the abominable fiend's weapons. He could not overcome this villain alone.

"This one has no exploitable weakness!" he told Adwen. "Help me."

She wept within her heart, as she watched him failing. "I can't do it."

Thrown against another wall like a toy, Oryn managed to stay on his feet. He squeezed his sword tighter, snarling.

"I know you," he growled. "Your tone betrays you. You can help me fight. Help me now!" The knight hound dodged a devastating attack, then slashed. His blade did not even scratch the dense armor. The demon backhanded him, sending him in a backward tumble.

Adwen's heart cringed, seeing and feeling his pain.

Oryn picked himself up as the monster returned. "I need you, now!"

She refused to even speak.

"Now, Adwen!" He ducked, dodged and deflected several swings of blades before being struck again. This time he was stunned. Fighting to get up again, the knight begged, "Help me, Adwen."

"I don't want to hurt you!" she cried.

The dark juggernaut sheathed a sword and grabbed Oryn by his sword arm, pinning him high against the wall. Though he realized why she denied him assistance, he did not change his mind. The hound knight bared his fangs at the mighty demon, as it took aim to impale him.

He barked urgently, "Just do it!"

Adwen cried out in despair. Her energy swelled and spread through Oryn's body, using it as a conduit. She blasted out a mighty tendril of light, striking the evil swords. Though she stopped the blades, she felt what her power did to the knight.

While watching Adwen's light strike the demon it felt as if a thousand blades ripped at his insides. The hound gasped wide-eyed and quivered in agony. When she sent out another blast at the monster, her incredible energy made Oryn squirm. His breaths became short and rapid. It was almost unbearable. She used multiple tendrils of light to swat away the monster's arms, forcing it drop her knight. When Oryn slumped onto the floor, he shifted into his elf-like form.

The demon bellowed and pounced, thrusting its swords toward both hearts at once.

Adwen no longer hesitated. She ensnared all four of the monster's arms. Yet another tendril gripped the horns on its helm to hold it still.

The pain was too much for Oryn. He whimpered, unable to take the easy kill. With no alternative, Adwen took command of his body. She made him rise to his feet and drive the Rose Thorne deep through one of the only openings in the armor – the eye holes.

The knight was just aware enough to perceive what was happening. She did as he had asked. It felt as if they both drove the sword in together. Because he wanted to twist his blade to finish off the demon more quickly, she sensed his desire and made his hand give a hard, merciless twist. The monster roared, and they drove the sword deeper, forcing the fiend to slump to its knees.

It was not dead yet, and they hollered in unison, enduring the pain together. They withdrew the sword and punched it through the other eye with all their might. Their grip held firm, waiting for the juggernaut to fall.

For a long moment, the demon shuddered on the end of the blade. At last, it gasped and rolled backward off the sword, collapsing in a heap of dark flesh and metal. It tumbled into the ballroom doors, throwing them wide open.

Adwen withdrew her energy. The pain did not end, and they both dropped to their knees. She relinquished control gradually because she could sense Oryn was weakened. The knight coughed violently, struggling to breathe. Feeling sick, he buckled and spat up on the floor and down his front. Both were startled to see a puddle of blood.

Her weeping renewed, and he shivered, beginning to see how little time they had left.

Gaining control of his breaths, Oryn felt relief at seeing the way clear. "It will be alright. I can last long enough to put you back."

Nevertheless, Adwen was inconsolable after what she put him through.

On wobbly legs, the knight hiked over the body of the slain

demon. Dropping down on the other side, they looked out across the ballroom to the pedestal. What was there made them freeze.

Jack blinked and shook his head to dispel the strange fog. Then he flinched at the sight of Alexander lying against a pile of wooden debris. Dozens of black blades, spears and arrows penetrated the planks. The Marine lay in human form, eyes wide, staring at the ceiling. Jack panicked.

"Alex!"

Leaping to his friend's side, the warrior became frantic. "No, no, no!"

Alexander's head slowly turned to gaze at him in horror.

Weakly, Jack asked, "Jarhead?"

The Marine blinked in disbelief. "Jack?"

Confounded, he stared in silence. Then Jack received a hard punch to the face and he barked and whined. "What the hell was that for!"

Alexander heaved a sigh. "Oh, good. You're you again."

"Wait a minute. You're not hurt? I thought you were dead."

"Yes, and remind me to never make you mad."

The ground under them began to tremble. They stared at each other in realization, just as Kai ran in to find them.

"Come on, you lot! It's time to go!"

The ballroom lay bare and burnt from the previous battle. Adwen's body sealed in stone was gone.

At a loss, the knight's face slackened, and his stare grew vacant. Beginning to walk slowly toward the pedestal, his grip on the sword grew weak. Dazed, the knight could no longer hold his blade, and it fell with a resounding clang. His weary feet kept walking sluggishly. A familiar silence filled his head, as chills of fear washed over him.

Coming to the pedestal, Oryn stumbled and braced himself on it, gazing at the emptiness it held – much like what he felt inside. The knight screwed his face up and wailed a deafening cry that rang in the windy ballroom. He felt Adwen crying within her heart.

Oryn drew a deep rattling breath and continued to stare into an invisible abyss. His mind became hushed.

A coarse, bitter voice muttered from nearby, "So, it comes down to this."

The knight wobbled as he turned and snarled up at Impurus. The abomination sat atop a stone facet like a gargoyle. Arms folded, he watched the knight with the golden heart attached to his now severely bruised neck. A passive smile spread across the fiend's face.

"I can relate to that desolate feeling I see in you both."

Oryn scowled, and Adwen's heart stopped weeping, as the monster jumped and fluttered to a spot several paces away. Impurus did not attack, so they both wondered what his intentions were.

After studying them, he added with a bitter scoff, "That's right. I'm not attacking – not just yet. I hate you, Conrad, and I hate the Tame One even more."

The knight growled, and a small flame puffed from the heart of gold.

"But I hate my masters the most. They control me much like she can control you. Ironic, isn't it? I'll make you both a deal. If you can free me from their control, I will tell you where they took her body."

Oryn growled, "You lie."

Adwen spoke with a grim tone: "He's telling the truth."

The knight stared in shock. Impurus could see in Oryn's face that he understood.

"My binding makes it impossible for me to simply tell you where her body is. I must be free from them. Free my will. Free my soul, and I will betray them for you both to spite them."

Adwen and Oryn's wills fused, and they spoke as one: "We can free your will, but not your soul. It is theirs. That cannot be undone. You must die."

The vile creature shrugged. "That suits me just as well. However, I cannot simply let you kill me. You understand. Not to mention, you and I have a score to settle, Sir Oryn Reynard Conrad."

Oryn continued to growl, and Adwen's energy fluctuated in anger. It tore at him a little more, making him heave wet coughs. Blood droplets flew past his chapped lips.

Summoning his jagged sword, Impurus grinned. "End me, then end them for me." He lunged to attack.

They spoke in unison with combined wills: "Not for you or

for spite." Adwen and Oryn dove aside and sprung up again. Impurus missed them and instead destroyed the pedestal. "But for everything against such things."

Impurus continued to grin. "Either way, my wish will be granted. Now, face me and slay me."

The knight spat, "Fine."

Adwen hardened. With righteous wrath she coldly replied as well: "Fine."

She summoned all her power, and the knight endured the agony. The immense energy made his body transform and ripped at him until he grew numb. No longer in anguish, they unified their wills, sharing command over a vast amount of light power.

Impurus sneered, shielding his eyes, while energy flowed out from the heart. It wrapped about the hound warrior's armor, cloaking his whole form. Streaming ribbons like auroras extended from his back in waving strands. Oryn and Adwen combined bore the likeness of a white dragon. The golden heart at his throat shone like a luminous pendant, and the angry green eyes burned just as bright.

The demon bellowed, taking flight.

The combined beings roared and leaped after him.

While Impurus breathed balls of fire, the shining creature's claws raked marble as easily as loose soil. Blood wept from the crushing jaws, and the intense light made it shine, sparkling like wispy stars on every breath. The noble creature cloaked in light and fire swatted the purple flames away with green barriers, and continued to give chase. When they drew closer to the demon, the rainbow streams of light on their back whipped forward like many scorpion stingers. They punched holes in the demon's broad venous wings, making the fiend shriek.

Impurus rolled in midflight, swinging his blade at the deadly ribbons. No matter how many he cut back, the extensions mended, while the rest continued to strike. There were too many. Like a frightened swallow, he darted upward to escape their reach.

The white creature clung to a pillar, roaring up at their prey. The monster puffed fireballs over and over at them to no effect. While they held fast to the stones the flowing ribbons deflected the attacks. Angry, Impurus bellowed and dove at them to breathe a column of fire. They took a deep breath as well.

Impurus flinched and swallowed his flames. He realized what

they intended and tried to fly away. His wings beat vigorously, straining to get clear.

The white creature blew a pillar of gold and blue flames. Blood turned pale and sparkled about the column while it surged. As the demon flew wildly to avoid the holy fire, they turned their head, continuing to unleash a storm upon the fiend.

Impurus tried to escape their reach. His wings beat as hot wind swept up from beneath. The draft was followed by searing pain along his tail and legs. He continued to fly higher, face set in a grimace. But his wings were burning. Then the monster began to fall.

While the demon dropped as a mess of burnt flesh, the white shining creature leaped from the pillar. Landing on two feet, the light tendrils on its back waved as it waited to see if Impurus could still resist. Once the monster landed with a dull thud and his blood splattered the ground, they saw he was but a head and torso. Both forearms were burnt away up to the elbows. The purple demon flesh that remained began to liquify.

Adwen and Oryn relinquished the light powers. Bright white and colors faded into the confines of the golden heart, and the knight took on his more human guise. Skin across most of his face was black and blue. Emerald eyes were severely bloodshot but remained bright and focused on Impurus, dying in a pool of his own tainted fluids.

They watched him as he breathed in rattling gasps. The demon flesh melted away, revealing his human face beneath it. Raising his head with great effort, Jacques smiled sickeningly, reaching out with a mutilated arm to beckon them close.

The knight sneered, but Adwen made him approach, kneel low and take hold of the demonic chest-armor. Drawing near, both listened to the damned human whisper with his final breath, "They took her ... to where Vlad was made."

Oryn wore an icy cold look of indifference.

Jacques tried to laugh but did not have the strength. He choked on more blood as his eyes started to roll back. A long, relaxed gasp issued from his lips. His head hung limp, lolling.

As they set him down, the ground shook violently. Adwen and Oryn were not bothered; it no longer mattered. As the castle began to plummet toward the sea, they took brisk strides to the hole in the wall, where turbulent winds increased with the speed of the structure's descent. To signal their feathery allies, they howled.

It took a moment for two harpy warriors to arrive. Adwen and Oryn leaped out into their friendly talons. As soon as they were being carried away, they closed their eyes. Adwen let the knight's world go dark once more.

Kai called out to his brother as the harpies set him down on the ledge by the aerie. He and the other Holy Hounds gathered around, while the bird warriors laid the knight down. Oryn had the look of a man who had been beaten and left for dead.

Most of the harpies survived the mission including the oldest. The ancient immortal warrior approached Kai.

"I must deliver word: Our leader commanded that you are still guests and should be treated as such. What is your wish?"

Kai was unable to tear his gaze from his brother. Blood trickled from Oryn's nose to his mouth, and Kai weakly answered, "We must not move him any farther."

The noble harpy nodded. "Those who wish to rest within are welcome." Trilling to his warriors, the creature led them inside to report to the grand harpy.

Jack knelt low over the knight and reached to check his vitals. Before he could touch him, Kai snapped. "Don't." He swallowed a lump in his throat and added, "I don't want to know."

Grimacing, Jack touched Oryn's forehead instead. "He's still warm."

This was some relief. "Thank you, Jack. Would the two of you prefer to wait inside?"

Jack and Alexander understood he was asking to be left alone. Neither wanted to impose and obliged without argument. The pair entered the tunnel to the inner sanctum.

Kai stood at Oryn's feet, gazing down. The knight lay reclined against a stone covered in moss and vines, as if asleep. It was easier for the moment to believe that his brother slumbered in peace free of pain. The warrior mage took a seat on another stone padded with moss. His eagle stare watched Oryn for a while, then looked away to the jungle. Winds whistled, dulling the clamor of animal calls below.

"It's strange," Kai murmured to Oryn regardless of whether he could hear. "We've had many days alongside each other, but it feels like I've only had you back for a moment." He shook his head. "Vaughn warned me. He said not to waste time. I cannot help but think that I've squandered it somehow. I could have tried harder to tell you. Maybe then it would not feel like your presence had been spoiled by my being so afraid – afraid of you hating me. Did I let you down by not believing that you could believe me?"

The knight was unresponsive, while the golden heart at his throat glimmered softly. Kai could not read Oryn's mind or sense Adwen's will. No reply came, so he looked away. "Perhaps I have. I know you take the blame for not realizing who I was. I am more to blame. I failed to tell you." Tears shone like glass. "I wasted our time."

"Kai." Oryn's voice was weak and hoarse.

Astonished, the mage warrior gave a start and stared at the knight's deathly face. He was aghast he was able to speak.

The knight's face was sad and confused. "Kai, where are the stars?"

He held his breath at the strange question. Looking up at the sky, it was late afternoon. Sunset would not come for almost an hour. Tears filled Kai's gaze, as he turned to stare, ashamed for squandering their days. Oblivious to Kai's actions, Oryn's eyes saw only darkness. The pupils and whites of his eyes were scarlet around his green glowing irises. Bloody teardrops trailed down his cheeks and were chilled by a passing breeze.

Confused by the emptiness, the knight murmured, "I can't see them."

Chapter 33
DEATH CANNOT KILL

Adwen wept unseen within her heart. She alone bore the horror of knowing what she had done. Watching the brothers, as Kai lamented that Oryn was rendered blind, filled her with sorrow. Only she sustained his life force. Like the knight's eyes, the rest of him was destroyed beyond repair. Inside, much of him was reduced to swirling reservoirs of blood. When Oryn exhaled with ragged lungs, red vapor suspended on his breath.

The knight felt nothing of his mortal condition. All pain was gone. He began to understand when it dawned on him why the stars were gone. Oryn sensed both Adwen and Kai's distress. Knowing the simple question brought them pain made him feel guilty. He took pity on them and did not ask anything more. He tried to stand, and his body could not move.

Adwen took control, entwining their wills so he could get up. Kai leapt to brace his twin but found he was stable. Oryn felt the hands about his shoulders. He paused to sniff but only smelled blood. By instinct, he knew it was his brother. Speaking was difficult, as the tender cords in his throat were severely damaged.

With a faint raspy voice, he said, "We must go."

Unsure if it were his brother speaking, Kai hesitated. "Adwen?"

The knight sensed her feelings. "She will not speak."

She wept silently.

Frowning, Kai cautiously released him.

"Where are the others?" Oryn asked.

"They entered the aerie to wait."

The knight was determined and his faint voice firm: "Enough

waiting. We know where they took her body."

Kai blanched at the news. Again, Oryn sensed Kai's reactions. His frown deepened into one of frustration. "We must act quickly, before they realize that her location has been betrayed."

Snapping out of the daze, Kai weakly replied, "Of course." He could not help but gasp when Oryn walked as if he could see and entered the tunnel.

Adwen guided his movements. They heard Kai following and their feelings diverged from each other. She was very solemn, but Oryn chose indifference. The knight's mind set on one thing only: restore Adwen so she may defeat the demon overlord. It was the single reason he still drew breath, and Oryn embraced that purpose proudly.

Jack and Alexander smelled them coming and jumped to their feet. The harpies stared. The companions were glad to reunite, but then they grimaced. All who looked upon the knight knew he was already dead. Crimson tears traced fine lines down his battered face. Dried blood collected around his nostrils and lips. Adwen halted her knight, so he knew they had arrived.

Detecting the air about the chamber, Oryn's hard frown held. "Grand Harpy, we must leave this place. We are grateful for all you and your flock have done."

Though the bird woman's face was as blank as a mask, her stare glinted with admiration for the noble creature bound for death. There was no fear in him, no reluctance. She nodded, then smiled. "Same to you and especially to the Heir of Darien. Child of Light, we thank you for your efforts and that of your brave warriors. May the Great Light shine bright on you all."

Adwen sufficed to reply by flickering rather than using Oryn for speech. The harpy woman nodded, recognizing the gesture.

Jack watched Oryn apprehensively. He could not read his mind. It was as if he was not there. The discovery disturbed him. "Where are we going?"

"Back."

Before the many faces of the earie, Adwen extended streams of light from her place at Oryn's neck. As she summoned the powers of the Gray Blade to make a portal, even more blood ran from the knight's eyes. Blue fire appeared out of thin air, slowly expanding into a large ring. Through it they saw sunset colors washing over the abandoned manufacturing facility. Orange and gold masked the building with warmth that vastly contradicted the darkness within.

The knight walked through the portal and into bright afternoon sunshine. The others joined him on the other side, and he came to a stop. As the portal vanished, Oryn's eyes blindly set on the evil place. Fine crimson lines ran down his face.

The three other warriors studied the facility's windows, then looked to the knight. Kai remained somber, Jack wore a pitying expression, and Alexander frowned. They waited for the knight's final instruction.

His faint voice was stern as he spoke: "We will enter alone."

Everyone flinched but did not argue.

"Once it is done, she must be taken far from this place. Adwen will attain her full potential upon being returned to her body. However, she is in no condition to fight – not now."

The warriors understood. Jack nodded, and the light flickered in the heart as Adwen sobbed soundlessly.

"Be swift in taking her away. I am certain she will not be easily coaxed into leaving without a fight. Adwen is in no state to listen to reason."

Intense emotions made her energy swell as she wanted to scream. Strings of golden light emerged from the heart, winding about the knight's neck, shoulders and chest. Adwen did not want to let him go. The others saw the way the light clung to his armor, though he showed no reaction.

Kai did not want to ask but knew he must: "And what of you?"

Oryn took pity on them, but remained stern: "My body is of no value. Leave it."

Everyone grimaced, and Kai wept a few tears. Immediately, the knight sensed this and was angry.

"I am not dead yet. I feel no pain! Do not forget our purpose. If you fail to protect her, so help me, I will find you all in the afterlife and make you wish for the Void!"

They were still as stone, gazing back in shock.

"Am I understood?"

Jack growled miserably, and Alexander whimpered.

Kai muttered with a cracking voice, "Yeah."

The knight spat, "Good." Taking a moment to query

Adwen's will, he sensed it was frail. Because she was so entwined with him, the strength to walk became his own. Without a word, Oryn began the blind trek, letting Adwen keep the course true.

They approached the tall chain-link fence, and fine tendrils of energy lashed out. The tendrils cut the wires and tore the fence open wide. Sharp ends glowed red hot and smoked as he walked past. After crossing the parking lot, he came to the doors. The knight saw only darkness, and Adwen burned a hole through steel and glass so he could enter.

He strode purposefully through the darkness as if he were in the depths of the Void. He felt no fear. Adwen led him through the invisible maze. Oryn heard her powers working, keeping the way clear; he felt the warm streams of energy embracing him. The tendrils could cut most anything like butter, yet they were gentle to him. Oryn doubted that even the Gray Kingdom could strip away his memories of his time in the dark realm. Yet in this journey through nothingness, Adwen was with him. She had been and still was his light in the dark.

Reaching the supply lift in the smelting factory, she stopped Oryn and commanded the platform to take them below. Red lights flashed and buzzers sounded before the enormous lift jarred to life. Their descent began with the silencing of the alarms. With nothing to do, Adwen quaked.

He sensed her lament. Finally, he began to soften. "So, this is why."

She spoke to him at last: "What is?"

"Why you can control our bodies. It was in case you might need us for this purpose."

Adwen was stunned. Realizing he was correct made her pain all the greater. Oryn smiled contentedly. Perhaps, he thought, the Light Spirits designed his fate because he was the one who was closest to her heart. All the Holy Hounds were willing to lay down their lives for her, but he would always be the first to leap at the chance. It seemed appropriate. By being this willing sacrifice, he could atone at long last.

The lift reached bottom, and the doors opened wide. Adwen let him continue forward and could not keep silent any longer.

"Oryn?"

"Yes, Adwen."

She wished to cry. Her strings of light swayed like dragon

whiskers about the knight's body. They illuminated him in the unlit underground hallways.

"I ... I don't want you to go."

"I know."

They were almost to the bay doors. Both could sense pure darkness waiting beyond.

"What am I supposed to do? Please, Oryn, ask me not to let go."

He was silent.

"Tell me not to let you go."

"You must let me go."

Oryn heard her start to cry.

He insisted, "This cannot continue. You must be able to wield the Gray Blade, and I cannot stay. Borrowed time not returned becomes stolen. Neither of us can afford to pay for such an atrocity. I must go. Please, Adwen. When the moment comes, let me go."

"I can't."

The knight walked into the vast facility, filled with burnt corpses and scorched metal. It stank of rotting flesh and smoke, but Oryn could not smell it. Instead, he sensed the arrival of the kings among demons. Five white-eyed shadows with fearsome shapes emerged from portals on the floor and walls. They stood tall like wicked monuments as high as watchtowers. Horns, spikes and sinister wings grazed the ceiling crossbeams.

Beyond the terrible gathering, Adwen's pearly stone body glowed, frozen in a desperate reaching pose. Her hand extended toward them and past the demon lords brandishing evil weapons. Oryn came to a halt of his own accord and frowned.

They hissed, anticipating the wrath of the light within the heart he carried. She grew uncertain, but her knight did not waver.

He spoke to the great shadows defiantly: "You know no fear, demons."

Whispered curses buzzed on their voices. The knight smiled slyly.

"In your own way, you do fear. I can smell nothing else beside that stench. Every one of you reeks of it."

His accusations riled the shadows, making them spit more vile words.

"You are responsible for the awakening of everyone's nightmares. Now it is time to awaken your own. I'll waste no more precious breath on such filth."

They began to creep forward but recoiled at the sight of Adwen's heart, shining like a star. Some shielded their eyes shrieking in anger. Adwen flashed brightly to keep them back a little longer. Every second Oryn remained she felt her fire burning. Adwen needed him and desperately wanted to keep him always.

Oryn cupped a gentle hand over the warm golden heart. Feeling her, he smiled happily. "I'm such a damned fool, Adwen. No matter what happens, promise me you will remember something for me. Even if I forget, I want you to remember."

She wept, breathless, "What?"

He dug the sharp points of his gauntlets into his own flesh and pulled hard. Adwen's light burst loose and his blood flowed down his armor in a cascade of red. The heart in his fist turned to a ball of condensed light brighter than a sun, emitting streams of light that waved wildly. As he pulled his arm back to throw her, he felt at peace.

"I love you."

Adwen screamed as the knight threw her. Tendrils of light ran through his fingers, as she took flight like a bird. She tried to keep hold of him, but all her power could not grab his hand quickly enough. The final strands of light slipped between his fingers, and his life went with her.

She watched him fall in what seemed like slow motion. The demon lords tried to strike her out of the air. They were swift but could not catch her with blades, spears or whips. In an instant, she reached her body, and an explosion shook the earth. The demons shielded themselves with black shrouds against the blast. When it ended, they shrieked in outrage.

Adwen picked herself up, gazing franticly at the fallen warrior. She gave no care to the shadows that wanted to kill her. They did not matter anymore.

The demon lords summoned flasks of darkness drawn from the Black Lake. They lobbed them at her to blind her. She made no effort to flee or retaliate. Instead, her power flared, and the evil containers shattered over a powerful barrier of hidden flames. Anything that struck it evaporated, leaving her free to stare at the knight. The monsters paused, appalled at their failure.

Adwen could not accept the loss of Oryn. Tears filled her eyes while she stared at him, lying on the floor among the burnt and impaled victims. In a blinding flash, she blinked, instantly reappearing at Oryn's side, beyond the reach of the towering monsters. The swiftness and brightness of the action angered the shadows, making them shriek, bellow and hiss.

It was difficult for Adwen to breathe. Oryn lay on his face at her feet. Blood continued to flow. The growing crimson pool stopped before her toes, boiling away in contact with her barrier. Adwen could not sense him. Once before, she had thought he was dead. Slowly she knelt low, begging the Light Spirits that this might be like that time again. Her heart yearned to hear him draw breath and reach for her as she reached for him. Slowly reaching out for his head, Adwen anticipated the knight to stir in her presence.

The demon lords kept their distance but could not resist chuckling at her anguish.

Her fingers hovered an inch above his hair. She could not bring herself to touch him. For a moment, she waited, but nothing happened. Oryn did not move. There was no life left.

Adwen gasped rapidly, and breaths quickly became heaving. Agony leaped from her throat to a wail of anger. In an instant, the Gray Blade roared with fire into her outstretch hand. She clutched it tightly. Unable to set it to his body, Adwen's pain turned into blinding wrath. She blinked through the air screaming at the top of her voice, swinging the sword at the demons who jeered and laughed.

They deflected her deadly blows. She leaped to and fro, fighting all of them at once. The bereft frenzy rendered Adwen senseless. Tears floated about her face within the flaming light barrier. The monstrous fiends smashed and slashed in retaliation, laughing, feeding her ravenous lament. Each strike that hit the barrier sent Adwen tumbling, but she rebounded, sobbing and bellowing battle cries. Their glee and her pain fanned the fire and darkness until Adwen was vulnerable. The barrier began to crack, and flames flicked wildly at the edges. With every devastating hit that she failed to block, her defense grew weaker.

Adwen did not care. All the tears in the world could not drown this sorrow. The one thing that could stand against it was the rage she felt for the evil ones. That fire devoured her, blinding her. If they slew her, she did not care. The others were coming, though she wished they would not arrive until her own fire extinguished, as well.

A giant blade crashed into Adwen's barrier, shattering it into a million fragments. The explosion sent her tumbling across the floor. Panting, Adwen snarled and picked herself back up, but she staggered. The pain would be gone in a few moments, when she would cease to exist. Screaming as the demons came at once from all sides, she raised her sword.

There was the loud clang of metal on metal. She blocked only three of the enemy's weapons. Regardless, she remained standing and untouched. Stunned to be alive, she watched the demon lords flinch and hiss. Something stood at her back between her and the other two monsters. While the demon lords stood frozen in shock, she looked over her shoulder and was dumbfounded.

Light coursed over the body of the eerie warrior defending her. Blood evaporated from him, as his skin turned to olive copper. His hair turned pale white, fading to emerald green at the tips. The color matched his fierce glowing eyes. Armor turned from black to gray, then green and gold under ripples of light. He held his sword high, pushing back wicked blades. The gray knight with an emerald mark on his throat roared at the monsters.

As the shadows recoiled, Adwen turned to face them once more, beginning to smile. More tears streamed from her eyes. Sorrow died, and joy roared to life within her beating heart.

Adwen roared also, transforming into her true form. While the renewed warrior pushed back at the Taskmaster and the Weaver, she assailed the Reaper, the Whisperer and the Tormentor. In a series of blinks through the air, the white Holy Hound vanished and reappeared from all sides. She slashed at the demon lords, forcing them to recoil.

Leaving her to contend with the three, Oryn snarled and transformed, as well. As a great grey and white hound, he gnashed his jaws at the demons. Degah'lee shrieked in outrage, and the Weaver hissed. Both charged again.

Beating the weapons away, the great grey hound with green runes across his coat took a deep breath. As he exhaled, a ball of green fire flew. It struck the fiend responsible for hurting Kai directly in the face. As the monster screamed, backing away, the Weaver became far more cautious. The demon lord had no desire to be made a similar example.

Oryn rumbled like a dragon, smoke issuing from wrinkled jaws.

With Degah'lee having fled, four demons remained in the underground factory. Witnessing the full power of Adwen made them desperate. The Tormenter was next to flee through a portal. The instant the fiend vanished, Adwen appeared overhead to strike at the Reaper. Kahli'nah bellowed in excitement at the grand battle, but as he swung a sickle, he found the barrier had been restored. The curved black metal bounced back, and her sword caught the exposed wrist.

In a flash of blue fire, the hand evaporated. More flames caught hold of the severed limb. The Reaper tried to flee through a portal, but the fire barred him from entering. The demon's fickle allies watched in astonishment as the fire consumed him. When Adwen rebounded to cut him down, the Reaper was unable to stop her. The white Holy Hound pounced, stabbing Kahli'nah through his core, where a heart should be. The monster fell with her and vanished in a burst of glittering dust. Pale particles shimmered in the air like crystal flecks. She looked up and snarled at the Whisperer. Her barrier and sword radiated with pale light.

The fiend leaped through a portal. A second, later the Weaver did the same, unwilling to face the shining creatures and their fire on his own. After the demons departed, the darkness eased. Peaceful stillness filled the underground chamber despite the wanton carnage.

Adwen dismissed the sword and turned with ears erect, staring at the pale hound warrior. He faced her from across the metal battlefield. The warmth in his emerald eyes was unmistakable, though disbelief gnawed at her still.

She reverted to woman form and ran to confirm that he was no illusion. Stopping a few feet away, she watched him transform. She thought he was a ghost of the departed like Tamis – that he had lingered to save her and stayed long enough to bid farewell. But as she watched, her heart raced. He did not speak, but neither did he vanish as a wisp. Surely, he would leave her again in a moment.

Oryn watched her and began to smile. Tears started to fill his eyes. The scents were real. Despite the intense stench all around, she smelled him and knew he was no ghost. No otherworldly spirit other than her had a scent.

Adwen could not move as he came close and held her face

in his hands. He dismissed the armor over them so his skin would touch hers. The hands were warm and real.

Numb with disbelief, she uttered, "How?"

Smiling with happy tears, he spoke softly. "I saw them."

She could not understand and did not care. Adwen threw herself into his arms and held him tightly, sobbing with joy.

Holding her close, he shed thankful tears. "Adwen, I saw them."

Chapter 34
MOMENT OF TRUTH

The moment the earth shook, Kai barked to his companions, and they darted into the complex. They tracked Oryn's blood trail, and more thundering booms shook the ground. Bursting into the factory and toward the lift, each warrior summoned his weapon. Leaping into the pitch-black shaft, they could feel incredible power flooding their bodies. Adwen's increased strength fed theirs. Armor and weapons shimmered with the influx.

When they reached the bottom, they prayed they were not too late. Through a series of concrete passages, the stench of decomposing burnt flesh reached them. Fearing the worst, the three dashed into the cavernous chamber and stopped to look about. Nothing moved.

Kai panted heavily from the dash, as well as panic at finding nothing. Then his mind picked up faint activity. Eyes wide, he strained to see past the poles and corpses. There was a little movement, and he gasped and bolted toward it. Jack and Alexander were on his heels, then nearly ran into him when he skidded to a stop. All three were unsure whether they were seeing a figment of their imaginations. Unable to smell anything beyond decomposing bodies, the friends inched closer.

It was Adwen, and she was with a stranger. Jack and Alexander thought it might be Darien, returned to help them. After a moment, the figures in pale armor both looked at the three warriors. Adwen, with her tearful sapphire stare, and the knight, with brilliant emerald eyes, gazed at them. Glassy droplets hung from his lashes and cheeks.

Dumbstruck, Kai dropped his sword and shuddered. He

inched forward. As he came within arm's reach, he could smell him. The smell was not the same, but the knight carried a scent, proving he was no ghost. Gasping as he grabbed the knight's arm, a gentle breeze could have knocked him flat.

Adwen began to smile when she saw how happy Kai was. She released Oryn to let him embrace his brother and keep him from falling to the floor. The knight watched his twin scarcely breathing. There was only one thing Oryn could think to say: "It is good to see you."

Kai squeezed his brother tightly. He gasped as he felt such joy that it bordered on pain. His heart quaked to be with his brother again.

Jack came closer, still confounded.

Alexander stood beside him and asked, "Oryn, is that you?"

Their gazes met, and the knight smiled. "Indeed."

The familiar response nearly bowled over the Marine. Jack swayed, so Alexander braced his short friend. Patting the cop's shoulder, he reassured him, "It's okay. We'll get through this one together, somehow."

Jack could say nothing and merely nodded.

"Many things throughout our journeys have bound me to Adwen. Some things were set into motion long before either of us were born. That is all I know as to why I have become like her."

They sat together in the sunny overlook the next morning, and Kai beamed at his brother. "I wish I could have been there to see it. You actually spat spirit fire into Degah'lee's face?"

Oryn wore a clever expression.

"Bloody brilliant."

Adwen enjoyed having Oryn's arm around her while they sat.

"Now two of the demon lords are destroyed," Kai reminded his companions. "That leaves four and the overlord."

"Sounds like a level playing field to me," Jack added. "Where do we hit them next?"

She sighed and admitted what Kai already knew: "The demon lords aren't stupid. I'm too big a threat, so they retreated to safety. We have just one place left to go."

Frowning, Kai agreed. "Beyond the Veil. We have to find a

way to enter the Gray Kingdom."

Alexander felt uneasy. "All of us?"

"Yes," Adwen replied. "All of us together. I'm strong, and so is Oryn, but we can't do it alone."

The knight grimaced. "No one has yet to enter that realm physically."

His brother chided, "Ah, but we all entered the Void in bodies and lived to tell the tale."

Jack chuckled. "Who have you told?"

Playfully shoving the warrior, Kai muttered through a grin, "Oh, come off it."

Adwen giggled, and the knight ceased frowning at Jack's poor joke to beam at her. How he enjoyed that sound.

"We need to find the door." Adwen was certain. "If the Void has one, then the Gray Kingdom does, too."

"Well, yeah, but how did you leave that realm?" Kai asked. "That would give us an idea of how to get there."

Adwen's smile wilted into a thoughtful frown. "I can't remember."

The response made Kai fall silent. When he spoke again he was gently insistent: "Could you try a might harder to remember?"

Oryn growled, smoke curdling on his breath.

His brother defended himself: "Well, this is quite serious, isn't it? Just because the Reaper is dead doesn't mean this is over. You lot saw what the Dark Heart did to the harpies."

Jack was disturbed. "He did that?"

"He's the only one who can, and, mark me, he will do it again. That shadow is having a right fit that she is whole and at full power. How are demons when they're bonkers with rage?"

Adwen replied, "We get the point, Kai. We need to finish this fast."

Satisfied, but not at ease, the warrior continued: "Only you and Darien know what is at the border between that realm and those of the living. We can't ask him for directions, can we?"

Alexander huffed. "He disappeared as quick as he showed up."

Stunned by the insinuation, Kai gawked. "You are pulling my leg? You've met Darien? Well, come on, you lot, where'd he go?"

Oryn growled again to quell Kai's berating.

"He's gone for good this time," Adwen answered ruefully. "The Master Knight isn't coming back. It's up to us now. Yet there is someone else who might know something."

Kai turned from anxious to bemused. "Are you about to say you know Arianwyn?"

She nodded.

"I'll be buggered. You know where he is?"

Adwen frowned. "I know where he was."

He got to his feet, urging her to stand. "Well, get a move on! Let's go!"

Getting up and sighing heavily, she summoned her sword and created a portal. The other side shone bright in the early morning. Trees grew taller, their leaves rustling gently as they shaded green grass. The companions walked through it and into a wild meadow.

As soon as the portal closed their faces drooped and Kai was aghast. In the young forest, they stood before the charred ruins of the gigantic Elf tree sanctuary.

"Aw, bugger it all!" Kai turned about, quickly getting his bearings. "This was the spot where the Dragon Mother first breathed her fire!"

Adwen muttered, "Yes, it is."

Alexander grimaced. "I hope he wasn't inside."

Aggravated at the dashing of his hopes, Kai growled, "He is a bloody Elf king. Not to mention, this one could see the future. Of course, he wasn't here when it happened. Probably buggered off a long while ago before any of this mess started."

"Enough, Kai," Adwen admonished her friend. "None of us is happy to find this."

He huffed and calmed himself. "Sorry."

"Let's go take a look around," she added.

They entered the burnt-out remains and spread out to search the rooms. Those who visited this place before remembered how warm and clean it was. The scents of dried herbs were gone. Everything smelled of damp soil and charcoal. Moments later, they gathered in the gutted lounge.

Adwen shook her head. "I thought so; there's nothing here."

Kai could not settle his nerves. Oryn took him to the fields below the sanctuary overlook. To distract his twin, he engaged him in an intense round of sparring. Before long, they were darting back and forth in a titanic struggle to outwit each other. Green and yellow barriers flashed in and out, and swords clashed. The twins darted about faster than any mortal eye could follow.

Jack and Alexander watched and exchanged remarks whenever one brother managed an incredible maneuver. Sitting atop a fallen log, they enjoyed the show.

Adwen did not join the two spectators. She sat high above on the ledge of the overlook. Her gaze locked with the western horizon. Deep in thought, she struggled to reimagine the spirit realm of peace. All Adwen could recall was running from demons, climbing a glowing white tree filled with wisps, and a bright light at the top flashing like a beacon.

What was that light, she wondered? No matter how long she sat contemplating hazy memories, the answers would not come. Lack of progress left Adwen dejected.

Meanwhile, the brothers clashed. Kai tried to tap into Oryn's mind, but he was changed. It was difficult to whittle his way into the knight's thoughts, much like Adwen's. The difficulty of placing illusions into Oryn's mind made for a challenging battle.

When the knight stood waiting for Kai to resume sword play, Adwen leaped down and called to them. Her voice was a distraction for a moment, as the knight looked back. Kai's eagle eyes lit up, and he lunged.

The knight's attention was not totally preoccupied. Oryn deflected the sword swing, as Kai vaulted overhead. While his twin flipped through the air, the knight saw the wild smile and knew the sparring wasn't over. The grey knight puffed green energy from his lips.

A look of shock replaced Kai's clever smile. The spirit fire wrapped around his neck. An instant later, he lay flat on the ground, pinned by spirit energy that had become as heavy as a house. Watching helplessly as Oryn pointed the sword at his throat, the warrior mage was irate.

"You bloody cheater!" Then another thought struck him. "You could have done that all the time? What a sour sod you are!"

Oryn scoffed at the protest.

Jack groaned in defeat. Alexander chuckled.

"Alright, Bad Dog. Pay up."

Adwen smiled as she approached the twins. She secretly wished she had not interrupted. They were having so much fun.

"What is it?" Oryn asked.

She shook her head. "I can't remember anything. We might as well do something else. Let's do the rounds and visit the kingdoms. I want to check on Toth and Eyrie first."

Kai picked himself up and dusted off dirt. "It would be good to pay Toady another visit."

Oryn rolled his eyes. "We both should have known who you were the moment you called him that."

He shrugged. "Not my fault you're both thick."

Jack stepped forward. "Now that I'm out fifty bucks because of you, why not? Let's have a field trip."

Adwen giggled and opened a portal.

Toth stood at the doors to the palace sanctuary thanking three harpies who had brought more fish and game. He was about to bid farewell when a portal opened a few yards away. They stared at the blue ring of fire, while Adwen and her companions stepped through.

He called to them happily, "Adwen! Oryn! It is good to see you all."

The long feathers atop the harpies' heads flicked in shock at seeing the knight. They chattered, then darted off as fast as they could to their aerie to report the news.

Toth paused to watch them go. They had been formal up until now and had never forgotten to greet or bid good-bye. Then, as his friends drew near, he too was astounded. The cloak of vines on his mantle rustled.

Adwen smiled and made way for the pleasantly surprised Elf as he came to inspect the twins. She and the brothers found this greeting amusing. Toth did not know which twin to examine first. Oryn seemed so different, and yet the other one's appearance was just as shocking. Going to Kai, Toth reached to put a hand on him.

Kai reached out faster. He clapped a hand on Toth's shoulder, making him flinch.

Chuckling at Toth's look of astonishment, Kai smiled. "Your

eyes don't deceive anyone, Toady. It's really me. And you don't need to touch me to believe it."

Toth muttered weakly through a happy smile, "Stars above ..." Then he looked at Oryn. "You are just as changed, my friend."

"Only in some ways," the knight replied.

"Words escape me. This is ... this is beyond anything I could have imagined."

Adwen called his attention to the present before it could wander: "How is everyone doing?"

"Better," Toth replied. "Very well, in fact. There are no sick or injured who have not been cured since Oryn's help. What brings you here?"

She became visibly perplexed. "We need help."

"Whatever it is, I will do anything I can to help."

"Thank you. We need to try to open a portal to the Gray Kingdom."

Toth wished he had not made such a promise. "Oh, dear."

"We don't know if a portal even exists," she added. "It's probably more of a door than a portal. We might even need a key."

Toth's face flushed ghostly white.

Kai asked, "You alright, Toady?"

He stood frozen. Scarce of breath, their Elf friend felt weak. "I need you to come with me."

The Holy Hounds studied his suspicious manner closely.

"I have something to show you."

The princess called from inside the sanctuary, "Toth! Are you finished? We have need of you."

"Adwen and the rest have returned," Toth replied. "I'll be back as soon as I am able."

She dashed to the door and stopped, astonished by the twins. "What is going on?"

Toth looked ill. "Everything is alright. Please go back inside. I will return shortly."

Though Princess Eyrie did not believe it, she nodded to the companions and retreated through the door.

Once she was gone, Toth beckoned to follow. "Come with me."

Following Fedius Toth through the overgrown passages, their friend was uncommonly silent.

Adwen strode alongside. "Toth, what's wrong?"

With fear in his eye as he glanced at her, the quill flower on his patch rustled. "I have something to give to you."

A few vines on his mantle drew out a small wooden box hidden in the tamed vegetation. They presented it to her gently, then withdrew as she accepted the token.

As they walked, she examined the tiny chest but didn't know what to make of it. "Should I open it now?"

He turned away. "I believe you may."

The hinges squeaked. Lying at the bottom was a neatly folded piece of silk. She tugged at the fabric but froze as she smelled a lovely medley of herbs. Snapping the box shut tight, her eyes widened in uncertainty. As they neared their destination, Adwen smelled him and bolted for what was once the private guest lounge. She barged into the chamber, lined with oil troughs, and stopped dead.

A cloaked figure stood by the steps before the Mirror of Truth. The being quietly watched her enter. Everyone else came in to stare, as well. Only then did the visitor draw back the hood on his black robe, adorned with golden embroidery. When none found the mind to speak, Elf King Arianwyn nodded.

"Well done. You have my deepest thanks for all your efforts in the war for the Gray Kingdom. Each of you has the gratitude of those who reside in the living worlds, including myself and my people."

Clutching the little box tightly, Adwen was confused. "Why are you giving this to me?"

"It is yours. I was to keep it until you were ready, and now you are." The deep, ancient gaze of the Elf king turned to lock with Kai's. The smile reached his eyes, making them twinkle.

Kai was breathless. "You've been watching all of us."

Arianwyn sighed. "Not all." He looked to Toth, whose mantle of protective plants hung limp, subdued like his demeanor. "I was barred from watching one of you for the longest time."

The one-eyed Elf prince gazed longingly at his kinsman.

"There is much to talk about between us ... nephew."

Toth gasped and staggered.

"It will have to wait for another time. My purpose in this turning of the age is unfinished. That is why I have come and why you are all here."

Adwen still did not understand. "But why do I need the silver oak leaf?"

The Elf king was amused. "Do you not have need of a key ... for a door that has yet to reappear in this world?"

His question left her aghast. "Yes."

"To allow the door to appear, the two seals must be broken." He looked to the golden mirror with the lion's head and ruby eyes.

Kai could not restrain himself. "That's what the mirrors are? Seals?"

"Yes, and they have served their purpose. When the balance was breached by the spawn from the Black Lake, Darien was allowed passage through the Veil. At the breaking of the balance, two seals were made by the Light Spirits to represent that balance lost."

Oryn scowled. "The Mirror of Lies is evil incarnate."

"According to whom?" When the knight held his tongue, the king continued: "The mirrors only reflect what is within. Unobtainable desires are a farce. It is not the mirror that consumed those mortals; rather, the lookers consumed themselves with false dreams. They stared into their deepest of envies and fell prey to a bottomless pit. Only the Golden Heart would have the power to break free from such wants. And so, the first of the two seals were broken."

Jack asked, "How does she break this one?"

"This seal reflects the beholder's true self. The seal of the spider was undone by Adwen rejecting the web. She must look upon her true self and accept it entirely. Reject the lie and behold the truth. With the seals unlocked, the door to the beyond will come. It is her true image alone and her acceptance of it that can break the seal of the lion."

Adwen grew hesitant. What would she see this time? The unknown frightened her. She felt frail. "Now?"

King Arianwyn nodded.

A part of her thought to look for the guidance of her friends, yet she did not. Adwen knew this invitation could not be denied. Steeling herself, she strode nervously yet confidently to the golden mirror. At the steps, she did not pause. Bare feet padded coolly up hard marble, littered with leaves fallen from rampant vines. She stood expectantly before her reflection.

The two elves and the Holy Hounds watched with little doubt.

Before Adwen's eyes alone, the room's reflections faded away. The visage in the surface stretched taller, glowed and looked back at her with the same stunned expression. While her body began to glow, as well, the mirror started to crack. A smile flickered on Adwen's face, and the glass exploded.

Oryn yelped and leaped to her side to ensure she was unharmed. While the bent metal frame creaked and toppled backward, Adwen remained in awe. The broken mirror crashed to the floor in pieces. She let the knight place an arm around her, and they both stared at the mess of gold and broken glass.

It was done, and the Elf king heaved a sigh of satisfaction. His role was complete. While the two spirit warriors descended the steps, he greeted them.

"The door has come. Adwen, the Light Spirits will guide you when you reach the threshold." To Oryn, he nodded. "It is good to see you come into your own at long last, Sir Oryn, the Silver Heart."

The knight nodded respectfully to the king.

"The Light Spirits have entrusted you with keeping your oaths, vows and promises. Do well by them."

Jack braced himself, as King Arianwyn turned and approached. Arching an eyebrow in scrutiny, he considered the warrior. "Do not abuse your gifts, Jack Towers. It is most unbecoming of someone who cares for virtue."

"I'll work on that, Your Highness."

At this, the king laughed. "You might, to be more correct."

Leaving the sheepish warrior to meet with the Marine, his smile warmed. "You, Alexander Greeves, have come a long way, as well."

"Thank you, sir." Immediately after speaking, he felt foolish for using the wrong honorific.

Arianwyn chuckled. "I see you reunited one day with the one you love most. Until that day, do not forget to wake for the sunrise."

A happy look came over him. "Thank you, Your Highness."

"And Kai."

He stared breathlessly at the ancient king.

"Kai Groenendael Conrad, the Windwalker. Your journey was the most harrowing of all. Despite that, your soul remained true."

A voice belonging to a young woman called from the door of the chamber, "Father."

Everyone turned and stared at a beautiful young Elf woman who looked the age of a teen. Her hazel eyes locked on the king, while the others stared in shock. The instant Kai saw her, his complexion turned whiter than cream.

After giving his daughter a smile, Arianwyn took a moment to admire the warrior again. "Was her promise worth the wait?"

Kai could not speak and remained scarce of breath. Then a tall blonde Elf woman joined the girl.

Oryn gasped and froze like his brother. Those hazel eyes still seemed to burn. The Elf queen only briefly glanced at the knight before addressing her husband: "You are late. Time is short."

The king chuckled. "Indeed." To the companions, he bid his final farewell: "I must go."

Toth protested, "You're leaving?" He was aghast. After such a short time, his only relations were leaving him.

"Yes."

"Where are you going?"

Arianwyn sighed, smiling at his wife and child. "Home."

Toth's heart leaped to his throat, and the vines on his mantle rustled. "Take me with you."

The king turned to frown. "I cannot."

Toth trembled. Then Arianwyn smiled as he looked into the future.

"I will not be a thief and steal away from Dargadia the greatest king it shall ever know."

Toth froze, and a tear fell from behind his eye patch.

"We will see each other again one day. Until then, keep the trees tame. Farewell, Fedius, my dear sweet nephew."

The king headed for the door and was about to extend a hand to his family when he stopped and frowned. Turning back to face them again, he gave Adwen a concerned expression.

"Dear, Adwen. I have a question to ask you before I go."

"Yes?"

"When faced with the choice, will you save the Gray Kingdom and restore the balance?"

It seemed outrageous. "Of course, I will. I promise."

Another vision came to him, dispelling the more frightening possibility. The future was set, and he smiled. "Thank you, Adwen Andredan. Good-bye."

King Arianwyn joined his queen and held the hand of his daughter as he departed for places unknown.

Toth darted for the door and skidded into the hall. "Wait!" The passage was empty. The uncle he had never known before was gone like the wind. Defeated and feeling abandoned, he slumped to his knees. The others joined him quickly. Kai braced his childhood best friend.

"It's alright, Toady. He'll be back if he said he would be."

Prince Fedius Toth had a vison of his own and wanted to weep even more. "It will be almost a hundred years till then." He hung his head lamenting the truth.

Kai was undeterred. Hoisting Toth up by his sides, the warrior shushed him: "Come on, now. It's not so long as you think. How long do you think he waited to only get to see you for a minute?"

That had not occurred to the prince. Feeling ashamed, he shook his head. "Just short of an eternity."

Adwen came close, as well. "You won't be alone, and you never have been. A lot of Elves are going to return when the new forests of Dargadia have grown tall."

"How do you know this?"

She beamed warmly. "The Light tells me so. It's going to be alright."

Oryn was firmly supportive. "It seems you are to prepare for their return."

Feeling better, he smiled. "It certainly does."

Jack chuckled. "No pressure."

Alexander elbowed him in the ribs to make him shut up and was pleased to have caught him off guard. It was satisfying to hear sorry whimpers.

Adwen rolled her eyes then stated what must be done: "We have to go now. This time, there really is no telling what will happen."

Toth nodded. "I understand. There is no guarantee that even if you succeed that any of you can leave that place. I wish I could, but I cannot keep you."

She chided, "But I do want to sit and talk when I get back. We'll tell you all about our adventures together – add them to the history texts you've started."

"That will be lovely. I look forward to it."

With that, Adwen faced her warriors. "Let's go."

Kai sent her mind the directions where to open a portal. She summoned the Gray Blade, and white blue flames flew from the tip to create another oblong window. Wild Elf forests in the northeast beckoned. Before going through, Adwen glanced at Toth, the first friend she ever made in her travels. His expression showed peaceful admiration.

With a clever grin, she warned, "We shouldn't be gone long."

"I've learned to be prepared for anything with regards to you, my friend. Fare you well, and may the Light Spirits guide your feet."

"Same to you. See you later."

He watched as they went through without another backward glance, and the spirit flames shrank. When the floating tongues of fire died off, Toth sighed ruefully. Another vision had flitted through his mind as he watched them go. There was work for him to do, and like his uncle, now he too knew how the War for the Gray Kingdom would end.

Chapter 35
BEYOND THE VEIL

Once in the untamed Elf-woods, Kai took the lead.

Jack asked, "The darkness knew where Darien came through?"

Traveling by vague second-hand memory, the warrior replied, "Oh, yeah. They knew alright. There was a scuffle as soon as he emerged. King Arianwyn was out for a hunt with some of his royal court. They saw the whole thing. Not all the demons who attacked died. At least one survived to share the knowledge with the Black Lake. Then all demons connected directly to the darkness of the waters learned."

Adwen added, "It's comforting to know that the demons don't know anything about how Darien passed through."

Kai smiled. "Too, right. That's what I call a silver lining."

Everyone agreed.

"We should be getting close," Kai replied thoughtfully.

Adwen detected a strange energy. "Wait."

They paused, and Oryn felt it as well. Both scanned the woods through dense ferns, underbrush and curtains of hanging moss. Neither could deny the urge to dart toward the source as fast as they could. The others raced to keep up. In seconds, the dash ended in a clearing.

The threshold before the portal felt like a temple. The air was one of serene awe. Dangling moss and vines hung as tattered tapestries high overhead. Golden rays of sunshine streamed through with a subtle breeze. As Adwen went nearer, a translucent silver portal shimmered like a ghostly mirror. The edges refracted the light of day, throwing faint rainbow hues into the boughs of trees. She and her warriors gazed at the pale door.

She murmured and was breathless. "This is it."

Oryn wore a firm expression, and Kai agreed, "Yeah, it is."

Adwen sensed in her heart what needed to be done. She summoned the little chest. For a moment, she felt the weight of it. Then her fire evaporated the box and fittings, leaving the silk cloth untouched. Gently unfolding it, the silver oak leaf shimmered in the light.

She summoned the Gray Blade. Its flames roared to life, and Adwen gave the silver artifact one final look before touching it to the sword. The little leaf burned away immediately. Once it was gone, the sword shone and its flames turned blue and gold. Her friends watched, while she became hesitant.

Adwen let the rippling fire hypnotize her. This was the final step. Oryn placed a hand on her shoulder, making her gasp in surprise.

He reassured her: "We are with you."

Adwen was grateful. "Thank you." Still frightened, she asked, "Is everybody ready?"

To this, Jack scoffed. "No."

The knight and the mage gave the cop identical sardonic frowns.

"Wow. That's like looking at a mirror trick. It's kind of creepy."

Alexander elbowed him.

"Easy!" Jack snapped then addressed Adwen firmly: "What's on the other side, exactly? I want a good idea of what I'm walking into."

Kai was incredulous: "Why?"

Jack scowled. "You can't fool me, Big Guy. We might not come back. I'm the only one with someone waiting on me back home. Let me ask questions, so it's easier to jump through the portal to the land of the dead. Adwen?"

Her gaze lowered. "Kai?"

The mage sympathized with his friends and spoke on her behalf: "The sky and earth are blank. There's an endless black forest with nothing growing – they aren't trees; they are hives for demons to dwell in. The only source of light is the Great White Oak."

"Are the demon lords going to show up?"

Kai paused to give Adwen a supportive glance. "Yes, all of them. If she were to enter that realm unopposed, it would become hers. Darkness would lose its footing, and Adwen would succeed."

"Why doesn't the Overlord just lie low, let her do it, then strike again later?"

Still watching Adwen, Kai elaborated: "Because she is too powerful. There would be no taking it back from her afterward. Those who came before were naïve to battle. Had they known how to fight, the Gray Kingdom never would have been lost in the first place."

Alexander grew curious. "What's it like?"

Kai rolled his eyes. "I just said."

The Marine turned to their leader. "I'm asking Adwen: What is it like being in that world? How does it feel?"

Her voice was low, as she tried to muster her courage. "Weightless. It's quiet and feels like floating, suspended in water. It's like flying."

Jack liked the sound of that. "Sounds nice."

She found herself beginning to smile. "It is."

"I'm ready." The cop nodded firmly.

Alexander nodded.

Oryn and Kai turned to her at once with identical determined expressions.

The support of her four warriors dispelled any uncertainty. Adwen's heart fluttered. "Me too. Let's go end this."

She pointed her sword at the silver door, and its gold and blue fire washed over the portal, making it glow. A blinding white flash burst from the portal. Their world vanished in an instant, as they were momentarily blinded. The four felt strange and then saw they were no longer in the living worlds.

Indeed, they felt lighter than air. The sky high above was black and misty, and beneath their feet was a glowing white bough on a colossal tree. Adwen's warriors gasped, as the impossibly large thing shimmered with countless silvery wisps. Beside her, something was blinking and it caught all their attention.

Flickering atop the highest branch was a single silver leaf. It flashed brilliantly in the dark far brighter than the tree. The twinkling somehow was greeting the adventurers. It made them smile. The Holy Hounds' hair floated as if they were submerged in water.

"How is everyone feeling?" Adwen asked.

The three living beings smiled.

"Euphoric," Kai said happily.

Jack shrugged. "Same here."

Alexander heaved a long-winded sigh of contentment. Feeling better as well, though not so heavily affected, Adwen and Oryn exchanged glances.

"That feeling won't stay," she warned. "The power within the tree is thanking us for coming. It will provide support by easing our fears, but only so far as necessary."

Already she felt the energy withdrawing to let her focus on the task at hand.

The knight looked far out over the infinite nightmare scape. "I see fortifications."

A wicked formation like thorns and blades protruded from the hazy horizon. From such a distance, it appeared small, but they knew it was massive.

Kai huffed, scowling. "It's a bridge, an extension of the Void."

It made Adwen frown and Oryn snarl with smoke on his breath. The emerald mark on his throat glowed like his eyes. A dense cloud of black began to swirl over the evil basilica.

Adwen lost all fear. "They know we are here. Let's go."

She leaped far out and seemed to fly for miles over the misty landscape. Oryn and Kai darted after her, followed closely by Jack and Alexander. Adwen transformed before landing like a feather among the black trees. The other warriors did the same and drew weapons just as demon hordes emerged. Waves of jaws and claws leaped from misshapen hives.

As the warriors joined Adwen's side, she unleashed her fire. Gold and blue flames burst in a sphere from her pale form. She snarled, willing the fire to expand far and wide. Lesser demons evaporated, shrieking, though they did not flee. Like dumb insects, the spawns rushed into the blaze as it swept outward. Their twisted forms burst like dry fungus in a shower of dark mist.

The flames purged the land, turning it from black to gray. Wakes of flames rolled outward faster and farther. Drawing nearer to the parasitic monument, the fire slowed. Finally, it struck the dark walls of the evil temple like water against a rocky shore. Though the holy fire continued to spread, it could not burn the monstrous structure.

Adwen ran up the fortifications. The twins stayed at her sides, and the two friends raced behind them. Reaching the battlements, they flew up high. Demons shrieked as the Holy Hounds descended. Oryn breathed pale green flames to clear their way. The monsters writhed while the warriors claimed the ramparts.

The fortress held a city made of slivers. Demon numbers beyond count began to climb, so Adwen and Oryn used breath and sword flames. Green, white, blue and gold billowed across the black surface, incinerating thousands. Silvery fragments like ash and cinders floated away, while she and her warriors leaped down from the fortifications. When they landed, Kai, Jack and Alexander slew stronger fiends who had survived the flames.

With a path open, they took their chance and bolted. Adwen set her sights on the tallest tower. She could sense the Dark Heart watching from the pinnacle and growled. A large black mass flew from a pillar. Degah'lee laughed maniacally as he tackled Oryn. The two crashed through many rows of dark shards, and the other warriors saw flashes of the knight hound's green fire. More gales of wicked laughter echoed out from the tunnel they had plowed through the shards.

Adwen yelped in dismay. She was about to go back for him, but Kai cut her off. He barked aggressively snapping his jaws, "No! He can handle himself. We must get you to the top. Kill Umbradonus, and they all die or leave this world."

Her ears folded, as her eyes flickered with intense worry. She could feel Oryn taking lashings from Degah'lee's whips but knew his brother was right. She nodded and put newfound urgency into racing through the demon swarm. A storm of shrieks and bellows filled their ears. While Adwen continuously carved a path, Kai worked hard to protect her flank.

The Tormentor crashed down from above, and Jack was first to see the fiend. Before anyone else could react, the roaring warrior leaped at the terrible demon. They tumbled through the air into more of the black spikes, smashing through and out of sight.

None could go to his aid. Kai barked, "No matter what, Adwen, keep going. Don't stop until you reach the top."

Screams and insidious murmurs filled the air, as the Whisperer lunged. His tongues extended from open jaws. Rather than attacking Adwen, the monster targeted the yellow hound warrior. Alexander roared when it pressed him into a wall. The Marine could no longer follow Adwen.

Kai stayed close to her. With his magic barriers and her holy fire, no enemy could touch them. The two eventually reached broad stairs, where the minions did not dare to follow. The race along the steep path became eerily quiet, and they passed into swirling black mist. They ran deep into foreboding structures that gave way to more ominous silhouettes. At the top stood a monumental arch. When they were nearly beneath it, both Adwen and Kai stopped dead. What they had mistaken for a fixture atop the arch blinked and moved. It opened pale white eyes at them.

The Holy Hounds snarled.

Nephalos the Weaver extended spindly spider appendages out like wings, then raised four arms holding swords and scythes. The second in command stood silently, challenging Kai to a duel. The large brown hound warrior rumbled with a sly glint in his eagle eyes.

Adwen heard and sensed his eagerness to answer the challenge but hesitated to leave him.

Kai gave the white Holy Hound a warm look. "You believed in me, Adwen. Now it's our turn to believe in you. Go. Let me take care of this one."

She tossed the Weaver a deadly scowl with back-folded ears.

The warrior insisted with an excited pant, "Go on, now. I owe him for spinning the plans that hurt each of you, and he owes me for ruining them. Oryn and the rest are counting on you."

Adwen bolted through the arch. Nephalos let her pass. His sights never left the reborn being who had spoiled his hard work.

Excited to face the demon tactician, Kai growled, flashing sharp fangs, "What do yah say, Weaver? Is it time to dance?"

The demon lord's spindly appendages retracted and extended. Long cutting threads flashed in the gloom as tight razor-sharp nets. "These webs will kill you where my plans failed, knowledge thief."

Kai's long tail flicked. His gaze remained fiery and unafraid. "Overconfident, are we?"

Nephalos scoffed. "Your own arrogance is just as hot."

Twirling Horizon as it glowed, the warrior replied, "Then

let's dance."

The demon hissed, and Kai snarled, leaping up high to meet the monster.

Adwen pressed on through the mist, which grew thick like a noxious gas. She burst through it and ran along a passage to an opening. She emerged in a wide arena with rising levels like a tower. A hive network of arches encircled her in the eye of the storm. Coming to the center of the misty battleground, Adwen sensed Umbradonus.

She growled, ears pricked and sword at the ready. The air grew cold. A subtle humming began. It sounded as lovely as it was threatening. The tones emanated from the hundreds of dark arches filled with swirling black fog.

A low, soft voice spoke from a shrouded arch: "Is my song not lovely, child? I know you like music. All of your kind did."

Glaring at the shadow, she saw Umbradonus had taken on a human-like shape for their meeting. The Dark Heart did not fully show himself, and Adwen knew better than to drop her guard.

When she did not answer, the overlord cocked his crowned head quizzically. "Rudeness does not become you, little one. I sing for your pleasure. Is that not kind?"

In a blinding flash, she reappeared before the monster's ledge and swung her sword. Adwen barked and snapped in irritation when he vanished. Landing on the ground far below, she waited for him to taunt her again.

The humming continued. Eventually, the Dark Heart spoke, sounding disappointed: "Come now. I've greeted you warmly, started beautiful music to entertain you, and engaged in a peaceful conversation. There's no need for violence when I merely wish to speak."

"I'm not interested in talking, and neither are you!"

The fiend wore a saccharine smile as he appeared from yet another archway. "Oh, but I am. I am interested in a great many things, daughter of paradise. Mainly, my intentions are to reach a mutually beneficial agreement. It would be worth your while to listen."

Discovering his new perch, she gnashed her jaws ravenously. "Nothing you say matters!"

This entertained the demon greatly. "Is that a claim you can make, little candle? I am not so certain."

Adwen lobbed a ball of flame and watched the demon vanish into the fog before it could find him. The fire burst in a flashy spray of blue and gold. "Only someone with their back to the wall tries to make a deal."

"I warn you, neither of us shall have what we want this day if you try to defeat me."

There was a note of truth to the monster's words. It put Adwen on edge even more than the haunting melody.

"Let me help you, child. It is plain to see that you are still naïve."

Finding the demon's next station in an arch on the ground level, the hair on her body bristled. She growled, "I want nothing from you."

"Oh, dear, that was a bold lie. You wish to rob me of existence. That is something you want very badly and which I will not give to anyone. There is no need for lies here. I wish to help you."

Adwen gnashed her jaws angrily. "That's the biggest lie you've told yet!"

Umbradonus paused, smiling kindly from within his protective shadow. "You can hear lies, but can you hear the truth?"

She thought hard for a way to separate the demon from the mist.

"Whether I leave this realm by choice or by destruction, it makes no difference. The result would be the same: You, the Heir, would inherit this world. You, Adwen Andredan, would be trapped here for all time."

The ring of absolute truth stunned Adwen. All thoughts of the battle were dashed from her mind. A nauseating chill swept over the white Holy Hound, and her eyes flashed. Long ears flicked, while her heart shivered.

Umbradonus elaborated with his smooth, sweet low voice: "After you inherit your kingdom, your friends will all die."

Wanting to cry, she yelped and snarled, "That's a lie!"

"Not right away, but they will eventually. For a short while, you will have them back, but then they will forget – just like your passed-on family has already forgotten you. Then you shall be alone, the only one who remembers in the land of forgetfulness, Daughter to the Land of the Dead."

Adwen growled louder, shuddering with wrinkled jaws and

flattened ears.

"You see? Neither of us will get what we truly want. You can let me have this world and keep your friends, but I know you refuse to see reason. So that leaves a single outcome: despair. Slaying or driving me out would mean never feeling the wind or smelling green grass crowned with dew at dawn. You would bid farewell to ever seeing the sunshine again."

Her grip on the sword was so firm it turned the hilt hot from the immense pressure.

Watching with passive amusement at her suffering, the Dark Heart put on a concerned look. "Tell me, does it still not matter?"

Adwen disappeared in a flash, and the demon slunk away to another lofty arch. When Umbradonus materialized again, she appeared before him, sword raised. The demon hissed in surprise at her predicting his movements. Canine face set in a pained snarl, her sapphire eyes shone.

"It doesn't matter!" she shouted.

She sent a wave of fire from her magical force field, swiftly blowing back the shroud and exposing the demon. The monster resisted being burned, then drew a narrow black sword to block the Gray Blade. Holy flame and corrupt darkness collided when their swords clashed, sending smoke and streams of bent light flying. The Dark Heart scowled, making his face shift repeatedly into the likenesses of those she knew and loved.

Using Oryn's voice and face, the demon overlord sounded sad. "Then you are better off alone."

Adwen howled in determination and misery. A brilliant flash of light blasted from her body, banishing the rest of the shadow from the arches. Fire danced across white fur and blue cloth, while her heart raced, building even more resolve until there was no reproach left.

She snarled past their crossed blades, "If it means saving them from you, fine by me."

The demon put on the face of her mother and spoke with her voice: "Either way, I will be pleased. My blade will kill you, or regret will fester in your heart. One day you will fall to that darkness and sour your kingdom into a second Void." At this, his smile became a grin. "Then all will fall, and the will of the Black Lake will be done!"

"That won't happen!" she insisted. "That's a promise."

Umbradonus took on the face of her father and sneered. "You're so disappointing."

A burst of dark energy knocked Adwen back. She rebounded in mid-air and reappeared overhead in a bright flash. Roaring, she smashed the arch to pieces.

The demon leaped at her, and barriers of light and dark collided. Their orbs swirled with pale fire and dark fog across the arena, demolishing archways. Back and forth they darted like swallows. When they came together, sparks flew from their swords. All the while, the song in the air grew louder.

"Spiteful child, why won't you see what is true? You yearn for life!"

"I died three years ago. Since then I've lived on borrowed time. Now I have to give it back." Lunging at the demon once more, she growled, "And that's okay."

Deflecting and returning the slash, the fiend took on her brother's face and voice. "But you lie to yourself. Your heart wants what it wants. Go home. That's what you really want."

With that, the demon slashed at her barrier and she at his. Both barriers dissipated in a fiery explosion, knocking them away from each other. Standing on opposite sides, the combatants snarled and hissed. Adwen sent a wave of flames, and Umbradonus retaliated with darkness to cancel it out. The forces nullified each other, leaving a wall of smoky vapor.

Standing tall and more certain than before, Adwen calmly replied, "I am home."

The demon wore the face and voice of her sister. "But in your own private hell."

She brandished the Gray Blade, becoming ever calmer. "It won't be that way. I won't let it. And you won't be around to watch, so take that as another promise."

Umbradonus rumbled and sneered.

At peace with her destiny, Adwen stared down the frustrated overlord. "Say what you want. I don't care. You have no power over me."

Angry, the demon spoke in the voices of all her warriors at once. His face rapidly flashed with theirs as he bellowed, "You would sacrifice your heart's desires for both damned worlds? You who were used by the Light Spirits, cursed with a short life full of nothing but misery? How can you still obey a master who deals so unfairly?"

Nothing the monster shouted could make her waver. Stalking coolly across the arena, she growled, "What has been no longer matters. I have no reason to look back."

The overlord stood his ground defiantly. "Why should you pay the price for the pleasure of others?"

"Life and happiness are not pleasures. A shadow like you can never understand."

"I understand quite well. Creatures of the light are fools who chase false promises such as happiness. What drivel."

"The only thing that is false is fear. Light is greater than darkness. It always has been and will always be. And I am their fire."

"There is much you do not understand, child slave. Let me tell you what you do not know."

Standing tall a few paces from the demon's reach, Adwen growled, "Fire does not bend to the whispers of the dark. It is night that cringes from the flame. If I am a candle, then how much smaller does that make you, shadow?"

Umbradonus seethed. Fog undulated from his shoulders and down his back, creating a fountain of black vapor.

"Darkness always flees from light. You know that. That's why you have no power over me."

"You know little of the dark."

"I don't need to know. Faith is enough."

"Faith? Faith is empty. You and your fire are hollow; empty and weak."

"So says the shadow who shrinks from me and my sword."

Umbradonus only just realized he had taken a step backward. It angered him greatly until the black fog from his back solidified into waving tendrils. The fiend hissed.

She lowered her jaws and glared. "Done talking yet?"

Recomposing himself, the fiend fell silent. The humming in the air ceased. A cold hush fell about them. Adwen waited for a reply.

Eventually, the demon smirked, donning his one true face. It was a lovely form with seductive features. Terrible hypnotic designs flowed like water across the smooth surfaces. The demon's eyes were white at the center, while evil runes from many languages flashed in and out in them like subliminal images.

Umbradonus sighed heavily and shook his spike-crowned head. Chuckling coolly, he spoke again with no voice but his own: "Poor simple creature. I'll end your ignorant suffering."

Adwen wrinkled her jaws, muzzle quivering threateningly. "Shut up and fight me, devil."

"With absolute pleasure."

She roared, and the demon shrieked. They clashed together in a storm of ringing swords. They performed a deadly dance, flames and dark mist spraying across the arena. The only music left was their battle. Adwen's weapon rang sublime tones with each strike, and the demon's fine sword made ear-piercing whines. Sparks flew. Embers sprayed from each clash of weapons.

Their duel appeared evenly matched. They darted to and fro. Barriers to deflect were gone. Neither tired in the fearsome waltz of blades. Adwen remained patient, and Umbradonus brooded. They drew close once more. Pale and dark blades rang loudly in their ears.

Adwen stared unblinkingly at the monster. Umbradonus took his moment. The demon opened his mouth wide like a snake. He split the beautiful face into rows of short, pointy teeth that glinted as if made of glass. Black water from the lake of the Void belched forth at Adwen.

Beating the demon's sword away, she renewed her barrier of fire at the last second. The fluids evaporated, and she thrust the Gray Blade. The demon hissed and glared. Umbradonus' monstrous serpentine grin froze in place.

Adwen snarled, holding the Gray Blade tight. Flames lapped at the demon's chest armor, where the sword tip pierced through. She held it still, baring fangs at the stunned nemesis.

For a quiet moment, the overlord stared. Then he grew angry. A roaring shriek came, as he bellowed, resisting the flames. Shadows everywhere screamed with Umbradonus.

She snarled and stabbed again and again, while the demon stood frozen. More burning holes with pale flames appeared at every strike.

As the fiend wailed, all the darkness cried out. The Void screamed with the fiend, and the Black Lake boiled and frothed. Lost souls flickered at the momentary reprieve from their torment, as demons howled. Shadows in the living worlds danced like the fire that fed on their master. They writhed like worms, making mortals cringe not knowing what to make of the sight. In her cave, the Mother Dragon and her brood smiled, as the shadows danced with pain.

Within the palace sanctuary, Toth and Princess Eyrie consoled the panicked refugees as the darkest reaches screamed in agony.

The Dwarves of the north stood in awe with their newly crowned king as he stood over the fallen body of his wicked father. The shadows wailed and fled for a moment, making the dwarf city glow brighter than ever before. Onlookers took it as a sign that hope was reborn, and they knew in their hearts that it was true.

Survivors in Jenkirk marveled and smiled, knowing the enemy was at last defeated. Finally, they could go home.

Adwen twisted the Gray Blade and stepped forward, plunging it deeper until it ran Umbradonus through. Still he cried out and refused to die, though the fire spread faster.

With her nose close to his, she blew breath on him, and it entered his mouth. Fire within him caught the air, creating a spark that ignited. Light flashed up the overlord's throat. To the very last second before he exploded, the demon was defiant. A colossal blast rocked the realm. Everything quaked. Dark structures crumbled and faded in crashing roars. Shadows melted, falling away to nothing. The black mount that the castle was built upon withered. It wore away into a blank, gray plane.

Adwen's warriors stood in pale mist. They were covered in gashes and bleeding wounds. In a flash, all the demons were gone, leaving them dazed. The lords vanished. With the shadows gone, their wounds rapidly mended.

Lost in a hazy fog, Kai called out, "Oy! Anybody hear me?" When he heard nothing, he yelled even louder, "Is anybody there?"

"Is that you, Big Guy?" Jack shouted from a long distance.

Kai breathed a sigh of relief. Dashing through the mist, the short warrior came into view supporting a wounded Alexander. The Marine healed rapidly and was able to stand unassisted by the time Kai reached them. Happy to see them, Kai could not restrain a laugh.

"You lot are alive!"

Jack scoffed. "You're surprised? That hurts my feelings."

Kai laughed and called through the mist, "Oryn! We're over here! Where are you, brother?"

They waited a long while. No answer came.

Beginning to worry, he called again, "Oryn, don't toy with me right now. It's not funny."

Again, they heard and sensed nothing of the gray knight.

Kai flew into a panic. "ORYN!"

There was still nothing. Kai fell quiet, while Jack and Alexander looked on with pity.

Something shone through the mist, catching their attention. The warrior mage ran toward it hoping to find his brother. While he sprinted, the fog began to dissipate, and the source of the light grew more defined. Stunned by the discovery, he slowed to a walk. Awe filled him. Jack and Alexander chased after him, and they too walked closer to the shining figure in the gray world.

Adwen stood alone in the stillness. The last of the shadows was gone. White fur and skin turned to misty fragments, unveiling her true form. The hound being fell away from the shining spirit of a tall woman, robed in sky-blue cloth. Golden ribbons fluttered from sapphire gems. Snow-white hair flowed in waves, and golden bangs draped over cheeks and a pale hound pelt mantle. The Gray Blade in her hand shone brightly like the blue gem atop the pale diadem on her brow.

Sensing the three staring, her blue spirit eyes turned to them. The centers shone brilliant gold. The powerful swirling light in them held a sad shine, and she frowned. Her warriors would need to leave soon. Knowing she could not go with them weighed on her. Tears brimmed in her fiery opal-blue eyes like silvery diamond dust. Kai frowned too. He knew what made her so sad.

Behind the trio, a shape moved out of the fading mist. Once Adwen saw green eyes with silver light at the centers, she gasped. Then Kai and the others sensed him. Turning around, the warriors froze.

The skin and armor of the Gray Hound fell away, as he joined them. While the creature shape fell away, a human shape appeared beneath it. A silvery fur cloak covered broad shoulders and draped across his chest. Pale gray hair with green tips flowed as if there were a breeze. Gladness and relief filled his expression. Oryn's spirit eyes never blinked nor looked away from hers. Silver armor shone like stars.

Adwen felt weak, as he came close. Joy drew many glittery

tears when the knight touched her cheek, and both smiled.

His true voice echoed, "I made a promise. I aim to keep it."

She dismissed the fiery sword and wrapped her arms around him. Kai, Jack and Alexander were pleased to see them together.

Oryn took a moment to gently kiss Adwen's forehead, and she laughed weakly. Then their attention turned to the living warriors. The new guardians of the spirit realm beamed proudly. None spoke. Even Jack and Alexander knew this was good-bye. Somehow, it did not make them somber.

Adwen Andredan turned from Oryn Conrad and quietly approached. He stood at her side, while she nodded and spoke. Her voice echoed subtly like a sweet choir: "Thank you, guys. We did it." She sighed, and Oryn placed a proud arm around her. "The balance is restored."

Alexander was confused. "No more demons?"

Kai scoffed incredulously. "There'll always be more, Yank."

Adwen nodded. "Correct. That is why you three will still be needed. Others like you will always be needed. However ..."

Jack raised an eyebrow. He could not read the minds of spirits like these. "What?"

"Just this once, I can offer each of you a new chance. The Light Spirits are very happy with your actions. They want me to give each of you a choice, a wish. There are limits but many possibilities. What desires are on your hearts? Tell me, and I will say if it can be done."

The short warrior did not hesitate. "Can I be human again?"

Adwen smiled warmly and nodded.

He almost wept with joy. Jack watched her lean forward and kiss his brow. Warm energy surged through his body. By the time she stood back, he felt different. Touching his face, he felt stubble with the return of his natural five o'clock shadow. Fangs and Elf ear tips withdrew to human proportions. He could no longer smell his friends. Instead, there was the scent of milk and honey on the air. Then he noticed he still wore his magical garments and froze. She and Oryn frowned at his hesitation.

Looking up, Jack stared blankly, then chuckled. "I get to keep the rest?"

Relieved that he was not angry, Adwen replied, "You are a warrior bound to me and the Light. I can never take that from you.

No one can. You're human. Is that enough?"

He finally did shed joyful tears. "More than you know." Jack bowed then stood beaming.

She faced Alexander. "What does your heart ask for, soldier?"

The Marine pondered. As much as he wanted to be with the spirit of his love, something in him was not ready. "I'd like to stay this way."

Jack was shocked, but Kai was not.

Perplexed, Adwen tilted her head. "Is there nothing you could think to ask for?"

"No, not really. I just need to know: Will we live forever? If so, then I don't want that."

Adwen laughed, shaking her head. "Of course not. You all will live very long lives, but not forever. That is a promise."

"How long?"

She thought then sighed, "I cannot say."

The Marine pondered anew then decided. "Then promise me one thing: When I come back here, make sure Emily and I are always together like the both of you."

Adwen and Oryn exchanged glances, smiling. "Of course, we will. That's our job."

Alexander was satisfied. "Good. Then I'll take a pass. I don't need anything else."

She laughed, and it sounded like many children giggling. "But I promise anyway."

When the two spirit guardians faced Kai, he admired them both and chuckled. "I doubt somehow that you lot are going to give me the same choices."

Jack and Alexander grew worried.

The guardians of the Gray Kingdom exchanged clever looks. "Why would you say something like that?"

"Because I know what's in my heart, and you can see it clear as crystal. Can you give it to me, or is it to bold a wish?"

Adwen smiled, "What is written on all of your hearts is what your souls know to be true. The Light Spirits are telling you what is ahead, and you are given the choice to heed the call or turn away. Are you accepting this new task, Kai Groenendael Conrad?"

"With all my heart and soul, sweet lady."

Adwen summoned the Gray Blade. Gently, she tapped his shoulders, and the blue and gold flames rested there. They spread, becoming a mantle. "Summon Horizon."

He did. As soon as the silver and gold sword appeared in Kai's hand, the gentle fire sent embers to the hilt. They burned the hand guard and sloughed away metal, revealing a blue gem that flashed with gold light. Ghostly flames cloaked the blade.

"I, Adwen Andredan, Pure White Guardian of the Gray Kingdom, appoint you the task of Gate Walker. Your body and sword now hold the power to pass freely between the worlds. Your life will be long. You may visit the Gray Kingdom once a year at the dawn of the longest day until you can finally pass your task to another. Watch over the living and wayward spirits. Guard against the dark forces you know so well. Know all you have been through has molded you for this task."

Kai smirked. "Oh, that thought occurred to me, Lady Adwen."

She laughed. "Please, just keep calling me Adwen."

"Please yourself, then." The flames on his shoulders dissipated.

Jack bid his farewell to the transformed knight: "I'm going to miss you, Cujo."

He scoffed. "I'll not miss your impish antics."

"Aw, yes, you will."

The emerald and silver eyes shone over a smile.

"Yes, I will."

"How do we get back?" Jack asked.

Kai answered, "When I'm good and ready, blighter."

Alexander sighed, enjoying the last moments in Adwen and Oryn's company. "I'm ready to go back. I look forward to coming here someday."

"We will be glad to welcome you."

"Indeed," Oryn added.

"Alright, Kai. Take them home."

The warrior slung fire through the air. A silvery portal like a mirror appeared, glinting with pale colors.

Alexander looked back at Adwen and Oryn one last time. "See you soon."

She waved and he nodded. The soldier walked through to

the other side.

Jack was close behind. "If there's any way to write, don't forget to."

Adwen chortled. "We'll see."

Sighing heavily, the human warrior passed beyond the veil.

Kai moved to stand by the silver gate. Looking up at his brother, the guardian of worlds nodded, "This destiny suits you, don't you think? Living forever at her side?"

Oryn glanced at Adwen. "I never imagined it any other way."

"Until we meet again ... and before I go, be sure to tidy up a bit before my next visit. Perhaps curtains. I leave you to it then."

Kai walked through the portal and vanished from the Gray Kingdom. All was still. Suddenly Adwen felt uncertain. The realm was bare. Only they and the tree in the distance stood in the blank world.

Oryn sensed her feelings and touched his lips to her cheek, dispelling them in an instant. She felt so warm that her form glowed with delight. Then they saw that green ghostly grass had sprung up about their feet. The sight made them share excited looks. Locking in a tight embrace, they poured out love into each other, letting the feelings overflow like a fountain.

Light shone from them in bright beams as if they were a star. Wherever the light touched, a new world appeared. A verdant spirit paradise of rolling hills and outcroppings of wild red lilies sprung. When the green reached the base of the White Oak and spread beyond, the wisps flitted down at last.

As the multitudes touched ground, their bodily shapes returned. Laughing and cheering, the spirits of man and creature raced around. Among them, Tamis ran through the field and sat by some children to play his flute.

Lithus, free from undeath, manifested in knight armor and looked about expectantly. Sensing his old friend, he whistled shrilly, calling a great black steed. Champion the battle horse high-stepped up to greet him, letting the noble master pet his nose. Reunited, he rode across the hills to a beautiful woman who still remembered her dashing warrior. Sweeping her off her feet, the two rode on horseback into eternity.

Adwen and Oryn looked out at the world their hearts had created. It was filled with joy like a dream. Then she paused. It was missing something. Looking up, Adwen used her sword and sent a fireball far aloft. The flames roared through the air high over paradise. Then it burst, transforming into a sun that cast stars of many colors across the sky. Night was day in their world, and everyone basked in the sun forever after.

Epilogue
ON THE WIND

Kai walked up behind Jack and Alexander on volcanic rock along the California coast. Wind lashed as waves crashed on the shore. Jack was bemused.

"How did you know to take us here?"

Rolling his eyes, Kai tapped one temple. "You must be thicker than I thought. Did you forget?"

Jack frowned. "Reading my mind without letting me know? That's rude."

The Marine growled, and Jack only heard canine sounds. "Now you know how it feels."

The human warrior shot his friend a sardonic glance. "I can still read your mind, Jarhead. I understood you." He turned to Kai. "So, what's next, Big Guy? Come with us. I'd love to introduce you to Ashley. She'd get a real kick out of you."

Caressing the ornamental groves on Horizon, Kai replied, "Can't. I have work to do."

"You had better visit at some point."

Alexander agreed, "We're the only ones left. And you're our new superior officer."

Irate, Jack turned to argue. "Hey! I was third in line! What am I, chopped liver?"

Kai gave a deadpan look. "You're you, and all that that implies."

Giving up, he sighed, "Figures."

Nodding to the camo blanket masking the motor bikes, Kai chuckled. "Get a move on and behave yourselves. I'll come when the wind blows me your way."

"Will you give us fair warning?"

He laughed. "Not a chance." Making another ghostly portal, Kai departed for places they could only guess.

Jack shrugged. "Well, come on, Jarhead. Help me uncover the bikes."

Several months passed since mysterious silver portals opened wide in the magical world. They linked the Kingdoms of Day, allowing free travel from one to the next. Dargadia grew greener than since the dawn of time. Magic flowed through the air with the fairies so thick that it materialized as white wisps that murmured songs and stories to those willing to listen.

On the north beach, Moira held a swaddled bundle tightly to her chest and carried a pack on her back. Her feet were weary and her face worn from sorrow at returning to this place. She stood at the brink, where the waves broke before her shoes. Alone, the mage stared out across the sea.

Nearby atop a rock by the cliffs, Kai watched with Horizon in hand. Smiling, he spoke to the wind. "Are you going to let her keep standing there like that, or are you going to talk to her?"

A harsh breeze lashed at the side of his face angrily. Kai was unfazed and chuckled.

"So, you'd rather I tell her the truth?"

For a moment, the gales ceased, and a doldrum took its place. A sly look came over him.

"Well, then, bloody talk to her."

The wind blew again much smoother and subdued.

By the washing waves, Moira felt eyes watching. It frightened her, and she spun around. As soon as she saw the Guardian of fire and ice, there was no question. Shock gave way to tears of joy, and the mage woman wept, clinging tightly to the gurgling bundle.

Upon the rocky ledge, Kai smiled, then made another portal to go on his way.

Toth and Eyrie walked into the ruined castle of her late father. After entering the throne room, he knew she wished to be left alone. Watching as the princess walked steadily down the steps, Toth waited patiently by the passage.

After a few moments, a feeling of a mind touching his let him know they were not alone. Regardless, the soon-to-be-crowned Elf king watched his bride face her fears.

"What a sad mess this is," a voice murmured nearby.

Fedius Toth agreed, "It is, my friend. It is sad."

Kai stood in the shadows, where the princess would never see him. "But not all sad."

Toth's tone was somber: "Adwen and Oryn won't be coming back, will they?"

"They are very happy."

"Tamis is there, as well?"

Kai replied, "You knew before coming back to Dargadia that he was gone, too."

Toth sighed heavily. "There is so much to do."

"Things are going to be so much better, though."

"Yes, they will be better."

"Jack and Alexander are safely returned to their home," Kai added. "I'm performing my rounds. I'm going to keep an eye on things for a long time."

Toth smiled. "It is good to know one friend will be by my side for a while yet."

"You'll never be alone, Toady."

The Elf prince glanced at the eagle-eyed Holy Hound.

Kai smiled. "That's a promise."

Chuckling and feeling much better, the Elf replied, "Don't you have somewhere to be?"

"Always. I'll take the hint and toddle off then. There is going to be a lot of happiness."

Toth said nothing. He already knew.

The Order of the Gargoyle worked hard to transform the blessed overlook caves into a bastion of hope. Workers, creatures and mages used all their gifts and strength to carve and build a noble stronghold into the cliff face. Gargoyles flew in and out through the overlook transporting goods, tools and equipment. Everyone worked under the guidance of their three commanders.

Out on the green grass, Remy used a piece of charcoal and

parchment to draw. His skills had grown great over the years. A prodigy in the arts, he was tasked with designing a flag crest befitting of the new order. A winged gargoyle warrior, armed with spear and shield, stood between two pillars on the paper. The young boy studied the symbols, contemplating how to decorate the pillars to represent their cause.

"Are you done yet?"

Collin sat beside him on the grass under the bright sunshine.

He shook his head. "Something is missing. I don't know what."

The cousin studied the work closely. He thought of something and grinned. "May I?"

Remy insisted with a gesturing hand. Rather than taking up the charcoal, Collin pulled a scrap of cloth from his pocket. Using the handkerchief, he scrubbed away one of the gargoyles wings.

Both admired the banner design and Remy laughed. "It's perfect."

"Yeah, now it's perfect."

Atop the ledge of the overlook, where the gargoyles came and went, the one-winged gargoyle commander shouted orders.

The two human knight brothers discussed plans for their future.

"We need to keep in touch with the new royal family," Raglan cautioned his companions. "It will be different having an Elf for a king, and there could be resistance to this vast change in having an immortal on the throne."

Admiring the diversity of their organization, Dynic mused aloud: "Somehow, I doubt that will be such a problem."

Raglan shrugged. "Perhaps, but it pays to be prepared."

A voice beside a wall agreed, "Too right, it does."

Startled, they whirled around to see the eagle-eyed warrior and froze.

"Sir ... Oryn?"

Kai smiled. "Not quite. At least you didn't call me it, again."

Both knights swayed with shock. "You ...?"

"Yeah, you got it right. I'm not Oryn. I am his brother."

Dynic muttered breathlessly, "This is a rather lot of twisted nonsense. How are you not a dark creature anymore, and not Sir Oryn? Where is he? Where is Lady Adwen? We've searched high and low for all of them."

"They are home. Jack and Alexander are returned to their own realm, as well. They are very happy. You'll both get to see them again someday."

The brothers smiled.

"Tamis is with Adwen and Oryn. He is well taken care of."

Raglan frowned. "I suspected as much. What might your name be? Is it not Kale?"

Walking up to the knights, he extended a hand. "The name is Kai."

Staring unblinkingly, both knights shook it in greeting. "Pleasure is ours, sir."

"Whatever happens from now on, I'll be around to help sort it out. If things get bad, use this. Adwen slipped it into my possession."

Accepting a white uncut diamond, Dynic mused. "What is this stone?"

"It's special to me. Keep it here somewhere. If the need is great, touch it, speak and I will hear you. If whatever I am doing is not more important, I will come."

Raglan remained stunned by his face. "I never knew the great Sir Oryn had a brother."

Kai admired the noble knights. "We'll have to talk about it sometime. But I have to go. There's one more thing I need to do before I get to work."

"What might that be, Sir Kai?"

"Don't worry about it. It's personal."

In the world without magic, the sun blazed in the heat of day. A lush green park rested on the bank of a steady flowing river. Near the water's edge on a lonely park bench sat a man in a suit and tie. He was short, lean and clean-shaven. Taking out his wallet methodically opening it, the middle-aged man studied his badge and card identifying him as an FBI agent.

It frustrated him to look at it for some reason. After some of the stranger things he had seen, heard and felt, he pondered whether he should be proud to have it or would be better off lobbing it into the water. He was lucky to still have his badge at all. If the situation had not been so strange, he would be locked up with some of the men he had helped send to prison. Yet he knew he had made questionable decisions, and it gnawed at him that the case had gone ice cold. Still, he hoped and prayed it would stay that way.

"Afternoon."

The sudden appearance of a stranger near the bench shocked the agent, and he nearly reached for his gun. The odd man wore a black vest suit with a golden tie. His long unkempt brown hair contrasted with his otherwise well-groomed appearance. The way the man with the distinctly London accent watched with yellow piercing eyes made the detective uncomfortable.

Deciding this man was strange but no threat, he relaxed. "Afternoon."

"Might I join you?"

The detective did not care. It would give him time to decide if this man was trouble or not. There was a sly look to him. The odd well-dressed man joined him on the bench and watched the light dance on the river. Moments of calm passed.

The odd man sighed contentedly. "Lovely day, isn't it?"

Giving a searching glance, the detective frowned. "Yes, it is."

"It's perfect."

Becoming suspicious, the agent turned in his seat to face the stranger. "I'm sorry, but do I know you?"

Kai wore a clever smile. "I don't know. Do you know me ... Agent?"

The agent almost gasped as he realized the truth. Wide-eyed, he turned back and sat straight, staring at nothing. The fear he had for the damned case file that plagued him day and night were gone in an instant.

"How is the case coming along, Joe?"

Further confirmation both excited and reassured the agent. "It's not. The trail ended that night. Nothing has happened since ... except for that massacre in Vegas. Did he ... were you there?"

"Yeah, that was a living nightmare. Helped put a fire out before it could spread."

"Kale?"

He chuckled. "Nah, he's long gone. That poor creature won't be coming back."

Detective Joe Castellani looked confused.

"I'm Kai."
They extended hands and shook.
Joe muttered, short of breath, "Nice to meet you."